PENGUIN BOOKS

I AM NUMBER FOUR

Pittacus Lore is a Lorien elder who was entrusted with the story of the Lorien Nine. His whereabouts are unknown.

I am Number Four

PITTACUS LORE

PENGUIN BOOKS

PENGUIN BOOKS

Published by the Penguin Group
Penguin Books Ltd, 80 Strand, London WC2R ORL, England
Penguin Group (USA) Inc., 375 Hudson Street, New York, New York 10014, USA
Penguin Group (Canada), 90 Eglinton Avenue East, Suite 700, Toronto, Ontario, Canada M4P 2Y3
(a division of Pearson Penguin Canada Inc.)
Penguin Ireland, 25 St Stephen's Green, Dublin 2, Ireland (a division of Penguin Books Ltd)
Penguin Group (Australia), 250 Camberwell Road, Camberwell, Victoria 3124, Australia
(a division of Pearson Australia Group Pty Ltd)
Penguin Books India Pvt Ltd, 11 Community Centre, Panchsheel Park, New Delhi – 110 017, India
Penguin Group (NZ), 67 Apollo Drive, Rosedale, Auckland 0632, New Zealand
(a division of Pearson New Zealand Ltd)
Penguin Books (South Africa) (Pty) Ltd, 24 Sturdee Avenue, Rosebank, Johannesburg 2196, South Africa

Penguin Books Ltd, Registered Offices: 80 Strand, London WC2R ORL, England

www.penguin.com

First published in the United States of America by HarperCollins Publishers 2010
First published in Great Britain by Michael Joseph and Razorbill 2010
Published in Penguin Books 2011
016

Typeset by Palimpsest Book Production Limited, Falkirk, Stirlingshire
Printed in England by Clays Ltd, St Ives plc

ISBN: 978-0-141-04784-3

www.greenpenguin.co.uk

MIX
Paper from
responsible sources
FSC www.fsc.org
FSC™ C018179

Penguin Books is committed to a sustainable
future for our business, our readers and our planet.
This book is made from Forest Stewardship
Council™ certified paper.

The door starts shaking. It's a flimsy thing made of bamboo shoots held together with tattered lengths of twine. The shake is subtle and stops almost immediately. They lift their heads to listen, a fourteen-year-old boy and a fifty-year-old man, who everyone thinks is his father but who was born near a different jungle on a different planet hundreds of lightyears away. They are lying shirtless on opposite sides of the hut, a mosquito net over each cot. They hear a distant crash, like the sound of an animal breaking the branch of a tree, but in this case, it sounds like the entire tree has been broken.

'What was that?' the boy asks.

'Shh,' the man replies.

They hear the chirp of insects, nothing more. The man brings his legs over the side of the cot when the shake starts again. A longer, firmer shake, and another crash, this time closer. The man gets to his feet and walks slowly to the door. Silence. The man takes a deep breath as he inches his hand to the latch. The boy sits up.

'No,' the man whispers, and in that instant the blade of a sword, long and gleaming, made of a shining white metal that is not found on Earth, comes through the door and sinks deeply into the man's chest. It protrudes six inches out through his back, and is quickly pulled free. The man grunts. The boy gasps. The man takes a single breath, and utters one word: 'Run.' He falls lifeless to the floor.

The boy leaps from the cot, bursts through the rear wall. He doesn't bother with the door or a window; he literally runs through the wall, which breaks apart as if it's paper, though it's made of strong, hard African mahogany. He tears into the Congo night, leaps over trees, sprints at a speed somewhere around sixty miles per hour. His sight and hearing are beyond human. He dodges trees, rips through snarled vines, leaps small streams with a single step. Heavy footsteps are close behind him, getting closer every second. His pursuers also have gifts. And they have something with them. Something he has only heard hints of, something he never believed he would see on Earth.

The crashing nears. The boy hears a low, intense roar. He knows whatever is behind him is picking up speed. He sees a break in the jungle up ahead. When he reaches it, he sees a huge ravine, three hundred feet across and three hundred feet down, with a river at the bottom. The river's bank is covered with huge boulders. Boulders that would break him apart if he fell on them. His only chance is to get across the ravine. He'll have a short running start, and one chance. One chance to save his own life. Even for him, or for any of the others on Earth like him, it's a near impossible leap. Going back, or going down, or trying to fight them means certain death. He has one shot.

There's a deafening roar behind him. They're twenty, thirty feet away. He takes five steps back and runs – and just before the ledge, he takes off and starts flying across the ravine. He's in the air three or four seconds. He screams, his arms outstretched in front of him, waiting for either safety or the end. He hits the ground and tumbles forward, stopping at the base of a mammoth tree. He smiles. He can't believe he made it, that he's going to survive. Not wanting them to see him, and knowing he needs to get farther away from them, he stands. He'll have to keep running.

He turns towards the jungle. As he does, a huge hand wraps itself around his throat. He is lifted off the ground. He struggles, kicks, tries to pull away, but knows it's futile, that it's over. He should have expected that they'd be on both sides, that once they found him, there would be no escape. The Mogadorian lifts him so that he can see the boy's chest, see the amulet that is hanging around his neck, the amulet that only he and his kind can wear. He tears it off and puts it somewhere inside the long black cloak he is wearing, and when his hand emerges it is holding the gleaming white metal sword. The boy looks into the Mogadorian's deep, wide, emotionless black eyes, and he speaks.

'The Legacies live. They will find each other, and when they're ready, they're going to destroy you.'

The Mogadorian laughs, a nasty, mocking laugh. It raises the sword, the only weapon in the universe that can break the charm that until today protected the boy, and still protects the others. The blade ignites in a silver flame as it points to the sky, as if it's coming alive, sensing its mission and grimacing in anticipation. And as it falls, an arc of light speeding through the blackness of the jungle, the boy still believes that some part of him will survive, and some part of him will make it home. He closes his eyes just before the sword strikes. And then it is over.

I

In the beginning there were nine of us. We left when we were young, almost too young to remember.

Almost.

I am told the ground shook, that the skies were full of light and explosions. We were in that two-week period of the year when both moons hang on opposite sides of the horizon. It was a time of celebration, and the explosions were at first mistaken for fireworks. They were not. It was warm, a soft wind blew in from off the water. I am always told the weather: it was warm. There was a soft wind. I've never understood why that matters.

What I remember most vividly is the way my grandmother looked that day. She was frantic, and sad. There were tears in her eyes. My grandfather stood just over her shoulder. I remember the way his glasses gathered the light from the sky. There were hugs. There were words said by each of them. I don't remember what they were. Nothing haunts me more.

It took a year to get here. I was five when we arrived. We were to assimilate ourselves into the culture before returning to Lorien when it could again sustain life. The nine of us had to scatter, and go our own ways. For how long, nobody knew. We still don't. None of them know where I am, and I don't know where they are, or what they look like now. That is how we protect ourselves because of the charm that was placed upon us when we left, a charm guaranteeing that we can only be killed in the order of our numbers, so long as we stay apart. If we come together, then the charm is broken.

When one of us is found and killed, a circular scar wraps around the right ankle of those still alive. And residing on our left ankle, formed when the Loric charm was first cast, is a small scar identical to the amulet each of us wears. The circular scars are another part of the charm. A warning system so that we know where we stand with each other, and so that we know when they'll be coming for us next. The first scar came when I was nine years old. It woke me from my sleep, burning itself into my flesh. We were living in Arizona, in a small border town near Mexico. I woke screaming in the middle of the night, in agony, terrified as the scar seared itself into my flesh. It was the first sign that the Mogadorians had finally found us on Earth, and the first sign that we were in danger. Until the scar showed up, I had almost convinced myself that my memories were wrong, that what Henri told me was wrong. I wanted to be a normal kid living a normal life, but I knew then, beyond any doubt or discussion, that I wasn't. We moved to Minnesota the next day.

The second scar came when I was twelve. I was in school, in Colorado, participating in a spelling bee. As soon as the pain started I knew what was happening, what had happened to Number Two. The pain was excruciating, but bearable this time. I would have stayed on the stage, but the heat lit my sock on fire. The teacher who was conducting the bee sprayed me with a fire extinguisher and rushed me to the hospital. The doctor in the ER found the first scar and called the police. When Henri showed, they threatened to arrest him for child abuse. But because he hadn't been anywhere near me when the second scar came, they had to let him go. We got in the car and drove away, this time to Maine. We left everything we had except for the Loric Chest that Henri brought along on every move. All twenty-one of them to date.

The third scar appeared an hour ago. I was sitting on a pontoon boat. The boat belonged to the parents of the most popular kid at my school, and unbeknownst to them, he was having a party on it. I had never been invited to any of the parties at my school before. I had always, because I knew we might leave at any minute, kept to myself. But it had been quiet for two years. Henri hadn't seen anything in the news that might lead the Mogadorians to one of us, or might alert us to them. So I made a couple friends. And one of them introduced me to the kid who was having the party. Everyone met at a dock. There were three coolers, some music, girls I had admired from afar but never spoken to, even though I wanted to. We pulled out from the dock and went half a mile into the Gulf of Mexico. I was sitting on the edge of the pontoon with my feet in the water, talking to a cute, dark-haired, blue-eyed girl named Tara, when I felt it coming. The water around my leg started boiling, and my lower leg started glowing where the scar was imbedding itself. The third of the Lorien symbols, the third warning. Tara started screaming and people started crowding around me. I knew there was no way to explain it. And I knew we would have to leave immediately.

The stakes were higher now. They had found Number Three, wherever he or she was, and Number Three was dead. So I calmed Tara down and kissed her on the cheek and told her it was nice to meet her and that I hoped she had a long beautiful life. I dove off the side of the boat and started swimming, underwater the entire time, except for one breath about halfway there, as fast as I could until I reached the shore. I ran along the side of the highway, just inside of the tree line, moving at speeds as fast as any of the cars. When I got home, Henri was at the bank of scanners and monitors that he used to research news around the world, and police activity in our area. He knew without me saying a word, though he did lift my soaking pants to see the scars.

In the beginning we were a group of nine.

Three are gone, dead.

There are six of us left.

They are hunting us, and they won't stop until they've killed us all.

I am Number Four.

I know that I am next.

2

I stand in the middle of the drive and stare up at the house. It is light pink, almost like cake frosting, sitting ten feet above the ground on wooden stilts. A palm tree sways in the front. At the back of the house a pier extends twenty yards into the Gulf of Mexico. If the house were a mile to the south, the pier would be in the Atlantic Ocean.

Henri walks out of the house carrying the last of the boxes, some of which were never unpacked from our last move. He locks the door, then leaves the keys in the mail slot beside it. It is two o'clock in the morning. He is wearing khaki shorts and a black polo. He is very tanned, with an unshaven face that seems downcast. He is also sad to be leaving. He tosses the final boxes into the back of the truck with the rest of our things.

'That's it,' he says.

I nod. We stand and stare up at the house and listen to the wind come through the palm fronds. I am holding a bag of celery in my hand.

'I'll miss this place,' I say. 'Even more than the others.'

'Me too.'

'Time for the burn?'

'Yes. You want to do it, or you want me to?'

'I'll do it.'

Henri pulls out his wallet and drops it on the ground. I pull out mine and do the same. He walks to our truck and comes back with passports, birth certificates, social security cards, checkbooks, credit cards and bank cards, and drops them on the ground. All of the documents and materials related to our identities here, all of them forged and manufactured. I grab from the truck a small gas can we keep for emergencies. I pour the gas over the small pile. My current name is Daniel Jones. My story is that I grew up in California and moved here because of my dad's job as a computer programmer. Daniel Jones is about to disappear. I light a match and drop it, and the pile ignites. Another one of my lives, gone. As we always do, Henri and I stand and watch the fire. *Bye, Daniel,* I think, *it was nice knowing you.* When the fire burns down, Henri looks over at me.

'We gotta go.'

'I know.'

'These islands were never safe. They're too hard to leave quickly, too hard to escape from. It was foolish of us to come here.'

I nod. He is right, and I know it. But I'm still reluctant to leave. We came here because I wanted to, and for the first time, Henri let me choose where we were going. We've been here nine months, and it's the longest we have stayed in any one place since leaving Lorien. I'll miss the sun and the warmth. I'll miss the gecko that watched from the wall each morning as I ate breakfast. Though there are literally millions of geckos in south Florida, I swear this one follows me to school and seems to be everywhere I am. I'll miss the thunderstorms that seem to come from out of nowhere, the way everything is still and quiet in the early-morning hours before the terns arrive. I'll miss the dolphins that sometimes feed when the sun sets. I'll even miss the smell of sulfur from the rotting seaweed at the base of the shore, the way that it fills the house and penetrates our dreams while we sleep.

'Get rid of the celery and I'll wait in the truck,' Henri says. 'Then it's time.'

I enter a thicket of trees off to the right of the truck. There are three Key deer already waiting. I dump the bag of celery out at their feet and crouch down and pet each of them in turn. They allow me to, having long gotten over their skittishness. One of them raises his head and looks at me. Dark, blank eyes staring back. It almost feels as though he passes something to me. A shudder runs up my spine. He drops his head and continues eating.

'Good luck, little friends,' I say, and walk to the truck and climb into the passenger seat.

We watch the house grow smaller in the side mirrors until Henri pulls onto the main road and the house disappears. It's a Saturday. I wonder what's happening at the party without me. What they're saying about the way that I left and what they'll say on Monday when I'm not at school. I wish I could have said good-bye. I'll never see anyone I knew here ever again. I'll never speak to any of them. And they'll never know what I am or why I left. After a few months, or maybe a few weeks, none of them will probably ever think of me again.

Before we get on the highway, Henri pulls over to gas up the truck. As he works the pump, I start looking through an atlas he keeps on the middle of the seat. We've had the atlas since we arrived on this planet. It has lines drawn to and from every place we've ever lived. At this point, there are lines crisscrossing all of the United States. We know we should get rid of it, but it's really the only piece of our life together that we have. Normal people have photos and videos and journals; we have the atlas. Picking it up and looking through it, I can see Henri has drawn a new line from Florida to Ohio. When I think of Ohio, I think of cows and corn and nice people. I know the license plate says THE HEART OF IT ALL. What 'All' is, I don't know, but I guess I'll find out.

Henri gets back into the truck. He has bought a couple of sodas and a bag of chips. He pulls away and starts heading toward U.S. 1, which will take us north. He reaches for the atlas.

'Do you think there are people in Ohio?' I joke.

He chuckles. 'I would imagine there are a few. And we might even get lucky and find cars and TV there, too.'

I nod. Maybe it won't be as bad as I think.

'What do you think of the name 'John Smith'?' I ask.

'Is that what you've settled on?'

'I think so,' I say. I've never been a John before, or a Smith.

'It doesn't get any more common than that. I would say it's a pleasure to meet you, Mr Smith.'

I smile. 'Yeah, I think I like "John Smith".'

'I'll create your forms when we stop.'

A mile later we are off the island and cruising across the bridge. The waters pass below us. They are calm and the moonlight is shimmering on the small waves, creating dapples of white in the crests. On the right is the ocean, on the left is the gulf; it is, in essence, the same water, but with two different names. I have the urge to cry, but I don't. It's not that I'm necessarily sad to leave Florida, but I'm tired of running. I'm tired of dreaming up a new name every six months. Tired of new houses, new schools. I wonder if it'll ever be possible for us to stop.

3

We pull off for food and gas and new phones. We go to a truck stop, where we eat meat loaf and macaroni and cheese, which is one of the few things Henri acknowledges as being superior to anything we had on Lorien. As we eat, he creates new documents on his laptop, using our new names. He'll print them when we arrive, and as far as anyone will know, we'll be who we say we are.

'You're sure about John Smith?' he says.

'Yeah.'

'You were born in Tuscaloosa, Alabama.'

I laugh. 'How did you come up with that?'

He smiles and motions towards two women sitting a few booths away. Both of them are extremely hot. One of them is wearing a T-shirt that reads **WE DO IT BETTER IN TUSCALOOSA**.

'And that's where we're going next,' he says.

'As weird as it may sound, I hope we stay in Ohio for a long time.'

'Really. You like the idea of Ohio?'

'I like the idea of making some friends, of going to the same school for more than a few months, of maybe actually having a life. I started to do it in Florida. It was sort of great, and for the first time since we've been on Earth, I felt almost normal. I want to find somewhere and stay somewhere.'

Henri looks thoughtful. 'Have you looked at your scars today?'

'No, why?'

'Because this isn't about you. This is about the survival of our race, which was almost entirely obliterated, and about keeping you alive. Every time one of us dies – every time one of *you*, the Garde, dies – our chances diminish. You're Number Four; you're next in line. You have an entire race of vicious murderers hunting you. We're leaving at the first sign of trouble, and I'm not going to debate it with you.'

Henri drives the entire time. Between breaks and the creation of the new documents, it takes about thirty hours. I spend most of the time napping or playing video games. Because of my reflexes, I can master most of the games quickly. The longest it has taken me to beat any of them is about a day. I like the alien war and space games the best. I pretend I'm back on Lorien, fighting Mogadorians, cutting them down, turning them to ash. Henri thinks it's weird and tries to discourage me from doing it. He says we need to live in the real world, where war and death are a reality, not pretend. As I finish my latest game, I look up. I'm tired of sitting in the truck. The clock on the dash reads 7:58. I yawn, wipe my eyes.

'How much farther?'

'We're almost there,' Henri says.

It is dark out, but there is a pale glow to the west. We pass by farms with horses and cattle, then barren fields, and beyond those, it's trees as far as the eye can see. This is exactly what Henri wanted, a quiet place to go unnoticed. Once a week he scours the internet for six, seven, eight hours at a time to update a list of available homes around the country that fit his criteria: isolated, rural, immediate availability. He told me it took four tries – one call to South Dakota, one to New Mexico, one to Arkansas – until he had the rental where we're going to live now.

A few minutes later we see scattered lights that announce the town. We pass a sign that reads:

WELCOME TO PARADISE, OHIO
POPULATION 5,243

'Wow,' I say. 'This place is even smaller than where we stayed in Montana.'

Henri is smiling. 'Who do you think it's paradise for?'

'Cows, maybe? Scarecrows?'

We pass by an old gas station, a car wash, a cemetery. Then the houses begin, clapboard houses spaced thirty or so feet apart. Halloween decorations hang in the windows of most of them. A sidewalk cuts through small yards leading to the front doors. A traffic circle sits in the center of town, and in the middle of it is a statue of a man on horseback holding a sword. Henri stops. We both look at it and laugh, though we're laughing because we hope no one else with swords ever shows up here. He continues around the circle and once we're through it, the dashboard GPS system tells us to make a turn. We begin heading west, out of town.

We drive for four miles before turning left onto a gravel road, then pass open cut fields that are probably full of corn in the summer, then through a dense forest for about a mile. And then we find it, tucked away in overgrown vegetation, a rusted silver mailbox with black lettering painted on the side of it that reads 17 OLD MILL RD.

'The closest house is two miles away,' he says, turning in. Weeds grow throughout the gravel drive, which is littered with potholes filled with tawny water. He comes to a stop and turns the truck off.

'Whose car is that?' I ask, nodding to the black SUV Henri has just parked behind.

'I'm assuming the real-estate agent's.'

The house stands silhouetted by trees. In the dark there is an eerie look to it, like whoever last lived in it was scared away, or was driven away, or ran away. I get out of the truck. The engine ticks and I can feel the heat coming off of it. I grab my bag from the bed and stand there holding it.

'What do you think?' Henri asks.

The house is one story. Wooden clapboard. Most of the white paint has been chipped away. One of the front windows is broken. The roof is covered with black shingles that look warped and brittle. Three wooden stairs lead to a small porch covered with rickety chairs. The yard itself is long and shaggy. It's been a very long time since the grass was last mowed.

'It looks like Paradise,' I say.

We walk up together. As we do, a well-dressed blond woman around Henri's age comes out of the doorway. She's wearing a business suit and is holding a clipboard and folder; a BlackBerry is clipped to the waist of her skirt. She smiles.

'Mr Smith?'

'Yes,' says Henri.

'I'm Annie Hart, the agent from Paradise Realty. We spoke on the phone. I tried calling you earlier but your phone seemed to be turned off.'

'Yes, of course. The battery unfortunately died on the way here.'

'Ah, I just hate when that happens,' she says, and walks towards us and shakes Henri's hand. She asks me my name and I tell her, though I am tempted, as I always am, to just say 'Four.' As Henri signs the lease she asks me how old I am and tells me she has a daughter at the local high school about my age. She's very warm, friendly, and clearly loves to chat. Henri hands the lease back and the three of us walk into the house.

Inside most of the furniture is covered with white sheets. Those that aren't covered are coated with a thick layer of dust and dead insects. The screens in the windows look brittle to the touch, and the walls are covered with cheap plywood paneling. There are two bedrooms, a modest-sized kitchen with lime green linoleum, one bathroom. The living room is large and rectangular, situated at the front of the house. There's a fireplace in the far corner. I walk through and toss my bag on the bed of the smaller room. There is a huge faded poster of a football player wearing a bright orange uniform. He's in the middle of throwing a pass, and it looks like he's about to get crushed by a massive man in a black and gold uniform. It says BERNIE KOSAR, QUARTERBACK, CLEVELAND BROWNS.

'Come say good-bye to Mrs Hart,' Henri yells from the living room.

Mrs Hart is standing at the door with Henri. She tells me I should look for her daughter at school, that maybe we could be friends. I smile and say yes, that would be nice. After she leaves we immediately start unpacking the truck. Depending on how quickly we leave a place, we either travel very lightly – meaning the clothes on our back, Henri's laptop and the intricately carved Loric Chest that goes everywhere with us – or we bring a few things – usually Henri's extra computers and equipment, which he uses to set up a security perimeter and search the web for news and events that might be related to us. This time we have the Chest, the two high-powered computers, four TV monitors, and four cameras. We also have some clothes, though not many of the clothes we wore in Florida are appropriate for life in Ohio. Henri carries the Chest to his room, and we lug all of the equipment into the basement, where he'll set it up so no visitors will see it. Once everything is inside, he starts placing the cameras and turning on the monitors.

'We won't have the internet here until the morning. But if you want to go to school tomorrow, I can print all of your new documents for you.'

'If I stay will I have to help you clean this place and finish the setup?'

'Yes.'

'I'll go to school,' I say.

'Then you better get a good night's sleep.'

4

Another new identity, another new school. I've lost track of how many there have been over the years. Fifteen? Twenty? Always a small town, a small school, always the same routine. New students draw attention. Sometimes I question our strategy of sticking to the small towns because it's hard, almost impossible, to go unnoticed. But I know Henri's rationale: it is impossible for *them* to go unnoticed as well.

The school is three miles away from our house. Henri drives me in the morning. It's smaller than most of the others I've attended and is unimpressive looking, one story, long and low-slung. A mural of a pirate with a knife between his teeth covers the outside wall beside the front door.

'So you're a Pirate now?' Henri says beside me.

'It looks like it,' I reply.

'You know the drill,' he says.

'This ain't my first rodeo.'

'Don't show your intelligence. It'll make them resent you.'

'Wouldn't dream of it.'

'Don't stand out or draw too much attention.'

'Just a fly on the wall.'

'And don't hurt anybody. You're far stronger than they are.'

'I know.'

'Most importantly, always be ready. Ready to leave at a moment's notice. What's in your backpack?'

'Five days' worth of dried fruit and nuts. Spare socks and thermal underwear. Rain jacket. A handheld GPS. A knife disguised as a pen.'

'On you at all times.' He takes a deep breath. 'And keep an eye out for signs. Your Legacies are going to appear any day now. Hide them at all costs and call me immediately.'

'I know, Henri.'

'Any day, John,' he reiterates. 'If your fingers start to disappear, or if you start to float, or shake violently, if you lose muscular control or begin to hear voices even when nobody is talking. Anything at all, you call.'

I pat my bag. 'Got my phone right here.'

'I'll be waiting here after school. Good luck in there, kiddo,' he says.

I smile at him. He is fifty years old, which means he was forty when we arrived. Being his age made for a harder transition. He still speaks with a strong Loric accent that is often mistaken for French. It was a good alibi in the beginning, so he named himself Henri, and he has stuck with it ever since, just changing his last name to match mine.

'Off I go to rule the school,' I say.

'Be good.'

I walk towards the building. As is the case with most high schools, there are crowds of kids hanging around outside. They're divided into their cliques, the jocks and the cheerleaders, the band kids carrying instruments, the brains in their glasses with their textbooks and BlackBerries, the stoners off to one side, oblivious to everyone else. One kid, gangly with thick glasses, stands alone. He's wearing a black NASA T-shirt and jeans, and can't weigh more than a hundred pounds. He has a handheld telescope and is scanning the sky, which is mostly obscured by clouds. I notice a girl taking pictures, moving easily from one group to the next. She's shockingly beautiful with straight blond hair past her shoulders, ivory skin, high cheekbones, and soft blue eyes. Everyone seems to know her and says hello to her, and no one objects to her taking their picture.

She sees me, smiles and waves. I wonder why and turn to see if someone is behind me. There are, two kids discussing math homework, but no one else. I turn back around. The girl walks towards me, smiling. I've never seen a girl so good-looking, much less spoken to one, and I've definitely never had one wave and smile as if we're friends. I'm immediately nervous, and start blushing. But I'm also suspicious, as I've been trained to be. As she nears me, she lifts the camera and starts snapping pictures. I raise my hands to block my face. She lowers the camera and smiles.

'Don't be shy.'

'I'm not. Just trying to protect your lens. My face might break it.'

She laughs. 'With that scowl it might. Try smiling.'

I smile, slightly. I'm so nervous I feel like I'm going to explode. I can feel my neck burning, my hands getting warm.

'That's not a real smile,' she says, teasingly. 'A smile involves showing your teeth.'

I smile broadly and she takes pictures. I usually don't allow anyone to take my picture. If it ended up on the internet, or in a newspaper, it would make finding me much easier. The two times it happened, Henri was furious, got hold of the pictures, and destroyed them. If he knew I was doing this now, I'd be in huge trouble. I can't help it, though – this girl is so pretty and so charming. As she's taking my picture, a dog comes running up to me. It's a beagle with tan floppy ears, white legs and chest, a slender black body. He's thin and dirty as if he's been living on his own. He rubs against my leg, whines, tries to get my attention. The girl thinks it's cute and has me kneel down so she can take a picture of me with the dog. As soon as she starts snapping shots, he backs away. Whenever she tries again, he moves farther away. She finally gives up and shoots a few more of me. The dog sits about thirty feet away watching us.

'Do you know that dog?' she asks.

'Never seen him before.'

'He sure likes you. You're John, right?'

She holds out her hand.

'Yeah.' I say. 'How'd you know?'

'I'm Sarah Hart. My mother is your real-estate agent. She told me you'd probably be starting school today, and I should look out for you. You're the only new kid to show up today.'

I laugh. 'Yeah, I met your mom. She was nice.'

'You gonna shake my hand?'

She's still holding her hand out. I smile and take it, and it is literally one of the best feelings I've ever had.

'Wow,' she says.

'What?'

'Your hand feels hot. Really hot, like you have a fever or something.'

'I don't think so.'

She lets go.

'Maybe you're just warm-blooded.'

'Yeah, maybe.'

A bell rings in the distance and Sarah tells me that it's the warning bell. We have five minutes to get to class. We say good-bye and I watch her walk away. A moment later, something hits the back of my elbow. I turn and a group of football players, all wearing letterman jackets, sweep by me. One of them is glaring at me and I realize that he hit me with his backpack as he walked past. I doubt it was an accident and I start to follow them. I know I'm not going to do anything, even though I could. I just don't like bullies. As I do, the kid in the NASA shirt walks next to me.

'I know you're new, so I'll fill you in,' he says.

'On what?' I ask.

'That's Mark James. He's a big deal around here. His dad is the town sheriff and he's the star of the football team. He used to date Sarah, when she was a cheerleader, but she quit cheerleading and dumped him. He hasn't gotten over it. I wouldn't get involved if I were you.'

'Thanks.'

The kid hurries away. I make my way to the principal's office so I can register for classes and get started. I turn and look back to see if the dog is still around. He is, sitting in the same spot, watching me.

The principal's name is Mr Harris. He's fat and mostly bald, except for a few long hairs at the back and sides of his head. His belly reaches over his belt. His eyes are small and beady, set too close together. He grins at me from across the desk, and his smile seems to swallow his eyes.

'So you're a sophomore from Santa Fe?' he asks.

I nod, say yes even though we've never been to Santa Fe, or New Mexico, for that matter. A simple lie to keep from being traced.

'That explains the tan. What brings you to Ohio?'

'My dad's job.'

Henri isn't my father, but I always say he is to allay suspicion. In truth he is my Keeper, or what would be better understood on Earth as my guardian. On Lorien there were two types of citizens, those who develop Legacies, or powers, which can be extremely varied, anything from invisibility to the ability to read minds, from being able to fly to using natural forces like fire, wind or lightning. Those with the Legacies are called the Garde, and those without are called Cêpan, or Keepers. I am a member of the Garde. Henri is a Cêpan. Every Garde is assigned a Cêpan at an early age. Cêpans help us understand our planet's history and develop our powers. The Cêpan and the Garde – one group to run the planet, the other group to defend it.

Mr Harris nods. 'And what does he do?'

'He's a writer. He wanted to live in a small, quiet town to finish what he's working on,' I say, which is our standard cover story.

Mr Harris nods and squints his eyes. 'You look like a strong young man. Are you planning on playing sports here?'

'I wish I could. I have asthma, sir,' I say, my usual excuse to avoid any situation that might betray my strength and speed.

'I'm sorry to hear that. We're always looking for able athletes for the football team,' he says, and casts his eyes to the shelf on the wall, on top of which a football trophy sits engraved with last year's date. 'We won the Pioneer Conference,' he says, and beams with pride.

He reaches over and pulls two sheets of paper from a file cabinet beside his desk and hands them to me. The first is my student schedule with a few open slots. The second is a list of the available electives. I choose classes and fill them in, then hand everything back. He gives me a sort of orientation, talking for what seems like hours, going over every page of the student manual with painstaking detail. One bell rings, then another. When he finally finishes he asks if I have any questions. I say no.

'Excellent. There is a half hour left of second period, and you've chosen astronomy with Mrs Burton. She's a great teacher, one of our very best. She won an award from the state once, signed by the governor himself.'

'That's great,' I say.

After Mr Harris struggles to free himself from his chair, we leave his office and walk down the hall. His shoes click upon the newly waxed floor. The air smells of fresh paint and cleaner. Lockers line the walls. Many are covered with banners supporting the football team. There can't be more than twenty classrooms in the whole building. I count them as we pass.

'Here we are,' Mr Harris says. He extends his hand. I shake it. 'We're happy to have you. I like to think of us as a close-knit family. I'm glad to welcome you to it.'

'Thank you,' I say.

Mr Harris opens the door and sticks his head in the classroom. Only then do I realize that I'm a little nervous, that a somewhat dizzy feeling is creeping in. My right leg is shaking; there are butterflies in the pit of my stomach. I don't understand why. Surely it's not the prospect of walking into my first class. I've done it far too many times to still feel the effect of nerves. I take a deep breath and try to shake them away.

'Mrs Burton, sorry to interrupt. Your new student is here.'

'Oh, great! Send him in,' she says in a high-pitched voice of enthusiasm.

Mr Harris holds open the door and I walk through. The classroom is perfectly square, filled with twenty-five people, give or take, sitting at rectangular desks about the size of kitchen tables, three students to each. All eyes are on me. I look back at them before looking at Mrs Burton. She is somewhere around sixty, wearing a pink wool sweater and red plastic glasses attached to a chain around her neck. She smiles widely, her hair graying and curly. My palms are sweaty and my face feels flushed. I hope it isn't red. Mr Harris closes the door.

'And what is your name?' she asks.

In my unsettled mood I almost say 'Daniel Jones' but catch myself. I take a deep breath and say, 'John Smith.'

'Great! And where are you from?'

'Fl— ,' I begin, but then catch myself again before the word fully forms. 'Santa Fe.'

'Class, let's give him a warm welcome.'

Everybody claps. Mrs Burton motions for me to sit in the open seat in the middle of the room between two other students. I am relieved she doesn't ask any more questions. She turns around to go to her desk and I begin walking down the aisle, straight towards Mark James, who is sitting at a table with Sarah Hart. As I pass, he sticks his foot out and trips me. I lose my balance but stay upright. Snickers filter throughout the room. Mrs Burton whips around.

'What happened?' she asks.

I don't answer her, and instead glare at Mark. Every school has one, a tough guy, a bully, whatever you want to call him, but never has one materialized this quickly. His hair is black, full of hair gel, carefully styled so it goes in all directions. He has meticulously trimmed sideburns, stubble on his face. Bushy eyebrows over a set of dark eyes. From his letterman jacket I see that he is a senior, and his name is written in gold cursive stitching above the year. Our eyes stay locked, and the class emits a taunting groan.

I look to my seat three desks away, then I look back at Mark. I could literally break him in half if I wanted to. I could throw him into the next county. If he tried to run away, and got into a car, I could outrun his car and put it in the top of a tree. But aside from that being an extreme overreaction, Henri's words echo in my mind: 'Don't stand out or draw too much attention.' I know that I should follow his advice and ignore what has just happened, as I always have in the past. That is what we're good at, blending into the environment and living within its shadows. But I feel slightly off, uneasy, and before I have a chance to think twice, the question is already asked.

'Did you want something?'

Mark looks away and glances around the rest of the room, scoots his weight up the chair, then looks back at me.

'What are you talking about?' he asks.

'You stuck your foot out when I passed. And you bumped into me outside. I thought you might have wanted something.'

'What's going on?' Mrs Burton asks behind me. I look over my shoulder at her.

'Nothing,' I say. I turn back to Mark. 'Well?'

His hands tighten around the desk but he remains silent. Our eyes stay locked until he sighs and looks away.

'That's what I thought,' I say down at him, and continue walking. The other students aren't sure how to respond and most of them are still staring when I take my seat between a redheaded girl with freckles and an overweight guy who looks at me with his mouth agape.

Mrs Burton stands at the head of the class. She seems a

little flustered, but then shrugs it off and describes why there are rings around Saturn, and how they're made mostly of ice particles and dust. After a while I tune her out and look at the other students. A whole new group of people that I'll yet again try to keep at a distance. It's always a fine line, having just enough interaction with them to remain mysterious without becoming strange and thus sticking out. I've already done a horrible job of that today.

I take a deep breath and slowly exhale. I still have butterflies in my stomach, still the nagging shake in my leg. My hands feel warmer. Mark James sits three tables in front of me. He turns once and looks at me, then whispers something into Sarah's ear. She turns around. She seems cool, but the fact that she used to date him and is sitting with him makes me wonder. She gives me a warm smile. I want to smile back but I'm frozen. Mark again tries to whisper to her but she shakes her head and pushes him away. My hearing is much better than human hearing if I focus it, but I'm so flustered by her smile that I don't. I wish I could have heard what was said.

I open and close my hands. My palms are sweaty and beginning to burn. Another deep breath. My vision is blurring. Five minutes pass, then ten. Mrs Burton is still talking but I don't hear what she is saying. I squeeze my fists shut, then reopen them. When I do my breath catches in my throat. A slight glow is coming from my right palm. I look down at it, dumbfounded, amazed. After a few seconds the glow begins to brighten.

I close my fists. My initial fear is that something else has happened to one of the others. But what could happen? We can't be killed out of order. That is the way the charm works. But does that mean that some other harm can't befall them? Has somebody's right hand been cut off? I have no way of knowing. But if something had happened, I would have felt it in the scars on my ankles. And only then does it dawn on me. My first Legacy must be forming.

I pull my phone out of my bag, and send Henri a text that says CMEE, though I meant to type COME. I'm too dizzy to send anything else. I close my fists and place them in my lap. They're burning and shaking. I open my hands. My left palm is bright red, my right is still glowing. I glance at the clock on the wall and see that class is almost over. If I can get out of here I can find an empty room and call Henri and ask him what's going on. I start counting the seconds: sixty, fifty-nine, fifty-eight. It feels like something is going to explode in my hands. I focus on the counting. Forty, thirty-nine. They're tingling now, as though little needles are being stuck into my palms. Twenty-eight, twenty-seven. I open my eyes and stare ahead, focusing on Sarah with the hope that looking at her will distract me. Fifteen, fourteen. Seeing her makes it worse. The needles feel like nails now. Nails that have been put in a furnace and heated until they're glowing. Eight, seven.

The bell rings and in an instant I'm up and out of the room, rushing past the other students. I'm feeling dizzy, unsteady on my feet. I continue down the hall and have no idea where to go. I can feel someone following me. I pull my schedule from my back pocket and check my locker number. As luck would have it, my locker is just to my right. I stop at it and lean my head against the metal door. I shake my head, realizing that in my rush to get out of the classroom I left behind my bag with my phone inside of it. And then someone pushes me.

'What's up, tough guy?'

I stumble a few steps, look back. Mark is standing there, smiling at me.

'Something wrong?' he asks.

'No,' I reply.

My head is spinning. I feel like I'm going to pass out. And my hands are on fire. Whatever is happening couldn't be happening at a worse time. He pushes me again.

'Not so tough without any teachers around, are you?'

I'm too unbalanced to stay standing, and I trip over my own feet and fall to the ground. Sarah steps in front of Mark.

'Leave him alone,' she says.

'This has nothing to do with you,' he says.

'Right. You see a new kid talking to me and you try immediately to start a fight with him. *This* is just one example of why we aren't together anymore.'

I start to stand up. Sarah reaches down to help me, and as soon as she touches me, the pain in my hands flares up and it feels like lightning strikes through my head. I turn around and start rushing away, in the opposite direction from the astronomy class. I know that everyone will think I'm a coward for running, but I feel like I'm about to pass out. I'll thank Sarah, and deal with Mark, later. Right now I just need to find a room with a lock on the door.

I get to the end of the hall, which intersects with the school's main entrance. I think back to Mr Harris's orientation, which included where the various rooms were located in the school. If I remember correctly, the auditorium, band rooms, and art rooms are at the end of this hall. I run towards them as fast as I can in my current state. Behind me I can hear Mark yelling to me, and Sarah yelling at him. I open the first door I find, and shut it behind me. Thankfully there is a lock, which I click into place.

I'm in a dark room. Strips of negatives hang on drying lines. I collapse onto the floor. My head spins and my hands are burning. Since first seeing the light, I have kept my hands clenched into fists. I look down at them now and see my right hand is still glowing, pulsating. I start to panic.

I sit on the floor, sweat stinging my eyes. Both hands are in terrible pain. I knew to expect my Legacies, but I had no idea it would include this. I open my hands and my right palm is shining brightly, the light beginning to concentrate. My left is dimly flickering, the burning sensation almost unbearable. I wish Henri was here. I hope he's on his way.

I close my eyes and fold my arms across my body. I rock back and forth on the floor, everything inside of me in pain. I don't know how much time is passing. One minute? Ten minutes? The bell rings, signaling the start of the next period. I can hear people talking outside the door. The door shakes a couple times, but it's locked and nobody will be able to get in. I just keep rocking, eyes closed tightly. More knocks begin to fall on the door. Muffled voices that I can't understand. I open my eyes and can see that the glow from my hands has lit up the entire room. I squeeze my hands into fists to try and stop the light but it streams out between my fingers. Then the door really starts shaking. What will they think of the light in my hands? There is no hiding it. How will I explain it?

'John? Open the door – it's me,' a voice says.

Relief floods through me. Henri's voice, the only voice in the whole world that I want to hear.

5

I crawl to the door and unlock it. It swings open. Henri is covered in dirt, wearing gardening clothes as though he had been working outside on the house. I'm so happy to see him that I have the urge to jump up and wrap my arms around him, and I try to, but I'm too dizzy and I fall back onto the floor.

'Is everything okay in there?' asks Mr Harris, who is standing behind Henri.

'Everything is fine. Just give us a minute, please,' Henri says back.

'Do I need to call an ambulance?'

'No!'

The door shuts. Henri looks down at my hands. The light in the right one is shining brightly, though the left dimly flickers as though trying to gain confidence in itself. Henri smiles widely, his face shining like a beacon.

'Ahh, thank Lorien,' he sighs, then pulls a pair of leather gardening gloves from his back pocket. 'What dumb luck that I've been working in the yard. Put these on.'

I do and they completely hide the light. Mr Harris opens the door and sticks his head through. 'Mr Smith? Is everything okay?'

'Yes, everything is fine. Just give us thirty seconds,' Henri says, then looks back to me. 'Your principal meddles.'

I take a deep breath and exhale. 'I understand what is happening, but why this?'

'Your first Legacy.'

'I know that, but why the lights?'

'We'll talk about it in the truck. Can you walk?'

'I think so.'

He helps me up. I am unsteady, still shaking. I grab hold of his forearm for support.

'I have to get my bag before we leave,' I say.

'Where is it?'

'I left it in the classroom.'

'What number?'

'Seventeen.'

'Let's get you to the truck and I'll go get it.'

I drape my right arm over his shoulders. He supports my weight by putting his left arm around my waist. Even though the second bell has rung I can still hear people in the hall.

'You need to walk as straight and as normal as you can.'

I take a deep breath. I try to gather any bit of strength I might have in reserve to tackle the long walk out of the school.

'Let's do this,' I say.

I wipe the sweat from my forehead and follow Henri out of the darkroom. Mr Harris is still in the hallway.

'Just a bad case of asthma,' Henri tells him, and walks past.

A crowd of twenty or so people are still in the hallway, and most of them are wearing cameras around their necks, waiting to get into the darkroom for photography class. Thankfully Sarah isn't among them. I walk as steadily as I can, one foot in front of the other. The school's exit is a hundred feet away. That is a lot of steps. People are whispering.

'What a freak.'

'Does he even go to school here?'

'I hope so, he's cute.'

'What do you think he was doing in the darkroom to make his face so red?' I hear, and everyone laughs. Just like we can focus our hearing, we can close it off, which helps when you're trying to concentrate amidst noise and confusion. So I shut out the noise and follow closely behind Henri. Each step feels like ten, but finally we reach the door. Henri holds it open for me and I try to walk on my own to his truck, which is parked up front. For the last twenty steps I drape my arm around his shoulders again. He opens the truck door and I scoot in.

'You said seventeen?'

'Yes.'

'You should have kept it with you. It's the little mistakes that lead to big mistakes. We can't make any.'

'I know. I'm sorry.'

He shuts the door and walks back into the building. I hunch over in the seat and try to slow my breathing. I can still feel the sweat on my forehead. I sit up and flip down the sun visor so I can look into the mirror. My face is redder than I thought, my eyes a little watery. But through the pain and exhaustion, I smile. *Finally*, I think. After years of waiting, after years of my only defense against the Mogadorians being intellect and stealth, my first Legacy has arrived. Henri comes out of the school carrying my bag. He walks around the truck, opens the door, tosses my bag on the seat.

'Thank you,' I say.

'No problem.'

When we're out of the lot I remove the gloves and take a closer look at my hands. The light in my right hand is beginning to concentrate itself into a beam like a flashlight, only brighter. The burning is beginning to lessen. My left hand still flickers dimly.

'You should keep those on until we're home,' Henri says.

I put the gloves back on and look over at him. He is smiling proudly.

'Been a shit long wait,' he says.

'Huh?' I ask.

He looks over. 'A shit long wait,' he says again. 'For your Legacies.'

I laugh. Of all the things Henri has learned to master while on Earth, profanity is not one of them.

'A *damn* long wait,' I correct him.

'Yeah, that's what I said.'

He turns down our road.

'So, what next? Does this mean I'll be able to shoot lasers from my hands or what?'

He grins. 'It's nice to think so, but no.'

'Well, what am I going to do with light? When I'm getting chased am I going to turn and flash it in their eyes? Like that's supposed to make them cower from me or something?'

'Patience,' he says. 'You aren't supposed to understand it yet. Let's just get home.'

And then I remember something that nearly makes me jump out of my seat.

'Does this mean we'll finally open the Chest?'

He nods and smiles. 'Very soon.'

'Hell, yes!' I say. The intricately carved wooden Chest has haunted me my entire life. It's a brittle-looking box with the Loric symbol on its side that Henri has remained completely secretive about. He's never told me what's in it, and it's impossible to open, and I know, because I've tried more times than I can count, never with any luck. It's held shut with a padlock with no discernible slot for a key.

When we get home I can tell that Henri has been working. The three chairs from the front porch have been cleared away and all the windows are open. Inside, the sheets over the furniture have been removed, some of the surfaces wiped clean. I set my bag atop the table in the living room and open it. A wave of frustration passes over me.

'The son of a bitch,' I say.

'What?'

'My phone is missing.'

'Where is it?'

'I had a slight disagreement this morning with a kid named Mark James. He probably took it.'

'John, you were in school for an hour and a half. How in the hell did you have a disagreement already? You know better.'

'It's high school. I'm the new kid. It's easy.'

Henri removes his phone from his pocket and dials my number. Then he snaps his phone shut.

'It's turned off,' he says.

'Of course it is.'

He stares at me. 'What happened?' he asks in that voice I recognize, the voice he uses when pondering another move.

'Nothing. Just a stupid argument. I probably dropped it on the floor when I put it into my bag,' I say, even though I know I didn't. 'I wasn't in the best frame of mind. It's probably waiting for me in lost and found.'

He looks around the house and sighs. 'Did anyone see your hands?'

I look at him. His eyes are red, even more bloodshot than

they were when he dropped me off. His hair is tousled and he has a slumped look as though he may collapse in exhaustion at any moment. He last slept in Florida, two days ago. I'm not sure how he is even still standing.

'Nobody did.'

'You were in school for an hour and a half. Your first Legacy developed, you were nearly in a fight, and you left your bag in a classroom. That's not exactly blending in.'

'It was nothing. Certainly not a big enough deal to move to Idaho, or Kansas, or wherever the hell our next place is going to be.'

Henri narrows his eyes, pondering what he just witnessed and trying to decide whether it's enough to justify leaving.

'Now is not the time to be careless,' he says.

'There are arguments in every single school every single day. I promise you, they aren't going to track us because some bully messed with the new kid.'

'The new kid's hands don't light up in every school.'

I sigh. 'Henri, you look like you're about to die. Take a nap. We can decide after you've had some sleep.'

'We have a lot to talk about.'

'I've never seen you this tired before. Sleep a few hours. We'll talk after.'

He nods. 'A nap would probably do me some good.'

Henri goes into his bedroom and closes the door. I walk outside, pace around the yard for a bit. The sun is behind the trees with a cool wind blowing. The gloves are still on my hands. I take them off and tuck them into my back pocket. My hands are the same as before. Truth be told, only half of me is thrilled that my first Legacy has finally arrived after so many years of impatiently waiting. The other half of me is crushed. Our constant moving has worn me down, and now it'll be impossible to blend in or to stay in one place for any period of time. It'll be impossible to make friends or feel like I fit in. I'm sick of the fake names and the lies. I'm sick of always looking over my shoulder to see if I'm being followed.

I reach down and feel the three scars on my right ankle. Three circles that represent the three dead. We are bound to each other by more than mere race. As I feel the scars I try to imagine who they were, whether they were boys or girls, where they were living, how old they were when they died. I try to remember the other kids on the ship with me and give each of them numbers. I think about what it would be like to meet them, hang out with them. What it might have been like if we were still on Lorien. What it might be like if the fate of our entire race wasn't dependent on the survival of so few of us. What it might be like if we weren't all facing death at the hands of our enemies.

It's terrifying to know that I'm next. But we've stayed ahead of them by moving, running. Even though I'm sick of the running I know it's the only reason we're still alive. If we stop, they will find us. And now that I'm next in line, they have undoubtedly stepped up the search. Surely they must know we are growing stronger, coming into our Legacies.

And then there is the other ankle and the scar to be found there, formed when the Loric charm was cast in those precious moments before leaving Lorien. It's the brand that binds us all together.

6

I walk inside and lie on the bare mattress in my room. The morning has worn me out and I let my eyes close. When I reopen them the sun is lifted over the tops of the trees. I walk out of the room. Henri is at the kitchen table with his laptop open and I know he's been scanning the news, as he always does, searching for information or stories that might tell us where the others are.

'Did you sleep?' I ask.

'Not much. We have internet now and I haven't checked the news since Florida. It was gnawing at me.'

'Anything to report?' I ask.

He shrugs. 'A fourteen-year-old in Africa fell from a fourth-story window and walked away without a scratch. There is a fifteen-year-old in Bangladesh claiming to be the Messiah.'

I laugh. 'I know the fifteen-year-old isn't us. Any chance of the other?'

'Nah. Surviving a four-story drop is no great feat, and besides, if it was one of us they wouldn't have been that careless in the first place,' he says, and winks.

I smile and sit across from him. He closes his computer and places his hands on the table. His watch reads 11:36. We've been in Ohio for slightly over half a day and already this much has happened. I hold my palms up. They've dimmed since the last time I looked.

'Do you know what you have?' he asks.

‘Lights in my hands.’

He chuckles. ‘It’s called Lumen. You’ll be able to control the light in time.’

‘I sure hope so, because our cover is blown if they don’t turn off soon. I still don’t see what the point is, though.’

‘There’s more to Lumen than mere lights. I promise you.’

‘What’s the rest?’

He walks into his bedroom and returns with a lighter in his hand.

‘Do you remember much of your grandparents?’ he asks. Our grandparents are the ones who raise us. We see little of our parents until we reach the age of twenty-five, when we have children of our own. The life expectancy for the Loric is around two hundred years, much longer than that of humans, and when children are born, between the parents’ ages of twenty-five and thirty-five, the elders are the ones who raise them while the parents continue honing their Legacies.

‘A little. Why?’

‘Because your grandfather had the same gift.’

‘I don’t remember his hands ever glowing,’ I say.

Henri shrugs. ‘He might never have had reason to use it.’

‘Wonderful,’ I say. ‘Sounds like a great gift to have, one I’ll never use.’

He shakes his head. ‘Give me your hand.’

I give him the right one and he flicks the lighter on, then moves it to touch the tip of my finger with the flame. I jerk my hand away.

‘What are you doing?’

‘Trust me,’ he says.

I give my hand back to him. He takes hold of it and flicks the lighter on again. He looks into my eyes. Then he smiles. I look down and see that he is holding the flame over the tip of my middle finger. I don't feel a thing. Instinct causes me to jerk my hand free anyway. I rub my finger. It feels no different than it did before.

'Did you feel that?' he asks.

'No.'

'Give it back,' he says. 'And tell me when you do feel something.'

He starts at my fingertip again, then moves the flame very slowly up the back of my hand. There is a slight tickle where the flame touches the skin, nothing more. Only when the fire reaches my wrist do I begin to sense the burn. I pull my arm free.

'Ouch.'

'Lumen,' he says. 'You're going to become resistant to fire and heat. Your hands come naturally, but we'll have to train the rest of your body.'

A smile spreads across my face. 'Resistant to fire and heat,' I say. 'So I'll never be burned again?'

'Eventually, yes.'

'That's awesome!'

'Not such a bad Legacy after all, huh?'

'Not bad at all,' I agree. 'Now what about these lights? Are they ever going to turn off?'

'They will. Probably after a good night's sleep, when your mind forgets they're on,' he says. 'But you'll have to be careful not to get worked up for a while. An emotional imbalance will cause them to come right back on again, if you get overly nervous, or angry, or sad.'

'For how long?'

'Until you learn to control them.' He closes his eyes and rubs his face with his hands. 'Anyway, I'm going to try to sleep again. We'll talk about your training in a few hours.'

After he leaves I stay at the kitchen table, opening and closing my hands, taking deep breaths and trying to calm everything inside of me so the lights will dim. Of course it doesn't work.

Everything in the house is still a mess aside from the few things Henri did while I was at school. I can tell that he is leaning towards leaving, but not to the point that he couldn't be persuaded to stay. Maybe if he wakes and finds the house clean and in order it'll tip him in the right direction.

I start with my room. I dust, wash the windows, sweep the floor. When everything is clean I throw sheets, pillows, and blankets on the bed, then hang and fold my clothes. The dresser is old and rickety, but I fill it and then place the few books I own on top of it. And just like that, a clean room, everything I own put away and in order.

I move to the kitchen, putting away dishes and wiping down the counters. It gives me something to do and takes my mind off of my hands, even though while cleaning I think about Mark James. For the first time in my life I stood up to somebody. I've always wanted to but never did because I wanted to heed Henri's advice to keep a low profile. I've always tried to delay another move for as long as I could. But today was different. There was something very satisfying about being pushed by somebody and responding by pushing back. And then there's the issue of my phone, which was stolen. Sure, we could easily get a new one, but where is the justice in that?

7

I wake before the alarm. The house is cool and silent. I lift my hands from under the covers. They are normal, no lights, no glow. I lumber out of bed and into the living room. Henri is at the kitchen table reading the local paper and drinking coffee.

'Good morning,' he says. 'How do you feel?'

'Like a million bucks,' I say.

I pour myself a bowl of cereal and sit across from him.

'What are you going to do today?' I ask.

'Errands mostly. We're getting low on money. I'm thinking of putting in a transfer at the bank.'

Lorien is (or was, depending on how you look at it) a planet rich with natural resources. Some of those resources were precious gems and metals. When we left, each Cêpan was given a sack full of diamonds, emeralds and rubies to sell when we arrived on Earth. Henri did, and then deposited the money into an overseas bank account. I don't know how much there is and I never ask. But I know it's enough to last us ten lifetimes, if not more. Henri makes withdrawals from it once a year, give or take.

'I don't know, though,' he continues. 'I don't want to stray too far in case something else happens today.'

Not wanting to make a big deal of yesterday, I wave the notion away. 'I'll be fine. Go get paid.'

I look out the window. Dawn is breaking, casting a pale light over everything. The truck is covered with dew. It's been a while since we've been through a winter. I don't even own a jacket and have outgrown most of my sweaters.

'It looks cold out,' I say. 'Maybe we can go clothes shopping soon.'

He nods. 'I was thinking about that last night, which is why I need to go to the bank.'

'Then go,' I say. 'Nothing is going to happen today.'

I finish the bowl of cereal, drop the dirty dish into the sink, and jump into the shower. Ten minutes later I'm dressed in a pair of jeans and a black thermal shirt, the sleeves pulled to my elbows. I look in the mirror, and down at my hands. I feel calm. I need to stay that way.

On the way to school Henri hands me a pair of gloves.

'Make sure you keep these with you at all times. You never know.'

I tuck them into my back pocket.

'I shouldn't need them. I feel pretty good.'

At the school, buses are lined up in front. Henri pulls up to the side of the building.

'I don't like you not having a phone,' he says. 'Any number of things could go wrong.'

'Don't worry. I'll have it back soon.'

He sighs and shakes his head. 'Don't do anything stupid. I'll be right here at the end of the day.'

'I won't,' I say, and get out of the truck. He pulls away.

Inside, the halls are bustling with activity, students loitering at lockers, talking, laughing. A few look at me and whisper. I don't know whether it's because of the confrontation or because of the darkroom. It's likely that they are whispering about both. It is a small school, and in small schools there is little that isn't readily known by everyone else.

When I reach the main entrance, I turn right and find my locker. It's empty. I have fifteen minutes before sophomore composition begins. I walk by the classroom just to make sure I know where it is and then head to the office. The secretary smiles when I enter.

'Hi,' I say. 'I lost my phone yesterday and I was wondering if anyone turned it in to lost and found?'

She shakes her head. 'No, I'm afraid no phone's been turned in.'

'Thank you,' I say.

Out in the hallway I don't see Mark anywhere. I pick a direction and begin walking. People still stare and whisper, but that doesn't bother me. I see him fifty feet ahead of me. All at once the thrill of adrenaline kicks in. I look down at my hands. They're normal. I'm worried about them turning on, and that worry might just be the thing that does it.

Mark's leaning against a locker with his arms crossed, in the middle of a group, five guys and two girls, all of them talking and laughing. Sarah is sitting on a windowsill about fifteen feet away. She looks radiant again today with her blond hair pulled into a ponytail, wearing a skirt and a gray sweater. She's reading a book, but looks up as I walk towards them.

I stop just outside of the group, stare at Mark, and wait. He notices me after about five seconds.

'What do you want?' he asks.

'You know what I want.'

Our eyes stay locked. The crowd around us swells to ten people, then twenty. Sarah stands and walks to the edge of the crowd. Mark is wearing his letterman jacket, and his black hair is carefully styled to look like he rolled straight out of bed and into his clothes.

He pushes away from the locker and walks towards me. When he is inches away he stops. Our chests nearly touch and the spicy scent of his cologne fills my nostrils. He is probably six one, a couple inches taller than I am. We have the same build. Little does he know that what is inside of me is not what is inside of him. I am quicker than he is and far stronger. The thought brings a confident grin to my face.

'You think you can stay in school a little longer today? Or are you going to run off again like a little bitch?'

Snickers spread through the crowd.

'I guess we'll see, won't we?'

'Yeah, I guess we will,' he says, and moves even closer.

'I want my phone back,' I say.

'I don't have your phone.'

I shake my head at him. 'There are two people who saw you take it,' I lie.

By the way his brows crinkle I know I have guessed correctly.

'Yeah, and what if it was me? What are you going to do?'

There are probably thirty people around us now. I have no doubt that the entire school will know what has happened within ten minutes of the start of first period.

'You've been warned,' I say. 'You have till the end of the day.'

I turn and leave.

'Or what?' he yells behind me. I don't acknowledge it. Let him dwell on the answer. My fists have been clenched and I realize I had mistaken adrenaline for nerves. Why was I so nervous? The unpredictability? The fact that this is the first time I've confronted somebody? The possibility of my hands glowing? Probably all three.

I go to the bathroom, enter an empty stall, and latch the

door behind me. I open my hands. A slight glow in the right one. I close my eyes and sigh, focus on breathing slowly. A minute later the glow is still there. I shake my head. I didn't think the Legacy would be that sensitive. I stay in the stall. A thin layer of sweat covers my forehead; both of my hands are warm, but thankfully the left is still normal. People filter in and out of the bathroom and I stay in the stall, waiting. The light stays on. Finally the first-period bell rings and the bathroom is empty.

I shake my head in disgust and accept the inevitable. I don't have my phone and Henri is on his way to the bank. I'm alone with my own stupidity and I have no one to blame but myself. I pull the gloves from my back pocket and slip them on. Leather gardening gloves. I couldn't look more foolish if I were wearing clown shoes with yellow pants. So much for blending in. I realize I have to stop with Mark. He wins. He can keep my phone; Henri and I will get a new one tonight.

I leave the bathroom and walk the empty hallway to my classroom. Everybody stares at me when I enter, then at the gloves. There is no point trying to hide them. I look like a fool. I am an alien, I have extraordinary powers, with more to come, and I can do things that no human would dream of, but I still look like a fool.

I sit in the center of the room. Nobody says anything to me and I'm too flustered to hear what the teacher says. When the bell rings I gather my things, drop them into my bag, and pull the straps over my shoulder. I'm still wearing the gloves. When I exit the room I lift the cuff of the right one and peek at my palm. It's still glowing.

I walk the hall at a steady pace. Slow breathing. I try to

clear my mind but it isn't working. When I enter the classroom Mark is sitting in the same spot as the day before, Sarah beside him. He sneers at me. Trying to act cool, he doesn't notice the gloves.

'What's up, runner? I heard the cross-country team is looking for new members.'

'Don't be such a dick,' Sarah says to him. I look at her as I pass, into her blue eyes that make me feel shy and self-conscious, that make my cheeks warm. The seat I sat in the day before is occupied, so I head to the very back. The class fills and the kid from yesterday, the one who warned me about Mark, sits next to me. He's wearing another black T-shirt with a NASA logo in the center, army pants, and a pair of Nike tennis shoes. He has disheveled, sandy blond hair, and his hazel eyes are magnified by his glasses. He pulls out a notepad filled with diagrams of constellations and planets. He looks at me and doesn't try to hide the fact that he is staring.

'How goes it?' I ask.

He shrugs. 'Why are you wearing gloves?'

I open my mouth to answer, but Mrs Burton starts the class. During most of it the guy beside me draws pictures that seem to be his interpretation of what Martians look like. Small bodies; big heads, hands, and eyes. The same stereotypical representations that are usually shown in movies. At the bottom of every drawing he writes his name in small letters: SAM GOODE. He notices me watching, and I look away.

As Mrs Burton lectures on Saturn's sixty-one moons, I look at the back of Mark's head. He's hunched over his desk, writing. Then he sits up and passes a note to Sarah. She flicks it back at him without reading it. It makes me smile.

Mrs Burton turns off the lights and starts a video. The rotating planets being projected on the screen at the front of the class make me think of Lorien. It is one of the eighteen life-sustaining planets in the universe. Earth is another. Mogadore, unfortunately, is another.

Lorien. I close my eyes and allow myself to remember. An old planet, a hundred times older than Earth. Every problem that Earth now has – pollution, overpopulation, global warming, food shortages – Lorien also had. At one point, twenty-five thousand years ago, the planet began to die. This was long before the ability to travel through the universe, and the people of Lorien had to do something in order to survive. Slowly but surely they made a commitment to ensure that the planet would forever remain self-sustaining by changing their way of life, doing away with everything harmful – guns and bombs, poisonous chemicals, pollutants – and over time the damage began to reverse itself. With the benefit of evolution, over thousands of years, certain citizens – the Garde – developed powers in order to protect the planet, and to help it. It was as though Lorien rewarded my ancestors for their foresight, for their respect.

Mrs Burton flicks the lights on. I open my eyes and look at the clock. Class is almost over. I feel calm again, and had completely forgotten about my hands. I take a deep breath and flip open the cuff of the right glove. The light is off! I smile and remove both gloves. Back to normal. I have six periods left in the day. I have to remain at peace through all of them.

The first half of the day passes without incident. I remain calm, and likewise have no further encounters with Mark. At lunch I fill my tray with the basics, then find an empty table at the back of the room. When I'm halfway through a slice of pizza, Sam Goode, the kid from astronomy class, sits across from me.

'Are you really fighting Mark after school?' he asks.

I shake my head. 'No.'

'That's what people are saying.'

'They're wrong.'

He shrugs, keeps eating. A minute later he asks, 'Where'd your gloves go?'

'I took them off. My hands aren't cold anymore.'

He opens his mouth to respond but a giant meatball that I'm sure is aimed for me comes out of nowhere and hits him in the back of the head. His hair and shoulders are covered with bits of meat and spaghetti sauce. Some of it has splattered onto me. While I start cleaning myself off a second meatball flies through the air and hits me square on the cheek. *Ooh*s filter throughout the cafeteria.

I stand and wipe the side of my face with a napkin, anger coursing through me. In that instant I don't care about my hands. They can shine as brightly as the sun, and Henri and I can leave this afternoon if that's what it comes to. But there isn't a chance in hell I'm letting this slide. It was over after this morning . . . but not now.

'Don't,' Sam says. 'If you fight then they'll never leave you alone.'

I start walking. A hush falls over the cafeteria. A hundred sets of eyes focus on me. My face twists into a scowl. Seven people are sitting at Mark James's table, all guys. All seven of them stand as I approach.

'You got a problem?' one of them asks me. He is big, built like an offensive lineman. Patches of reddish hair grow on his cheeks and chin as though he's trying to grow a beard.

It makes his face look dirty. Like the rest of them he's wearing a letterman jacket. He crosses his arms and stands in my way.

'This doesn't concern you,' I say.

'You'll have to go through me to get to him.'

'I will if you don't get out of my way.'

'I don't think you can,' he says.

I bring my knee straight up into his crotch. His breath catches in his throat, and he doubles over. The whole lunchroom gasps.

'I warned you,' I say, and I step over him and walk straight for Mark. Just as I reach him I'm grabbed from behind. I turn with my hands clenched into fists, ready to swing, but at the last second I realize it's the lunchroom attendant.

'That'll be enough, boys.'

'Look what he just did to Kevin, Mr Johnson,' Mark says. Kevin is still on the ground holding himself. His face is beet red. 'Send him to the principal!'

'Shut up, James. All four of you are going. Don't think I didn't see you throw those meatballs,' he says, and looks at Kevin still on the floor. 'Get up.'

Sam appears from nowhere. He has tried to wipe the mess from his hair and shoulders. The big pieces are gone, but the sauce has only smeared. I'm not sure why he's here. I look down at my hands, ready to flee at the first hint of light, but to my surprise they're off. Was it because of the urgency of the situation, allowing me to approach without preemptive nerves? I don't know.

Kevin stands and looks at me. He is shaky, still having trouble breathing. He grips the shoulder of the guy beside him for support.

'You'll get yours,' he says.

'I doubt it,' I say. I'm still scowling, still covered in food. To hell with wiping it away.

The four of us walk to the principal's office. Mr Harris is sitting behind his desk eating a microwavable lunch, a napkin tucked into the neck of his shirt.

'Sorry to interrupt. We just had a slight disruption during lunch. I'm sure these boys will be happy to explain,' the lunchroom attendant says.

Mr Harris sighs, pulls the napkin from his shirt, and throws it in the trash. He pushes his lunch to the side of his desk with the back of his hand.

'Thank you, Mr Johnson.'

Mr Johnson leaves, closing the office door behind him, and the four of us sit.

'So who wants to start?' the principal asks, irritation in his voice.

I stay silent. The muscles in Mr Harris's jaw are flexed. I look down at my hands. Still off. I place them palms down on my jeans just in case. After ten seconds of silence, Mark starts. 'Somebody hit him with a meatball. He thinks it was me, so he kneed Kevin in the balls.'

'Watch your language,' Mr Harris says, and then turns to Kevin. 'You okay?'

Kevin, whose face is still red, nods.

'So who threw the meatball?' Mr Harris asks me.

I say nothing, still seething, irritated at the whole scene. I take a deep breath to try to calm myself.

'I don't know,' I say. My anger has reached new levels. I don't want to have to deal with Mark through Mr Harris, and would rather take care of the situation myself, away from the principal's office.

Sam looks at me in surprise. Mr Harris throws his hands up in frustration. 'Well then, why in the hell are you boys here?'

'That's a good question,' says Mark. 'We were simply eating our lunch.'

Sam speaks. 'Mark threw it. I saw him and so did Mr Johnson.'

I look over at Sam. I know he didn't see it because his back was turned the first time, and the second time he was busy cleaning himself off. But I'm impressed at him saying so, for his taking my side knowing it will put him in danger with Mark and his friends. Mark scowls at him.

'Come on, Mr Harris, ' Mark pleads. 'I have the interview with the *Gazette* tomorrow, and the game on Friday. I don't have time to worry about crap like this. I'm being accused of something I didn't do. It's hard to stay focused with this shit going on.'

'Watch your mouth!' Mr Harris yells.

'It's true.'

'I believe you,' the principal says, and sighs very heavily. He looks at Kevin, who's still struggling to catch his breath. 'Do you need to go to the nurse?'

'I'll be fine,' Kevin says.

Mr Harris nods. 'You two forget about the lunchroom incident, and Mark, get your mind straight. We've been trying to get this article for a while now. They might even put us on the front page. Imagine that, the front page of the *Gazette*,' he says, and smiles.

'Thank you,' Mark says. 'I'm excited about it.'

'Good. Now, you two can leave.'

They go, and Mr Harris gives a hard look at Sam. Sam holds his gaze.

'Tell me, Sam. And I want the truth. Did you see Mark throw the meatball?'

Sam's eyes narrow. He doesn't look away.

'Yes.'

The principal shakes his head. 'I don't believe you, Sam. And because of that, here is what we are going to do.' He looks at me. 'So a meatball was thrown—'

'Two,' Sam interjects.

'What?!' Mr Harris asks, again glowering at Sam.

'There were two meatballs thrown, not one.'

Mr Harris slams his fist on the desk. 'Who cares how many there were! John, you assaulted Kevin. An eye for an eye. We'll let it go at that. Do you understand me?'

His face is red and I know it's pointless to argue.

'Yep,' I say.

'I don't want to see you two in here again,' he says. 'You're both dismissed.'

We leave his office.

'Why didn't you tell him about your phone?' Sam asks.

'Because he doesn't care. He just wanted to go back to his lunch,' I say. 'And be careful,' I tell him. 'You'll be on Mark's radar now.'

I have home economics after lunch – not because I necessarily care about cooking, but because it was either that or choir. And while I have many strengths and powers that are considered exceptional on Earth, singing is not one of them. So I walk into home ec and take a seat. It is a small room, and just before the bell rings Sarah walks in and sits beside me.

'Hi,' she says.

'Hi.'

Blood rushes to my face and my shoulders stiffen. I grab a pencil and begin to twirl it in my right hand while my left bends back the corners of my notepad. My heart is pounding. Please don't let my hands be glowing. I peek at my palm and breathe a sigh of relief that it's still normal. *Stay calm,* I think. *She's just a girl.*

Sarah is looking at me. Everything inside of me feels as though it is turning to mush. She may be the most beautiful girl I have ever seen.

'I'm sorry Mark is being a jerk to you,' she says.

I shrug. 'It's not your fault.'

'You guys aren't really going to fight, are you?'

'I don't want to,' I say.

She nods. 'He can be a real dick. He always tries to show he's boss.'

'It's a sign of insecurity,' I say.

'He's not insecure. Just a dick.'

Sure he is. But I don't want to argue with Sarah. Besides, she speaks with such certainty that I almost doubt myself.

She looks at the spots of spaghetti sauce that have dried on my shirt, then reaches over and pulls a hardened piece from my hair.

'Thanks,' I say.

She sighs. 'I'm sorry that happened.' She looks me in the eye. 'We're not together, you know?'

'No?'

She shakes her head. I'm intrigued that she felt the need to make that clear to me. After ten minutes of instruction on how to make pancakes – none of which I actually hear – the teacher, Mrs Benshoff, pairs Sarah and me together. We enter a door at the back of the room that leads to the kitchen, which is about three times the size of the actual classroom. It contains ten different kitchen units, complete with refrigerators, cabinets, sinks, ovens. Sarah walks into one, grabs an apron from a drawer, and puts it on.

'Will you tie this for me?' she asks.

I pull too much on the bow and have to tie it again. I can feel the contours of her lower back beneath my fingers. When hers is tied I put mine on and start to tie it myself.

'Here, silly,' she says, and then takes the straps and does it for me.

'Thanks.'

I try cracking the first egg but do it too hard, and none of the egg actually makes it into the bowl. Sarah laughs. She places a new egg in my hand and takes my hand in hers and shows me how to crack it on the rim of the bowl. She leaves her hand on mine for a second longer than is necessary. She looks at me and smiles.

'Like that.'

She mixes the batter and strands of hair fall into her face while she works. I desperately want to reach over and tuck the loose strands behind her ear, but I don't. Mrs Benshoff comes into our kitchen to check our progress. So far so good, which is all thanks to Sarah, since I have no idea what I'm doing.

'How do you like Ohio so far?' Sarah asks.

'It's okay. I could have used a better first day of school.'

She smiles. 'What happened, anyway? I was worried about you.'

'Would you believe it if I told you I was an alien?'

'Shut up,' she says playfully. 'What really happened?'

I laugh. 'I have really bad asthma. For some reason I had an attack yesterday,' I say, and feel regret at having to lie. I don't want her to see weakness within me, especially weakness that is untrue.

'Well, I'm glad you feel better.'

We make four pancakes. Sarah stacks all of them onto one plate. She dumps an absurd amount of maple syrup over them and hands me a fork. I look at the other students. Most are eating off of two plates. I reach over and cut a bite.

'Not bad,' I say while chewing.

I'm not hungry in the least, but I help her eat all of them. We alternate bites until the plate is empty. I have a stomachache when we finish. After, she cleans the dishes and I dry them. When the bell rings, we walk out of the room together.

'You know, you're not so bad for a sophomore,' she says, and nudges me. 'I don't care what they say.'

'Thanks, and you're not so bad yourself for a – whatever you are.'

'I'm a junior.'

We walk in silence for a few steps.

'You're not really going to fight Mark at the end of the day, are you?'

'I need my phone back. Besides, look at me,' I say, and motion to my shirt.

She shrugs. I stop at my locker. She takes note of the number.

'Well, you shouldn't,' she says.

'I don't want to.'

She rolls her eyes. 'Boys and their fights. Anyway, I'll see you tomorrow.'

'Have a good rest of the day,' I say.

After my ninth-period class, American history, I take slow steps to my locker. I think of just leaving the school quietly, without looking for Mark. But then I realize I will forever be labeled a coward.

I get to my locker and empty my bag of the books I don't need. Then I just stand there and feel the nervousness that begins to course through me. My hands are still normal. I think of throwing the gloves on as a precaution, but I don't. I take a deep breath and close the locker door.

'Hi,' I hear, the voice startling me. It's Sarah. She glances behind her, and looks back at me. 'I have something for you.'

'It's not more pancakes, is it? I still feel like I'm about to burst.'

She laughs nervously.

'It's not pancakes. But if I give it to you, you have to promise me you won't fight.'

'Okay,' I say.

She looks behind her again and quickly reaches into the front pocket of her bag. She pulls out my phone and gives it to me.

'How did you get this?'

She shrugs.

'Does Mark know?'

'Nope. So are you still going to be a tough guy?' she asks.

'I guess not.'

'Good.'

'Thank you,' I say. I can't believe she went to such lengths to help me – she barely knows me. But I'm not complaining.

'You're welcome,' she says, then turns and rushes down the hall. I watch her the whole way, unable to stop smiling. When I head out, Mark James and eight of his friends meet me in the lobby.

'Well, well, well,' Mark says. 'Actually made it through the day, huh?'

'Sure did. And look what I found,' I say, holding my phone up for him to see. His jaw drops. I pass by him, head down the hall and walk out of the building.

8

Henri is parked exactly where he said he would be. I jump in the truck, still smiling.

'Good day?' he asks.

'Not bad. Got my phone back.'

'No fighting?'

'Nothing major.'

He looks at me suspiciously. 'Do I even want to know what that means?'

'Probably not.'

'Did your hands come on at all?'

'No,' I lie. 'How was your day?'

He follows the driveway around the school. 'It was good. I drove an hour and a half to Columbus after dropping you off.'

'Why Columbus?'

'Big banks there. I didn't want to draw suspicion by requesting a transfer for an amount of money larger than what is collectively contained within the entire town.'

I nod. 'Smart thinking.'

He pulls onto the road.

'So are you going to tell me her name?'

'Huh?' I ask.

'There has to be a reason for that ridiculous smile of yours. The most obvious reason is a girl.'

'How'd you know?'

'John, my friend, back on Lorien this ol' Cêpan was quite the ladies' man.'

'Get out of here,' I say. 'There is no such thing as a ladies' man on Lorien.'

He nods approvingly. 'You've been paying attention.'

The Loric are a monogamous people. When we fall in love, it's for life. Marriage comes around the age of twenty-five, give or take, and has nothing to do with law. It's based more on promise and commitment than anything else. Henri was married for twenty years before he left with me. Ten years have passed but I know he still misses his wife every single day.

'So who is she?' he asks.

'Her name is Sarah Hart. She's the daughter of the real-estate agent you got the house from. She's in two of my classes. She's a junior.'

He nods. 'Pretty?'

'Absolutely. And smart.'

'Yeah,' he draws out slowly. 'I've been expecting this for a long time now. Just keep in mind that we might have to leave at a moment's notice.'

'I know,' I say, and the rest of the trip home is made in silence.

When I get home, the Loric Chest is sitting on the kitchen table. It's the size of a microwave oven, almost perfectly square, a foot and a half by a foot and a half. Excitement shoots through me. I walk up to it and grab the lock in my hand.

'I think I'm more excited about learning how this is unlocked than about what's actually in it,' I say.

'Really? Well, I can show you how it's unlocked and then we can just relock it and forget about what's inside.'

I smile at him. 'Let's not be rash. Come on. What's inside?'

'It's your Inheritance.'

'What do you mean, my Inheritance?'

'It's what's given to each Garde at birth to be used by his or her Keeper when the Garde is coming into his or her Legacy.'

I nod with exhilaration. 'So what's in it?'

'Your Inheritance.'

His coy response frustrates me. I pick up the lock and try to force it open as I've always tried doing. Of course it doesn't budge.

'You can't open it without me, and I can't open it without you,' Henri says.

'Well, how do we open it? There isn't a keyhole.'

'By will.'

'Oh, come on, Henri. Quit being secretive.'

He takes the lock from me. 'The lock only opens when we're together, and only after your first Legacy appears.'

He walks to the front door and sticks his head out, then he closes and locks it. He walks back. 'Press your palm against the side of the lock,' he says, and I do.

'It's warm,' I say.

'Good. That means you're ready.'

'Now what?'

He presses his palm against the other side of the lock and interlocks his fingers with mine. A second passes. The lock snaps open.

'Amazing!' I say.

'It's protected by a Loric charm, just like you are. It can't be broken. You could run over it with a steamroller and it wouldn't even be dented. Only the two of us can open it together. Unless I die; then you can open it yourself.'

'Well,' I say, 'I hope that doesn't happen.'

I try to lift the top of the box, but Henri reaches over and stops me.

'Not yet,' he says. 'There are things in here you aren't ready to see. Go sit on the couch.'

'Henri, come on.'

'Just trust me,' he says.

I shake my head and sit down. He opens the box and removes a rock that is probably six inches long, two inches thick. He relocks the box, then brings the rock over to me. It is perfectly smooth and oblong, clear on the outside but cloudy in the center.

'What is it?' I ask.

'A Loric crystal.'

'What's it for?'

'Hold it,' he says, handing it to me. The second my hands come into contact with it both lights snap on in my palms. They are even brighter than the day before. The rock begins to warm. I hold it up to look more closely at it. The cloudy mass in the center is swirling, turning in on itself like a wave. I can also feel the pendant around my neck heating up. I'm thrilled by all this new development. My whole life has been spent impatiently waiting for my powers to arrive. Sure, there were times when I hoped they never would, mainly so we could finally settle somewhere and live a normal life; but for now – holding a crystal that contains what looks like a ball of smoke in its center, and knowing my hands are resistant to heat and fire, and that more Legacies are on the way that will then be followed by my major power (the power that will allow me to fight) – well, it's all pretty cool and exciting. I can't wipe the smile from my face.

'What is happening to it?'

'It's tied to your Legacy. Your touch activates it. If you

weren't developing Lumen, then the crystal itself would light up the way your hands are. Instead it's the other way around.'

I stare at the crystal, watching the smoke circle and glow.

'Shall we start?' Henri asks.

I nod my head rapidly. 'Hell, yes.'

The day has turned cold. The house is silent aside from the occasional gust of wind rattling the windows. I lie on my back on top of the wooden coffee table. My hands dangle over the sides. At some point Henri will build a fire beneath them both. My breathing is slow and steady, as Henri has instructed.

'You have to keep your eyes closed,' he says. 'Just listen to the wind. There might be a slight burning in your arms when I drag the crystal up them. Ignore it as best as you can.'

I listen to the wind blow through the trees outside. I can somehow feel them sway and bend.

Henri begins with my right hand. He presses the crystal against the back of it, then pushes it up my wrist and onto my forearm. There is a burn as he has predicted, but not enough of one to make me pull my arm free.

'Let your mind drift, John. Go where you need to go.'

I don't know what he's talking about, but I try to clear my mind and breathe slowly. All at once I feel myself drift away. From somewhere I can feel the sun's warmth upon my face, and a wind far warmer than what is blowing beyond our walls. When I open my eyes I'm no longer in Ohio.

I'm above a vast expanse of treetops, nothing but jungle as far as I can see. Blue sky, the sun beating down, a sun almost double the size of Earth's. A warm, soft wind blows through my hair. Down below, rivers forge deep ravines that cut through the greenery. I am floating above one of them. Animals of all shapes and sizes – some long and slender, some with short arms and stout bodies, some with hair and some with dark-colored skin that looks rough to the touch – are drinking from the cool waters at the river's bank. There is a bend in the horizon line far off in the distance, and I know that I am on Lorien. It's a planet ten times smaller than Earth, and it's possible to see the curve of its surface when looking from far enough away.

Somehow I'm able to fly. I rush up and twist in the air, then torpedo down and speed along the river's surface. The animals lift their heads and watch with curiosity, but not with fear. Lorien in its prime, covered with growth, inhabited by animals. In a way, it looks like what I imagine Earth looked like millions of years ago, when the land ruled the lives of its creatures, before humans arrived and started ruling the land. Lorien in its prime; I know that it no longer looks like this today. I must be living a memory. Surely it isn't my own?

And then the day skips ahead to darkness. Off in the distance a great display of fireworks begins, rising high in the sky and exploding into shapes of animals and trees with the dark sky and the moons and a million stars serving as a brilliant backdrop.

'I can feel their desperation,' I hear from somewhere. I turn and look around me. There is nobody there. 'They know where one of the others is, but the charm still holds. They can't touch her until they've killed you first. But they continue to track her.'

I fly up high, then dip low, seeking the source of the voice. Where is it coming from?

'Now is when we have to be most cautious. Now is when we have to stay ahead of them.'

I push forward towards the fireworks. The voice unnerves me. Perhaps the loud booms will drown it out.

'They had hoped to kill us all well before your Legacies developed. But we've kept hidden. We have to stay calm. The first three panicked. The first three are dead. We have to stay smart and cautious. When we panic is when mistakes are made. They know it will only get harder for them the more developed the rest of you are, and when you are all fully developed, the war will be waged. We will hit back and seek our revenge, and they know it.'

I see the bombs fall from miles above Lorien's surface. Explosions shake the ground and the air, screams carry on the wind, bursts of fire sweep across the land and the trees. The forest burns. There must be a thousand different aircraft, all dropping from high in the sky to land on Lorien. Mogadorian soldiers pour out, carrying guns and grenades that hold powers far greater than what is used in warfare here. They are taller than we are, and still look similar except in the face. They have no pupils and their irises are a deep magenta color, some of them black. Dark, heavy circles rim their eyes and there's a pallor to their skin – an almost discolored, bruised quality to it. Their teeth glint between lips that never seem to close, teeth that look filed, coming to an unnatural point.

The beasts of Mogadore come off the planes close behind, the same cold look in their eyes. Some of them are as big as houses, razor teeth showing, roaring so loud that it hurts my ears.

'We got careless, John. That is how we were defeated so easily,' he says. I know now that the voice I'm hearing is

Henri's. But he is nowhere to be seen, and I can't take my eyes off the killing and the destruction below me to look for him. People are running everywhere, fighting back. As many Mogadorians as Loric are being killed. But the Loric are losing the battle against the beasts, which are killing our people by the dozens: breathing fire, gnashing teeth, viciously swinging arms and tails. Time is speeding along, going much faster than normal. How much has passed? An hour? Two?

The Garde lead the fight, their Legacies on full display. Some are flying, some able to run so fast that they become a blur, and some disappear entirely. Lasers shoot from hands, bodies become engulfed in flames, storm clouds are brewed coupled with harsh winds above those able to control the weather. But they are still losing. They are outnumbered five hundred to one. Their powers are not enough.

'Our guard had dropped. The Mogadorians had planned well, picking that exact moment when they knew we were at our most vulnerable, when the planet's Elders were gone. Pittacus Lore, the greatest of them, their leader, had assembled them before the attack. Nobody knows what happened to them, or where they went, or if they are even still alive. Perhaps the Mogadorians took them out first, and once the Elders were out of the way, that is when they attacked. All we really know is that there was a column of shimmering white light that shot into the sky as far as anyone could see on the day the Elders assembled. It lasted the entire day, then vanished. We, as a people, should have recognized it as a sign that something was amiss, but we didn't. We have no one to blame but ourselves for what happened. We were lucky to get anyone off the planet, much less nine young

Garde who might someday continue the fight, and keep our race alive.'

Off in the distance a ship shoots high and fast into the air, a blue stream following behind it. I watch it from my vantage point in the sky until it disappears. There is something familiar about it. And then it dawns on me: I am in that ship, and Henri is, too. It's the ship carrying us to Earth. The Loric must have known they were beaten. Why else would they send us away?

Useless slaughter. That is how it all looks to me. I land on the ground and walk through a ball of fire. Rage sweeps through me. Men and women are dying, Garde and Cêpan, along with defenseless children. How can this be tolerated? How can the hearts of the Mogadorians be so hardened as to do all this? And why was I spared?

I lunge at a nearby soldier but go straight through him and fall down. Everything I am witnessing has already happened. I'm a spectator of our own demise and there's nothing I can do.

I turn around and face a beast that must be forty feet tall, broad shouldered, with red eyes and horns twenty feet in length. Drool falls from its long, sharp teeth. It lets out a roar, and then lunges.

It passes through me but takes out dozens of Loric around me. Just like that, every one of them gone. And the beast keeps going, taking out more Loric.

Through the scene of destruction I hear a scratching noise, something separate from the carnage on Lorien. I am drifting away, or drifting back. Two hands press down upon my shoulders. My eyes snap open and I'm back in our home in Ohio. My arms are dangling over the coffee table. Inches below them are two cauldrons of fire, and both of my hands and wrists are completely submerged in the flames. I don't feel the effects at all. Henri stands over me. The scratching I heard a minute ago is coming from the front porch.

'What is that?' I whisper, sitting up.

'I don't know,' he says.

We are both silent, straining to listen. Three more scratches at the door. Henri looks down at me.

'There's somebody out there,' he says.

I look at the clock on the wall. Nearly an hour has passed. I'm sweating, out of breath, unsettled by the scenes of slaughter I just witnessed. For the first time in my life I truly understand what happened on Lorien. Before tonight the events were just part of another story, not all that different from the many I have read in books. But now I have seen the blood, the tears, the dead. I have seen the destruction. It's a part of who I am.

Outside, darkness has set in. Three more scratches at the door, a low groan. We both jump. I immediately think of the low groans I heard coming from the beasts.

Henri rushes into the kitchen and grabs a knife from the drawer beside the sink. 'Get behind the couch.'

'What, why?'

'Because I said so.'

'You think that little knife is going to take down a Mogadorian?'

'If I hit them straight in the heart it will. Now get down.'

I scramble off the coffee table and crouch behind the sofa. The two cauldrons of fire are still going, faint visions of Lorien still moving through my mind. An impatient growl comes from the other side of the front door. There is no mistaking that somebody, or something, is out there. My heart races.

'Keep down,' Henri says.

I lift my head so that I can peer over the back of the couch. All that blood, I think. Surely they knew they were outmatched. But they fought to the end anyway, dying to save each other, dying to save Lorien. Henri grips the knife tightly. He slowly reaches for the brass knob. Anger sweeps through me. I hope it *is* one of them. Let a Mogadorian come through that door. He'll meet his match.

There's no way I'm staying behind this couch. I reach over and grab one of the cauldrons, thrust my hand into it and pull out a burning piece of wood with a pointed end. It's cool to the touch, but the fire burns on, sweeping over and around my hand. I hold the piece of wood like a dagger. *Let them come,* I think. *There will be no more running.* Henri looks over at me, takes a deep breath and rips the front door open.

9

Every muscle in my body is flexed, everything tense. Henri jumps through the doorway and I am ready to follow. I can feel the *thud-thud-thud* in my chest. My fingers are white-knuckled around the piece of wood still burning. A gust of wind bursts through the door and the fire dances in my hand and crawls up my wrist. No one is there. All at once Henri's body relaxes and he chuckles, looking down at his feet. There, looking up at Henri through the tops of his eyes, is the same beagle I saw yesterday at school. The dog wags his tail and paws at the ground. Henri reaches down and pets him; then the dog pushes past and trots into the house with his tongue dangling.

'What's he doing here?' I ask.

'You know this dog?'

'I saw him at school. He was following me around yesterday after you dropped me off.'

I put the piece of wood back and wipe my hand on my jeans, leaving a trail of black ash down the front. The dog sits at my feet and looks up expectantly, his tail thumping against the hardwood floor. I sit on the couch and watch both fires burn. Now that the excitement of the situation is over, my mind goes back to what I just saw in my vision. I can still hear the screams in my ears, still see the way the blood shimmered in the grass in the moonlight, still see the bodies and fallen trees, the red glow in the eyes of the beasts of Mogadore and the terror in the eyes of the Loric.

I look at Henri. 'I saw what happened. At least the beginning of it.'

He nods. 'I thought you might.'

'I could hear your voice. Were you talking to me?'

'Yes.'

'I don't understand,' I say. 'It was a massacre. There was too much hatred for them to only be interested in our resources. There was more to it than that.'

Henri sighs and sits on the coffee table across from me. The dog jumps into my lap. I pet him. He's filthy, his coat stiff and oily under my hand. There is a tag in the shape of a football attached to the front of his collar. It's an old tag, most of the brown paint worn away. I take it in my hand, the number 19 on one side, the name BERNIE KOSAR on the other.

'Bernie Kosar,' I say. The dog wags his tail. 'I guess that's his name, same as that dude in the poster on my wall. Popular guy around here, I guess.' I run my hand down his back. 'He doesn't seem like he has a home,' I say. 'And he's hungry.' Somehow I can tell.

Henri nods. He looks down at Bernie Kosar. The dog stretches out, rests his chin on his paws, and closes his eyes. I flip open the lighter and hold the flame over my fingers, then my palm, then run it up the underside of my arm. Only when the flame is an inch or two away from my elbow do I feel the burn. Whatever Henri has done has worked, and my resistance has spread. I wonder how long it will take until all of me becomes resistant.

'So what happened?' I ask.

Henri takes a deep breath. 'I've had those visions, too. So real it's like you're there.'

'I never realized how bad it all was. I mean, I know you

had told me, but I didn't truly understand it until I saw it with my own eyes.'

'The Mogadorians are different than we are, secretive and manipulative, untrusting of almost everything. They have certain powers, but they're not powers like ours. They are gregarious and thrive in crowded cities. The more densely populated, the better. That is why you and I stay out of cities now, even when living in one might make it easier to blend in. It would make it a hell of a lot easier for them to blend in as well.

'About a hundred years ago Mogadore began to die, much like Lorien did twenty-five thousand years before that. They didn't respond the way we did, though – didn't understand it the way the human population is beginning to now. They ignored it. They killed their oceans and flooded their rivers and lakes with waste and sewage to keep adding to their cities. The vegetation started to die, which caused the herbivores to die, and then the carnivores weren't far behind. They knew they had to do something drastic.'

Henri closes his eyes, remains silent for a full minute.

'Do you know the closest life-sustaining planet to Mogadore?' he finally asks.

'Yes, it's Lorien. Or was, I guess.'

Henri nods. 'Yes, it *is* Lorien. And I'm sure you know now that it was our resources they were after.'

I nod. Bernie Kosar lifts his head and lets out a deep yawn. Henri heats a cooked chicken breast in the microwave, cuts it into strips, then carries the plate back to the couch and sets it in front of the dog. He eats with ferocity, as though he hasn't eaten in days.

'There are a large number of Mogadorians on Earth,' Henri continues. 'I don't know how many are here, but I can feel them when I sleep. Sometimes I can see them in my dreams. I can never tell where they are, or what they are saying. But I see them. And I don't think the six of you are the only reason there are so many of them here.'

'What do you mean? Why else would they be here?'

Henri looks me in the eye. 'Do you know what the second-closest life-sustaining planet is to Mogadore?'

I nod. 'It's Earth, isn't it?'

'Mogadore is double the size of Lorien, but Earth is five times the size of Mogadore. In terms of defense Earth is better prepared for an offensive because of its size. The Mogadorians will need to understand this planet better before they can attack. I can't necessarily tell you how we were defeated so easily because there's much of it I still don't understand. But I can say for sure that part of it was a combination of their knowledge of our planet and our people, and the fact that we had no defense other than our intelligence and the Garde's Legacies. Say what you will about the Mogadorians, but they are brilliant strategists when it comes to war.'

We sit through another silence, the wind still roaring outside.

'I don't think they're interested in taking Earth's resources,' Henri says.

I sigh and look up at him. 'Why not?'

'Mogadore is still dying. Even though they've patched the more pressing matters, the planet's death is inevitable, and they know it. I think they're planning to kill the humans. I think they want to make Earth their permanent home.'

I bathe Bernie Kosar after dinner, using shampoo and conditioner. I brush him with an old comb left in one of the drawers from the last tenant. He looks and smells much better, but his collar still stinks. I throw it away. Before going to bed I hold open the front door for him, but he isn't interested in going back outside. Instead he lies down on the floor and rests his chin on his front paws. I can feel his desire to stay in the house with us. I wonder if he can feel my desire for the same.

'I think we have a new pet,' Henri says.

I smile. As soon as I saw him earlier I was hoping Henri would let me keep him.

'Looks like it,' I say.

A half hour later I crawl into bed and Bernie Kosar jumps up with me and curls into a ball at my feet. He is snoring within minutes. I lie on my back for a while, staring into the darkness, a million different thoughts swimming in my head. Images from the war: the greedy, hungry look of the Mogadorians; the angry, hard look of the beasts; the death and the blood. I think of the beauty of Lorien. Will it again sustain life, or will Henri and I go on waiting here on Earth forever?

I try to push the thoughts and images from my mind, but they don't stay gone for very long. I get up and pace for a while. Bernie Kosar lifts his head and watches me, but then drops it and falls back to sleep. I sigh, grab my phone from the nightstand and go through it to make sure Mark James didn't mess with anything. Henri's number is still there, but it is no longer the only entry. Another number, listed under the name of 'Sarah Hart' has been added. After the last bell rang, and before coming to my locker, Sarah added her number to my phone.

I close the phone, set it on the nightstand, and smile. Two minutes pass and I check my phone again to make sure I wasn't seeing things. I wasn't. I snap it shut and set it down, only to lift it again five minutes later just to look at her number again. I don't know how long it takes to fall asleep, but eventually I do. When I wake in the morning my phone is still in my hand, resting against my chest.

10

Bernie Kosar is scratching at my bedroom door when I wake. I let him outside. He patrols the yard, rushing along with his nose to the ground. Once he's covered all four corners he bolts across the yard and disappears into the woods. I close the door and jump into the shower. I walk out ten minutes later and he's back inside, sitting on the couch. His tail wags when he sees me.

'You let him in?' I ask Henri, who is at the kitchen table with his laptop open and four newspapers stacked in front of him.

'Yes.'

After a quick breakfast, we head out. Bernie Kosar rushes ahead of us, then stops and sits looking up at the passenger door of the truck.

'That's kind of weird, don't you think?' I say.

Henri shrugs. 'Apparently he's no stranger to car rides. Let him in.'

I open the door and he jumps in. He sits in the middle seat with his tongue dangling. When we pull out of the driveway he moves into my lap and paws at the window. I roll it down and he sticks half his body out, mouth still open, the wind flapping his ears. Three miles later Henri pulls in to the school. I open the door and Bernie Kosar jumps out ahead of me. I lift him back into the truck but he jumps right back out. I lift him back in again and have to block him from jumping out while I close the truck door.

He stands on his hind legs with his front paws on the ledge of the door, the window still down. I pat him on the head.

'Have your gloves?' Henri asks.

'Yep.'

'Phone?'

'Yep.'

'How do you feel?'

'I feel good,' I say.

'Okay. Call me if you have any sort of trouble.'

He pulls away and Bernie Kosar watches from the back window until the truck disappears around the turn.

I feel a similar nervousness as I did the day before, but for different reasons. Part of me wants to see Sarah right away, though part of me hopes that I don't see her at all. I'm not sure what I'll say to her. What if I can't think of anything at all and stand there looking foolish? What if she's with Mark when I see her? Should I acknowledge her and risk another confrontation, or just walk by and pretend that I don't see either of them? At the very least I'll see them both in second period. There's no getting around that.

I head to my locker. My bag is filled with books I was supposed to read the night before but never opened. Too many thoughts and images running through my head. They haven't gone away and it's hard to imagine they ever will. It was all so different from what I expected. Death isn't like what they show you in the movies. The sounds, the looks, the smells. So different.

At my locker I notice immediately that something's off. The metal handle is covered with dirt, or what looks like dirt. I'm not sure if I should open it, but then I take a deep breath and force the handle up.

The locker is half filled with manure and as I swing the

door open, much of it comes pouring out onto the floor, covering my shoes. The smell is horrendous. I slam the door shut. Sam Goode was standing behind it and his sudden appearance from out of nowhere startles me. He is looking forlorn, wearing a white NASA T-shirt only slightly different from the one he wore yesterday.

'Hi, Sam,' I say.

He looks down at the pile of manure on the floor, then back at me.

'You, too?' I ask.

He nods.

'I'm going to the principal's office. Do you want to come?'

He shakes his head, then turns and walks away without saying a word. I walk to Mr Harris's office, knock on his door, then enter without waiting for his reply. He is sitting behind his desk, wearing a tie that is tiled with the school mascot, no less than twenty tiny pirate heads scattered across the front of it. He smiles proudly at me.

'It's a big day, John,' he says. I don't know what he is talking about. 'The reporters from the *Gazette* should be here within the hour. Front page!'

Then I remember, Mark James's big interview with the local paper.

'You must be very proud,' I say.

'I'm proud of each and every one of Paradise's students.' The smile doesn't leave his face. He leans back in his chair, locks his fingers together, and rests his hands on his stomach. 'What can I do for you?'

'I just wanted to let you know that my locker was filled with manure this morning.'

'What do you mean "filled"?'

'I mean the whole thing was full of manure.'

'With manure?' he asks confusedly.

'Yes.'

He laughs. I'm taken aback by his total lack of regard, and anger surges through me. My face is warm.

'I wanted to let you know so it could be cleaned. Sam Goode's locker is filled with it, too.'

He sighs and shakes his head. 'I'll send Mr Hobbs, the janitor, down immediately and we'll make a full investigation.'

'We both know who did it, Mr Harris.'

He flashes a patronizing grin at me. 'I'll handle the investigation, Mr Smith.'

There's no point in saying anything further, so I walk out of his office and head to the bathroom to run cold water over my hands and face. I have to calm down. I don't want to have to wear the gloves again today. Maybe I should do nothing at all, just let it slide. Will that end it? And besides, what other choice is there? I'm outmatched and my only ally is a hundred-pound sophomore with a penchant for the extraterrestrial. Maybe that isn't the whole truth – maybe I have another ally in Sarah Hart.

I look down. My hands are fine, no glow. I walk out of the bathroom. The janitor is already sweeping the manure from my locker, lifting out books and placing them in the trash. I walk past him and into the classroom and wait for class to start. Rules of grammar are discussed, the main topic being the difference between a gerund and a verb, and why a gerund is not a verb. I pay closer attention than I did the day before, but as the end of the period nears I start to get nervous about the next class. But not because I might see Mark . . . because I might see Sarah. Will she smile at me again today? I think it'll be best to arrive before she does so I can find my seat and watch her walk in. That way I can see if she says hello to me first.

When the bell rings, I dash out of class and rush down the hall. I'm the first one to enter astronomy. The classroom fills and Sam sits beside me again. Just before the bell rings Sarah and Mark enter together. She's dressed in a white button-up shirt and black pants. She smiles at me before sitting down. I smile back. Mark doesn't look my way at all. I can still smell the manure on my shoes, or maybe the odor is coming from Sam's.

He pulls a pamphlet from his bag with the title *They Walk Among Us* on the cover. It looks as though it was printed in somebody's basement. Sam flips to an article in the center and starts reading intently.

I look at Sarah four desks in front of me, at her hair pulled back in a ponytail. I can see the nape of her slender neck. She crosses her legs and sits straight in her chair. I wish I were sitting beside her, that I could reach over and take her hand in mine. I wish it were eighth period already. I wonder if I'll be her partner in home ec again.

Mrs Burton begins lecturing. She's still on the topic of Saturn. Sam takes out a sheet of paper and begins scribbling wildly, pausing at times to consult an article in the magazine he has opened beside him. I look over his shoulder and read the title: 'Entire Montana Town Abducted by Aliens.'

Before last night I would never have pondered such a theory. But Henri believes the Mogadorians are plotting to take over Earth, and I must admit, even though the theory in Sam's publication is ludicrous, at its most basic level there might be something there. I know for a fact that the Loric have visited Earth many times over the life of this planet. We watched Earth develop, watched it through the times of growth and abundance when everything moved, and through the times of ice and snow when nothing did. We helped the humans, taught them to make fire, gave them the tools to develop speech and language, which is why our language is so similar to the languages of Earth. And even though we never abducted humans, that doesn't mean it's never been done. I look at Sam. I've never met somebody with a fascination in aliens to the point of reading and taking notes on conspiracy theories.

Just then the door opens and Mr Harris sticks his smiling face in.

'Sorry to interrupt, Mrs Burton. I'm going to have to snag Mark from you. The *Gazette* reporters are here to interview him for the paper,' he says loudly enough so everyone in the class can hear.

Mark stands, grabs his bag and casually strolls out of the room. From the doorway I see Mr Harris pat him on the back. Then I look back at Sarah, wishing I could sit in the empty seat beside her.

Fourth period is physical education. Sam is in my class. After changing we sit beside each other on the gymnasium floor. He is wearing tennis shoes, shorts, a T-shirt two or three sizes too large. He looks like a stork, all knees and elbows, somewhat lanky even though he's short.

The gym teacher, Mr Wallace, stands firmly in front of us, his feet shoulder width apart, his hands clenched into fists on his hips.

'All right, guys, listen up. This is probably the last chance we'll get to work outdoors, so make it count. One-mile run, as hard as you can. Your times will be noted and saved for when we run the mile again in the spring. So run hard!'

The outside track is made of synthetic rubber. It circles around the football field, and beyond it are some woods that I imagine might lead to our house, but I'm not sure. The wind is cool and goose bumps traverse the length of Sam's arms. He tries to rub them away.

'Have you run this before?' I ask.

Sam nods. 'We ran it the second week of class.'

'What was your time?'

'Nine minutes and fifty-four seconds.'

I look at him. 'I thought skinny kids are supposed to be fast.'

'Shut up,' he says.

I run side by side with Sam towards the back of the crowd. Four laps. That is how many times I must circle the track to have run a mile. Halfway around I begin to pull away from Sam. I wonder how fast I could run a mile if I really tried. Two minutes, maybe one, maybe less?

The exercise feels great, and without paying much attention, I pass the lead runner. Then I slow and feign exhaustion. When I do I see a brown and white blur come dashing out of the bushes by the entrance of the grandstand and head straight towards me. *My mind is playing tricks on me*, I think. I look away and keep running. I pass the teacher. He is holding a stopwatch. He yells words of encouragement but he is looking behind me, away from the track. I follow his eyes. They are fixated on the brown and white blur. It is still coming straight for me and all at once the images from the day before come rushing back. The Mogadorian beasts. There were small ones too, with teeth that glinted in the light like razor blades, fast creatures intent on killing. I start sprinting.

I run halfway around the track in a dead sprint before I

turn back around. There is nothing behind me. I have outrun it. Twenty seconds have passed. Then I turn back around and the thing is right in front of me. It must have cut across the field. I stop dead in my tracks and my perspective corrects itself. It's Bernie Kosar! He's sitting in the middle of the track with his tongue dangling, tail wagging.

'Bernie Kosar!' I yell. 'You scared the hell out of me!'

I resume running at a slow pace and Bernie Kosar runs alongside me. I hope nobody noticed how fast I ran. Then I stop and bend over as though I have cramps and can't catch my breath. I walk for a bit. Then I jog a little. Before I finish the second lap two people have passed me.

'Smith! What happened? You were dusting everyone!' Mr Wallace yells when I run by him.

I breathe heavily, for show. 'I – have – asthma,' I say.

He shakes his head in disapproval. 'And here I thought I had this year's Ohio state track champion in my class.'

I shrug and keep going, stopping every so often to walk. Bernie Kosar stays with me, sometimes walking, sometimes trotting. When I start the last lap Sam catches up to me and we run together. His face is bright red.

'So what were you reading in astronomy today?' I ask. 'An entire Montana town abducted by aliens?'

He grins at me. 'Yeah, that's the theory,' he says somewhat shyly, as though embarrassed.

'Why would an entire town be abducted?'

Sam shrugs, doesn't answer.

'No, really?' I ask.

'Do you really want to know?'

'Of course.'

'Well, the theory is that the government has been allowing alien abductions in exchange for technology.'

'Really? What kind of technology?' I ask.

'Like chips for supercomputers and formulas for more bombs and green technologies. Stuff like that.'

'Green technology for live specimens? Weird. Why do aliens want to abduct humans?'

'So they can study us.'

'But why? I mean, what reason could they possibly have?'

'So that when Armageddon comes they'll know our weaknesses and be able to easily defeat us by exposing them.'

I'm kind of taken aback by his answer, but only because of the scenes still playing in my head from the night before, remembering the weapons I saw the Mogadorians use, and the massive beasts.

'Wouldn't it be easy for them if they already have bombs and technologies far superior to our own?'

'Well, some people seem to think that they're hoping we'll kill ourselves first.'

I look at Sam. He is smiling at me, trying to decide whether I'm taking the conversation seriously.

'Why would they want us to kill ourselves first? What is their incentive?'

'Because they're jealous.'

'Jealous of us? Why, because of our rugged good looks?'

Sam laughs. 'Something like that.'

I nod. We run in silence for a minute and I can tell Sam is having a tough time, breathing heavily. 'How did you get interested in all this?'

He shrugs. 'It's just a hobby,' he says, though I get the distinct feeling that he's keeping something from me.

We finish the mile at eight minutes fifty-nine seconds, better than the last time Sam ran it. Bernie Kosar follows the class back to the school. The others pet him, and when we walk in he tries to come in with us. I don't know how he knew where I was. Could he have memorized the way to the school this morning on the ride in? The thought seems ridiculous.

He stays at the door. I walk to the locker room with Sam and the second he catches his breath he rattles off a ton of other conspiracy theories, one right after another, most of which are laughable. I like him, and find him amusing, but sometimes I wish he would stop talking.

When home ec begins Sarah isn't in class. Mrs Benshoff gives instruction for the first ten minutes and then we head to the kitchen. I enter the station alone, resigned to the fact that I'll be cooking alone today, and as soon as that thought occurs to me, Sarah walks in.

'Did I miss anything good?' she asks.

'About ten minutes of quality time with me,' I say with a smile.

She laughs. 'I heard about your locker this morning. I'm sorry.'

'You put the manure there?' I ask.

She laughs again. 'No, of course not. But I know they're picking on you because of me.'

'They're just lucky I didn't use my superpowers and throw them into the next county.'

She playfully grabs my biceps. 'Right, these huge muscles. Your superpowers. Boy, they are lucky.'

Our project for the day is to make blueberry cupcakes. As we start mixing the batter, Sarah begins telling me about her history with Mark. They dated for two years, but the longer they were together, the more she drifted from her parents and her friends. She was Mark's girlfriend, nothing else. She knew she had started to change, to adopt some of his attitudes towards people: being mean and judgmental, thinking she was better than them. She also started drinking and her grades slipped. At the end of the last school year, her parents sent her to live with her aunt in Colorado for the summer. When she got there, she started taking long hikes in the mountains, taking pictures of the scenery with her aunt's camera. She fell in love with photography and had the best summer ever, realizing there was far more to life than being a cheerleader and dating the quarterback of the football team. When she got home she broke up with Mark and quit cheerleading, and made a vow that she was going to be good, and kind, to everyone. Mark hasn't gotten over it. She says he still considers her his girlfriend, and believes she's going to come back to him. She says the only thing she misses about him are his dogs, which she hung out with whenever she was at his house. I then tell her about Bernie Kosar, and how he showed up at our doorstep unexpectedly after that first morning at the school.

We work as we talk. At one point I reach into the oven without the oven mitts and pull out the cupcake pan. She sees me do it and asks if I'm okay, and I pretend to be hurt, shake my hand as if it's burned, though I don't actually feel a thing. We go to the sink and Sarah runs lukewarm water to help with the burn that isn't there. When she sees my hand, I just shrug. As we're frosting the cupcakes, she asks about my phone, and tells me she noticed there was only one number in it. I tell her it's Henri's number, that I lost my old phone with all of my contacts. She asks if I left a girlfriend behind when we moved. I say no, and she smiles, which just about ruins me. Before class ends, she tells me about the upcoming Halloween festival in town, and says she hopes to see me there, that maybe we can hang out. I say yeah, that would be great, and pretend to be cool, even though I'm flying inside.

11

Images come to me, at random times, usually when I least expect them. Sometimes they are small and fleeting – my grandmother holding a glass of water and opening her mouth to say something – but I never know the words because the image vanishes as quickly as it came. Sometimes they are longer, more lifelike: my grandfather pushing me on a swing. I can feel the strength in his arms as he pushes me up, the butterflies in the pit of my stomach as I race down. My laughter carries on the wind. Then the image is gone. Sometimes I explicitly remember the images from my past, remember being a part of them. But sometimes they are as new to me as though they never happened before.

In the living room, with Henri running the Loric crystal up each of my arms, my hands suspended over flames, I see the following: I am young – three, maybe four – running through our front yard of newly clipped grass. Beside me is an animal with a body like a dog, but with a coat like a tiger. His head is round, his body barrel chested atop short legs. Unlike any animal I have ever seen. He crouches, poised to leap at me. I can't stop laughing. Then he jumps and I try to catch him but I'm too small and both of us fall to the grass. We wrestle. He is stronger than I am. Then he jumps in the air, and instead of falling back to the ground as I expect, he turns himself into a bird and flies up and around me, hovering just beyond my reach. He circles, then comes down, shoots between my legs, lands twenty feet away. He changes into an animal that looks like a monkey without a tail. He crouches low to lunge at me.

Just then a man comes up the walk. He is young, dressed in a silver and blue rubber suit that is tight on his body, the kind of suit I've seen divers wear. He speaks to me in a language that I don't understand. He says the name 'Hadley' and nods to the animal. Hadley runs over to him, his shape changing from a monkey to something larger, something bearlike with a lion's mane. Their heads are level, and the man scratches Hadley beneath the chin. Then my grandfather comes out of the house. He looks young, but I know that he must be at least fifty.

He shakes hands with the man. They speak but I don't understand what they are saying. Then the man looks at me, smiles, lifts his hand out, and all of a sudden I'm off the ground and flying through the air. Hadley follows, as a bird again. I'm in full control of my body, but the man controls where I go, moving his hand to the left or to the right. Hadley and I play in midair, him tickling me with his beak, me trying to get a grip on him. And then my eyes snap open and the image is gone.

'Your grandfather could make himself invisible at will,' I hear Henri say, and I close my eyes again. The crystal continues up my arm, spreading the fire repellent to the rest of my body. 'One of the rarest Legacies there is, developing only in one per cent of our people, and he was one of them. He could make himself and whatever he was touching completely disappear.

'There was one time he wanted to play a joke on me, before I knew what his Legacies were. You were three years old and I had just started working with your family. I came to your house for the first time the day before, and as I came up the hill for my second day the house wasn't there. There was a driveway, and a car, and the tree, but no house. I thought I was losing my mind. I continued past it. Then when I knew I had gone too far I turned back and there, some distance away, was the house that I swore wasn't there before. So I started walking back, but when I came close enough the house again vanished. I just stood there looking at the spot where I knew it must be, but seeing only the trees beyond it. So I walked on. Only on my third time by did your grandfather make the house reappear for good. He couldn't stop laughing. We laughed about that day for the next year and a half, all the way till the very end.'

When I open my eyes I am back on the battlefield. More explosions, fire, death.

'Your grandfather was a good man,' Henri says. 'He loved to make people laugh, loved to tell jokes. I don't think there was ever a time that I left your house without having a stomachache from laughing so hard.'

The sky has turned red. A tree rips through the air, thrown by the man in silver and blue, the one I saw at the house. It takes out two of the Mogadorians and I want to cheer in victory. But what use is there in celebrating? No matter how many Mogadorians I see killed, the outcome of that day will not change. The Loric will still be defeated, every last one of them killed. I will still be sent to Earth.

'I never once saw the man get angry. When everyone else lost their temper, when stress encompassed them, your grandfather stayed calm. It was usually then that he would bring out his best jokes, and just like that everyone would be laughing again.'

The small beasts target the children. They are defenseless, holding sparklers in their hands from the celebration. That is how we are losing – only a few of the Loric are fighting the beasts, and the rest are trying to save the children.

'Your grandmother was different. She was quiet and reserved, very intelligent. Your elders complemented each other that way, your grandfather the carefree one, your grandmother working behind the scenes so that everything went off as planned.'

High in the sky I can still see the trail of blue smoke from the airship carrying us to Earth, carrying us Nine and our Keepers. Its presence unnerves the Mogadorians.

'And then there was Julianne, my wife.'

Far off in the distance there is an explosion, this one like the kind that comes from the liftoff of Earth's rockets. Another ship rises in the air, a trail of fire behind it. Slowly at first, then building speed. I'm confused. Our ships didn't use fire for liftoff; they didn't use oil or gasoline. They emitted a small blue trail of smoke that came from the crystals used to power them, never fire like this one. The second ship is slow and clumsy compared to the first, but it makes it, rising through the air, gaining speed. Henri never mentioned a second ship. Who is on it? Where is it going? The Mogadorians shout and point at it. Again, it causes them anxiety, and for a brief moment the Loric surge.

'She had the greenest eyes I'd ever seen, bright green like emeralds, plus a heart as big as the planet itself. Always helping others, constantly bringing in animals and keeping them as pets. I'll never know what it was she saw in me.'

The large beast has returned, the one with the red eyes and enormous horns. Drool mixed with blood falls from razor-sharp teeth so large they can't be contained within its mouth. The man in silver and blue is standing directly in front of it. He tries to lift the beast with his powers, and he gets it a few feet off the ground but then struggles and lifts no farther. The beast roars, shakes, and falls back to the ground. It forces ahead against the man's powers, but it can't break them. The man lifts it again. Sweat and blood glisten in the moonlight on his face. Then he doubles his hands over and the beast crashes to its side. The ground shakes. Thunder and lightning fill the sky but there's no rain to go with them.

'She was a late sleeper, and I always woke before she did. I would sit in the den and read the paper, make breakfast, go for a walk. Some mornings I would come back and she would still be sleeping. I was impatient, couldn't wait to start the day together. She made me feel good just to be around her. I would go in and try to rouse her. She would pull the covers over her head and growl at me. Almost every morning, always the same thing.'

The beast flails but the man is still in control. Other Garde have joined in, every one of them using a power on the mammoth beast, fire and lightning raining down upon it, streaks of lasers coming from all directions. Some Garde are doing damage unseen, standing away from it and holding their hands out in concentration. And then high up a collective storm brews, one major cloud growing and glowing in an otherwise cloudless sky, some sort of energy collecting within it. All Garde are in on it, all of them helping to create this cataclysmic haze. And then a final, massive bolt of lightning drops down and hits the beast where it lies. And there it dies.

'What could I do? What could anyone do? In total there were nineteen of us on that ship. You nine children and us nine Cêpan, chosen by no means other than where we happened to be that night, and the pilot who brought us here. We Cêpan couldn't fight, and what difference would it have made if we could? The Cêpan are bureaucrats, meant to keep the planet running, meant to teach, meant to train new Garde how to understand and manipulate their powers. We were never meant to be fighters. We would have been ineffective. We would have died like the rest. All we could do was leave. Leave with you to live and to one day restore to glory the most beautiful planet in all of the universe.'

I close my eyes and when I reopen them the fight has ended. Smoke rises from the ground among the dead and the dying. Trees broken, the forests burned, nothing standing save the few Mogadorians that have lived to tell the tale. The sun rising to the south and a pale glow growing on the barren land bathed in red. Mounds of bodies, not all of them intact, not all of them whole. On top of one mound is the man in silver and blue, dead like the rest. There are no discernible marks on his body, but he is dead all the same.

My eyes snap open. I can't breathe, and my mouth is dry, parched.

'Here,' Henri says. He helps me off the coffee table, guides me into the kitchen and pulls out a chair for me. Tears are coming to my eyes though I try to blink them back. Henri brings me a glass of water and I drink every bit of it without stopping. I give him the glass and he refills it. I drop my head, still struggling to breathe. I drink the second glass, then look at Henri.

'Why didn't you ever tell me about a second ship?' I ask.

'What are you talking about?'

'There was a second ship,' I say.

'Where was there a second ship?'

'On Lorien, the day we left. A second ship that took off after ours.'

'Impossible,' he says.

'Why is it impossible?'

'Because the other ships were destroyed. I saw it with my own eyes. When the Mogadorians landed they took out our ports first. We traveled in the only ship that survived their offensive. It was a miracle that we made it off.'

'I saw a second ship. I'm telling you. It wasn't like the others, though. It ran on fuel, a ball of fire following behind it.'

Henri watches me closely. He is thinking hard, his brows crinkled.

'Are you sure, John?'

'Yes.'

He leans back in his chair, looks out the window. Bernie Kosar is on the ground, staring up at us both.

'It made it off Lorien,' I say. 'I watched it the whole way until it disappeared.'

'That makes no sense,' Henri says. 'I don't see how it could be possible. There was nothing left.'

'There was a second ship.'

We sit through a long silence.

'Henri?'

'Yes?'

'What was on that ship?'

He fixes me with a stare.

'I don't know,' he says. 'I truly don't know.'

We sit in the living room, a fire in the hearth, Bernie Kosar in my lap. An occasional pop from the logs breaks the silence.

'On!' I say, and snap my fingers. My right hand illuminates, not as brightly as I've seen it before, but close. In the short amount of time since Henri started coaching me I've learned to control the glow. I can concentrate it, making it wide, like the light in a house, or narrow and focused, like a flashlight. My ability to manipulate it is coming more quickly than I expected. The left hand is still dimmer than the right, but it's catching up. I snap my fingers and say 'on' just to show off, but I don't need to do either to control the light, or to have it come on. It just happens from within, as effortlessly as twitching a finger or blinking an eye.

'When do you think the other Legacies will develop?' I ask.

Henri looks up from the paper. 'Soon,' he says. 'The next one should start within the month, whatever it is. You just have to keep a close watch. Not all the powers will be obvious like your hands.'

'How long will it take for them all to come?'

He shrugs. 'Sometimes all is complete within two months, sometimes it takes up to a year. It varies from Garde to Garde. But however long it takes, your major Legacy will be the last to develop.'

I close my eyes and lean back against the couch. I think about my major Legacy, the one that will allow me to fight. I'm not sure what I want it to be. Lasers? Mind control? The ability to manipulate the weather as I had seen the man in silver and blue do? Or do I want something darker, more sinister, like the ability to kill without touching?

I run my hand down Bernie Kosar's back. I look over at Henri. He's wearing a nightcap and a pair of spectacles on the tip of his nose like a storybook rat.

'Why were we at the airfield that day?' I ask.

'We were there for an air show. After it was over we took a tour of some of the ships.'

'Was that really the only reason?'

He turns back to me and nods. He swallows hard, and it makes me think that he's keeping something from me.

'Well, how was it decided that we would leave?' I ask. 'I mean, surely a plan like that would've needed more time than a few minutes' notice, right?'

'We didn't take off until three hours after the invasion started. Do you not remember any of it?'

'Very little.'

'We met your grandfather at the statue of Pittacus. He gave you to me and told me to get you to the airfield, that that was our only chance. There was an underground compound beneath the airfield. He said there had always been a contingency plan in case something of the sort occurred, but it was never taken seriously because the threat of an attack seemed ludicrous. Just like it would be here, on Earth. If you were to tell any human now that there is a threat of an attack by aliens, well, they would laugh at you. It was no different on Lorien. I asked him how he knew about the plan and he didn't answer, just smiled, and said good-bye. It makes sense that no one would really know about the plan, or only a few would.'

I nod. 'So just like that, you guys came up with a plan to come to Earth?'

'Of course not. One of the planet's Elders met us at the airfield. He's the one who cast the Loric charm that branded your ankles and tied you all together, and gave you each an amulet. He said you were special children, blessed children, by which I assume he meant you were getting a chance to escape. We originally planned to take the ship up and wait out the invasion, wait for our people to fight back and win. But that never happened . . . ,' he says, trailing off. Then he sighs. 'We stayed in orbit for a week. That was how long it took for the Mogadorians to strip Lorien of everything. After it became clear that there would be no going back, we set our course for Earth.'

'Why didn't he cast a charm so that none of us could be killed, regardless of numbers?'

'There's only so much that can be done, John. What you are talking about is invincibility. It's not possible.'

I nod. The charm only does so much. If one of the Mogadorians tries killing us out of order, whatever damage it attempts is reversed and done to it instead. If one had tried shooting me in the head the bullet would have gone through its own head. But not anymore. Now if they catch me, I die.

I sit in silence for a moment thinking about it all. The airfield. Lorien's lone remaining Elder who cast the charm on us, Loridas, now dead. The Elders were the first inhabitants of Lorien, those beings who made it what it was. There were ten of them in the beginning, and they contained all Legacies within them. So old, so long ago that they seem more of a myth than anything based in reality. Aside from Loridas, no one knew what had happened to the rest of them, if they were dead.

I try to remember what it was like orbiting the planet waiting to see if we could go back, but I don't remember any of it. I can recall bits and pieces of the journey. The interior of the ship we traveled in was round and open aside from the two bathrooms that had doors. There were cots pushed to one side; the other side was devoted to exercise and games to keep us from getting too antsy. I can't remember what the others look like. I can't remember the games we played. I remember being bored, an entire year being spent inside an airship with seventeen others. There was a stuffed animal I slept with at night, and though I'm sure the memory is wrong, I seem to recall the animal playing back.

'Henri?'

'Yes?'

'I keep having images of a man in a silver and blue suit. I saw him at our house, and on the battlefield. He could control the weather. And then I saw him dead.'

Henri nods. 'Every time you travel back it'll only be to those scenes holding relevance to you.'

'He was my father, wasn't he?'

'Yes,' he says. 'He wasn't supposed to come around much, but he did anyway. He was around a lot.'

I sigh. My father had fought valiantly, killing the beast and many of the soldiers. But in the end it still wasn't enough.

'Do we really have a chance to win?'

'What do you mean?'

'We were defeated so easily. What hope is there for a different outcome if we're found? Even when we have all developed our powers, and when we finally come together and are ready to fight, what hope do we have against things like those?'

'Hope?' he says. 'There is always hope, John. New developments have yet to present themselves. Not all the information is in. No. Don't give up hope just yet. It's the last thing to go. When you have lost hope, you have lost everything. And when you think all is lost, when all is dire and bleak, there is always hope.'

12

Henri and I go into town on Saturday for the Halloween parade, almost two weeks after arriving in Paradise. I think the solitude is getting to us both. Not that we aren't used to solitude. We are. But the solitude in Ohio is different from that of most other places. There is a certain silence to it, a certain loneliness.

It's a cold day, the sun peeking intermittently through thick white clouds gliding by overhead. The town is bustling. All the kids are in costume. We have bought a leash for Bernie Kosar, who is wearing a Superman cape draped over his back, a large 'S' on his chest. He seems unimpressed with it. He's not the only dog dressed as a superhero.

Henri and I stand on the sidewalk in front of the Hungry Bear, the diner just off the circle in the center of town, to watch the parade. In its front window hangs a clipping of the *Gazette* article on Mark James. He's pictured standing on the fifty-yard line of the football field, wearing his letter-man jacket, his arms crossed, his right foot resting atop a football, a wry, confident grin on his face. Even I have to admit he looks impressive.

Henri sees me staring at the paper.

'It's your friend, right?' he asks with a smile. Henri now knows the story, from the near fight to the cow manure to the crush I have on his ex-girlfriend. Since finding out all this information he has only referred to Mark as my 'friend'.

'My *best* friend,' I correct him.

Just then the band starts. It's at the head of the parade, followed by various Halloween-themed floats, one of which is carrying Mark and a few of the football players. Some I recognize from class, some I don't. They throw handfuls of candy to the kids. Then Mark catches sight of me and he nudges the guy beside him – Kevin, the kid I kneed in the groin in the cafeteria. Mark points at me and says something. They both laugh.

'That's him?' Henri asks.

'That's him.'

'Looks like a dick.'

'I told you.'

Then come the cheerleaders, walking, all in uniform, hair pulled back, smiling and waving to the crowd. Sarah is walking alongside them, taking pictures. She gets them in action, while they're jumping, doing their cheers. Despite the fact that she's wearing jeans and no makeup, she's far more beautiful than any of them. We've been talking more and more at school, and I can't stop thinking about her. Henri sees me staring at her.

Then he turns back to the parade. 'That's her, huh?'

'That's her.'

She sees me and waves, then points to the camera, meaning she'd come over but wants to take pictures. I smile and nod.

'Well,' Henri says. 'I can certainly see the appeal.'

We watch the parade. The mayor of Paradise passes by, sitting on the back of a red convertible. He throws more candy to the children. There will be a lot of hyper kids today, I think.

I feel a tap on my shoulder and turn around.

'Sam Goode. What's the word?'

He shrugs. 'Nothin'. What's up with you?'

'Watching the parade. This is my dad, Henri.'

They shake hands. Henri says, 'John has told me a lot about you.'

'Really?' Sam asks with a crooked grin.

'Really,' Henri responds. Then he pauses a minute and a smile takes shape. 'You know, I've been reading. Maybe you've heard it already, but did you know that aliens are the reason we have thunderstorms? They create them in order to enter our planet unnoticed. The storm creates a diversion, and the lightning you see is really coming from the spaceships entering Earth's atmosphere.'

Sam smiles and scratches his head. 'Get out of here,' he says.

Henri shrugs. 'That's what I've heard.'

'All right,' Sam says, more than willing to oblige Henri. 'Well, did you know that the dinosaurs really didn't go extinct? Aliens were so fascinated by them that they decided to gather them all up and take them to their own planet.'

Henri shakes his head. 'I didn't know that,' he says. 'Did you know that the Loch Ness monster was really an animal from the planet Trafalgra? They brought him here as an experiment, to see if he could survive, and he did. But when he was discovered the aliens had to take him back, which is why he was never spotted again.'

I laugh, not at the theory, but at the name Trafalgra. There is no planet named Trafalgra and I wonder if Henri has made it up on the fly.

'Did you know the Egyptian pyramids were built by aliens?'

'I've heard that,' Henri says, smiling. This is funny to him because though the pyramids weren't actually built by aliens, they were built using Lorien knowledge and with Lorien help. 'Did you know the world is supposed to end on December 21, 2012?'

Sam nods and grins. 'Yeah, I've heard that. Earth's supposed expiration date, the end of the Mayan calendar.'

'Expiration date?' I chime in. 'Like, a "best if used before" date that's printed on milk cartons? Is Earth going to curdle?'

I laugh at my own joke, but Sam and Henri pay me no attention.

Then Sam says, 'Did you know crop circles were originally used as a navigational tool for the Agharian alien race? But that was thousands of years ago. Today they are only created by bored farmers.'

I laugh again. I have the urge to ask what sorts of people create alien conspiracies if it is bored farmers who create crop circles, but I don't.

'How about the Centuri?' asks Henri. 'Do you know of them?'

Sam shakes his head.

'They're a race of aliens living at Earth's core. They are a contentious race, in constant discord with one another, and when they have civil wars Earth's surface is thrown off-kilter. That's when things such as earthquakes and volcanic eruptions occur. The tsunami of 2004? All because the Centuri king's daughter went missing.'

'Did they find her?' I ask.

Henri shakes his head, looks at me, then back at Sam, who is still smiling at the game. 'They never did. Theorists believe she is able to shift her shape, and that she is living somewhere in South America.'

Henri's theory is so good, I think there's no way he made it up that quickly. I stand there and actually ponder it, even though I've never heard of aliens called the Centuri, even when I know for a fact that nothing lives at Earth's core.

'Did you know . . .' Sam pauses. I think Henri has stumped him, and as soon as that thought pops into my mind Sam says something so frightening that a wave of terror shoots through me.

'Did you know that the Mogadorians are on a quest for universal domination, and that they have already wiped out one planet and are planning to wipe Earth out next? They're here seeking human weakness so that they can exploit us when the war begins.'

My mouth drops open and Henri stares at Sam, dumbfounded. He's holding his breath. His hand tightens around his coffee cup until I'm afraid that if it tightens any further the cup will crumple. Sam glances at Henri, then at me.

'You guys look like you've seen a ghost. Does this mean I win?'

'Where did you hear that?' I ask. Henri looks at me so fiercely that I wish I had remained silent.

'From *They Walk Among Us*.'

Henri still can't think of how to respond. He opens his mouth to speak but nothing comes. Then a petite woman standing behind Sam interrupts.

'Sam,' she says. He turns and looks at her. 'Where have you been?'

Sam shrugs. 'I was standing right here.'

She sighs, then says to Henri, 'Hi, I'm Sam's mother.'

'Henri,' he says, and shakes her hand. 'Pleased to meet you.'

She opens her eyes in surprise. Something in Henri's accent has excited her.

'Ah bon! Vous parlez français? C'est super! J'ai personne avec qui je peux parler français depuis longtemps.'

Henri smiles. 'I'm sorry. I don't actually speak French. I know my accent sounds like it, though.'

'No?' She is disappointed. 'Well hell, here I thought some dignity had finally come to town.'

Sam looks at me and rolls his eyes.

'All right, Sam, let's get going,' she says.

He shrugs. 'You guys gonna go to the park and the hayride?'

I look at Henri, then at Sam. 'Yeah, sure,' I say. 'Are you?'

He shrugs.

'Well, try to come meet us if you can,' I say.

He smiles and nods. 'Okay, cool.'

'Time to go, Sam. And you might not be able to go on the hayride. I need your help at home,' his mother says. He starts to say something but she walks away. Sam follows her.

'Very nice woman,' Henri says sarcastically.

'How did you make all that up?' I ask.

The crowd begins migrating up Main Street, away from the circle. Henri and I follow it up to the park, where cider and food are being served.

'You lie long enough and you start to get used to it.'

I nod. 'So what do you think?'

He takes a deep breath and exhales. The temperature is cold enough so that I can see his breath. 'I have no idea. I don't know what to think at this point. He caught me off guard.'

'He caught us both off guard.'

'We're going to have to look into the publication he's getting his information from, find out who is writing it and where it's being written.'

He looks over at me expectantly.

‘What?’

‘You’re going to have to get a copy,’ he says.

‘I will,’ I say. ‘But still, it makes no sense. How could somebody know that?’

‘It’s being supplied from somewhere.’

‘Do you think it’s one of us?’

‘No.’

‘Do you think it’s them?’

‘It could be. I’ve never thought to check the conspiracy-theory rags. Perhaps they think we read them and can root us out by leaking information like that. I mean . . .’ He pauses, thinks about it for a minute. ‘Hell, John, I don’t know. We’ll have to look into it, though. It’s not a coincidence, that’s for sure.’

We walk in silence, still a little stunned, turning possible explanations over in our minds. Bernie Kosar trots along between us, tongue dangling, his cape falling to one side and dragging on the sidewalk. He’s a big hit with the kids and many of them stop us to pet him.

The park is situated on the southern edge of town. At the far border are two adjacent lakes separated by a narrow strip of land leading into the forest beyond them. The park itself is made up of three baseball fields, a playground, and a large pavilion where volunteers serve cider and slices of pumpkin pie. Three hay wagons are off to the side of the gravel drive, with a large sign reading:

BE SCARED OUT OF YOUR WITS!
HALLOWEEN HAUNTED HAYRIDES
START @ SUNDOWN
$5 PER PERSON

The drive segues from gravel to dirt before it reaches the woods, the entrance to which is decorated with cutouts of ghost and goblin caricatures. It appears that the haunted hayride travels through the woods. I look around for Sarah but don't see her anywhere. I wonder if she'll be going on it.

Henri and I enter the pavilion. The cheerleaders are off to the side, some of them doing Halloween-themed face paintings for the kids, the others selling raffle tickets for the drawing to be held at six p.m.

'Hi, John,' I hear behind me. I turn around and there's Sarah, holding her camera. 'How did you like the parade?'

I smile at her and slide my hands into my pockets. There's a small white ghost painted on her cheek.

'Hey, you,' I say. 'I liked it. I think I'm getting used to this small-town Ohio charm.'

'Charm? You mean boringness, right?'

I shrug. 'I don't know, it isn't bad.'

'Hey, it's the little guy from school. I remember you,' she says, bending down to pet Bernie Kosar. He wags his tail wildly, jumps up and tries to lick her face. Sarah laughs. I look over my shoulder. Henri is twenty feet away, talking to Sarah's mom at one of the picnic tables. I'm curious to know what they're talking about.

'I think he likes you. His name is Bernie Kosar.'

'Bernie Kosar? That's no name for an adorable dog. Look at this cape. It's, like, cute overload.'

'You know if you keep that up I'm going to be jealous of my own dog,' I say.

She smiles and stands.

'So are you going to buy a raffle ticket from me or what? It's to rebuild a not-for-profit animal shelter destroyed in a fire last month in Colorado.'

'Really? How does a girl from Paradise, Ohio, learn of an animal shelter in Colorado?'

'It's my aunt's. I've convinced all the girls on the cheerleading squad to participate. We're going to take a trip and assist in the construction. We'll be helping the animals and getting out of school and Ohio for a week. It's a win-win situation.'

I picture Sarah dressed in a hard hat, wielding a hammer. The thought brings a grin to my face. 'So you're saying I'm going to have to cover the kitchen alone for a whole week?' I fake an exasperated sigh and shake my head. 'I don't know if I can support such a trip now, even if it is for the animals.'

She laughs and punches me in the arm. I take out my wallet and give her five dollars for six tickets.

'These six are good luck,' she says.

'They are?'

'Of course. You bought them from me, silly.'

Just then, over Sarah's shoulder, I see Mark and the rest of the guys from the float walk into the pavilion.

'Are you going on the haunted hayride tonight?' Sarah asks.

'Yeah, I was thinking about it.'

'You should, it's fun. Everybody does it. And it actually gets pretty scary.'

Mark sees Sarah and me talking and scrunches his face into a scowl. He comes walking our way. Same outfit as always – letterman jacket, blue jeans, hair full of gel.

'So you're going?' I ask Sarah.

Before she can respond Mark interrupts. 'How'd you like the parade, Johnny?' he asks. Sarah quickly turns around and glares at him.

'I liked it a lot,' I reply.

'You going on the haunted hayride tonight, or are you going to be too scared?'

I smile at him. 'As a matter of fact, I am going.'

'You going to have a freak-out like in school and run out of the woods crying like a baby?'

'Don't be an ass, Mark,' Sarah says.

He looks at me, seething. With the crowd around there is nothing he can do without causing a scene – and I don't think he would do anything anyway.

'All in due time,' Mark says.

'You think?'

'Yours is coming,' he says.

'That might be true,' I say. 'But it won't be coming from you.'

'Stop it!' Sarah yells. She works her way in between us, pushing us away from each other. People are watching. She glances around as though embarrassed by the attention, then scowls at Mark first, then at me.

'Fine, then. You guys fight if that's what you want to do. Good luck with it,' Sarah says, and turns and walks away. I watch her go. Mark doesn't.

'Sarah,' I call, but she keeps walking and disappears past the pavilion.

'Soon,' Mark says.

I look back to him. 'I doubt it.'

He retreats to his group of friends. Henri walks up to me.

'I don't suppose he was inquiring about yesterday's math homework?'

'Not quite,' I say.

'I wouldn't worry about him,' Henri says. 'He looks to be all talk.'

'I'm not,' I say, and then glance at the spot where Sarah

disappeared. 'Should I go after her?' I ask, and look at him, pleading to the part of him that was once married and in love, that part that still misses his wife every day, and not the part of him that wants to keep me safe and hidden.

He nods his head. 'Yeah,' he says with a sigh. 'As much as I hate to admit it, you should probably go after her.'

13

Kids running, screaming, on slides and jungle gyms. Every kid with a bag of candy in his or her hand, with a mouth stuffed full of sweets. Kids dressed as cartoon characters, monsters, ghouls and ghosts. Every resident of Paradise must be at the park right now. And in the midst of all the madness I see Sarah, sitting alone, gently pushing herself on the swing.

I weave my way through the screams and shrieks. When Sarah sees me she smiles, those big blue eyes of hers like a beacon.

'Need a push?' I ask.

She nods to the swing that has just opened beside her and I sit.

'Doing okay?' I ask.

'Yeah, I'm fine. He just wears me down. He always has to act so tough and he's downright mean when he's around friends.'

She twists herself on the swing until the rope becomes taut, then she lifts her feet and it spins her around, slowly at first, then gaining speed. She laughs the whole time, her blond hair a trail behind her. I do the same thing. When the swing finally stops the world keeps spinning.

'Where is Bernie Kosar?'

'I left him with Henri,' I say.

'Your dad?'

'Yes, my dad.' I am constantly doing that, calling Henri by his name when I should be saying 'Dad'.

The temperature is quickly dropping, and my hands are white knuckled on the rope chain, becoming cold. We watch the kids run amok around us. Sarah looks at me and her eyes seem bluer than ever in the coming dusk. Our gaze stays locked, each of us just staring at the other, no words being said but much passing between us. The children seem to fade into the background. Then she smiles shyly and looks away.

'So what are you going to do?' I ask.

'About what?'

'Mark.'

She shrugs. 'What can I do? I've already broken up with him. I keep telling him I have no interest in getting back together.'

I nod. I'm not sure how to respond to that.

'But anyway, I should probably try to sell the rest of these tickets. Only an hour before the raffle.'

'Do you want any help?'

'No, that's okay. You should go have fun. Bernie Kosar is probably missing you right now. But you should definitely stick around for the hayride. Maybe we can go on it together?'

'I will,' I say. A happiness blooms inside of me, but I try to keep it hidden.

'I'll see you in a little while, then.'

'Good luck with the tickets.'

She reaches over and grabs my hand and holds it for a good three seconds. Then she lets go, jumps off the swing, and hurries away. I sit there, gently swinging, enjoying the brisk wind that I haven't felt in a very long time because we spent the last winter in Florida, and the one before that in south Texas. When I head back to the pavilion Henri is sitting at a picnic table eating a slice of pie with Bernie Kosar lying at his feet.

'How'd it go?'

'Good,' I say with a smile.

From somewhere an orange and blue firework shoots up and explodes in the sky. It makes me think of Lorien and of the fireworks I saw on the day of the invasion.

'Have you thought any more about the second ship I saw?'

Henri looks around to make sure there's nobody within earshot. We have the picnic table to ourselves, positioned in the far corner away from the crowd.

'A little. I still have no idea what it means, though.'

'Do you think it could have traveled here?'

'No. It wouldn't be possible. If it ran on fuel, like you say, it wouldn't have been able to travel far without refueling.'

I sit for a moment.

'I wish it could have.'

'Could have what?'

'Traveled here, with us.'

'It's a nice thought,' says Henri.

An hour or so passes and I see all the football players, Mark in front, walk across the grass. They are dressed up as mummies, zombies, ghosts, twenty-five of them in total. They sit in the bleachers of the nearest baseball field and the cheerleaders who were drawing on the children begin applying makeup to complete the costumes of Mark and his friends. It's only then that I realize the football players will be the ones doing the scaring on the haunted hayride, the ones waiting for us in the woods.

'See that?' I ask Henri.

Henri looks at them all and nods, then picks up his coffee and takes a long drink.

'Think you should still go on the ride?' he asks.

'No,' I say. 'But I'm going to anyway.'

'I figured you would.'

Mark is dressed as a zombie of sorts, wearing dark tattered clothes, with black and gray makeup on his face, splotches of red in random places to simulate blood. When his costume is complete Sarah walks up to him and says something. His voice becomes raised but I can't hear what he's saying. His movements are animated and he talks so fast that I can tell he's stumbling over his words. Sarah crosses her arms and shakes her head at him. His body tenses. I move to stand, but Henri grabs my arm.

'Don't,' he says. 'He's only pushing her further away.'

I look at them and wish with everything that I could hear what is being said, but there are too many screaming kids around to focus in. When the yelling stops they both stand looking at each other, a hurtful scowl on Mark's face, an incredulous grin on Sarah's. Then she shakes her head and walks away.

I look at Henri. 'What should I do now?'

'Not a thing,' he says. 'Not a thing.'

Mark walks back to his friends, head hung, scowling. A few of them look in my direction. Smirks appear. Then they start walking towards the forest. A slow methodical march, twenty-five guys in costume receding in the distance.

To kill time I walk back to the center of town with Henri and we eat dinner at the Hungry Bear. When we walk back the sun has set and the first trailer piled with hay and pulled by a green tractor takes off for the woods. The crowd has thinned considerably and those left are mostly high schoolers and free-spirited adults who total a hundred or so people. I look for Sarah among them but I don't see her. The next trailer leaves in ten minutes. According to the pamphlet the whole ride is half an hour long, the tractor going through the woods slowly, the anticipation building, and then it stops and the riders are to get off and follow a different trail on foot, at which point the scares begin.

Henri and I stand beneath the pavilion and I again scan the long line of people waiting their turn. I still don't see her. Just then my phone vibrates in my pocket. I can't remember the last time my phone rang when it wasn't Henri calling. The caller ID reads SARAH HART. Excitement rushes through me. She must have entered my number into her phone the same day she entered hers into mine.

'Hello?' I say.

'John?'

'Yeah.'

'Hey, it's Sarah. Are you still at the park?' she says. She sounds as though her calling me is normal, that I shouldn't think twice about her already having my number despite my never having given it to her.

'Yes.'

'Great! I'm going to be back there in about five minutes. Have the rides started?'

'Yeah, a couple minutes ago.'

'You haven't gone yet, have you?'

'No.'

'Oh, good! Wait so we can ride together.'

'Yeah, definitely,' I say. 'The second one is about to leave now.'

'Perfect. I'll be there in time for the third.'

'See you then.'

I hang up, a huge smile on my face.

'Be careful out there,' Henri says.

'I will.' Then I pause and try to bring lightness to my voice. 'You don't have to stick around. I'm sure I can get a ride home.'

'I'm willing to stay and live in this town, John. Even when it's probably smarter for us to leave given the events that have already happened. But you're going to have to meet me halfway on things. And this is one of them. I don't like the looks those guys gave you earlier one bit.'

I nod. 'I'll be fine,' I say.

'I'm sure you will. But just in case I'm going to be right here waiting.'

I sigh. 'Fine.'

Sarah pulls up five minutes later with a pretty friend who I've seen before but have never been introduced to. She has changed into jeans, a wool sweater, and a black jacket. She has wiped away the painted ghost that was on her right cheek and her hair is down, falling past her shoulders.

'Hey, you,' she says.

'Hi.'

She wraps her arms around me in a tentative hug. I can smell the perfume wafting up from her neck. Then she pulls away.

'Hi, John's dad,' she says to Henri. 'This is my friend Emily.'

'Pleased to meet you both,' Henri says. 'So you guys are off into the unknown terror?'

'You bet,' Sarah says. 'Will this one be okay out there? I don't want him getting too scared on me,' Sarah says to Henri, motioning to me with a smile.

Henri grins and I can tell he already likes Sarah. 'You better stay close just in case.'

She looks over her shoulder. The third trailer is a quarter full. 'I'll keep him safe,' she says. 'We better get going.'

'Have a great time,' Henri says.

Sarah surprises me by taking my hand and the three of us rush off towards the hay wagon a hundred yards away from the pavilion. There is a line about thirty people long. We get to the back of it and start talking, though I'm feeling a little shy and mostly just listen to the two girls talk. As we're waiting I see Sam hovering off to the side as though contemplating whether or not to approach us.

'Sam!' I yell with more enthusiasm than I intended. He stumbles over. 'You coming on the ride with us?'

He shrugs. 'Do you mind?'

'Come on,' Sarah says, and motions him in. He stands next to Emily, who smiles at him. He immediately starts blushing and I'm ecstatic he's along for the ride. Suddenly a kid holding a walkie-talkie comes over. I recognize him from the football team.

'Hi, Tommy,' Sarah says to him.

'Hey,' he says. 'There are four spots left on this wagon. You guys want them?'

'Really?'

'Yeah.'

We skip the line and jump up onto the trailer, where the four of us sit on a bale of hay together. I find it odd that Tommy doesn't ask us for tickets. I'm curious as to why he let us skip the line altogether. Some of the people waiting look at us with disgust. I can't say that I blame them.

'Enjoy the ride,' Tommy says with a grin, the kind I've

seen people wear when told something bad has happened to someone they despise.

'That was weird,' I say.

Sarah shrugs. 'He probably has a crush on Emily.'

'Oh God, I hope not,' Emily says, and then fake-gags.

I watch Tommy from the bale of hay. The trailer is only half full, which is another thing that strikes me as strange since there are so many people waiting.

The tractor pulls away, bumps along the pathway, and drives through the entrance of the forest, where ghastly sounds come through hidden speakers. The forest is thick and no light penetrates other than what shines from the front of the tractor. *Once that is off,* I think, *there will be nothing but darkness.* Sarah takes hold of my hand again. She's cold to the touch, but a sense of warmth floods through me. She leans over to me and whispers, 'I'm a little scared.'

Figures of ghosts hang just over us from the low branches, and off the drive grimacing zombies lean against various trees. The tractor stops and kills its headlight. Then come intermittent strobes that flash for ten seconds. There is nothing scary about them and only when they stop do I understand their effect: our eyes take a few seconds to adjust and we can't see a thing. Then a scream shoots through the night and Sarah tenses against me as figures sweep around us. I squint to focus and I see that Emily has moved next to Sam, and that he is smiling widely. I'm actually a little scared myself. I put my arm carefully around Sarah. A hand grazes our backs and Sarah grips tightly to my leg. Some of the others scream. With a jolt the tractor turns back on and continues forward, nothing but the outlines of the trees in its light.

We drive for another three or four minutes. The anticipation builds, the foreboding fear of having to walk the distance we just drove. Then the tractor pulls into a circular clearing and stops.

'Everybody off,' the driver yells.

When the last person is off, the tractor pulls away. Its light recedes in the distance, then disappears, leaving nothing but the night and not a single sound other than what we make.

'Shit,' somebody says, and all of us laugh.

In total there are eleven of us. A path of lights turns on, showing us the way, then turns off. I close my eyes to focus on the feel of Sarah's fingers interlocked with mine.

'I have no idea why I do this every year,' Emily says nervously, her arms wrapped around herself.

The other people have started down the trail and we follow. The pathway of lights occasionally flickers on to keep us on our way. The others are far enough ahead that we can't see them. I can barely see the ground at my feet. Three or four screams suddenly ring out in front of us.

'Oh no,' Sarah says, and squeezes my hand. 'Sounds like trouble ahead.'

Just then something heavy falls on us. Both girls scream and so does Sam. I trip and hit the ground, scraping my knee, tangled in whatever the hell the thing is. Then I realize it's a net!

'What the hell?' Sam asks.

I tear straight through the twisted rope but the second I'm free I get shoved hard from behind. Someone grabs me and drags me away from the girls and Sam. I break free and stand, but am immediately hit from behind again. This isn't part of the ride.

'Let go of me!' one of the girls yells. A guy laughs in

response. I can't see a thing. The girls' voices are moving away from me.

'John?' Sarah calls.

'Where are you, John?' shouts Sam.

I stand to go after them but am hit again. No, that's not right. I am tackled. The wind is knocked out of me when I'm plowed to the ground. I rush up and try to catch my breath, my hand against a tree for support. I pick dirt and leaves from my mouth.

I stand there a few seconds and don't hear a single sound other than my own labored breathing. Just when I think I've been left alone, somebody shoulders into me and sends me flying into a nearby tree. My head slams against the trunk and I briefly see stars. I'm surprised by the person's strength. I reach up and touch my forehead and feel blood on my fingertips. I look around again but can't see anything other than the silhouetted trees.

I hear a scream from one of the girls, followed by the sounds of struggle. I grit my teeth. I am shaking. Are there people mixed in with the wall of trees around me? I can't tell. But I feel a set of eyes on me, somewhere.

'Get off of me!' Sarah yells. She is being pulled away, I can tell that much.

'Okay,' I say to the darkness, to the trees. Anger surges through me. 'You want to play games?' I say, loudly this time. Somebody laughs nearby.

I take a step towards the sound. I get shoved from behind but I catch my balance before I fall. I throw a blind punch and the back of my hand scrapes against the bark of a tree. There is nothing left to do. What point is there in having Legacies if they are never used when needed? Even if it means Henri and I load the truck tonight and drive off to yet another town, at least I will have done what I needed to do.

'You want to play games?' I yell again. 'I can play games too!'

A trickle of blood runs down the side of my face. Okay, I think, let's do this. They can do all they want to me, but they will not harm a single hair on Sarah's head. Or Sam's, or Emily's.

I take a deep breath and adrenaline races through me. A malicious smile takes shape and my body feels as though it has grown bigger, stronger. My hands come on and glow brilliantly with bright light that sweeps through the night, the world suddenly ablaze.

I look up. I flash my hands across the trees and sprint off into the night.

14

Kevin steps from the trees, dressed as a mummy. He's the one who tackled me. The lights stun him and he seems dumbfounded, trying to figure out where they're coming from. He's wearing night-vision goggles. *So that is how they are able to see us*, I think. Where did they get them?

He charges me and at the last second I step out of the way and trip him.

'Let go of me!' I hear from down the trail. I look up and sweep my lights across the trees but nothing moves. I can't tell if the voice is Emily's or Sarah's. A guy's laughter follows.

Kevin tries to stand but I kick him in the side before he gets to his feet. He falls back to the ground with an 'Ummpf!' I rip the goggles from his face and throw them as far as I can and know they will land at least a mile away, maybe two or three because I'm so angry that my strength is out of control. Then I race off through the woods before Kevin can even sit up.

The trail winds left, then right. My hands glow only when I need to see. I sense that I'm close. Then I see Sam up ahead, standing with a zombie's arms around him. Three others are close by.

The zombie lets go of him. 'Chill out, we're just kidding around. If you don't resist, you won't get hurt,' he says to Sam. 'Sit down or something.'

I snap my hands on and flash the lights in their eyes to blind them. The closest person steps towards me and I swing and hit him in the side of the face and he falls motionless to the ground. His goggles sail into the overgrown brambles and disappear. The second person tries to bear-hug me, but I break his grip and lift him off the ground.

'What the hell?' he says, confused.

I throw him and he hits the side of a tree twenty feet away. The third guy sees this and runs away. That just leaves the fourth, the one who was holding Sam. He lifts his hands in front of him as though I'm aiming a gun at his chest.

'It wasn't my idea,' he says.

'What does he have planned?'

'Nothing, man. We just wanted to play a joke on you guys, scare you a little.'

'Where are they?'

'They let Emily go. Sarah is up ahead.'

'Give me your goggles,' I say.

'No way, man. We're borrowing them from the police. I'll get in trouble.'

I step towards him.

'Fine,' he says. He takes them off and hands them to me. I throw them even harder than I did the previous pair. I hope they land in the next town. Let them explain that one to the police.

I grab Sam's shirt with my right hand. I can't see a thing without turning on my light. Only then do I realize I should have kept the two pairs of goggles for us to wear. But I didn't, so I take a deep breath and let my left hand glow and begin guiding us up the path. If Sam finds it suspicious, he doesn't let on.

I stop to listen. Nothing. We continue on, weaving through the trees. I turn the light off.

'Sarah!' I yell.

I stop to listen and hear nothing but the wind blowing through the branches and Sam's heavy breathing.

'How many people are with Mark?' I ask.

'Five or so.'

'Do you know which way they went?'

'I didn't see.'

We push on and I have no idea in which direction we are headed. From far off I hear the groan of the tractor motor. The fourth ride is starting. I feel frantic inside and want to sprint, but I know that Sam can't keep up. He's breathing heavily already and even I'm sweating despite the temperature being only forty-five degrees. Or maybe I'm mistaking blood for sweat. I can't tell.

As we pass a thick tree with a knotted trunk I get tackled from behind. Sam yells as a fist hits me in the back of the head and I'm momentarily stunned, but then I pivot and grab the guy by the throat and shine the light in his face. He tries to peel my fingers away but it's useless.

'What is Mark planning?'

'Nothing,' he says.

'Wrong answer.'

I thrust him into the nearest tree five feet away, then I pick him up and lift him a foot off the ground with my hand again around his throat. His legs kick wildly, hitting me, but I tighten my muscles so that the kicks do no damage.

'What is he planning to do?'

I lower him until his feet touch solid ground, loosening my grip to allow him to speak. I sense Sam watching, drinking all of this in, but there is nothing I can do about it.

'We just wanted to scare you guys,' he gasps.

'I swear I will break you in half if you don't tell me the truth.'

'He thinks that the others are dragging you two to Shepherd Falls. That's where he took Sarah. He wanted her to see him beat the crap out of you, and then he was going to let you go.'

'Lead me,' I say.

He shuffles forward and I turn my light off. Sam takes hold of my shirt and follows behind us. When we walk through a small clearing lit by the moonlight overhead I can see that he's looking at my hands.

'They're gloves,' I say. 'Kevin Miller was wearing them. Some sort of Halloween prop.'

He nods but I can tell he's freaked out. We walk for nearly a minute until we hear the sound of running water just ahead of us.

'Give me your goggles,' I say to the guy leading us.

He hesitates and I twist his arm. He writhes in pain and quickly rips them from his face.

'Take them, take them,' he yells.

When I put them on the world turns to a shade of green. I push him hard and he falls to the ground.

'Come on,' I say to Sam, and we walk ahead, leaving the guy behind.

Up ahead I see the group. I count eight guys, plus Sarah.

'I can see them now. Do you want to wait here or come with me? It might get ugly.'

'I want to come,' Sam says. I can tell he's scared, though I'm not sure if it's because of what he's seen me do or the football players ahead of us.

I walk the rest of the way as silently as I can, Sam tiptoeing behind me. When we are just a few feet away a twig snaps beneath Sam's foot.

'John?' Sarah asks. She's sitting on a large rock with her

knees to her chest and her arms wrapped around them. She isn't wearing goggles and squints in our direction.

'Yes,' I say. 'And Sam.'

She smiles. 'Told you,' she says, and I assume she's talking to Mark.

The water I heard is nothing more than a small babbling brook. Mark steps forward.

'Well, well, well,' he says.

'Shut up, Mark,' I say. 'Manure in my locker was one thing, but you've gone way too far with this one.'

'You think? It's eight on two.'

'Sam has nothing to do with this. You scared to face me alone?' I ask. 'What are you expecting to happen? You've tried kidnapping two people. Do you really think they'll keep silent?'

'Yeah, I do. When they see me whip your ass.'

'You're delusional,' I say, then turn to the others. 'For those of you who don't want to go into the water, I suggest you leave now. Mark is going in no matter what. He's lost his chance to barter.'

All of them snicker. One of them asks what 'barter' means.

'Now's your last chance,' I say.

Every one of them stands firm.

'So be it,' I say.

A nervous excitement plants itself in the center of my chest. As I take one step forward Mark steps back and trips over his own feet, falling to the ground. Two of the guys come at me, both bigger than me. One swings but I duck his punch and send one of my own into his gut. He doubles over with his hands holding his stomach. I shove the second guy and his feet leave the ground. He lands with a thud five feet away and the momentum pushes him into the water. He comes up splashing. The others stand rooted, shocked. I sense Sam moving over toward Sarah. I grab hold of the first guy and drag him across the ground. His errant kicks slice through the air but hit nothing. When we are at the bank of the brook I lift him by the waistband of his jeans and throw him into the water. Another guy lunges at me. I merely sidestep him and he lands face-first in the brook. Three down, four to go. I wonder how much of this Sarah and Sam can see without goggles on.

'You guys are making it too easy for me,' I say. 'Who's next?'

The biggest of the group throws a punch that comes nowhere near hitting me, though I counter so swiftly that his elbow catches me in the face and the goggle strap snaps. The goggles fall to the ground. I can only see slight shadows now. I throw a punch and hit the guy in the jaw and he falls to the ground like a sack of potatoes. He looks lifeless, and I fear that I've hit him too hard. I rip his goggles from his face and put them on.

'Any volunteers?'

Two of them hold their hands up in front of them in surrender; the third stands with his mouth gaping open like an idiot.

'That leaves you, Mark.'

Mark turns as though he intends to run, but I lunge forward and grab him before he can, pulling his arms up into a full nelson. He writhes in pain.

'This ends right now, do you understand me?'

I squeeze tighter and he grunts in pain. 'Whatever you have against me, you drop it now. That includes Sam and Sarah. You understand?'

My grip tightens. I fear that if I squeeze any tighter his shoulder will pop from its socket.

'I said, do you understand me?'

'Yes!'

I drag him over to Sarah. Sam is sitting on the rock beside her now.

'Apologize.'

'Come on, man. You've proven your point.'

I squeeze.

'I'm sorry!' he yells.

'Say it like you mean it.'

He takes a deep breath. 'I'm sorry,' he says.

'You're an asshole, Mark!' Sarah says, and slaps him hard across the face. He tenses, but I'm holding him firmly and there isn't a thing he can do about it.

I drag him to the water. The rest of the guys stand watching in shock. The guy I had knocked out is sitting up scratching his head as though trying to figure out what has happened. I breathe a sigh of relief that he isn't badly hurt.

'You're not going to say a word to anybody about this, you understand me?' I say, my voice so low that only Mark can hear me. 'Everything that has happened tonight, it dies here. I swear, if I hear one word about it in school next week this is nothing compared to what will happen to you. Do you understand me? Not a single word.'

'Do you really think I would say anything?' he asks.

'You make sure you tell your friends the same. If they tell a single soul it will be *you* that I come for.'

'We won't say anything,' he says.

I let go, put my foot on his butt, and push him face-first into the water. Sarah is standing at the rock with Sam beside her. She hugs me tightly when I get to her.

'Do you know kung fu or something?' she asks.

I laugh nervously. 'Could you see much?'

'Not a lot, but I could tell what was happening. I mean, have you been training in the mountains your whole life or what? I don't understand how you did that.'

'I was just scared something would happen to you, I guess. And yeah, there was the past twelve years of martial arts training high in the Himalayas.'

'You're amazing,' Sarah laughs. 'Let's get out of here.'

None of the guys say a word to us. After ten feet I realize I have no idea where I'm going so I give the goggles to Sarah to lead the way.

'I can't friggin' believe that,' Sarah says. 'I mean, what an asshole. Wait till they try to explain it to the police. I'm not letting him get away with it.'

'Are you really going to the police? Mark's dad is the sheriff, after all,' I say.

'Why wouldn't I after that? It was bullshit. Mark's dad's job is to enforce law, even when his son breaks it.'

I shrug in the darkness. 'I think they received their punishment.'

I bite my lip, terrified of the police getting involved. If they do I'll have to leave, no way around it. We'll be packed up and headed out of town within the hour of Henri knowing. I sigh.

'Don't you think?' I ask. 'I mean, they've already lost several of the night-vision goggles. They'll have to explain that. And that's not to mention the icy cold water.'

Sarah doesn't say anything. We walk in silence and I pray that she is debating the merits of letting it go.

Eventually the end of the woods comes into view. Light reaches in from the park. When I stop, Sarah and Sam both look at me. Sam has been silent the entire time and I'm hoping that it's because he couldn't really see what was happening, the dark for once serving as an unexpected ally, that maybe he's a little shaken up by everything.

'It's up to you guys,' I say, 'but I'm all for just letting the matter die. I really don't want to have to talk to police about what happened.'

The light falls on Sarah's skeptical face. She shakes her head.

'I think he's right,' Sam says. 'I don't want to have to sit and write a stupid statement for the next half hour. I'll be in deep crap; my mom thinks I went to bed an hour ago.'

'You live nearby?' I ask.

He nods. 'Yeah, and I gotta go before she checks my room. I'll see you guys around.'

Without another word, Sam hurries away. He's clearly rattled. He's probably never been in a fight and certainly never one where he was kidnapped and attacked in the woods. I'll try talking to him tomorrow. If he did see something he shouldn't have, I'll convince him his eyes were playing tricks on him.

Sarah turns my face to hers and traces the line of my cut with her thumb, moving it very gently across my forehead. Then she traces both my brows, staring into my eyes.

'Thank you for tonight. I knew you were going to come.'

I shrug. 'I wasn't going to let him scare you.'

She smiles and I can see her eyes glistening in the moonlight. She moves towards me and as I realize what's about to happen my breath catches in my throat. She presses her lips to mine and everything inside of me turns to rubber. It's a soft kiss, lingering. My first. Then she pulls away and her eyes take me in. I don't know what to say. A million different thoughts run through my head. My legs feel wobbly and I'm barely able to stay upright.

'I knew you were special the first time I saw you,' she says.

'I felt the same with you.'

She reaches up and kisses me again, her hand lightly pressed to my cheek. For the first few seconds I'm lost in the feel of her lips on mine and in the idea that I'm with this beautiful girl.

She pulls away and both of us smile at each other, saying nothing, staring into each other's eyes.

'Well, I think we better go see if Emily is still here,' Sarah says after about ten seconds. 'Or else I'll be stranded.'

'I'm sure she is,' I say.

We hold hands on the walk to the pavilion. I can't stop thinking about our kisses. The fifth tractor chugs along the trail. The trailer is full and there's still a line ten or so people long waiting their turn. And after everything that happened in the woods, with Sarah's warm hand in mine, the smile doesn't leave my face.

15

The first snowfall comes two weeks later. A slight dusting, just enough to cover the truck with a fine powder. Since just after Halloween, once the Loric crystal spread the Lumen throughout my body, Henri has begun my real training. We've worked every day, without fail, through the cold weather and the rain and now the snow. Though he doesn't say it I believe he's impatient for me to be ready. It started with disconcerted looks, his brows crinkled while he chewed on his bottom lip, followed by deep sighs and eventually sleepless nights, the floorboards creaking under his feet while I lay awake in my room, to where we are now, an inherent desperation in Henri's strained voice.

We stand in the backyard, ten feet apart, facing each other.

'I'm not really in the mood today,' I say.

'I know you're not, but we have to anyway.'

I sigh and look at my watch. It's four o'clock.

'Sarah will be here at six,' I say.

'I know,' Henri says. 'That's why we must hurry.'

He holds a tennis ball in each hand.

'Are you ready?' he asks.

'As ready as I'll ever be.'

He throws the first ball high in the air, and as it reaches its apex, I try to conjure a power deep within me to keep it from falling. I don't know how I'm supposed to do it, only that I should be *able* to do it, with time and practice, says Henri. Each Garde develops the ability to move objects with their mind. Telekinesis. And instead of letting me discover it on my own – as I did my hands – Henri seems hell-bent on waking the power from whatever cave it's hibernating in.

The ball drops just as the thousand or so balls before it did, without a single interruption, bouncing twice, then lying motionless in the snow-covered grass.

I let out a deep sigh. 'I'm not feeling it today.'

'Again,' Henri says.

He throws the second ball. I try to move it, to stop it, everything inside of me straining to just make the damn thing move a single inch to the right or left, but no luck. It hits the ground as well. Bernie Kosar, who has been watching us, walks out to it, picks it up, and walks away.

'It'll come in its own time,' I say.

Henri shakes his head. The muscles in his jaw are flexed. His moods and impatience are getting to me. He watches Bernie Kosar trot off with the ball, then he sighs.

'What?' I ask.

He shakes his head again. 'Let's keep trying.'

He walks over and picks up the other ball. Then he flings it high in the air. I try to stop it but of course it just falls.

'Maybe tomorrow,' I say.

Henri nods and looks at the ground. 'Maybe tomorrow.'

I am covered in sweat and mud and melted snow after our workout. Henri pushed me harder than normal today and came at me with an aggression that could only be steeped in panic. Beyond the telekinesis practice, most of our session was spent drilling technique in fighting – hand-to-hand combat, wrestling, mixed martial arts – followed by elements of composure – grace under pressure, mind control, how to spot fear in the eyes of an opponent and then know how best to expose it. It wasn't Henri's hard training that got to me, but rather the look in his eyes. A distressed look, tinged with fear, despair, disappointment. I don't know if he's just concerned about progress, or if it's something deeper, but these sessions are becoming very exhausting – emotionally and physically.

Sarah arrives right on time. I walk outside and kiss her as she's coming up to the front porch. I take her coat from her and hang it when we're inside. Our home-ec midterm is a week away, and it was her idea to cook the meal before we'll have to prepare it in class. As soon as we begin cooking Henri grabs his jacket and goes for a walk. He takes Bernie Kosar with him and I'm thankful for the privacy. We make baked chicken breasts and potatoes and steamed vegetables, and the meal comes out far better than I had hoped. When all is ready the three of us sit and eat together. Henri is silent through most of it. Sarah and I break the awkward silence with small talk, about school, about our going to the movies the following Saturday. Henri rarely looks up from his plate other than to offer how wonderful the meal is.

When dinner is over Sarah and I wash the dishes and retreat to the couch. Sarah brought a movie over and we watch it on our small TV, but Henri mostly stares out the window. Halfway through he gets up with a sigh and walks outside. Sarah and I watch him go. We hold hands and she leans against me with her head on my shoulder. Bernie Kosar sits beside her with his head in her lap, a blanket draped over both of them. It may be cold and blustery outside, but it's warm and cozy in our living room.

'Is your dad okay?' Sarah asks.

'I don't know. He's been acting weird.'

'He was really quiet during dinner.'

'Yeah, I'm going to go check on him. I'll be right back,' I say, and follow Henri outside. He's standing on the porch – looking out into the darkness.

'So what's going on?' I ask.

He looks up at the stars in contemplation.

'Something doesn't feel right,' he says.

'What do you mean?'

'You're not going to like it.'

'Okay. Let's have it.'

'I don't know how much longer we should stay here. It doesn't feel safe to me.'

My heart sinks and I stay silent.

'They're frantic, and I think they're getting close. I can feel it. I don't think we're safe here.'

'I don't want to leave.'

'I knew you wouldn't.'

'We've kept hidden.'

Henri looks at me with a raised brow. 'No offense, John, but I hardly think you've stayed in the shadows.'

'I have where it counts.'

He nods. 'I guess we'll see.'

He walks to the edge of the porch and places his hands on the rail. I stand beside him. New snowflakes start falling, sifting down, specks of white shimmering on an otherwise dark night.

'That's not all,' Henri says.

'I didn't think it was.'

He sighs. 'You should have already developed telekinesis. It almost always comes with your first Legacy. Very rarely does it come after, and when it does, it's never longer than a week later.'

I look over at him. His eyes are full of concern, and creases of worry traverse the length of his forehead.

'Your Legacies come from Lorien. They always have.'

'So what are you telling me?'

'I don't know how much we can expect from here on out,' he says, and pauses. 'Since we're no longer on the planet, I don't know if the rest of your Legacies will come at all. And if that is true, we have no hope of fighting the Mogadorians, much less defeating them. And if we can't defeat them, we'll never be able to go back.'

I watch the snowfall, unable to decide whether I should be worried or relieved, relieved since perhaps that would bring an end to our moving and we could finally settle. Henri points at the stars.

'Right there,' he says. 'Right there is where Lorien is.'

Of course I know full well where Lorien is without having to be told. There is a certain pull, a certain way that my eyes always gravitate towards the spot where, billions of miles away, Lorien sits. I try to catch a snowflake on the tip of my tongue, then close my eyes and breathe in the cold air. When I open them I turn around and look at Sarah through the window. She's sitting with her legs beneath her, Bernie Kosar's head still in her lap.

'Have you ever thought of just settling here, of saying to hell with Lorien and making a life here on Earth?' I ask Henri.

'We left when you were pretty young. I don't imagine you remember much of it, do you?'

'Not really,' I say. 'Bits and pieces come to me from time to time. Though I can't necessarily say whether they are things I remember or things I've seen during our training.'

'I don't think you would feel that way if you could remember.'

'But I don't remember. Isn't that the point?'

'Maybe,' he says. 'But whether or not you want to go back doesn't mean the Mogadorians are going to stop searching for you. And if we get careless and settle, you can be assured they'll find us. And as soon as they do, they'll kill us both. There's no way to change that. No way.'

I knows he's right. Somehow, like Henri, I can sense that much, can feel it in the dead of night when the hairs on my arms stand at attention, when a slight shiver crawls up my spine even though I'm not cold.

'Do you ever regret sticking with me for this long?'

'Regret it? Why do you think I would regret it?'

'Because there's nothing for us to go back to. Your family is dead. So is mine. On Lorien there is only a life of rebuilding. If it wasn't for me you could easily create an identity here and spend the rest of your days becoming a part of someplace. You could have friends, maybe even fall in love again.'

Henri laughs. 'I'm already in love. And I'll continue to be until the day that I die. I don't expect you to understand that. Lorien is different from Earth.'

I sigh with exasperation. 'But still, you could be a part of somewhere.'

'I am a part of somewhere. I'm a part of Paradise, Ohio, right now, with you.'

I shake my head. 'You know what I mean, Henri.'

'What is it that you think I'm missing?'

'A life.'

'You are my life, kiddo. You and my memories are my only ties to the past. Without you I have nothing. That's the truth.'

Just then the door opens behind us. Bernie Kosar comes trotting out ahead of Sarah, who is standing in the doorway half in and half out.

'Are you two really going to make me watch this movie all by my lonesome?' she asks.

Henri smiles at her. 'Wouldn't dream of it,' he says.

After the movie Henri and I drive Sarah home. When we get there I walk her to her front door and we stand on the stoop smiling at each other. I kiss her good night, a lingering kiss while holding both her hands gently in mine.

'See you tomorrow,' she says, giving my hands a squeeze.

'Sweet dreams.'

I walk back to the truck. Henri pulls out of Sarah's driveway and steers towards home. I can't help feeling a sense of fear while remembering Henri's words the day he picked me up from my first full day of school: 'Just keep in mind we might have to leave at a moment's notice.' He's right, and I know it, but I've never felt this way about anyone before. Like I'm floating on air when we're together, and I dread the times when we're apart, like now, despite having just spent the last couple of hours with her. Sarah gives some purpose to our running, and hiding, a reason that transcends mere survival. A reason to win. And to know that I may be putting her life in danger by being with her – well, it terrifies me.

When we get back, Henri walks into his bedroom and comes out carrying the Chest. He drops it on the kitchen table.

'Really?' I ask.

He nods. 'There's something in here I've wanted to show you for years.'

I can't wait to see what else is in the chest. We pop the lock together and he lifts the lid in such a way that I can't peer in. Henri removes a velvet bag, closes the Chest, and relocks it.

'These aren't part of your Legacy, but the last time we opened the Chest I slipped them in because of the bad feeling I've been having. If the Mogadorians catch us, they'll never be able to open this,' he says, and motions to the Chest.

'So what's in the bag?'

'The solar system,' he says.

'If they aren't part of my Legacy then why have you never shown me?'

'Because you needed to develop a Legacy in order to activate them.'

He clears the kitchen table and then sits across from me with the bag in his lap. He smiles at me, sensing my enthusiasm. Then he reaches down and removes seven glass orbs of varying sizes from the bag. He holds them up to his face in his cupped hands and blows on the glass orbs. Tiny flickers of light come from within them, then he tosses them up in the air and all at once they come to life, suspended above the kitchen table. The glass balls are a replica of our solar system. The largest of them is the size of an orange – Lorien's sun – and it hangs in the middle emitting the same amount of light as a lightbulb while looking like a self-contained sphere of lava. The other balls orbit around it. Those closest to the sun move at a faster rate, while those farthest away seem to only creep by. All of them spinning, days beginning and ending at hyperspeed. The fourth globe from the sun is Lorien. We watch it move, watch the surface of it begin to form. It is about the size of a racquetball. The replica must not be to scale because in reality Lorien is far smaller than our sun.

'So what's happening?' I ask.

'The ball is taking on the exact form of what Lorien looks like at this moment.'

'How is this even possible?'

'It's a special place, John. An old magic exists at its very core. That's where your Legacies come from. It's what gives life and reality to the objects contained within your Inheritance.'

'But you just said that this isn't part of my Legacy.'

'No, but they come from the same place.'

Indentations form, mountains grow, deep creases cut across the surface where I know rivers once ran. And then it stops. I look for any sort of color, any movement, any wind that might blow across the land. But there is nothing. The entire landscape is a monochromatic patch of gray and black. I don't know what I had hoped to see, what I had expected. Movement of some kind, a hint of fertileness. My spirits fall. Then the surface dims away so that we can see through it and at the very core of the globe a slight glow begins to form. It glows, then dims, then glows again as though replicating the heartbeat of a sleeping animal.

'What is that?' I ask.

'The planet still lives and breathes. It has withdrawn deep into itself, biding its time. Hibernating, if you will. But it will wake one of these days.'

'What makes you so sure?'

'That little glow right there,' he says. 'That is hope, John.'

I watch it. I find an odd pleasure in seeing it glow. They tried to wipe away our civilization, the planet itself, and yet it still breathes. *Yes*, I think, *there is always hope, just as Henri has said all along.*

'That isn't all.'

Henri stands and snaps his fingers and the planets stop moving. He moves his face to within inches of Lorien, then cups his hands around his mouth and again breathes onto it. Hints of green and blue sweep across the ball and begin to fade almost immediately as the mist from Henri's breath evaporates.

'What did you do?'

'Flash your hands on it,' he says.

I make them glow and when I hold them over the ball the green and blue come back, only this time they stay as my hands shine upon it.

'It's how Lorien looked the day before the invasion. Would you look how beautiful it all is? Sometimes even I forget.'

It *is* beautiful. Everything green and blue, plush and verdant. The vegetation seems to waver beneath gusts of wind that I can somehow feel. Slight ripples appear on the water. The planet is truly *alive*, flourishing. But then I turn my glow back off and it all fades away, back to shades of gray.

Henri points at a spot on the globe's surface.

'Right here,' he says, 'is where we took off from on the day of the invasion.' Then he moves his finger half an inch from the spot. 'And right here is where the Loric Museum of Exploration used to be.'

I nod and look at the spot he is pointing to. More gray.

'What do museums have to do with anything?' I ask. I sit back in the chair. It's hard to look at this without feeling sad.

He looks back at me. 'I've been thinking a lot about what you saw.'

'Uh-huh,' I say, urging him on.

'It was a huge museum, devoted entirely to the evolution of space travel. One of the wings of the building held early rockets that were thousands of years old. Rockets that used to run on a kind of fuel known only to Lorien,' he says, and stops, looking back to the small glass orb hanging two feet above our kitchen table. 'Now, if what you saw did in fact happen, if a second ship managed to take off and escape from Lorien during the height of the war, then it would have to have been housed at the space museum. There's no other explanation for it. I'm still having a tough time believing that it would have worked, and even if it did, that it would have gotten very far.'

'So if it wouldn't have gotten very far, then why are you still thinking about it?'

Henri shakes his head. 'You know, I'm not really sure. Maybe because I've been wrong before. Maybe because I'm hoping I am wrong now. And, well, if it *had* made it anywhere, then it would have made it here, the closest life-sustaining planet aside from Mogadore. And that's to assume that there was life on it in the first place, that it wasn't just full of artifacts, or that it wasn't just empty, meant to confuse the Mogadorians. But I think there had to have been at least one Loric manning the ship because, well, as I'm sure you know, ships of that nature couldn't steer themselves.'

Another night of insomnia. I stand shirtless in front of the mirror, staring into it with both lights in my hands turned on. 'I don't know how much we can expect from here on out,' Henri said today. The light at Lorien's core still burns, and the objects we brought from there still work, so why would that magic have ended there? And what about the others: are they now running into the same problems? Are they without their Legacies?

I flex in front of the mirror, then punch the air, hoping that the mirror will break, or a thud will be heard on the door. But there is nothing. Just me looking like an idiot standing shirtless, shadowboxing with myself while Bernie Kosar watches from the bed. It's nearly midnight and I'm not tired in the least. Bernie Kosar jumps off the bed, sits beside me, and watches my reflection. I smile at him and he wags his tail.

'How about you?' I ask Bernie Kosar. 'Do you have any special powers? Are you a superdog? Should I put your cape back on so you can go flying through the air?'

His tail keeps wagging and he paws the ground while looking at me through the tops of his eyes. I lift him up and over my head and fly him around the room.

'Look! It's Bernie Kosar, the magnificent superdog!'

He squirms under my grip, so I set him down. He plops on his side with his tail thumping against the mattress.

'Well, buddy, one of us should have superpowers. And it doesn't look like it's going to be me. Unless we go back to the Dark Ages and I can supply the world with light. Otherwise, I'm afraid I'm useless.'

Bernie Kosar rolls onto his back and stares at me with big eyes, wanting me to rub his belly.

16

Sam is avoiding me. At school he seems to disappear when he sees me, or always makes sure we're in a group. At the urging of Henri – who's desperate to get his hands on Sam's magazine after combing through everything that came up on the internet and finding nothing like Sam's magazine – I decide to just go over to his place unannounced. Henri drops me off after we've trained for the day. Sam lives on the outskirts of Paradise in a small, modest house. There's no answer when I knock so I try the door. It's unlocked and I open it and walk through.

Brown shag carpet covers the floors, and family photographs from when Sam was very young hang on wood-paneled walls. Him, his mother, and a man who I assume is his father, who is wearing glasses every bit as thick as Sam's. Then I look closer. They look like the exact same pair of glasses.

I creep down the hallway until I find the door that must be to Sam's bedroom; a sign reading ENTER AT YOUR OWN RISK hangs from a tack. The door is open a crack and I peer inside. The room is very clean, everything consciously put in a place. His twin bed is made, has a black comforter with the planet Saturn repeated across it. Matching pillowcases. The walls are covered with posters. There are two NASA ones, the movie poster from *Alien*, a movie poster from *Star Wars*, and one that is a blacklight poster of a green alien head surrounded by dark felt. In the center of the room, hanging from clear thread, is the solar system, all nine planets and the sun. It makes me think of what Henri showed me earlier in the week. I think that Sam would lose his mind if he were to see the same thing. And then I see Sam, hunched over a small oak desk, with headphones on. I push the door open and he looks over his shoulder. He isn't wearing his glasses, and without them his eyes look very small and beady, almost cartoonlike.

'What's up?' I ask casually, as if I'm at his house every day.

He looks shocked and scared and he frantically pulls the headphones off to reach in one of the drawers. I look at his desk and see that he's reading a copy of *They Walk Among Us*. When I look back up he is pointing a gun at me.

'Whoa,' I say, instinctively lifting my hands in front of me. 'What's going on?'

He stands up. His hands are shaking. The gun is pointed at my chest. I think that he's lost his mind.

'Tell me what you are,' he says.

'What are you talking about?'

'I saw what you did in those woods. You're not human.'

I was afraid of this, that he saw more than I had hoped.

'This is crazy, Sam! I got into a fight. I've been doing martial arts for years.'

'Your hands lit up like flashlights. You could throw people around like they were nothing. That's not normal.'

'Don't be stupid,' I say, my hands still in front of me. 'Look at them. Do you see any lights? I told you, they were gloves that Kevin was wearing.'

'I asked Kevin! He said he wasn't wearing gloves!'

'Do you really think he would tell you the truth after what happened? Put the gun down.'

'Tell me! What are you?'

I roll my eyes. 'Yes, I'm an alien, Sam. I'm from a planet hundreds of millions of miles away. I have superpowers. Is that what you want to hear?'

He stares at me, his hands still shaking.

'Do you realize how stupid that sounds? Quit being crazy and put the gun down.'

'Is what you just said true?'

'That you're being stupid? Yes, it's true. You're too obsessed with this stuff. You see aliens and alien conspiracies in every part of your life, including in your only friend. Now quit pointing that damn gun at me.'

He stares at me, and I can tell he's thinking about what I said. I drop my hands. Then he sighs and lowers the gun. 'I'm sorry,' he says.

I take a deep, nervous breath. 'You should be. What the hell were you thinking?'

'It wasn't actually loaded.'

'You should have told me that earlier,' I say. 'Why do you want so badly to believe in this stuff?'

He shakes his head and puts the gun back in the drawer. I take a minute to calm myself down and try to act casual, like what just happened is no big deal.

'What are you reading?' I ask.

He shrugs. 'Just more alien stuff. Maybe I should cool it a bit.'

'Or just read it as fiction instead of fact,' I say. 'The stuff must be pretty convincing, though. Can I see it?'

He hands me the latest copy of *They Walk Among Us* and I sit tentatively on the edge of his bed. I think he's calmed down enough to not spring a gun on me again at least. Again, it is a bad photocopy, the print slightly unaligned with the paper. It isn't very thick – eight pages, twelve at the most, printed on legal-sized sheets. The date at the top reads DECEMBER. It must be the newest issue.

'This is weird stuff, Sam Goode,' I say.

He smiles. 'Weird people like weird stuff.'

'Where do you get this?' I ask.

'I subscribe to it.'

'I know, but how?'

Sam shrugs. 'I don't know. It just started arriving one day.'

'Are you subscribed to some other magazine? Perhaps they pulled your contact info from there.'

'I went to a convention once. I think I signed up for some contest or something while I was there. I can't remember. I've always assumed that's where they got my address.'

I scan the cover. There's no website listed anywhere on it, and I didn't expect there to be, considering that Henri has already searched the internet high and low. I read the headline of the top story:

IS YOUR NEIGHBOR AN ALIEN?
TEN FAILSAFE WAYS TO TELL!

In the middle of the article there's a picture of a man holding a bag of trash in one hand and the lid to the trash can in the other. He is standing at the end of the driveway and we're to assume he's in the process of dropping the bag into the can. Though the whole publication is in black-and-white, there is a certain glow to the man's eyes. It's a horrible image – as though somebody took a picture of an unsuspecting neighbor and then drew around his eyes with a crayon. It makes me laugh.

'What?' Sam asks.

'This is a terrible picture. It looks like something from *Godzilla*.'

Sam looks at it. Then he shrugs. 'I dunno,' he says. 'It could be real. Like you said, I see aliens everywhere, and in everything.'

'But I thought aliens looked like that,' I say, and nod to the blacklight poster on his wall.

'I don't think all of them do,' he says. 'Like you said, you're an alien with superpowers and you don't look like that.'

We both laugh, and I wonder how I'm going to get myself out of that one. Hopefully Sam never finds out I was telling him the truth. Part of me wants to tell him, though – about me, about Henri, about Lorien – and I wonder what his reaction would be. Would he believe me?

I flip the paper open to look for the publishing page that all newspapers and magazines have. There isn't one here, only more stories and theories.

'There isn't a publisher info page.'

'What do you mean?'

'You know how magazines and newspapers always have that page listing staff, editors, writers, where it's being printed, and all that? You know, "For questions, contact so and so." All publications have them, but this doesn't.'

'They have to protect their anonymity,' Sam says.

'From what?'

'Aliens,' he says, and smiles, as though acknowledging the absurdity of it.

'Do you have last month's issue?'

He grabs it from his closet. I quickly flip through it, hoping that the Mogadorian article is in this one and not an earlier month. And then I find it on page 4.

THE MOGADORIAN RACE SEEK TO TAKE OVER EARTH

The Mogadorian alien race, from the planet Mogadore of the 9th Galaxy, have been on Earth for over ten years now. They are a vicious race on a quest for universal domination. They are rumored to have wiped out another planet not unlike Earth, and are planning to expose Earth's weaknesses in a quest to inhabit our planet next.

(more to follow next issue)

I read the article three times. I was hoping there might be more to it than what Sam already said, but no such luck. And there is no Ninth Galaxy. I wonder where they got that from. I flip through the new issue twice. There is no mention of the Mogadorians. My first thought is that there was nothing left to report, that more news failed to present itself. But I don't believe that's the case. My second thought is that the Mogadorians read the issue and then fixed the problem, whatever the problem was.

'Do you mind if I borrow this?' I ask, holding up last month's issue.

He nods. 'But be careful with it.'

Three hours later, at eight o'clock, Sam's mother still isn't home. I ask Sam where she is and he shrugs as though he doesn't know and her absence is nothing new. Mostly we just play video games and watch TV and for dinner we eat microwavable meals. The whole time I'm there he doesn't once wear his glasses, which is odd since I've never seen him without them before. Even when we ran the mile in gym class, he kept them on. I grab them from the top of his dresser and put them on. The world becomes an instant blur and they give me a headache almost immediately.

I look at Sam. He's sitting cross-legged on the floor, his back against his bed, with a book of aliens in his lap.

'Jesus, is your vision really this bad?' I ask.

He looks up at me. 'They were my dad's.'

I take them off.

'Do you even need glasses, Sam?'

He shrugs. 'Not really.'

'So why do you wear them?'

'They were my dad's.'

I put them back on. 'Wow, I don't see how you can even walk straight with these on.'

'My eyes are used to them.'

'You know these will screw up your vision if you continue wearing them, right?'

'Then I'll be able to see what my dad saw.'

I take them off and put them back where I found them. I don't really understand why Sam wears them. For sentimental reasons? Does he really think it's worth it?

'Where is your dad, Sam?'

He looks up at me.

'I don't know,' he says.

'What do you mean?'

'He disappeared when I was seven.'

'You don't know where he went?'

He sighs, drops his head, and resumes reading. Obviously he doesn't want to talk about it.

'Do you believe in any of this stuff?' he asks after a few minutes of silence.

'Aliens?'

'Yeah.'

'Yes, I believe in aliens.'

'Do you think they really abduct people?'

'I have no idea. I guess we can't rule it out. Do you believe they do?'

He nods. 'Most days. But sometimes the idea just seems stupid.'

'I can understand that.'

He looks up at me. 'I think my dad was abducted,' he says.

He tenses the second the words leave his mouth and a look of vulnerability crosses his face. It makes me believe that he has shared his theory before, with someone whose response was less than kind.

'Why do you think that?'

'Because he just disappeared. He went to the store to buy milk and bread, and he never came back. His truck was parked right outside the store but nobody there had seen him. He just vanished, and his glasses were on the sidewalk beside his truck.' He pauses for a second. 'I was worried you were here to abduct me.'

It's a hard theory to believe. How could nobody have seen his father abducted if the incident occurred in the middle of town? Perhaps his dad had reason to leave and he plotted his own disappearance. It's not hard to make yourself disappear; Henri and I have been doing it for ten years now. But all of a sudden Sam's interest in aliens makes perfect sense. Perhaps Sam just wants to see the world as his dad did, but maybe part of him truly believes that his dad's final sight is captured in the glasses, somehow etched into the lenses. Maybe he thinks that with persistence one day he'll eventually come to see it as well, and that his dad's last vision will confirm what is already in his head. Or maybe he believes that if he searches long enough he'll finally come across an article that proves his father was abducted, and not only that, but that he can be saved.

And who am I to say that he won't one day find that proof?

'I believe you,' I say. 'I think alien abductions are very possible.'

17

The next day I wake earlier than normal, crawl out of bed, and walk out of my room to find Henri sitting at the table scanning the papers with his laptop open. The sun is still hidden, and the house is dark, the only light coming from his computer screen.

'Anything?'

'Nah, nothing really.'

I turn on the kitchen light. Bernie Kosar paws at the front door. I open it and he shoots out into the yard and patrols as he does every morning, head up, trotting around the perimeter looking for anything suspicious. He sniffs at random places. Once satisfied that everything is as it should be, he bolts into the woods and disappears.

Two issues of *They Walk Among Us* are lying atop the kitchen table, the original and a photocopy that Henri has made to keep for himself. A magnifying glass lies between them.

'Anything unique on the original?'

'No.'

'So, now what?' I ask.

'Well, I have had some luck. I cross-referenced some of the other articles in the issue and got a few hits, one of which led me to a man's personal website. I sent him an email.'

I stare at Henri.

'Don't worry,' he says. 'They can't track emails. At least not the way I send them.'

'How do you send them?'

'I reroute them through various servers in cities across the world, so that the original location is lost along the way.'

'Impressive.'

Bernie Kosar scratches at the door and I let him in. The clock on the microwave reads 5:59. I have two hours before I have to be at school.

'Do you really think we want to go digging around in all this?' I ask. 'I mean, what if it's all a trap? What if they are simply trying to root us out of hiding?'

Henri nods. 'You know, if the article had mentioned anything about us, that might have given me pause. But it didn't. It was about their invading Earth, much the same way they did Lorien. There is so much about it that we don't understand. You were right a few weeks ago when you said we were defeated so easily. We were. It doesn't make sense. The entire situation with the disappearance of the Elders also doesn't make sense. Even getting you and the other children off of Lorien, which I have never questioned, seems odd. And while you've seen what happened – and I've had the same visions, too – something is still missing from the equation. If we one day make it back, I think it's imperative to understand what happened in order to prevent it from happening again. You know the saying: he who doesn't understand history is doomed to repeat it. And when it's repeated, the stakes are doubled.'

'Okay,' I say. 'But according to what you said Saturday night, the chance of us going back seems slimmer every day. So, with that, do you think it's worth it?'

Henri shrugs. 'There are still five others out there. Perhaps they've received their Legacies. Perhaps yours are merely delayed. I think it's best to plan for all possibilities.'

'Well, what are you planning to do?'

'Just make a phone call. I'm curious to hear what this person knows. I wonder what caused him to not follow up. One of two possibilities: either he found no other information and lost interest in the story, or somebody got to him after the publication.'

I sigh. 'Well, be careful,' I say.

I pull on a pair of sweatpants and a sweatshirt over two T-shirts, tie my tennis shoes and stand and stretch. I toss into my backpack the clothes I plan to wear to school, along with a towel, a bar of soap and a small bottle of shampoo so I can shower when I get there. I'll now be running to school each morning. Henri ostensibly believes the additional exercise will help in my training, but the real reason is that he hopes it will help my body's transition and pull my Legacies from their slumber, if that is indeed what they are doing.

I look down at Bernie Kosar. 'Ready for a run, boy? Huh? Want to go for a run?'

His tail wags and he turns in circles.

'See you after school.'

'Have a good run,' says Henri. 'Be careful on the road.'

We walk out the door and cold, brisk air meets us. Bernie Kosar barks excitedly a few times. I start at a slight jog, down the drive, out onto the gravel road, the dog trotting beside me as I thought he would. It takes a quarter of a mile to warm up.

'Ready to step it up a notch, boy?'

He pays me no attention, just keeps trotting along with his tongue dangling, looking happy as can be.

'All right then, here we go.'

I kick it into high gear, moving into a run, and then into a dead sprint shortly after, going as fast as I can. I leave Bernie Kosar in the dust. I look behind me and he is running as fast as he can, yet I am pulling ahead of him. The wind through my hair, the trees passing in a blur. It all feels great. Then Bernie Kosar bolts into the woods and disappears from sight. I'm not sure if I should stop and wait for him. Then I turn around and Bernie Kosar jumps out of the woods ten feet in front of me.

I look down at him and he looks up at me, tongue to the side, a sense of glee in his eyes.

'You're an odd dog, you know that?'

After five minutes the school comes into view. I sprint the remaining half mile, exerting myself, running as hard as I can because it is so early that there is no one out and about to see me. Then I stand with my fingers interlocked behind my head, catching my breath. Bernie Kosar arrives thirty seconds later and sits watching me. I kneel down and pet him.

'Good job, buddy. I think we have a new morning ritual.'

I pull my bag from over my shoulders, unzip it, and remove a package with a few strips of bacon and I give them to him. He scarfs them down.

'Okay, boy, I'm heading in. Go on home. Henri's waiting.'

He watches me for a second, and then goes off trotting towards home. His comprehension completely amazes me. Then I turn and walk into the building and head for the shower.

I am the second person to enter astronomy. Sam is the first, already sitting in his normal seat at the back of the class.

'Whoa,' I say. 'No glasses. What gives?'

He shrugs. 'I thought about what you said. It's probably stupid for me to wear them.'

I sit beside him and smile. It's hard to imagine I'll ever get used to his eyes looking so beady. I give him back the issue of *They Walk Among Us*. He tucks it into his bag. I hold up my fingers like a gun and nudge him.

'Bang!' I say.

He starts laughing. Then I do, too. Neither of us can stop. Every time one of us is close the other starts laughing and it begins all over again. People stare at us when they enter. Then comes Sarah. She walks in by herself, saunters up to us with a look of confusion and sits in the seat beside me.

'What are you guys laughing at?'

'I'm not really sure,' I say, and then laugh a little more.

Mark is the last person to walk in. He sits in his usual seat, but instead of Sarah sitting beside him today there's another girl. I think she's a senior. Sarah reaches beneath the table and grabs hold of my hand.

'There is something I need to talk to you about,' she says.

'What?'

'I know it's last-minute, but my parents want to have you and your dad over for Thanksgiving dinner tomorrow.'

'Wow. That would be awesome. I have to ask, but I know we don't have plans, so I assume the answer is yes.'

She smiles. 'Great.'

'Since it's just the two of us, we don't usually even do Thanksgiving.'

'Well, we really go all out. And my brothers will both be home from college. They want to meet you.'

'How do they know about me?'

'How do you think?'

The teacher walks in and Sarah winks, then we both start taking notes.

Henri is waiting for me as usual, Bernie Kosar propped up on the passenger seat with his tail wagging, thumping the side of the door the second he sees me. I slide in.

'Athens,' says Henri.

'Athens?'

'Athens, Ohio.'

'Why?'

'That's where the issues of *They Walk Among Us* are being written, and printed. It's where they are being mailed.'

'How did you find that out?'

'I have my ways.'

I look at him.

'Okay, okay. It took three emails and five phone calls, but now I have the number.' He looks over at me. 'That is to say, it wasn't all that hard to find with a little effort.'

I nod. I know what he is telling me. The Mogadorians would have found it just as easily as he did. Which means, of course, that the scale now tips in favor of Henri's second possibility – that somebody got to the publisher before the story further developed.

'How far away is Athens?'

'Two hours by car.'

'Are you going?'

'I hope not. I'm going to call first.'

When we get home Henri immediately picks up the phone and sits at the kitchen table. I sit down across from him and listen.

'Yes, I'm calling to inquire about an article in last month's issue of *They Walk Among Us.*'

A deep voice responds on the other end. I can't hear what is said.

Henri smiles. 'Yes,' he says, then pauses.

'No, I'm not a subscriber. But a friend of mine is.'

Another pause. 'No, thank you.'

He nods his head.

'Well, I'm curious about the article written on the Mogadorians. There was never a follow-up in this month's issue as expected.'

I lean in and strain to hear, my body tense and rigid. When the reply comes the voice sounds shaken, disturbed. Then the phone goes dead.

'Hello?'

Henri pulls the phone away from his ear, looks at it, then brings it back in.

'Hello?' he says again.

Then he closes the phone and sets it on the table. He looks at me.

'He said, "Don't call here again." Then he hung up on me.'

18

After debating it for several hours, Henri wakes up the next morning and prints door-to-door directions from here to Athens, Ohio. He tells me he'll be home early enough so we can go to Thanksgiving dinner at Sarah's house, and he hands me a slip of paper with the address and the phone number of where he's going.

'Are you sure this is worth it?' I ask.

'We have to figure out what's going on.'

I sigh. 'I think we both know what is going on.'

'Maybe,' he says, but with full authority and none of the uncertainty usually accompanying the word.

'You do realize what you would tell me if the roles were reversed, right?'

Henri smiles. 'Yes, John. I know what I would say. But I think this will help us. I want to find out what they have done to scare this man so badly. I want to know if they have mentioned us, if they are searching for us by means that we haven't yet thought of. It will help us to stay hidden, stay ahead of them. And if this man has seen them, we'll learn what they look like.'

'We already know what they look like.'

'We knew what they looked like when they attacked, over ten years ago, but they might have changed. They've been on Earth a long time now. I want to know how they're blending in.'

'Even if we know what they look like, by the time we see them on the street, it's probably going to be too late.'

'Maybe, maybe not. I see one, I'm going to try and kill it. There's no guarantee it's going to be able to kill me,' he says, this time with the uncertainty and none of the authority.

I give up. I don't like a single thing about him driving to Athens while I sit around at home. But I know my objections will continue to fall on deaf ears.

'You sure you'll be back on time?' I ask.

'I'm leaving now, which puts me there about nine. I doubt I'll stay more than an hour, two at the most. I should be back by one.'

'So why do I have this?' I ask, and hold up the slip of paper with the address and phone number.

He shrugs. 'Well, you never know.'

'Which is precisely why I don't think you should go.'

'Touché,' he says, bringing an end to the discussion. He gathers his papers, stands from the table, and pushes in the chair.

'I'll see you this afternoon.'

'Okay,' I say.

He walks out to the truck and gets inside. Bernie Kosar and I walk out to the front porch and watch him drive away. I don't know why, but I have a bad feeling. I hope he makes it back.

It's a long day. One of those days where time slows down and every minute seems like ten, every hour seems like twenty. I play video games and surf the internet. I look for news that might be related to one of the other children. I don't find anything, which makes me happy. That means we're staying under the radar. Avoiding our enemies.

I periodically check my phone. I send a text message to Henri at noon. He doesn't reply. I eat lunch and feed Bernie, and then I send another. No reply. A nervous, unsettled feeling creeps in. Henri has never failed to text back immediately. Maybe his phone is off. Maybe his battery has died. I try to convince myself of these possibilities, but I know that neither of them is true.

At two o'clock I start to get worried. Really worried. We're supposed to be at the Harts' in an hour. Henri knows the dinner is important to me. And he would never blow it off. I get in the shower with the hope that by the time I get out, Henri will be sitting at our kitchen table drinking a cup of coffee. I turn the hot water all the way up and don't bother with the cold at all. I don't feel a thing. My entire body is now impervious to heat. It feels like lukewarm water is streaming over my skin, and I actually miss the feeling of heat. I used to love taking hot showers. Standing under the water for as long as it lasted. Closing my eyes and enjoying the water hitting my head and running down. It took me away from my life. It let me forget about who and what I am for a little while.

When I get out of the shower, I open my closet and look for the nicest clothes I have, which are nothing special: khakis, a button-down shirt, a sweater. Because we live our life on the run, all I have are running shoes, which is so ridiculous it makes me laugh – the first time I've laughed all day. I go to Henri's room and look in his closet. He has a pair of loafers that fit me. Seeing all his clothes makes me more worried, more upset. I want to believe he's just taking longer than he should, but he would have contacted me. Something has to be wrong.

I walk to the front door, where Bernie is sitting, staring

out the window. He looks up at me and whines. I pat him on the head and go back to my room. I look at the clock. It's just after three. I check my phone. No messages, no texts. I decide to go to Sarah's and if I don't hear from Henri by five, I'll figure out a plan then. Maybe I'll tell them Henri is sick and that I'm not feeling well either. Maybe I'll tell them Henri's truck broke down and I need to go help him. Hopefully he shows up and we can just have a nice Thanksgiving dinner. It will actually be the first one we've ever had. If not, I'll tell them something. I'll have to.

Without the truck I decide I'll run. I probably won't even break a sweat, and I will be able to get there faster than I would in the truck. And because of the holiday, the roads should be empty. I say good-bye to Bernie, tell him I'll be home later, and take off. I run on the edges of the fields, through woods. It feels good to burn some energy. It takes the edge off my anxiety. A couple times I get up near full speed, which is probably somewhere around sixty or seventy miles per hour. The cold air feels amazing whipping across my face. The sound of it is great, the same sound I hear when I stick my head out the window of the truck as we're driving down a highway. I wonder how fast I'll be able to run when I'm twenty, or twenty-five.

I stop running about a hundred yards from Sarah's house. I'm not short of breath at all. As I walk up the driveway I see Sarah peek out the window. She smiles and waves, opening the front door just as I step onto her porch.

'Hey, handsome,' she says.

I turn and look over my shoulder to pretend she's talking to somebody else. Then I turn back around and ask her if she's talking to me. She laughs.

'You're silly,' she says, and punches me in the arm before

pulling me close to give me a lingering kiss. I take a deep breath and can smell the food: turkey and stuffing, sweet potatoes, brussels sprouts, pumpkin pie.

'Smells great,' I say.

'My mom has been cooking all day.'

'Can't wait to eat.'

'Where is your dad?'

'He got held up. He should be here in a little while.'

'Is he okay?'

'Yeah, it's not a big deal.'

We go inside and she takes me on a tour. It's a great house. A classic family home with bedrooms on the second floor, an attic where one of her brothers has his room, and all of the living spaces – the living room, dining room, kitchen and family room – on the first floor. When we get to her room, she closes the door and kisses me. I'm surprised, but thrilled.

'I've been looking forward to doing that all day,' she says softly when she pulls away. As she walks towards the door, I pull her back to me and kiss her again.

'And I'm looking forward to kissing you again later,' I whisper. She smiles and punches me on the arm again.

We head back downstairs and she takes me to the family room, where her two older brothers, home from college for the weekend, are watching football with her father. I sit with them, while Sarah goes to the kitchen to help her mother and her younger sister with dinner. I've never been that into football. I guess, because of the way Henri and I have lived, I've never really gotten into anything outside of our life. My concerns were always with trying to fit into wherever we were, and then getting ready to go somewhere else. Her brothers, and her father, all played football in high school.

They love it. And in today's game, one of her brothers and her father like one of the teams, while her other brother likes the other team. They argue with each other, taunt each other, cheer and groan depending on what's happening in the game. They've clearly been doing this for years, probably for their entire lives, and they're clearly having a great time. It makes me wish Henri and I had something, besides my training and our endless running and hiding, that we were both into and that we could enjoy with each other. It makes me wish I had a real father and brothers to hang out with.

At halftime Sarah's mother calls us in for dinner. I check my phone and still nothing. Before we sit down I go to the bathroom and try to call Henri and it goes straight to voice mail. It's almost five o'clock, and I'm starting to panic. I come back to the table, where everyone is sitting. The table looks amazing. There are flowers in the center, with place mats and table settings meticulously placed in front of each of the chairs. Serving dishes of food are spread around the inside of the table, with the turkey sitting in front of Mr Hart's place. Just after I sit down, Mrs Hart comes into the room. She has taken off her apron and is wearing a beautiful skirt and sweater.

'Have you heard from your dad?' she says.

'I just tried calling him. He, uh, is running late and asked us not to wait. He's very sorry for the inconvenience,' I say.

Mr Hart starts carving the turkey. Sarah smiles at me from across the table, which makes me feel better for about half a second. The food starts being passed, and I take small portions of everything. I don't think I'm going to be able to eat very much. I keep my phone out and on my lap, and have it set to vibrate if a call or text comes through. With each passing second, however, I don't believe anything is going to come through, or that I will ever see Henri again. The idea of living by myself – with my Legacies developing, and without anyone to explain them to me or train me, of running on my own, of hiding on my own, of finding my own way, of fighting the Mogadorians, fighting them until they are defeated or I am dead – terrifies me.

Dinner takes forever. Time is moving slowly again. Sarah's whole family peppers me with questions. I've never been in a situation where I've been asked so many things by so many people in such a short period of time. They ask about my past, the places I've lived, about Henri, about my mother – who, I say as I always do, died when I was very young. It's the only answer I give that has even the smallest sliver of truth. I have no idea if my answers even make sense. The phone on my leg feels like it weighs a thousand pounds. It doesn't vibrate. It just sits there.

After dinner, and before dessert, Sarah asks everyone to go out to the backyard so she can take some pictures. As we go outside, Sarah asks if something is wrong. I tell her I'm worried about Henri. She tries to calm me down and tell me everything is fine, but it doesn't work. If anything, it makes me feel worse. I try to imagine where he is and what he's doing, and the only image I can bring is him standing before a Mogadorian, looking terrified, and knowing he's about to die.

As we gather for the pictures, I start to panic. How could I get to Athens? I could run, but it might be hard to find my way, especially because I would have to avoid traffic and stay off the major highways. I could take a bus, but it would take too long. I could ask Sarah, but that would involve a huge amount of explaining, including telling her I was an alien and that I believed Henri had been either captured or killed by hostile aliens who were searching for me so that they could kill me. Not the best idea.

As we pose I get a desperate urge to leave, but I need to do it in a way that doesn't make Sarah or her family mad at me. I focus on the camera, staring directly into it while trying to think of an excuse that will get the least amount of questions. I'm wracked with full-on panic now. My hands begin to shake. They feel hot. I look down at them to make sure they aren't glowing. They're not, but when I look back up I see that the whole camera is shaking in Sarah's hands. I know that somehow I'm doing it, but I have no idea how or what I can do to make it stop. A chill shoots up my back. My breath catches in my throat and at the same time the glass lens of the camera cracks and shatters. Sarah screams, then pulls the camera down and stares at it in confusion. Her mouth drops open and tears well up in her eyes.

Her parents rush over to her to see if she's okay. I just stand there in shock. I'm not sure what to do. I'm bummed about her camera, and that she's upset about it, but I'm also thrilled because my telekinesis has clearly arrived. Will I be able to control it? Henri will be beside himself when he finds out. Henri. The panic returns. I clench my hands into fists. I need to get out of here. I need to find him. If the Mogadorians have him, which I hope they don't, I'll kill every damn one of them to get him back.

Thinking quickly, I walk over to Sarah and pull her away from her parents, who are examining the camera to figure out what has just happened.

'I just got a message from Henri. I'm really sorry, but I need to go.'

She's clearly distracted, glancing from me to her parents.

'Is he all right?'

'Yes, but I have to go – he needs me.' She nods and we kiss gently. I hope it's not for the last time.

I thank her parents and her brothers and sister and I leave before they can ask me too many questions. I walk through the house and as soon as I'm out the front door, I start running. I take the same route home that I took to get to Sarah's house earlier. I stay off the main roads, run through the trees. I'm back in a few minutes. I hear Bernie Kosar scratching at the door as I sprint up the drive. He's clearly anxious, as though he also senses something amiss.

I go straight to my room. I retrieve from my bag the piece of paper containing the phone number and address Henri gave me before leaving. I dial the number. A recording comes on. 'I'm sorry, the number you are trying to reach has been disconnected or is no longer in service.' I look down at the piece of paper and try the number again. The same recording.

'Shit!' I yell. I kick a chair and it sails across the kitchen and into the living room.

I walk into my room. I walk out. I walk back in again. I stare in the mirror. My eyes are red; tears have surfaced but none are falling. Hands shaking. Anger and rage and a terrible fear that Henri is dead consume me. I squeeze my eyes shut and squeeze all the rage into the pit of my stomach. In a sudden burst I scream and open my eyes and thrust my hands towards the mirror and the glass shatters though I am ten feet away. I stand looking at it. Most of the mirror is still attached to the wall. What happened at Sarah's was no fluke.

I look at the shards on the floor. I reach a hand out in front of me and while concentrating on one particular shard, I try to move it. My breathing is controlled, but all the fear and anger remain within me. Fear is too simple a word. Terror. That is what I feel.

The shard doesn't move at first, but then after fifteen seconds it begins to shake. Slowly at first, then rapidly. And then I remember. Henri said that it's usually emotions that trigger Legacies. Surely that is what is happening now. I strain to lift the shard. Beads of sweat stand out on my forehead. I concentrate with everything that I have and everything that I am despite all that is going on. It's a struggle to breathe. Ever so slowly the shard begins to rise. One inch. Two inches. It is a foot above the floor, continuing up, my right arm extended and moving with it until the shard of glass is at eye level. I hold it there. *If only Henri could see this,* I think. And in a flash, through the excitement of my newly discovered happiness, panic and fear return. I look at the shard, at the way it reflects the wood-paneled wall looking old and brittle in the glass. Wood. Old and brittle. And then my eyes snap open wider than they ever have before in all of my life.

The Chest!

Henri had said it: 'Only the two of us can open it together. Unless I die; then you can open it yourself.'

I drop the shard and sprint from my bedroom into Henri's. The Chest is on the floor beside his bed. I snatch it, run into the kitchen, and throw it on the table. The lock in the shape of the Loric emblem is looking me in the face.

I sit at the table and stare at the lock. My lip is quivering. I try to slow my breathing but it is useless; my chest is heaving as though I just finished a ten-mile sprint. I'm scared of feeling a click beneath my grip. I take a deep breath and close my eyes.

'Please don't open,' I say.

I grab hold of the lock. I squeeze as tightly as I can, my breath held, vision blurry, the muscles in my forearm flexed and straining. Waiting for the click. Holding the lock and waiting for the click.

Only there is no click.

I let go and slouch in the chair and hold my head in my hands. A small glimmer of hope. I run my hands through my hair and stand. On the counter five feet away is a dirty spoon. I focus on it and sweep my hand across my body and the spoon goes flying. Henri would be so happy. *Henri,* I think, *where are you? Somewhere, and still alive, too. And I'm going to come get you.*

I dial Sam's number, the only friend besides Sarah I've made in Paradise, the only friend I've ever had, if I'm to be honest. He answers on the second ring.

'Hello?'

I close my eyes and pinch the bridge of my nose. I take a deep breath. The shaking has returned, if it ever left in the first place.

'Hello?' he says again.

'Sam.'

'Hey,' he says, then, 'You sound like hell. Are you okay?'

'No. I need your help.'

'Huh? What's happened?'

'Is there any way your mom can bring you over?'

'She's not here. She's working a shift at the hospital because she gets paid double time on holidays. What's going on?'

'Things are bad, Sam. And I need help.'

Another silence, then, 'I'll get there as quickly as I can.'

'You sure?'

'I'll see you soon.'

I close my phone and drop my head to the table. Athens, Ohio. That is where Henri is. Somehow, some way, that is where I have to go.

And I need to get there fast.

19

While I wait for Sam I walk through the house lifting inanimate objects up in the air without touching them: an apple from the kitchen counter, a fork in the sink, a small potted plant sitting beside the front window. I can only lift the small things, and they rise in the air somewhat timidly. When I try for something heavier – a chair, a table – nothing happens.

The three tennis balls Henri and I use for training sit in a basket on the other side of the living room. I bring one of them to me, and as it crosses his line of sight Bernie Kosar stands at attention. Then I throw it without touching it and he sprints after it; but before he can get to it, I pull it back, or when he does manage to get it, I pull it from his mouth, all while sitting in the chair in the living room. It keeps my mind from Henri, from the harm that may have found him, and from the guilt of the lies I'll have to tell Sam.

It takes him twenty-five minutes to ride his bike the four miles to my house. I hear him ride up the drive. He jumps off of it and it crashes to the ground while he runs through the front door without knocking, out of breath. His face is streaked with sweat. He looks around and surveys the scene.

'So what's up?' he asks.

'This is going to sound absurd to you,' I say. 'But you have to promise to take me seriously.'

'What are you talking about?'

What am I talking about? I'm talking about Henri. He has disappeared because of carelessness, the same carelessness he has always preached against. I'm talking about the fact that when you had that gun on me, I told you the truth. I am an alien. Henri and I came to Earth ten years ago, and we are being hunted by a malicious race of aliens. I'm talking about Henri thinking that he could somehow evade them by understanding them a little more. And now he is gone. That is what I'm talking about, Sam. Do you understand? But no, I can't tell him any of these things.

'My dad's been captured, Sam. I'm not entirely sure by who, or what is being done to him. But something has happened, and I think he's being held prisoner. Or worse.'

A grin spreads on his face. 'Get out of here,' he says.

I shake my head and close my eyes. The gravity of the situation again makes it difficult to breathe. I turn and stare pleadingly at Sam. Tears well up in my eyes.

'I'm not kidding.'

Sam's face becomes stricken. 'What do you mean? Who has captured him? Where is he?'

'He tracked the writer of one of the articles in your magazine back to Athens, Ohio, and he went there today. He went there and he hasn't come back. His phone is off. Something has happened to him. Something bad.'

Sam becomes more confused. 'What? Why would he care? I'm missing something. It's just some stupid paper.'

'I don't know, Sam. He's like you – he loves aliens and conspiracy theories and all that stuff,' I say, thinking quickly. 'It's always been a stupid hobby of his. One of the articles piqued his interest and I guess he wanted to know more, so he drove down.'

'Was it the article on the Mogadorians?'

I nod. 'How did you know?'

'Because he looked like he had seen a ghost when I mentioned it on Halloween,' he says, and he shakes his head. 'But why would somebody care if he asked questions about a stupid article?'

'I don't know. I mean, I would imagine these people aren't the sanest in the world. They're probably paranoid and delusional. Maybe they thought he was an alien, the same reason you aimed a gun at me. He was supposed to be home by one and his phone is off. That's all I can say.'

I stand and walk to the kitchen table. I grab the slip of paper with the address and phone number of where Henri has gone.

'This is where he went today,' I say. 'Do you have any idea where it is?'

He looks at the slip, then at me.

'You want to go there?'

'I don't know what else to do.'

'Why can't you just call the cops and tell them what happened?'

I sit down on the couch, thinking of the best way to respond. I wish I could tell him the truth, that the best-case scenario with the cops getting involved would be Henri and I leaving. The worst case would be Henri being questioned, maybe fingerprinted, thrust into the sluggish-paced bureaucracy, which would give the Mogadorians the chance to move. And once they find us, death is imminent.

'Call which cops? The ones in Paradise? What do you think they would do if I told them the truth? It would take days for them to take me seriously, and I don't have days.'

Sam shrugs. 'They might take you seriously. Besides, what if he just got held up, or his phone broke? He might be on his way home now.'

'Maybe, but I don't think so. Something feels off, and I have to get there as soon as possible. He was supposed to be home hours ago.'

'Maybe he got into an accident.'

I shake my head. 'Maybe you're right, but I don't think you are. And if he's being harmed, then we're wasting time.'

Sam looks at the sheet of paper. He bites his lip and remains silent for fifteen seconds.

'Well, I know vaguely how to get to Athens. No idea how to get to this address once we're there, though.'

'I can print directions from the internet. I'm not worried about that. The thing I am worried about is transportation. I have a hundred and twenty dollars in my room. I can pay someone to drive us, but I have no idea who I would ask. There aren't exactly a whole lot of taxis in Paradise, Ohio.'

'We can take our truck.'

'What truck?'

'I mean my dad's truck. We still have it. It's sitting in the garage. It hasn't been touched since he disappeared.'

I look at him. 'Are you serious?'

He nods.

'How long has it been? Does it even still run?'

'Eight years. Why wouldn't it still run? It was nearly new when he bought it.'

'Wait, let me get this right. You're suggesting we drive there ourselves, me and you, two hours to Athens?'

Sam's face twists into a devious smile. 'That's exactly what I'm suggesting.'

I lean forward on the sofa. I can't help but smile as well.

'You know we'll be in deep shit if we get caught, right? Neither of us has our license.'

Sam nods. 'My mom will kill me, and she'll maybe kill you, too. And then there is the law. But yeah, if you really think your dad is in trouble, what other choice do we have? If the roles were reversed, and it was my dad who was in trouble, I would go in a second.'

I look at Sam. There isn't an ounce of hesitation on his face in his suggesting that we drive illegally to a town two hours away, and that's not to mention that neither of us knows how to drive and that we have no idea what to expect once getting there. And yet Sam is on board. It was his idea even.

'All right then, let's drive to Athens,' I say.

I throw my phone in my bag, make sure everything is zipped and in order. Then I walk through the house, taking everything in as though it will be the last time I see any of it. It's foolish thinking, and I know I'm merely being sentimental, but I'm nervous and there is a sort of calming sensation to it. I pick things up, then I set them down. After five minutes I am ready.

'Let's go,' I say to Sam.

'You want to ride on the back of my bike?'

'You ride; I'll jog alongside.'

'What about your asthma?'

'I think I'll be okay.'

We leave. He gets on his bike. He tries to ride as fast as he can, but he is not in great shape. I jog a few feet behind and pretend that I'm winded. Bernie follows us as well. By the time we get to his house, Sam is dripping with sweat. Sam runs into his room and comes out with a backpack. He sets it on the kitchen counter and goes to change his clothes. I peer inside of it. There is a crucifix, a few cloves of garlic, a wooden stake, a hammer, a blob of Silly Putty, and a pocketknife.

'You do realize these people aren't vampires, right?' I say when Sam walks back in.

'Yeah, but you never know. They're probably crazy, like you said.'

'And even if we were hunting vampires, what the hell is the Silly Putty for?'

He shrugs. 'Just want to be prepared.'

I pour a bowl of water for Bernie Kosar and he laps it all up immediately. I change clothes in the bathroom and remove the door-to-door directions from my bag. Then I walk out and through the house and into the garage, which is dark and smells of gasoline and old grass clippings. Sam flips on the light. Various tools have rusted with disuse and hang on the Peg-Board walls. The truck sits in the center of the garage, covered with a large blue tarp that's coated with a thick layer of dust.

'How long has it been since this tarp was removed?'

'Not since Dad went missing.'

I grab one corner, Sam takes the other, and together we peel it away and I set it in the corner. Sam stares at the truck, his eyes big, a smile on his face.

The truck is small, dark blue, room inside for only two people, or maybe a third if they don't mind an uncomfortable ride sitting in the center. It will be perfect for Bernie Kosar. None of the dust from the past eight years has made it onto the truck, so it sparkles as though it was recently waxed. I throw my bag onto the bed.

'My dad's truck,' Sam says proudly. 'All these years. It looks exactly the same.'

'Our golden chariot,' I say. 'Do you have the keys?'

He walks to the side of the garage and lifts a set of keys from a hook on the wall. I unlock the garage door and open it.

'Do you want to paper-rock-scissors to see who drives?' I ask.

'Nope,' Sam says, and then he unlocks the driver's side door and gets in behind the wheel. The engine cranks over and finally starts. He rolls down the window.

'I think my dad would be proud to see me driving it,' he says.

I smile. 'I think so, too. Pull it out and I'll close the door.'

He takes a deep breath, and then puts the truck in drive and slowly, timidly, inches it out of the garage. He hits the brakes too hard too soon and the truck slams to a stop.

'You aren't all the way out yet,' I say.

He eases his foot off the brake and then inches the rest of the way out. I close the garage door behind him. Bernie Kosar jumps up and in of his own volition and I slide in beside him. Sam's hands are white knuckled at the ten and two positions of the wheel.

'Nervous?' I ask.

'Terrified.'

'You'll be fine,' I say. 'We've both seen it done a thousand times before.'

He nods. 'Okay. Which way do I turn out of the driveway?'

'We really going to do this?'

'Yes,' he says.

'We turn right, then,' I say, 'and head in the direction away from town.'

We both buckle our seat beats. I crack the window enough

so that Bernie Kosar can fit his head out, which he does immediately, standing with his hind legs in my lap.

'I'm scared shitless,' Sam says.

'Me too.'

He takes a deep breath, holds the air in his lungs, and then slowly exhales.

'And . . . away . . . we . . . go,' he says, taking his foot off the brake when he says the last word. The truck goes bouncing down the driveway. He hits the brakes once and we skid to a stop. Then he starts again and inches down the drive more slowly this time until he stops at the end of it, looks both ways, and then turns out onto the road. Again, slow at first, then gaining speed. He is tense, leaning forward, and then after a mile a grin begins to form on his face and he leans back.

'This isn't so hard.'

'You're a natural.'

He keeps the truck close to the painted line on the right side of the road. He tenses every time a car passes in the opposite direction, but after a while he relaxes and pays the other cars little attention. He makes one turn, then another, and in twenty-five minutes we pull onto the interstate.

'I can't believe we're doing this,' Sam finally says. 'This is the craziest shit I've ever done.'

'Me too.'

'Do you have any plan when we get there?'

'None whatsoever. I'm hoping we'll be able to scope the place out and go from there. I have no idea if it's a house or an office building or what. I don't even know if he is there.'

He nods. 'Do you think he's okay?'

‘I have no idea,’ I say.

I take a deep breath. We have an hour and a half to go. Then we’ll reach Athens.

Then we’ll find Henri.

20

We drive south until, nestled in the foothills of the Appalachian Mountains, Athens comes into view: a small city sprouting through the trees. In the waning light I can see a river curling gently around that seems to cup the city, serving as the border to the east, south and west, and to the north lie hills and trees. The temperature is relatively warm for November. We pass the college football stadium. A white-domed arena stands a little beyond it.

'Take this exit,' I say.

Sam guides the truck off the interstate and turns right onto Richland Avenue. Both of us are elated we made it in one piece, and without being caught.

'So this is what a college town looks like, huh?'

'I guess so,' Sam says.

Buildings and dorms are on each side of us. The grass is green, meticulously trimmed even though it is November. We drive up a steep hill.

'At the top of this is Court Street. We want to turn left.'

'How far are we?' Sam asks.

'Less than a mile.'

'Do you want to drive by it first?'

'No. I think we should park the first opportunity we get and walk.'

We drive down Court Street, which is the main artery in the center of town. Everything is closed for the holiday

– bookstores, coffeehouses, bars. Then I see it, standing out like a jewel.

'Stop!' I say.

Sam slams on the brakes.

'What?!'

A car honks behind us.

'Nothing, nothing. Keep driving. Let's park.'

We drive another block until we find a lot to park in. By my guess we are a five-minute walk at most from the address.

'What was that? You scared the crap out of me.'

'Henri's truck is back there,' I say.

Sam nods. 'Why do you sometimes call him Henri?'

'I don't know, I just do. Sort of a joke between us,' I say, and look at Bernie Kosar. 'Do you think we should take him?'

Sam shrugs. 'He might get in the way.'

I give Bernie Kosar a few treats and leave him in the truck with the window cracked. He is not happy about it and begins whining and scratching at the window, but I don't think we'll be long. Sam and I walk back up Court Street, the straps of my bag pulled over my shoulders, Sam holding his in his hand. He has removed the Silly Putty and is squeezing it like people do with those foam balls when they're stressed. We reach Henri's truck. The doors are locked. There is nothing of importance on the seats or dash.

'Well, this means two things,' I say. 'Henri is still here, and whoever has him hasn't discovered his truck yet, which means he hasn't talked. Not that he ever would.'

'What would he say if he talked?'

For a brief moment I had forgotten that Sam knows nothing of Henri's true reasons for being here. I've already slipped and called him Henri. I need to be careful not to reveal anything else.

'I don't know,' I say. 'I mean, who knows what sorts of questions these weirdos are asking.'

'Okay, now what?'

I pull out the map to the address Henri had given me that morning. 'We walk,' I say.

We walk back the way we came. The buildings end and houses begin. Unkempt and dirty looking. In no time at all we reach the address and stop.

I look at the slip of paper, then at the house. I take a deep breath.

'This is us,' I say.

We stand looking up at the two-story house with gray vinyl siding. The front walk leads to an unpainted front porch with a broken swing hanging unevenly to the side. The grass is long and untended. It looks uninhabited, but there is a car in the driveway at the rear. I don't know what to do. I remove my phone. It is 11:12. I call Henri even though I know he won't answer. It's an attempt to establish my wits, to come up with a plan. I hadn't thought this far ahead, and now that the reality is here my mind is blank. My call goes straight to voice mail.

'Let me go knock on the door,' Sam says.

'And say what?'

'I don't know, whatever comes to my mind.'

But he doesn't get a chance to because just then a man walks out of the front door. He is huge, at least six feet six, two hundred and fifty pounds. He has a goatee and his head is shaved. He's wearing work boots, blue jeans, and a black sweatshirt pulled up to his elbows. There is a tattoo on his right forearm, but I am too far away to see what it is. He spits into the yard, then turns around and locks the front door, walking off the porch and heading our way. I stiffen as he approaches. The tattoo is of an alien holding a bouquet of tulips in one hand as though offering them to some unseen entity. Then the man walks right past us without saying a word. Sam and I turn and watch him go.

'Did you see his tattoo?' I ask.

'Yeah. And so much for the stereotype of scrawny nerds being the only ones fascinated by aliens. That man is huge, and mean looking.'

'Take my phone, Sam.'

'What? Why?' he asks.

'You have to follow him. Take my phone. I'll go into the house. It's obvious there is nobody there or he wouldn't have locked the door. Henri might be in there. I'll call you as soon as I can.'

'How are you going to call me?'

'I don't know. I'll find a way. Here.' He reluctantly takes it.

'What if Henri isn't in there?'

'That's why I want you to follow that guy. He might be going to Henri now.'

'What if he comes back?'

'We'll figure it out. But you have to go now. I promise, I'll call you the first chance I get.'

Sam turns and looks at the man. He is fifty yards away from us now. Then he looks back at me.

'Okay, I'll do it. But be careful in there.'

'You be careful, too. Don't let him out of your sight. And don't let him see you.'

'Not a chance.'

He turns and hurries after the man. I watch them go and,

once they vanish from sight, I walk up to the house. The windows are dark, each one covered with a white shade. I can't see in. I walk around to the back. There is a small concrete patio leading to a back door, which is locked. I walk the rest of the way around the house. Overgrown weeds and bushes left over from summer. I try a window. Locked. All of them are locked. Should I break one? I look for rocks among the brambles, and the second I see one and lift it from the ground with my mind an idea occurs to me, an idea so crazy that it just might work.

I drop the rock and walk to the back door. It has a simple lock, no deadbolt. I take a deep breath, close my eyes in concentration, and grab hold of the doorknob. I give it a shake. My thoughts move from head to heart to stomach; everything is centered there. My grip tightens, my breath is held in anticipation as I try to envision the inner workings. Then I feel and hear a click in the hand holding the knob. A smile forms on my face. I turn the knob and the door swings open. I can't believe I can unlock doors by imagining what is inside of them.

The kitchen is surprisingly clean, the surfaces wiped down, the sink free of dirty dishes. A new loaf of bread sits on the counter. I walk through a narrow corridor into a living room with sports posters and banners on the walls, a big-screen TV sitting in a corner. The door to a bedroom is off to the left side. I poke my head in. It's in a state of disarray, covers thrown aside on the bed, clutter atop the dresser. The foul stench of dirty laundry covered in sweat that has never dried.

At the front of the house, beside the door, a flight of stairs ascends to the second level. I begin walking up them. The third step groans under my foot.

‘Hello?’ a voice yells from the top of the stairs.

I freeze, holding my breath.

‘Frank, is that you?’

I stay silent. I hear somebody stand from a chair, the creak of footsteps on a hardwood floor approaching. A man appears at the top of the stairs. Dark shaggy hair, sideburns, an unshaven face. Not as big as the man who left earlier, but not exactly small either.

‘Who the hell are you?’ he asks.

‘I’m looking for a friend of mine,’ I say.

He screws his face up into a scowl, vanishes and reappears five seconds later holding a wooden baseball bat in his hand.

‘How did you get in here?’ he asks.

‘I would put the bat down if I were you.’

‘How did you get in here?’

‘I am faster than you are and I am far stronger.’

‘Like hell you are.’

‘I’m looking for a friend of mine. He came here this morning. I want to know where he is.’

‘You’re one of them, aren’t you?’

‘I don’t know who you are talking about.’

‘You’re one of them!’ he screams. He holds the bat as a baseball player would, both white-knuckled hands at the thin base poised to swing. There is genuine fear in his eyes. His jaw is tightly clenched. ‘You’re one of them! Why don’t you just leave us alone already!?’

‘I am not one of them. I’ve come for my friend. Tell me where he is.’

‘Your friend is one of them!’

‘No he isn’t.’

‘So you know who I’m talking about?’

‘Yes.’

He takes a step down.

'I'm warning you,' I say. 'Drop the bat and tell me where he is.'

My hands are shaking from the uncertainty of the situation, from the fact that he has a bat in his hands while I have nothing but my own abilities. I'm unnerved by the fear in his eyes. He takes another step down. There are only six stairs between us.

'I'm going to take your head off. That'll send your friends a message.'

'They aren't my friends. And I assure you, you'd be doing them a favor if you hurt me.'

'Let's see then,' he says.

He comes racing down the stairs. There is nothing I can do but react. He swings the bat. I duck and it hits the wall with a thud, leaving a large splintered hole in the wood panel. I come up after him and lift him in the air, one hand gripping his throat, the other in his armpit, carrying him back up the stairs. He flails, landing kicks to my legs and groin. The bat drops from his hands. It bounces hollowly down the stairs and I hear one of the windows break behind me.

The second floor is a wide-open loft. It is dark. The walls are covered with issues of *They Walk Among Us*, and where the issues end, alien paraphernalia takes up the rest – but unlike Sam's, the posters are actual photographs taken over the years, blown up and grainy so that it is hard to make them out, mostly white blips on black backdrops. A rubber alien dummy with a noose around its neck sits in the corner. Somebody has added a Mexican sombrero to its head. Glow-in-the-dark stars are stuck to the ceiling. They seem out of place, more like something belonging in a ten-year-old girl's room.

I throw the man to the ground. He scoots away from me and stands up. When he does I put all my power into the pit of my stomach and direct it towards him with a hard forward-thrusting motion, and he goes flying backwards and crashes into the wall.

'Where is he?' I ask.

'I'll never tell you. He's one of you.'

'I'm not who you think I am.'

'You guys will never succeed! Just leave Earth alone!'

I lift my hand and choke him. I can feel the flexed tendons beneath my hand even though I am not touching him. He can't breathe and his face turns red. I let go.

'I'll ask again.'

'No.'

I choke him once more, but this time when his face turns red I squeeze tighter. When I let go he begins to cry and I feel bad for him, for what I've done to him. But he knows where Henri is, has done something to him, and my sympathy ends almost as soon as it began.

After he catches his breath, and between sobs, he says, 'He's downstairs.'

'Where? I didn't see him.'

'In the basement. The door is behind the Steelers banner in the living room.'

I dial my phone number from the telephone atop the middle desk. Sam doesn't answer. Then I pull the phone from the wall and break it in half.

'Give me your cell phone,' I say.

'I don't have one.'

I walk to the dummy and remove the noose from around its neck.

'Come on, man,' he pleads.

'Shut up. You've kidnapped my friend. You're holding him against his will. You're lucky all I'm doing is tying you up.'

I pull his arms behind him and tie the rope tightly around them, then tie him to one of the chairs. I don't think that it will hold him for very long. Then I duct-tape his mouth shut so that he can't yell and I sweep down the stairs and rip the Steelers banner from the wall, revealing a black door that is locked. I unlock it as I did the other. A set of wooden stairs leads down to total darkness.

The smell of mildew reaches my nose. I flip the light switch on and begin walking down, slowly, terrified at what I might find. The rafters are littered with cobwebs. I reach the bottom and immediately feel the presence of somebody else, somebody there with me. I stiffen, take a deep breath, and then turn.

There, in the corner of the basement, sits Henri.

'Henri!'

He is squinting from the light, his eyes adjusting. A length of duct tape is across his mouth. His hands are bound behind him, his ankles tied to the legs of the chair in which he is sitting. His hair is tousled, and down the right side of his face is a line of dried blood that looks almost black. The sight of it fills me with rage.

I rush over to him and rip the piece of tape from his mouth. He takes a deep breath.

'Thank God,' he says. His voice is weak. 'You were right, John. It was foolish to come here. I'm sorry. I should have listened.'

'Shh,' I say.

I bend down and begin untying his ankles. He smells like urine.

'I was ambushed.'

'How many are there?' I ask.

'Three.'

'I've tied one of them up upstairs,' I say.

I free his ankles. He stretches his legs out and sighs with relief.

'I've been in this damn chair all day.'

I begin working his hands free.

'How in the hell did you get here?' he asks.

'Sam and I came together. We drove down.'

'You're kidding me?'

'I had no other way.'

'What did you drive?'

'His father's old truck.'

Henri is silent a minute while he ponders what that means.

'He doesn't know anything,' I say. 'I told him aliens are a hobby of yours, nothing more.'

He nods. 'Well, I'm happy you made it. Where is he now?'

'Trailing one of them. I don't know where they went.'

The creak of a floorboard comes from above us. I stand, Henri's hands only halfway untied.

'Did you hear that?' I whisper.

We both watch the door with our breaths held. A foot steps onto the top stair, and then a second, and all at once the large man I passed earlier, the one Sam was trailing, comes into view.

'The party's over, fellas,' he says. He is holding a gun aimed at my face. 'Now, step away.'

I hold my hands up in front of me and take a step back. I think of using my powers to pull the gun away, but what if I somehow cause it to fire by accident? I'm not confident in my abilities just yet. It's too risky.

'They told us you might be coming. That you would look like humans. That you were the real enemy,' the man says.

'What are you talking about?' I ask.

'They're delusional,' Henri says. 'They think we're the enemy.'

'Shut up!' the man screams.

He takes three steps towards me. Then he moves the gun from me and fixes it straight on Henri.

'One false move by you and he gets it. You understand?'

'Yes,' I say.

'Now, catch this,' he says. He pulls down a roll of duct tape from the shelf beside him and throws it towards me. As it moves through the air, I stop it, suspended about eight feet off the ground, halfway between us. I start spinning it very quickly. The man stares at it, confused.

'What the . . .'

While he's distracted, I move my arm towards him with a throwing motion. The roll of tape flies back and slams him in the nose. Blood starts gushing, and as he reaches for it he drops the gun, which hits the ground and goes off. I point my hand towards the bullet and I make it stop, and behind me I hear Henri laugh. I move the bullet so that it hangs in front of the man's face.

'Hey, fat boy,' I say.

He opens his eyes and sees the bullet in the air in front of his face.

'You're gonna need to bring more.'

I let the bullet fall to the ground at his feet. He turns to run, but I bring him back across the room and slam him against a large support pole. It knocks him out and he slumps to the floor. I grab the tape and tie him to the pole.

After I'm sure he's secured, I turn to Henri and finish freeing him.

'John, I think that's the best surprise I've ever seen in my entire life,' he says in a whisper, such relief in his voice that I think tears might come next.

I smile proudly. 'Thanks. It showed at dinner.'

'Sorry I missed it.'

'I told them you were tied up.'

He smiles.

'Thank God the Legacy came,' he says, and I realize that the stress of my Legacies forming – or the fear of them not forming – took a far greater toll on Henri than I imagined.

'So what happened to you?' I ask.

'I knocked on the door. All three of them were home. When I walked in one of them clubbed me in the back of the head. Then I woke up in this chair.' He shakes his head and says a long string of words in Loric that I know are curses. I finish untying him and he stands and stretches his legs.

'We need to get out of here,' he says.

'We have to find Sam.'

And then we hear him.

'John. You down there?'

21

Everything slows. I see a second person at the top of the stairs. Sam yelps in surprise and I turn to him, silence filling my ears with the discordant hum that comes with slow motion. The man behind him gives him a hard shove that causes his feet to leave the ground, and, when he hits, it will be at the bottom of the stairs, where the concrete floor awaits. I watch him sail through the air, flailing his arms with a look of terror on his anguished face. Without giving it a single thought, my instinct takes over and I lift my hands at the very last second and catch him, his head a mere two inches above the basement floor. I set him down gently.

'Shit,' Henri says.

Sam sits up and crawls backwards like a crab until he reaches the cinder-block wall. His eyes are wide-open, staring at the steps, his mouth moving but no words coming out. The figure who pushed him stands at the top of the stairs trying to figure out, like Sam, what just happened. It must be the third one.

'Sam, I tried to—' I say.

The man at the top of the stairs turns and tries to sprint away but I force him down two of the stairs. Sam looks at the man being held by an unseen force, then looks at my one arm extended towards him. He is shocked and speechless.

I grab the duct tape and lift the man in the air and carry him up to the second floor, keeping him suspended the entire way. He yells obscenities while I tape him into a chair, but I hear none of them because my mind is racing to figure out what we will say to Sam about what just happened.

'Shut up,' I say.

He unloads another string of cuss words. I decide I've had enough so I tape his mouth shut and walk back to the basement. Henri is standing near Sam, who is still sitting there, with the same blank stare on his face.

'I don't get it,' he says. 'What just happened?'

Henri and I look at each other. I shrug.

'Tell me what's happening,' Sam says, his voice pleading with us, tinged with desperation to know the truth, to know that he's not crazy and that he didn't imagine what he just saw.

Henri sighs and shakes his head. Then he says, 'What the hell's the point?'

'The point in what?' I ask.

He ignores me, and instead turns to Sam. He purses his lips together, looks at the man slumped in the chair to make sure he is still out, and then at Sam. 'We aren't who you think we are,' he says, and pauses. Sam stays silent, staring at Henri. I can't read his face, and I have no idea what Henri is about to tell him – if he will again make up some elaborate story or, for once, tell him the truth – and it's this latter that I'm truly hoping for. He looks at me and I nod my head in agreement.

'We came to Earth ten years ago from a planet named Lorien. We came because it was destroyed by the inhabitants of another planet named Mogadore. They destroyed Lorien for its resources because they had turned their own planet into a cesspool of decay. We came here to hide until we could return to Lorien, which we will one day do. But we were followed by the Mogadorians. They are here hunting us. And I believe they are here to take over Earth, and that is why I came here today, to find out a little more.'

Sam says nothing. Had it been me who told him as much, I'm sure that he wouldn't believe me, that he might become angry, but it is Henri who has told him, and there is a certain integrity within Henri that I have always felt, and I have no doubt that Sam feels it also. He looks over at me.

'I was right: you're an alien. You weren't joking when you admitted it,' Sam says to me.

'Yes, you were right.'

He looks back at Henri. 'And those stories you told me on Halloween?'

'No. Those were just that,' Henri says. 'Ridiculous stories that made me smile when I stumbled across them on the internet, nothing more. But what I told you now is the honest truth.'

'Well . . .' Sam says, and trails off, grasping for words. 'What happened just now?'

Henri nods to me. 'John is in the process of developing certain powers. Telekinesis is one of them. When you were pushed, John saved you.'

Sam still smiles beside me, watching me. When I look at him he nods his head.

'I knew you were different,' he says.

'Needless to say,' Henri says to Sam, 'you're going to have to be quiet about this.' Then he looks over at me. 'We need information and we need to get out of here. They're probably nearby.'

'The guys upstairs might still be conscious.'

'Let's go talk to them.'

Henri walks over and picks the gun up from the floor and

pulls the clip. It's full. He removes all the bullets and sets them on a nearby shelf, then snaps the clip back in and tucks the gun in the waistband of his jeans. I help Sam to his feet and we all go upstairs to the second floor. The man I brought up with my telekinesis is still struggling. The other one is sitting still. Henri walks over to him.

'You were warned,' Henri says.

The man nods.

'Now you're going to talk,' Henri says, and he pulls the tape from the man's mouth. 'And if you don't . . .' He pulls the slide back on the gun and aims it at the man's chest. 'Who visited you?'

'There were three of them,' he says.

'Well, there are three of us. Who cares? Keep talking.'

'They told me if you showed up and I said anything, they'd kill me,' the man says. 'I won't tell you anything more.'

Henri presses the barrel of the gun against the man's forehead. For some reason it makes me uncomfortable. I reach out and move the gun down so it points only at the floor. Henri looks at me curiously.

'There are other ways,' I say.

Henri shrugs and sets the gun down. 'The floor is yours,' he says.

I stand five feet in front of the man. He looks at me with fear. He is heavy, but after catching Sam as he sailed through the air, I know that I can lift him. I hold my arms out, my body straining in concentration. Nothing at first, and then very slowly he begins to rise off the floor. The man struggles but he is taped to the chair and there is nothing he can do. I concentrate with everything I have, and yet in my peripheral vision I can see that Henri is smiling proudly, and that Sam is, too. Yesterday I couldn't lift a tennis ball; now I'm lifting a chair with a two-hundred-pound man sitting in it. How quickly the Legacy has developed.

When I have raised him to face level, I flip the chair over and he hangs upside down.

'Come on!' he yells.

'Start talking.'

'No!' he yells. 'They said they'd kill me.'

I let go of the chair and it falls. The man screams but I catch him before he hits the ground. I raise him back up.

'There were three of them!' he yells, talking fast. 'They showed up the same day we sent out the magazines. They showed up that night.'

'What did they look like?' Henri asks.

'Like ghosts. They were pale, almost like albinos. They wore sunglasses, but when we wouldn't talk one of them took the sunglasses off. They had black eyes and pointy teeth, but they didn't look natural like an animal's would. Theirs looked as though they had been broken and chiseled. They all wore long coats and hats like some shit out of an old spy movie. What the hell more do you want?'

'Why did they come?'

'They wanted to know our source for the story. We told them. A man had called, said he had an exclusive for us, starting raging about a group of aliens that wanted to destroy our civilization. But he called on the day we were printing, so instead of writing the full story, we put in a small quip and said more to follow next month. He talked so fast that we hardly grasped what he was saying. We were planning on calling him the next night, only that didn't happen, because the Mogadorians showed up instead.'

'How did you know they were Mogadorians?'

'What the hell else could they have been? We wrote a story

about the Mogadorian race of aliens and lo and behold a group of aliens shows up on our doorstep the same day wanting to know where we got the story. It wasn't hard to figure out.'

The man is heavy and I'm having trouble holding him. My forehead is beaded with sweat and it's a struggle to breathe. I flip him back over, begin to lower him. When he is within a foot of the floor I drop him the rest of the way and he lands with an *Oomphf.* I bend over with my hands on my knees to catch my breath.

'What the hell, man? I'm answering your questions,' he says.

'I'm sorry,' I say. 'You're too heavy.'

'And that's the only time they came?' says Henri.

The man shakes his head. 'They came back.'

'Why?'

'To make sure we didn't print anything else. I don't think they trusted us, but the man who called us never answered his phone again, so we had nothing else to print.'

'What happened to him?'

'What do you think happened?' the man asks.

Henri nods. 'So they knew where he lived?'

'They had the phone number we were supposed to call him back on. I'm sure they could have figured it out.'

'Did they threaten you?'

'Hell, yes. They trashed our office. They screwed with my mind. I haven't been the same since.'

'What'd they do to your mind?'

He closes his eyes and takes another deep breath.

'They didn't even look real,' he says. 'I mean, here are these three men standing in front of us talking in deep, raspy voices, all in trench coats and hats and sunglasses even though it was nighttime. It looked like they were dressed up for a Halloween party or something. They looked funny and out of place, so at first I laughed at them . . .' he says, his voice trailing off.

'But the second I laughed I knew I had made a mistake. The other two Mogadorians started towards me with their sunglasses off. I tried to look away, but I couldn't. Those eyes. I had to look, as though something was pulling me there. It was like seeing death. My own death, and the deaths of all the people I know and love. Things weren't so funny anymore. Not only did I have to witness the deaths, but I could feel them, too. The uncertainty. The pain. The complete and utter terror. I wasn't in that room anymore. And then came things I've always feared as a kid. Images of stuffed animals that came to life, with sharp teeth as mouths, razor blades for claws. The usual stuff all kids are afraid of. Werewolves. Demonic clowns. Giant spiders. I viewed them all through the eyes of a child, and they absolutely terrified me. And every time one of those things bit into me, I could feel its teeth rip the flesh from my body, I could feel the blood pour from the wounds. I couldn't stop screaming.'

'Did you try to fight back at all?'

'They had two of these little weasel-looking things, fat, with short legs. No bigger than a dog. They were frothing at the mouth. One of the men was holding them on a leash, but you could tell they were hungry for us. They said they would turn them loose if we resisted. I'm telling you, man, these things weren't from Earth. If they were dogs, big deal, we would have fought back. But I think those things would have eaten us whole despite our size. And they were pulling against the leash, growling, trying to get to us.'

'So you talked?'

'Yes.'

'When did they come back?'

'The night before the next magazine went out, a little over a week ago.'

Henri gives me a concerned look. Only one week ago the Mogadorians were within a hundred miles of where we live. They could still be here somewhere, maybe monitoring the paper. Perhaps that is why Henri has felt their presence of late. Sam stands beside me, taking everything in.

'Why didn't they just kill you like they did your source?'

'How the hell do I know? Maybe because we publish a respectable paper.'

'How did the man who called know about the Mogadorians?'

'He said he had captured one of them and tortured it.'

'Where?'

'I don't know. His phone number was from the area code near Columbus. So north of here. Maybe sixty or eighty miles north.'

'You spoke to him?'

'Yeah. And I wasn't sure if he was crazy or not, but we had heard rumors about something like this before. He started talking about them wanting to wipe out civilization as we know it, and sometimes he talked so fast that it was hard to make sense of anything he said. One thing he kept repeating was that they were here hunting something, or somebody. Then he started spouting numbers.'

My eyes open wide. 'What numbers? What did they mean?'

'I have no idea. Like I said, he was talking so fast that it was all we could do to write it all down.'

'You wrote while he talked?' Henri says.

'Of course we did. We're journalists,' he says incredulously. 'Do you think we make up the stories we write?'

'Yeah, I do,' says Henri.

'Do you still have the notes that you wrote?' I say.

He looks at me and nods. 'I'm telling you, they're worthless. Most of what I wrote are scribbles on their plan to destroy the human race.'

'I need to see them,' I nearly bellow. 'Where, where are they?'

He motions towards a desk against one of the walls.

'On the desk. On sticky notes.'

I walk over to the desk, which is covered with papers, and start looking through the sticky notes. I find some very vague notes on the Mogadorians' hope to conquer Earth. Nothing concrete, no plans or details, just a few indistinct words:

'Overpopulation.'

'Earth's resources.'

'Biological warfare?'

'The Planet Mogadore.'

I come to the note I'm looking for. I read it carefully three or four times.

PLANET LORIEN? THE LORIC?

1–3 DEAD

4?

7 TRAILED IN SPAIN.

9 ON THE RUN IN SA

(WHAT IS HE TALKING ABOUT? WHAT DO THESE NUMBERS HAVE TO DO WITH INVADING EARTH?)

'Why is there a question mark after the number 4?' I ask.

'Because he said something about it but he talked too fast and I didn't get it.'

'You've got to be kidding me?'

He shakes his head. I sigh. *Just my luck,* I think. *The one thing said about me is the one thing that wasn't written.*

'What does "SA" mean?' I ask.

'South America.'

'Did he say where in South America?'

'No.'

I nod, stare at the slip of paper. I wish I could have heard the conversation, that I could have asked questions of my own. Do the Mogadorians really know where Seven is? Are they really following him or her? If so, the Loric charm still holds. I fold the sticky notes and slip them into my back pocket.

'Do you know what the numbers mean?' he asks.

I shake my head. 'I have no idea.'

'I don't believe you,' he says.

'Shut up,' Sam says, and pokes him in the gut with the heavy end of the bat.

'Is there anything else you can tell me?' I ask.

He thinks about it for a moment, then says, 'I think bright light bothers them. It seemed to cause them pain when they took their sunglasses off.'

We hear a noise downstairs. Like someone trying to slowly open the door. We look at each other. I look to the man in the chair.

'Who is that?' I quietly say.

'Them.'

'What?'

'They said they'd be watching. That they knew someone might be coming.'

We hear quiet footsteps on the first floor.

Henri and Sam look at each other, both terrified.

'Why didn't you tell us?'

'They said they'd kill me. And my family.'

I run to the window, look out the back. We're on the second floor. It's a twenty-foot drop to the ground. There's a fence around the yard. Eight feet of wood slats. I move quickly back to the stairs, and peer down. I see three huge figures, in long black trench coats, black hats, and sunglasses. They're carrying long gleaming swords. There's no way we're going to make it down the stairs. My Legacies are growing stronger, but they aren't strong enough to take on three Mogadorians. The only way out is through one of the windows or over a small porch at the front of the room. The windows are smaller but the backyard will allow us to escape unseen. If we go out the front, we will most likely be visible. I hear noise coming from the basement and the Mogadorians talking to each other in an ugly, guttural language. Two of them move towards the basement while the third starts walking towards the stairs that lead to us.

I have a second or two to act. The windows will break if we go through them. Our only chance is the doors leading to the second-floor porch. I open them using telekinesis. It's black outside. I hear footsteps coming up the stairs. I pull Sam and Henri over to me and I throw each of them over my shoulders like sacks of potatoes.

'What are you doing?' whispers Henri.

'I have no idea,' I say. 'But I hope it works.'

Just as I see the top of the first Mogadorian's hat, I sprint towards the doors, and right before the ledge of the porch, I jump. We go flying into the night sky. For two or three seconds we're floating. I see cars moving down the street beneath us. I see people on the sidewalk. I don't know where we're going to land, or if my body will support all the weight I'm carrying when we do. When we hit the roof of a house across the street I collapse, with Sam and Henri on top of me. I get my breath knocked out of me, and it feels like my legs are broken. Sam starts to stand, but Henri keeps him down. He drags me to the far end of the roof and asks if I can use my telekinesis to get him and Sam onto the ground. I can and I do. He tells me I need to jump. I stand on legs that are wobbly and still hurt, and just before I jump, I turn and see the three Mogadorians are standing on the porch across the street, looking confused. Their swords are gleaming. Without a second to spare, we got away without them seeing us.

We get to Sam's truck. Henri and Sam have to help me walk. Bernie is there waiting for us. We decide to leave Henri's truck because they most likely know what it looks like and would track it. We pull out of Athens and Henri starts driving back to Paradise, which it really might be after the night we just had.

Henri starts from the beginning, telling Sam everything. He doesn't stop until we are pulling into our driveway. It's still dark. Sam looks over at me.

'Unbelievable,' he says, and smiles. 'It's the coolest thing I've ever heard of.' I look at him and I see the validation he has always looked for in his life, an affirmation that the time he's spent with his nose in the conspiracy rags, looking for clues to his father's disappearance, wasn't in vain.

'Are you really resistant to fire?' he asks.

'Yes,' I say.

'God, that's awesome.'

'Thanks, Sam.'

'Can you fly?' he asks. At first I think he is joking, but then I see that he isn't.

'I can't fly. I'm resistant to fire and can turn my hands into lights. I have telekinesis, which I only learned to use yesterday. More Legacies are supposed to come soon. We think so, anyhow. But I have no idea what they will be until they actually develop.'

'I hope you learn to make yourself invisible,' Sam says. 'My grandfather could. And anything he touched also became invisible.'

'Seriously?'

'Yes.'

He starts laughing.

'I still can't believe you two drove all the way to Athens by yourselves,' Henri says. 'You guys are really something. When we stopped for gas I saw that the plates have been expired for four years. I really don't see how you made it without getting stopped.'

'Well, you can count on me from now on,' says Sam. 'I'll do whatever it takes to help stop them. Especially because I bet they're the ones who took my dad.'

'Thanks, Sam,' says Henri. 'The most important thing you could do is stay quiet with our secret. If anyone else finds out about this it could lead to our deaths.'

'Don't worry. I'll never tell anyone. I don't want John using his powers on me.'

We laugh and thank Sam again and he pulls away. Henri and I go inside. Even though I slept on the drive back, I'm still exhausted. I lie down on the couch. Henri sits in a chair across from me.

'Sam won't say anything,' I say.

He doesn't respond, just stares at the floor.

'They don't know we're here,' I say.

He looks up at me.

'They don't,' I say. 'If they knew they'd be following us now.'

He stays silent. I can't take it.

'I'm not leaving Ohio on nothing more than speculation.'

Henri stands.

'I'm happy that you've made a friend. And I think Sarah is great. But we can't stay. I'm going to start packing,' he says.

'No.'

'When we're packed I'll go into town and buy a new truck. We need to get out of here. They might not have followed us, but they know how close they were to catching us, and that we might still be nearby. I believe the man who called the magazine did in fact capture one of them. That was his story, that he captured one and tortured it until it talked and then he killed it. We don't know what kind of tracking technology they have, but I don't think it will take them long to find us. And when they do, we'll die. Your Legacies are emerging, and your strength is growing, but you're nowhere near ready to fight them.'

He walks out of the room. I sit up. I don't want to leave. I have a real friend for the first time in my life. A friend who knows what I am and isn't scared, doesn't think I'm a freak. A friend who is willing to fight with me, and go into danger with me. And I have a girlfriend. Someone who wants to be with me, even without knowing who I am. Someone who makes me happy, someone I would fight for, or go into danger in order to protect. My Legacies haven't all emerged yet, but enough of them have. I took down three grown men. They didn't stand a chance. It was like fighting with little kids. I could do anything I wanted to them. We also now know that humans can also fight, and capture, and hurt, and kill Mogadorians. If they can, then I definitely can. I don't want to leave. I have a friend, and I have a girl-friend. I am not going to leave.

Henri walks back out of his room. He is carrying the Loric Chest that is our most prized possession.

'Henri,' I say.

'Yes?'

'We're not leaving.'

'Yes we are.'

'You can if you want, but I'll go live with Sam. I'm not leaving.'

'This is not your decision to make.'

'It's not? I thought I was the one being hunted. I thought I was the one in danger. You could walk away right now and the Mogadorians would never look for you. You could live a nice, long, normal life. You could do whatever you want. I can't. They will always be after me. They will always be trying to find me and kill me. I'm fifteen years old. I'm not a kid anymore. It is my decision to make.'

He stares at me for a minute. 'That was a good speech, but it doesn't change anything. Pack your stuff. We're leaving.'

I raise my hand and point it at him and lift him off the ground. He's so shocked that he doesn't say anything. I stand and move him into the corner of the room, up near the ceiling.

'We're staying,' I say.

'Put me down, John.'

'I'll put you down when you agree to stay.'

'It's too dangerous.'

'We don't know that. They're not in Paradise. They might not have any idea where we are.'

'Put me down.'

'Not until you agree to stay.'

'PUT ME DOWN.'

I don't say anything back. I just hold him there. He struggles, tries to push off the wall and the ceiling, but he can't move. My power holds him in place. And I feel strong doing it. Stronger than I've ever felt in my life. I am not leaving. I am not running. I love my life in Paradise. I love having a real friend, and I love my girlfriend. I'm ready to fight for what I love, be it with the Mogadorians, or be it with Henri.

'You know you're not coming down until I bring you down.'

'You're acting like a child.'

'No, I'm acting like someone who is starting to realize who he is and what he can do.'

'And you're really going to keep me up here?'

'Until I fall asleep or get tired, but I'll just do it again once I get some rest.'

'Fine. We can stay. With certain conditions.'

'What?'

'Put me down and we'll talk about it.'

I lower him, set him on the floor. He hugs me. I'm surprised; I expected him to be pissed. He lets go of me and we sit down on the couch.

'I'm proud of how far you've come. I've spent many years waiting and preparing for these things to happen, for your Legacies to arrive. You know my entire life is devoted to keeping you safe, and making you strong. I would never forgive myself if something happened to you. If you died on my watch, I'm not sure how I would go on. In time the Mogadorians will catch up with us. I want to be ready for them when they come. I don't think you are yet, even though you do. You have a long way to go. We can stay here, for now, if you agree that training comes first. Before Sarah, before Sam, before everything. And at the first sign that they're nearby, or are on our trail, we leave, no questions asked, no fighting about it, no levitating me up to the ceiling and holding me there.'

'Deal,' I say, and smile.

22

Winter comes early and with full force to Paradise, Ohio. First the wind, then the cold, then the snow. Light dustings to start, then a storm blows through and buries the land so that the scraping sound of snowplows is as consistently heard as the wind itself, leaving a coat of salt over everything. School is canceled for two days. The snow near the roads segues from white to dingy black and eventually melts to standing puddles of slush that refuse to drain. Henri and I spend my time off training, indoors, outdoors. I can now juggle three balls without touching them, which also means I can lift more than one thing at a time. The heavier and larger objects have come, the kitchen table, the snowblower Henri bought the week before, our new truck, which looks almost exactly like the old one and like millions of other pickup trucks in America. If I can lift it physically, with my body, then I can lift it with my mind. Henri believes that the strength of my mind will eventually transcend that of my body.

In the backyard the trees stand sentinel around us, frozen branches like figurines of hollow glass, an inch of a fine white powder piled atop each one. The snow is up to our knees aside from the small patch Henri has cleared away. Bernie Kosar sits watching from the back porch. Even he wants nothing to do with the snow.

'Are you sure about this?' I ask.

'You need to learn to embrace it,' Henri says. Over his

shoulder, watching with morbid curiosity, stands Sam. It is his first time watching me train.

'How long will this burn?' I ask.

'I don't know.'

I am wearing a highly combustible suit made mostly of natural fibers soaked in oils, some of which are slow burning, some of which are not. I want to set it on fire just to be rid of the smells that are making my eyes water. I take a deep breath.

'Are you ready?' he asks.

'As ready as I'll ever be.'

'Don't breathe. You're not immune to the smoke or fumes and your internal organs will burn.'

'This seems foolish to me,' I say.

'It's part of your training. Grace under pressure. You need to learn to multitask while consumed in flames.'

'But why?'

'Because when the battle comes, we're going to be greatly outnumbered. Fire will be one of your great allies in war. You need to learn to fight while burning.'

'Ugh.'

'If you get in trouble, jump into the snow and start rolling.'

I look at Sam, who has a big grin spread across his face. He is holding a red fire extinguisher in his hand just in case it's needed.

'I know,' I say.

Everyone is silent while Henri messes with the matches.

'You look like Sasquatch wearing that suit,' Sam says.

'Eat it, Sam,' I say.

'Here we go,' says Henri.

I take a deep breath just before he touches a match to the

suit. Fire sweeps across my body. It feels unnatural for me to keep my eyes open, but I do. I look up. The fire rises eight feet above me. The whole world is shrouded in shades of orange, red, yellow that dance in my line of sight. I can feel the heat, but only slightly as one feels the sun's rays on a summer day. Nothing more than that.

'Go!' Henri yells.

I hold my arms out to my sides, eyes wide-open, breath held. I feel as though I'm hovering. I enter the deep snow and it begins to sizzle and melt underfoot, a slight steam rising while I walk. I reach my right hand forward and lift a cinder block, which feels heavier than normal. Is it because I'm not breathing? Is it the stress of the fire?

'Don't waste time!' Henri yells.

I hurl the block as hard as I can against a dead tree fifty feet away. The force causes it to smash into a million little pieces, leaving an indentation in the wood. Then I raise three tennis balls soaked in gasoline. I juggle them in midair, one over the other. I bring them in towards my body. They catch fire, and still I juggle them – and while doing so I lift a long, thin broomstick. I close my eyes. My body is warm. I wonder if I'm sweating. If I am, the sweat must be evaporating the second it reaches the skin's surface.

I grit my teeth, open my eyes, thrust my body forward and direct all of my powers into the stick's very core. It explodes, splintering into small bits. I don't let any of them fall to the ground; instead I keep them suspended, collectively looking like a cloud of dust hovering in midair. I pull them to me and let them burn. The wood pops through the flicker and hum of the flames. I force them back together into a tightly compacted spear of fire that looks as though it has sprung straight from the depths of hell.

'Perfect!' Henri yells.

One minute has passed. My lungs begin to burn from the fire, from my breath still held. I put everything that I am into the spear and I hurl it so hard that it speeds through the air like a bullet and hits the tree, and hundreds of tiny fires spread throughout the vicinity and extinguish almost immediately. I had hoped the dead wood would catch fire but it does not. I have also dropped the tennis balls. They sizzle in the snow five feet away from me.

'Forget the balls,' Henri yells. 'The tree. Get the tree.'

The dead wood looks ghastly with its arthritic limbs silhouetted against the world of white beyond it. I close my eyes. I can't hold my breath much longer. Frustration and anger begin to form, fueled by the fire and the discomfort of the suit and the tasks that are left undone. I focus on the large branch coming off the tree's trunk and I try to break that branch away but it won't come. I grit my teeth and furrow my brows and finally a loud snap rings through the air like a shotgun blast and the branch comes sailing towards me. I catch it in my hands and hold it straight above me. *Let it burn,* I think. It must be twenty feet long. It finally catches fire and I lift it into the air forty or fifty feet above me and, without touching it, I drive it straight into the ground as though I'm staking my claim like some old-world swordsman standing atop the hill after winning the war. The stick totters back and forth smoking, flames dancing along the upper half of it. I open my mouth and instinctively take a breath, and the flames come rushing in; an instant burning spreads throughout my body. I'm so shocked and it hurts so much that I don't know what to do.

'The snow! The snow!' Henri yells.

I dive in headfirst and begin rolling. The fire goes out

almost immediately but I keep rolling and the sizzle of snow touching the tattered suit is all I hear while wisps of steam and smoke rise off of me. And then Sam finally pulls the clip from the extinguisher and unloads with a thick powder that makes it even harder to breathe.

'No,' I yell.

He stops. I lie there trying to catch my breath, but each inhalation brings about a pain in my lungs that reverberates throughout my body.

'Damn, John. You weren't supposed to breathe,' Henri says, standing over me.

'I couldn't help it.'

'Are you okay?' Sam asks.

'My lungs are burning.'

Everything is blurry but slowly the world comes into focus. I lie there looking up into the low gray sky at the flakes of snow sifting sullenly down upon us.

'How'd I do?'

'Not bad for your first try.'

'We're going to do it again, aren't we?'

'In time, yes.'

'That was wicked cool,' Sam says.

I sigh, then take a deep, labored breath. 'That sucked.'

'You did well for your first time,' Henri says. 'You can't expect everything to come easily.'

I nod from the ground. I lie there a good minute or two, and then Henri extends a hand and helps me up, bringing about the end of training for the day.

I wake in the middle of the night two days later, 2:57 on the clock. I can hear Henri working at the kitchen table. I crawl out of bed and walk out of the room. He is hunched over a document, wearing bifocals and holding some sort of stamp with a pair of tweezers. He looks up at me.

'What are you doing?' I ask.

'Creating forms for you.'

'For what?'

'I got to thinking about you and Sam driving down to get me. I think it's foolish of us to keep using your real age when we can just as easily change it according to our needs.'

I pick up a birth certificate that he has already finished. The name written is James Hughes. The date of birth would make me a year older. I'd be sixteen and able to drive. Then I bend over and look at the one he is in the process of creating. The name listed is Jobie Frey, age eighteen, a legal adult.

'Why didn't we ever think to do this before?' I ask.

'We never had reason to.'

Papers of different shapes and sizes and densities are scattered across the table, a large printer off to the side. Bottles of ink, rubber stamps, notary stamps, metal plate-looking things, various tools that look as though they belong in a dentist's office. The process of document creation has always remained foreign to me.

'Are we going to change my age now?'

Henri shakes his head. 'It's too late to change your age in Paradise. These are mostly for the future. Who knows what will happen that will give you reason to use them.'

The thought of moving in the future makes me nauseous. I would rather stay fifteen and unable to drive forever than move someplace new.

Sarah returns from Colorado a week before Christmas. I haven't seen her in eight days. It feels as though it's been a month. The van drops all the girls off at the school and one of her friends drives her straight to my house without first taking her home. When I hear the tires come up the drive I meet her with a hug and a kiss and I lift her off the ground and twirl her in the air. She has just been in a plane and a car for ten hours and she is wearing sweatpants and no makeup with her hair pulled into a ponytail and yet she is the most beautiful girl I have ever seen and I don't want to let go of her. We stare into each other's eyes beneath the moonlight and all either of us can do is smile.

'Did you miss me?' she asks.

'Every second of every day.'

She kisses the tip of my nose.

'I missed you, too.'

'So do the animals have a shelter again?' I ask.

'Oh, John, it was amazing! I wish you could have been there. There were probably thirty people helping out at all times, around the clock. The building went up so fast and it's so much nicer than it was before. We built this cat tree in one of the corners, and I swear the whole time we were there, there were cats playing on it.'

I smile. 'It sounds great. I wish I could have been there, too.'

I take her bag and we walk into the house together.

'Where's Henri?' she asks.

'Grocery shopping. He left about ten minutes ago.'

She walks through the living room and drops her coat onto the back of a chair on her way into my bedroom. She sits on the edge of my bed and kicks her shoes off.

'What should we do?' she asks.

I stand there watching her. She is wearing a red hooded sweatshirt with a zipper down the front. It is only halfway zipped. She smiles and looks at me through the tops of her eyes.

'Come here,' she says, and holds her hand out to me.

I walk to her and she takes my hand in hers. She looks up at me and squints her eyes from the light shining overhead. I snap my fingers with my free hand and the light turns off.

'How'd you do that?'

'Magic,' I say.

I sit beside her. She tucks a few loose strands of hair behind her ear, then leans over and kisses me on the cheek. Then she cups my chin and pulls my head to hers and kisses me again, softly, delicately. My whole body tingles in response. She pulls away, her hand still on my cheek. She traces my brow with her thumb.

'I really did miss you,' she says.

'Me, too.'

A silence passes between us. Sarah bites her lower lip.

'I couldn't wait to get here,' she says. 'The whole time I was in Colorado, you were all I could think of. Even when playing with the animals, I was wishing you were there with me playing with them, too. And then when we finally left this morning, the entire trip was hell even though every mile we traveled was another mile I was closer to you.'

She smiles, mostly with her eyes, her lips a thin upturned crescent that keeps her teeth hidden. She kisses me again, a kiss that starts as slow and lingering and goes from there. Both of us are sitting on the edge of the bed, her hand on the side of my face, mine on the small of her back. I can feel the tight contours beneath the tips of my fingers, can taste the berry gloss on her lips. I pull her to me. I feel as though I can't get close enough to her despite our bodies being pressed tightly together. My hand running up her back, the smooth porcelain feel of her skin. Her hands through my hair, both of us breathing heavily. We fall back on the bed, on our sides. Our eyes are closed. I keep opening mine to see her. The room is dark aside from the moonlight entering through the windows. She catches me watching her and we stop kissing. She puts her forehead to mine and stares at me.

She places her hand on the back of my neck and pulls me to her and all at once we're kissing again. Entangled. Meshed. Our arms tightly around the other. My mind clear of every plague that normally visits and every thought of other planets, my mind free of the hunt and pursuit by the Mogadorians. Sarah and I on the bed kissing each other, falling into each other. Nothing else in the world matters.

And then the door opens in the living room. We both jump up.

'Henri's home,' I say.

We stand and quickly brush the wrinkles from our clothes, smiling, a secret shared between us that makes us giggle as we walk out of the bedroom holding hands. Henri is setting a bag of groceries on the kitchen table.

'Hi, Henri,' Sarah says.

He smiles at her. She lets go of my hand and walks over and hugs him and they start talking about her trip to Colorado. I walk outside to get the rest of the groceries. I breathe in the cold air, try to shake my limbs free of the tension of what just happened, and the disappointment of Henri coming home when he did. I'm still breathing heavily as I grab the rest of the groceries and carry them into the house. Sarah is telling Henri about some of the cats that were at the shelter.

'And you didn't bring one of them back for us?'

'Now Henri, you know I would have happily brought you one if you had told me,' Sarah says, her arms folded across her chest with her hip cocked to the side.

He smiles at her. 'I know you would've.'

Henri puts the groceries away and Sarah and I head out into the frigid air to go for a walk before her mom arrives to take her home. Bernie Kosar comes with us. He takes the lead and runs ahead. Sarah and I hold hands, walking through the yard, the temperature slightly above freezing. The snow melting, the ground wet and muddy. Bernie Kosar disappears for a time into the woods and then comes running back out. His bottom half is filthy.

'What time is your mom coming?' I ask.

She looks at her watch. 'Twenty minutes.'

I nod. 'I'm so happy you're back.'

'Me too.'

We go to the edge of the woods but it is too dark for us to enter. We instead walk along the perimeter of the yard, hand in hand, occasionally stopping to kiss with the moon and stars as witnesses. Neither of us talks about what just happened, but it's obvious that it is on both of our minds. When we make the first lap Sarah's mother pulls into the drive. She's ten minutes early. Sarah runs up and hugs her. I walk inside and grab Sarah's bag. After we say good-bye, I walk to the road and watch their taillights recede in the distance. I stand outside for a while and then Bernie Kosar and I go back into the house. Henri is halfway through making dinner. I give the dog a bath. When I'm finished dinner is ready.

We sit at the table and eat, not a word passing between us. I can't stop thinking of her. I stare blankly into my plate.

I'm not hungry but I try to force the food down anyhow. I manage a few bites, and then I push the plate out in front of me and I sit there in silence.

'So are you going to tell me?' Henri asks.

'Tell you what?'

'What's on your mind.'

I shrug. 'I don't know.'

He nods, goes back to eating. I close my eyes. I can still smell Sarah on the collar of my shirt, can still feel her hand on my cheek. Her lips to mine, the texture of her hair when I ran my hand through it. All I can think about is what she must be doing, and how I wish she were still here.

'Do you think it's possible for us to be loved?' I ask.

'What are you talking about?'

'By humans. Do you think we can be loved, like, truly be loved by them?'

'I think they can love us the way they love each other, especially if they don't know what we are, but I don't think it's possible to love a human the way you would love a Loric,' he says.

'Why?'

'Because deep down we're different from them. And we love differently. One of the gifts our planet gave us is to love completely. Without jealousy or insecurity or fear. Without pettiness. Without anger. You may have strong feelings for Sarah, but they aren't what you would feel for a Loric girl.'

'There aren't many Loric girls available for me.'

'Even more reason to be careful with Sarah. At some point, if we last long enough, we will need to regenerate our race and repopulate our planet. Obviously you're a long way from having to worry about that, but I wouldn't count on Sarah being your partner.'

'What happens if we try to have children with humans?'

'It's happened many times before. Usually it results in an exceptional and gifted human. Some of the greatest figures in Earth's history were actually the product of humans and the Loric, including Buddha, Aristotle, Julius Caesar, Alexander the Great, Genghis Khan, Leonardo da Vinci, Isaac Newton, Thomas Jefferson, and Albert Einstein. Many of the ancient Greek gods, who most people believe were mythological, were actually the children of the humans and Loric, mainly because it was much more common then for us to be on this planet and we were helping them develop civilizations. Aphrodite, Apollo, Hermes, and Zeus were all real, and had one Loric parent.'

'So it is possible.'

'It was possible. In our current situation it's reckless and impractical. In fact, though I don't know her number, or have any idea where she is, one of the children who came to Earth with us was the daughter of your parents' best friends. They used to joke that it was fate that the two of you would end up together. They may well have been right.'

'So what do I do?'

'Enjoy your time with Sarah, but don't get too attached to her, and don't let her get too attached to you.'

'Really?'

'Trust me, John. If you never believe another word I say, then believe that.'

'I believe all the words you say even if I don't want to.'

Henri winks at me. 'Good,' he says.

Afterwards I go into my room and call Sarah. I think

about what Henri said to me before I do it, but I can't help myself. I am attached to her. I think I'm in love with her. We talk for two hours. It is midnight when the call ends. Then I lie in bed smiling through the darkness.

23

The day has grown dark. The warm night carries a soft wind and the sky is scattered with intermittent flashes of light, clouds turning to brilliant colors of blue and red and green. Fireworks at first. Fireworks that segue to something else, louder, more menacing, the *oohs* and *aahs* turning to shrieks and screams. A chaos erupts. People running, children crying. Me, standing in the middle of it all, watching without the benefit of being able to do anything to help. The soldiers and the beasts pour onto the scene from all directions as I have seen before, the continuous fall of bombs so loud that it hurts the ears, the reverberations felt in the pit of my stomach. So deafening it makes my teeth ache. Then the Loric charge back with such intensity, with such courage, that it makes me proud to be among them, to be one of them.

Then I am gone, sweeping through the air at a rate that causes the world beneath to pass in a blur so that I can't focus on any one thing. When I stop I am standing on the tarmac of an airfield. A silver airship is fifteen feet away and forty or so people stand at the ramp leading up to its entrance. Two people have already entered, standing in the doorway with their eyes on the sky, a very young girl and a woman Henri's age. And then I see myself, four years old, crying, shoulders slumped. A much younger version of Henri just behind me. He, too, is watching the sky. On bended knee in front of me is my grandmother, gripping me by the shoulders. My grandfather stands behind her, his face set hard, distracted, the lenses of his glasses gathering the light from the sky.

'Come back to us, you hear? Come back to us,' my grandmother says, finishing speaking. I wish I could have heard the words that came before them. Up until now I have never remembered anything that was spoken to me that night. But now I have something. My four-year-old self doesn't respond. My four-year-old self is too scared. He doesn't understand what is happening, why there is urgency and fear in the eyes of everyone around him. My grandmother pulls me to her and then she lets go. She stands and turns her back to keep me from seeing her cry. My four-year-old self knows that she is crying, but he doesn't know why.

Next is my grandfather, who is covered in sweat, grime, and blood. He has clearly been fighting, and his face is twisted as though he is straining, ready to fight more, ready to go and do all he can in the struggle to survive. His, and the planet's. He drops to a knee as my grandmother did before him. For the first time I look around. Twisted heaps of metal, chunks of concrete, large holes in the ground where the bombs have fallen. Scattered fires, shattered glass, dirt, splintered trees. And in the middle of it all a single airship, unharmed, the one that we are boarding.

'We gotta go!' somebody yells out. A man, dark hair and eyes. I don't know who he is. Henri looks at him and nods. The children walk up the ramp. My grandfather fixes me with a hard stare. He opens his mouth to speak. But before the words come I am again swept away, hurled up through the air, the world below again passing in a blur. I try to make it out, but I am moving too fast. The only discernible sights are the bombs, continually falling, large displays of fire of all colors that sweep through the night sky and the perpetual explosions that follow.

Then I stop again.

I am inside of a large, open building that I have never seen before. It is silent. The ceiling is domed. The floor is one great slab of concrete the size of a football field. There are no windows, but the sounds of the bombs still penetrate, echoing off the walls around me. Standing in the very middle of the building, tall and proud, alone, is a white rocket that extends all the way to the apex of the ceiling.

Then a door slams open in the far corner. My head snaps around to it. Two men enter, frantic, talking quickly and loudly. All at once a herd of animals rush in behind the men. Fifteen, give or take, continually changing shape. Some flying, some running, on two legs, then on four. Bringing up the rear, a third man follows and the door is shut. The first man reaches the spacecraft, opens a sort of hatch on the ship's bottom, and begins ushering the animals in.

'Go! Go! Up and in, up and in,' he yells.

The animals go, all of them changing their shapes in order to do so. Then the last animal enters and one of the men pulls himself in. The other two begin throwing bags and boxes up to him. It takes them a good ten minutes to get everything on board. Then all three scatter around the rocket, preparing it. The men are sweating, moving frantically until everything is ready. Just before the three of them climb inside the rocket, someone runs up with a bundle that looks like a swaddled child, though I can't see well enough to tell. They take whatever it is and go inside. Then the door snaps shut behind them and is sealed. Minutes pass. The bombs must be just outside the walls now. And then from nowhere an explosion occurs inside the building and I see the beginnings of fire shoot from the bottom of the rocket, a fire that quickly grows, a fire that consumes everything inside the building. A fire that consumes even me.

My eyes snap open. I am back home, in Ohio, lying in bed. The room is dark, but I can sense that I am not alone. A figure moves, a shadow thrown across the bed. I tense myself to it, ready to snap my lights on, ready to hurl it against the wall.

'You were talking,' Henri says. 'In your sleep just now, you were talking.'

I turn on my lights. He is standing beside the bed, wearing pajamas pants and a white T-shirt. His hair is tousled; his eyes are red with sleep.

'What was I saying?'

'You said, "Up and in, up and in." What was happening?'

'I was just on Lorien.'

'In a dream?'

'I don't think so. I was there, just like before.'

'What did you see?'

I scoot up the bed so my back rests against the wall.

'The animals,' I say.

'What animals?'

'In the spaceship I saw take off. The old one, at the museum. In the rocket that left after ours. I watched animals being loaded into it. Not many. Fifteen, maybe. With three other Loric. I don't think they were Garde. And something else. A bundle. It looked like a baby, but I couldn't tell.'

'Why don't you think they were Garde?'

'They loaded the rocket with supplies, fifty or so boxes and duffel bags. They didn't use telekinesis.'

'Into the rocket inside the museum?'

'I think it was the museum. I was inside a large, domed

building with nothing inside of it but a rocket. I can only assume it was the museum.'

Henri nods. 'If they worked at the museum then they would have been Cêpan.'

'Loading animals,' I say. 'Animals that could change their shape.'

'Chimæra,' Henri says.

'What?'

'Chimæra. Animals on Lorien that could change their shape. They were called Chimæra.'

'Is that what Hadley was?' I ask, remembering back to the vision I had a few weeks ago, the vision of playing in the yard of my Elders' home when I was lifted in the air by the man wearing a silver and blue suit.

Henri smiles. 'You remember Hadley?'

I nod. 'I've seen him the way that I've seen everything else.'

'You're having the visions even when we're not training?'

'Sometimes.'

'How often?'

'Henri, who cares about the visions? Why were they loading animals into a rocket? What was a baby doing with them, or was it even a baby? Where did they go? What purpose could they possibly have had?'

Henri thinks about it a moment. He shifts the weight of his body to his right leg. 'Probably the same purpose we had. Think about it, John. How else could animals repopulate Lorien? They too would have to go to some sort of sanctuary. Everything was wiped out. Not just the people, but also the animals, and all plant life. Maybe the bundle was just another animal. A fragile one, or maybe a young one.'

'Well, where would they go? What other sanctuary exists besides Earth?'

'I think they went to one of the space stations. A rocket with Loric fuel would have been able to make it that far. Maybe they thought the invasion would be short-lived, and they thought they could wait it out. I mean, they would have been able to live on the space station for as long as their supplies lasted.'

'There are space stations close to Lorien?'

'Yes, two of them. Well, there *were* two of them. I know for sure the larger of the two was destroyed at the same time as the invasion. We lost contact with it less than two minutes after the first bomb fell.'

'Why didn't you mention that before, when I first told you about the rocket?'

'I had assumed that it was empty, that it went up in the air as a decoy. And I think that if one space station was destroyed, then the other was as well. Their trip, unfortunately, was probably done in vain, whatever their goal was.'

'But what if they came back when their supplies ran out? Do you think they could survive on Lorien?' I ask in desperation. I already know the answer, already know what Henri will say, but I ask anyway in order to hold on to some sort of hope that we aren't alone in all this. That maybe, somewhere far away, there are others like us, waiting, monitoring the planet so that they, too, might one day return and we won't be alone when we go back.

'No. There is no water there now. You saw that for yourself. Nothing but a barren wasteland. And nothing can survive without water.'

I sigh and scoot back down into the bed. I drop my head onto the pillow. What's the point in arguing? Henri is right and I know it. I saw it for myself. If the globes that he pulled from the Chest are to be trusted, then Lorien is nothing more than wasteland, a dump. The planet still lives but on the surface there is nothing. No water. No plants. No life. Nothing but dirt and rocks and the rubble of the civilization that once existed.

'Did you see anything else?' Henri asks.

'I saw us on the day we left. All of us at the airship right before we took off.'

'It was a sad day.'

I nod. Henri crosses his arms and gazes out the window, lost in thought. I take a deep breath. 'Where was your family during it all?' I ask.

My lights have been off for a good two or three minutes, but I can see the whites of Henri's eyes staring back at me.

'Not with me, not on that day,' he says.

We are both silent for a time and then Henri shifts his weight.

'Well, I better get back to bed,' he says, bringing an end to the conversation. 'Get some sleep.'

After he leaves I lie there thinking of the animals, of the rocket, of Henri's family and how I'm sure he never got the chance to say good-bye to them. I know I won't be able to go back to sleep. I never can when the images visit me, when I feel Henri's sadness. It must be a thought constantly on his mind, as it would be for anyone who left under the same circumstances, leaving the only home you've ever known, all the while knowing you will never see the people you love again.

I grab my cell phone and text Sarah. I always text her when I can't sleep, or she texts me if it's the other way around. Then we'll talk for as long as it takes to become tired. She calls me twenty seconds after I hit the send button.

'Hey, you,' I answer.

'You can't sleep?'

'No.'

'What's the matter?' she asks. She yawns on the other end of the line.

'Was just missing you is all. Been lying in bed staring at the ceiling for like an hour now.'

'You're silly. You saw me like six hours ago.'

'I wish you were still here,' I say. She moans. I can hear her smile through the darkness. I roll onto my side and hold the phone between my ear and the pillow.

'Well, I wish I was still there, too.'

We talk for twenty minutes. The last half of the call is both of us just lying there listening to the other breathe. I feel better after having talked to Sarah, but I find it even harder to fall back asleep.

24

For once, since we arrived in Ohio, things seem to slow for a time. School ends quietly and for winter break we have eleven days off. Sam and his mother spend most of it visiting his aunt in Illinois. Sarah stays home. We spend Christmas together. We kiss when the ball drops at midnight on New Year's Eve. Despite the snow and the cold, or maybe even in retaliation against it, we go for long walks through the woods behind my house, holding hands, kissing, breathing in the chilly air beneath the low gray skies of winter. We spend more and more time together. Not a day passes during that whole break that we don't see each other at least once.

We walk hand in hand beneath an umbrella of white from the snow piled atop the tree branches overhead. She has her camera with her and occasionally stops to take pictures. Most of the snow on the ground lies undisturbed aside from the tracks we have made on the walk out. We follow them back now, Bernie Kosar in the lead, darting in and out of the brambles, chasing rabbits into small groves and thickets of thorny bush, chasing squirrels up trees. Sarah wears a pair of black earmuffs. Her cheeks and the tip of her nose are red with the cold, making her eyes look bluer. I stare at her.

'What?' she asks, smiling.

'Just admiring the view.'

She rolls her eyes at me. For the most part the woods are

dense aside from sporadic clearings we continually stumble upon. I'm not sure how far in any one direction the woods extend, but in all of our walks we have yet to reach their end.

'I bet it's beautiful here in the summer,' Sarah says. 'We can probably picnic in the clearings.'

An ache forms in my chest. Summer is still five months away and if Henri and I are here in May, we will have made it seven months in Ohio. That is very nearly the longest we have ever stayed in one place.

'Yeah,' I agree.

Sarah looks at me. 'What?'

I look at her questioningly. 'What do you mean, "What?"'

'That wasn't very convincing,' she says. A mess of crows fly by overhead, squawking noisily.

'I just wish it was summer now.'

'Me too. I can't believe we have to go back to school tomorrow.'

'Ugh, don't remind me.'

We enter another clearing, larger than the others, an almost perfect circle a hundred feet in diameter. Sarah lets go of my hand, runs into the middle of it, and drops into the snow, laughing. She rolls to her back and begins making a snow angel. I drop beside her and do the same. The tips of our fingers just barely touch while we make the wings. We get up.

'It's like we're holding wings,' she says.

'Is that possible?' I ask. 'I mean, how would we fly if we're holding wings?'

'Of course it's possible. Angels can do anything.'

Then she turns and nuzzles into me. Her cold face against my neck makes me squirm away from her.

'Ahh! Your face is like ice.'

She laughs. 'Come warm me up.'

I take her in my arms and kiss her beneath the open sky, the trees surrounding us. There are no sounds save the birds and the occasional pack of snow falling from the nearby branches. Two cold faces pressed tightly together. Bernie Kosar comes trotting up, out of breath, tongue dangling, tail wagging. He barks and sits in the snow staring at us, his head cocked to the side.

'Bernie Kosar! Were you off chasing rabbits?' Sarah asks.

He barks twice and runs over and jumps up on her. He barks again and pushes off and then looks up expectantly. She grabs a stick from the ground, shakes the snow off it, and then hurls it into the trees. He races after it and disappears from sight. He emerges from the trees ten seconds later, but instead of returning to the clearing where he had exited it, he comes from the opposite side. Sarah and I both spin around to watch him.

'How'd he do that?' she asks.

'Don't know,' I say. 'He's a peculiar dog.'

'Did you hear that, Bernie Kosar? He just called you peculiar!'

He drops the stick at her feet. We walk towards home, holding hands, the day nearing dusk. Bernie Kosar trots beside us the whole way out, his head on a swivel as though ushering us along, keeping us safe from what may or may not lurk in the outer dark beyond our line of sight.

Five newspapers are stacked on the kitchen table, Henri at his computer, the overhead light on.

'Anything?' I ask out of habit, nothing more. There hasn't been a promising story in months, which is a good thing, but I can't help but always hope for something every time I ask.

'Actually, yes, I think so.'

I perk up, then walk around the table and look over Henri's shoulder at the computer screen. 'What?'

'There was an earthquake in Argentina yesterday evening. A sixteen-year-old girl pulled an elderly man free from a pile of rubble in a tiny town near the coast.'

'Number Nine?'

'Well, I certainly think she's one of us. Whether she's Number Nine or not remains to be seen.'

'Why? There's nothing really extraordinary about pulling a man from rubble.'

'Look,' Henri says, and then scrolls to the top of the article. There is a picture of a large slab of concrete at least a foot thick, eight feet long and wide. 'This is what she lifted to save him. It must weigh five tons. And look at this,' he says, and scrolls back to the bottom of the page. He highlights the very last sentence. It reads: 'Sofia García could not be found for comment.'

I read the sentence three times. 'She couldn't be found,' I say.

'Exactly. She didn't *decline* to comment; she simply couldn't be found.'

'How did they know her name?'

'It's a small town, less than a third the size of Paradise. Almost everyone would know her name there.'

'She left, didn't she?'

Henri nods. 'I think so. Probably before the paper was even published. That's the downfall of small towns; it's impossible to remain unnoticed.'

I sigh. 'Hard for the Mogadorians to go unnoticed too.'

'Precisely.'

'Sucks for her,' I say, and stand up. 'Who knows what she must have left behind.'

Henri gives me a skeptical look, opens his mouth to say something, but then thinks better of it and goes back to the computer. I return to my bedroom. I pack my bag with a fresh change of clothes and the books I'll need for the day. Back to school. I'm not looking forward to it, though it'll be nice to see Sam again, whom I haven't seen in nearly two weeks.

'Okay,' I say. 'I'm off.'

'Have a good day. Be safe out there.'

'See you this afternoon.'

Bernie Kosar rushes out of the house ahead of me. He's a ball of energy this morning. I think he's come to look forward to our morning runs, and the fact that we haven't done one in a week and a half has him chomping at the bit to get back to it. He keeps up with me for most of the run. Once we make it I give him a good pet and scratch behind his ears.

'All right, boy, go home,' I say. He turns and starts trotting back to the house.

I take my time in the shower. By the time I finish, other students are beginning to arrive. I walk the hall, stop by my locker, then go to Sam's. I slap him on the back. It startles him, then he flashes a big toothy grin when he sees that it's me.

'I thought I was going to have to whip somebody's ass there for a minute,' he says.

'Just me, my friend. How was Illinois?'

'Ugh,' he says, and rolls his eyes. 'My aunt made me drink tea and watch reruns of *Little House on the Prairie* nearly every day.'

I laugh. 'That sounds awful.'

'It was, trust me,' he says, and reaches into his bag. 'This was waiting in the mail when we got back.'

He hands me the latest issue of *They Walk Among Us*. I begin flipping through it.

'There is nothing on us or the Mogadorians,' he says.

'Good,' I say. 'They must fear us after you visited them.'

'Yeah, right.'

Over Sam's shoulder I see that Sarah is coming our way. Mark James stops her in the middle of the hallway and hands her a few sheets of orange paper. Then she continues on her way.

'Hi, gorgeous,' I say when she reaches us. She stands on her toes to kiss me. Her lips taste like strawberry lip balm.

'Hi, Sam. How are you?'

'Good. How're you?' he asks. He seems at ease with her now. Before the incident with Henri, which was a month and a half ago, being in Sarah's presence would have made him uncomfortable, and he wouldn't have been able to meet her eye or know what to do with his hands. But now he looks at her and smiles, speaking with confidence.

'Good,' she says. 'I'm supposed to give you both one of these.'

She hands us each one of the orange sheets Mark just gave her. It's a party invitation for this upcoming Saturday night at his house.

'I'm invited?' Sam asks.

Sarah nods. 'All three of us are.'

'Do you want to go?' I ask.

'Maybe we could give it a shot.'

I nod. 'You interested, Sam?'

He looks past Sarah and me. I turn to see what he is

looking at, or rather who. At a locker across the hall is Emily, the girl who was on the hayride with us, and who Sam has been pining for ever since. When she walks past she sees that Sam is watching her and she smiles politely.

'Emily?' I say to Sam.

'Emily what?' Sam asks, looking back at me.

I look at Sarah. 'I think Sam likes Emily Knapp.'

'I do not,' he says.

'I could ask her to come to the party with us,' Sarah says.

'Do you think she would go?' Sam asks.

Sarah looks at me. 'Well, maybe I shouldn't invite her since Sam doesn't like her.'

Sam smiles. 'Okay, fine. I just, I don't know.'

'She kept asking why you never called after the hayride. She kind of likes you.'

'That is true,' I say. 'I've heard her say it.'

'Why didn't you tell me?' says Sam.

'You never asked.'

Sam looks down at the flyer. 'So it's this Saturday?'

'Yes.'

He looks up at me. 'I say we go.'

I shrug. 'I'm in.'

Henri is waiting for me when the final bell rings. As always, Bernie Kosar is in the passenger seat, and when he sees me, his tail begins wagging a hundred miles an hour. I jump into the truck. Henri puts it into gear and drives away.

'There was a follow-up article on the girl in Argentina,' Henri says.

'And?'

'Just a short article saying that she has disappeared. The mayor of the town is offering a modest reward for information on her whereabouts. It sounds like they believe she's been kidnapped.'

'Are you worried about the Mogadorians having gotten to her first?'

'If she's Nine, like the note we found indicated, and the Mogadorians were tracking her, it's a good thing that she vanished. And if she's been captured, the Mogadorians can't kill her – they can't even hurt her. That gives us hope. The good thing, aside from the news itself, is that I imagine every Mogadorian on Earth has poured into Argentina.'

'Speaking of which, Sam had the latest issue of *They Walk Among Us* today.'

'Was there anything in it?'

'Nope.'

'I didn't think there would be. Your levitation trick seemed to affect them rather profoundly.'

When we arrive home I change clothes and meet Henri in the backyard for our day of training. Working while consumed with fire has gotten easier. I don't get as flustered as I did on that first day. I can hold my breath longer, close to four minutes. I have more control over the objects I lift, and I can lift more of them at the same time. Little by little, the look of worry I saw on Henri's face during the first days has melted away. He nods more. He smiles more. On the days it goes really well he gets a crazed look in his eyes and he raises his arms in the air and yells 'Yes!' as loudly as he can. In that way I am gaining confidence in my Legacies. The rest have yet to come, but I don't think they're far off. And the major one, whatever it will be. The anticipation of it keeps me up most nights. I want to fight. I hunger for a Mogadorian to saunter into the backyard so that I may finally seek revenge.

It's an easy day. No fire. Mostly just me lifting things and manipulating them while they are suspended in the air. The last twenty minutes pass with Henri throwing objects at me – sometimes just allowing them to fall to the ground, other times deflecting them in a way that emulates a boomerang so that they twist in the air and go blazing back towards Henri. At one point a meat tenderizer flies back so fast that Henri dives face-first into the snow to keep from being hit by it. I laugh. Henri does not. Bernie Kosar lies on the ground the whole time watching us, seeming to offer his own encouragement. After we are done I shower, do my homework, and sit at the kitchen table for dinner.

'So there is a party this Saturday that I'm going to go to.'

He looks up at me, stops chewing. 'Whose party?'

'Mark James's.'

Henri looks surprised.

'All that's over,' I say before he can object.

'Well, you know best, I suppose. Just remember what's at stake.'

25

And then the weather warms. Brisk winds, bitter cold, and continuous snow showers are followed by blue skies and fifty-degree temperatures. The snow melts. At first there are standing puddles in the driveway and the yard, the road wet with the sounds of splashing tires, but after a day all the water drains and evaporates and the cars pass as they do on any other day. A lull in the action, a brief reprieve before old man winter takes up the reins again.

I sit on the porch waiting for Sarah, staring up at the night sky full of twinkling stars and a full moon. A thin, knifelike cloud cuts the moon in two and then quickly disappears. I hear the crunch of gravel under tires; then headlights come into view and the car pulls into the driveway. Sarah gets out of the driver's side. She's dressed in dark gray pants flared at the ankles, a navy blue cardigan sweater beneath a beige jacket. Her eyes are accentuated by the blue shirt peeking out where the jacket's zipper ends. Her blond hair falling past her shoulders. She smiles coyly and looks at me, fluttering her eyelashes as she approaches. There are butterflies in my stomach. Almost three months together and yet I still grow nervous when I see her. A nervousness that's hard to imagine time will ever assuage.

'You look gorgeous,' I say.

'Well, thank you,' she says, and bobs a curtsy. 'You don't look so bad yourself.'

I kiss Sarah on the cheek. Then Henri walks out of the

house and waves to Sarah's mom, who is sitting in the passenger seat of the car.

'So you'll call when you're ready to be picked up, right?' Henri asks me.

'Yes,' I say.

We walk to the car and Sarah gets behind the wheel. I sit in the back. She's had her learner's permit for a few months now, which means she can drive so long as a licensed driver sits in the passenger seat beside her. Her actual driver's test is on Monday, two days away. She's been anxious about it ever since making the appointment over winter break. She backs out of the driveway and pulls away, eventually flipping the visor down and smiling at me through the mirror. I smile back.

'So how was your day, John?' her mother turns and asks me. We make small talk. She tells me of the trip to the mall that the two of them made earlier in the day, and how Sarah drove. I tell her about playing with Bernie Kosar in the yard, and about the run we went on after. I *don't* tell her about the training session that lasted for three hours in the backyard after the run. I don't tell her how I split the dead tree's trunk straight down the middle through telekinesis, or how Henri threw knives at me that I deflected into a sandbag fifty feet away. I don't tell her about being lit on fire or the objects that I lifted and crushed and splintered. Another kept secret. Another half-truth that feels like a lie. I would like to tell Sarah. I somehow feel that I'm betraying her by keeping myself hidden, and over the last few weeks the burden has really begun to weigh on me. But I also know I have no other choice. Not at this point, anyhow.

'So it's this one?' Sarah asks.

'Yes,' I say.

She pulls into Sam's driveway. He paces at the end of it, dressed in jeans and a wool sweater. He looks up at us with a deer-caught-in-the-headlights blank stare. There is gel in his hair. I've never seen gel in his hair before. He walks to the side of the car, opens the door, and slides in beside me.

'Hi, Sam,' Sarah says, then introduces him to her mom.

Sarah reverses the car out of the driveway and pulls onto the road. Both of Sam's hands are planted firmly on the seat in nervousness. Sarah turns down a road I've never seen before and makes a right turn into a winding driveway. Thirty or so cars are parked along the side of it. At the end of the driveway, surrounded by trees, is a large, two-story house. We can hear the music well before we reach the house.

'Jeez, nice house,' Sam says.

'You guys be good in there,' Sarah's mom says. 'And be safe. Call if you need anything, or if you can't get ahold of your father,' she says, looking at me.

'Will do, Mrs Hart,' I say.

We get out of the car and begin walking to the front door. Two dogs run up to us from the side of the house, a golden retriever and a bulldog. Their tails are wagging and they're sniffing spastically at my pants, smelling the scent of Bernie Kosar. The bulldog is carrying a stick in his mouth. I wrestle it away from him and throw it across the yard and both dogs sprint after it.

'Dozer and Abby,' Sarah says.

'I take it Dozer is the bulldog?' I ask.

She nods and smiles at me as though in apology. I'm reminded how well she must know this house. I wonder if it's odd for her to be back now, with me.

'This is a horrible idea,' Sam says. He looks at me. 'I'm only now realizing that.'

'Why do you think so?'

'Because only three months ago the guy who lives here filled both our lockers with cow manure and hit me in the back of the head with a meatball during lunch. And now we're here.'

'I bet Emily is already here,' I say, and nudge him with my elbow.

The door opens into the foyer. The dogs come rushing in past us and disappear into the kitchen, which lies straight ahead. I can see that Abby is now holding the stick. We're met with loud music that we have to yell over to be heard. People are dancing in the living room. There are cans of beer in most of their hands, a few people drinking bottled water or soda. Apparently Mark's parents are out of town. The whole football team is in the kitchen, half of them wearing their letterman jackets. Mark comes up and hugs Sarah. Then he shakes my hand. He holds my gaze for a second and then looks away. He doesn't shake Sam's hand. He doesn't even look at him. Perhaps Sam is right. This may have been a mistake.

'Happy you guys could make it. Come on in. Beer's in the kitchen.'

Emily stands in the far corner talking to other people. Sam looks her way, then asks Mark where the bathroom is. He points the way.

'Be right back,' Sam says to me.

Most of the guys are standing around the island in the middle of the kitchen. They look at me when Sarah and I enter. I look at each of them in turn, and then grab a bottle of water from the ice bucket. Mark hands Sarah a beer and opens it for her. The way he looks at her makes me realize yet again just how little I trust him. And I realize now just how bizarre this whole situation is. Me, being in his house now, with Sarah, his ex-girlfriend. I'm happy that Sam is with me.

I reach down and play with the dogs until Sam comes out of the bathroom. By then Sarah has made her way to the corner of the living room and is talking to Emily. Sam tenses beside me when he realizes that there is nothing else for us to do but walk up to them and say hello. He takes a deep breath. In the kitchen two of the guys have lit a corner of the newspaper on fire for no other reason than to watch it burn.

'Make sure you compliment Emily,' I say to Sam as we approach. He nods.

'There you guys are,' Sarah says. 'I thought you had left me all by my lonesome.'

'Wouldn't dream of it,' I say. 'Hi, Emily. How are you?'

'I'm good,' she says, then to Sam, 'I like your hair.'

Sam just looks at her. I nudge him. He smiles.

'Thank you,' he says. 'You look very nice.'

Sarah gives me a knowing look. I shrug and kiss her on the cheek. The music has grown even louder. Sam talks to Emily, somewhat nervously, but she laughs and after a while he eases a little.

'So are you okay?' Sarah asks me.

'Of course. I'm with the prettiest girl at the party. How could things be better?'

'Oh shush,' she says, and pokes me in the stomach.

The four of us dance for an hour or so. The football players keep drinking. Somebody shows up with a bottle of vodka and not long after that one of them – I don't know which – throws up in the bathroom so that the smell of vomit wafts throughout the whole downstairs. Another one passes out on the living-room sofa and some of the others draw with marker on his face. People keep filtering in and out of the doorway leading to the basement. I have no idea what is going on down there. I haven't seen Sarah for the past ten minutes. I leave Sam and walk through the living room and the kitchen, then walk up the stairs. White, thick carpet, walls lined with art and family portraits. Some of the bedroom doors are open. Some are closed. I don't see Sarah. I walk back downstairs. Sam is standing sullenly by himself in the corner. I walk over to him.

'Why the long face?' I ask.

He shakes his head.

'Don't make me lift you in the air and turn you upside down like the guy in Athens.'

I smile, Sam doesn't.

'I just got cornered by Alex Davis,' he says.

Alex Davis is another of Mark James's brood, a wide receiver for the team. He's a junior, tall and thin. I've never talked to him before, and likewise know little else about him.

'What do you mean by "cornered"?'

'We just talked. He saw that I've been talking to Emily. I guess they dated over the summer.'

'So what. Why does that bother you?'

He shrugs. 'It just sucks, and it bothers me, okay?'

'Sam, do you know how long Sarah and Mark dated?'

'For a long time.'

'Two years,' I say.

'Does it bother you?' he asks.

'Not in the least. Who cares about her past? Besides, look

at Alex,' I say, and nod to him standing in the kitchen. He is slumped against the kitchen counter, his eyes aflutter, a thin layer of sweat glistening on his forehead. 'Do you really think she misses being with that?'

Sam looks at him, shrugs.

'You're a good dude, Sam Goode. Don't get down on yourself.'

'I'm not down on myself.'

'Well then, don't worry about Emily's past. We don't have to be defined by the things we did or didn't do in our past. Some people allow themselves to be controlled by regret. Maybe it's a regret, maybe it's not. It's merely something that happened. Get over it.'

Sam sighs. He's still wrestling with it.

'Go on. She likes you. There's nothing to be scared of,' I say.

'I am, though.'

'Best way to deal with fear is to confront it. Just walk up to her and kiss her. I bet you she kisses you back.'

Sam looks at me and nods, then goes to the basement, where Emily is hanging out. The two dogs come wrestling into the living room. Tongues dangling. Tails wagging. Dozer drops his chest to the ground and waits for Abby to come near enough and then he jumps at her and she jumps away. I watch them until they disappear up the stairs, playing tug-of-war with a rubber toy. It's a quarter till midnight. A couple is making out on the couch across the room. The football players are still drinking in the kitchen. I'm starting to get sleepy. I still can't find Sarah.

Just then one of the football players comes rushing up the basement stairs, a crazed, frantic look in his eyes. He rushes to the kitchen sink, turns on the water as high as it will go, and begins throwing open the kitchen-cupboard doors.

'There's a fire downstairs!' he says to the guys nearby.

They begin filling pots and pans with water, and one by one they rush down the stairs.

Emily and Sam come up the stairs. Sam looks shaken.

'What's wrong?' I say.

'The house is on fire!'

'How bad?'

'Is any fire good? And I think we started it. We, uh, knocked a candle into a curtain.'

Sam and Emily both look disheveled and have clearly been making out. I make a mental note to congratulate Sam later.

'Have you seen Sarah?' I ask Emily.

She shakes her head.

More guys rush up the stairs, Mark James with them. There is fear in his eyes. For the first time I smell smoke. I look at Sam.

'Go outside,' I say.

He nods and takes Emily's hand and they leave together. Some of the others follow, but some stay where they are, watching with drunken curiosity. A few people stand around stupidly patting the football players on the back as they rush up and down the basement stairs, cheering them on as though it's all a joke.

I go to the kitchen and grab the largest thing left, a medium-sized metal pot. I fill it with water and then go downstairs. Everybody has evacuated aside from us battling the blaze, which is far bigger than I expected. Half the basement is consumed in flames. Dousing it with the little water I have left is completely futile. I don't try, and instead drop the pot and dash back up. Mark comes flying down. I stop him in the middle of the stairway. His eyes are swimming in booze but through it I can see that he is terrified, that he is desperate.

'Forget about it,' I say. 'It's too big. We have to get everyone out.'

He looks down the stairs at the fire. He knows that what I've said is true. The tough-guy front is gone. There is no more pretending.

'Mark!' I yell.

He nods and drops the pot and we go back up together.

'Everybody out! Now!' I yell when I get to the top of the stairs.

Some of the drunker ones don't move. Some of them laugh. One person says, 'Where's the marshmallows?' Mark slaps him across the face.

'Get out!' he screams.

I rip the cordless phone from the wall and shove it into Mark's hand.

'Dial 911,' I yell over the loud voices and the music that still blares from somewhere like a sound track to the erupting pandemonium. The floor is getting warm. Smoke begins to billow up from beneath us. Only then do people take it seriously. I start pushing them towards the door.

I dart past Mark as he begins dialing and rush through the house. I take the stairs three at a time and kick through the open doors. One couple is making out on a bed. I yell at them both to get out. Sarah's nowhere to be found. I sprint back down the stairs and through the door into the dark, cold night. People are standing around, watching. Some of them I can tell are excited by the prospect of the house burning down. Some laugh. I can feel myself begin to panic. Where is Sarah? Sam stands at the back of the crowd, which must total a hundred people. I run to him.

'Have you seen Sarah?' I ask.

'No,' he says.

I look back at the house. People are still coming out. The basement windows glow red, flames licking against the panes of glass. One of them is open. Black smoke pours out of it and floats high in the air. I weave through the crowd. Just then an explosion rattles the house. All the basement windows shatter. Some of the people cheer. The flames have reached the first floor, and they're moving fast. Mark James stands at the front of the crowd, unable to divert his gaze away from it. His face is illuminated by the orange glow. There are tears in his eyes, a look of despair, the same look that I saw in the eyes of the Loric on the day of the invasion. What an odd thing it must be to watch everything you've ever known be destroyed. The fire spreads with hostility, with disregard. All Mark can do is watch. Flames are beginning to rise up past the first-floor windows. We can feel the heat on our faces from where we stand.

'Where's Sarah?' I ask him.

He doesn't hear me. I shake him by the shoulder. He turns and looks at me with a blankness that suggests he still doesn't believe what his own eyes are telling him.

'Where's Sarah?' I ask again.

'I don't know,' he says.

I start to weave through the crowd looking for her, getting more and more frantic. Everyone is watching the blaze. The vinyl siding has begun to bubble and melt. The curtains in the windows have all burned away. The front door stands open, smoke pouring out of the top of it like an upside-down waterfall. We can see all the way into the kitchen, which is an inferno. On the left side of the house the fire has reached the second floor. And that's when we all hear it.

A long terrible scream. And dogs barking. My heart drops. Every person there strains to listen while hoping like hell we didn't hear what we all know we did. And then it comes again. Unmistakable. It comes in a torrent and this time it doesn't let up. Gasps filter throughout the crowd.

'Oh no,' Emily says. 'Oh God no, please no.'

26

Nobody speaks. All eyes are wide-open, staring up in shock. Sarah and the dogs must be somewhere in the back. I close my eyes and lower my head. All I can smell is the smoke. 'Just remember what's at stake,' Henri had warned. I know damn well what's at stake, but still his voice echoes. My life, and now Sarah's life. There is another scream. Terrified. Severe.

I feel Sam's eyes on me. He has seen firsthand my resistance to fire. But he also knows how I am hunted. I glance around. Mark is on his knees, rocking himself back and forth. He wants it over with. He wants the dogs to stop barking. But they don't stop, and he takes each bark as though being stabbed in the gut with a knife.

'Sam,' I say so that only he can hear, 'I'm going in.' He closes his eyes, takes a deep breath, fixes me with a stare.

'Go get her,' he says.

I hand him my phone and tell him to call Henri if for some reason I don't make it out. He nods. I begin moving to the back of the crowd, weaving in and out of the mass of bodies. Nobody pays me any attention. When I finally reach the back I make a mad dash for the yard's perimeter and then sprint to the rear of the house so that I can enter without being seen. The kitchen is completely submerged in flame. I watch it for a brief moment. I can hear Sarah and the dogs. They sound closer now. I take a deep breath and with that breath other things come. Anger.

Determination. Hope and fear. I let them in, I feel them all. And then I lunge forward and sweep across the yard and burst into the house. I am swallowed by the inferno immediately, hearing nothing but the crackle and hum of the flames. My clothes catch fire. There is no end to the blaze. I move to the front of the house and half of the stairs have burned away. What is left is on fire, looking brittle, but there isn't time to test them. I rush up but they collapse under my weight when I reach the halfway point. I tumble down with them, the fire rising as though someone has stoked the flames. Something pierces my back. I grit my teeth, still holding my breath. I stand from the rubble and listen to Sarah screaming. She's screaming and she's scared and she's going to die, die a hideous miserable death if I don't get to her. Time is short. I'll have to jump to the second floor.

I jump and grab hold of the edge of the floor and pull myself up. The fire has spread to the other side of the house. She and the dogs are somewhere to my right. I leap down the hallway, checking rooms. The pictures on the walls have burned in their frames, nothing more than blackened silhouettes melted to the wall. Then my foot falls through the floor and my breath catches in surprise and I breathe in. Nothing but smoke and flame enter. I begin coughing. I cover my mouth with my arm but it does little to help. Smoke and fire are burning my lungs. I drop to a knee, coughing, gasping. Then a fury surges through me and I stand back up and I move on, hunched over, gritting my teeth, determined.

And then I find them in the last room on the left. Sarah is screaming, 'HELP!' The dogs are whining and crying. The door is closed and I kick it open, send it flying off its hinges. All three of them are huddled tightly against one another as far into the corner as they can get. Sarah sees me and yells my name and starts to stand. I motion to her to stay where she is, and as I step into the room, a huge flaming support beam falls between us. I raise my hand and send it upwards, crashing through what remains of the roof. Sarah seems confused by what she's just seen. I leap towards her, covering twenty feet in a single bound, moving straight through the flames without them affecting me at all. The dogs are at her feet. I push the bulldog into her arms and pick up the retriever. With my other arm I help her stand.

'You came,' she says.

'No one, and nothing, will ever hurt you as long as I'm alive,' I say back to her.

Another huge beam falls and takes out part of the floor, landing in the kitchen below us. We need to get out the back of the house so no one sees me, or sees what I think I'm going to need to do. I hold Sarah tight against my side and the dog against my chest. We take two steps, then leap over the flaming chasm created by the fallen beam. As we start to move down the hall, a huge explosion below takes out most of it. The hallway is gone; where it used to be are a wall and a window, quickly being consumed by flames. Our only chance is through the window. Sarah is screaming again, clutching my arm, and I can feel the dog's claws digging into my chest. I lift my hand towards the window, stare at it, and focus – and it blows out of its frame, leaving us the opening we need. I look at Sarah, pulling her securely against my side.

'Hold on tight,' I say.

I take three steps and dive forward. The flames swallow us whole but we fly through the air like a bullet, heading straight towards the opening. I'm worried we're not going to make it. We barely clear it, and I feel the edge of the shattered frame scrape against my arms and the tops of my legs. I hold Sarah and the dog as best as I can, and twist my body so that I'll land on my back and everyone else will be on top of me. We hit the ground with a thud. Dozer goes rolling. Abby yelps. I hear the breath go out of Sarah. We're about thirty feet behind the house. I feel a cut on the top of my head from the broken glass of the window. Dozer is the first one up. He seems fine. Abby is a little slower. She limps on her front paw, but I don't think it is anything serious. I lie on my back and hold Sarah. She is starting to cry. I can smell her singed hair. Blood drips down the side of my face and gathers in my ear.

I sit in the grass to catch my breath. Sarah is in my arms. The bottoms of my shoes have melted. My shirt has completely burned away, and so have most of my jeans. Small cuts traverse the length of both arms. But I am not burned at all. Dozer walks over and licks my hand. I pet him.

'You're a good boy,' I say between Sarah's sobs. 'Go on. Get your sister and go back up front.'

There are sirens in the distance that should be here within the next minute or two. The woods are about a hundred yards from the back of the house. Both dogs sit watching me. I nod to the front of the house and they get up as if they understand and both begin walking that way. Sarah is still in my arms. I turn her so she is cradled in them and I stand and head to the woods, carrying her as she cries on my shoulder. Just as I enter them I hear the whole crowd erupt in cheers. Dozer and Abby must have been seen.

The woods are dense. The full moon still shines but there is little light coming from it. I turn my hands on so we can see. I start to shiver. Panic sweeps through me. How will I explain this to Henri? I'm wearing what now look like singed cutoffs. My head is bleeding. So is my back, along with various cuts on my arms and legs. My lungs feel as though they are on fire with every breath I take. And Sarah is in my arms. She now must know what I can do, what I am capable of, or at least some of it. I'm going to have to explain everything to her. I'll have to tell Henri she knows. I already have too many strikes against me. He'll say someone will slip at some point. He'll insist we leave. There's no way around it.

I set Sarah down. She's stopped crying. She looks at me, confused, scared, bewildered. I know I need to get some clothes and get back to the party so that people aren't suspicious. I need to get Sarah back so people don't think she's dead.

'You're okay to walk?' I say.

'I think so.'

'Follow me.'

'Where are we going?'

'I need to get some clothes. Hopefully, one of the football players has a change of clothes for after practice.'

We start walking through the woods. I'm going to circle around and look inside people's cars for something to wear.

'What just happened, John? What is happening?'

'You were in a fire, and I got you out of it.'

'What you did isn't possible.'

'It is for me.'

'What's that supposed to mean?'

I look at her. I had hoped never to have to tell her what I'm about to tell her. Even though I knew it probably wasn't realistic, I had hoped to stay hidden in Paradise. Henri has always said never to get too close to anyone. Because if you do, at some point they're going to notice that you're different, and that will require an explanation. And that means we have to leave. My heart is pounding, my hands are shaking, but not because I'm cold. If I have any hope of staying, or of getting away with what I did tonight, I have to tell her.

'I am not who you think I am,' I say.

'Who are you?'

'I am Number Four.'

'What's that supposed to mean?'

'Sarah, it's going to sound stupid and crazy, but what I'm about to say is the truth. You have to believe me.'

She touches her hand to the side of my face. 'If you say it's the truth, then I'll believe you.'

'It is.'

'Then tell me.'

'I'm an alien. I am the fourth of nine kids sent to Earth after our planet was destroyed. I have powers, powers unlike any human, powers that allow me to do things like I did in the house. And there are other aliens here on Earth who are hunting me, the ones who attacked my planet, and if they find me they will kill me.'

I expect her to slap me, or laugh at me, or scream, or turn and run away from me. She stops and looks at me. Looks right into my eyes.

'You're telling me the truth,' she says.

'Yes, I am.' I look into her eyes, willing her to believe me. She stares searchingly at me for a long moment, and then nods.

'Thank you for saving my life. I don't care what you are or where you're from. To me you're John, the boy I love.'

'What?'

'I love you, John, and you saved my life, and that's all that's important.'

'I love you too. And I always will.'

I wrap my arms around her and kiss her. After a minute or so, she pulls away.

'Let's go find you some clothes and get back so people know we're okay.'

Sarah finds a change of clothes in the fourth car we check. They're close enough to what I was wearing – jeans and a button-down shirt – that no one will notice the difference. When we reach the house we stand as far away as possible while still being able to see. The house has collapsed in on itself and is now nothing more than a twisted heap of blackened coals soggy with water. Wisps of smoke sporadically rise, looking ghastly in the night sky. There are three fire trucks. I count six cop cars. Nine sets of flashing lights but no sound to go with them. Few people, if any, have left. They've been pushed back, the house cordoned off with yellow tape. The police officers are questioning some of them. Five firemen stand in the middle of it all, sifting through the rubble.

Then I hear 'There they are!' yelled from behind me. Every set of eyes in the crowd turns my way. It takes me a full five seconds to realize that it is me the person is referring to.

Four police officers walk towards us. Behind them is a man holding a notepad and tape recorder. While we were looking for the clothes, Sarah and I agreed on a story. I came around the back of the house where she was watching the fire. She had jumped out of the second-floor window with the dogs, who had run away. We had watched away from the crowd, but eventually drifted over and joined it. I explained to her that we couldn't tell anyone about what happened, not even Sam or Henri, that if anyone found out the truth, I would have to leave immediately. We agreed that I would answer the questions and she would agree with whatever I said.

'Are you John Smith?' one of the cops asks me. The officer is of medium height, and stands with his shoulders hunched. He isn't overweight but is far from being in shape, with a slight paunch and an overall look of softness.

'Yes, why?'

'Two people said they saw you run into that house and then come flying out the back of it like Superman, with the dogs and the girl in your arms.'

'Seriously?' I ask in disbelief. Sarah stays beside me.

'That's what they said.'

I fake a laugh. 'The house was on fire. Do I look like I was inside a burning house?'

He scrunches his eyebrows together and rests his hands on his hips. 'So you're telling me you didn't go in there?'

'I came around the back to try and find Sarah,' I say. 'She had gotten out with the dogs. We stayed back there and watched the fire and then came over here.'

The officer looks at Sarah. 'Is that true?'

'Yes.'

'Well, who ran into that house, then?' the reporter beside him chimes in. It's his first time speaking. He watches me with shrewd, judging eyes. I can already tell that he doesn't believe my story.

'How do I know?' I say.

He nods his head and writes something in his notebook. I can't read what it says.

'So you're telling me these two witnesses are liars?' the reporter asks.

'Baines,' the officer says, shaking his head at him.

I nod. 'I didn't go into the house and save her or the dogs. They were outside.'

'Who said anything about saving her or the dogs?' Baines asks.

I shrug. 'I thought that's what you were implying.'

'I didn't imply anything.'

Sam walks up with my phone. I try to fix him with a stare to tell him the timing is bad, but he doesn't understand and he hands me my phone anyway.

'Thanks,' I say.

'I'm happy you're okay,' he says. The officers glare at him and he slinks away.

Baines watches with his eyes squinted. He's chewing gum, trying to piece the information together. He nods to himself.

'So you handed your phone to your friend before you went for a walk?' he asks.

'I handed him my phone during the party. It was uncomfortable in my pocket.'

'I bet it was,' Baines says. 'So where did you go?'

'All right, Baines, that's enough questions,' the officer says.

'Can I leave?' I ask him. He nods his head. I walk away with my phone in my hand, dialing Henri's number with Sarah at my side.

'Hello,' answers Henri.

'I'm ready to be picked up,' I say. 'There's been a terrible fire here.'

'What?'

'Can you just pick us up?'

'Yes. I'll be right there.'

'So how do you explain the cut on the top of your head?' Baines asks from behind me. He had been following me, listening to my call to Henri.

'I cut it on a branch in the woods.'

'How convenient,' he says, and again writes something in his notebook. 'You know I can tell when I'm being lied to, right?'

I ignore him, keep walking away with Sarah's hand in mine. We head over to Sam.

'I'll find the truth, Mr Smith. I always do,' Baines yells behind me.

'Henri is on the way,' I say to Sam and Sarah.

'What the hell was that all about?' Sam asks.

'Who knows? Somebody thinks they saw me run in, probably somebody who drank too much,' I say more at Baines than Sam.

We stand at the end of the driveway until Henri arrives. When he pulls up he steps out of the truck and looks at the smoldering house far off in the distance.

'Ah, hell. Promise me you weren't a part of this,' he says.

'I wasn't,' I say.

We get into the truck. He pulls away while looking at the smoking rubble.

'You guys smell like smoke,' Henri says.

None of us reply, making the drive in silence. Sarah sits on my lap. We drop Sam off first, then Henri pulls out of the driveway and points the truck towards Sarah's home.

'I don't want to leave you tonight,' Sarah says to me.

'I don't want to leave you either.'

When we arrive at her house I get out with her and walk her to the door. She won't let go of me when I hug her good night.

'Will you call me when you get home?'

'Of course.'

'I love you.'

I smile. 'I love you too.'

She goes inside. I walk back to the truck, where Henri is waiting. I have to figure out a way to keep him from finding out the truth about tonight, from making us leave Paradise. Henri pulls out and drives home.

'So what happened to your jacket?' he asks.

'It was in Mark's closet.'

'What happened to your head?'

'I hit it trying to get out when the fire first started.'

He looks over at me doubtfully. 'You're the one who smells like smoke.'

I shrug. 'There was a lot of it.'

'So what started it?'

'Drunkenness is my guess.'

Henri nods and turns down our road.

'Well,' he says, 'it will be interesting to see what's in the papers on Monday.' He turns and looks at me, studying my reaction.

I keep silent.

Yes, I think, *it most certainly will be.*

27

I can't sleep. I lie in bed staring through the darkness at the ceiling. I call Sarah and we talk until three; I hang up and lie there with my eyes wide-open. At four I crawl out of bed and walk out of the room. Henri sits at the kitchen table, drinking coffee. He looks up at me, bags beneath his eyes, hair tousled.

'What are you doing?' I ask.

'I couldn't sleep either,' he says. 'Scouring the news.'

'Find anything?'

'Yes, but I'm not sure what it means to us yet. The men who wrote and published *They Walk Among Us*, the men we met, were tortured and killed.'

I sit across from him. 'What?'

'Police found them when the neighbors called after hearing screams coming from the house.'

'They didn't know where we lived.'

'No, they didn't. Thankfully. But it means the Mogadorians are getting bolder. And they're close. If we see or hear anything else out of the ordinary, we're going to need to leave immediately, no questions asked, no discussion.'

'Okay.'

'How's your head?'

'Sore,' I say. It took seven stitches to close the cut. Henri did it himself. I'm wearing a baggy sweatshirt. I'm certain one of the cuts on my back needs stitches as well, but that would require me to take my shirt off, and how would I explain the other cuts and scrapes to Henri? He'll know for sure what has happened. My lungs still burn. If anything, the pain has grown worse.

'So, the fire started in the basement?'

'Yes.'

'And you were in the living room?'

'Yes.'

'How did you know it started in the basement?'

'Because all the guys came running up.'

'And you knew everyone was out of the house by the time you went outside?'

'Yes.'

'How?'

I can tell he's trying to get me to contradict myself, that he's skeptical of my story. I'm certain he doesn't believe that I merely stood out front watching like everyone else.

'I didn't go in,' I say. It pains me to do so, but I look him in the eye and I lie.

'I believe you,' he says.

I wake close to noon. Birds are chirping beyond the window, and sunlight is pouring in. I breathe a sigh of relief. The fact that I was allowed to sleep this late means that there was no news to incriminate me. If there had been, I would have been pulled from bed and told to pack.

I roll off my back and that's when the pain hits. My chest feels as though somebody is pushing down on it, squeezing me. I can't take full breaths. When I try there is a sharp pain. It scares me.

Bernie Kosar is snoring in a ball at my side. I wake him by wrestling with him. He groans at first, then wrestles back. That is the beginning to our day. Me rousing the snoring dog beside me. His wagging tail, his dangling tongue immediately make me feel better. Never mind the pain in my chest. Never mind what the day might bring.

Henri's truck is gone. On the table is a note that reads: 'Ran to the store. Be back at one.' I walk outside. I have a headache and my arms are red and splotchy, the cuts slightly raised as though I've been scratched by a cat. I don't care about the cuts, or my headache, or the burning in my chest. What I care about is that I'm still here, in Ohio, that tomorrow I'll be going back to the same school I've gone to for three months now, and that I will see Sarah tonight.

Henri gets home at one. There is a haggard look in his eyes that tells me he still hasn't slept. After he unloads the groceries he goes into his bedroom and closes the door. Bernie Kosar and I go for a walk in the woods. I try to run, and I'm able to for a little while, but after a half mile or so the pain is too great and I have to stop. We walk on for what must be five miles. The woods end at another country road that looks similar to ours. I turn around and walk back. Henri is still in his room with the door closed when I return. I sit on the porch. I tense every time a car passes. I keep thinking one of them will stop, but none of them do.

The confidence I felt when I woke up is slowly chipped away as the day wanes. The *Paradise Gazette* isn't printed on Sunday. Will there be a story tomorrow? I suppose I expected a call to arrive, or the same reporter to show up at our doorstep, or one of the officers to ask more questions. I don't know why I'm so worried about a small-time reporter, but he'd been persistent – too persistent. And I know he didn't believe my story.

But nobody comes to our house. No one calls. I expected

something, and when that something doesn't come, a dread creeps in that I'm about to be exposed. 'I'll find the truth, Mr Smith. I always do,' Baines said. I consider running into town, trying to find him to dissuade him from any such truth, but I know that would only encourage suspicion. All I can do is hold my breath and hope for the best.

I wasn't in that house.

I have nothing to hide.

Sarah comes over that night. We go to my room and I hold her in my arms, lying on my back on the bed. Her head is against my chest and her leg is draped over me. She asks me questions about who I am, my past, about Lorien, about the Mogadorians. I'm still amazed at how quickly, and easily, Sarah believed everything, and how she's accepted it. I answer everything truthfully, which feels good after all the lies I've told over the last few days. But when we talk about the Mogadorians, I start to get scared. I'm worried that they'll find us. That what I did will expose us. I would do it again, for if I didn't Sarah would be dead, but I'm scared. I'm also scared of what Henri is going to do if he finds out. Though he is not biologically, for all intents and purposes he is my father. I love him and he loves me and I don't want to disappoint him. And as we lie there, my fear begins to reach new levels. I can't take not knowing what the next day will bring – the uncertainty is sawing me in two. The room is dark. A flickering candle burns on the window ledge a few feet away. I take a deep breath, which is to say, as deep a breath as I *can* take.

'Are you okay?' Sarah asks.

I wrap my arms around her. 'I miss you,' I say.

'You miss me? But I'm right here.'

'That's the worst way to miss somebody. When they're right beside you and you miss them anyway.'

'You're talking crazy. She reaches up and pulls my face to hers and kisses me, her soft lips on mine. I don't want her to stop. I don't ever want her to stop kissing me. As long as she is, then everything is fine. Everything is right. I would stay in this room forever if I could. The world can pass by without me, without us. Just as long as we can stay here, together, in each other's arms.

'Tomorrow,' I say.

She looks up at me. 'Tomorrow, what?'

I shake my head. 'I don't really know,' I say. 'I guess I'm just scared.'

She flashes a confused look at me. 'Scared of what?'

'I don't know,' I say. 'Just scared.'

When Henri and I get home after dropping her off I go back into my bedroom and lie in the same spot where she was. I can still smell her on my bed. I won't sleep tonight. I won't even try. I pace the room. When Henri goes to bed I walk out and sit at the kitchen table and write under candlelight. I write about Lorien, about Florida, about the things that I've seen when our training first began – the war, the animals, childhood images. I hope for some sort of cathartic release, but there isn't one. It only makes me sadder.

When my hand cramps I walk out of the house and stand on the porch. The cold air helps ease the pain of breathing. The moon is nearly full, a side of it ever so subtly shaved away. Sunrise is two hours away, and with that sunrise comes a new day, and the news of the weekend. The paper falls on our doorstep at six, sometimes six thirty. I'll already be at the school by the time it arrives and, if I'm in the news,

I refuse to leave without seeing Sarah again, without saying good-bye to Sam.

I walk into the house, change clothes, and pack my bag. I tiptoe back through and quietly close the door behind me. I take three steps on the porch when I hear a scratching at the door. I turn around and open it and Bernie Kosar comes trotting out. *Okay,* I think, *let us go together.*

We walk, stopping often, standing and listening to the silence. The night is dark but after a while a pale glow grows in the eastern sky just as we enter the school grounds. There are no cars in the lot and all the lights are off inside. At the very front of the school, in front of the pirate mural, sits a large rock that has been painted by previous graduating classes. I sit on it. Bernie Kosar lies in the grass a few feet away from me. I'm there for half an hour before the first vehicle arrives, a van, and I assume it's Hobbs, the janitor, arriving early to get the school in order, but I'm wrong. The van pulls up to the front doors and the driver gets out and leaves it idling. He's carrying a stack of newspapers bound by wire. We nod at each other and he drops the stack by the door and then drives off. I stay on the rock. I glance contemptuously at the papers. In my mind I'm hurling curses at them, threatening them to deliver the bad news I'm terrified of.

'I wasn't in that house on Saturday,' I say out loud, and as soon as I do I feel stupid. Then I look away, sigh, and jump off the rock.

'Well,' I say to Bernie Kosar. 'This is it, for good or bad.'

He opens his eyes briefly, then closes them and resumes his nap on the cold ground.

I tear the binding away and lift the top paper. The story has made the front page. At the very top is a picture of the burned rubble taken the next morning at dawn. There is a gothic, foreboding feel to it. Blackened ash is forefront to naked trees and frost-covered grass. I read the headline:

JAMES HOUSE GOES *UP IN SMOKE*

I hold my breath, a miserable feeling centered in my gut as though horrible news is about to find me. I race through the article. I don't read it, only look for my name. I reach the end. I blink my eyes and shake my head to rid myself of the cobwebs. A cautious smile forms. Then I scan through it again.

'No way,' I say. 'Bernie Kosar, my name isn't here!'

He pays me no attention. I run across the grass and jump back on the rock.

'My name isn't here!' I yell again, this time as loudly as I can.

I sit back down and read the story. The headline is a play on Cheech and Chong's *Up in Smoke*, which is apparently a movie about drugs. What the police believe started the blaze was a marijuana joint being smoked in the basement. How that information was discovered, I have no idea, especially because it is so wrong. The article itself is callous and mean, almost an attack on the James family. I didn't like the reporter. It's apparent that he doesn't like the Jameses. Who knows why?

I sit on the rock and read the article three times before the first person arrives to unlock the doors. I can't stop smiling. I'm staying in Ohio, in Paradise. The town name doesn't seem so foolish to me anymore. Through my excitement I feel as though I'm overlooking something, that I've forgotten a key component. But I'm so happy that I don't care. What harm can come now? My name isn't in the article. I didn't run into that house. The proof is right here, in my hands. Nobody can say otherwise.

'What are you so happy about?' Sam asks in astronomy class. I haven't stopped smiling.

'Didn't you read the paper this morning?'

He nods.

'Sam, I wasn't in it! I don't have to leave.'

'Why would they put you in the paper?' he asks.

I'm dumbfounded. I open my mouth to argue with him but just then Sarah walks into the room. She comes sauntering up the aisle.

'Hey, gorgeous,' I say.

She bends down and kisses me on the cheek, something I'll never take for granted.

'Somebody's in a happy mood today,' she says.

'Happy to see you,' I say. 'Nervous about your driver's test?'

'Maybe a little. Just can't wait until it's over.'

She sits down beside me. *This is my day,* I think. *This is where I want to be and this is where I am. Sarah on one side, Sam on the other.*

I go to class as I've done all the other days. I sit with Sam at lunch. We don't talk about the fire. We must be the only two in the whole school not talking about it. The same story, over and over. I never hear my name spoken once. As I expected, Mark isn't in school. A rumor spreads that he and several of the others will be suspended for the theory the paper has spouted. I don't know if it's true or not. I don't know if I care.

By the time Sarah and I enter the kitchen for eighth-period home ec, my certainty that I'm safe has taken a firm hold. Such a strong certainty that I'm confident I must be wrong, that something has been overlooked. The doubt has been creeping up throughout the day but I've been quick to push it back down.

We make tapioca pudding. An easy day. In the middle of class, the kitchen door opens. It's the hall monitor. I look at him and I know immediately what it means. The harbinger of bad news. The messenger of death. He walks straight up to me and hands me a slip of paper.

'Mr Harris wants to see you,' he says.

'Now?'

He nods.

I look at Sarah and shrug. I don't want her to see my fear. I smile at her and walk to the door. Before I leave I turn around and look at her again. She's bent over the table mixing our ingredients, wearing the same green apron that I tied on her my first day, the day we made pancakes and ate them off the same plate. Her hair is in a ponytail and loose strands dangle in front of her face. She tucks them behind her ear and as she does she sees me standing in the doorway watching her. I keep staring, trying to remember every minute detail of this moment, the way she grips the wooden spoon in her hand, the ivory look to her skin with the light coming in the windows behind her, the tenderness in her eyes. Her shirt has a loose button at the collar. I wonder if she knows about it. Then the hall monitor says something behind me. I wave at Sarah, shut the door, and walk down the hall. I take my time, trying to convince myself that it's just a formality, some document we forgot to sign, some question about transcripts. But I know it's not just a formality.

Mr Harris sits at his desk when I enter the office. He is

smiling in a way that terrifies me, the same prideful smile that he had on the day he pulled Mark from class to do the interview.

'Sit down,' he says. I sit. 'So, is it true?' he asks. He glances at his computer screen, then he looks back at me.

'Is what true?'

On his desk there is an envelope with my name handwritten in black ink. He sees me looking at it.

'Oh yes, this was faxed to you about half an hour ago.'

He picks the envelope up and tosses it to me. I catch it.

'What is it?' I ask.

'No idea. My secretary sealed it in the envelope as soon as it arrived.'

Several things happen at once. I open the envelope and remove its contents. Two sheets of paper. The top is a cover page with my name on it and 'CONFIDENTIAL' written in large black letters. I shuffle it behind the second sheet. A single sentence written in capitals. No name. Just four black words on a white canvas.

'So, Mr Smith, is it true? Did you run into that burning house to save Sarah Hart and those dogs?' Mr Harris asks. Blood rushes to my face. I look up. He turns his computer monitor towards me so that I can read the screen. It's the blog affiliated with the *Paradise Gazette*. I don't need to look at the name of the author to know who has written it. The title is more than enough.

THE JAMES HOUSE FIRE:
THE UNTOLD STORY

My breath catches in my throat. My heart races. The world stops, or at least it seems to. I feel dead inside. I look back down at the sheet of paper I'm holding. White paper, smooth in my fingertips. It reads:

ARE YOU NUMBER 4?

Both sheets fall from my hands, drift away, and float to the floor, where they lie motionless. *I don't understand,* I think. *How can this be?*

'So is it?' Mr Harris asks.

My mouth drops open. Mr Harris is smiling, proud, happy. But it's not him that I see. It's what's behind him, seen through the windows of his office. A blur of red coming around the corner, moving faster than what is normal, than what is safe. The squeal of tires as it zips into the lot. The pickup truck throwing gravel as it makes a second turn. Henri leaning over the wheel like some crazed maniac. He hits the brakes so forcefully that his whole body jerks and the truck comes screeching to a stop.

I close my eyes.

I place my head in my hands.

Through the window I hear the truck door open. I hear it close.

Henri will be in this office within the minute.

28

'Are you okay, Mr Smith?' the Principal asks. I look up at him. He attempts his best look of concern, a look that lasts only a second before the toothy grin returns to his face.

'No, Mr Harris,' I say. 'I'm not okay.'

I pick the sheet up off the floor. I read it again. Where did it come from? Are they merely screwing with us now? There is no phone number or address, no name. Nothing but four words and a question mark. I look up and out the window. Henri's truck is parked, fumes rising from the exhaust. In and out as quickly as he can. I look back at the computer screen. The article was posted at 11:59 a.m., almost two hours ago. I'm amazed it took Henri this long to arrive. A sense of vertigo seeps in. I feel myself sway.

'Do you need the nurse?' Mr Harris asks.

The nurse, I think. *No, I don't need the nurse.* The nurse's station is the room beside the home economics kitchen. *What I need, Mr Harris, is to go back there, fifteen minutes ago, before the hall monitor arrived.* Sarah must have the pudding on the stove by now. I wonder if it's boiling yet. Is she looking towards the door, waiting for me to return?

The faint echo of the school doors slamming shut reaches the principal's office. Fifteen seconds until Henri is here. Then to his truck. Then home. Then where? To Maine? Missouri? Canada? A different school, a new beginning, another new name.

I haven't slept in almost thirty hours and only now do I

feel the exhaustion. But then something else enters with it, and in that split second between instinct and action, the reality that I'm going away forever without the chance to say good-bye is suddenly too much to bear. My eyes narrow, my face twists in agony, and – without thinking, without truly knowing what it is that I'm doing – I lunge over Mr Harris's desk and crash through the plate-glass window, which shatters into a million little pieces behind me. A scream of shock follows.

My feet land in the outside grass. I turn right and run across the schoolyard, the classrooms passing in a blur to my right, across the lot and into the woods that lie beyond the baseball field. There are cuts on my forehead and left elbow from the glass. My lungs are burning. The hell with the pain. I keep going, the sheet of paper still in my right hand. I shove it into my pocket. Why would the Mogadorians send a fax? Wouldn't they just show up? That is their main advantage, to arrive unexpectedly, without warning. The benefit of surprise.

I take a hard left in the middle of the woods, weaving in and out of the forest's density until it ends and a field begins. Cows chewing cud watch with blank eyes as I streak past. I beat Henri to the house. Bernie Kosar is nowhere to be seen. I burst through the door and stop dead in my tracks. My breath catches in my throat. At the kitchen table, in front of Henri's open laptop, sits a person I immediately think is one of them. They've beaten me here, have worked it out so that I am alone, without Henri. The person turns around and I clench my hands into fists and am ready to fight.

But it's Mark James.

'What are you doing here?' I ask.

'I'm trying to figure out what's going on,' he says, a look of fright evident in his eyes. 'Who the hell *are* you?'

'What are you talking about?'

'Look,' he says, pointing to the computer screen.

I walk to him, but I don't look at the screen, my eyes instead focusing on the white sheet of paper sitting beside the computer. It's an exact replica of the sheet in my pocket except for the paper that it's printed on, which is thicker than the fax. And then I notice something else. At the bottom of Henri's, in very small handwriting, is a phone number. Surely they can't expect us to call? 'Yes, it's me, Number Four. I am here waiting for you. We've been running for ten years, but please, come kill us now; we won't put up a fight.' It makes no sense at all.

'Is this yours?' I ask.

'No,' he says. 'But it was delivered by UPS at the same time that I got here. Your dad read it as I showed him the video, and then he sprinted out of the house.'

'What video?' I ask.

'Watch,' he says.

I look at the computer and see that he's pulled up YouTube. He presses the play button. It's a grainy video, of poor quality as though it has been shot on somebody's cell phone. I recognize his house immediately, the front of which is in flames. The camera is shaky, but through it can be heard the dogs bark and the filtered gasps throughout the crowd. Then the person begins walking away from the crowd, to the side of the house, and eventually to the back. The camera zooms in to the rear window where the bark is coming from. The bark stops and I close my eyes because I know what is coming. About twenty seconds pass, and in the moment that I fly through the window with Sarah in one arm and the dogs in the other, Mark hits the pause button on the video. The camera is zoomed in, and our faces are unmistakable.

'Who are you?' Mark asks.

I ignore his question, instead ask one of my own: 'Who took this?'

'I have no idea,' he answers.

The gravel pops beneath the truck tires in the front of the house as Henri pulls in. I stand straight and my first instinct is to run, get out of the house and get back to the school, where I know Sarah will be staying late to develop photos – until her driver's test at four thirty. Her face is just as obvious as mine is in that video, which puts her in as much danger as me. But something keeps me from fleeing, and I instead move around to the other side of the table and wait. The truck door slams shut. Henri walks into the house five seconds later, Bernie Kosar dashing in ahead of him.

'You lied to me,' he says in the doorway, his face set hard, the muscles in his jaw flexed.

'I lie to everybody,' I say. 'I learned that from you.'

'We don't lie to each other!' he screams.

Our eyes stay locked.

'What's going on?' Mark asks.

'I'm not leaving without finding Sarah,' I say. 'She's in danger, Henri!'

He shakes his head at me. 'Now isn't the time for sentimentality, John. Do you not see this?' he says, and walks across the room and lifts the sheet of paper and begins waving it at me. 'Where the hell do you think this came from?'

'What in the hell is going on?' Mark nearly bellows.

I ignore the sheet and Mark, and keep my eyes on Henri's. 'Yes, I've seen it, and that's why I need to get back to the school. They'll see her and go after her.'

Henri starts towards me. After his second step I lift my hand and stop him where he stands, ten or so feet away. He tries to keep walking but I hold him in place.

'We need to get out of here, John,' he says, a hurt, almost pleading tone in his voice.

While holding him at a distance, I begin walking backwards towards my bedroom. He stops trying to walk. He says nothing, standing there watching me with pain in his eyes, a look that makes me feel worse than I've ever felt before. I have to look away. When I get to my doorway our eyes meet again. His shoulders are slumped, arms at his sides as though he doesn't know what to do with himself. He just stares at me, looking as though he may cry.

'I'm sorry,' I say, giving myself enough of a head start to get away, and turn and sprint across my bedroom, grab from my drawer a knife I used to scale fish when we still lived in Florida, and jump out the window and race into the woods. Bernie Kosar's bark follows, nothing else. I run for a mile and stop in the big clearing where Sarah and I made snow angels. Our clearing, she had called it. The clearing in which we would have our summer picnics. A pain in my chest at the thought that I won't be here for summer, a pain so great that I bend over and grit my teeth. If only I could call her and warn her to get out of the school. My phone, along with everything else I took to school, is in my locker. I'll get her out of harm's way and then I'll get back to Henri and we'll leave.

I turn and run towards school, run as hard as my lungs will permit me. I reach the school just as the buses have begun pulling out of the lot. I watch them from the border of the woods. At the front of the school Hobbs is standing outside the front window measuring a large sheet of plywood to cover the window I broke. I slow my breathing, try my best to clear my mind. I watch the cars trickle out until there are only a few left. Hobbs covers the hole, disappears into the school. I wonder if he has been warned about me, if he has been instructed to call the police if he sees me. I look at my watch. Though it is only 3:30, the darkness seems to have come on faster than normal, a darkness steeped in density, a darkness that is heavy, consuming. The lights in the lot have come on, but even they seem dulled and stunted.

I leave the woods and walk across the baseball field and into the lot. Ten or so cars stand alone. The door to the school is already locked. I grab hold of it and close my eyes and focus and the lock clicks. I walk inside, and I don't see anyone. Only half of the hallway lights are on. The air is still and quiet. Somewhere I hear the floor polisher running. I turn into the lobby and the door to the photography darkroom comes into view. Sarah. She was going to develop some pictures today before her test. I pass by my locker and open it. My phone isn't there; the locker is completely empty. Somebody, hopefully Henri, has it. By the time I reach the darkroom I haven't seen a single person. Where are the athletes, the members of the band, the teachers who often stay late to grade papers or do whatever it is they do? A bad feeling creeps into my bones, and I'm terrified that something awful has already happened to Sarah. I press my ear against the darkroom door to listen, but hear nothing aside from the drone of the floor polisher coming from far down the hallway. I take a deep breath and try the door. It's locked.

I press my ear to it again and gently knock. There's no answer, but I hear a slight rustling on the other side. I take a deep breath, tense myself to what I might find inside, and unlock the door.

The room is pitch-black. I turn on my lights and sweep my hands one way, then the other. I see nothing and think the room is empty, but in the corner, I see a very slight movement. I crouch down to look, and beneath the counter, trying to remain unseen, is Sarah. I dim my lights so that she can see it's me. From the shadows, she looks up and smiles, and breathes a sigh of relief.

'They're here, aren't they?'

'If they aren't yet, they will be soon.'

I help her up from off the floor and she wraps her arms around me and squeezes me so tightly that I don't think she intends to ever let go.

'I came in here right after eighth period, and as soon as school ended, all these weird noises started coming from the halls. And it got really dark, so I locked myself in here and stayed beneath the counter, too scared to move. I just knew something was wrong, especially after I heard about you jumping through the window and you weren't answering your phone.'

'That was smart, but now we have to get out of here, and fast.'

We leave the room, holding hands. The hallway lights flicker off, the whole school is engulfed in darkness, even though dusk is still an hour or so away. After about ten seconds, they come back on.

'What's happening?' Sarah whispers.

'I don't know.'

We move down the hallway as quietly as we can, and any

noise we do make seems deadened, muffled. The quickest way out is the back door that opens onto the teachers' lot, and as we head that way, the sound of the floor polisher grows. I assume that we'll run into Hobbs. I assume he knows that I'm the one who broke the window. Will he fend me off with a broomstick and call the police? I guess at this point it doesn't matter.

When we reach the back hallway the lights turn off again. We stop and wait for them to come back on, but they don't. The floor polisher continues, a steady hum. I can't see it, but it is only twenty or so feet away in the impenetrable darkness. I find it odd that the machine keeps running, that Hobbs keeps polishing in the dark. I turn on my lights, and Sarah lets go of my hand and stands behind me with her hands on my hips. I find the plug in the wall first, then the cord, then the machine itself. It stands in one place, bumping against the wall, unmanned, running itself. Panic sweeps through me, with fear close behind. Sarah and I have to get out of the school.

I rip the cord from the outlet and the polisher stops, replaced by the soft hum of silence. I turn my lights off. Somewhere far down the hall a door slowly creaks open. I crouch down, my back against the wall, Sarah holding tightly to my arm. Both of us are too scared to say a word. Instinct caused me to pull the cord to stop the polisher, and I have the urge to plug it back in, but I know it'll give us away if they're here. I close my eyes and strain to listen. The creaking door stops. A soft wind seems to materialize from nowhere. Surely there isn't a window open. I think that maybe the wind is entering from the window I broke. Then the door slams shut and glass breaks and shatters on the floor.

Sarah screams. Something sweeps by us but I don't see what it is and I don't care to find out. I pull Sarah by the hand and sprint down the hall. I shoulder the door and rush out into the parking lot. Sarah gasps and both of us stop dead in our tracks. My breath catches in my throat and chills shoot up my spine. The lights are still on but dimmed and looking ghastly in the heavy dark. Beneath the nearest light we both see it, trench coat swaying in the breeze, hat pulled low so that I can't see its eyes. It lifts its head and grins at me.

Sarah's grip tightens on my hand. We both take one step backwards and trip in our rush to get away. We move the rest of the way back in a crab walk until we hit the door.

'Come on,' I yell as I rush to my feet. Sarah stands. I try the latch but the door automatically locked behind us.

'Shit!' I yell.

I see another in the corner of my eye, standing still at first. I watch as it takes its first step towards me. There is another one behind it. The Mogadorians. All these years and they are finally here. I try to focus but my hands are shaking too badly to open the door. I feel them bearing down, closing in. Sarah presses close to me and I can feel her trembling.

I can't focus to get the door unlocked. What happened to grace under pressure, to all those days of training in the backyard? *I don't want to die,* I think. *I don't want to die.*

'John,' Sarah says, and in her voice there is such fear that it causes my eyes to open wide, and twist in determination.

The lock clicks. The door opens. Sarah and I push through and I slam it shut. There is a thud on the other side as though one of them has kicked it. We run down the hall. Noises follow. I don't know if any of the Mogadorians are in the school. Another window breaks off to the side and Sarah screams in surprise.

'We have to be quiet,' I say.

We try opening classroom doors but all of them are locked. I don't think there is enough time for me to open one of them. Somewhere a door is slammed shut and I can't tell if it was ahead of us or behind us. Noises follow close behind, closing in, filling our ears. Sarah takes my hand and we run faster, my mind rushing ahead to remember the layout of the building so I can keep my lights off, keep from being seen. Finally a door opens and we fall headlong into it. It's the history classroom, at the left of the school overlooking a slight hill, and because of the twenty-foot drop, there are bars over the windows. Darkness is pressing firmly against the glass and no light enters. I silently shut the door and hope they didn't see us. I sweep my lights across the room and quickly turn them off. We're alone and we hide beneath the teacher's desk. I try to catch my breath. Sweat runs down the sides of my face and stings my eyes. How many of them are here? I saw at least three. Surely those aren't the only ones out there. Did they bring the beasts with them, the small weasels that the writers in Athens were so scared of? I wish that Henri were here, or even Bernie Kosar.

The door slowly opens. I hold my breath, listening. Sarah leans into me and we put our arms around each other. The door closes very quietly and clicks into place. No footsteps follow. Did they merely open the door and stick their heads in to see if we were inside? Did they move on without entering? They found me after all this time; surely they aren't that lazy.

'What are we going to do?' Sarah whispers after thirty seconds.

'I don't know,' I whisper back.

The room is wrapped in silence. Whatever opened the door must have left, or is out in the hall waiting. I know, though, the longer we sit, the more of them will arrive. We need to get out of here. We'll have to risk it. I take a deep breath.

'We have to leave,' I whisper. 'We're not safe here.'

'But they're out there.'

'I know, and they aren't going to leave. Henri is at home, and is in just as much danger as we are.'

'But how are we going to get out?'

I have no idea, don't know what to say. Only one way out and that's the way we came in. Sarah's arms stay around me.

'We're sitting ducks, Sarah. They'll find us, and when they do, it will be with all of them. At least we'll have the element of surprise this way. If we can get out of the school, I think I can start a car. If I can't, we'll have to fight our way back.'

She nods in agreement.

I take a deep breath and move out from underneath the desk. I reach for Sarah's hand and she stands with me. Together we take one step, quietly as possible. Then another. It takes a full minute to cross the room and nothing meets us in the darkness. A very slight glow comes from my hands, emitting almost no light, only enough to keep from running into a desk. I stare at the door. I'll open it and have Sarah jump on my back and I'll run as hard and as fast as I can, lights on, down the hall, out of the school and into the lot or, failing that, into the woods. I know the woods and the way home. There are more of them, but Sarah and I will have the home-field advantage.

As we near the door, I can feel my heart pounding so hard that I fear the Mogadorians can hear it. I close my eyes and slowly reach for the knob. Sarah tenses, gripping my hand as tightly as she can. When my hand is an inch away, so close to the knob that I can feel the cold coming off of it, we are both grabbed from behind and pulled to the ground.

I try to scream but a hand covers my mouth. Fear rushes through me. I can feel Sarah struggling beneath the grip and I do the same thing but the grip is too strong. I never anticipated this, the Mogadorians being stronger than I am. I've greatly underestimated them. There is no hope now. I've failed. I have failed Sarah and Henri and I'm sorry. *Henri, I hope you put up a better fight than I did.*

Sarah is breathing heavily and with all my might I try to free myself but I can't.

'Shhh, stop struggling,' the voice whispers in my ear. A girl's voice. 'They're out there waiting. Both of you have to be quiet.'

It's a girl, every bit as strong as I am, maybe even stronger. I don't understand. Her grip loosens and I turn and face her. We take each other in. Above the glow of my hands I see a face slightly older than mine. Hazel eyes, high cheekbones, long dark hair pulled into a ponytail, a wide mouth and strong nose, olive-toned skin.

'Who are you?' I ask.

She looks to the door, still silent. *An ally,* I think. Somebody besides the Mogadorians knows we exist. Somebody is here, to help.

'I am Number Six,' she says. 'I tried to get here before they did.'

29

'How did you know it was me?' I ask.

She looks to the door. 'I've been trying to find you ever since Three was killed. But I'll explain it all later. First, we have to get out of here.'

'How did you get in without them seeing you?'

'I can make myself invisible.'

I smile. The same Legacy my grandfather had. Invisibility. The ability to make those things he touches invisible as well, like the house on Henri's second day of work.

'How far do you live from here?' she asks.

'Three miles.'

I feel her nod through the darkness.

'Do you have a Cêpan?' she asks.

'Yes, of course. Don't you?'

Her weight shifts and she pauses before speaking, as though drawing strength from some unseen entity. 'I did,' she says. 'She died three years ago. I've been on my own since then.'

'I'm sorry,' I say.

'It's a war, people are going to die. Right now we have to get out of here or we'll die as well. If they're in the area, then they already know where you live, which means they're already there, so it's pointless to try to be secretive once we're out of here. These are only scouts. The soldiers are on the way. They have the swords. The beasts won't be far behind. Time is short. At best we have a day. At worst they're already here.'

My first thought: *They already know where I live.* I panic. Henri is at home, with Bernie Kosar, and the soldiers and beasts may already be there. My second thought: her Cêpan, dead three years now. Six has been alone that long, alone on a foreign planet since what, the age of thirteen? Fourteen?

'He's at home,' I say.

'Who?'

'Henri, my Cêpan.'

'I'm sure he's fine. They won't touch him as long as you're free. It's you they want, and they'll use him to try to lure you,' Six says, then lifts her head towards the barred window. We turn and look with her. Speeding around the bend coming towards the school, very faintly so that nothing else can be seen, is a pair of headlights that slow, pass the exit, then turn into the entrance and quickly disappear. Six turns back to us. 'All the doors are blocked. How else can we get out?'

I think about it, figuring that one of the unbarred windows in a different classroom is our best bet.

'We can get out through the gymnasium,' Sarah says. 'There's a passageway beneath the stage that opens like a cellar door in the back of the school.'

'Really?' I ask.

She nods, and I feel a sense of pride.

'Each of you take a hand,' Six says. I take her right, Sarah her left. 'Be as quiet as possible. As long as you hold my hands, you'll both be invisible. They won't be able to see us, but they'll hear us. Once we're outside we'll run like hell. We'll never be able to escape them, not since they've found us. The only way to escape is to kill them, every last one of them, before the others arrive.'

'Okay,' I say.

'Do you know what that means?' Six says.

I shake my head. I'm not sure what she is asking me.

'There's no escaping them now,' she says. 'It means you're going to have to fight.'

I mean to respond, but the shuffling I had heard earlier stops outside the door. Silence. Then the doorknob is jiggled. Number Six takes a deep breath and lets go of my hand.

'Never mind sneaking out,' she says. 'The war starts now.'

She rushes up and thrusts her hands forward and the door breaks away from the jamb and crashes across the hallway. Splintered wood. Shattered glass.

'Turn your lights on!' she yells.

I snap them on. A Mogadorian stands amid the rubble of the broken door. It smiles, blood seeping from the corner of its mouth, where the door has hit it. Black eyes, pale skin as though the sun has never touched it. A cave-dwelling creature risen from the dead. It throws something that I don't see and I hear Six grunt beside me. I look into its eyes and a pain tears through me so that I'm stuck where I am, unable to move. Darkness falls. Sadness. My body stiffens. A haze of pictures of the day of the invasion flicker through my mind: the death of women and children, my grandparents; tears, screams, blood, heaps of burning bodies. Six breaks the spell by lifting the Mogadorian in the air and hurling it against the wall. It tries standing and Six lifts it again, this time throwing it as hard as she can against one wall and then the other. The scout falls to the ground twisted and broken, its chest rising once and then becoming still. One or two seconds pass. Its entire body collapses into a pile of ash, accompanied by a sound similar to a bag of sand being dropped to the ground.

'What the hell?' I ask, wondering how it's possible for the body to completely disintegrate like it just did.

'Don't look into their eyes!' she yells, ignoring my confusion.

I think of the writer of *They Walk Among Us*. I now understand what he went through when looking into their eyes. I wonder if he welcomed death when the time finally came, welcomed it just to be rid of the images that perpetually played in his mind. I can only imagine how intense they would have become had Six not broken the spell.

Two other scouts sweep towards us from the end of the hall. A shroud of darkness surrounds them, as though they consume everything around them and turn it into black. Six stands tall in front of me, firm, chin held high. She is two inches shorter than I am, but her presence makes her seem two inches taller. Sarah stands behind me. Both Mogadorians stop where the hallway intersects with another, their teeth bared in a sneer. My body is tense, muscles burning with exhaustion. They take deep, rasping breaths, which is what we heard outside the door, their breathing, not their walking. Watching us. And then a different noise fills the hallway, and the Mogadorians both turn their attention to it. A door being shaken as though somebody is trying to force it open. From out of nowhere there comes the sound of a gun blast, followed by the school door being kicked open. They both look surprised, and as they turn to flee, two more blasts boom through the hallway and both scouts are blown backwards. We hear the approaching sound of two sets of shoes and the click of a dog's toenails. Six tenses beside me, ready for whatever is coming our way. Henri! It was his truck's lights we saw enter the school grounds. He has a double-barreled shotgun I have never seen before. Bernie Kosar is at his side, and he comes sprinting towards me. I crouch down and lift him off the floor. He licks wildly at my face, and I'm so excited to see him that I almost forget to tell Six who the man with the shotgun is.

'It's Henri,' I say. 'My Cêpan.'

Henri comes walking down, vigilant, looking at the classroom doors as he passes them, and behind him, carrying the Loric Chest in his arms, is Mark. I have no idea why Henri has brought him along. There is a crazed look in Henri's eyes, one of exhaustion, full of fear and worry. I expect the worst after the way I left the house, some sort of scolding, perhaps a slap across the face, but he instead switches the shotgun to his left hand and hugs me as tightly as he can. I hug him back.

'I'm sorry, Henri. I didn't know this would happen.'

'I know you didn't. I'm just happy you're okay.' He says, 'Come on, we have to get out of here. The whole damn school is surrounded.'

Sarah leads us to the safest room she can think of, which is the home economics kitchen down the hall. We lock the door behind us. Six moves three refrigerators in front of it to keep anything from entering while Henri rushes to the windows and pulls the blinds down. Sarah walks straight into the kitchen we normally use, opens the drawer, and removes the biggest butcher's knife she can find. Mark watches her, and when he sees what she has done, he drops the Chest to the floor and grabs a knife of his own. He rifles through other drawers and removes a meat-tenderizer hammer and tucks it into the waistband of his pants.

'You guys okay?' Henri asks.

'Yes,' I say.

'Aside from the dagger in my arm, yes, I'm fine,' Six says.

I turn my lights on dimly and look at her arm. She wasn't kidding. Where the biceps meets the shoulder a small dagger is sticking out. That was why I heard her gasp before she killed the scout. It had thrown a knife at her. Henri reaches up and pulls it free. She grunts.

'Thankfully it's just a dagger,' she says, looking at me. 'The soldiers will have swords that glow with different sorts of powers.'

I mean to ask what kind of powers, but Henri interrupts.

'Take this,' he says, and holds the shotgun out for Mark to take. He accepts it in his free hand without protest, staring in awe at everything he is witnessing around him. I wonder how much Henri has told him. I wonder why Henri brought him along in the first place. I look back at Six. Henri presses a rag to her arm and she holds it in place. He steps over and lifts the Chest and sets it on the nearest table.

'Here, John,' he says.

Without explanation I help him unlock it. He throws the top open, reaches in, removes a flat rock every bit as dark as the aura surrounding the Mogadorians. Six seems to know what the rock is for. She takes her shirt off. Beneath it she is wearing a black and gray rubber suit very similar to the silver and blue suit I saw my father wear in my flashbacks. She takes a deep breath, offers Henri her arm. Henri thrusts the rock against the gash, and Six, with her teeth clenched tightly, grunts and writhes in pain. Sweat beads across her forehead, her face bright red under the strain, tendons standing out on her neck. Henri holds it there for nearly a full minute. He pulls the stone away and Six bends over at the waist, taking deep breaths to compose herself. I look at her arm. Aside from a bit of blood still glistening, the cut is completely healed, no scars, nothing aside from the small tear in the suit.

'What is that?' I ask, nodding to the rock.

'It's a healing stone,' says Henri.

'Stuff like that really exists?'

'On Lorien it does, but the pain of healing is double that of the original pain caused by whatever has happened, and the stone only works when the injury was done with the intent to harm or kill. And the healing stone has to be used right away.'

'Intent?' I ask. 'So, the stone wouldn't work if I tripped and cut my head by accident?'

'No,' Henri says. 'That's the whole point of Legacies. Defense and purity.'

'Would it work on Mark or Sarah?'

'I have no idea,' Henri says. 'And I hope we don't have to find out.'

Six catches her breath. She stands straight, feeling her arm. The red in her face begins to fade. Behind her, Bernie Kosar is running back and forth from the blocked door to the windows, which are placed too high off the ground for him to see out of, but he stands on his hind legs and tries anyway, growling at what he feels is out there. *Maybe nothing,* I think. Occasionally he bites at the air.

'Did you get my phone today when you were at the school?' I ask Henri.

'No,' he says. 'I didn't grab anything.'

'It wasn't there when I went back.'

'Well, it wouldn't work here anyway. They've done something to our house and the school. The power is off, and no signals penetrate whatever sort of shield they've set up. All the clocks have stopped. Even the air seems dead.'

'We don't have much time,' Six interrupts.

Henri nods. A slight grin appears while he looks at her, a look of pride, maybe even relief.

'I remember you,' he says.

'I remember you, too.'

Henri reaches out his hand and Six shakes it. 'It's shit good to see you again.'

'*Damn* good,' I correct him, but he ignores me.

'I've been looking for you guys for a while,' Six says.

'Where is Katarina?' Henri asks.

Six shakes her head. A mournful look crosses her face. 'She didn't make it. She died three years ago. I've been looking for the others since, you guys included.'

'I'm sorry,' Henri says.

Six nods. She looks across the room at Bernie Kosar, who has just begun to growl ferociously. He seems to have grown tall enough so that his head is able to peek out the bottom of the window. Henri picks the shotgun up off the floor and walks to within five feet of the window.

'John, turn your lights off,' he says. I comply. 'Now, on my word, pull the blinds.'

I walk to the side of the window and wrap the cord twice around my hand. I nod to Henri, and over his shoulder I see that Sarah has placed her palms against her ears in anticipation of the blast. He cocks the shotgun and aims it.

'It's payback time,' he says, then, 'Now!'

I pull the cord and the blind flies up. Henri fires the shotgun. The sound is deafening, echoing in my ears for seconds after. He cocks the gun again, keeps it aimed. I twist my body to look out. Two fallen scouts are lying in the grass, unmoving. One of them is reduced to ash with the same hollow thud as the one in the hallway. Henri shoots the other a second time and it does the same. Shadows seem to swarm around them.

'Six, bring a fridge over,' Henri says to her.

Mark and Sarah watch with amazement as the fridge floats in the air towards us and is positioned in front of the window to block the Mogadorians from entering or seeing into the room.

'Better than nothing,' Henri says. He turns to Six. 'How much time do we have?'

'Time is short,' she says. 'They have an outpost three hours from here, in a hollowed-out mountain in West Virginia.'

Henri snaps the gun open, slides in two new cartridges, snaps it shut.

'How many bullets does that hold?' I ask.

'Ten,' he says.

Sarah and Mark whisper to each other. I walk over to them.

'You guys okay?' I ask.

Sarah nods, Mark shrugs, neither really knowing quite what to say in the terror of the situation. I kiss Sarah on the cheek and take hold of her hand.

'Don't worry,' I say. 'We'll get out of this.'

I turn to Six and Henri. 'Why are they just out there waiting?' I ask. 'Why don't they break a window and rush in? They know they have us outnumbered.'

'They only want to keep us here, inside,' Six says. 'They have us exactly where they want us, all together, confined to one place. Now they're waiting for the others to arrive, the soldiers with the weapons, the ones who are skilled at killing. They're desperate now because they know we're developing our Legacies. They can't afford to screw it up and risk us getting stronger. They know that some of us can now fight back.'

'We have to get out of here then,' Sarah pleads, her voice soft and shaky.

Six nods reassuringly to her. And then I remember something I had forgotten in all the excitement.

'Wait, your being here, us being together, that breaks the charm. All the others are fair game now,' I say. 'They can kill us at will.'

I can see by the look of horror on Henri's face that it had slipped his mind as well.

Six nods. 'I had to risk it,' she says. 'We can't keep running, and I'm sick of waiting. We're all developing, all of us are ready to hit back. Let's not forget what they did to us that day, and I'm not going to forget what they did to Katarina. Everybody we know is dead, our families, our friends. I think they're planning to do the same thing to Earth as they did to Lorien, and they are almost ready. To sit back and do nothing is to allow that same destruction, that same death and annihilation. Why stand back and let it happen? If this planet dies, we die with it.'

Bernie Kosar is still barking at the window. I almost want to let him outside, see what he can do. His mouth is frothing with his teeth bared, hair standing tall down the center of his back. *The dog is ready,* I think. *The question is, are the rest of us?*

'Well, you're here now,' Henri says. 'Let's hope the others are safe; let's hope they can fend for themselves. Both of you will know immediately if they can't. As for us, war has come to our doorstep. We didn't ask for it, but now that it's here we have no choice but to meet it, head on, with full force,' he says. He lifts his head and looks at us, the whites of his eyes glistening through the dark of the room.

'I agree with you, Six,' he says. 'The time has come.'

30

Wind from the open window rushes into the home economics room, the refrigerator in front of it doing little to prevent the cold air. The school is already chilly from the electricity being off. Six is now wearing only the rubber suit, which is entirely black aside from a gray band slicing diagonally down the front of it. She is standing in the middle of our group with such poise and confidence that I wish I had a Loric suit of my own. She opens her mouth to speak but is interrupted by a loud boom from outside. All of us rush to the windows but can see nothing of what is happening. The crash is followed by several loud bangs, and the sounds of tearing, gnashing, something being destroyed.

'What's happening?' I ask.

'Your lights,' Henri says over the sounds of destruction.

I turn them on and sweep them across the yard outside. They reach but ten feet before being swallowed by the darkness. Henri steps back and tilts his head, listening to the sounds in extreme concentration, and then he nods in resigned acceptance.

'They are destroying all the cars out there, my truck included,' he says. 'If we survive this and escape this school, it'll have to be on foot.'

Terror sweeps across both Mark's and Sarah's faces.

'We can't waste any more time,' Six says. 'Strategy or no strategy, we have to go before the beasts and soldiers arrive.

She said we can get out through the gymnasium,' Six says, and nods at Sarah. 'It's our only hope.'

'Her name is Sarah,' I say.

I sit in a nearby chair, unnerved by the urgency in Six's voice. She seems to be the steady one, the one who has remained calm under the weight of the terrors we have seen thus far. Bernie Kosar is back at the door, scratching at the fridges that are blocking it, growling and whining in impatience. Since my lights are on, Six has a good look at him for the first time. She stares at Bernie Kosar, then squints her eyes and inches her face forward. She walks over and bends down to pet him. I turn and look at her. I find it odd that she is grinning.

'What?' I ask.

She looks up at me. 'You don't know?'

'Know what?'

Her grin widens. She looks back at Bernie Kosar, who races away from her and charges back to the window, scratching at it, growling, the occasional bark in frustration. The school is surrounded, death imminent, almost certain, and Six is grinning. It irritates me.

'Your dog,' she says. 'You really don't know?'

'No,' says Henri. I look at him. He shakes his head at Six.

'What the hell?' I ask. 'What?'

Six looks at me, then at Henri. She emits a half laugh and opens her mouth to speak. But just before any words escape something catches her eye and she rushes back to the window. We follow and, as before, the very subtle glow of a set of headlights sweeps around the bend in the road and into the lot of the school. Another car, maybe a coach or teacher. I close my eyes and take a deep breath.

'It could mean nothing,' I say.

'Turn your lights off,' Henri says to me.

I turn them off, clench my hands into fists. Something about the car outside causes anger within me. The hell with the exhaustion, with the shakes that have been present ever since I jumped through the principal's window. I can't take being confined in this room any longer, knowing that the Mogadorians are out there, waiting, and plotting our doom. That car outside may be the first of the soldiers arriving on the scene. But just when that thought pops into my mind, we see the lights quickly retreat from the lot, and speed away in a hurry, down the same road they came.

'We have to get out of this damn school,' Henri says.

Henri sits in a chair ten feet away from the door with the shotgun aimed right at it. He is breathing slowly though he is tense and I can see the muscles flexed in his jaw. None of us say a word. Six made herself invisible and slipped out to do some exploring. We're just waiting, and finally it comes. Three slight taps on the door, Six's knock so that we know it's her and not a scout trying to enter. Henri lowers the gun and she walks in and I return one of the fridges to block the door behind her. She was gone for a full ten minutes.

'You were right,' she says to Henri. 'They've destroyed every car in the lot, and have somehow moved the wreckage to block every door from being opened. And Sarah is right; they've overlooked the stage hatch. I counted seven scouts outside and five inside walking the halls. There was one outside this door but it's been disposed of. They seem to be getting antsy. I think that means the others should have been here already, which means they can't be far.'

Henri stands and grabs the Chest and nods at me. I help him open it. He reaches in and pulls out a few small round pebbles that he sticks in his pocket. I have no idea what they are. Then he closes and locks the Chest and slides it into one of the ovens and closes the door. I move a refrigerator up against the oven to keep it from being opened. There really is no other choice. The Chest is heavy, it would be impossible to fight while carrying it, and we need every available hand to get out of this mess.

'I hate to leave it behind,' Henri says, shaking his head. Six nods uneasily. Something in the thought of the Mogadorians getting ahold of the Chest terrifies them both.

'It'll be fine here,' I say.

Henri lifts the shotgun and pumps it once, looks at Sarah and Mark.

'This isn't your fight,' he tells them. 'I don't know what to expect out there, but if this thing goes badly you guys get back in this school and stay hidden. They aren't after you, and I don't think they'll care to come looking if they already have us.'

Sarah and Mark both look stricken with fear, both holding their respective knives with white-knuckled grips in their right hands. Mark has lined his belt with everything from the kitchen drawers that might be of use – more knives, the meat tenderizer, cheese grater, a pair of scissors.

'We go left out of this room, and when we reach the end of the hall, the gymnasium is past double doors twenty or so feet to the right,' I say to Henri.

'The hatch is in the very middle of the stage,' Six says. 'It's covered with a blue mat. There were no scouts in the gym, but that doesn't mean they won't be there this time around.'

'So we're just going to go outside and try to outrun them?' Sarah asks. Her voice is full of panic. She's breathing heavily.

'It's our only choice,' says Henri.

I grab her hand. She is shaking badly.

'It'll be okay,' I say.

'How do you know that?' she says in a more demanding tone than a questioning one.

'I don't,' I say.

Six moves the fridge from the door. Bernie Kosar immediately starts scratching at the door, trying to get out, growling.

'I can't make you all invisible,' Six says. 'If I disappear, I'll still be nearby.'

Six grabs hold of the doorknob and Sarah takes a deep, shaky breath beside me, squeezing my hand as tightly as she can. I can see the knife quivering in her right hand.

'Stay close to me,' I say.

'I'm not leaving your side.'

The door swings open and Six jumps out into the hall, Henri close behind. I follow and Bernie Kosar races ahead of us all, a ball of fury speeding away. Henri points the shotgun one way, then the other. The hallway is empty. Bernie Kosar has already reached the intersection. He disappears. Six follows suit and makes herself invisible and the rest of us run towards the gym, Henri in the lead. I make Mark and Sarah go ahead of me. None of us can really see a thing, can only hear each other's footsteps. I turn my lights on to help guide the way, and that's the first mistake I make.

A classroom door to my right swings open. Everything happens in a split second and, before I have a chance to react, I am hit in the shoulder with something heavy. My lights shut off. I crash straight through a glass display window. I'm cut on the top of my head and blood runs down the side of my face almost immediately. Sarah screams.

Whatever it was that hit me clubs me again, a hollow thud in my ribs that knocks the wind from me.

'Turn your lights on!' Henri yells. I do. A scout stands over me, holding a six-foot-long piece of wood that it must have found in the industrial arts classroom. It raises it in the air to hit me again, but Henri, standing twenty feet away, fires the shotgun first. The scout's head disappears, blown to pieces. The rest of its body turns to ash before it even hits the floor.

Henri lowers the gun. 'Shit,' he says, catching sight of the blood. He takes a step towards me and then from the corner of my eye I see another scout, in the same doorway, a sledgehammer raised over its head. It comes charging forward and, with telekinesis, I throw the nearest thing to me without even knowing what that thing is. A golden glinting object that speeds through the air with violence. It hits the scout so hard that its skull cracks on impact, and then it falls to the ground and lies motionless. Henri, Mark, and Sarah rush over. The scout is still alive and Henri takes Sarah's knife and thrusts it through its chest, reducing it to a pile of ash. He hands Sarah back her knife. She holds it out in front of her, between thumb and forefinger, as though she's just been handed a pair of somebody's dirty underwear. Mark bends down and lifts the object I had thrown, now in three separate pieces.

'It's my all-conference trophy,' he says, and then can't help but chuckle to himself. 'It was given to me last month.'

I stand. It was the trophy case that I crashed through.

'You okay?' Henri asks, looking at the cut.

'Yeah, I'm fine. Let's keep going.'

We rush down the hall and into the gymnasium, sprint across the floor, jump up onto the stage. I flip my lights on to see the blue mat being moved away as though of its own volition. Then the hatch is thrown up. Only then does Six make herself visible again.

'What happened back there?' she asks.

'Ran into a little bit of trouble,' Henri says, climbing down the ladder first to make sure the coast is clear. Then Sarah and Mark go.

'Where is the dog?' I ask.

Six shakes her head.

'Go on,' I say. She goes down first, leaving only me on the stage. I whistle as loudly as I can, knowing full well that I'm giving away my position by doing so. I wait.

'Come on, John,' Henri calls up from below.

I crawl into the hatch, my feet on the ladder, but from the waist up I'm still on the stage, watching.

'Come on!' I say to myself. 'Where are you?' And in that split second when I have no choice but to give up, but just before I drop down, Bernie Kosar materializes on the far side of the gym and comes sprinting my way, ears pinned to the sides of his head. I smile.

'Come on!' Henri yells this time.

'Hold on!' I yell back.

Bernie Kosar jumps onto the stage and into my arms.

'Here!' I yell, and hand the dog to Six. I drop down, close and lock the hatch and turn my lights on as brightly as they'll go.

The walls and floor are made of concrete, reeking of mildew. We have to walk in a low crouch to keep from hitting our heads. Six leads the way. The tunnel is about a hundred feet long and I have no idea what purpose this could have served at one time. We reach the end; a short flight of steps leads to a pair of metal cellar doors. Six waits until everyone is together.

'Where does this open?' I ask.

'Behind the faculty lot,' Sarah says. 'Not far from the football field.'

Six presses her ear to listen in the small crack between the closed doors. Nothing but the wind. Everyone's face is streaked with sweat, dust, and fear. Six looks at Henri and nods. I turn my lights off.

'All right,' she says, and makes herself invisible.

She inches the door up just enough to stick her head out and have a look around. The rest of us watch with bated breath, waiting, listening, all of us wracked with nerves. She turns one way, then the other. Satisfied we've made it unnoticed, she pushes the door all the way open and we file out one by one.

Everything is dark and silent, no wind, the forest trees to our right standing motionless. I look around, can see the busted silhouettes of the twisted cars piled in front of the doors of the school. No stars or moon. No sky at all, almost as though we're beneath a bubble of darkness, some sort of dome where only shadows remain. Bernie Kosar begins to growl, low at first so that my initial thought is that it's done for reasons of anxiety only; but the growl grows into something more ferocious, more menacing, and I know that he senses something out there. All of our heads turn to see what he is growling at but nothing moves. I take a step forward to put Sarah behind me. I think to turn on my lights but I know that will give us away even more so than the dog's growl. Suddenly, Bernie Kosar takes off.

He charges ahead thirty yards before leaping through the air and sinking his teeth deeply into one of the unseen scouts, who materializes from out of nowhere as though some spell of invisibility has been broken. In an instant, we're able to see them all, surrounding us, no fewer than twenty of them, who begin closing in.

'It was a trap!' Henri yells, and fires twice and drops two scouts immediately.

'Get back in the tunnel!' I scream to Mark and Sarah.

One of the scouts comes charging towards me. I lift it in the air and hurl it as hard as I can against an oak tree twenty yards away. It hits the ground with a thud, quickly stands, and hurls a dagger my way. I deflect it and lift the scout again and throw it even harder. It bursts into ash at the base of the tree. Henri unloads more rounds, the shots echoing. Two hands grab me from behind. I almost deflect them until I realize that it's Sarah. Six is nowhere to be seen. Bernie Kosar has brought a Mogadorian to the ground, his teeth now sunk deeply into its throat, hell ablaze in the dog's eyes.

'Get into the school!' I yell.

She doesn't let go. A clap of thunder breaks through the silence and a storm begins to brew, dark clouds now forming overhead with flashes of lightning and thunder tearing through the night sky, loud pounding thunder that makes Sarah jump each time one booms. Six has reappeared, standing thirty feet away, her eyes to the sky and her face twisted in concentration with both arms raised. She's the one creating the storm, controlling the weather. Bolts of lightning begin raining down, striking the scouts dead where they stand, creating small explosions that form clouds of ash that drift listlessly across the yard. Henri stands off to the side, loading more shells into the shotgun. The scout that Bernie Kosar is choking finally succumbs to death and bursts into a heap of ash covering the dog's face. He sneezes once, shakes the ash from his coat and then rushes off and chases the closest scout until they both disappear into the dense woods fifty yards away. I have this unbearable fear that I've seen him for the very last time.

'You have to go into the school,' I say to Sarah. 'You have to go now and you have to hide. Mark!' I yell. I look up and don't see him. I snap around. I catch sight of him sprinting towards Henri, who is still loading his gun. At first I don't understand why, and then I see what is happening: a Mogadorian scout has snuck up on Henri without his knowing it.

'Henri,' I scream to get his attention. I lift my hand to stop the scout with its knife raised high in the air, but Mark tackles the thing first. A wrestling match ensues. Henri snaps the shotgun closed, and Mark kicks the scout's knife away. Henri fires and the scout explodes. Henri says something to Mark. I yell for Mark again and he sprints over, breathing heavily.

'You have to take Sarah into the school.'

'I can help here,' he says.

'It's not your fight. You have to hide! Get in the school and hide with Sarah!'

'Okay,' he says.

'You have to stay hidden, no matter what!' I yell over the storm. 'They won't come for you. It's me they want. Promise me, Mark! Promise me you'll stay hidden with Sarah!'

Mark nods rapidly. 'I promise!'

Sarah is crying and there's no time to comfort her. Another clap of thunder, another shotgun blast. She kisses me one time on the lips, her hands holding tightly to my face and I know she would stay like this forever. Mark pulls her off, begins leading her away.

'I love you,' she says, and in her eyes she is staring at me in the same way that I had stared at her earlier, before I left home ec, as though she may be seeing me for the final time, wanting to remember it so that this last image might last a lifetime.

'I love you too,' I mouth back just as the two of them reach the steps of the tunnel, and as soon as the words leave my lips, Henri cries out in pain. I turn. One of the scouts has thrust a knife into his gut. Terror sweeps through me. The scout pulls the knife from Henri's side, the blade glistening with his blood. It thrusts down to stab Henri a second time. My hand reaches out for it and I rip the knife away at the last second so that it is only a fist that hits Henri. He grunts, gathers himself, and presses the barrel of the shotgun to the chin of the scout and fires. The scout drops, headless.

The rain starts, a cold, heavy rain. In no time at all I'm soaked to the bone. Blood leaks from Henri's gut. He's aiming the shotgun into the darkness, but all of the scouts have moved into the shadows, away from us, so that Henri can't get a good enough aim. They're no longer interested in attacking, knowing that two of us have retreated and a third has been wounded. Six is still reaching for the sky. The storm has grown; the wind is beginning to howl. She seems to be having trouble controlling it. A winter storm, thunder in January. As quickly as everything started, it all seems to stop – the thunder, the lightning, the rain. The wind dies away and a low groan begins to grow from off in the distance. Six lowers her arms, all of us straining to listen. Even the Mogadorians turn. The groan grows, unmistakably coming our way, some sort of deep mechanical groan. The scouts step from the shadows and begin to laugh. Despite our killing at least ten of them, there are many more than before.

From far off a cloud of smoke rises over the tops of the trees as if a steam engine is coming around the bend. The scouts nod to one another, smiling their wicked smiles, and re-form their circle around us in what is an apparent attempt to get us back into the school. And it's obvious that that is our only choice. Six walks over.

'What is it?' I ask.

Henri hobbles, the shotgun hanging limply at his side. He's breathing heavily, a gash on his cheek below his right eye, a circular puddle of blood on his gray sweater from the knife wound.

'It's the rest of them, isn't it?' Henri asks Six.

Six looks at him, stricken, her hair wet and clinging to the sides of her face.

'The beasts,' she says. 'And the soldiers. They're here.'

Henri cocks the shotgun and takes a deep breath. 'And so the real war begins,' he says. 'I don't know about you two, but if this is it, then this is it. I, for one . . .' he says, and trails off. 'Well, I'll be damned if I'll go down without a fight.'

Six nods. 'Our people fought back till the end. And so shall I,' she says.

A mile off the smoke still rises. *Live cargo,* I think. *That is how they transport them, by oversized semitrucks.* Six and I follow Henri back down the steps. I yell for Bernie Kosar but he's nowhere to be seen.

'We can't wait for him again,' Henri says. 'There isn't time.'

I look around one final time, and slam the cellar doors shut. We rush back through the tunnel, up onto the stage, across the gymnasium. We don't see a single scout, nor do we see Mark and Sarah, and I'm relieved by that. I hope they are well hidden, and I hope Mark keeps his promise and that they stay that way. When we make it back to the home-ec room I slide the fridge out of the way and grab the Chest. Henri and I open it. Six takes the healing stone out and thrusts it against Henri's gut. He is silent, his eyes closed, holding his breath. His face is red under the strain but not a single sound escapes. A minute of this and Six pulls the stone away. The cut has healed. Henri exhales, his forehead covered in sweat. Then it's my turn. She presses it to the gash on my head and a pain far greater than anything I've ever felt before rips through me. I grunt and groan, every muscle in my body flexing. I can't breathe until it's over, and when it finally is, I bend over and catch my breath for a full minute.

Outside the mechanical groan has stopped. The semi is hidden from view. While Henri closes up the Chest and places it back in the same oven as before, I look out the window hoping to catch sight of Bernie Kosar. I don't see him. Another set of headlights passes by the school. As before, I can't tell if it's a car or truck, and it slows as it drives by the entrance, then quickly speeds away without turning in. Henri pushes his shirt down, picks up the shotgun. As we move towards the door, a sound stops the three of us dead in our tracks.

A roar comes from outside, loud, animal-like, a sinister roar unlike anything I have ever heard before, followed by the sound of the metallic clicks of a gate being unlocked, lowered, and opened. A loud bang snaps us all back to attention. I take another deep breath. Henri shakes his head and sighs in what is an almost hopeless gesture, a gesture made when the fight is lost.

'There's always hope, Henri,' I say. He turns and looks at me. 'New developments have yet to present themselves.

Not all the information is in. Don't give up hope just yet.'

He nods and the tiniest trace of a smile forms. He looks at Six, a new development that I don't think either of us could have imagined. Who's to say that there aren't more waiting? And then he picks up where I left off, quoting the exact words he spoke to me when I was the one who was discouraged, the day I asked how we could possibly expect to win this fight, alone and outnumbered, far from home – against the Mogadorians, who seem to take great joy in war and death. 'It's the last thing to go,' Henri says. 'When you have lost hope, you have lost everything. And when you think all is lost, when all is dire and bleak, there is always hope.'

'Exactly,' I say.

31

Another roar cuts through the night air, through the walls of the school. A roar that makes my blood turn cold. The ground begins to rumble under the footsteps of the beast that must now be on the loose. I shake my head. I saw first-hand how big they were during the flashbacks of the war on Lorien.

'For your friends' sake and ours,' Six says, 'we better get the hell out of this school while there's still time. They'll destroy the entire building trying to get to us.'

We nod to one another.

'Our only hope is to get to the woods,' Henri says. 'Whatever that thing is, we might be able to escape it if we can stay invisible.'

Six nods. 'Just keep ahold of my hands.'

Needing no other motivation than that, Henri and I each take a hand.

'As quietly as we can,' Henri says.

The hallway is dark and silent. We walk with a quiet urgency, moving as swiftly as we can while making little noise. Another roar, and in the middle of it, another roar begins. We stop. Not one beast, but *two*. We continue on and enter the gymnasium. No sign of the scouts. When we reach the very center of the court, Henri stops. I look over but can't see him.

'Why are we stopped?' I whisper.

'Shh,' he says. 'Listen.'

I strain to listen, but hear nothing aside from the steady hum of blood filling my ears.

'The beasts have stopped moving,' Henri says.

'So what?'

'Shh,' he says. 'There's something else out there.'

And then I hear it too, slight high-pitched yipping sounds as though coming from small animals. The sounds are muffled, though obviously growing louder.

'What the hell?' I ask.

Something begins banging at the stage hatch, the hatch we are hoping to escape through.

'Turn your lights on,' he says.

I let go of Six's hand, snap them on, and aim them towards the stage. Henri looks down the end of the shotgun barrel. The hatch bounces up as though something is trying to force itself through but lacks the strength to do so. *The weasels,* I think, *the stout-bodied little creatures that the guys in Athens were terrified of.* One of them hits the hatch so hard that it breaks away from the stage and rattles across the floor. So much for thinking they lacked strength. Two of them come bursting forth, and upon catching sight of us, come racing our way so swiftly that I can hardly make them out. Henri stands watching with the gun aimed, an amused grin on his face. Their paths diverge and both leap from about twenty feet away, one jumping at Henri, the other coming at me. Henri fires once and the weasel explodes and covers him with its blood and guts; and just as I'm about to rip apart the second with telekinesis, it is snatched out of midair by Six's unseen hand and spiked to the ground like a football, killing it instantly.

Henri cocks the shotgun. 'Well, that wasn't so bad,' he says, and before I can respond, the entire wall along the stage is smashed in by the fist of a beast. It draws back and punches again, smashing the stage to smithereens and exposing the night sky. The impact pushes both Henri and me backwards.

'Run!' Henri yells, and he immediately unloads every shell in the shotgun into the beast. They have no effect upon it. The beast leans forward and roars so loudly that I feel my clothes flutter. A hand reaches out and grabs hold of me, turning me invisible. The beast charges ahead, moving straight for Henri, and I'm gripped with terror at what it might do.

'No!' I scream. 'To Henri, get to Henri!' I twist under Six's grip, finally grabbing hold of her and pushing her away. I become visible; she stays hidden. The beast surges towards Henri, who stands firm and watches it come. Out of bullets. Out of options. 'Get to him!' I scream again. 'Get to him, Six!'

'Go to the woods!' she yells back.

All I can do is watch. The beast must stand thirty feet tall, maybe forty, towering over Henri. It roars, pure wrath in its eyes. Its muscled and bulging fist rushes high in the air, so high that it breaks straight through the rafters and the roof of the school gymnasium. And then it falls, speeding down with such swiftness that it becomes a blur, like the blades of a spinning fan. I cry out in horror, knowing that Henri is about to be crushed. I can't look away, Henri seeming tiny standing there with the shotgun limply at his side. When the fist of the beast is a split second from him, Henri disappears. The fist crashes through the gymnasium floor, the wood splintering, the impact sending me crashing into the stands twenty feet away. The beast turns to me, blocking from view the place where Henri had just stood.

'Henri!' I yell. The beast roars so that any response that might have come is drowned out. It takes one step towards me. To the woods, Six had said. Go to the woods. I stand and run as fast as I can to the back of the gym, where the beast had just broken through. I turn to see if the beast is following. It is not. Perhaps Six has done something to divert its attention. All I know is that I'm on my own now, alone.

I leap over the pile of rubble and sprint away from the school, running as hard as I can for the woods. The shadows swarm around me, following like villainous wraiths. I know that I can outrun them. The beast roars and I hear another wall crumble. I reach the trees and the swarming shadows seem to have disappeared. I stop and listen. The trees sway under a light breeze. There is a wind here! I've escaped whatever dome the Mogadorians have created. Something warm collects at the waistband of my pants. The cut I suffered at Mark James's has reopened on my back.

The school's silhouette is faint from where I stand. The entire gymnasium is gone, a pile of brick. The beast's shadow stands tall in the rubble of the cafeteria. Why hasn't it run after me? And where is the second beast we all heard? The beast's fist falls again, another room demolished. Mark and Sarah are there somewhere. I told them to go back and I realize how foolish it was. I didn't anticipate the beast destroying the school if it knew I wasn't there. I have to do something to get the beast away. I take a deep breath to gather my strength, and as soon as I take that first step, something hard hits me in the back of the head. I fall face-first into the mud. I touch where I've been hit and my hand is covered in blood, drips of it falling from my fingertips. I turn around and see nothing at first, and then it steps out of the shadows and grins.

A soldier. This is what they look like. Taller than the scouts – seven, maybe eight feet tall – its muscles bulging beneath a black ragged cloak. Large, raised veins traverse the length of each arm. Black boots. Nothing covering its head, and its hair falling to its shoulders. The same pale, waxy skin as the scouts. A grin of self-assurance, of finality. In one of its hands is a sword. Long and shimmering, made of some kind of metal I've never seen here on Earth or in my visions of Lorien, and it appears to be pulsing, as if it is somehow alive.

I begin to crawl away, the blood dripping down my neck. The beast at the school lets out another roar, and I reach for the low branches of a nearby tree and pull myself up. The soldier is ten feet away. I grip both hands into fists. It motions the sword nonchalantly towards me, and something comes out of its tip, something that looks like a small dagger. I watch the dagger twist in an arc, leaving a slight trail behind it like smoke from a plane. The light casts a spell that I can't look away from.

A flash of bright light devours everything, the world dimming away into a soundless void. No walls. No sound. No floor or ceiling. Very slowly the shapes of things return, the trees standing like ancient effigies whispering of the world that once was in some alternate realm where only shadows reside.

I reach out to feel the nearest tree, the only touch of gray in an otherwise white world. My hand goes through it and for a moment the tree shimmers as if it were liquid. I take a deep breath. When I exhale the pain returns to the gash on the back of my head and the tears down my arms and body from the James house fire. A sound of dripping water comes from somewhere. Slowly, the soldier takes form, twenty or thirty feet away. Giantlike. We take each other in. Its sword glowing more brightly in this new world. Its eyes narrow and my hands again clench into fists. I've lifted objects far heavier than it; I've split trees and I've caused destruction. Surely I can match its strength with my own. I push everything that I feel into the core of my being, everything that I am and everything that I will be, until it feels as though I'm about to burst.

'Yahhhh!' I yell, and I thrust my arms forward. The brute force leaves my body, raging towards the soldier. At the same time it sweeps the sword across its body as though swatting a fly. The power deflects into the trees, which dance for a brief moment like the grain in a wheat field waving in a light wind, and then they become still. It laughs at me, a deep, guttural laugh meant to taunt. Its red eyes begin to glow, swirling as though lava filled. It lifts its free hand and I tense myself against the unknown. And without my knowing what has happened, my throat is in its grip, the gap that had separated us closed in the blink of an eye. It lifts me, one handed, breathing with its mouth open so that I can smell the sour stench of its breath, the smell of decay. I thrash, try to pry its fingers from around my throat, but they are like iron.

And then it throws me.

I land on my back forty feet away. I stand and it charges, swinging the sword at my head, which I duck and counter by pushing it as hard as I can. It stumbles back but stays standing. I try to lift it with telekinesis but nothing happens. In this alternate world my powers are dimmed, almost ineffectual. The Mogadorian has the advantage here.

It smiles at my futility and raises the sword with both hands. The sword comes alive, turning from shimmering silver into ice blue. Blue flames lick across the blade. A sword that glows with power, just as Six had talked about. It swings the sword in my direction and another dagger comes flying off the tip, straight at me. *This I can do,* I think. All the hours in the backyard with Henri preparing for this very thing. Always the knives, more or less the same as a dagger. Did Henri know they would use them? Certainly, though in my flashbacks of the invasion I had never seen them. But I had never seen these creatures, either. They were different on Lorien, not quite as sinister looking. On the day of the invasion they looked sickly and starved. Is it Earth's fault for this convalescence, have the resources here caused them to grow stronger and healthier?

The dagger literally screams as it rages towards me. It grows and becomes consumed in flames. Just when I am about to deflect it, it explodes into a ball of fire, and the flames jump to me. I'm trapped within it, consumed in a perfect sphere of fire. Anyone else would burn, but not me, and somehow it causes my strength to return. I'm able to breathe. Without the soldier knowing it, it has made me stronger. Now it's my turn to smile at its own futility.

'Is this all you've got?' I yell.

Its face turns into rage. It defiantly reaches one hand over its shoulder and returns with a cannonlike gun that begins conforming to its body, the gun wrapping around its forearm. Its arm and the gun becoming one and the same. I pull the knife from my back pocket, the knife that I grabbed from home before returning to school. Small, ineffectual, but better than nothing. I open the blade and charge. The ball of fire charges with me. The soldier squares its body and brings down its sword with force. I deflect it with the pocketknife but the weight of the sword snaps the blade in two. I drop the remaining pieces and swing as hard as I can. My fist slams into the soldier's gut. It doubles over but comes right back up and swings the sword again. I duck beneath the blade at the last second. It singes the hair on top of my head. Right behind the sword comes the cannon. No time to react. It hits me in my shoulder and I grunt and fall backwards. The soldier regroups and points the cannon in the air. I'm confounded at first. The gray from the trees is being pulled away and sucked into the gun. Then I understand. The gun. It needs to be charged before it can be fired, needs to steal Earth's essence in order to be used. The gray in the trees isn't shadows; the gray is the life of the trees at its most elemental level. And now those lives are being stolen, consumed by the Mogadorians. A race of aliens that depleted their planet's resources in the quest for advancement, now doing the same thing here. That is the reason they attacked Lorien. The same reason they will attack Earth. One by one the trees fall and crumble into heaps of ash. The gun glows brighter and brighter, so bright that it hurts the eyes to look at. No time to spare.

I charge. It keeps the gun pointed at the sky and swings the sword. I duck and plow straight into it. Its body tenses and it writhes in agony. The fire surrounding me burns it where it stands. But I've left myself open. It swings the blade feebly, not enough to cut me, but there is nothing I can do to prevent its fall. It hits me and my body is hurled backwards fifty feet as though I've been struck by a bolt of lightning. I lie there, my body shaking with post-electrocution tremors. I lift my head. Thirty piles of ash from the fallen trees surround us. How many times will that allow him to fire? A slight wind kicks up and the ash begins filtering across the empty space between us. The moon returns. This world to which it has brought me is beginning to fail. It knows it. The gun is ready. I wrestle myself up from the ground. Sitting a couple feet away, still glowing, is one of the daggers it fired at me. I pick it up.

It lowers the cannon and aims. The white surrounding us is beginning to dim, color returning. And then the cannon fires, a bright flash of light containing the ghoulish forms of everyone I have ever known – Henri, Sam, Bernie Kosar, Sarah – all of them dead in this alternate realm and the light so bright that they are all I can see, trying to take me with them, raging forward in a ball of energy growing as it nears. I try to deflect the blast but it's too strong. The white makes it as far as the fiery enclosure, and when the two touch an explosion erupts and the power sends me backwards. I land with a thud. I take inventory. I am unharmed. The ball of fire has extinguished. Somehow it has absorbed the blast, has saved me from what I am certain would have been death. Surely that is how the cannon works, the death of one thing for the death of another. The power of mind control, manipulation that plays on fear, possible through the destruction of the elements of the world. The scouts have learned to do this weakly with their minds. The soldiers rely on weapons that produce a much greater effect.

I stand, the glowing knife still in my hand. The soldier pulls some sort of lever on the side of the cannon as though to reload it. I sprint towards it. When I'm close enough, I aim for its heart and hurl the knife as hard as I can. It fires a second shot. A torpedo of orange raging its way, the certainty of a white death coming – mine. They cross in midair without touching. Just when I expect that second shot to hit, to bring upon that death, something else happens instead.

My knife strikes first.

The world vanishes. The shadows fade and the cold and the dark return as though they had never left. A vertiginous transition. I take a step backwards and fall. My eyes adjust to the dearth of light. I fix them on the dark figure of the soldier hovering over me. The cannon blast didn't travel with us. The glowing knife did, the blade sunk deeply into its heart, the handle pulsating orange beneath the moonlight overhead. The soldier staggers, and then the knife is sucked in deeper and disappears. It grunts. Spurts of black blood pump from the open wound. Its eyes go blank, then roll back into its head. It falls to the ground, lies motionless, and then explodes into a cloud of ash that covers my shoes. A soldier. I've killed my first. May it not be the last.

Something about being in the alternate realm has weakened me. I place my hand on a nearby tree to steady myself and catch my breath, only the tree is no longer there. I look around. All the trees surrounding us have collapsed into heaps of ash just as they did in the other realm, just as the Mogadorians do when they die.

I hear the roar of the beast and I look up to see how much of the school is left standing. But instead of the school there is something else, fifteen feet away, standing tall with a sword in one hand and a similar-looking cannon in the other. The cannon is aimed right at my heart, a cannon that has already been charged, glowing with power. Another soldier. I don't think I have the strength to fight this one as I did the last.

There is nothing I can throw, and the gap between us is too great to charge before it fires. And then its arm twitches and the sound of a gunshot rings through the air. My body instinctively jerks, expecting the cannon to rip me in half. But I am fine, unharmed. I look up confused, and there, in the soldier's forehead, is a hole the size of a quarter spurting its hideous blood. Then it drops and disintegrates.

'That's for my dad,' I hear behind me. I turn. Sam, holding a silver pistol in his right hand. I smile at him. He lowers the gun. 'They passed right through the center of town,' he says. 'I knew it was them as soon as I saw the trailer.'

I try to catch my breath, staring in awe at Sam's figure. Just moments before, in the first soldier's blast, he was a decaying corpse sprung from hell to take me away. And now he just saved me.

'You okay?' he asks.

I nod. 'Where did you just come from?'

'I followed them in my dad's truck after they passed my house. I pulled in fifteen minutes ago and got swarmed by the ones that were already here. So I left and parked in a field a mile away and walked through the woods.'

The second set of lights we had seen from the window of the school came from Sam's truck. I open my mouth to respond but a clap of thunder shakes the sky. Another storm begins to brew, and relief courses through me that Six is still alive. A bolt of lightning cuts the sky and clouds begin rushing in from all directions, being pulled together into one giant mass. An even greater darkness falls, followed by a rain so heavy that I have to squint to see Sam five feet away from me. The school is blotted out. But then a great bolt of lightning strikes and everything brightens for a split second, and I see that the beast has been hit. An agonizing roar follows.

'I have to get to the school!' I yell. 'Mark and Sarah are somewhere inside.'

'If you're going, then I'm going,' he yells back over the rumble of the storm.

We take no more than five steps before the wind comes howling, pushing us back, torrential rain stinging our faces. We're soaked, shivering and cold. But if I'm shivering then I know I'm alive. Sam drops to a knee, then lies on his stomach to keep from being blown backwards. I do the same. Through squinted eyes I look into the clouds – heavy, dark, ominous – swirling in small concentric circles and, in the center, the center I'm trying mightily to reach, a face begins to form.

It's an old, weathered face, bearded, tranquil looking as though it sleeps. A face that looks older than Earth itself. The clouds begin to lower, slowly nearing the surface and consuming everything, everything darkening, a dark so deep and impenetrable that it's hard to imagine that somewhere, anywhere, a sun still exists. Another roar, a roar of anger and doom. I try to stand but am quickly knocked back down, the wind too great. The face. It's coming alive. An awakening. The eyes opening, the face upturned into a grimace. Is this Six's creation? The face becomes the look of rage itself, a look of revenge. Coming down fast. Everything seems to hang in the balance. And then the mouth opens, hungry, its lips curling to show teeth and its eyes squinted in what can only be described as pure malice. A complete and utter wrath.

And then the face touches down and a sonic blast shakes the ground, an explosion reaching out over the school, everything illuminated in red, orange, and yellow. I'm thrust backwards. Trees break in half. The ground rumbles. I land with a thud, branches and mud falling atop me. My ears ring as they've never rung before. A boom so loud that it must have been heard fifty miles away. And then the rain stops, and everything falls silent.

I lie in the mud, listening to the beat of my heart. The clouds clear away, revealing a hanging moon. Not a single gust of wind. I look around but don't see Sam. I yell for him but get no response. I yearn to hear something, anything, another roar, Henri's shotgun, but there is nothing.

I pull myself up off the forest floor, wipe away the mud and the twigs as best as I can. I exit the woods for the second time. The stars have reappeared, a million of them twinkling high in the night sky. Is it over? Have we won? Or is it just a lull in the action? The school, I think. I have to get to the school. I take one step forward, and that's when I hear it.

Another roar, coming from within the woods behind me.

Sound returns. Three successive gunshots ring through the night, echoing so that I have no idea from which direction they have come. I hope with everything inside of me that they are from Henri's shotgun, that he is still alive, still fighting.

The ground begins to shake. The beast is on the run, coming for me, no mistaking it now, trees broken and uprooted behind me. They don't seem to slow it down at all. Is this one even bigger than the other? I don't care to find out. I take off running for the school, but then realize that's the absolute worst place I can go. Sarah and Mark are still there, still hiding. Or at least I hope they are.

Everything returns to the way it was before the storm, the shadows following, looming. Scouts. Soldiers. I veer to the right and sprint along the tree-lined path that leads to the football field, the beast hot on my trail. Can I really expect to outrun it? If I can make it to the woods beyond the field, maybe I can. I know those woods, the woods that lead to our house. Within them I'll have the home-field advantage. I look around and see the figures of the

Mogadorians in the schoolyard. There are too many of them. We're greatly outnumbered. Did we ever really believe we could win?

A dagger flies by me, a flash of red missing my face by mere inches. It sticks into the trunk of a tree beside me and the tree ignites in flame. Another roar. The beast is keeping pace. Which of us has the greater endurance? I enter the stadium, sprint straight across the fifty-yard line and pass through the visiting team's side. Another knife whizzes by, a blue one this time. The woods are near, and when I finally sprint into them a smile forms on my face. I've led it away from the others. If everyone else is safe then I've done my job. Just when a sense of triumph blooms within me, the third dagger strikes.

I cry out, fall face-first into the mud. I can feel the dagger between my shoulder blades. A pain so sharp that it paralyzes me. I try to reach to pull it free but it is up too high. It feels as though it's moving, digging itself deeper, the pain spreading as if I've been poisoned. On my stomach, in agony. I can't pull it free with telekinesis, my powers somehow failing me. I begin dragging myself forward. One of the soldiers – or maybe it's a scout; I can't tell which – places a foot on my back, reaches down, and pulls the knife free. I grunt. The knife is gone but the pain stays. It takes its foot off of me but I can still feel its presence, and I wrestle myself onto my back to face it.

Another soldier, standing tall and smiling with hatred. The same look as the one before, the same type of sword. The dagger that was in my back twists in its grip. That is what I felt, the blade turning while imbedded in my flesh. I lift a hand towards the soldier to move it but I know it's in vain. I can't focus, everything blurry. The soldier raises its sword in the air. The blade tastes death, starts glowing in the night sky behind it. *I'm gone,* I think. *Nothing I can do.* I look into its eyes. Ten years on the run and this is how easily it ends, how quietly. But behind it lurks something else. Something far more menacing than a million soldiers with a million swords. Teeth every bit as long as the soldier is tall, teeth glowing white in a mouth too small to hold them. The beast with its evil eyes hovering over us.

A sharp intake of breath catches in my throat, and my eyes open wide in terror. It'll take us both out, I think. The soldier is oblivious. It tenses and grimaces at me and starts to bring the sword down to split me in two. But it is too slow and the beast strikes first, its jaws clamping down like a bear trap. The bite doesn't stop until the beast's teeth come together, the soldier's body cut cleanly in half just below the hips, leaving nothing behind but two stumps still standing. The beast chews twice and swallows. The soldier's legs fall hollowly to the ground, one dropping to the right, the other to the left, and quickly disintegrate.

It takes every ounce of strength I have to reach out and grab the dagger that has fallen at my feet. I tuck it into the waistband of my jeans, and begin crawling away. I feel the beast hovering over me, feel its breath upon the nape of my neck. The smell of death and rotting meat. I enter a small clearing. I expect the beast's wrath to fall any second, expect its teeth and claws to rip me to shreds. I pull myself forward until I can go no more, my back against an oak tree.

The beast stands in the very center of the clearing, thirty feet away from me. I look at it fully for the first time. A looming figure, hazy in the dark and the cold of the night. Taller and bigger than the beast at the school, forty feet, standing upright on two hind legs. Thick, gray skin stretched tightly over slabs of bulging muscle. No neck, its head sloped so that its lower jaw protrudes farther out than its upper. A set of fangs points towards the sky, another set points to the ground, dripping blood and drool. Long, thick arms hang a foot or two above the ground even while the beast stands straight, giving it the appearance of slightly leaning forward. Yellow eyes. Round disks at the sides of its head that pulsate with the beating of its heart, the only sign that it has any sort of heart at all.

It leans forward and brings its left hand to the ground. A hand, complete with stubby short fingers with claws like a raptor, claws meant to rip apart anything they touch. It sniffs at me, and roars. An ear-splitting roar that would have pushed me backwards if I weren't already against a tree. Its mouth opens, showing what must be fifty other teeth, each one every bit as sharp as the next. Its free hand thrusts away from its side and splits in half every tree that it strikes, ten, fifteen of them.

No more running. No more fighting. Blood from the knife wound runs down my back; my hands and legs are both shaking. The dagger is still tucked into the waistband of my jeans, but what's the point in grabbing it? What faith is there in a four-inch blade against a forty-foot beast? It would be the equivalent of a splinter. It'll only make it angrier. My only hope is to bleed to death before I am killed and eaten.

I close my eyes and accept death. My lights are off. I don't want to see what is about to happen. I hear movement behind me. I open my eyes. One of the Mogadorians must be moving in for a closer look, I think at first, but I know immediately that I am wrong. There is something familiar about the loping gait, something I recognize in the sound of his breathing. And then he enters the clearing.

Bernie Kosar.

I smile, but the smile quickly fades. If I am doomed, there is no point in him dying too. *No, Bernie Kosar. You can't be here. You need to leave and you need to run like the wind, get as far away as you can. Pretend you've just finished our early-morning jog to school and that it's time to return home.*

He looks at me as he walks up. *I am here,* he seems to say. *I am here and I will stand with you.*

'No,' I say aloud.

He stops long enough to give my hand a reassuring lick. He looks up at me with his big, brown eyes. *Get away, John,* I hear in my mind. *Crawl if you have to crawl, but get away now.* The blood loss has made me delusional. Bernie seems to be communicating with me. Is Bernie Kosar even here, or am I imagining that as well?

He stands in front of me as though in protection. He begins to growl, low at first, but it grows to a growl every bit as ferocious as the beast's own roar. The beast fixates on Bernie Kosar. A staredown. Bernie Kosar's hair is raised down the center of his back, his tan ears pinned to his head. His loyalty, his bravery very nearly make me weep. He's a hundred times smaller than the beast yet he stands tall, vowing to fight. One quick strike from the beast and all is done.

I reach my hand out to Bernie Kosar. I wish I could stand and grab him and get away. His growls are so fierce that his whole body shakes, tremors coursing through him.

And then something begins to happen.

Bernie Kosar begins to grow.

32

After all this time, only now do I understand. The morning runs when I would run too fast for him to keep pace. He would disappear into the woods, reappear seconds later in front of me. Six tried to tell me. Six took one look at him and she knew immediately. On those runs Bernie Kosar went into the woods to change himself, to turn himself into a bird. The way he would rush outside each morning, nose to the ground, patrolling the yard. Protecting me, and Henri. Looking for signs of the Mogadorians. The gecko in Florida. The gecko that used to watch from the wall while I ate breakfast. How long has he been with us? The Chimæra, the ones I watched being loaded into the rocket – did they make it to Earth after all?

Bernie Kosar continues to grow. He tells me to run. I can communicate with him. No, that's not all. I can communicate with all animals. Another Legacy. It started with the deer in Florida on the day that we left. The shudder that ran up my spine as it passed something along to me, some feeling. I attributed it to the sadness of our leaving, but I was wrong. Mark James's dogs. The cows I passed on my morning runs. The same thing. I feel like such a fool to discover it only now. So blatantly obvious, right in front of my face. Another of Henri's adages: Those things that are most obvious are the very things we're most likely to overlook. But Henri knew. That is why he said no to Six when she tried to tell me.

Bernie Kosar is done growing; his hair has fallen away, replaced by oblong scales. He looks like a dragon, but without the wings. His body is thick with muscle. Jagged teeth and claws, horns that curl like a ram's. Thicker than the beast, but far shorter. Looking every bit as menacing. Two giants on opposite sides of the clearing, roaring at one another.

Run, he tells me. I try to tell him that I can't. I don't know if he can understand me. *You can,* he says. *You must.*

The beast swings. A hammer swing that starts in the clouds and pours down with brutality. Bernie Kosar blocks it with his horns and then charges before the beast can swing again. A colossal collision in the very center of the clearing. Bernie Kosar thrusts up, sinks his teeth into the beast's side. The beast knocks him back. Both of them so quick that it defies all logic. Bleeding gashes already down the sides of each. I watch with my back against the tree. I try to help. But my telekinesis is still failing me. Blood still pours down my back. My limbs feel heavy, as though my blood has turned to lead. I can feel myself fading.

The beast is still upright on two legs while Bernie Kosar must fight on four. The beast makes a charge. Bernie Kosar lowers his head and they smash into one another, crashing through the trees off to my right side. Somehow the beast ends up on top. It sinks its teeth deep in Bernie Kosar's throat. It thrashes, trying to tear his throat out. Bernie Kosar twists under the beast's bite but he can't shake free. He tears at the beast's hide with his paws but the beast doesn't let go.

Then a hand reaches out behind me, grabs my arm. I try to push it away but I'm incapable of doing even that. Bernie Kosar's eyes are closed tightly. He is straining under the beast's jaws, his throat constricted, unable to breathe.

'No!' I yell.

'Come on!' the voice yells behind me. 'We need to get out of here.'

'The dog,' I say, not comprehending whose voice it is. 'The dog!'

Bernie Kosar is being bitten and choked, about to die, and there isn't a damn thing I can do about it. I won't be far behind. I would sacrifice my own life for his. I scream out. Bernie Kosar twists his head around and looks at me, his face scrunched tightly in pain and agony and the oncoming death he must feel.

'We have to go!' the voice behind me yells, the hand pulling me up from off the forest floor.

Bernie Kosar's eyes stay fixed on mine. *Go,* he says to me. *Get out of here, now, while you can. There isn't much time.*

I somehow reach my feet. Dizzy, the world cast in a haze around me. Only Bernie Kosar's eyes remain clear. Eyes that scream 'Help!' even while his thoughts say otherwise.

'We have to go!' the voice yells again. I don't turn to face it, but I know whose it is. Mark James, no longer hiding in the school, trying to save me from this clash. His being here must mean that Sarah is okay, and for a brief moment I allow myself to be relieved, but then that relief vanishes as quickly as it came. In this exact moment only one thing matters. Bernie Kosar, on his side, looking at me with glassy eyes. He saved me. It's my turn to save him.

Mark reaches his hand across my chest, begins pulling me backwards, out of the clearing, away from the fight. I twist myself free. Bernie Kosar's eyes slowly begin to close. He's fading, I think. *I won't watch you die,* I tell him. *I'm willing to watch many things in this world but I'll be damned if I'll watch you die.* There's no response. The beast's bite hardens. It can sense that death is near.

I take one wobbly step and pull the dagger from the waistband of my jeans. I close my fingers tightly around it and it comes alive and starts glowing. I'll never be able to hit the beast by throwing the dagger, and my Legacies have all but vanished. An easy decision. No choice but to charge.

One deep, shaky breath. I rock my body backwards, everything tensing through the ache of exhaustion, not an inch anywhere on me that doesn't feel some sort of pain.

'No!' Mark yells behind me.

I lunge forward and sprint for the beast. The beast's eyes are closed, jaws clamped tightly around Bernie Kosar's throat so that the moonlight glows in the pools of blood around it. Thirty feet away. Then twenty. The beast's eyes snap open at the exact moment I jump. Yellow eyes that twist in rage the second they focus upon me, sailing through the air towards them, dagger in both hands held high over my head as though in some heroic dream I never want to wake from. The beast lets go of Bernie Kosar's throat and moves to bite, but surely it knows that it has sensed me too late. The blade of the dagger glows in anticipation, and I jam it deeply into the eye of the beast. A liquid ooze immediately bursts out. The beast lets out a blood-curdling scream so loud that it's hard to imagine the dead being able to sleep through it.

I fall flat on my back. I lift my head and watch the beast totter over me. It tries in vain to pull the dagger from its eye, but its hands are too big and the dagger is too small. The Mogadorian weapons function in some way that I don't think I'll ever understand, because of the mystical gateways between the realms. The dagger is no different, the black of the night rushing into the eye of the beast in a vortexlike funnel cloud, a tornado of death.

The beast falls silent as the last of the great black cloud enters its skull, and the dagger is sucked in with it. The beast's arms fall limply to its sides. Its hands begin to shake. A violent shake that reverberates throughout the entirety of its massive body. When the convulsions end the beast hunches over and then falls to the ground with its back against the trees. Sitting, but yet still towering some twenty-five feet over me. Everything silent, hanging in anticipation of what is to come. A gun fires once, very close so that my ears ring for seconds afterward. The beast takes a great breath and holds it in as though in meditation, and suddenly its head explodes, raining down pieces of brain and flesh and skull over everything, all of which quickly turn to ash and dust.

The woods fall silent. I turn my head and look at Bernie Kosar, who still lies motionless on his side, his eyes closed. I can't tell if he's alive or not. As I look at him, he begins to change again, shrinking down to his normal size, while remaining lifeless. I hear the sound of crunching leaves and snapping twigs nearby.

It takes all the strength I have just to lift my head an inch off the ground. I open my eyes and peer up into the haze of night, expecting to see Mark James. But it's not him standing over me. My breath catches in my throat. A looming figure, indistinct with the moon's light hovering just over it. Then he takes one step forward, blotting out the moon, and my eyes widen in anticipation and dread.

33

The hazy image sharpens. Through the exhaustion and pain and fear, a smile comes to my face, coupled with a sense of relief. Henri. He throws the shotgun into the bushes and drops to one knee beside me. He face is bloodied, his shirt and jeans in tatters, cuts down the length of both arms and on his neck, and beyond that I see that his eyes are fear-stricken from what he sees in mine.

'Is it over?' I ask.

'Shhh,' he says. 'Tell me, have you been stabbed by one of their daggers?'

'My back,' I say.

He closes his eyes and shakes his head. He reaches into his pocket and removes one of the small round stones I watched him grab from the Loric Chest before we left the home-ec room. His hands are shaking.

'Open your mouth,' he says. He inserts one of the stones. 'Keep it under your tongue. Don't swallow it.' He hefts me up with his hands beneath my armpits. I get to my feet and he keeps an arm on me while I regain balance. He turns me around to look at the gash on my back. My face feels warm. A sort of rejuvenation blooms through me from the stone. My limbs still ache with exhaustion, but enough strength has returned so that I'm able to function.

'What is this?'

'Loric salt. It'll slow and numb the dagger's effects,' he says. 'You'll feel a burst of energy, but it won't last long and we have to get back to the school as quickly as we can.'

The pebble is cold in my mouth, tastes nothing like salt – tastes like nothing at all, actually. I look down and take inventory, and then brush off with my hands the ashen residue left from the fallen beast.

'Is everyone okay?' I ask.

'Six has been badly hurt,' he says. 'Sam is carrying her back to the truck as we speak; then he is going to drive to the school to pick us up. That's why we have to get back there.'

'Have you seen Sarah?'

'No.'

'Mark James was just here,' I say, and look at him. 'I thought you were him.'

'I didn't see him.'

I look past Henri at the dog. 'Bernie Kosar,' I say. He is still shrinking, the scales fading away – tan, black, and brown hair taking their place – returning to the form in which I have known him most recently: floppy ears, short legs, long body. A beagle with a cold wet nose always ready to run. 'He just saved my life. You knew, didn't you?'

'Of course I knew.'

'Why didn't you tell me?'

'Because he watched over you when I couldn't.'

'But how is he here?'

'He was on the ship with us.'

And then I remember what I thought was a stuffed animal that used to play with me. It was really Bernie Kosar I was playing with, though back then his name was Hadley.

We walk to the dog together. I crouch down and run my hand along Bernie Kosar's side.

'We have to hurry,' Henri says again.

Bernie Kosar isn't moving. The woods are alive, swarming with shadows that can only mean one thing, but I don't care. I move my head to the dog's rib cage. Ever so faintly I hear the *th-tump* of his beating heart. Some glimmer of life is still left. He is covered in deep cuts and gashes, and blood seems to seep from everywhere. His front leg is twisted at an unnatural angle, broken. But he is still alive. I lift him as gently as I can, cradling him like a child in my arms. Henri helps me up, then reaches into his pocket, grabs another salt pebble, and plops it into his own mouth. It makes me wonder if he was talking about himself when he said there was little time. Both of us are unsteady. And then something catches my eye in Henri's thigh. A wound glowing navy blue through the gathering blood around it. He's also been stabbed by a soldier's knife. I wonder if the salt pebble is the only reason he's now standing, as it is for me.

'What about the shotgun?' I ask.

'I'm out of ammo.'

We walk out of the clearing, taking our time. Bernie Kosar doesn't move in my arms but I can feel that life hasn't left him. Not yet. We exit the woods, leaving behind us the overhanging branches and bushes and the smell of wet and rotting leaves.

'Do you think you can run?' Henri asks.

'No,' I say. 'But I'll run anyway.'

Up ahead of us we hear a great commotion, several grunts followed by clanking of chains.

And then we hear a roar, not quite as sinister as the others, but loud enough so that we know it can only mean one thing: another beast.

'You're kidding me,' Henri says.

Twigs snap behind us, coming from the woods. Henri and I both twist around, but the woods are too dense to see. I snap the light on in my left hand and sweep it through the trees to see. There must be seven or eight soldiers standing at the entrance of the woods, and when my light hits them they all draw their swords, which come alive, glowing their various colors the second they do.

'No!' Henri yells. 'Don't use your Legacies; it'll weaken you.'

But it's too late. I snap the light off. Vertigo and weakness return, then the pain. I hold my breath and wait for the soldiers to come charging at us. But they don't. There follows no sound aside from the obvious struggle happening straight ahead of us. Then an uproar of yells behind us. I turn to look. The glowing swords begin swaggering forward from forty feet away. A confident laugh comes from one of the soldiers. Nine of them armed and full of strength versus three of us broken and battered and armed with nothing more than our valor. The beast one way, the soldiers the other. That is the choice that we now face.

Henri seems unfazed. He removes two more pebbles from his pocket and hands one to me.

'The last two,' he says, his voice shaky as though it requires a great effort just to speak.

I plop the new pebble into my mouth and bury it beneath my tongue despite a small bit of the first still remaining. Renewed strength rushes through me.

'What do you think?' he asks me.

We are surrounded. Henri and Bernie Kosar and I are the only three left. Six badly hurt and carried away by Sam. Mark just here but now nowhere to be found. And that leaves Sarah, who I pray is tucked away safely in the school that lies a tenth of a mile ahead of us. I take a deep breath and I accept the inevitable.

'I don't think it matters, Henri,' I say, and look at him. 'But the school is ahead of us, and that is where Sam will be shortly.'

What he does next catches me off guard: he smiles. He reaches his hand out and gives my shoulder a squeeze. His eyes are tired and red but in them I see relief, a sense of serenity as though he knows it's all about to end.

'We've done all we could. And what's done is done. But I'm damn proud of you,' he says. 'You did amazing today. I always knew you would. There was never a doubt in my mind.'

I drop my head. I don't want him to see me cry. I squeeze the dog. For the first time since I grabbed him he shows a slight sign of life, lifting his head just enough so that he can lick the side of my face. He passes one word to me and one word only, as if that is all his strength will allow. *Courage*, he says.

I lift my head. Henri steps forward and hugs me. I close my eyes and bury my face in his neck. He is still shaking, his body frail and weak beneath my grip. I'm sure mine is no stronger. *So this is it,* I think. With our heads held high we will walk across the field to whatever awaits there. At least there is dignity in that.

'You did damn good,' he says.

I open my eyes. From over his shoulder I see the soldiers are near, twenty feet away now. They have stopped walking. One of them is holding a dagger that pulsates silver and gray. The soldier tosses it in the air, catches it, and hurls it at Henri's back. I lift my hand and deflect it away and it misses by a foot. My strength leaves me almost immediately even though the pebble is only half dissolved.

Henri takes my free arm and drapes it over his shoulders and places his right arm around my waist. We stagger forward. The beast comes into view, looming just ahead in the center of the football field. The Mogadorians follow behind us. Perhaps they are curious to see the beast in action, to see the beast kill. Each step I take becomes more of an effort than the one that preceded it. My heart thuds in my chest. Death is forthcoming and of that I am terrified. But Henri is here. And so is Bernie Kosar. I'm happy not to have to face it alone. Several soldiers stand on the other side of the beast. Even if we could get past the beast, we would then have to walk straight into the soldiers, who stand with drawn swords.

We have no choice. We reach the field and I expect the beast to pounce at any moment. But nothing happens. When we are within fifteen feet of it we stop. We stand leaning against each other for support.

The beast is half the size of the other but still big enough to kill us all with no great effort of its own. Pale, almost translucent skin stretched over protruding ribs and knobby joints. Various pinkish scars down its arms and sides. White, sightless eyes. It shifts its weight and lowers itself, then swings its head low over the grass to smell what its eyes fail to see. It can sense us in front of it. It lets out a low groan. I feel none of the rage and malice that the other beasts radiated, no desire for blood and death. There is a sense of fear, a sense of sadness. I open myself to it. I see images of torture and starvation. I see the beast locked up for all its life here on Earth, a damp cave where little light reaches. Shivering through the night to stay warm, always cold and wet. I see the way the Mogadorians pit the beasts against one another, force them to fight in order to train, to toughen them and make them mean.

Henri lets go of me. I can't hold Bernie Kosar any longer. I gently place him in the grass at my feet. I haven't felt him move in minutes and I can't tell if he's still alive. I take one step forward and drop to my knees. The soldiers yell around us. I don't understand their language but I can tell by their tones that they are impatient. One swings his sword and a dagger just misses me, a flash of white that flutters and tears the front of my shirt. I stay on my knees and I look up at the beast hovering over me. Some weapon is fired but it sails over our heads. A warning shot, meant to move the beast to action. The beast quivers. A second dagger darts through the air and hits the beast below the elbow of its left arm. It lifts its head and roars in pain.

I am sorry, I try to tell it. *I am sorry for the life you've been forced to live. You've been wronged. No living creature deserves such treatment. You've been forced to endure hell, plucked from your own planet to fight a war that isn't yours. Beaten and tortured and starved. The blame for all the pain and agony you've experienced lies with them. You and I share a common bond. Both wronged by these monsters.*

I try with everything to pass along my own images, the things that I've seen and felt. The beast doesn't look away. My thoughts, on some level, are reaching it. I show it Lorien, the vast ocean and thick forests and verdant hills teeming with life and vitality. Animals drinking from the cold blue waters. A proud people content to pass the days in harmony. I show it the hell that followed, the slaying of men, women, and children. The Mogadorians. Cold-blooded murderers. Draconian killers destroying all that lies within their path due to their own recklessness and pathetic beliefs. Destroying even their own planet. Where does it end? I show it Sarah, show it every emotion that I've ever felt with her. Happiness and bliss, this is how I feel with her. And this is the pain I feel in having to leave her, all because of them. *Help me,* I say. *Help me end this death and slaughter. Let us fight together. I have so little left but if you stand with me, I'll stand with you.*

The beast lifts its head to the sky and it roars. A roar both long and deep. The Mogadorians can sense what is happening and have seen enough. Their weapons begin firing. I look over and one of the cannons is aimed right at me. It fires and the white death surges forth, but the beast drops its head in time and absorbs the shot instead. Its face twists in pain, its eyes squeeze tightly shut, but almost immediately they snap back open. This time I see the rage.

I fall face-first in the grass. I'm grazed by something but I don't see what it is. Henri cries out in pain behind me and he is flung thirty feet away, his body lying in the mud, face up, smoking. I have no idea what has hit him. Something big and deadly. Panic and fear hit me. *Not Henri,* I think. *Please not Henri.*

The beast throws a hard sweeping blow that takes out several of the soldiers and quiets many of their guns. Another roar. I look up and see the beast's eyes have turned red, ablaze with fury. Retribution. Mutiny. It looks my way once and swiftly rushes off to follow its captors. Guns blaze but many of them are quick to be silenced. *Kill them all,* I think. *Fight nobly and honorably and may you kill them all.*

I lift my head. Bernie Kosar is motionless in the grass. Henri, thirty feet away, is motionless as well. I place a hand in the grass and pull myself forward, across the field, inch by inch, dragging myself to Henri. When I get there his eyes are open slightly; each breath is a fight. Trails of blood run from his mouth and nose. I take him into my arms and I pull him into my lap. His body is frail and weak and I can feel him dying. His eyes flutter open. He looks at me and lifts his hand and presses it to the side of my face. The second he does I begin to cry.

'I'm here,' I say.

He tries to smile.

'I'm so sorry, Henri.' I say. 'I'm so sorry. We should have left when you wanted to.'

'Shh,' he says. 'It's not your fault.'

'I'm so sorry,' I say between sobs.

'You did great,' he says in a whisper. 'You did so great. I always knew you would.'

'We have to get you to the school,' I say. 'Sam could be there.'

'Listen to me, John. Everything,' he says. 'Everything you need to know, it's all in the Chest. The letter.'

'It's not over. We can still make it.'

I can feel him begin to go. I shake him. His eyes reluctantly reopen. A trail of blood runs from his mouth.

'Coming here, to Paradise, it wasn't by chance.' I don't know what he means. 'Read the letter.'

'Henri,' I say, and reach down and wipe the blood off his chin.

He looks me in the eye.

'You are Lorien's Legacy, John. You and the others. The only hope the planet has left. The secrets,' he says, and is gripped by a fit of coughs. More blood. His eyes close again. 'The Chest, John.'

I pull him more tightly to me, squeezing him. His body is going slack. Breaths so shallow that they are hardly breaths at all.

'We'll make it back together, Henri. Me and you, I promise,' I say, and close my eyes.

'Be strong,' he says, and is overtaken by slight coughs, though he tries to speak through them. 'This war . . . Can win . . . Find the others . . . Six . . . The power of . . .' he says, and trails off.

I try to stand with him in my arms but I have nothing left, hardly enough strength to even breathe. Off in the distance I hear the beast roar. Cannons are still being fired, the sounds and lights of which reach out over the stadium bleachers, but as each minute passes less and less of them are being fired until there is only one. I lower Henri in my arms. I place my hand to the side of his face and he opens his eyes and looks at me for what I know will be the final time. He takes a weak breath and exhales and then slowly closes his eyes.

'I wouldn't have missed a second of it, kiddo. Not for all of Lorien. Not for the whole damn world,' he says, and when that last word leaves his mouth I know that he is gone. I squeeze him in my arms, shaking, crying, despair and hopelessness taking hold. His hand drops lifelessly to the grass. I cup his head in my hand and hold it close to my chest, and I rock him back and forth and I cry like I've never cried before. The pendant around my neck glows blue, grows heavy for just a split second, and then dims to normal.

I sit in the grass and I hold Henri while the last cannon falls silent. The pain leaves my body and with the cold of the night I feel my own self begin to fade. The moon and the stars shine overhead. I hear a cackle of laughter carried on the wind. My ears attune to it. I turn my head. Through the dizziness and blurry vision I see a scout fifteen feet away from me. Long trench coat, hat pulled to its eyes. It drops the coat and takes off the hat to reveal a pale and hairless head. It reaches to the back of its belt and removes a bowie knife, the blade of which is no less than twelve inches long. I close my eyes. I don't care anymore. The scout's raspy breathing comes my way, ten feet, then five. And then the footsteps end. The scout grunts in pain, and begins gurgling.

I open my eyes, the scout so close that I can smell it. The bowie knife falls from its hand, and there in its chest, where I assume its heart must be, is the end of a butcher's knife. The knife is pulled free. The scout drops to its knees, falls to its side, and explodes into a puff of ash. Behind it, holding the knife in her shaky right hand, with tears in her eyes, stands Sarah. She drops the knife and rushes over to me, wrapping her arms around me with my arms around Henri. I hold Henri as my own head falls and the world dims away into nothingness. The aftermath of war, the school destroyed, the trees fallen and heaps of ash piled in the grass of the football field and I still hold Henri. And Sarah holds me.

34

Images flicker, each one bringing its own sorrow or its own smile. Sometimes both. At the very worst an impenetrable and sightless black and at best a happiness so bright that it hurts the eyes to see, coming and going on some unseen projector perpetually turned by an invisible hand. One, then another. The hollow click of the shutter. Now stop. Freeze this frame. Pluck it down and hold it close and be damned by what you see. Henri always said: the price of a memory is the memory of the sorrow it brings.

A warm summer day in the cool grass with the sun high in the cloudless sky. The air coming off the water, carrying the freshness of the sea. A man walks up to the house, briefcase in hand. A younger man, brown hair cut short, freshly shaven, dressed casually. A sense of nervousness by the way he switches his briefcase from one hand to the other and the thin layer of sweat glistening on his forehead. He knocks at the door. My grandfather answers, opens the door for the man to enter, then closes it behind him. I resume my romping in the yard. Hadley changing forms, flying, then dodging, then charging. Wrestling with one another and laughing until it hurts. The day passing as time only can under the reckless abandon of childhood's invincibility, of its innocence.

Fifteen minutes pass. Maybe less. At that age a day can last forever. The door opens and closes. I look up. My grandfather is standing with the man I had seen approach, both of them looking down at me.

‘There is somebody I would like you to meet,’ he says.

I stand from the grass and clap my hands together to knock away the dirt.

‘This is Brandon,’ my grandfather says. ‘He is your Cêpan. Do you know what that means?’

I shake my head. Brandon. That was his name. All these years and only now does it come back to me.

‘It means he’s going to be spending a lot of time with you from here on out. The two of you, it means you are connected. You are bound to one another. Do you understand?’

I nod and walk to the man and I offer him my hand as I have seen done many times by grown men before. The man smiles and drops to one knee. He takes my small hand in his right and he closes his fingers around it.

‘Pleased to meet you, sir,’ I say.

Bright, kind eyes full of life look into mine as though offering a promise, a bond, yet I’m too young to know what that promise or bond really means.

He nods and brings his left hand on top of his right, my tiny hand lost somewhere in the middle. He nods at me, still smiling.

‘My dear child,’ he says. ‘The pleasure is all mine.’

I am jolted awake. I lie on my back, my heart racing, breathing heavily as though I had been running. My eyes stay closed but I can tell the sun has just risen by the long shadows and the crispness of air in the room. Pain returns, my limbs still heavy. With the pain comes another pain, a pain far greater than any physical ailment I could ever be afflicted with: the memory of the hours before.

I take a deep breath and exhale. A single tear rolls down

the side of my face. I keep my eyes closed. An irrational hope that if I don't find the day then the day won't find me, that the things in the night will be nullified. My body shudders, a silent cry turning into a hard one. I shake my head and let it in. I know that Henri is dead and that all the hope in the world won't change it.

I feel movement beside me. I tense myself, try to remain motionless so as not to be detected. A hand reaches up and touches the side of my face. A delicate touch done with love. My eyes come open, adjusting to the postdawn light until the ceiling of a foreign room comes into focus. I have no idea where I am, nor how I could have gotten here. Sarah is sitting next to me. She brings her hand to the side of my face and traces my brow with her thumb. She leans down and kisses me, a soft lingering kiss that I wish I could bottle and save for all time. She pulls away and I take a deep breath and close my eyes and kiss her on the forehead.

'Where are we?' I ask.

'A hotel thirty miles from Paradise.'

'How did I get here?'

'Sam drove us,' she says.

'I mean from the school. What happened? I remember that you were with me last night, but I don't remember a thing after,' I say. 'It almost seems like a dream.'

'I waited on the field with you until Mark arrived and he carried you to Sam's truck. I couldn't stay hidden any longer. Being in the school without knowing what was happening out there was killing me. And I felt like I could help somehow.'

'You certainly helped,' I say. 'You saved my life.'

'I killed an alien,' she says, as though the fact still hasn't settled in.

She wraps her arms around me, her hand resting on the back of my head. I try to sit up. I make it halfway on my own and then Sarah helps me the rest of the way, pushing on my back but being careful not to touch the wound left by the knife. I swing my feet over the edge of the bed and reach down and feel the scars around my ankle, counting them with the tips of my fingers. Still only three, and in this way I know that Six has survived. I had already accepted the fate of the rest of my days being spent alone, an itinerant wanderer with no place to go. But I won't be alone. Six is still here, still with me, my tie to a past world.

'Is Six okay?'

'Yes,' she says. 'She's been stabbed and shot but she seems to be doing okay now. I don't think she would have survived had Sam not carried her to the truck.'

'Where is she?'

'In the room next door, with Sam and Mark.'

I stand. My muscles and joints ache in protest, everything stiff and sore. I am wearing a clean T-shirt, a pair of mesh shorts. My skin is fresh with the smell of soap. The cuts have been cleaned and bandaged, a few of them stitched.

'Did you do all of this?' I ask.

'Most of it. The stitches were hard. We only had the ones Henri put in your head to go on as an example. Sam helped with them.'

I look at Sarah sitting on the bed, her legs pulled underneath her. Something else catches my eye, a small mass that has shifted beneath the blanket at the foot of the bed. I tense, and immediately my mind returns to the weasels that sped across the gym. Sarah sees what I am looking at and smiles. She crawls to the bottom of the bed on her hands and knees.

'There's somebody here who wants to say hello,' she says, then takes the corner of the blanket and gently peels it back to reveal Bernie Kosar, sleeping away. A metal splint goes the length of his front leg, and his body is covered with cuts and gashes that, like mine, have been cleaned and are already beginning to heal. His eyes slowly open and adjust, eyes rimmed with red, full of exhaustion. He keeps his head on the bed but his tail gives a subtle wag, softly thumping against the mattress.

'Bernie,' I say, and drop to my knees before him. I place my hand softly on his head. I can't stop smiling and tears of joy surface. His small body is curled into a ball, head resting on his front paws, his eyes taking me in, battle scarred and wounded but still here to tell the tale.

'Bernie Kosar, you made it through. I owe my life to you,' I say, and kiss the top of his head.

Sarah runs her hand down the length of his back.

'I carried him to the truck while Mark carried you.'

'Mark. I'm sorry I ever doubted him,' I say.

She lifts one of Bernie Kosar's ears. He turns and sniffs at her hand and then licks it. 'So, is it true what Mark said, that Bernie Kosar grew to thirty feet tall and killed a beast almost double his size?'

I smile. 'A beast triple his size.'

Bernie Kosar looks at me. *Liar*, he says. I look down and wink at him. I stand back up and look at Sarah.

'All of this,' I say. 'All of this has happened so fast. How are you handling it?'

She nods. 'Handling what? The fact that I've fallen in love with an alien, which I only found out about three days ago, and then just happened to walk headlong into the middle of a war? Yeah, I'm handling that okay.'

I smile at her. 'You're an angel.'

'Nah,' she says. 'I'm just a girl crazy in love.'

She gets up from the bed and wraps her arms around me and we stand in the center of the room holding one another.

'You really have to leave, don't you?'

I nod.

She takes a deep breath and exhales shakily, willing herself not to cry. More tears in the past twenty-four hours than I have ever witnessed in all the years of my life.

'I don't know where you have to go or what you have to do, but I'll wait for you, John. Every bit of my heart belongs to you, whether you ask for it or not.'

I pull her to me. 'And mine belongs to you,' I say.

I walk across the room. Sitting on top of the desk are the Loric Chest, three packed bags, Henri's computer, and all the money from the last withdrawal he made at the bank. Sarah must have rescued the Chest from the home-ec room. I place my hand on it. All the secrets, Henri had said. All of them contained within this. In time I'll open it and discover them, but that time is certainly not now. And what did he mean about Paradise, that our coming wasn't by chance?

'Did you pack my bags?' I ask Sarah, who is standing behind me.

'Yes, and it was probably the hardest thing I ever had to do.'

I lift my bag from the table. Beneath it is a manila envelope carrying my name across the front of it.

'What is this?' I ask.

'I don't know. I found it in Henri's bedroom. We went there after leaving the school and tried to grab everything we could, then we came here.'

I open the envelope and pull out the contents. All of the documents Henri had created for me: birth certificates, social security cards, visas, and so on. I count through them. Seventeen different identities, seventeen different ages. On the very front sheet is a sticky note in Henri's writing. It reads, 'Just in case.' After the last sheet is another sealed envelope, across which Henri has written my name. A letter, the one he must have been talking about just before he died. I don't have the heart to read it now.

I look out the window of the hotel room. A light snow sifts down from the low, gray clouds overhead. The ground is too warm for any of it to stick. Sarah's car and Sam's father's blue truck are parked beside each other in the lot. As I stand looking down at them a knock sounds at the door. Sarah opens it and Sam and Mark walk into the room; Six limps behind them. Sam hugs me, says he's sorry.

'Thank you,' I say.

'How do you feel?' Six asks. She is no longer wearing the suit but is now dressed in the pair of jeans she wore when I first saw her, and one of Henri's sweatshirts.

I shrug. 'I'm okay. Sore and stiff. My body feels heavy.'

'The heaviness is from the dagger. It'll eventually wear off, though.'

'How badly were you stabbed?' I ask.

She lifts her shirt and shows me the gash in her side, then a different one on her back. All told, she was stabbed three times last night, and that's not to mention the various cuts along the rest of her body, or the shot that left a deep gash in her right thigh, now wrapped tightly with gauze and tape, the reason for her limp. She tells me that by the time we made it back it was too late to be healed by the stone. It amazes me that she is even alive.

Sam and Mark are wearing the same clothes as the day before, both filthy and covered in mud and dirt with smatterings of blood mixed in. Both with heavy eyes as though they've yet to sleep. Mark stands behind Sam, shifting his weight uncomfortably.

'Sam, I always knew you were a wrecking machine,' I say.

He laughs uncertainly. 'Are you okay?'

'Yeah, I'm fine,' I say. 'How about you?'

'Doing okay.'

I look over his shoulder at Mark.

'Sarah told me you carried me off the field last night.'

Mark shrugs. 'I was happy to help.'

'You saved my life, Mark.'

He looks me in the eye. 'I think every one of us saved somebody at some point last night. Hell, Six saved me on three separate occasions. And you saved my two dogs on Saturday. I say we're even.'

I somehow manage to smile. 'Fair enough,' I say. 'I'm just happy to find out you're not the dick I thought you were.'

He half grins. 'Let's just say that had I known you were an alien and could kick my ass at will, I might have been a little nicer to you that first day.'

Six walks across the room and looks at my bags atop the table.

'We really should get going,' she says, and then looks at me with implicit concern, her face softening. 'There's really only one thing left undone. We weren't sure what you wanted us to do.'

I nod. I don't need to ask to know what she is talking about. I look at Sarah. It's going to happen much sooner than I thought. My stomach turns. I feel as though I could vomit. Sarah reaches out and takes hold of my hand.

'Where is he?'

The ground is damp with the melting snow. I hold Sarah's hand in mine and we pass through the woods in silence, a mile away from the hotel. Sam and Mark walk in the lead, following the muddy footprints they created a few hours before. Up ahead I see a slight clearing, in the center of which Henri's body has been laid out on a slab of wood. He is wrapped in the gray blanket pulled from his bed. I walk to him. Sarah follows and places a hand on my shoulder. The others stand behind me. I pull the blanket down to see him. His eyes are closed, his face is ashen gray, and his lips are blue from the cold. I kiss his forehead.

'What do you want to do, John?' Six asks. 'We can bury him if you want. We can also cremate him.'

'How can we cremate him?'

'I can create a fire.'

'I thought you could only control the weather.'

'Not the weather. The elements.'

I look up at her soft face, concern written upon it but also the stress of time at our having to leave before reinforcements arrive. I don't answer. I look away and squeeze Henri a final time with my face close to his and I lose myself to grief.

'I'm so sorry, Henri,' I whisper in his ear. I close my eyes. 'I love you. I wouldn't have missed a second of it, either. Not for anything,' I whisper. 'I'm going to take you back yet. Somehow I am going to get you back to Lorien. We always joked about it but you were my father, the best father I could have ever asked for. I'll never forget you, not for a minute for as long as I live. I love you, Henri. I always did.'

I let go of him, pull the blanket back over his face, and lay him gently on the wooden slab. I stand and hug Sarah. She holds me until I stop crying. I wipe the tears away with the back of my hand and I nod at Six.

Sam helps me clear away the sticks and leaves and then we lay Henri's body on the ground so as not to dilute his ash with anything else. Sam lights an edge of the blanket and Six makes the fire rage from there. We watch it burn, not a dry eye among us. Even Mark cries. Nobody says a word. When the flames end I gather the ashes in a coffee can that Mark was astute enough to bring from the hotel. I'll get something better the second we stop. When we walk back I put the can on the dashboard of Sam's dad's truck. I feel comforted to know that Henri will still travel with us, that he'll look out over the roads while we leave another town as the two of us have done so many times before.

We load our belongings into the back of the truck. Along with Six's things and mine, Sam has also loaded in two bags of his own. At first I'm confused, but then I realize that between him and Six some agreement has been made that Sam will come with us. And I'm happy for that. Sarah and I walk back into the hotel room. The second the door closes she takes my hand and turns me towards her.

'My heart is breaking,' she says. 'I want to be strong for you right now but the thought of you leaving is killing me inside.'

I kiss her on the head.

'My heart is broken already,' I say. 'The second I get settled I'll write. And I'll do my best to call when I know it is safe.'

Six pokes her head in the doorway.

‘We really have to go,’ she says.

I nod. She closes the door. Sarah lifts her face to mine and we kiss standing there in the hotel room. The thought of the Mogadorians returning before we’ve left, and thus putting her in danger yet again, is the only source of strength I can find. Else I might collapse. Else I might stay forever.

Bernie Kosar still lies waiting at the foot of the bed. He wags his tail when I carefully take him into my arms and carry him outside to the truck. Six starts the truck and lets it idle. I turn and look up at the hotel and am saddened that it’s not the house, and that I know I’ll never see it again. Its peeling wooden clapboards, broken windows, black shingles warped from excessive sun exposure and rain. It looks like Paradise, I once told Henri. But that will no longer hold true. Paradise lost.

I turn and nod to Six. She climbs into the truck, closes the door, and waits.

Sam and Mark shake hands but I don’t hear what they say to each other. Sam climbs into the truck and waits with Six. I shake Mark’s hand.

‘I owe you more than I’ll ever be able to repay,’ I say to Mark.

‘You don’t owe me a thing,’ Mark says.

‘Not true,’ I say. ‘Someday.’

I look away. I can feel myself wanting to collapse under the sadness of leaving. My resolve is being held by a tattered string ready to snap.

I nod. ‘I’ll see you again someday.’

‘Be safe out there.’

I take Sarah into my arms and squeeze her tightly, never wanting to let go.

'I'll come back to you,' I say. 'I promise you, if it's the last thing I do I'll come back to you.'

Her face is buried in my neck. She nods.

'I'll count the minutes until you do,' she says.

One last kiss. I set her on the ground and I open the door to the truck. My eyes never leave hers. She covers her mouth and her nose with her hands pressed together, neither one of us able to look away. I close the door. Six puts the truck in reverse and pulls out of the parking lot, comes to a stop, puts it in gear. Mark and Sarah walk to the end of the lot to watch us on our way, tears streaming down both sides of Sarah's face. I turn in my seat and watch from the rear window. I lift my hand to wave and Mark waves back but Sarah just watches. I watch her for as long as I can, growing smaller, one indistinct blur fading in the distance. The truck slows and turns and both of them vanish from sight. I turn back around and I watch the fields pass and I close my eyes and I picture Sarah's face and I smile. *We'll be together yet,* I tell her. *And until that day you'll be in my heart and my every thought.*

Bernie Kosar lifts his head and rests it in my lap and I place my hand upon his back. The truck bounces down the road, driving south. The four of us, together, heading for the next town. Wherever that might be.

The battle continues in the second thrilling instalment of The Lorien Legacies, *The Power of Six*. Read on to find out what happens next . . .

My name is Marina, as of the sea, but I wasn't called that until much later. In the beginning I was known merely as Seven, one of the nine surviving Garde from the planet Lorien, the fate of which was, and still is, left in our hands. Those of us who aren't lost. Those of us still alive.

I was six when we landed. When the ship jolted to a halt on Earth, even at my young age I sensed how much was at stake for us – nine Cêpan, nine Garde – and that our only chance waited for us here. We had entered the planet's atmosphere in the midst of a storm of our own creation, and as our feet found Earth for the very first time, I remember the wisps of steam that rolled off the ship and the goose bumps that covered my arms. I hadn't felt the wind in a year and it was freezing outside. Somebody was there waiting for us. I don't know who he was, only that he handed each Cêpan two sets of clothes and a large envelope. I still don't know what was in it.

As a group we huddled together, knowing we might never see one another again. Words were said, hugs were given, and then we split up, as we knew we must, walking in pairs in nine different directions. I kept peering over my shoulder as the others receded in the distance until, very slowly, one by one, they all disappeared. And then it was just Adelina and I, trudging alone in a world we knew next to nothing about. I realize now just how scared Adelina must have been.

I remember our aimless march that went on for days, maybe weeks, then Adelina rushing us aboard a ship headed to some unknown destination. I remember two or three different trains after that. Adelina and I kept to ourselves, huddled against one another in obscure corners, away from whoever might be around. We hiked from town to town, over mountains and across fields, knocking on doors that were quickly slammed in our faces. We were hungry, tired, and scared. I remember sitting on a sidewalk begging for change. I remember crying instead of sleeping. I'm certain that Adelina gave away some of our precious gems from Lorien for nothing more than warm meals, so great was our need. Perhaps she gave them all away. And then we found this place in Spain.

A stern-looking woman I would come to know as Sister Lucia answered the heavy oak door. She squinted at Adelina, her gaze moving from head to toe, surely taking in her desperation, the way her shoulders drooped.

'Do you believe in the word of God?' the woman asked in Spanish, pursing her lips and narrowing her eyes in scrutiny.

'The word of God is my vow,' Adelina replied with a solemn nod. I don't know how she knew this response, perhaps she learned it when we stayed in a church basement weeks ago, but it was the right one. Sister Lucia opened the door.

We've been here ever since, eleven years in this stone cathedral with its musty rooms, drafty hallways, and hard floors like slabs of ice. Aside from the few visitors, the internet is my only source to the world outside our small town, and I search it constantly, looking for some indication that the others are out there, that they're searching, maybe fighting. Some sign that I'm not alone, because at this point I can't say that Adelina still believes, that she's still with me. Her attitude changed somewhere over the mountains. Maybe it was with the slam of one of the doors that shut a starving woman and her child out in the cold for another night. Whatever it was, Adelina seems to have lost the urgency of staying on the move, and her faith in the resurgence of Lorien seems to have been replaced by the faith shared by the convent's Sisters. I remember a distinct shift in Adelina's eyes, her sudden speeches on the need for guidance and structure if we were to survive.

Not mine. In India, a year and a half ago, four different people witnessed a boy move objects with his mind. Not once, but twice. While the significance behind the event was small at first, the boy's abrupt disappearance shortly thereafter created much buzz in the region, and a hunt for him began. As far as I know, he hasn't been found.

A few months ago there was news of a girl in Argentina who, in the wake of an earthquake, lifted a five-ton slab of concrete to save a man trapped beneath it, and when news of this heroic act spread, she disappeared. Like the boy in India, she's still missing.

And then there's the father/son duo making all the news now in America, in Ohio, who the police are hunting after the two allegedly demolished an entire school by themselves, killing five people in the process. They left no trace behind other than mysterious heaps of ash. The authorities have no leads.

'It looks like a battle took place here. I don't know how else to explain it,' the head investigator was quoted. 'But make no mistake, we will get to the bottom of this, and we will find Henri Smith and his son, John. You have my word on that.'

Perhaps John Smith, if that's his real name, is merely a boy with a grudge who was pushed too far. But I don't think that's the case. My heart races whenever his picture appears on my screen. My breathing becomes labored and I'm gripped with a profound desperation that I can't quite explain. I can feel it in my bones that he is one of us. And I know, somehow, that I must find him.

I perch my arms on the cold windowsill and watch the snowflakes fall from the dark sky and settle on the side of the mountain, which is dotted with pine, cork-oak, and beech trees, with patches of craggy rock mixed throughout. The snow hasn't let up all day, and they say it will continue through the night. I can barely see beyond the edge of town to the north – the world lost in a white haze. During the day, when the sky is clear, it's possible to see the watery blue smudge of the Bay of Biscay. But not in this weather, and I can't help but wonder what might lurk in all that white beyond my line of sight.

I look behind me. In the high-ceilinged and drafty room, there are two computers. To use one we must add our name to a list and wait our turn. At night, there is a ten-minute time limit if somebody is waiting, twenty minutes if there isn't. The two girls using them now have been on for a half hour each and my patience is thin. I haven't checked the news since this morning when I snuck in before breakfast. At that time nothing new about John Smith had been reported, but I'm almost shaking in anticipation over what might have sprung up since then. Some new discovery has been uncovered each day since the story first broke.

Santa Teresa is a convent that doubles as an orphanage for girls. Though I'm told it was a once-respected orphanage, it has since fallen into obscurity and few girls come anymore. Even fewer leave. I'm now the oldest out of thirty-seven, a distinction I've held for six months after the last girl who turned eighteen left. At eighteen we must all make the choice to strike out on our own or to forge a life within the church. Of all who've reached eighteen, not a single girl has stayed. I can't blame them. The birthday Adelina and I created for me when we arrived, when I will turn eighteen, is less than five months away. Like the others, I have every intention to leave this prison behind, whether or not Adelina comes with me. And it's hard to imagine she will.

The cathedral itself was built entirely of stone in 1510, and is much too large for the small number who live here. Most of the rooms stand empty, and those that aren't are imbued with a damp, earthy feel and our voices echo to the ceiling and back. The cathedral rests atop the highest hill overlooking the village that shares the same name, nestled deep within the Picos de Europa Mountains of northern Spain. The village, like the convent, is made of rock; with many structures built straight into the mountainside. Walking down the town's main road, Calle Principal, it's impossible not to be inundated by the disrepair. It's as though this place was forgotten by time and the passing centuries having turned most everything to shades of mossy green and brown, while the pervasive smell of mildew hangs in the air.

It's been five years since I started begging Adelina to leave, to keep moving like we were instructed to. 'I'm going to be getting my Legacies soon and I don't want to discover them here, with all of these girls and nuns around,' I said. She refused, quoting La Biblia Reina Valera that we must stand still for salvation. I've begged every year since, and every year she looks at me with blank eyes and talks me down with a different religious quote. But I know my salvation does not lie here.

Looking south now, past the church gates and down the gently sloping hill, I can see the faint dimness of the town lights. In the midst of this blizzard, they look like floating halos. Though I can't hear the music from either of the two cantinas, I'm sure both of them are packed. Aside from those, there is a restaurant, a café, a market, a bodega, and various vendors that line Calle Principal most mornings and afternoons. Towards the bottom of the hill, on the southern edge of town, is the brick school we all attend.

My head snaps around when the bell dings: prayers are five minutes away, followed directly by bed. Panic sweeps through me. I have to know if anything new has been reported. Perhaps John's been caught. Perhaps the police have found something else at the demolished school, something originally overlooked. Even if there's nothing new at all, I have to know. I'll never get to sleep otherwise.

I fix a hard stare on Gabriela García – Gabby for short – who scans photos of celebrities. Gabby's sixteen and very pretty with long dark hair and brown eyes, and she always dresses slutty when she's outside the convent, wearing tight shirts that show off her pierced navel. Every morning she dresses in loose, baggy clothes, but the second we're out of sight of the Sisters she removes them, revealing a tight, skimpy outfit underneath. Then she spends the rest of the walk to school applying makeup and redoing her hair. It's the same with her four friends, three of whom also live here. And when the day ends they wipe their faces clean on the walk back, and redress in their original clothes.

'What?' Gabby asks in a snotty voice, glaring at me. 'I'm writing an email.'

'I've been waiting longer than ten minutes,' I say. 'And

you're not writing an email. You're looking at guys with their shirts off.'

'So what? Are you gonna tell on me, tattle tale?' she asks mockingly, as though talking to a child.

The girl beside her, whose name is Hilda, but who most kids in school call La Gorda, 'the fat one,' (behind her back, never to her face) laughs.

They're an inseparable pair, Gabby and La Gorda. I bite my tongue and turn back to the window, folding my arms across my chest. They go back to typing, giggling and whispering to one another. I'm seething inside, partly because I need to get on the computer, and partly because I never know how to respond when Gabby mocks me. There are four minutes left. My impatience segues to full on desperation. There could be news right now – breaking news! – but I have no way of knowing because these selfish jerks won't give up one of the computers!

Three minutes left. I'm nearly shaking with anger. And then an idea pops into my head, and a grin plays across my lips. It's risky, but worth it if it works.

I pivot just enough to see Gabby's chair in my periphery. I take a deep breath and, focusing all my energy on her chair, use my telekinesis to jerk it to the left. Then I quickly thrust it right so hard it nearly topples over. Gabby jumps up and yelps. I look at her in mock surprise.

'What?' La Gorda asks.

'I don't know, it felt like somebody just kicked my chair or something. Did you feel anything?'

'No,' La Gorda says, and as soon as the word is uttered I move her chair a few centimeters backwards, then jerk it to the right, all while remaining at my spot by the window. Both of the girls scream this time. I thrust Gabby's chair, then

La Gorda's again, and without giving their computer screens a second glance, they flee the room, screaming as they go.

'Yes!' I say, rushing to the computer Gabby was using and quickly typing the web address of the news site I've deemed most reliable. Then I wait impatiently for the page to load. The old computers combined with the slow internet here are the bane of my existence.

The browser goes white, and line by line the page forms. When a quarter of it has loaded the final bell rings. One minute until prayers. I'm inclined to ignore the bell, even at the risk of being punished. At this point I don't really care. 'Five more months,' I whisper to myself.

Half of the page is now up, revealing the top half of John Smith's face, his upturned eyes, which are dark and confident, though within them there's a sense of discomfort that seems almost out of place. I lean on the edge of my seat, waiting, the excitement bubbling up inside me, causing my hands to tremble.

'Come on,' I say to the screen, trying in vain to hurry it. 'Come on come on come on.'

'Marina!' a voice barks from the open doorway. I jerk around and see Sister Dora, a portly woman who's the head cook in the kitchen, staring daggers at me. This is nothing new. She stares daggers at everyone who walks through the lunch line holding a tray, as though our needing sustenance is a personal affront towards her. She presses her lips together in a perfect straight line, then narrows her eyes. 'Come! Now! And I mean *right* now!'

I sigh, knowing I have no choice but to go; the punishment for insubordination is far more severe than truancy. I clear the browser's history and close it, then follow Sister Dora down the dark hallway. There was something new on that screen, I just know it. Why else would John's face have taken up the entire page? A week and a half is a long enough period for any news to turn stale, so for him to command so much of the screen means there's some significant piece of information.

We walk to Santa Teresa's nave, which is huge, with towering pillars leading to a high, vaulted ceiling and stained glass windows lining the walls. Wooden pews run the length of the open room and can seat nearly three hundred people. Sister Dora and I are the last to enter. I sit alone in one of the center pews. Sister Lucia, who opened the door to Adelina and me when we first arrived, and who is eighty-seven years old now and still runs the convent, stands at the pulpit and closes her eyes, lowers her head and presses her hands together in front of her. Everyone else does the same.

'*Padre divino*,' the prayer begins in somber unison. '*Que nos bendiga y nos proteje en su amor . . .*'

I tune it out and look at the back of the heads before me, all of which are bowed in concentration. Or just bowed. My eyes find Adelina, sitting in the very first row six pews in front of me and slightly to the right. She is on her knees, deeply meditative, her brown hair pulled into a tight braid that falls to the middle of her back. She doesn't look up once, doesn't try to find me at the back of the room like she used to during our first few years here, our eyes always meeting, a covert smile on each of our faces, acknowledging our shared secret that nobody else knew. We still share that secret, but somewhere along the way Adelina has stopped acknowledging it. Somewhere along the way the plan to bide our time until we felt strong enough and safe enough to leave has been replaced with Adelina's desire – or fear – to simply stay.

Before the news of John Smith, which I told Adelina

about when it broke, it had been months since we last talked about our mission. In September I showed her my third scar, the third warning that said another Garde has died and that she and I are one step closer to being hunted and killed by the Mogadorians, and she acted like it didn't exist. Like it didn't mean what we both know it means. Upon hearing the news about John, she merely rolled her eyes and told me to stop believing in fairy tales. She won't even look at the picture of John I had printed out for her.

'En el nombre del Padre, y del hijo, y del espíritu santo. Amén,' they say, and everyone in the room does the sign of the cross in harmony with this last sentence, myself included to keep up appearances: forehead, navel, left shoulder, right shoulder.

I had been asleep, dreaming of running down a mountain with my arms out at my sides as if I was about to take flight, when I was awoken by the pain and glow of the third scar wrapping itself around my lower leg. The light woke several girls in the room, but thankfully not the attending Sister. The girls thought I had a flashlight and a magazine under the covers and that I was breaking the rules of curfew. On the bed next to mine, Elena, a quiet sixteen-year-old with jet-black hair she often sticks in her mouth when speaking, threw a pillow at me. My flesh began to bubble and the pain was so intense I had to bite on the edge of my blanket to remain quiet. Still, I couldn't help but cry in silence because somewhere Number Three had lost his or her life. There were six of us left now.

Tonight I file out of the nave with the rest of the girls and head to our sleeping quarters, filled with creaky twin beds evenly spaced apart, but in my mind I'm hatching a plan. To compensate for the hard beds and the concretey chill of every room, the linens are soft and the blankets heavy, the only real luxury we're afforded. My bed is in the back corner, furthest from the door, which is the most sought-after spot; it's the quietest, and it took me a long time to get it, moving one bed closer as each girl left.

The lights are shut off once everyone is settled in. I lie on my back and stare at the faint, jagged outline of the high ceiling. An occasional whisper breaks the silence, followed immediately by the attending Sister shushing whomever it came from. I keep my eyes open, waiting impatiently for everyone to fall asleep. After a half hour the whispers fade, replaced by the soft sounds of sleep, but I don't dare risk it yet. Too soon. Another fifteen minutes and still no sounds. Then I can't stand it any longer.

I hold my breath and inch my legs over the edge of the bed, listening to the rhythm of Elena beside me. My feet find the icy floor and they turn cold instantly. I stand slowly to keep the bed from creaking and then tiptoe across the room and towards the door, taking my time, being careful not to bump any of the others. I reach the open doorway and rush out into the hall and down to the computer room. I pull out the chair and push the computer's power button. It springs to life. The fan whirs as the computer loads and I hope no one else hears it.

I fidget waiting for the computer to boot and keep peering towards the hallway to see if anyone has followed. I'm finally able to type in the web address. The screen goes white, then two pictures take shape in the center of the page, surrounded by text with a top headline in bold black letters too blurry to read. Two images now – I wonder what changed since I tried to check earlier. And then, at last, they come into focus:

INTERNATIONAL TERRORISTS?

John Smith, with his square jaw, shaggy dark blond hair, and his blue eyes, fills the left side of the screen, while his father – or more likely Cêpan – Henri takes up the right. What's there isn't a photo but a black-and-white artist's sketch done in pencil. I skim the details I already know – demolished school, five deaths, abrupt disappearance – and then come to the breaking news only now being reported:

In a bizarre twist, FBI investigators today uncovered what is believed to be the tools of a professional counterfeiter. Several machines typically used for the creation of fictitious documents were found in the Paradise, Ohio, home rented by Henri and John Smith, in a secret hatch beneath the floorboards of the master bedroom, leading investigators to consider possible links to terrorism. Creating local uproar within the Paradise community, Henri and John Smith are now considered a threat to national security, fugitives of the utmost importance, and investigators are encouraging any and all information that might lead to their whereabouts be directed to police.

I scroll back to John's image and when my gaze meets his, my hands begin to shake. His eyes – even in this sketch there's something familiar about them. How could I know them if not from the yearlong journey that brought us here? Nobody can convince me now that he isn't one of the six remaining Garde, still alive in this foreign world.

I lean back and blow my bangs out of my eyes, wishing I could go in search of John myself. Of course Henri and John Smith are able to elude police; they've kept hidden for eleven years now, just as Adelina and I have. But how can I possibly hope to be the one to find him when the whole world is looking? How can any of us hope to come together?

The eyes of the Mogadorians are everywhere. I have no idea how One or Three were found, but I know for sure they located Two because of a blog post he or she wrote. I had found it, and then I sat there for fifteen minutes thinking how best to respond without giving myself away. Though the message itself was obscure, it was very obvious to those of us looking: *'Nine, now eight. Are the rest of you out there?'* It was posted by an account called 'Two.' My fingers found the keyboard and I typed a quick response, and just before I hit the 'post' button, the page refreshed – and somebody else responded first.

'We are here,' it read.

My mouth dropped open and I stared in utter shock. Hope flooded through me from these two brief messages, but just as my fingers typed a different reply, a bright glow appeared at my feet and the sizzling sound of burning flesh reached my ears, followed closely by a searing pain so great that I dropped to the floor and writhed in agony, screaming at the top of my lungs for Adelina, holding my hands over my ankle so no one else would see. When Adelina arrived and realized what was happening, I pointed at the screen, but it was blank; both posts had been deleted. To this day I don't know who wrote that reply.

I look away from John Smith's familiar eyes alight on the screen. Beside the computer sits a small flower that's been forgotten. It's wilted and tired, shrunken down to half its normal height, a brown, crispy tinge at the edge of its leaves. Several petals have dropped, now dry and crinkled on the desk around the pot. I peer over my shoulder, listening for footsteps or voices, but hear only silence. The flower isn't dead yet, but it's not far off. I lean forward and cup my hands around it, move my face near enough so that my lips brush against the edge of its leaves, and then I blow hot air over it. An icy feeling shoots down my spine and in response life bursts through the small flower. It springs upward and a verdant green floods the leaves and stalk and new petals bloom, colorless at first, then turning a brilliant purple. A mischievous grin sprouts on my face, and I can't help but think of how the Sisters would react if they were to see such a thing. But I'll never let them see it. It would be misinterpreted, and I don't want to be cast out into the cold. I'm not ready for that just yet. Soon I will be, but not just yet.

I turn off the computer, and hurry back to bed while thoughts of John Smith, somewhere out there swim in my head.

Be safe and stay hidden, I think. *We'll find each other yet.*

PENGUIN BOOKS

Published by the Penguin Group
Penguin Books Ltd, 80 Strand, London WC2R 0RL, England
Penguin Group (USA) Inc., 375 Hudson Street, New York, New York 10014, USA
Penguin Group (Canada), 90 Eglinton Avenue East, Suite 700, Toronto, Ontario, Canada M4P 2Y3
(a division of Pearson Penguin Canada Inc.)
Penguin Ireland, 25 St Stephen's Green, Dublin 2, Ireland (a division of Penguin Books Ltd)
Penguin Group (Australia), 707 Collins Street, Melbourne, Victoria 3008, Australia
(a division of Pearson Australia Group Pty Ltd)
Penguin Books India Pvt Ltd, 11 Community Centre, Panchsheel Park, New Delhi – 110 017, India
Penguin Group (NZ), 67 Apollo Drive, Rosedale, Auckland 0632, New Zealand
(a division of Pearson New Zealand Ltd)
Penguin Books (South Africa) (Pty) Ltd, Block D, Rosebank Office Park,
181 Jan Smuts Avenue, Parktown North, Gauteng 2193, South Africa

Penguin Books Ltd, Registered Offices: 80 Strand, London WC2R 0RL, England

www.penguin.com

First published in the United States of America by HarperCollins Publishers 2011
First published in Great Britain by Michael Joseph and Razorbill 2011
Published in Penguin Books 2012

020

Set in 12.90/16.02 pt Garamond MT Std
Typeset by Jouve (UK), Milton Keynes
Printed in England by Clays Ltd, St Ives plc

ISBN: 978-0-141-04785-0

www.greenpenguin.co.uk

MIX
Paper from
responsible sources
FSC www.fsc.org
FSC™ C018179

Penguin Books is committed to a sustainable
future for our business, our readers and our planet.
This book is made from Forest Stewardship
Council™ certified paper.

I

My name is Marina, as of the sea, but I wasn't called that until much later. In the beginning I was known merely as Seven, one of the nine surviving Garde from the planet Lorien, the fate of which was, and still is, left in our hands. Those of us who aren't lost. Those of us still alive.

I was six when we landed. When the ship jolted to a halt on Earth, even at my young age I sensed how much was at stake for us – nine Cêpan, nine Garde – and that our only chance waited for us here. We had entered the planet's atmosphere in the midst of a storm of our own creation, and as our feet found Earth for the very first time, I remember the wisps of steam that rolled off the ship and the goose bumps that covered my arms. I hadn't felt the wind in a year, and it was freezing outside. Somebody was there waiting for us. I don't know who he was, only that he handed each Cêpan two sets of clothes and a large envelope. I still don't know what was in it.

As a group we huddled together, knowing we might never see one another again. Words were spoken, hugs were given, and then we split up, as we knew we must, walking in pairs in nine different directions. I kept

peering over my shoulder as the others receded in the distance until, very slowly, one by one, they all disappeared. And then it was just Adelina and me, alone. I realize now just how scared Adelina must have been.

I remember boarding a ship headed to some unknown destination. I remember two or three different trains after that. Adelina and I kept to ourselves, huddled against each other in obscure corners, away from whoever might be around. We hiked from town to town, over mountains and across fields, knocking on doors that were quickly slammed in our faces. We were hungry, tired, and scared. I remember sitting on a sidewalk begging for change. I remember crying instead of sleeping. I'm certain that Adelina gave away some of our precious gems from Lorien for nothing more than warm meals, so great was our need. Perhaps she gave them all away. And then we found this place in Spain.

A stern-looking woman I would come to know as Sister Lucia answered the heavy oak door. She squinted at Adelina, taking in her desperation, the way her shoulders drooped.

'Do you believe in the word of God?' the woman asked in Spanish, pursing her lips and narrowing her eyes in scrutiny.

'The word of God is my vow,' Adelina replied with a solemn nod. I don't know how she knew this response – perhaps she learned it when we stayed in a

church basement weeks before – but it was the right one. Sister Lucia opened the door.

We've been here ever since, eleven years in this stone convent with its musty rooms, drafty hallways, and hard floors like slabs of ice. Aside from the few visitors, the internet is my only source to the world outside our small town; and I search it constantly, looking for some indication that the others are out there, that they're searching, maybe fighting. Some sign that I'm not alone, because at this point I can't say that Adelina still believes, that she's still with me. Her attitude changed somewhere over the mountains. Maybe it was with the slam of one of the doors that shut a starving woman and her child out in the cold for another night. Whatever it was, Adelina seems to have lost the urgency of staying on the move, and her faith in the resurgence of Lorien seems to have been replaced by the faith shared by the convent's Sisters. I remember a distinct shift in Adelina's eyes, her sudden speeches on the need for guidance and structure if we were to survive.

My faith in Lorien remains intact. In India, a year and a half ago, four different people witnessed a boy move objects with his mind. While the significance behind the event was small at first, the boy's abrupt disappearance shortly thereafter created much buzz in the region, and a hunt for him began. As far as I know, he hasn't been found.

A few months ago there was news of a girl in

Argentina who, in the wake of an earthquake, lifted a five-ton slab of concrete to save a man trapped beneath it; and when news of this heroic act spread, she disappeared. Like the boy in India, she's still missing.

And then there's the father-son duo making all the news now in America, in Ohio, who the police are hunting after the two allegedly demolished an entire school by themselves, killing five people in the process. They left no trace behind other than mysterious heaps of ash.

'It looks like a battle took place here. I don't know how else to explain it,' the head investigator was quoted as saying. 'But make no mistake, we will get to the bottom of this, and we will find Henri Smith and his son, John.'

Perhaps John Smith, if that's his real name, is merely a boy with a grudge who was pushed too far. But I don't think that's the case. My heart races whenever his picture appears on my screen. I'm gripped with a profound desperation that I can't quite explain. I can feel it in my bones that he's one of us. And I know, somehow, that I must find him.

2

I perch my arms on the cold windowsill and watch the snowflakes fall from the dark sky and settle on the side of the mountain, which is dotted with pine, cork oak, and beech trees, with patches of craggy rock mixed throughout. The snow hasn't let up all day, and they say it will continue through the night. I can barely see beyond the edge of town to the north – the world lost in a white haze. During the day, when the sky is clear, it's possible to see the watery blue smudge of the Bay of Biscay. But not in this weather, and I can't help but wonder what might lurk in all that white beyond my line of sight.

I look behind me. In the high-ceilinged, drafty room, there are two computers. To use one we must add our name to a list and wait our turn. At night there's a ten-minute time limit if somebody is waiting, twenty minutes if there isn't. The two girls using them now have been on for a half hour each, and my patience is thin. I haven't checked the news since this morning when I snuck in before breakfast. At that time nothing new about John Smith had been reported, but I'm almost shaking in anticipation over what might have sprung up since then. Some new discovery has been uncovered each day since the story first broke.

Santa Teresa is a convent that doubles as an orphanage for girls. I'm now the oldest out of thirty-seven, a distinction I've held for six months, after the last girl who turned eighteen left. At eighteen we must all make the choice to strike out on our own or to forge a life within the Church. The birthday Adelina and I created for me when we arrived is less than five months away, and that's when I'll turn eighteen, too. Of all who've reached eighteen, not a single girl has stayed. I can't blame them. Like the others, I have every intention of leaving this prison behind, whether or not Adelina comes with me. And it's hard to imagine she will.

The convent itself was built entirely of stone in 1510 and is much too large for the small number of us who live here. Most of the rooms stand empty; and those that aren't are imbued with a damp, earthy feel, and our voices echo to the ceiling and back. The convent rests atop the highest hill overlooking the village that shares the same name, nestled deep within the Picos de Europa Mountains of northern Spain. The village, like the convent, is made of rock, with many structures built straight into the mountainside. Walking down the town's main road, Calle Principal, it's impossible not to be inundated by the disrepair. It's as though this place was forgotten by time, and the passing centuries have turned most everything to shades of mossy green and brown, while the pervasive smell of mildew hangs in the air.

It's been five years since I started begging Adelina

to leave, to keep moving like we were instructed to. 'I'm going to be getting my Legacies soon, and I don't want to discover them here, with all of these girls and nuns around,' I'd said. She had refused, quoting La Biblia Reina Valera that we must stand still for salvation. I've begged every year since, and every year she looks at me with blank eyes and talks me down with a different religious quote. But I know my salvation does not lie here.

Past the church gates and down the gently sloping hill, I can see the faint dimness of the town lights. In the midst of this blizzard, they look like floating halos. Though I can't hear the music from either of the two cantinas, I'm sure both of them are packed. Aside from those, there is a restaurant, a café, a market, a bodega, and various vendors that line Calle Principal most mornings and afternoons. Towards the bottom of the hill, on the southern edge of town, is the brick school we all attend.

My head snaps around when the bell dings: prayers are five minutes away, followed directly by bed. Panic sweeps through me. I have to know if anything new has been reported. Perhaps John's been caught. Perhaps the police have found something else at the demolished school, something originally overlooked. Even if there's nothing new at all, I have to know. I'll never get to sleep otherwise.

I fix a hard stare on Gabriela García – Gabby for short – who sits at one of the computers. Gabby's

sixteen and very pretty, with long dark hair and brown eyes; and she always dresses slutty when she's outside the convent, wearing tight shirts that show off her pierced navel. Every morning she dresses in loose, baggy clothes, but the second we're out of sight of the Sisters she removes them, revealing a tight, skimpy outfit underneath. Then she spends the rest of the walk to school applying makeup and redoing her hair. It's the same with her four friends, three of whom also live here. And when the day ends, they wipe their faces clean during the walk back and re-dress in their original clothes.

'What?' Gabby asks in a snotty voice, glaring at me. 'I'm writing an email.'

'I've been waiting longer than ten minutes,' I say. 'And you're not writing an email. You're looking at guys with their shirts off.'

'So what? Are you gonna tell on me, tattletale?' she asks mockingly.

The girl beside her, whose name is Hilda but who most kids in school call La Gorda – 'the fat one' – (behind her back, never to her face) laughs.

They're an inseparable pair, Gabby and La Gorda. I bite my tongue and turn back to the window, folding my arms across my chest. I'm seething inside, partly because I need to get on the computer and partly because I never know how to respond when Gabby mocks me. There are four minutes left. My impatience segues to full-on desperation. There could be news

right now – breaking news! – but I have no way of knowing because these selfish jerks won't give up one of the computers.

Three minutes left. I'm nearly shaking with anger. And then an idea pops into my head, and a grin plays across my lips. It's risky, but worth it if it works.

I pivot just enough to see Gabby's chair in my peripheral vision. I take a deep breath and, focusing all my energy on her chair, use my telekinesis to jerk it to the left. Then I quickly thrust it right so hard it nearly topples over. Gabby jumps up and yelps. I look at her in mock surprise.

'What?' La Gorda asks.

'I don't know; it felt like somebody just kicked my chair or something. Did you feel anything?'

'No,' La Gorda says; and as soon as the word is uttered, I move her chair a few centimeters backwards, then jerk it to the right, all the while remaining at my spot by the window. Both of the girls scream this time. I thrust Gabby's chair, then La Gorda's again; and without giving their computer screens a second glance, they flee the room, screaming as they go.

'Yes!' I say, rushing to the computer Gabby was using and quickly typing the web address of the news site I've deemed most reliable. Then I wait impatiently for the page to load. The old computers, combined with the slow internet here, are the bane of my existence.

The browser goes white and, line by line, the page forms. When a quarter of it has loaded, the final bell

rings. One minute until prayers. I'm inclined to ignore the bell, even at the risk of being punished. At this point I don't really care. 'Five more months,' I whisper to myself.

Half of the page is now up, revealing the top of John Smith's face, his upturned eyes, which are dark and confident, though within them there's a sense of discomfort that seems almost out of place. I lean on the edge of my seat, waiting, the excitement bubbling up inside me, causing my hands to tremble.

'Come on,' I say to the screen, trying in vain to hurry it. 'Come on come on come on.'

'Marina!' a voice barks from the open doorway. I jerk around and see Sister Dora, a portly woman who's the head cook in the kitchen, staring daggers at me. This is nothing new. She stares daggers at everyone who walks through the lunch line holding a tray, as though our needing sustenance is a personal affront. She presses her lips together in a perfect straight line, then narrows her eyes. 'Come! Now! And I mean *right* now!'

I sigh, knowing I have no choice but to go. I clear the browser's history and close it, then follow Sister Dora down the dark hallway. There was something new on that screen; I just know it. Why else would John's face have taken up the entire page? A week and a half is long enough for any news to turn stale, so for him to command so much of the screen means there's some significant new piece of information.

We walk to Santa Teresa's nave, which is huge. Towering pillars lead to a high, vaulted ceiling and stained glass windows line the walls. Wooden pews run the length of the open room and can seat nearly three hundred people. Sister Dora and I are the last to enter. I sit alone in one of the center pews. Sister Lucia, who opened the door to Adelina and me when we first arrived and who still runs the convent, stands at the pulpit, closes her eyes, lowers her head and presses her hands together in front of her. Everyone else does the same.

'*Padre divino*,' the prayer begins in somber unison. '*Que nos bendiga y nos proteja en su amor* . . .'

I tune it out and look at the back of the heads before me, all of which are bowed in concentration. Or just bowed. My eyes find Adelina, sitting in the very first row six pews in front of me and slightly to the right. She is on her knees, deeply meditative, her brown hair pulled into a tight braid that falls to the middle of her back. She doesn't look up once, doesn't try to find me at the back of the room like she used to during our first few years here, a covert smile on each of our faces as our eyes met, acknowledging our shared secret. We still share that secret, but somewhere along the way Adelina has stopped acknowledging it. Somewhere along the way the plan to bide our time until we felt strong enough and safe enough to leave has been replaced with Adelina's desire to simply stay – or her fear to leave.

Before the news of John Smith, which I'd told Adelina about when it broke, it had been months since we last talked about our mission. In September I had shown her my third scar, the third warning that said another Garde has died and that she and I are one step closer to being hunted and killed by the Mogadorians, and she had acted like it didn't exist. Like it didn't mean what we both know it means. Upon hearing the news about John, she merely rolled her eyes and told me to stop believing in fairy tales.

'En el nombre del Padre, y del Hijo, y del Espíritu Santo. Amén,' they say, and everyone in the room makes the sign of the cross in unison with this last sentence, myself included to keep up appearances: forehead, chest, left shoulder, right shoulder.

I had been asleep, dreaming of running down a mountain with my arms out at my sides as if I was about to take flight, when I had been awoken by the pain and glow of the third scar wrapping itself around my lower leg. The light had woken several girls in the room, but thankfully not the attending Sister. The girls thought I had a flashlight and a magazine under the covers and that I was breaking the rules of curfew. On the bed next to mine, Elena, a quiet sixteen-year-old with jet-black hair she often sticks in her mouth when speaking, had thrown a pillow at me. My flesh had begun to bubble, and the pain had been so intense I had to bite on the edge of my blanket to remain quiet. I couldn't help but cry, because somewhere Number

Three had lost his or her life. There were six of us left now.

Tonight I file out of the nave with the rest of the girls and head to our sleeping quarters filled with creaky twin beds evenly spaced apart, but in my mind I'm hatching a plan. To compensate for the hard beds and the concrete chill of every room, the linens are soft and the blankets heavy, the only real luxury we're afforded. My bed is in the back corner, farthest from the door, which is the most sought after spot; it's the quietest, and it took me a long time to get it, moving one bed closer as each girl left.

The lights are shut off once everyone is settled in. I lie on my back and stare at the faint, jagged outline of the high ceiling. An occasional whisper breaks the silence, followed immediately by the attending Sister shushing whoever it came from. I keep my eyes open, waiting impatiently for everyone to fall asleep. After a half hour the whispers fade, replaced by the soft sounds of sleep, but I don't dare risk it yet. Too soon. Another fifteen minutes and still no sounds. Then I can't stand it any longer.

I hold my breath and inch my legs over the edge of the bed, listening to the rhythm of Elena's breathing beside me. My feet find the icy floor, and turn cold instantly. I stand slowly to keep the bed from creaking and then tiptoe across the room and towards the door, taking my time, being careful not to bump any beds. I reach the open doorway and rush out into the hall and

down to the computer room. I pull out the chair and push the computer's power button.

I fidget waiting for the computer to boot up and keep peering towards the hallway to see if anyone has followed. I'm finally able to type in the web address and the screen goes white, then two pictures take shape in the center of the page, surrounded by text with a top headline in bold black letters too blurry to read. Two images now – I wonder what changed since I tried to check earlier. And then, at last, they come into focus:

INTERNATIONAL TERRORISTS?

John Smith, with his square jaw, shaggy dark blond hair, and blue eyes, fills the left side of the screen, while his father – or more likely Cêpan – Henri takes up the right. What's there isn't a photo but a black-and-white artist's sketch done in pencil. I skim the details I already know – demolished school, five deaths, abrupt disappearance – and then come to the breaking news only now being reported:

> In a bizarre twist, FBI investigators today uncovered what is believed to be the tools of a professional counterfeiter. Several machines typically used for the creation of documents were found in the Paradise, Ohio, home rented by Henri and John Smith in a hatch beneath the floorboards of the master bedroom, leading investigators to

consider possible links to terrorism. Creating local uproar within the Paradise community, Henri and John Smith are now considered a threat to national security, fugitives; and investigators are asking for any and all information that might lead to their whereabouts.

I scroll back to John's image, and when my gaze meets his, my hands begin to shake. His eyes – even in this sketch there's something familiar about them. How could I know them if not from the year-long journey that brought us here? Nobody can convince me now that he isn't one of the six remaining Garde, still alive in this foreign world.

I lean back and blow my bangs out of my eyes, wishing I could go in search of John myself. Of course Henri and John Smith are able to elude police; they've kept hidden for eleven years now, just as Adelina and I have. But how can I possibly hope to be the one to find him when the whole world is looking? How can any of us hope to come together?

The eyes of the Mogadorians are everywhere. I have no idea how One or Three were found, but I believe they located Two because of a blog post he or she had written. I had found it, and then I'd sat there for fifteen minutes thinking how best to respond without giving myself away. Though the message itself had been obscure, it was very obvious to those of us looking: Nine, now eight. Are the rest of you out there? It had been posted by an account called Two. My fingers

found the keyboard and I'd typed a quick response, and just before I hit the Post button, the page refreshed – somebody else had responded first.

We are here, it read.

My mouth had dropped open, and I'd stared in utter shock. Hope flooded through me from those two brief messages, but just as my fingers had typed a different reply, a bright glow appeared at my feet and the sizzling sound of burning flesh reached my ears, followed closely by a searing pain so great that I'd dropped to the floor and writhed in agony, screaming at the top of my lungs for Adelina, holding my hands over my ankle so no one else would see. When Adelina arrived and realized what was happening, I'd pointed at the screen, but it was blank; both posts had been deleted.

I look away from John Smith's familiar eyes on the screen. Beside the computer sits a small flower that's been forgotten. It's wilted and tired, shrunken down to half its normal height, a brown, crispy tinge at the edge of its leaves. Several petals have dropped, now dry and crinkled on the desk around the pot. The flower isn't dead yet, but it's not far off. I lean forward and cup my hands around it, move my face near enough so that my lips brush against the edge of its leaves, and then I blow hot air over it. An icy feeling shoots down my spine and, in response, life bursts through the small flower. It springs upward and a verdant green floods the leaves and stalk and new petals bloom, colorless at

first, then turning a brilliant purple. A mischievous grin sprouts on my face, and I can't help but think of how the Sisters would react if they were to see such a thing. But I'll never let them. It would be misinterpreted, and I don't want to be cast out into the cold. I'm not ready for that. Soon, but not just yet.

I turn off the computer and hurry back to bed while thoughts of John Smith, somewhere out there, swim in my head.

Be safe and stay hidden, I think. *We'll find each other yet.*

3

A low whisper finds me. The voice is cold. I can't seem to move but I listen intently.

I'm not asleep anymore, but I'm not awake either. I'm paralyzed, and as the whispers increase, my eyes are whisked away through the impenetrable darkness of my motel room. The electricity I feel as the vision breaks above my bed reminds me of when my first Legacy, Lumen, lit up my palms in Paradise, Ohio. Back when Henri was still here, still alive. But Henri's gone now. He's not coming back. Even in this state I can't escape that reality.

I completely enter the vision above me, blazing through its darkness with my hands turned on, but the glow is swallowed by the shadows. And then I snap to a halt. Everything falls silent. I lift my hands in front of me but touch nothing, my feet off the ground, floating in a great void.

More whispering in a language I don't recognize, but somehow still understand. The words burst forth anxiously. The darkness fades, and the world I'm in turns a shade of gray on its way to a white so bright I have to squint to see. A mist drifts in front of me and filters away, revealing a large open room with candles lining the walls.

'I – I don't know what went wrong,' a voice says, clearly shaken.

The room is long and wide, the size of a football field. The acrid smell of sulfur burns my nostrils, makes my eyes water. The air is hot and stuffy. And then I see them at the far end of the room: two figures shrouded in shadows, one much bigger than the other, and menacing even from a distance.

'They got away. Somehow they got away. I don't know how . . .'

I move forward. I feel the sort of calm that sometimes comes in dreams when you're aware you're asleep and that nothing can really hurt you. Step by step, nearing the growing shadows.

'All of them, all of them killed. Along with three piken and two krauls,' the smaller of the two says, standing with fidgeting hands beside the larger man.

'We had them. We were about to –,' comes the voice, but the other cuts him off. He scans the air to see what he's already sensed. I stop, stand motionless, and hold my breath. And then he finds me. A shudder runs up my spine.

'John,' somebody says, the voice a distant echo.

The larger figure comes towards me. He towers over me, twenty feet tall, muscular, a chiseled jaw. His hair isn't long like the others', but cut short instead. His skin is tan. Our eyes stay locked as he slowly approaches. Thirty feet away, then twenty. He stops ten feet short. My pendant grows heavy and the chain cuts into my

neck. Around his throat, like a collar, I notice a grotesque, purplish scar.

'I've been expecting you,' he says, his voice level and calm. He lifts his right arm and pulls a sword from the sheath on his back. It comes alive at once, keeping its shape while the metal turns nearly liquid. The wound in my shoulder, from the soldier's dagger during the battle in Ohio, screams with pain as though I'm being stabbed all over again. I fall to my knees.

'It's been a very long time,' he says.

'I don't know what you're talking about,' I say in a language I've never spoken before.

I want to leave immediately, wherever this place is. I try to rise, but it's as if I'm suddenly stuck to the ground.

'Don't you?' he asks.

'John,' I hear again from somewhere on the periphery. The Mogadorian doesn't seem to notice, and there's something about his gaze that holds my own. I can't look away.

'I'm not supposed to be here,' I say. My voice sounds watery. Everything dims until it's just the two of us and nothing else.

'I can make you disappear if that's what you want,' he says, slashing a figure eight with the sword, leaving a stark white streak hanging in the air where the blade passes through. And then he charges, his sword held high and cracking with power. He swings, and it comes down like a bullet, aimed for my throat, and I know that there's nothing I can do to stop the blow from decapitating me.

'John!' the voice screams again.

My eyes whip open. Two hands grip me hard by the shoulders. I'm covered in sweat and out of breath. I focus first on Sam standing over me, then on Six, with her stark hazel eyes that sometimes look blue and sometimes green, kneeling beside me, appearing tired and worn as though I just woke her, which I probably did.

'What was that all about?' Sam asks.

I shake my head, letting the vision dissipate, and I take in my surroundings. The room is dark with the curtains drawn, and I'm lying in the same bed I've spent the last week and a half in, healing from the battle wounds. Six has been recovering beside me, and neither she nor I have left this place since we arrived, relying on Sam to head out for food and supplies. A shabby motel room with two full beds off the main street in Trucksville, North Carolina. To rent the room, Sam had used one of the seventeen driver's licenses Henri created for me before he was killed, and luckily the old man at the front desk was too busy watching TV to study the photograph. Situated on the northwestern edge of the state, the motel is a fifteen-minute drive from both Virginia and Tennessee, a location chosen mainly because we had traveled as far as we could go given the extent of our injuries. But our wounds have slowly healed, and our strength is finally returning.

'You were talking in a foreign language I've never heard before,' Sam says. 'I think you made it up, dude.'

'No, he was talking in Mogadorian,' Six corrects him. 'And even a little Loric.'

'Really?' I ask. 'That's totally weird.'

Six walks to the window and pulls back the right side of the curtains. 'What were you dreaming about?'

I shake my head. 'I'm not really sure. I was dreaming, but I wasn't dreaming, you know. Having visions, I guess, and they were about them. We were about to have a battle; but I was, I don't know, too weak or confused or something.' I look up at Sam, who is frowning and looking at the TV. 'What?'

'Bad news.' He sighs, shaking his head.

'What?' I sit up, wipe the sleep from my eyes.

Sam nods to the front of the room, and I turn to the glow of the television. My face takes up the entire left half of the screen, while an artist's rendering of Henri's is on the right. The drawing looks nothing like him: his face seems sharp and haggard to the point of emaciation, giving him the appearance of being twenty years older than he really is. Or *was*.

'As if being called a threat to national security or a terrorist wasn't bad enough,' Sam says. 'They're now offering a reward.'

'For me?' I ask.

'For you and Henri. A hundred thousand dollars for any information leading to your and Henri's capture, and two hundred and fifty thousand if somebody brings either of you in on their own,' Sam says.

'I've been on the run all of my life,' I say, rubbing my eyes. 'What difference does it make?'

'Yeah, well, I haven't and they're offering a reward for

me, too,' Sam says. 'A measly twenty-five grand, if you can believe that. And I don't know how good a fugitive I am. I've never done this before.'

I gingerly scoot up the bed, still a little stiff. Sam sits on the other bed and places his head in his palms.

'You're with us, though, Sam. We have your back,' I say.

'I'm not worried,' he says into his chest.

I chew on the insides of my cheeks, thinking about how I'm going to keep him safe, and me and Six alive, without Henri. I turn to face Sam, who is stressed enough to be picking a hole in his black NASA T-shirt. 'Listen, Sam. I wish Henri was here. I can't even tell you how much I wish he was here, for so many reasons. Not only did he keep me safe when we were running from one state to the next, but he also had all this knowledge about Lorien and my family, and he had this amazing calming way about him that's kept us out of trouble for so long. I don't know if I'm ever going to be able to do what he did to keep us safe. I bet if he were alive today, he wouldn't have let you come with us. There's just no way he would have put you in this kind of danger. But, listen, you're here and that's that, and I promise that I won't let anything happen to you.'

'I want to be here,' Sam says. 'This is the coolest thing that's ever happened to me.' There is a pause, and then he looks me in the eyes. 'Plus you're my best friend, and I've never had a best friend.'

'Neither have I,' I say.

'Just hug already,' Six says. Sam and I laugh.

My face is still on the screen. The photo on the TV is the one Sarah took on my very first day of school, the day I'd met her; and I have an awkward, uncomfortable look on my face. The right side of the screen is now filled with smaller photos of the five people we're being accused of killing: three teachers, the men's basketball coach, the school janitor. And then the screen changes yet again to images of the wrecked school – and it really is wrecked; the entire right side of the building is nothing more than a heap of rubble. Next come various interviews with Paradise residents, the last being Sam's mom. When she comes on screen she's crying, and looking straight into the camera she desperately pleads with the 'kidnappers' to 'please please please return my baby safely to me.' When Sam sees this interview, I can tell something inside of him shifts.

Scenes from the past week's funerals and candlelight vigils come next. Sarah's face flashes on the screen, and she's holding a candle as tears stream down her cheeks. A lump forms in my throat. I'd give anything to hear her voice. It kills me to imagine what she must be dealing with. The video of us escaping Mark's burning house – which is what started all of this – has blown up on the internet, and while I was blamed for starting *that* blaze as well, Mark stepped in and swore up and down that I had no part in it, even though using me as a scapegoat would have let him off the hook completely.

When we had left Ohio, the damage to the school had

first been attributed to an out-of-season tornado; but then rescue crews filtered through the rubble, and in no time all five bodies had been found lying equal distances from each other – without a single mark on them – in a room untouched by the battle. Autopsies reported that they had died of natural causes, with no trace of drugs or trauma. Who knows how it really happened. When one of the reporters had heard the story of me jumping through the principal's window and running away from the school, and then when Henri and I couldn't be found, he'd run a story blaming us for everything; and the rest had been quick to follow. With the recent discovery of Henri's forgery tools, along with a few of the fake documents he had left at the house, the public outrage has grown.

'We're going to have to be very careful now,' Six says, sitting against the wall.

'More careful than staying inside a crummy motel room with the curtains drawn?' I ask.

Six goes back to the window and pulls aside one of the curtains to peer out. A sliver of sunlight cuts across the floor. 'The sun will set in three hours. Let's leave as soon as it's dark.'

'Thank God,' Sam says. 'There's a meteor shower tonight we can see if we drive south. Plus if I have to spend one more minute inside this crappy room, I'm going to go nuts.'

'Sam, you've been nuts since the first time I met you,' I kid. He throws a pillow at me, which I deflect without

lifting a hand. I twist the pillow over and over in the air with my telekenisis and then send it like a rocket at the television, shutting it off.

I know Six is right that we should keep moving, but I'm frustrated. It seems like there's no end in sight, no place where we'll be safe. At the foot of the bed, keeping my feet warm, is Bernie Kosar, who's hardly left my side since Ohio. He opens his eyes and yawns and stretches. He peers up at me, and through my telepathy communicates that he's also feeling better. Most of the small scabs that covered his body are gone, and the larger ones are healing nicely. He's still wearing the makeshift splint on his broken front leg, and he'll limp for a few more weeks; but he almost looks like his old self. He offers a subtle wag and paws at my leg. I reach down and pull him up to my lap and scratch his tummy.

'How about you, buddy? You ready to get out of this dump?'

Bernie Kosar thumps his tail against the bed.

'So where to, guys?' I ask.

'I don't know,' Six says. 'Preferably somewhere warm to ride out the winter. I'm pretty sick of this snow. Though I'm even more sick of not knowing where the others are.'

'For now it's just us three. Four plus Six plus Sam.'

'I love algebra,' Sam says. 'Sam equals *x*. Variable *x*.'

'Such a nerd, dude,' I say.

Six enters the bathroom and then exits a second later with a handful of toiletries. 'If there's any consolation in what happened, at least the other Garde know John not

only survived his first battle, but that he won it. Maybe they'll find a bit of hope in it. Our biggest priority now is finding the others. And training together in the meantime.'

'We will,' I say, then look at Sam. 'It's not too late to go back and put things straight, Sam. You can make up any story about us you want. Tell them we kidnapped you and held you against your will, and that you escaped the first chance you got. You'll be considered a hero. Girls will be all over you.'

Sam bites his lower lip and shakes his head. 'I don't want to be a hero. And girls are already all over me.'

Six and I roll our eyes, but I also see Six blush. Or maybe I imagine it.

'I mean it,' he says. 'I'm not leaving.'

I shrug. 'I guess that's settled. Sam equals *x* in this equation.'

Sam watches Six walk to her small duffel bag beside the TV, and his attraction to her is painted all over his face. She's wearing black cotton shorts and a white tank top with her hair pulled back. A few strands fall loose around her face. A purple scar is prominent on the front of her left thigh, and the stitch marks around it are a tender pink, still scabbed over. Stitches she not only sewed herself, but also removed. When Six looks up, Sam shyly diverts his gaze. Clearly there's another reason Sam wants to stick around.

Six bends down and reaches into her bag, removing a folded map. She opens it on the foot of the bed.

'Right here,' she says, pointing to Trucksville, 'is where we are. And here,' she continues, moving her finger from North Carolina to a tiny red star made in ink close to the center of West Virginia, 'is where the Mogadorians' cave is, the one I know of, anyhow.'

I look where she's pointing. Even on the map it's obvious the location is very isolated; there doesn't appear to be any sort of main road within five miles, nor any town within ten.

'How do you even know where the cave is?'

'That's a long story,' she says. 'Probably one better left for the road.'

Her finger takes up a new route on the map, heading southwest from West Virginia, traversing Tennessee, and coming to rest on a point in Arkansas near the Mississippi River.

'What's there?' I ask.

She puffs her cheeks and releases a deep breath, undoubtedly remembering something that happened. Her face takes on a special look when deep in concentration.

'This is where my Chest was,' she says. 'And some of the stuff Katarina brought from Lorien. This is where we hid it.'

'What do you mean, where it *was*?'

She shakes her head.

'It's not there anymore?'

'No. They were tracking us, and we couldn't risk them getting it. It was no longer safe with us, so we stowed it and Katarina's artifacts in Arkansas and fled as fast as

we could, thinking we could stay ahead of them . . .' She trails off.

'They caught up to you, didn't they?' I ask, knowing her Cêpan Katarina died three years ago.

She sighs. 'That's another story better left for the road.'

It takes minutes to throw my clothes into my duffel bag, and as I'm doing it I realize the last time this bag was packed, Sarah had done it. Only a week and a half has passed, but it feels like a year and a half. I wonder if she's been interrogated by police, or singled out at school. Where is she even going to school since the high school was destroyed? I'm certain she can hold her own, but still, it can't be easy on her, especially since she has no idea where I am, or even if I'm okay. I wish I could contact her without putting us both in danger.

Sam turns the TV back on the old-fashioned way – with the remote – and he watches the news while Six goes invisible to check on the truck. We assume Sam's mom noticed it missing, which surely means the police are keeping an eye out for it. Earlier in the week Sam stole the front license plate off another truck. It might help us until we get to where we're going.

I finish packing and set my bag beside the door. Sam smiles when his picture pops up on the television screen, again on the same news cycle, and I know he's enjoying his small bit of celebrity even at the risk of being considered a fugitive. Then they show my picture again, which

means they also show Henri's. It rips me apart to see him, even though the sketch looks nothing like him. Now isn't the time for guilt or misery, but I miss him so much. It's my fault he's dead.

Fifteen minutes later Six walks in carrying a white plastic bag.

She holds up the bag and shakes it at us. 'I bought you guys something.'

'Yeah, what is it?' I ask.

She reaches in and pulls out a pair of hair clippers. 'I think it's time for a haircut for you and Sam.'

'Oh come on, my head's too small. It's going to make me look like a turtle,' Sam objects. I laugh and try to picture him without his shaggy hair. He has a long, skinny neck, and I think he might be right.

'You'll be incognito,' Six replies.

'Well, I don't want to be incognito. I'm Variable *x*.'

'Stop being a wuss,' Six says.

He scowls. I try to be upbeat. 'Yeah, Sam,' I say, peeling off my shirt. Six follows me into the bathroom, ripping the packaging away from the clippers as I bend over the tub. Her fingers are a little cold, and goose bumps sprinkle down my spine. I wish it was Sarah who was holding my shoulder steady and giving me a makeover. Sam watches from the doorway, sighing loudly, making his displeasure known.

Six finishes, and I wipe away the loose hair with a towel, then stand and look in the mirror. My head is whiter than the rest of my face, but only because it's never seen the

sun. I think that a few days in the Florida Keys, where Henri and I lived before coming to Ohio, would fix the problem in no time.

'See, John looks tough and rugged like that. I'm going to look like a turd,' Sam groans.

'I *am* tough and rugged, Sam,' I reply.

He rolls his eyes while Six cleans the clippers. 'Down,' she says.

Sam obeys, dropping to his knees and bending over the tub. When she's done, Sam stands and flashes me a pleading look.

'How bad is it?'

'You look good, buddy,' I say. 'You look like a fugitive.'

Sam rubs his head a few times and finally looks in the mirror. He cringes. 'I look like an alien!' he exclaims in mock disgust, then glances at me over his shoulder. 'No offense,' he adds lamely.

Six collects all the hair from the tub and drops it in the toilet, careful to flush every strand. She coils the cord of the clippers into a neat, tight loop, then slips it back into its bag.

'No time like the present,' she says.

We strap our bags across her shoulders and she grabs them both with her hands, then makes herself invisible, causing the bags to disappear as well. She rushes out the door to take them to the truck without being seen. While she's gone I reach up into the far right corner of the closet, toss aside a few towels, and grab the Loric Chest.

'You ever going to open that thing or what?' Sam asks.

He's been excited to see what's inside ever since I told him about it.

'Yeah, I will,' I say. 'As soon as I feel safe.'

The motel door opens, then closes. Six reappears and glances at the Chest.

'I won't be able to make you and Sam disappear *and* that. Only what I hold in my hands. I'll run it back to the truck first.'

'No, that's okay. Take Sam with you, and I'll follow behind.'

'That's stupid, John. How are you going to follow behind?'

I pull on my hat and jacket, then zip it and pull the hood over my head so that only my face shows.

'I'll be fine. I have advanced hearing, like you,' I say.

She eyes me skeptically and shakes her head. I grab Bernie Kosar's leash and clip it to his collar.

'Only until we get to the truck,' I tell him, since he hates walking on a leash. On second thought, I lean down to carry him since his leg is still healing, but he tells me he'd rather walk himself.

'Ready when you are,' I say.

'All right, let's do this,' Six says.

Sam offers his hand to her a little too enthusiastically. I stifle a laugh.

'What?' he asks.

I shake my head. 'Nothing. I'll follow you as best I can, but don't get too far ahead.'

'Just cough if you can't follow and we'll stop. The truck is only a few minutes' walk from here, behind the abandoned barn,' Six says. 'Can't miss it.'

As the door flings open, Sam and Six disappear.

'That's our cue, BK. Just the two of us now.'

He follows me out, trotting happily with his tongue dangling. Aside from quick bathroom trips to the small plot of grass beside the motel, Bernie Kosar's been cooped up like the rest of us.

The night air is cool and fresh, carrying a scent of pine, and the wind on my face brings me instantly back to life. As I walk I close my eyes and try to sense Six by combing the air with my mind, reaching out and feeling the landscape with telekinesis, the same way I was able to stop the speeding bullet in Athens by grabbing everything in the air. I feel them, a few feet ahead of me and slightly to the right. I give Six a nudge and she startles, her breath catching in her throat. Three seconds later she shoulders into me, nearly causing me to fall. I laugh. And so does she.

'What are you guys doing?' Sam asks. He's annoyed with our little game. 'We're supposed to be quiet, remember?'

We make it to the truck, which is parked behind a dilapidated old barn that looks as though it's ready to collapse. Six releases Sam's hand and he climbs into the middle of the cab. Six jumps behind the wheel, and I slide in next to Sam with BK at my feet.

'Holy crap, dude, what happened to your hair?' I goad Sam.

'Shut up.'

Six starts the truck and I smile as she steers us onto the road, flicking on the headlights when the wheels touch the asphalt.

'What?' Sam asks.

'I was just thinking that, out of the four of us, three are aliens, two are fugitives with terrorist ties, and not a single one of us has a valid driver's license. Something tells me things might get interesting.'

Even Six can't help but smile at this.

4

'I was thirteen when they caught up to us,' Six says when we cross into Tennessee, fifteen minutes after leaving the Trucksville Motel behind. I'd asked her to tell us about how she and Katarina were captured. 'We were in West Texas after fleeing Mexico because of a stupid mistake. We had both been completely entranced by some stupid internet post that Two had written, though we didn't know it was by Two at the time, and we responded. We were lonely in Mexico, living in some dusty town in the middle of nowhere, and we just had to know if it really was a member of the Garde.'

I nod, knowing what she's talking about. Henri had also seen the blog post while we were in Colorado. I had been in a school spelling bee, and the scar had come while I was onstage. I'd been rushed to the hospital and the doctor saw the first scar, and the fresh burn all the way to the bone of the second. When Henri arrived, they'd accused him of child abuse, which was the catalyst behind our fleeing the state and assuming new identities, another new start.

'"Nine, now eight. Are the rest of you out there?"' I ask.

'That's the one.'

'So you guys are the ones who responded,' I say. Henri

had taken screen shots of the post so I could see it. He had tried furiously to hack the computer to delete it before the damage could be done, but he hadn't been quick enough. Two was killed. Somebody else deleted the post right after. We'd assumed it was the Mogadorians.

'We did, simply writing "We are here"; and not a minute later the scar appeared,' Six says, shaking her head. 'It was so stupid of Two to post that, knowing she was next. I still can't understand why she'd risk it.'

'Do you guys know where she was?' Sam asks.

I look at Six. 'Do you? Henri thought it was England, but he couldn't say for sure.'

'No idea. All we knew was that if they'd gotten to her that quickly, it wouldn't take long for them to get to us.'

'But, how do you even know she posted it?' Sam asks.

Six glances at him.

'What do you mean?'

'I don't know; you guys can't even say for sure where she was, so how do you know it *was* her?'

'Who else would it be?'

'Well, I mean, I watch the way you and John are so cautious. I can't imagine either of you doing something so stupid like that if you knew you were next. Especially with everything you know about the Mogadorians. I don't think you would have posted something to begin with.'

'True, Sam.'

'So maybe they had already captured Two and were trying to draw some of you guys out before they killed her, which could explain why she was killed seconds after

you responded. It could have been a bluff. Or maybe she knew what they were doing, and she killed herself to warn you guys away or something. Who knows. Those are just some guesses, right?'

'Right,' I say. But they are good guesses. Ones I hadn't thought about. Ones I wonder if Henri had.

We ride in silence thinking about it. Six drives the speed limit and a few cars cruise past us. The highway itself is lined with overhead lights that make the rolling hills beyond look spooky.

'She could have been scared and desperate,' I say. 'That could have led her to do something stupid, like write a careless post on the internet.'

Sam shrugs. 'Just seems kind of unlikely to me.'

'But they could have already killed her Cêpan, and she could have become frantic. She must have been twelve, maybe thirteen. Imagine being thirteen and on your own,' I say before I realize I'm describing Six's exact scenario. She glances at me, then turns back to the road.

'We never once thought it was a trick,' she says. 'Though it kind of makes sense. Back then we were just scared. And my ankle was on fire. Kind of hard to think straight when it feels as though your foot is being sawed off.'

I nod my head gravely.

'But even after the initial fear, we still didn't consider that angle. We replied, which is what put them on our tail. It was ridiculous for us to do. Maybe you're right, Sam. I can only hope we've grown a little wiser, those of us still left.'

Her last sentence hangs in the air. There are only six of us left. Six of us against any number of them. And no way of knowing how we might possibly find one another. We're the only hope. Strength in numbers. The power of six. The thought makes my heart pump at twice its normal speed.

'What?' Six asks.

'There're six of us left.'

'I know there are. So what?'

'Six of us, and maybe some of the others still have their Cêpans; maybe they don't. But six to fight who knows how many Mogadorians? A thousand? A hundred thousand? A *million*?'

'Hey, don't forget about me,' Sam says. 'And Bernie Kosar.'

I nod. 'Sorry, Sam; you're right. Eight of us.' And then all of a sudden I remember something else. 'Six, do you know about the second ship that left Lorien?'

'A ship aside from ours?'

'Yeah, it left after ours. Or, at least, I think it did. Loaded with Chimæra. Fifteen or so, and three Cêpan, and maybe a baby. I had visions of it when Henri and I were training, though he was skeptical. But so far all my visions have proven true.'

'I had no idea.'

'It took off in an old rocket that kind of looked like a NASA shuttle. You know, powered by fuel that left a trail of smoke behind it.'

'Then it wouldn't have made it here,' Six says.

'Yeah, that's what Henri said.'

'Chimæra?' Sam asks. 'The same kind of animal as Bernie Kosar?' I nod. He perks up. 'Maybe that's how Bernie made it here? Could you imagine if they *all* made it? After seeing what Bernie did during the fight?'

'It'd be amazing,' I agree. 'But I'm pretty sure old Bernie here was on our ship.'

I run my hand down the length of Bernie Kosar's back and can feel matted scabs still covering most of his body. Sam sighs, leans back in his seat with a look of relief on his face, probably imagining an army of Chimæra coming to our aid at the last minute to defeat the Mogadorians. Six looks into the rearview mirror, and the headlights from the car behind us illuminate a band of light across her face. She looks back to the road wearing the same introspective gaze that Henri always did when driving.

'The Mogadorians,' she begins softly, swallowing as Sam and I turn our attention to her. 'They caught up to us the day after we responded to Two's post, in a desolate town in West Texas. Katarina had driven fifteen straight hours from Mexico, and it was getting late and we were both exhausted because neither of us had slept. We stopped at a motel off the highway, not all that different from the one we just left. It was in a tiny town that looked like something out of an old Western movie, full of cowboys and ranchers. There were even hitching posts outside some of the buildings so that the people could

tie up their horses. It was very weird, but we had just come from a dusty town in Mexico, so we didn't think twice about stopping.'

She pauses as a car cruises past us. She follows it with her eyes and checks the speedometer before turning back to the road.

'We went to get something to eat at a diner. About halfway through our meal, a man entered and took a seat. He was wearing a white shirt and tie, but it was a Western tie and his clothes looked outdated. We ignored him, even though I noticed the others in the diner staring at him, the same way they were staring at us. At one point he turned and gazed our way, but since everyone else had done the same, I didn't piece it together. I was only thirteen then, and it was hard to think of anything at that point other than sleep and food. So we finished eating and went back to our room. Katarina jumped into the shower; and when she stepped out, wrapped in a robe, there was a knock at the door. We looked at each other. She asked who it was, and the man answered that he was the motel manager and had brought fresh towels and ice; and without thinking twice, I walked to the door and opened it.'

'Oh no,' Sam says.

Six nods. 'It was the man from the diner with the Western tie. He walked straight into the room and shut the door. I was wearing my pendant in plain view. He knew immediately who I was, and Katarina and I knew immediately who he was. In one fluid motion he pulled a knife

from the waistband of his trousers and swung for my head. He was fast, and I had no time to react. I had no Legacies yet, no defenses. I was dead. But then the weirdest thing happened. As the knife dug into my skull, it was *his* skull that split open. I didn't feel a thing. I learned later they had no idea how the charm worked, that he couldn't kill me until numbers one through five were dead. He dropped to the ground and burst into ash.'

'Wicked,' Sam says.

'Wait,' I interrupt. 'From what I've seen, Mogadorians are pretty recognizable. Their skin is so white it looks bleached. And their teeth and eyes . . .' I trail off. 'How could you not have known it in the diner? Why'd you let him into the room?'

'I'm pretty sure only the scouts and soldiers look like that. They're the Mogadorians' version of the military. That's what Katarina said, anyway. The rest of them look as much like normal humans as we do. The one who came into the diner looked like an accountant, wearing wire-rimmed glasses, black slacks, and a white short-sleeved dress shirt and that tie. He even had a really dorky mustache. I remember him being tan. We had no idea they had followed us.'

'That's reassuring,' I say sarcastically. I replay the image of the knife plunging into Six's skull and killing the Mogadorian instead. If one of them tried the same thing with a knife on me, right now, I would be killed. I push the thought away and ask, 'Do you think they're still in Paradise?'

She says nothing for a minute, and when she finally speaks, I wish she had stayed silent instead. 'I think they might be.'

'So Sarah's in danger?'

'Everyone's in danger, John. Every person we know in Paradise, every person we don't know in Paradise.'

All of Paradise is probably under surveillance, and I know it's not safe to go within fifty miles of it. Or to call. Or even to send a letter, or they'd learn the pull Sarah has on me, the connection we have.

'Anyway,' Sam says, wanting to get back to the story. 'The Mogadorian accountant falls to the floor and dies. Then what?'

'Katarina threw the Chest to me and grabbed our suitcase, and we sprinted out of the motel room, Katarina still in her robe. The truck was unlocked, and we jumped inside. Another Mog came charging out from behind the motel. Kat was so flustered that she couldn't find the keys. She locked the doors, though, and the windows were rolled up. But the guy wasted no time at all and punched straight through the passenger-side glass and grabbed me by the shirt. Katarina screamed, and some men nearby jumped into action.

'Others poured out of the diner to see what was happening. The Mogadorian had no choice but to let go of me to face the men.

'"The keys are in the motel room!" Katarina yelled. She looked at me with these big, huge, desperate eyes. She was panicking. We both were. I jumped out of the

truck and sprinted back to our room for the keys. Those men in Texas, they were the only reason we got away then; they saved our lives. When I came out of the motel room with the keys, one of the Texans was aiming a gun at the Mogadorian.

'We have no idea what happened after that because Katarina sped away and we didn't look back. We hid the Chest a few weeks later, right before they caught up to us for good.'

'Don't they already have the Chests from the first three?' Sam asks.

'I'm sure they do, but what use are they? The second we die the Chest unlocks itself, and everything inside becomes useless,' she says, and I nod, knowing that much from past conversations with Henri.

'Not only are the objects worthless,' I say, 'but they completely disintegrate the same way the Mogadorians do when they're killed.'

'Wicked,' Sam says.

And then I remember the sticky note I found when saving Henri in Athens, Ohio.

'Those guys Henri visited who ran the *They Walk Among Us* magazine?'

'Yeah?'

'They had this source who apparently caught a Mogadorian and tortured it for information, and he supposedly knew that Number Seven was being trailed in Spain and that Number Nine was somewhere in South America.'

Six thinks about it a moment. She bites her lip and

glances in the rearview mirror. 'I know for a fact that Number Seven is a girl; I remember that much from the ride in the ship.' The second this leaves her mouth, a siren blares behind us.

5

The snow stops on Saturday night. The scraping sound of shovels against asphalt fills the night air. From the window I can see the faint silhouettes of residents throwing snow to less cumbersome places, readying themselves for the morning walk for Sunday obligations. There's a certain tranquillity to the town at work on a quiet night, everyone bound by the same cause, and I wish I was out there among them. And then the bedtime bell tolls. In the room fourteen girls find their beds within the minute, and the lights are shut off.

The second I close my eyes the dream begins. I stand in a field of flowers on a warm summer day. To my right, in the distance, the outline of a jagged mountain range stands against the backdrop of the setting sun; to my left lies the sea. A girl dressed in black, with raven hair and striking gray eyes, appears out of nowhere. She wears a smile, both fierce and confident. It's just the two of us. Then a great disturbance kicks up behind me, as though an isolated earthquake has just begun, and the ground is split open and torn apart. I don't turn to see what's actually happening. The girl lifts her hand, beckoning me to take it, her eyes locked on mine. I reach for it. My eyes open.

Light streams in through the windows. While it feels as though minutes have passed, in reality the whole night has gone by. I shake my head free of the dream. Sunday is the day of rest, though ironically for us it's the busiest day of the week, starting with a long Mass.

Ostensibly the large Sunday crowd is because of religious devotion within the community, but really it's because of El Festín, the grand dinner that follows Mass. All of us who live here must work it. My place is in the cafeteria line. It's only after dinner that we're finally free. If I'm lucky we'll finish by four, then we're not due back until the sun sets. This time of year it comes a little after six.

We rush to the showers, quickly bathe, brush our teeth and our hair, then dress in our Sunday best, identical black-and-white outfits that leave only our hands and heads showing. When most of the other girls have fled the room, Adelina walks in. She stands in front of me and fixes the neck of my tunic. It makes me feel much younger than I really am. I can hear the throng of people filing into the nave. Adelina remains silent. So do I. I look at the gray streaks in her auburn hair, which I hadn't noticed before. There are wrinkles at her eyes and mouth. She's forty-two but looks ten years older.

'I had a dream about a girl with raven hair and gray eyes who reached her hand out to me,' I say, breaking the silence. 'She wanted me to take it.'

'Okay,' she says, unsure of why I'm telling her about a dream.

'Do you think she could be one of us?'

She gives the collar a final tug. 'I think you shouldn't read into your dreams so much.'

I want to argue with her, but I'm not sure what to say. So instead I utter, 'It felt real.'

'Some dreams do.'

'But you said a long time ago that on Lorien we could sometimes communicate with each other over long distances.'

'Yes, and right after that I would read you stories about a wolf who could blow down houses and a goose who laid golden eggs.'

'Those were fairy tales.'

'It's all one big fairy tale, Marina.'

I grit my teeth. 'How can you say that? We both know it's not a fairy tale. We both know where we came from and why we're here. I don't know why you act as if you didn't come from Lorien and you don't have a duty to teach me.'

She puts her hands behind her back and looks at the ceiling. 'Marina, since I've been here, since we've been here, we've been fortunate to learn the truth about creation and where we came from and what our real mission is on Earth. And that's all found in the Bible.'

'And the Bible isn't a fairy tale?'

Her shoulders stiffen. She furrows her brows and flexes her jaw.

'Lorien isn't a fairy tale,' I say before she can respond, and, using telekinesis, I lift a pillow from a nearby bed and spin it in the air. Adelina does something she's never done before: she slaps me. Hard. I drop the pillow and press my hand to my stinging cheek with my mouth wide-open.

'Don't you dare let them see you do that!' she says furiously.

'What I did right there, that's not a fairy tale. I am not part of a fairy tale. You are my Cêpan, and *you* are not part of a fairy tale.'

'Call it what you will,' she says.

'But haven't you read the news? You know the boy in Ohio is one of us; you have to! He could be our only chance!'

'Our only chance at what?' she asks.

'A life.'

'And what do you call this?'

'Spending our days living the lies of an alien race is no life,' I say.

She shakes her head. 'Give it up, Marina,' she says, and walks away. I have no choice but to follow.

Marina. The name sounds so normal now, so *me.* I don't think twice when Adelina hisses the name at me or when one of the other girls in the orphanage yells it on the way out the school doors, waving my forgotten math book. But it hasn't always been my name. Back when we were aimlessly looking for a warm meal or a bed, back before Spain and Santa Teresa, before

Adelina was Adelina, I had been Geneviève. Adelina was Odette. Those were our French names.

'We should change our names with every new country,' Adelina had whispered when she was Signy and we were in Norway, where our ship landed after months at sea. She'd chosen Signy because it had been written on the woman's shirt behind the counter.

'What should my name be?' I'd asked.

'Whatever you want it to be,' she'd said. We'd been at a café in the middle of a bleak village, enjoying the heat from the mug of hot chocolate we'd shared. Signy had stood and retrieved the weekend's newspaper from a nearby table. On the front page was the most beautiful woman I had ever seen. Blond hair, high cheekbones, deep blue eyes. Her name was Birgitta. My name had become Birgitta.

Even when we were on a train and the countries zipped past the window like trees, we'd always change our names, if just for a few hours. Yes, it was to stay hidden from the Mogadorians or anyone else who might be following us, but it was also the one thing that raised our spirits among so much disappointment. I'd thought it was so much fun, I wish we'd traveled over Europe several times. In Poland I was Minka and she chose Zali. She was Fatima in Denmark; I was Yasmin. I had two names in Austria: Sophie and Astrid. She fell in love with Emmalina.

'Why Emmalina?' I'd asked.

She laughed. 'I don't know exactly. I guess I love

that it's almost two names in one. Either one is beautiful, but you smash them together and you get something extraordinary.'

In fact, I wonder now if that was the last time I heard her laugh. Or the last time we hugged or made proclamations about our destinies. I believe it was the last time I sensed she cared about being my Cêpan or what happened to Lorien – what happened to me.

We arrive at Mass just before it begins. The only available seats are in the very last row, which is where I prefer to sit anyhow. Adelina shuffles to the front where the Sisters sit. Father Marco, the priest, begins with an opening prayer in his always-somber voice, and most of his words are muffled beyond recognition by the time they reach me. I like it this way, sitting through Mass with detached apathy. I try not to think about Adelina smacking me, filling my mind instead with what I will do when El Festín finally ends. None of the snow has melted, but I'm determined to make it to the cave anyway. I have something new to paint, and I want to finish the picture of John Smith that I started last week.

Mass drags on forever, or at least it feels that way, with rites, liturgies, communion, readings, prayers, rituals. When we reach the final prayer I'm exhausted and don't even bother pretending to pray like I normally do, and instead sit there with my head lifted and eyes open, scanning the backs of the heads of those in attendance. Almost all of them are familiar. One man

sleeps upright in his pew, arms crossed and chin touching his chest. I watch him until something in his dream startles him awake with a grunt. Several heads turn his way as he gathers his bearings. I can't help but smile; and as I look away, my eyes find Sister Dora scowling at me. I drop my head, close my eyes, and feign prayer, mouthing the words that Father Marco recites up front, but I know I've been caught. It's what Sister Dora thrives on. She goes out of her way to catch us in the act of doing something we shouldn't.

Prayer concludes with the sign of the cross, finally bringing an end to Mass. I'm up out of my seat before anyone else, and I hurry from the nave to the kitchen. Sister Dora may be the largest among all the Sisters, but she shows surprising agility when it's needed, and I don't want to give her the chance to catch me. If she doesn't, I might escape punishment. And I do, because when she enters the cafeteria five minutes later as I'm peeling potatoes beside a gangly fourteen-year-old named Paola and her twelve-year-old sister, Lucia, she only glares at me.

'What's up with her?' Paola asks.

'She caught me smiling during Mass.'

'Good thing you weren't paddled,' Lucia says out of the corner of her mouth.

I nod and go back to what I'm doing. As fleeting as they are, it's these small moments that bring us girls together, the fact that we share a common enemy. When I was younger, I thought commonalities like

this, and of being orphaned and living under this same tyrannical roof, would unite us all as immediate and lifelong friends. But really it only worked to further divide us, creating small factions within our already small group – the pretty girls huddling together (La Gorda excepted, but still a part of their crowd), the smart girls, the athletic ones, the young ones – until I was left all alone.

A half hour later when everything's ready, we carry the food from the kitchen to the serving line. The crowd of waiting people clap. At the back of the line I see my favorite person in all of Santa Teresa: Héctor Ricardo. His clothes are dirty and wrinkled, and his hair is tousled. He has bloodshot eyes, an almost scarlet complexion to his face and cheeks. Even from as far away as I am I notice he has a slight shake in each hand, as he always does on Sundays – the only day in the week he swears off drinking. He looks especially rough today, though when he finally approaches, he holds his tray out and fixes on his face the most optimistic smile he can muster.

'And how are you, my dear Queen of the sea?' he asks.

I curtsy in return. 'I'm doing well, Héctor. And you?'

He shrugs, then says, 'Life is but a fine wine, to be sipped and savored.'

I laugh. Héctor always has some old adage to share.

I first met Héctor when I was thirteen. He had been sitting outside the lone café on Calle Principal drinking a bottle of wine by himself. It was midafternoon,

and I had been on my way home from school. Our eyes met as I passed.

'Marina, as of the sea,' he had said, and I'd found it odd that he knew my name, though I shouldn't have since I'd seen him every week at the church pretty much since the day I'd arrived. 'Come keep a drunk man company a few minutes.'

I did. I'm not sure why. Maybe because there's something entirely agreeable about Héctor. He makes me feel relaxed, and doesn't pretend to be somebody he isn't like so many other people do. He exudes the attitude of 'This is who I am; take it or leave it.'

That first day we had sat and talked long enough for him to finish one bottle of wine and order a second.

'You stick with Héctor Ricardo,' he'd said when I had to get back to the convent. 'I'll take care of you; it's in my name. The Latin root of Hector means "to defend and hold fast." And Ricardo means "power and bravery,"' he'd said, thumping his chest twice with his right fist. 'Héctor Ricardo will take care of you!'

I could tell he meant it.

He'd gone on. 'Marina. "Of the sea." That's what your name means; did you know that?'

I'd told him I did not. I'd wondered what Birgitta meant. And Yasmin. What Emmalina was rooted in.

'That means you are Santa Teresa's own Sea Queen,' he'd said with a sideways grin.

I'd laughed at him. 'I think you've been drinking too much, Héctor Ricardo.'

'Yes,' he'd replied. 'I am the town drunk, dear Marina. But don't let that fool you. Héctor Ricardo is a defender all the same. And besides, show me a man without vice and I'll show you one without virtue!'

Years later, he's one of the few people I can call a friend.

It takes twenty-five minutes for the few hundred people to receive their due today; and after the last person leaves the line, it's our turn to eat, sitting away from the others. As a group we eat as fast as we can, knowing that the quicker we clean up and get everything put away, the sooner we'll be on our own.

Fifteen minutes later the five of us who work the line are scraping pots and pans and wiping counters. At its best, cleanup takes an hour, and that's only if everyone leaves the cafeteria after they're done eating, which rarely happens. As we're cleaning, when I know the others aren't looking, I throw into a bag the non-perishable items I plan to take to the cave today: dried fruits and berries, nuts, a can of tuna fish, a can of beans. This has become another weekly tradition of mine. For a long time I convinced myself I was doing it so I could snack when painting the cave's walls. But the truth is I'm creating a stockpile of food in case the worst arrives and I have to hide. And by the worst, I mean *them*.

6

When I finally walk outside after changing into warmer clothes and rolling my bed blanket under my arm, the sun is shifted to the west and there's not a cloud in the sky. It's half past four, which gives me an hour and a half at best. I hate the rushed quality of Sundays, the way the day creeps by until the very moment we're free, at which point time flies. I look to the east, and the light reflected off the snow causes me to squint. The cave is over two rocky hills. With as much snow as there is on the ground now, I'm not even sure I'll see the opening today. But I pull on my hat, zip up my jacket, tie the blanket around my neck like a cape, and head east.

Two tall birch trees mark the trail's start, and my feet turn cold the second I enter the deep drifts. The blanket-cape sweeps the snow behind me, erasing my footprints. I pass a few recognizable fixtures that show the way – a rock jutting out past the others, a tree that leans at a slightly different angle. After about twenty minutes I pass the rock formation identical to a camel's back, which tells me I'm almost there.

I have the faint sensation of being watched, possibly followed. I turn and scan the mountainside.

Silence. Snow, nothing else. The blanket around my neck has done a great job of hiding my tracks. A slow, prickly feeling crawls up the back of my neck. I've seen the way rabbits blend into the landscape, going unnoticed until you're almost on top of them, and I know that just because I can't see somebody doesn't mean they can't see me.

Five minutes later I finally spot the rounded shrub that blocks the entrance. The cave's mouth looks like an oversized groundhog hole cutting into the mountain, and that's exactly what I had mistaken it for years ago. But when I'd looked more closely I knew I was wrong. The cave was deep and dark, and back then I could see next to nothing in the little light that entered. There was an implicit desire to discover the cave's secrets, and I wonder if this is what caused the Legacy to develop: my ability to see in the dark. I can't see in the dark as easily as I can in the day, but even the deepest recesses of black glow as though lit by candlelight.

On my knees, I knock away just enough snow to be able to slip down and in. I drop the bag ahead of me, untie the blanket from my neck and sweep it across the snow to hide my footprints, then hang it on the other side of the opening to keep out the wind. The entrance is narrow for the first three meters, followed by a slightly wider passageway that winds down a steep decline large enough to navigate while standing; and after that the cave opens, revealing itself.

The ceiling is high and echoing, and its five walls smoothly transition into one another, creating an almost perfect polygon. A stream cuts through the back right corner. I have no idea where the water comes from or where it goes – springing up through one of the walls only to disappear into the earth's deeper depths – but the level never changes, offering a reservoir of icy cold water regardless of the time of day or season. With the constant fresh source of water, this is the perfect place to hide. From the Mogadorians, the Sisters, and the girls – even Adelina. It's also the perfect place to use and hone my Legacies.

I drop the bag beside the stream, remove the non-perishables, and place them on the rock ledge, which already holds several chocolate bars, small bags of granola, oatmeal, cereal, powdered milk, a jar of pea-nut butter, and various cans of fruits, vegetables, and soup. Enough for weeks. Only when everything is put away do I stand and allow myself to be greeted by the landscapes and faces I've painted on the walls.

From the very first time a brush was put into my hand at school, I fell in love with painting. Painting allows me to see things as I want to and not necessarily as they are; it's an escape, a way to preserve thoughts and memories, a way to create hopes and dreams.

I rinse the brushes, rubbing the stiffness from the bristles, and then mix the paint with water and sedi-ment from the creek bed, creating earthy tones that match the gray of the cave's walls. Then I walk to

where John Smith's partially completed face greets me with his uncertain grin.

I spend a lot of time on his dark blue eyes, trying to get them just right. There's a certain glint that's hard to replicate; and when I tire of trying, I start on a new painting, that of the girl with the raven hair I had dreamed about. Unlike John's eyes, I have no trouble at all with hers, letting the gray wall do its magic; and I think that if I were to wave a lighted candle in front of it, the color would slightly change, as I'm sure her eyes do depending on her mood and the light around her. It's just a feeling I get. The other faces I've painted are Hector's, Adelina's, a few of the town's vendors I see every weekday. Because this cave is so deep and dark, I believe my paintings are safe from anyone's eyes but mine. It's still a risk, I know, but I just can't help myself.

After a while I go up and push aside my blanket, poking my head out of the cave. I see nothing but drifts of white and the bottom of the sun kissing the horizon line – which tells me it's time to go. I haven't painted nearly as much or as long as I would have liked. Before cleaning the brushes I walk to the wall opposite John and look at the big red square I've painted there. Before it was a red square I'd done something foolish, something I know would have exposed me as a Garde, and painted a list.

I touch the square and think of the first three numbers that are underneath, running my fingertips over the dried, cracked paint, deeply saddened by what

those lines meant. If there is any consolation in their deaths, it's that they can now rest easy and no longer have to live in fear.

I turn from the square, from the hidden and destroyed list, clean the brushes, and put everything away.

'I'll see you guys next week,' I say to the faces.

Before leaving the cave I take in the landscape painted on the wall beside the passageway leading in and out. It's the first painting I'd ever attempted here, sometime around the age of twelve; and while I have touched it up a bit over the years, mostly it has remained the same. It's the view of Lorien from my own bedroom window and I still remember it perfectly. Rolling hills and grassy plains accentuated with tall trees. A thick slice of blue river that cuts across the terrain. Small bits of paint here and there that represent the Chimæra drinking from its cool waters. And then, off in the far distance at the very top, standing tall over the nine archways representing the planet's nine Elders, is the statue of Pittacus Lore, so small it's almost indistinct; but there's no mistaking it for what it really is, standing out among the others: a beacon of hope.

I hurry from the cave and back to the convent, keeping an eye open for anything out of place. The sun is just below the horizon when I leave the path, which means I'm running late. I push through the heavy oak doors to find the welcome bells ringing; somebody new has arrived.

I join the others on their way to our sleeping quarters. We have a welcoming tradition here, standing next to our beds with our hands behind our backs, facing the new girl and introducing ourselves one by one. I'd hated it when I had first arrived; hated feeling on display when all I wanted to do was hide.

In the doorway, standing beside Sister Lucia, is a small girl with auburn hair, curious brown eyes, and petite features not unlike a mouse. She stares at the stone floor, shifting her weight uncomfortably from one leg to the other. Her fingers fiddle with the waist of her gray wool dress, which is patterned with pink flowers. There's a small pink clip in her hair, and she wears black shoes with silver buckles. I feel sorry for her. Sister Lucia waits for us all to smile, all thirty-seven of us, and then she speaks.

'This is Ella. She's seven years old and will be staying with us from here on out. I trust that you will all make her feel welcome.'

A rumor is later whispered that her parents had been killed in an automobile accident and she's here because she has no other relatives.

Ella flutters her eyes up as each person says their name, but mostly she keeps her gaze on the floor. It's obvious she's scared and sad, but I can tell she's the kind of girl people will fall for. She won't be here for very long.

We all walk to the nave together so Sister Lucia can explain to Ella its importance to the orphanage. Gabby

García stands yawning in the back of the group, and I turn to look at her. Just beyond Gabby, framed in one of the clear panes of the stained glass window at the far wall, a dark figure stands outside looking in. I can just make him out in the oncoming nightfall, his black hair, heavy brows, and thick mustache. His eyes are trained on me; there's no doubt about it. My heart skips a beat. I gasp and take a step backwards. Everyone's head snaps around.

'Marina, are you okay?' Sister Lucia asks.

'Nothing,' I say, then shake my head. 'I mean, yes, I'm fine. Sorry.'

My heart pounds and my hands shake. I clasp them together so it's not noticeable. Sister Lucia says something else about welcoming Ella, but I'm too distracted to hear it. I turn back to the window. The figure is gone. The group's dismissed.

I rush across the nave and look outside. I don't see anyone, but I do see a single set of boot prints in the snow. I step away from the window. Perhaps it's a potential foster parent assessing the girls from afar, or perhaps it's one of the girl's real parents sneaking a glance at the daughter he can't provide for. But for some reason I don't feel safe. I don't like the way his eyes settled on me.

'Are you okay?' I hear behind me. I jump, then turn around. It's Adelina, standing with her hands clasped in front of her waist. A rosary dangles from her fingers.

'Yes, I'm fine,' I say.

'You look like you've seen a ghost.'

Worse than a ghost, I think, but I don't say that. I'm scared after this morning's slap, and I pocket my hands.

'There was somebody at the window watching me,' I whisper. 'Just now.'

Her eyes squint.

'Look. Look at the prints,' I say, turning back and motioning to the ground.

Adelina's back is straight and rigid, and for a moment I think she's actually concerned; but then she softens and steps forward. She takes in the prints.

'I'm sure it's nothing,' she says.

'What do you mean it's nothing? How can you say that?'

'I wouldn't worry. It could have been anyone.'

'He was looking right at me.'

'Marina, wake up. With today's new arrival there are thirty-eight girls here. We do the best we can keeping you girls safe, but that doesn't mean the occasional boy from town doesn't wander up here to sneak a peek. We've even caught some of them. And don't think for a minute we don't know the way that some of the others dress, changing clothes on the walk to school to look provocative. There are six of you turning eighteen soon, and everyone in town knows it. So, I wouldn't worry about the man you saw. He was probably nothing more than a boy from school.'

I'm sure this was no boy from school, but I don't say so.

'Anyway, I wanted to apologize for this morning. It was wrong of me to strike you.'

'It's okay,' I say, and for a minute I think of bringing John Smith up again, but I decide against it. It would create more friction, which I want to avoid. I miss the way we used to be. And it's hard enough living here without having Adelina angry at me.

Before she says anything further, Sister Dora hurries over and whispers something into Adelina's ear. Adelina looks at me and nods and smiles.

'We'll talk later,' she says.

They walk away, leaving me to myself. I look back down at the boot prints, and a shiver runs up my back.

For the next hour I pace from room to room looking down the hill at the dark town cast in shadow, but I don't see the looming figure again. Perhaps Adelina is right.

But no matter how hard I try convincing myself, I don't think she is.

7

Silence falls in the truck. Six glances in the rearview mirror. Flashing red and blue plays along her face.

'Not good,' Sam says.

'Shit,' Six says.

The bright lights and screaming siren rouse even Bernie Kosar, who peers out the back window.

'What do we do?' Sam asks, his voice frightened and desperate.

Six takes her foot off the accelerator and steers the truck to the right side of the highway.

'It might mean nothing,' she says.

I shake my head. 'Doubtful.'

'Wait. Why are we stopping?' Sam asks. 'Don't stop. Step on it!'

'Let's see what happens first. We'll never make it if we lead this cop on a high-speed chase. He'll call for backup and they'll get a helicopter. Then we'll never get away.'

Bernie Kosar begins growling. I tell him to chill out and he stops, but he keeps vigil out the window. Gravel pings against the truck as we slow along the shoulder. Cars speed past in the left lanes. The cop car pulls to within ten feet of our rear bumper, and its headlights fill the truck's interior. The cop flips them off, then aims a spotlight

straight through the rear window. The siren stops wailing but the lights still flash.

'What do you think?' I ask, watching from the side mirror. The spotlight is blinding; but when a car passes, I can see that the officer is holding the radio up in his right hand, probably running our license plate, or calling for backup.

'Our best bet is to flee on foot,' Six says. 'If that's what it comes to.'

'Turn off your vehicle and remove the key from the ignition,' the cop barks through a speaker.

Six turns off the truck. She looks at me and removes the key.

'If he radios us in, you have to assume that *they'll* hear it,' I say.

She nods, says nothing. From behind us the officer's car door creaks. His approaching boots click bleakly on the asphalt.

'Do you think he'll recognize us?' Sam asks.

'Shhh,' Six says.

When I look in the side mirror again, I realize the officer isn't walking towards the driver's side, and has instead veered right and is coming towards me. He taps my window with his chrome flashlight. I hesitate for a moment, then roll it down. He shines the light in my face, causing me to squint. Then he moves the beam to Sam, then Six. He forces his brows together, studying each of us closely while he tries to determine why we look so familiar.

'Is there a problem, officer?' I ask.

'You kids from around here?'

'No, sir.'

'Ya care tellin' me why y'alls drivin' through Tennessee in a Chevy S-10 with North Carolina plates belonging to a Ford Ranger?'

He glares at me, waiting for an answer. My face feels warm as I struggle to find one. I have nothing. The officer bends down and again flashes the light on Six. Then at Sam.

'Anyone wanna try me?' he asks.

He's met with silence, which causes him to chuckle.

'Of course not,' he says. 'Three kids from North Carolina driving through Tennessee in a stolen truck on a Saturday night. Ya kids are on a dope run, aren't ya?'

I turn and stare into his face, which is ruddy and clean shaven.

'What do you want to do?' I ask.

'What do *I* wanna do? Ha! Ya kids are going to jail!'

I shake my head at him. 'I wasn't talking to you.'

He leans forward with his elbows on the door.

'So where's the dope?' he says, and then sweeps the flashlight across the interior of the truck. He stops when the light hits the Chest at my feet, then a smug smile spreads along his lips. 'Well, never mind, looks like I found it myself.'

He reaches to open the door. In one lightning-quick motion I shoulder-open the door and knock the officer backwards. He grunts and moves for his gun before he even hits the ground. Using telekinesis, I rip it away, bringing it to me

as I step out. I open the chamber and empty the bullets into my hand and snap the gun shut.

'What the . . .' The officer is dumbfounded.

'We're not dealing dope,' I say.

Sam and Six are out of the truck now and standing beside me.

'Put these in your pocket,' I say to Sam, handing him the bullets. Then I hand him the gun.

'What do you want me to do with this?' Sam asks.

'I don't know; put it in your bag with your dad's gun.'

Off in the distance, two miles away, the whine of a second siren reaches me. The officer stares intently at me, his eyes wide in recognition.

'Aw hell, you the boys from the news, aren't ya? Y'all are those terrorists!' he says, and spits on the ground.

'Shut up,' Sam says. 'We're not terrorists.'

I turn around and grab Bernie Kosar, who's still in the cab because of his broken leg. As I'm lowering him to the ground, an agonizing scream rips through the night. I jerk around and see Sam convulsing, and it takes a second to realize what's happened. The officer has Tasered him. I tear the Taser from him while I'm ten feet away. Sam falls to the ground and shakes as though he's having a seizure.

'What the hell is the matter with you!' I yell at the officer. 'We're trying to save you; don't you see that!'

Confusion crosses his face. I press the button of the Taser as it hovers in the air. Blue currents snap across the top of it. The cop scrambles away. I use telekinesis to

drag him through the pebbles and trash on the side of the road. He kicks and tries in vain to get away.

'Please,' he begs. 'I'm sorry, I'm sorry.'

'Don't, John,' Six says.

I refuse to listen to her. I'm blind to anything other than retribution, and I don't feel a shred of remorse as I slam the Taser into the officer's gut and hold it there for a full two seconds.

'How do you like it, huh? Big, tough guy with a Taser? Why can't anyone see we're not the bad guys!'

He shakes his head, his face locked in a horrified grimace, sweat beads glistening on his forehead.

'We have to get out of here fast,' Six says as the red and blue lights of the second police car appear on the horizon.

I lift Sam and pull him over my shoulder. Bernie Kosar is able to run on his own on only three legs. I carry the Chest under my left arm while Six carries everything else.

'This way,' she says, jumping over the guardrail and entering a barren field leading to the dark hills a mile away.

I sprint as fast as I can with Sam and the Chest. Bernie Kosar tires of hobbling and morphs into a bird and speeds ahead of us. Not a minute later the second car arrives on the scene, followed by a third. I can't tell if the officers are pursuing us on foot; but if they are, Six and I can easily outrun them even as weighed down as we are.

'Put me down,' Sam finally says.

'Are you okay?' I put him down.

'Yeah, I'm fine.' Sam is a little unsteady. Sweat beads his forehead, and he wipes it away with the sleeve of his jacket and takes a deep breath.

'Come on,' Six says. 'They aren't going to let us go that easily. We have ten minutes, fifteen at the most, until we're hiding from a helicopter.'

We make for the hills, Six in the lead, then me, then Sam struggling to keep up. He moves much faster than when we ran the mile in gym class a few months ago. It feels like years ago. None of us looks back; but as soon as we reach the first incline, the howl of a bloodhound fills the air. One of the officers has brought a police dog.

'Any ideas?' I ask Six.

'I was hoping we could hide our stuff and go invisible. That would elude a copter, but the dog will still pick up our scent.'

'Shit,' I say. I look around. There's a hill to our right.

'Let's get to the top and see what's on the other side,' I say.

Bernie Kosar zips ahead and disappears into the night sky. Six leads, stumbling wildly up. I follow behind her; and Sam, who is breathing heavily yet still moving swiftly, brings up the rear.

We stop at the top. Faint outlines of more hills as far as I can see, nothing more. Very softly I hear the trickle of running water. I spin around. Eight sets of flashing lights line the highway, sandwiching Sam's father's truck. In the distance, coming from both directions, two more cop cars are speeding towards the scene. Bernie Kosar

lands beside me and turns back into a beagle, tongue dangling. The police bloodhound barks, closer than before. There's no doubt that it's following our scent, which means that officers on foot can't be far behind.

'We have to get the dog off our trail,' Six says.

'Can you hear that?' I ask her.

'Hear what?'

'The sound of water. I think there's some kind of stream at the bottom of this. Maybe a river.'

'I hear it,' Sam chimes in.

An idea pops into my head. I unzip my jacket and remove my shirt. I wipe it across my face, my chest, soaking up every bit of sweat and scent I might have. I throw it at Sam.

'Do what I just did,' I say.

'No way, that's disgusting.'

'Sam, the entire state of Tennessee is hot on our trail. We don't have much time.'

He sighs but obeys me. Six does too, unsure of what I have planned but willing to go along with it. I put on a new shirt and slip on my jacket. Six tosses me the soiled shirt and I rub it over Bernie Kosar's face and body.

'We're going to need your help, buddy. You up for it?'

I can hardly see him in the dark, but the sound of his tail thumping excitedly on the ground is unmistakable. Always eager to assist, happy to be alive. I can sense within him the odd thrill of being chased, and I can't help but feel it myself.

'What's your plan?' Six asks.

'We have to hurry,' I say, taking the first steps downhill towards the running water. Bernie Kosar again turns himself into a bird and we race down, occasionally hearing the bloodhound bark and howl. It's closing the gap. If my idea fails, I wonder if I might communicate with it and tell it to stop following us.

Bernie Kosar waits for us at the bank of the wide river, which has a still quality to its surface that tells me it's much deeper than it sounded from the top of the hill.

'We have to swim across,' I say. There's no other choice.

'What? John, do you understand what happens to the human body when it's in freezing water? Cardiac arrest from shock, for one. And if that doesn't kill you, then the loss of feeling in your arms and legs will make it impossible to swim. We'll freeze and drown,' Sam objects.

'It's the only way to get the dog from following our scent. At least we'll have a chance this way.'

'This is suicide. Remember for a second that I'm not an alien.'

I drop to a knee in front of Bernie Kosar. 'You have to take this shirt,' I say to him. 'Drag it across the ground as fast as you can, for two or three miles. We'll cross the river so the bloodhound loses our scent and follows this one instead. Then we'll run some more. You should have no trouble catching up to us if you fly.'

Bernie Kosar transforms into a large bald eagle, takes the shirt into his talons, and speeds off.

'No time to waste,' I say, gripping the Chest in my left

arm so I can swim with my right. Just as I'm about to jump into the water Six grabs my bicep.

'Sam's right; we'll *freeze*, John,' she urges. She looks afraid.

'They're too close. We have no other choice,' I say. She bites her lip, her eyes sweeping the river, and turns back to me, giving my arm another squeeze.

'Yes we do,' she says. She lets go of my arm, and the whites of her eyes glisten in the dark. She pushes me behind her and takes a step towards the water, then tilts her head in a gesture of concentration. The bloodhound barks, closer than before.

She exhales slowly. At the same time she lifts her hands out in front of her, and as they come up, the waters of the river begin to part right there before us. With a loud rushing sound, the water foams and churns as it recedes upward to reveal a muddy path five feet wide that cuts across to the other bank. The water hovers, looking like a wave ready to crash. But instead it hangs suspended while icy mist coats our faces.

'Go!' she orders, her face strained in concentration, her eyes on the water.

Sam and I jump down from the bank. My feet sink and the mud comes nearly to my knees, but it still beats swimming in forty-degree temperatures in the dead of night. We tramp through it, taking big steps and struggling to lift our feet from the heavy mud. Once we're across Six follows, rotating her hands as she passes through the massive waves ready to crash into each

other, waves of her own creation. She climbs up the bank and then lets it go. The waves smash down with a deep hollow thud as though someone has just done a cannonball into it. The water rises and falls, and then looks no different than it did before.

'Amazing,' Sam says. 'Just like Moses.'

'Come on, we have to get into the trees so the dog can't see us,' she says.

The plan works. After just a few minutes, the dog pauses at the riverbank and sniffs wildly. He circles several times and then rushes after Bernie Kosar. Sam, Six, and I take off in the opposite direction, just inside the tree line but near enough to still see the river, going as fast as Sam's legs will permit.

The sound of men's voices yelling to one another reaches us for the first few minutes until we outrun them. Ten minutes after that we hear the first whir of a helicopter. We stop and wait for it to appear. A minute later, a spotlight shines high in the sky a few miles away in the direction Bernie Kosar has flown. The light sweeps the hills, shining one way, rushing the other.

'He should have been back already,' I say.

'He's fine, John,' Sam says. 'He's BK, the most resilient beast I know.'

'He has a broken leg.'

'But two healthy wings,' Six counters. 'He's fine. We have to keep going. They'll figure it out soon, if they haven't already. We have to stay ahead. The longer we wait, the closer they'll get.'

I nod. She's right. We have to keep going.

After a half mile the river takes a sharp turn to the right, back towards the highway, away from the hills. We stop and huddle beneath the low branches of a tall tree.

'Now what?' Sam asks.

'No idea,' I say. We turn in the direction in which we had just fled. The helicopter is closer now, its spotlight still sweeping back and forth across the hills.

'We have to leave the river,' I say.

'Yes, we do,' Six says. 'He'll find us, John. I promise.'

We hear an eagle's scream high in the treetops not far off. It's too dark to see where he is, and perhaps too dark for him to see us. I don't think twice about it, even if it will give away our position – I aim my palms towards the sky and turn my lights on, letting them shine as brightly as I can for a full half second. We wait, listening with our breaths held and heads craned. And then I hear a dog's pant, and Bernie Kosar, changed back into a beagle, comes charging up from the riverbank. He's out of breath but excited, his tongue falling from his mouth and his tail whipping in the air a thousand miles an hour. I bend down and pet him.

'Good job, buddy!' I say, planting a kiss on the top of his head.

And then it happens, a quick end to a celebration that was only just beginning.

While I'm on bended knee, a second copter shoots up over the hill behind us, instantly hitting us with its bright spotlight.

I bolt to my feet, blinded at once by the glaring beam.

'Run!' Six says.

We do, sprinting up the nearest hill. The helicopter drops down and hovers so the wind off its rotors beats against our backs and causes the trees to bow. The forest floor is a haze of debris, and I drape my arm across my mouth to breathe, keeping my eyes squinted to alleviate the stinging dirt. How long until the FBI is called?

'Stay where you are!' a male voice blares from the copter. 'You're all under arrest.'

We hear shouts. The officers on foot can't be more than five hundred feet away.

Six stops running, which causes Sam and me to do the same.

'We're toast!' Sam yells.

'Okay, you bastards. We'll do this the hard way,' Six says under her breath. She drops the bags, and for a second I think she plans to make Sam and me invisible. While I have no problem with leaving the bags behind, what does she expect me to do with the Chest? She can't make all of us invisible and that, too.

A brilliant stroke of lightning splits the night sky in two, followed by the deep groan of rolling thunder.

'John!' she yells without looking away.

'Right here.'

'Take care of the cops. Keep them away from me.'

Now I understand. I shove the Chest into Sam's arms, who stands beside me, unsure of what to do. 'Guard this

with your life,' I tell him. 'And stay down!' I turn to Bernie Kosar and communicate that he needs to stay with Sam in case our plan falls apart.

I sprint down the hill as another bolt of lightning, chased by a clap of thunder dark and menacing in tone, flashes across the sky. *Good luck, fellas,* I think, knowing full well the power of Six's abilities. *You're going to need it.*

I reach the bottom and hide behind an oak. The voices draw near, moving swiftly towards both pillars of light. Rain begins to fall, cold and heavy. I glance up through the thick drops and see both helicopters struggling against the gale-force winds, but somehow still keeping their beams steady. That won't last for long.

The first two officers blow past me, followed closely behind by a third. I reach out with my mind when they're fifteen feet away, grab all three in midstride, and yank them towards the thick oak. They surge backwards so fast I have to leap out of the way to keep from being hit. Two of them fall lifelessly to the ground, knocked unconscious by the tree. The third lifts his head, confused, then reaches for his gun. I tear it from its holster before his hand even touches it. The metal feels cold against my palm, and I turn to the two copters and hurl it like a bullet at the nearest. That's when I see the eyes, doleful and black in the middle of the storm. Soon the old, withered face takes shape. The same face I saw in Ohio when Six killed the beast that wrecked the school.

'Don't move a muscle!' I hear behind me. 'Hands in the air!'

I turn to the officer. Without his gun, he aims his Taser straight at my chest.

'Which is it, hands in the air or don't move a muscle? I can't do both.'

He cocks the Taser. 'Don't be a smartass, kid,' he says.

Lightning cracks, followed by a roar of thunder that makes the officer jump in surprise. The officer looks towards the sound, and his eyes open wide in alarm. The face in the clouds, it's awoken.

I rip the Taser from his hand, then punch him hard in the chest. He sails thirty feet backwards and crashes into the side of a tree. While my back is still turned, the crack of a nightstick slams against my skull. I fall face-first in the mud and sparkling fuzz fills my vision. I turn as quickly as I can, lift my hand towards the cop who hit me, and get a firm grip around him before he's able to hit me again. He grunts, and with all of my might I throw him as hard as I can straight up in the air. He screams until he's up so high I can no longer hear him over the copter blades and rumbling thunder. I feel the back of my head and look at my hand. It's covered with blood. I catch the officer when he's within five feet of dying. I let him hover a few seconds before tossing him against a tree, knocking him unconscious.

A loud explosion tears through the night, and the whir of the copters cuts off. The wind stops. The rain stops, too.

'John!' Six screams from the top of the hill; and somehow in the pleading, desperate tone of her voice, I know what she needs me to do.

The lights in my hands snap on, two glowing spotlights every bit as bright as those just extinguished. Both helicopters are wrecked and twisted, and smoke pours from them as they free fall. I don't know what the face has done to them, but Six and I must save the people aboard.

As they torpedo down, the helicopter farthest from me jerks upwards. Six is trying to stop it. I don't think she'll be able to, and I know that I can't. It's too heavy. I close my eyes. *Remember the basement in Athens, the way you captured everything inside the room to stop the speeding bullet.* And that's what I do, feeling everything inside the cockpit's interior. The controls. The weapons. The chairs. The three men sitting in them. I grab hold of the men, and as the trees begin to snap under the weight of the falling copter, I yank all three out. The copter crashes to the ground.

Six's copter hits the ground at the same time as mine. The explosions reach out over the treetops, two red balls of fire floating up from the twisted steel. I hold the three men in the air a safe distance from the damage, and bring them carefully to the ground. Then I race back up the hill to Six and Sam.

'Holy crap!' Sam says, his eyes wide-open.

'Did you pull them free?' I ask Six.

She nods. 'Just in time.'

'Me too,' I say.

I grab the Chest from Sam and thrust it into Six's arms. Sam picks up our bags.

'Why are you giving me this?' Six asks.

'Because we have to get the hell out of here!' I say. I grab Sam and drape him across my shoulders. 'Hold on!' I yell.

We sprint away, deeper into the hills away from the river, Bernie Kosar in the lead as a hawk. *Let the cops try to keep up now,* I think.

It's hard running with Sam on my shoulders, but I still keep a pace three times faster than what he could run on his own. And a far faster pace than any of the officers. Their yelling voices fade away, and after both helicopters just crashed in a heaping mess, who's to say they're even following?

After twenty minutes of a full-on sprint, we stop in a small valley. Sweat runs down my face. I shrug Sam off and he drops the bags. Bernie Kosar lands.

'Well, I imagine we're going to be all over the news again after that,' Sam says.

I nod. 'Staying hidden is going to be a lot harder than I thought.' I bend over at the waist, catching my breath with my hands on my knees. I smile, which quickly changes to a kind of incredulous half laugh over what just happened.

Six grins crookedly, adjusts the Chest in her arms, and begins climbing the next hill.

'Come on, guys,' she says. 'We're far from out of the woods just yet.'

8

We hop a freight train in Tennessee, and once we are settled Six tells us about her and Katarina being captured while they were in upstate New York, just a month after narrowly escaping the Mogadorians in West Texas. This second time around, after botching the first attempt, the Mogadorians had planned well; and when they stormed the room, they totaled more than thirty in number. Six and Katarina had been able to take a few down, but they were quickly bound, gagged, and drugged. When Six woke up – having no idea how much time had passed – she was alone in a cell in a hollowed-out mountain. She didn't discover she was in West Virginia until some time later. Six learned the Mogadorians had been trailing them the entire time, observing, hoping the two might lead them to the others, because, in Six's words, 'Why kill one when the others might be near?' I shift uneasily when she says this. Maybe she is still being followed and they are waiting for the perfect time to kill us.

'They had bugged our car when we were eating in the diner in Texas, and it never once occurred to either of us to check,' she says, and then gives herself over to a long silence.

Aside from an iron door containing a sliding hatch in

its center for food to be delivered through, her tiny cell was made entirely of rock, measuring eight feet on each side. She had no bed or toilet, and the cell was pitch-black. The first two days passed in total darkness and silence, without food or water (though she never felt hungry or thirsty, which, she said she later learned, was due to the charm's effect), and she had started to believe she'd been forgotten. But her luck hadn't been that good, and on the third day they came for her.

'When they opened the door I was huddled in the far corner. They threw a bucket of cold water on me, picked me up, blindfolded me, and pulled me away.'

After being dragged down a tunnel, they'd let her walk on her own while surrounded by ten or so Mogs. She could see nothing, but heard plenty – screams and cries from other prisoners there for who knows what reasons (when he heard this, Sam perked up and seemed about to interrupt and ask questions, but said nothing), the roars of beasts locked away in their own cells, and metallic clanking. And then she had been thrust in a room, had her wrists chained to a wall, and been gagged. They'd ripped off her blindfold, and when her eyes finally adjusted, she saw Katarina on the opposite wall, also chained and gagged and looking far worse than Six felt.

'And then he finally entered, a Mogadorian who looked no different from someone you're likely to pass on the street. He was small, had hairy arms and a thick mustache. Almost all of them had mustaches, as though they had learned to blend in by watching movies from

the early eighties. He wore a white shirt, and the top button was undone; and for some reason my eyes focused on the thick tuft of black hair poking out. I looked into his dark eyes, and he smiled at me in a way that told me he was looking forward to doing what he was about to do, and I started to cry. I slid down the wall until I dangled from the shackles around my wrists, watching through my tears as he pulled razor blades, knives, pliers, and a drill from the desk they had in the center of the room.'

When the Mogadorian had finished removing over twenty instruments, he'd gone to Six and stood inches from her face so that she could smell his sour breath.

'Do you see all of these?' he'd asked. She didn't respond. 'I intend to use each and every one of them on you and your Cêpan, unless you truthfully answer every question I ask. If you don't, I assure you that both of you will wish you were dead.'

He picked one up – a thin razor blade with a rubber-coated handle – and caressed the side of Six's face with it.

'I've been hunting you kids for a very long time,' he'd said. 'We've killed two of you, and now we have one right here, whatever number you are. As you might imagine, I hope you are Number Three.'

Six had made no response, pushing herself against the wall as though she might disappear into it. The Mogadorian grinned, the flat end of the razor still touching her face. Then he twisted it so the blade pressed against her cheek, and while looking deep into her eyes, he jerked the razor down and made a long, thin gash along her

face. Or rather he tried to, but it had been his own face that was slit open. Blood instantly poured down his cheek and he screamed in pain and anger, kicking the desk over, sending all of his tools flying, and he stormed from the room. Six and Katarina had been dragged back to their cells, kept in darkness another two days before finding themselves again gagged and chained to the walls of the room. Sitting on the desk with his cheek bandaged sat the same Mog, looking far less certain of himself than he had before.

He'd jumped from the desk and removed Six's gag, grabbed the same razor he had tried cutting her with, and held it up in front of her face, twisting it so that the light glimmered along the blade. 'I don't know what number you are . . .' For a second she'd thought he would try to cut her again, but he turned and crossed the room to Katarina instead. He stood at her side while looking at Six, and then he touched the blade to Katarina's arm. 'But you're going to tell me right now.'

'No!' Six had screamed. And then very slowly the Mogadorian made an incision down Katarina's arm just to be certain he could. His grin widened, and beside the original cut he made another, this one deeper than the first. Katarina groaned in pain while the blood ran down her arm.

'I can do this all day. Do you understand me? You're going to tell me everything I want to know, starting with what number are you.'

Six had closed her eyes. When she reopened them

he was at the desk, turning over a dagger that changed colors with movement. He'd held it up, wanting Six to see the blade twist and glow as it came to life. Six could feel its hunger, its desperation for blood.

'Now . . . your number. Four? Seven? Are you lucky enough to be Number Nine?'

Katarina had shaken her head in an attempt to keep Six quiet, and Six knew that no amount of torture would ever cause her Cêpan to talk. But she also knew she preferred death to seeing Katarina maimed and mutilated.

The Mogadorian had gone to Katarina, lifted the dagger so the tip was just over her heart. It jerked in his hand, as though the heart was a magnet pulling it forward. He looked into Six's eyes.

'I have all the time in the galaxies for this,' he'd said without emotion. 'While you are in here with me, we are out there with the rest of you. Don't think anything has stopped us from moving forward because we have you. We know more than you think. But we want to know *everything*. If you don't want to see her sliced into little pieces, then you better start talking, and fast. And every single word that comes out better be true. I *will* know if you're lying.'

Six had told him everything she remembered about leaving Lorien and the trip here, the Chests, where they'd been hiding. She talked so fast that most of it came out jumbled. Six told him she was Number Eight – not wanting to tell him the whole truth – and there was something

about the desperation in her voice that caused him to believe it.

'You really are weak, aren't you? Your relatives on Lorien, as easy as they fell, at least they were fighters. At least they had some bravery and dignity. But you,' he'd said, and shook his head as if disappointed. 'You have nothing, Number Eight.'

And then he'd jammed the knife forward, through Katarina's heart. All Six could do was scream. Their eyes had met for a single second before Katarina drifted away, her mouth still gagged, slowly sliding down the wall until the chain had run out of slack and she hung limply by her wrists as the light drained from her eyes.

'They were going to kill her anyway,' Six says softly. 'Telling them what I did, at least I spared her from horrible torture, as if there's any comfort in that.'

Six wraps her arms around her knees and stares at some abstract point out the window of the train.

'Of course there's comfort in that,' I offer, wishing I were brave enough to stand and wrap my arms around her.

To my surprise, Sam is that brave. He stands, and makes his way over to her. He doesn't say a word when he sits down next to her, instead opening his arms. Six buries her face in Sam's shoulder and cries.

She eventually pulls back and wipes her cheeks. 'When Katarina was dead, they tried everything, and I mean everything, they could to kill me – electrocution, drowning, explosives. They injected me with cyanide, which did nothing – I didn't even feel the needle going into my arm.

They threw me in a chamber filled with poisonous gas, and it was like the air inside was the freshest I'd ever breathed. The Mogadorian who pushed the button on the other side of the door, though, he was dead within seconds.' Six takes another swipe at her cheek with the back of her hand. 'It's funny, you know, that I think I killed more Mogadorians when I was captured than I did at the school in Ohio. They finally threw me in another cell, and I think they'd planned on keeping me there until they killed Three through Seven.'

'I love that you told them you were Number Eight,' Sam says.

'I feel bad that I did it now. It's like I tarnished Katarina's legacy, or the real Number Eight's.'

Sam places his hands on both her shoulders. 'No way, Six.'

'How long were you in there?' I ask.

'One hundred and eighty-five days. I think.'

My mouth drops open. Over half a year locked away, completely and utterly alone, waiting to be killed. 'I'm so sorry, Six.'

'I was just waiting and praying for my Legacies to finally develop so I could get the hell out of there. And then one day, the first one finally did. It was after breakfast. I looked down and my left hand just wasn't there. Of course, I freaked out, but then I realized I could still feel my hand. I tried to pick up my spoon, and sure enough, I could. And that's when I understood what was happening – and invisibility was the thing I needed in order to escape.'

How it started for Six wasn't all that different from how it had started for me, when my hand began to glow in the middle of my first class at Paradise High.

Two days later Six had been able to make herself completely invisible, and when dinner rolled around that day, and the slot on the door was slid open and her meal pushed through, the Mogadorian guard saw an empty cell. He'd looked wildly around and then hit an alarm that sent a piercing wail through the cave. The iron door had been flung open and four Mogs charged in. While they stood there, dumbfounded as to how she'd escaped, she slid by and rushed out the door and down the tunnel, seeing the cave for the very first time.

It had been a massive labyrinthine network of long, interconnected tunnels that were dark and drafty. There were cameras everywhere. She'd passed thick glass windows revealing chambers that looked like scientific labs, clean and brightly lit. The Mogadorians inside had worn white plastic suits and goggles, but she'd raced by so swiftly she couldn't tell what they were doing. A sprawling room housed a thousand or so computer screens with a Mogadorian sitting in front of each, and Six assumed they were looking for signs of us. *Just like Henri*, I thought. One tunnel was lined with heavy steel doors she had been sure held other prisoners. But she sped on, knowing her Legacy was far from developed and terrified she wouldn't stay invisible for very long. The siren had continued to wail. And then she reached the

heart of the mountain, a great, cavernous hall a half mile wide and so dark and murky she could hardly see to its other side.

The air had been stifling and Six was already sweating. The walls and ceiling were lined with huge wooden trellises to keep the cave from collapsing, and narrow ledges chiseled into the rock face connected the tunnels dotting the dark walls. Above her, several long arches had been carved from the mountain itself to bridge the great divide from one side to the other.

She had pressed herself against a rocky crag, her eyes darting back and forth for a way out. The number of passageways had been endless. She'd stood there overwhelmed, her eyes sweeping across the hollow darkness, seeing nothing at all that looked promising. But then she did – far across the ravine, a pale pinprick of natural light at the end of a wider tunnel. Just before she climbed the wooden trellis to reach the stone bridge that led to it, something else caught her eye: the Mogadorian who had killed Katarina. She couldn't let him get away. She followed him.

He entered the room where he had killed Katarina.

'I went straight to his desk and took the sharpest razor I saw, then grabbed him from behind and slit his throat. And as I watched the blood gush and spread across the floor, followed by him bursting into ash, I found myself wishing that it would have been possible to kill him a little more slowly. Or to kill him again.'

'What did you do when you finally got out?' I ask.

'I hiked up the opposite mountain, and when I got up there I stared down at the cave for an hour, trying to remember every little detail I could. Once I was satisfied with that, I took note of everything I passed on the five-mile run to the nearest road, and from there I jumped on the back of a slow pickup truck. When it stopped a few miles down the road to get gas, I stole the driver's map, a notepad, and a couple of pens from the cab. Oh, and a bag of potato chips.'

'Niiiiice. What kind of chips?' Sam asks.

'Dude,' I say.

'What?'

'They were barbecue, Sam. I marked the cave's location on the map I showed you guys back at the motel, and in the notepad I drew a diagram of everything I remembered, like a chart that would lead whoever read it straight to its entrance. I kind of panicked and hid the diagram not far from the town but kept the map, then I stole a car and drove straight to Arkansas; but of course by then my Chest had long since been taken.'

'I'm so sorry, Six.'

'Me, too,' she says. 'But they can't open it without me anyway. Maybe I'll get it back someday.'

'At least we still have mine,' I reply.

'You should open it soon,' she says, and I know she's right. I should have opened it already. Whatever's in that Chest, whatever secrets it holds, Henri had wanted me to know them. *The secrets. The Chest.* He had said as

much in his final breaths. I feel stupid for having put it off this long; but whatever's in the Chest, I have a feeling it's going to set the four of us on a long, uphill journey.

'I will,' I say. 'Let's just get off this train and find a safe place first.'

9

I'm the first one out of bed when the morning bell rings. I always am. It's not necessarily because I'm a morning person but because I prefer being in and out of the bathroom before anyone else.

I rush through making my bed, which I've gotten very good at over time. The key is getting the sheet, blanket, and comforter tucked deeply in at the foot. From there it's just a matter of pulling the rest to the head, tucking the sides, and adding pillows to give it that clean, a-quarter-could-be-bounced-off-it finish.

By the time I'm done, across the room in the bed nearest to the door, Ella, the girl who arrived on Sunday, is the only other one up. Like the previous two mornings, she's trying to emulate the way I make my bed, though she's struggling with it. Her problem is that she's trying to work from the top down instead of the bottom up. While Sister Katherine has been lenient with Ella, her rotation ends today and Sister Dora's weeklong shift begins tonight. I know she won't allow Ella to skimp on perfection, regardless of how new she is or what she's going through.

'Would you like help?' I ask, crossing the room.

She looks at me with sad eyes. I can see she doesn't

care about the bed. I imagine she doesn't care about much of anything right now, and I can't blame her, given the death of her parents. I'd like to tell her not to worry, that unlike those of us who are 'lifers,' she'll be out of this place within the month, two at the most. But what consolation can that be to her now?

I bend down at the foot of the bed and pull the sheet and blanket until there's enough to tuck them both beneath the mattress, then I stretch her comforter over them both.

'Want to grab that side?' I ask, nodding to the left of the bed while I go to the right. Together we give the whole bed the same tight, clean look as my own.

'Perfect,' I say.

'Thank you,' she replies in her soft, timid voice. I look down into her big brown eyes and can't help but like her and feel some need to look after her.

'I'm sorry to hear about your parents,' I say.

Ella looks away. I think I've overstepped my boundaries, but then she offers me a slight smile. 'Thank you. I miss them a lot.'

'I'm sure they miss you, too.'

We leave the room together, and I notice she walks on the balls of her feet so as not to make a sound.

At the bathroom sink, Ella grips her toothbrush near the top, almost touching the bristles with her small fingers, making the toothbrush appear larger than it really is. When I catch her staring at me in the mirror, I grin. She grins back, showing two rows of tiny teeth. Tooth-

paste pours from her mouth and runs down her arm, dripping from her elbow. I watch it, thinking the *S* pattern it creates is familiar, and I let my mind wander.

A hot summer day in June. Clouds drift in the blue sky. Cool waters ripple in the sun. The fresh air carries hints of pine. I breathe it in and let the stress of Santa Teresa melt away into nothingness.

Though I believe my second Legacy developed shortly after the first, I didn't discover it until almost a full year later. It was an accident I discovered it at all, which makes me wonder if I have other Legacies waiting to be uncovered.

Every year when school lets out for summer, to reward those of us who have been what the Sisters deem 'good,' a four-day trip to a nearby mountain camp is organized. I've always loved the trip for the same reason I love the cave that sits hidden in the opposite direction. It's an escape – a rare opportunity to spend four days swimming in the huge lake nestled in the mountains, or a chance to hike, to sleep beneath the stars, to smell the fresh air away from the musty corridors of Santa Teresa. It is, in essence, a chance to act our age. I've even caught some of the Sisters laughing and smiling when they think nobody's looking.

In the lake, there's a floating dock. I'm a horrible swimmer, and for many summers I just sat and watched from shore while the others laughed and played and did flips off the dock into the water. It took a couple summers of practicing alone in the shallow water, but

the summer of my thirteenth year, I finally learned an imperfect and slow doggy paddle that kept my head above water. It got me to the dock, and that was enough for me.

At the dock, the game is to try to push each other off it. Groups team up until they're the only ones left, and then it's every girl for herself. As the biggest and strongest at Santa Teresa, I used to think it'd be an effortless victory for La Gorda, but it rarely is; she's often outsmarted by the smaller, more wily girls, and I don't think anyone has won as many times as a girl named Bonita.

I didn't want to play *La Reina del Muelle*, Queen of the Dock. I was content to sit on the side and let my feet dangle in the water, but Bonita shoves me hard from behind anyway, sending me headlong into the lake.

'Play the game or go back to shore,' Bonita says, flicking her hair over her shoulder.

I climb back up and rush straight towards her. I shove her as hard as I can, and she falls backwards and crashes into the lake.

I don't hear La Gorda behind me, and suddenly two strong hands shove me hard from behind. My feet slip on the wet wood, and the side of my head and shoulder smack against the edge of the dock, clouding my vision with stars. I'm knocked unconscious for a second, and when my eyes open I'm underwater. I see nothing but darkness and instinctively kick upward, flailing my arms to reach the surface. But my head

smacks against the bottom of the dock, and I realize there are only a few inches of space between the water and the wooden boards of the dock. I try to tilt my head backwards to put my nose and mouth above the surface, but water instantly laps into my nostrils. I panic, my lungs already burning. I scramble to the left but there's nowhere to go; I'm trapped by the dock's plastic barrels. Water fills my lungs while the absurdity of death by drowning pops into my head. I think of the others, how their ankles are about to be seared. Will they believe that Number Three has been killed, or will they somehow know it's me? Will it burn differently than if I'd died at the hands of the Mogadorians instead of my own stupidity? My eyes slowly close and I begin to sink. Just as I feel the last stream of bubbles escape my lips, my eyes snap open, and an odd sort of calm sweeps in. My lungs are no longer burning.

I'm breathing.

The water tickles my lungs, but at the same time satisfies every desperate need I have to breathe, and that's when I know I've discovered my second Legacy: the ability to breathe underwater. I've found it only because I was pushed to the brink of death.

I don't want to be found just yet by the girls diving into the water looking for me, so I let myself drift down to the deep bottom, the world slowly fading to black until my feet finally sink into the cold mud. I can see through the brown, murky water once my eyes adjust. Ten minutes pass. Then twenty. Finally the girls

swim away from the dock. I assume the lunch bell's been rung. I wait until I'm absolutely sure they've all left, then I walk slowly along on the lake's bottom towards shore, my feet sinking into the mud as I inch forward. After a while the icy water begins to warm and brighten and the mud segues to rocks and then to sand, and finally my head emerges. I listen to the girls, La Gorda and Bonita included, scream and splash towards me in relief. I take inventory of myself on shore, noticing a gash on my shoulder is bleeding, leaving a trail of blood down my arm in the shape of a subtle *S*.

The Sisters make me sit the rest of the afternoon at a picnic table under a tree, but I didn't mind. I had another Legacy.

In the bathroom, Ella catches me watching the toothpaste run down her arm in the mirror. She looks embarrassed, and as she tries to replicate the way I brush my teeth, even more frothy toothpaste pours from her mouth.

'You're like a bubble factory,' I say with a smile, grabbing a towel to clean her up.

We leave the bathroom as the others are arriving, dress quickly in the room and walk out of it as the others are coming in, keeping just ahead of the group, as I prefer to do. We grab our lunches from the cafeteria and head out into the cold morning. I eat my apple on the walk to school. Ella does the same. I'm about ten minutes early today, which will give me a

little time to get on the internet to see if there's anything new about John Smith. The thought of him makes me smile.

'Why are you smiling? Do you like school?' Ella asks. I look over at her. The half-eaten apple looks big in her small hand.

'It's a nice morning, I guess,' I say. 'And I have good company today.'

We walk through town as street vendors set up shop. The snow hasn't melted and is piled along both sides of Calle Principal, but the road itself is clear. Up ahead on the right Héctor Ricardo's front door opens, and out comes his mother in a wheelchair, being pushed by Héctor. She's had Parkinson's disease for a very long time. She's been in a wheelchair for the last five years, and she's been unable to speak for the last three. He positions her in a sliver of sunlight and applies her wheel brakes. While the sun seems to bring her some comfort, Héctor slinks away and sits in the shade, dropping his head.

'Good morning, Héctor,' I call out. He lifts his head and squints one eye open. He waves with a shaky hand.

'Marina, as of the sea,' he croaks. 'The only limits of tomorrow are the doubts we have today.'

I stop and smile. Ella stops, too.

'That's one of your better ones.'

'Don't doubt Héctor; he has a few nuggets left,' he says.

'Are you doing okay?'

'Strength, confidence, humility, love. Héctor Ricardo's four tenets of a happy life,' he says, which makes no sense whatsoever considering the question I asked, but it makes me feel good anyway. He turns his gaze on Ella. 'And who's this little angel?'

Ella grabs my hand and hides behind me.

'Her name is Ella,' I say, looking down at her. 'This is Héctor. He's my friend.'

'Héctor is one of the good guys,' he says, though Ella remains behind me.

He waves at us as we walk the rest of the way to school.

'Do you know where you're going?' I ask her.

'I have Señora Lopez's class,' she says, smiling.

'Ahh, you're a lucky girl. I had her, too. She's one of the good ones in this town, like Héctor,' I say.

I'm devastated; all three of the school computers are occupied, a trio of younger girls from town are desperately trying to finish a science assignment, their fingers flying across the keyboards. I coast through the day, keeping to myself as one thing runs through my mind. John Smith, on the run in America, somehow staying ahead of the law, and I'm stuck here, in Santa Teresa, an old, moldy town where nothing happens. I'd always thought I'd leave when I turned eighteen. But now that John Smith is out there, being hunted, I know I have to leave as soon as I can, to join him. The only question now is how to find him.

My last class is Spanish history. The teacher drones

on about General Francisco Franco and the Spanish Civil War of the 1930s. I tune her out and instead write in my notebook about John, what I know based on the most recent article I read.

John Smith
Lived 4 months in Paradise, OH
Pulled over by an officer in Tennessee, driving west in a pickup truck. Middle of the night, with 2 other people around the same age.
Where were they driving?
One of the two people he was with is believed to be Sam Goode, also from Paradise, originally thought to be a hostage, now considered an accomplice.
Who is the third person? A girl with black hair. Girl in my dream had black hair.
Where is Henri?
How did they get away from 2 helicopters and 35 police officers? How did the 2 copters crash?

How can I contact him OR the others?
Post something on internet?
Too dangerous. Is there a way to do so that eludes the Mogs? If so, will any of the others even see it?
John is on the run. Ever checking internet?
Does Adelina know something that I don't?
Can I bring it up to her without being obvious?

The pen hovers over the page. The internet and Adelina, my only two ideas, neither of which seems

promising. What more can I do, though? Everything else seems as futile as walking up the mountain and sending smoke signals into the air. But I can't help but feel like I'm missing something – some crucial element that's so obvious it's staring me right in the face.

The teacher drones on. I close my eyes and think it all through. Nine Garde. Nine Cêpan. An airship that brought us to Earth, the same airship to take us back eventually, hidden somewhere on Earth. All I remember about it is that we landed in a remote place in the midst of a thunderstorm. A charm was cast to protect us from the Mogadorians, which went into effect only when we scattered, and that only works if we stay away from each other. But why? A charm that keeps us apart seems pretty counterintuitive in helping us fight and defeat the Mogadorians. What's the point in it? While asking myself this question my mind stumbles on something else. I close my eyes and let the logic carry me.

We were meant to hide, but for how long? Until our Legacies developed and we had the tools to fight, to win. What's the one thing we're able to do when that first Legacy finally arrives?

The answer seems too obvious to be correct. With the pen still in my hand, I write the only answer I can come up with:

The Chest

10

I no longer sleep without nightmares. Every night I'm stricken by Sarah's face, there for only a second before it's swallowed by darkness, followed by her calling out for help. No matter how furiously I search, she's nowhere to be found. She keeps calling, a scared voice, bleak and alone, but I can never find her.

And then there's Henri, his body twisted and smoking as he looks at me, knowing our end together has finally come. It's never fear I see in his eyes, or regret, or sadness, but rather pride, relief, and love. He seems to tell me to go on, to fight, to win. Then, right at the end, his eyes widen in a plea for more time. 'Coming here, to Paradise, it wasn't by chance,' he says again, and I still have no idea what he means. Then, 'I wouldn't have missed a second of it, kiddo. Not for all of Lorien. Not for the whole damn world.' This is my curse, that every time I dream of Henri I'm forced to watch him die. Over and over again.

I see Lorien, the days before the war, the jungles and oceans I've dreamed of a hundred times. Myself as a kid, running wild through the tall grass while those around me smile and laugh, unaware of the horrors to come. Then I see the war, the destruction, the killing, and the

blood. Sometimes, on nights like tonight, I have distinct visions of what I believe is the future.

My eyes aren't closed for long before I'm whisked away. And even as it begins, I feel myself entering a landscape I know I've never seen before, but still find familiar.

I run down a pathway lined with litter and debris. Broken glass. Burned plastic. Twisted, rusted steel. Acrid mist fills my nose and causes my eyes to water. Decaying buildings stand tall against the gray sky. A dark, stagnant river lurks to my right. There's commotion up ahead. The sounds of yelling and metallic clattering swell in the thick air. I come to an angry mob surrounding a tarmac where a large airship prepares for takeoff. I go through a barbed-wire gate and enter the airstrip fenced off from the crowd.

The tarmac is marked with small rivulets the color of magma. Mogadorian soldiers keep the crowd at bay while swarms of scouts ready the ship, an onyx orb hovering in midair.

The crowd roars against the fence as soldiers knock them back. They're smaller than the soldiers, but have the same ashy skin tone. A low rumble grows from somewhere beyond the ship. The crowd hushes, taking panicked steps backwards, while those on the tarmac file into orderly lines.

Then something drops from the hazy sky. A dark vortex absorbs the surrounding clouds, leaving a thick, black discharge in its wake. I cover my ears before the object crashes to the ground, shooting vibrations through the

soil that nearly knock me off my feet. Everything falls silent as the dust clears, revealing a perfectly spherical ship, milky white like a pearl. A round door slides open, and a monstrous creature steps out. The same creature that tried to behead me in the rock castle.

A brawl breaks out along the fence, with everyone scrambling to get away from this monster. He's even more enormous than I remember, with muscular, chiseled features and short, cropped hair. Tattoos crawl up his arms, scars are branded into his ankles, the largest of which stands out on his neck, grotesque and purple. A soldier retrieves a golden cane from the ship, its head curved like a hammer, a black eye painted on its side. When the creature holds it in his hand, the eye comes alive, rolling left and then right, taking in its surroundings, until it finds me.

The Mogadorian scans the crowd, sensing me nearby. His eyes narrow. He takes a giant step towards me, lifting the golden cane. Its eye pulses.

Just then an onlooker shouts at the Mogadorian, furiously rattling the fence. The Mogadorian turns towards the protester, thrusting the rod in his direction. The rod's eye glows red and the man is instantly ripped to shreds, torn through the barbed-wired fence. Pandemonium erupts as everyone fights to get away.

The Mogadorian returns his attention to me, pointing the rod at my head. I'm hit with the sensation of falling. Weightlessness rises in my gut until I'm on the brink of vomiting. What I see around his neck is so disturbing, so

haunting, that I'm jolted awake as though struck by a bolt of blue lightning.

Early dawn breaks through the windows, bathing the small room in the hard morning light. The shapes of things return. I'm sweat covered and out of breath. And yet I'm here, the ache and confusion in my heart telling me I'm still alive, no longer in a dreadful place where a man can be ripped through the small holes of a barbed-wired fence.

We found an abandoned house bordering a conservation area a few miles from Lake George. The kind of house Henri would have loved: isolated, small and quiet, offering security without any personality. It's one story, the exterior painted lime green while the interior is various shades of beige, with brown carpeting. We couldn't be luckier that the water hasn't been turned off. By the heavy dust in the air, I can only assume it's been a while since anyone lived here.

I roll to my side and glance at the phone beside my head. Having seen what I just did, the only thing that could take it all away is Sarah. I remember the time in my room when she'd just returned from Colorado – the way we'd held one another. If I'm allowed to save a single moment with her then I choose that one. I close my eyes and imagine what she's doing at this very moment, what she's wearing, who she's talking to. The news reported that each of the six school districts surrounding Paradise absorbed a portion of the displaced students until a

new building is built. I wonder which of them Sarah's attending, if she's still taking photographs.

I reach for my cell phone, the one prepaid and registered under the name Julius Seazar. Henri's sense of humor. I turn it on for the first time in days. All I have to do is dial her number to hear her voice. It's that simple. I press the familiar numbers one by one until reaching the last. I close my eyes, take a deep breath, then turn the phone off and flip it shut. I know I can't punch the tenth number. Fear for Sarah's safety, for her life – and all of ours, too – stops me.

Out in the living room, Sam streams CNN with one of Henri's laptops on his thighs. Luckily Henri's wireless internet card, under whatever pseudonym he chose at the time, still works. Sam furiously scribbles notes on a legal pad. It's been three days since the mess in Tennessee, and we only arrived in Florida last night, having hopped aboard three different semis – one of which carried us two hundred miles in the wrong direction – before jumping a train that brought us here. Without the use of our Legacies – our speed, Six's invisibility – we would have never made it. It's our intent to lie low for a bit and let the news dissipate. We'll regroup, start training, and avoid any further mishaps like the one involving the helicopters at all costs. First order of business, find a new car. Second order of business, figure out what to do next. None of us really knows for sure. Again, I feel the enormity of Henri's absence.

'Where's Six?' I ask, stumbling into the living room.

'Out back swimming laps or something,' Sam replies.

The one cool thing about the house is the pool in the backyard, which Six immediately filled by directing a heavy rainstorm overhead.

'I'd think you'd want to catch a glimpse of Six in her bathing suit.' I nudge Sam.

His face reddens. 'Shut up, dude. I wanted to check the news. You know, be productive.'

'Anything?'

'Aside from now being considered an accomplice and having the reward for me increased to a half million dollars?' Sam asks.

'Oh come on, you know you love it.'

'Yeah, it's pretty cool,' he says, grinning. 'Anyway, no, nothing new. I don't see how Henri kept up with all this. There're literally thousands of stories every day.'

'Henri never slept.'

'Don't *you* want to go check out Six in her bathing suit?' Sam asks, turning back to the screen. I'm surprised by the lack of sarcasm in his voice. He knows how I feel about Sarah. And I know how he feels about Six.

'What's that supposed to mean?'

'I see the way you look at her,' Sam says. He clicks on a link about a plane crash in Kenya. One survivor.

'And how do I look at her, Sam?'

'Never mind.' The survivor is an old woman. Definitely not one of us.

'The Loric fall in love for life, man. And I love Sarah. You know that.'

Sam looks over the screen of the laptop. 'I know you

do. It's just that, I don't know. You're the kind of guy she'd go for, not some math nerd obsessed with aliens and outer space. I just don't see how Six could fall for someone like me.'

'You kick ass, Sam. And don't forget it.'

I walk out the rear sliding glass door leading to the pool. Beyond the pool lies an overgrown yard enclosed by a brick wall offering privacy from anyone who might wander by. The nearest neighbor is a quarter mile away. The nearest town is a ten-minute drive.

Six zips across the water, skimming the top like some water-borne insect, and beside her, going twice as fast, is a platypus-shaped mammal with long white hair and a beard – I have no idea what animal Bernie Kosar's copying. Six senses me and stops at the edge, pulling herself halfway out of the water and resting her arms on the deck. Bernie Kosar jumps out and returns to his beagle form, shaking himself dry and covering me with water. It's refreshing, and I can't help but think how nice it is to be down South again.

'You better not be killing my dog out here,' I say. I catch myself staring at her perfect shoulders, her slender neck. Maybe Sam is right. Maybe I am looking at Six the same way he does. I want more than ever to run back inside, turn on my phone, and hear Sarah's voice.

'More like he's killing me. The little guy swims like he's totally healed. Speaking of which, how's your head?'

'Still hurts,' I say, running a hand over it. 'But nothing I can't handle. I'm ready to start training today, if that's why you're asking.'

'Good,' she says. 'I'm getting antsy. It's been a long time since I've trained with somebody.'

'You're sure you want to train with me? You know you'll probably end up hurt, right?'

She laughs, and then spits a mouthful of water at me.

'Oh, it's on,' I say, visualizing the surface of the pool and forcing a blast of air over it. Water rushes towards her face. She dives beneath the surface to keep from being splashed, and when she comes up she rides the crest of a huge wave that nearly empties the pool, bringing her towards me. Before I can react she moves away, but the wave keeps coming, knocking me over and sending me crashing into the back of the house. I hear her laughing. The water recedes to the pool, and I stand and try pushing her backwards into it. She deflects my telekinesis, and all at once I'm upended and sailing through the air upside down where I flail helplessly.

'What the hell are you guys doing out here?' Sam asks. He's standing at the sliding glass door.

'Um. Six was talking smack, so I decided to put her in her place. Can't you tell?'

I remain upside down, hovering four feet over the pool's center. I can feel Six's grip around my right ankle, and the sensation is the same as if she were literally holding me up with one hand.

'Oh, totally. Got her right where you want her,' Sam replies.

'I was about to make my move, you know. Biding my time.'

'So what do you think, Sam?' Six asks. 'Should I let him have it?'

A smile breaks across Sam's face. 'Take it away.'

'Hey!' I say just before she lets go and I fall headfirst into the water. When I resurface, Six and Sam are laughing hysterically.

'That was only round one,' I say, climbing out. I peel off my shirt and slap it to the concrete. 'You caught me off guard. Just wait.'

'What happened to being tough and rugged?' Sam asks. 'Isn't that what you said when you buzzed your head?'

'Strategy,' I say. 'I'm just giving Six a false sense of security, then when she gets comfortable I'm going to pull the rug out from under her.'

'Ha! Yeah, right,' Sam says, then adds, 'God, I wish I had Legacies.'

Six stands between us in her solid black one-piece bathing suit. She's still laughing, and water runs down her arms and legs as she leans slightly forward and twists her hair to ring it out. The scar on her leg is still discolored, but it isn't nearly as purple as it was the week before. She whips her hair back over her head. Sam and I are both mesmerized.

'So, training this afternoon then?' Six asks. 'Or do you still feel like I might get hurt?'

I puff my cheeks and release the air slowly. 'Maybe I'll take it easy on you. I mean, that scar on your leg still looks kinda nasty. But, yeah, we're on.'

'Sam, is that a yes for you, too?'

'You guys want me to train? Seriously?'

'Of course. You're one of us now,' Six says.

He nods, rubbing his hands together. 'I'm in,' he says, grinning like a kid on Christmas morning. 'But if you just want me for target practice, I'm going home.'

We start at two o'clock, but by the look of the gloomy sky I don't anticipate training for very long. Sam bounces on the balls of his feet, wearing gym shorts and an oversized tee. He's all knees and elbows, but if heart and determination could be counted, I think he'd be nearly the size of the Mogadorian I'd seen aboard the ship.

To start, Six shows us what she's learned of combat techniques, which is far more than I know. Her body moves fluidly and with the precision of a machine when she throws a kick or punch, or when she does a back flip to evade an attack. She shows us how to counterassault and the merits of skill and coordination, and drills the same maneuvers until they come instinctively. Sam eats it up, even when Six pounds him backwards and he flips head over heels or has the wind knocked out of him. She does the same to me, and even though I try laughing it off like I'm playing around, I work my hardest and she still kicks the crap out of me. I can't fathom how she learned all this on her own. After my mouth is filled with grass and dirt for the second time, I realize just how much she can teach me.

The rain begins a half hour later. A light drizzle at first, but soon the skies open, sending us indoors for cover.

Sam paces through the house throwing kicks and punches at phantom enemies. I sit in the chair, my fist around my blue pendant, and stare out the front window for a very long time, simply watching it all happen while remembering that the last two storms I saw both raged because Six told them to.

When I turn back I see that she's sound asleep in the corner of the living room, curled around Bernie Kosar, holding him in her arms like a pillow. It's how she always sleeps, wrapping herself into a ball on her side, her features losing their sharp edges.

The white bottoms of her feet are aimed right at me, and I use telekinesis to lightly tickle the bottom of her right foot. She twitches it as though shooing a pesky fly. I tickle her again. She twitches her foot a little harder. I wait a few seconds and then, as softly as I can, I tickle the length of her foot, from her heel up to her big toe. Six pulls her foot back and kicks her leg straight out, the telekinetic force of which sends me flying into the nearest wall, leaving a hole revealing the interior wires and studs. Sam charges into the room and jumps into the perfect fighting position.

'What happened? Who's here?' he yells.

I stand, rubbing my elbow, which took the brunt of the hit.

'Jerk,' Six says, sitting up.

Sam looks from me to her.

'You guys are ridiculous,' he says, retreating back to the kitchen. 'Your flirting just scared the hell out of me.'

'Scared the hell out of me, too,' I say, ignoring the flirting comment; but he's already gone and doesn't hear it. Am I flirting? Would Sarah think that was flirting?

Six yawns, raising her arms to the ceiling. 'Still raining?'

'Totally, but look on the bright side; the weather saved you from any further bruises.'

She shakes her head. 'The tough-guy routine is pretty tired, Johnny. And don't forget what I can do with the weather.'

'Wouldn't dream of it,' I say. I try to change the subject. I hate myself for flirting with another girl. 'Hey, I've been meaning to ask you: who's the face in the clouds? Every time you whip up a storm I see this crazy, ominous face.'

She scratches the bottom of her right foot. 'I'm not sure, but ever since I've been able to mess with the weather, it's always the same face that appears. I assume it's Loric.'

'Yeah, probably. And here I thought it might be a crazy ex-boyfriend you've yet to get over.'

'Because obviously I have a weakness for ninety-year-old men. You know me so well, John.'

I shrug. Both of us smile.

That night I cook dinner on a rusty but serviceable grill left on the back patio. Or try to cook, I guess. Since I took home economics with Sarah in Paradise, I'm the only one who knows how to make anything remotely resembling a meal. Tonight: chicken breasts, potatoes, and a frozen pepperoni pizza.

We're sitting on the living-room carpet in a triangle.

Under the blanket Six has draped over her head and body, she wears a black tank top, and her pendant hangs in full view. The sight of it returns my mind to the vision I had. I long for a normal dinner around a table and a normal night's sleep where I'm not tortured by my Loric past. Was that what it was like on Lorien before we left?

'Do you think about your parents a lot?' I ask Six. 'Back on Lorien, I mean?'

'Not that much anymore. I can't even tell you what they look like, really. I remember how it felt being near them, though, if that makes any sense. I think about that feeling quite a bit, I guess. What about you?'

I pick at a burned slice of pizza. I resolve never to cook frozen pizza on the grill again. 'I see them a lot in my dreams. Which is really great, but at the same time it tears me up inside. Reminds me that they're dead.'

The blanket slides off the top of Six's head and rests on her shoulders. 'What about you, Sam? Do you miss your parents right now?'

Sam opens his mouth and closes it. I can tell he's considering telling Six that he thinks his dad was taken by aliens, abducted when he went out for milk and bread. Finally he says, 'I miss them both, my mom and dad, but I know that I'm better off here with you guys. Considering what I know about everything, I don't think I could be at home.'

'You know too much,' I say. I feel guilty he's eating my terrible meal on the floor of an abandoned house instead of feasting on his mother's food at a dining-room table.

'Sam, I'm sorry you got caught up in this with us,' Six says. 'But it's nice that you're here.'

He blushes. 'I don't know what it is, but I feel a weird connection to the whole situation. Can I ask you something? How far away is Mogadore from Earth?'

I think back to when Henri blew on the seven glass orbs, how they came to life. Soon we were looking at a floating replica of our solar system. 'It's a lot closer than Lorien is, why?'

Sam stands. 'How long would it take to get there?'

'A few months maybe,' Six says. 'Depends on what type of ship you're flying and what type of energy it uses.'

Walking in circles, Sam says, 'I think the U.S. government has to have a ship built somewhere that can handle that distance. I'm sure it's a prototype and top secret and hidden under a mountain that's hidden under another mountain, but I was just thinking about what would happen if we couldn't find your ship and needed to take the fight to them – go to Mogadore. We have to have a Plan B, right?'

'Sure. What's Plan A again?' I ask, biting my tongue. I can't fathom fighting the whole planet of Mogadore on their own turf.

'Getting my Chest,' Six says. She pulls the blanket back over her head.

'And then what?'

'Training?'

'And then what?' I ask.

'We go find the others, I guess.'

'It just sounds like a bunch of running and not much of anything else. I think Henri or Katarina would have us doing something more productive somehow. Like studying how to kill certain enemies. Do you know what a piken is?'

'Those are those huge beasts that destroyed the school,' Six says.

'What about a kraul?'

'Those are the smaller animal things that attacked us in the gymnasium,' she answers. 'Why?'

'In the dream that I had in North Carolina, when you and Sam heard me speaking Mogadorian, those two names were mentioned, but I'd never heard of them before. Henri and I simply called them "the beasts."' I pause. 'I had another dream earlier.'

'Maybe you aren't having dreams,' she says. 'Maybe you're having visions again.'

I nod. 'It's hard to tell the difference at this point. I mean, these dreams felt the same as the visions I had of Lorien, but I wasn't on Lorien during these two,' I say. 'Henri once said that when I have visions it's because they hold some sort of personal significance to me. And that's always been true – the past visions were always of things that had already happened. But I think what I witnessed in my dream this morning . . . I don't know. It's like I was seeing it as it was actually happening.'

'Wicked,' Sam says. 'You're like a TV.'

Six crumples her paper towel and tosses it up in the air above her head. Without thinking I set it on fire, and it wilts into nothing before landing on the carpet. Then Six

says, 'It's not impossible, John. Some of the Loric have been known to do it. That's what Katarina said, anyway.'

'But the thing is, I think I was on Mogadore, which, by the way, is just as disgusting as I imagined it would be. The air was so thick it made my eyes water. Everything was desolate and gray. But, how did I get there? And how could this one huge dude on Mogadore seem to sense when I was there?'

'How huge?' Sam asks.

'Huge, like more than double the size of the soldiers I saw, twenty feet tall, maybe more, far more intelligent and powerful. I can tell just by looking at him. He was definitely a leader of some sort. I've seen him twice now. The first time I was overhearing information relayed to him by some little peon, and it was all about us and what had happened at the school. This second time I saw him as he was preparing to board a ship; but before he was on it, one of the others ran up and handed him something. I didn't know what it was at first, but just before the ship's door closed, he turned towards me to make sure I could see exactly what it was.'

'What was it?' Sam asks.

I shake my head, ball up my paper towel, and burn it on the palm of my hand. I look out the back door at the setting sun, a blaze of orange and hot pink like the Florida sunsets Henri and I watched from our elevated porch. I wish he was still here to help make sense of all this now.

'John? What was it? What did he have?' Six asks.

I lift my hand and grab my pendant.

'This. These. He had pendants. Three of them. The Mogadorians must have taken them after each kill. And this massive leader guy, or whoever he is, he put them around his neck like Olympic medals, and then he stood there just long enough so I could see. Each one was glowing bright blue, and when I woke up, mine was too.'

'So are you saying it's a premonition, like you just saw your fate? Or could you have just had a weird dream because of how stressed out you are?' Sam asks.

I shake my head. 'I think Six is right and these are all visions. And I think they're all happening right now. But the thing that scares me the most is that when that guy got on that ship, there's a good chance he was headed this way. And, if Six is right about how fast a ship can travel, it won't be very long until he's here.'

11

The things I remember about coming to Santa Teresa are mostly just snippets of a long journey I thought would never end. I remember an empty stomach and sore feet and being impossibly tired most of the time. I remember Adelina begging for change, for food; remember the seasickness and the vomiting it caused. I remember disgusted looks from passersby. I remember every time we changed names. And I remember the Chest, as cumbersome as it was, that Adelina refused to part ways with no matter how dire our situation became. On the day we finally knocked at the door Sister Lucia answered, I remember it being on the ground tucked snug between Adelina's feet. I know she stowed it away in the shadows of some obscure corner of the orphanage. My days of searching have turned up nothing, but I still keep looking.

On Sunday, one week after Ella arrived, we sit together in the back pew during Mass. It's her first, and it holds her attention about as well as it holds mine: not at all. Aside from class, she's pretty much been by my side since the morning I helped her make her bed. We walk to and from school together, eat breakfast and dinner together, say our nightly prayers

together. I've grown very attached to her, and by the way she follows me around, I can tell she's grown attached to me as well.

Father Marco has droned on for a good forty-five minutes, and finally I close my eyes, thinking of the cave and debating whether I should bring Ella along with me today. There are several problems with it. First, there's zero light inside, and there's no way Ella will be able to see through the dark in the way that I can. Second, the snow has yet to melt, and I'm not sure she'd be able to make the trek through it. But most of all, I worry that bringing her would be putting her in harm's way. The Mogadorians could arrive at any moment, and Ella would be defenseless. But even with these obstacles and concerns, I'm eager to take her along anyway. I want to show her my paintings.

On Tuesday, minutes before we were to depart for school, I had found Ella hunched over on her bed. Still chewing on a breakfast biscuit, I looked over her shoulder to see her furiously shading a perfect drawing of our sleeping quarters. The details, the technical accuracy of each crack in the wall, her ability to capture the faintest of squares of sunrays that dropped through the windows in the morning, was astounding. It was as if I was looking at a black-and-white photograph.

'Ella!' I had blurted.

She had flipped the paper over, trapping it against her schoolbook with her tiny smudged hands. She knew it was me but didn't turn around.

'Where did you learn how to do that?' I'd whispered. 'How did you learn to draw so well?'

'My father,' she whispered back, keeping the drawing turned over. 'He was an artist. So was my mother.'

I'd sat down on her bed. 'And here I thought I was a pretty good painter.'

'My father was an incredible painter,' she'd said plainly. Before I could ask her more questions, we had been interrupted and then ushered out of the room by Sister Carmela. That night I'd found Ella's drawing under my pillow. It's the best present I've ever received.

Sitting in Mass, I think that maybe she can help me with my cave paintings. Surely I can find a flashlight or lantern somewhere here to take with us. And then my thoughts are interrupted by a fit of giggles beside me.

I open my eyes and look over. Ella's found a red-and-black furry caterpillar that's in the process of crawling up her arm. I bring my finger to my lips in a sign of silence. It stops her for a brief moment, but then the caterpillar climbs higher and she begins giggling again. Her face turns red while trying not to laugh, but the fact that she's trying to stifle it only makes it that much harder. And then she can't help herself and a string of laughs escape. Every head snaps around to see what's happening, and Father Marco stops his sermon in midsentence. I snatch the caterpillar from Ella's arm and sit upright, staring back at those staring at us. Ella stops laughing. Slowly the heads turn back around

and Father Marco, clearly flustered at having lost his spot, resumes his sermon.

I sit with my hand around the caterpillar. It tries wriggling free. After a minute I open my fist, and the sudden movement causes the furry little thing to curl into a ball. Ella raises her eyebrows and cups her hands together, and I place the caterpillar in them. She sits there smiling down at it.

I scan the front row. I'm not at all surprised to see Sister Dora glaring sternly in my direction. She shakes her head before turning back to Father Marco.

I lean over to Ella.

'When prayer ends,' I whisper into her ear, 'we have to get out of here as fast as we can. And keep away from Sister Dora.'

Before Mass I'd fixed Ella's hair into a tight braid; and now, gazing up at me with her big, brown eyes, it looks as though the heavy braid is weighing her head back.

'Am I in trouble?'

'We should be okay,' I tell her. 'But just in case, we'll rush out of here before Sister Dora can catch up to us. Got it?'

'Got it,' she says.

But we don't get the chance. When there are just a few minutes left, Sister Dora stands and casually strolls to the back, and then stands waiting at the door a few steps away. When my eyes reopen as the final prayer ends with the sign of the cross, Sister Dora places a hand on my left shoulder.

'Come with me, please,' she says to Ella, reaching across me to grab her by the wrist.

'What are you doing?' I say.

Sister Dora pulls Ella past me. 'It's none of your business, Marina.'

'Marina,' Ella pleads. As she's being dragged away, Ella looks back at me with scared eyes. I panic and rush to the front of the church where Adelina is standing, talking with a lady from town.

'Sister Dora just grabbed Ella and pulled her away,' I quickly say, interrupting her. 'You have to make her stop, Adelina!'

She looks incredulously at me. 'I will do no such thing. And it's *Sister* Adelina. If you'll excuse me, Marina, I was in the middle of a conversation,' she says.

I shake my head at her. Tears form in my eyes. Adelina doesn't remember what it feels like to ask for help and not receive it.

I turn and run from the room and up the winding staircase to the church offices. To the left, at the end of the hall, the only door closed is the one leading to Sister Lucia's office. I race towards it, trying to decide what I should do. Should I knock? Should I kick straight through it? But I don't get the chance to do either. When I'm within reaching distance of the knob, I hear the crack of the paddle, followed instantly by a scream. I'm frozen in shock. Ella cries on the other side of the door and a second later the door is opened by Sister Dora.

'What are you doing here?' she snaps at me.

'I came to see Sister Lucia,' I lie.

'She's not here, and you're due in the kitchen. Go on,' she says, shooing me the way I came. 'I'm headed there myself.'

'Is she okay?'

'Marina, it's none of your concern,' she says, and then grabs me by the bicep, spins me around, and gives me a shove.

'Go!' she orders.

I move away from the office, hating the fear that runs through me every time confrontation stares me in the face. It's always been that way – with the Sisters, with Gabriela García, with Bonita on the dock – I get the same feeling, the same nervousness that quickly segues to dread, that always causes me to walk away.

'Walk faster!' Sister Dora barks, following me down the staircase and towards the kitchen where El Festín duties await.

'I have to use the restroom,' I say before we reach the kitchen, which is a lie; I want to make sure Ella's okay.

'Fine. But you better make it fast. I'm timing you.'

'I will.'

I duck around the corner and wait thirty seconds to make sure she's gone. Then I rush back the way we came, up the staircase, down the hall. The office door is slightly ajar and I walk through it. The interior is dark, somber. A layer of dust covers the shelves that

line the walls, upon which sit ancient books. The only light enters through a dirty stained glass window.

'Ella?' I say, for some reason thinking she might be hiding. No answer. I walk away and poke my head in the rooms situated off the main hallway, all of which are empty. I call her name as I go. At the hall's opposite end is the Sisters' sleeping quarters. There's no sign of her in there either. I go back down the stairs. The crowd has made its way to the cafeteria. I walk to the nave looking around for Ella. She's not in there, nor is she in either of the two sleeping rooms, nor the computer room, nor any of the storage rooms. By the time I've looked in most places I can think to check, a half hour has passed and I know I'll be in trouble if I go to the cafeteria.

Instead I hurry out of my Sunday clothes, pull my coat off its hook, swipe the blanket from my bed, and dash outside. I trudge through the snow away from town, unable to push the sound of the paddle's crack and Ella's scream from my mind. I'm also unable to forgive Adelina's scorn towards me. My whole body tense, I focus my energy on some of the large rocks I pass, using telekinesis to lift and hurl them against the mountainside. It's a great way to blow off steam. The snow's surface has hardened, creating a thin layer of ice that crunches underfoot, but it doesn't keep the rocks from skidding downhill. I'm so mad I could let them go, careening towards town. But I stop them in

their tracks. My gripe isn't with the town but rather its namesake, and those who live within it.

I pass the camel's back – half a kilometer to go. The sun is warm on my face, situated high in the sky and slanted towards the east, which means I have at least five hours before I'm due back. I haven't had this much free time in a great while; and with the bright sun and crisp, fresh wind pulling me from my dismal mood, I hardly care that I'll be in trouble when I get back. I turn to see how effective my blanket cape is at hiding my prints in the hardened snow, and I'm afraid to see that it hasn't worked at all today.

Nevertheless, I push forward until I spot the rounded shrub sticking up over the snow, then I race towards it, at first not noticing the very thing my eyes should be attuned to: that the snow at the base of the cave is tossed up and pushed around. But as soon as I reach the cave's entrance, I know immediately that something is horribly off.

Approaching from the south, a single set of boot prints, double the size of my own, dot the mountain-side, a perfect straight line cut into the snow leading from town to the cave. They seem to tromp around its opening, as though circling it. I'm flustered, certain there's something else here I'm missing. And then it dawns on me. The prints – they lead into the cave, but they don't lead back out.

Whoever they belong to is still inside.

12

They're here! I think. *After all these years, the Mogadorians are finally here!*

I turn so fast I slip and fall into the snow. I quickly crawl backwards away from the cave's mouth, my shoes tangled in the blanket. Tears well up in my eyes. My heart races. I manage to right myself and sprint as hard and as fast as my legs will carry me. I don't even look behind me to see if I'm being followed, sweeping across the same snowy terrain I'd just hiked through, moving so fast I hardly take note of where my feet are falling. The trees below me begin to blur, as do the clouds above. I can feel the blanket hovering behind my shoulders, flapping in the wind like a superhero's cape. I trip once and slide across the ground, but immediately scramble to my feet and sprint onward, jumping straight over the camel's back, again crashing when I land. And then I finally dash past the birch trees and make it back to the convent; the hike there took nearly twenty-five minutes; the sprint back took less than five. Like the ability to breathe underwater, the Legacy of superspeed presents itself when I need it to.

I untie the blanket from around my neck, burst through the double doors, and hear the lunchtime

clatter coming from the dining room. I hurry up the winding staircase and down the narrow hall, knowing it's Adelina's turn to take Sunday off. I enter the open room where the Sisters sleep. Adelina sits regally in one of the two high-back chairs, Bible in her lap. She closes it when she sees me coming.

'Why aren't you at lunch?' she asks.

'I think they're here,' I say, out of breath, my hands violently shaking. I bend over and rest them on my knees.

'Who?'

'You know who!' I yell. Then, between my closed teeth: 'Mogadorians.'

Her eyes narrow in disbelief. 'Where?'

'I went to the cave –'

'What cave?' she interrupts.

'Who cares what cave! There was a set of boot prints outside of it, huge boot prints –'

'Slow down, Marina. Boot prints outside of a cave?'

'Yes,' I say.

She smirks, and I instantly realize coming to her was a mistake. I should have known she wouldn't believe me, and I can't help feeling foolish and vulnerable standing in front of her. I straighten. I don't know what to do with my hands.

'I want to know where my Chest is,' I say, not exactly in a confident voice, but not in a timid one either.

'What Chest?'

'You know exactly what Chest!'

'What makes you think I held on to that old thing?' she asks calmly.

'Because you would be turning against your own people if you didn't,' I say.

She reopens her Bible and pretends to read. I think of leaving, but then my mind returns to the boot prints in the snow.

'Where is it?' I ask.

She continues to ignore me, so I reach out with my mind and feel the contours of the book, its thin, dusty pages, its rough-hewn cover. I snap the book shut. Adelina jumps.

'Tell me where it is.'

'How dare you! Who do you think you are?'

'I'm a member of the Garde, and the fate of the entire race of Loriens depends on my survival, Adelina! How could you turn your back on them? How could you turn your back on the humans, too? John Smith, who I believe is a member of the Garde, is on the run in the United States; and when he was pulled over recently he was able to move the officer without touching him. Just like I can do. Like I just did with your book. Don't you see what's happening, Adelina? If we don't start helping, not only will Lorien be lost forever, but so will Earth and this stupid orphanage and stupid town!'

'How dare you call this place stupid!' Adelina steps towards me with clenched fists. 'This is the only place that let us in, Marina. It's the only reason we're still alive. What did the Loric do for us? They pushed us onto a

ship for a year, and then they pushed us out onto a cruel planet without any kind of plan or any instructions other than to stay hidden and train. Train for what?'

'To defeat the Mogadorians. To take back Lorien.' I shake my head. 'The others are probably out there right now, battling, figuring out how to come together and how to get us home, while we're stuck in this prison doing nothing.'

'I'm living my life with purpose, helping the human race with my prayers and service. And you should be, too.'

'Your sole purpose on Earth was to help *me*.'

'You're alive, aren't you?'

'Only in the literal sense of the word, Adelina.'

She sits back in her chair and opens the Bible on her lap. 'Lorien is dead and buried, Marina. What does it matter?'

'Lorien isn't dead; it's hibernating. You said so yourself. And the point is, we're not dead.'

She swallows hard. 'A death sentence has been handed down to us all,' she says, and her voice slightly cracks. Then, in a much softer tone, she says, 'Our lives were doomed from the beginning. We should do good while we're here, so we may have a good afterlife.'

'How can you say that?'

'Because that's the reality. We're the last of a dying race, and soon we'll be gone, too. And may God help us when that time comes.'

I shake my head at her. I have no interest in talking about God.

'Where is my Chest? In this room?' I walk around the room, casting my gaze along the ceiling's edges, and then I crouch and peer beneath a few of the beds.

'Even if you had it, you can't open it without me,' she says. 'You know that.'

She's right. If I'm to believe what she'd told me years before, when I could still trust the things she said, then I can't open it without her. The futility of it hits me all at once. The boot prints in the snow; John Smith on the run; the sheer and utter claustrophobia of Santa Teresa; and Adelina, my Cêpan, meant to help and assist in developing my Legacies, who has given up on our mission. She doesn't even know what Legacies of mine have developed. I have the ability to see in the dark, breathe underwater, to run at superspeeds; to move things with my mind; and the means to bring plants back from the brink of death. Anxiety sweeps over me, and at the worst possible moment, Sister Dora enters the room. She props her fists on her hips.

'Why aren't you in the kitchen?'

I look at her and mirror the same scowl she's giving me.

'Oh, shut up,' I say, and march out of the room before she responds. I run down the hall, down the stairs, grab my coat again and push through the double doors.

I look wildly around as I move within the shadows lining the side of the road. Though I still feel as though I'm being watched, outside nothing seems amiss. I race down the hill without letting my guard down, and when

I reach the café, I enter because it's the only place open. About half of its twenty tables are occupied, which I'm thankful for; I have the urge to be surrounded by people. I'm about to sit when I notice Héctor, alone in the corner, drinking wine.

'Why aren't you at El Festín?'

He glances up. He's clean shaven, and his eyes appear clear and sharp. He seems well rested; he's even well dressed. I haven't seen him this way in quite a while. I wonder how long it will last.

'I thought you didn't drink on Sunday,' I say, and immediately wish I hadn't. Héctor and Ella are my only friends at the moment, and one has already disappeared today. I don't want to upset Héctor as well.

'I thought so, too,' he says, not taking offense. 'If you ever know a man who tries to drown his sorrows, kindly inform him his sorrows know how to swim. Here, sit down, sit down,' he says, kicking out the chair across from him. I plop down in it. 'How are you?'

'I hate this place, Héctor. I hate it with everything inside of me.'

'Bad day?'

'Every day is a bad day here.'

'Eh, this place isn't so terrible.'

'How are you always so cheerful?'

'Alcohol,' he says with a sideways grin. He pours himself what looks to be his first glass from the bottle. 'I wouldn't recommend it to others. But it seems to work for me.'

'Oh, Héctor,' I say. 'I wish you wouldn't drink so much.'

He chuckles. Takes a sip. 'You know what I wish?'

'What?'

'That you didn't look so sad all the time, Marina of the sea.'

'I didn't know that I did.'

He shrugs. 'It's something I've noticed, but Héctor is a very perceptive man.'

I look to my left and to my right, pausing to focus on each person here. Then I take the napkin off the table and put it on my lap. I put it back on the table. Then I put it back on my lap.

'Tell me what is troubling you,' Héctor says, then takes a larger sip.

'Absolutely everything.'

'Everything? Even me?'

I shake my head. 'Okay, not everything.'

His eyebrows rise and then furrow. 'Now tell me.'

I have a deep urge to tell him my secret, the reason I'm here and where it is I really come from. I want to tell him about Adelina and what her role was supposed to be, and what it has instead become. I want him to know about the others, out there on the run or fighting, maybe sitting idly like me, collecting dust. If there's one person I'm certain would be my ally, who would help me in any way he could, then surely it's Héctor. He is, after all, a defender who's meant to hold fast and who was born into power and bravery by such simple means as the name he was given.

'You ever feel like you don't belong here, Héctor?'

'Sure. Some days.'

'Why do you stay, then? You could go anywhere.'

He shrugs. 'Several reasons.' He pours more wine into his glass. 'For one, there's no one else to take care of my mother. Plus, this place is my home, and I'm not convinced there's much better out there. My experiences have taught me that things rarely improve with a simple change of scenery.'

'Maybe so, but I still can't wait to leave. I only have a little over four months left at the orphanage, you know? And you can't tell anyone this, but I think that I'm going to leave sooner than that.'

'I don't think that's a good idea, Marina. You're very young to be on your own. Where will you go?'

'America,' I say without hesitation.

'America?'

'There's somebody there I need to find.'

'If you're so determined, then why haven't you already left?'

'Fear,' I say. 'Mostly fear.'

'You're not the first,' he says, taking a moment to empty his entire glass. His eyes have lost their sharpness. 'The key to change is letting go of fear.'

'I know.'

The door to the café opens, and a tall man wearing a long coat and carrying an old book enters. He moves past us and takes a table in the far corner. He has dark hair and bushy brows. A thick mustache covers his upper

lip. I've never seen him before; but when he lifts his head and meets my gaze, there's something I immediately don't like about him and I quickly look away. From the corner of my eye, I can see he's still staring at me. I try ignoring it. I resume talking to Héctor, or rather I babble, hardly making sense, watching him refill his glass with red wine; and I hear next to nothing of what he says in reply.

Five minutes later the man's still staring, and I'm so bothered by it that the café seems to spin. I lean across the table and whisper to Héctor, 'Do you know who the person in the far corner is?'

He shakes his head. 'No, but I've noticed him watching us, too. He was in here on Friday, sitting in the same seat and reading the same book.'

'There's something about him I don't like, but I don't know what it is.'

'Don't worry, you have me here,' he says.

'I really should leave,' I say. An odd desperation to get away has come over me. I try not to look at the man, but I do anyway. He's reading the book now, the cover of which is angled toward me as though he wants me to see it. It's brittle and worn, a dusty shade of gray.

PITTACUS OF MYTILENE
AND THE
ATHENIAN WAR

Pittacus? *Pittacus?* The man is watching me again, and though I can't see the bottom half of his face, his

eyes suggest a knowing grin on his lips. All at once I feel as though I've been struck by a train. Could this be my first Mogadorian?

I jump up, smacking my knee against the bottom of the table and nearly knocking over Héctor's wine bottle. My chair falls backwards, crashing to the ground. Everybody in the café turns.

'I gotta go, Héctor,' I say. 'I gotta go.'

I stumble through the doorway and make a mad dash for home, running faster than a speeding car, not caring if anyone sees. I'm back at Santa Teresa in seconds. I crash through the double doors and quickly slam them shut. I put my back against them and close my eyes. I try to slow my breathing, the twitching in my arms and legs, my quivering bottom lip. Sweat runs down the side of my face.

I open my eyes. Adelina stands in front of me, and I fall headlong into her arms, not caring about the tension from an hour before. She tentatively hugs me back, probably confused by my sudden display of affection, which I haven't shown her in years. She pulls away and I open my mouth to tell her what I've just seen, but she brings a finger to her lips the same way I did to Ella at Mass. Then she turns and walks away.

That night, after dinner and before prayers, I stand at the bedroom window gazing out as darkness falls, scanning the landscape for anything suspicious.

'Marina? What are you doing?'

I turn around. Ella stands behind me; I hadn't heard her approach. She moves through these halls like a shadow.

'There you are,' I say, relieved. 'Are you okay?'

She nods, but her big brown eyes tell me otherwise. 'What are you doing?' she repeats.

'Just looking outside, that's all.'

'What for? You're always looking out the windows at bedtime.'

She's right; every night since she arrived, since I saw the man watching me in the nave window, I've been looking outside at bedtime for any signs of him. I'm now certain he's the same man I saw in the café today.

'I'm looking for bad men, Ella. There are bad men out there sometimes.'

'Really? What do they look like?'

'It's hard to say,' I reply. 'I think they're very tall, and they're usually very dark and mean looking. And some might even be muscular, like this,' I add, doing my best bodybuilder pose.

Ella giggles, going to the window. She stands on her tippy toes and pulls herself up to see out.

It's been several hours since I was in the café, and I've managed to calm down a bit.

I place my index finger on the foggy window and trace a figure onto it with two quick squeaks.

'That's the number three,' Ella says.

'That's right, kiddo. I bet you can do better than that, huh?'

She smiles, sticks her finger onto the bottom of the window, and soon there is the beginning of a beautiful farmhouse and backyard barn. I watch as my number three is absorbed by Ella's perfect silo.

Three is the only reason I was allowed to leave that café today, it's the distance from John Smith to myself. I'm now absolutely convinced that he is Number Four by the way he is being hunted; just as I'm convinced the man at the café was a Mogadorian. This town is so small I rarely see someone I don't recognize, and his book – *Pittacus of Mytilene and the Athenian War* – plus his constant stare, are no coincidence. The name 'Pittacus' is one I've heard since childhood, since long before we made it to Santa Teresa.

My number: Seven. It's my only refuge now, my greatest defense. As unfair as it might be, I'm separated from death by the three others who all must die before me. So long as the charm holds, which, I assume, is why I was left alone and not attacked right at the café table. But one thing is certain: if he is a Mogadorian, they know where I am and they could take me any time they choose and hold me until they kill Four through Six. I wish I knew what's keeping them at bay and why I'm allowed to sleep in my bed again tonight. I know the charm ensures that we can't be killed out of order, but perhaps there's more to it than that.

'You and I, we're a team now,' I say. Ella puts the finishing touches on her window drawing, curling her

fingernails over the heads of a few cows to give them horns.

'You want to be a team with me?' she asks in a tone of disbelief.

'You bet,' I say, and hold out my pinky. 'Let's pinky-swear on it.'

She smiles widely and hooks her pinky around mine. I shake it once.

'There, that settles it,' I say.

We turn back to the window, and Ella wipes her picture away with the heel of her palm. 'I don't like it here.'

'I don't like it here either, believe me. But don't worry, we'll both be out of here soon enough.'

'You think so? We'll leave together?'

I turn and look at her. That wasn't what I had meant at all, but without thinking twice I nod in agreement. I hope it isn't something I'll regret promising. 'If you're still here when I leave, then we'll leave together. Deal?'

'Deal! And I won't let them hurt you.'

'Who?' I ask.

'The bad men.'

I smile. 'I would appreciate that very much.'

She leaves the window and walks to another, again pulling herself up to look out. As always, she moves like a ghost, making no sound. I still have no idea where she might have hidden today, but wherever it was, it was clearly a place no one would think to look. And then an idea occurs to me.

'Hey, Ella? I need your help,' I say. Ella drops from

the window and looks at me expectantly. 'I'm trying to find something here, but it's hidden.'

'What is it?' she asks, leaning forward in excitement.

'It's a chest. It's wooden and looks very old, like you might expect to see on a pirate ship.'

'And it's here?'

I nod. 'It's here somewhere, but I have no idea where. Somebody did a very good job of hiding it. You're just about the most clever girl I know. I bet you can find it in no time.'

She beams, rapidly nodding her head. 'I'll find it for you, Marina! We're a team!'

'That's right,' I agree. 'We *are* a team.'

13

Six drives our charcoal-colored SUV, which we saw for sale in a yard two miles down the road for fifteen hundred dollars, into town to buy groceries. While she's gone, Sam and I spar together in the backyard. The three of us have spent a week training, and I'm amazed at how good Sam's gotten in the short amount of time. Despite his small size, he's a natural; and what he lacks in strength, he makes up for in technique, which is much better than my own.

At the end of each day as Six and I retreat to the corners of the living room or to our empty rooms, Sam stays up studying fighting techniques on the internet. What Six learned from Katarina and I learned from Henri is a method of combat that loosely resembles a blend of jujitsu, Tae Kwon Do, karate and Bojuka here on Earth, a system designed to be committed to muscle memory, including grappling, blocks, fluid body movements, joint manipulation and strikes to vital points of a person's central nervous system. For Six and me, having the benefit of telekinesis, it's a matter of sensing the subtlest of motions in a radius around us and then reacting to them. Sam, however, needs to keep his enemies in front of him.

While Six ends each session without a mark, Sam and I both finish with new scrapes and bruises. But despite

them, Sam never loses passion or drive. Today is no different. He comes at me, chin tucked and eyes alert. He throws a right cross that I block, then a left side kick that I counter by sweeping his right leg out from under him, sending him crashing to the ground. He stands, then charges me again. Though he connects often, with my strength, his shots aren't very effective. But sometimes I feign pain to boost his confidence.

Six gets home an hour later. She changes into shorts and a T-shirt and joins us. We drill for a while, slowly doing the same block-counterkick over and over until it becomes second nature. But while I take it somewhat easy against Sam, Six goes all out against me, thrusting me backwards with such force that the wind is knocked out of me. Sometimes I get irritated, but I can still tell I'm getting better. She's no longer able to deflect my telekinesis with a casual flick of the wrist. Now she's required to throw her whole body into it.

Sam takes a break and watches from the side with Bernie Kosar.

'You're better than that, Johnny. Show me the good stuff already,' she says after she upends me when I threw a sloppy roundhouse kick.

I charge her, closing the gap between us in a tenth of a second. I throw a left hook but Six blocks it, taking hold of my bicep and using my momentum to toss me over her head. I brace myself for a painful landing, but she doesn't let go of my arm, instead twisting me back over her shoulder so my feet hit the ground.

She wraps her arms around my arms; my back is smashed against her chest. She sticks her face against mine and playfully kisses me on the cheek. Before I can react she kicks the back of my knees and my butt hits the grass. My arms are swept out from under me and I'm flat on my back. Six easily pins me, and she's so close I can count the hairs on her brow. Butterflies flood my stomach.

'Okay,' Sam finally interrupts. 'I think you got him pretty good. You can let him up now.'

Six's smile widens, and mine does, too. We stay that way for a second longer before she leans back and hefts me up by my shoulders.

'My turn with Six,' Sam says.

I take a deep breath, then shake my arms to rid them of their jitters.

'She's all yours,' I say, making a beeline towards the house.

'John?' Six says just as I reach the back door.

I turn, trying to tamp down a strange fluttery sensation at the sight of her. 'Yeah?'

'We've been in this house for a week now. I think it's time to lose whatever sentimentality or fear you've been holding on to.'

For a second, after what just happened I think she's talking about Sarah.

'The Chest,' she says.

'I know,' I say, and I enter the house, sliding the door behind me.

*

I go to my room and pace, taking deep breaths, trying to figure out what just happened out in the yard.

I go to the bathroom and splash cold water on my face. I stare into the mirror. Sarah would kill me if she caught me looking at Six like that. I tell myself again that I have nothing to worry about because Loriens love one person for life. If Sarah is my one love, then Six is simply a crush.

Back in my room I lie on my back, fold my hands across my stomach, and close my eyes. I take deep breaths, holding each one in for a five-count before exhaling out my nose.

Thirty minutes later I open the door and creep down the hall, hearing Sam and Six milling about in the living room. The only place I could find to hide my Chest in the house was in the utility closet, on top of the hot water heater. I struggle getting it out, making as little noise as possible. Then I tiptoe back to my room, gently closing and locking the door behind me.

Six is right. It's time. No more waiting. I grab hold of the lock. It quickly warms, then squirms against the palm of my hand, taking on an almost liquid form, and snaps open. The inside glows brightly. It's never done that before. I reach in and remove the coffee can containing Henri's ashes and his letter, still in its sealed envelope. I close the lid and relock it. I know it's stupid, but I feel like I'm somehow keeping Henri alive by not reading the letter he left behind. Once the Chest is open, and once the letter is read, he'll have nothing left to tell me, nothing left to teach – and then he'll become nothing more than a memory. I'm not ready for it yet.

I open the closet where my clothes sit in a pile, and I bury the coffee can and letter under them. Then I grab the Chest and leave the room, hovering in the hallway to listen to Sam and Six streaming a show online called *Ancient Aliens*. Sam is asking Six about all the alien theories he knows and Six quickly confirms or denies them based on the teachings of Katarina. Sam furiously scribbles answers on his legal pad, which then breeds more questions that Six patiently answers or shrugs her shoulders at. Sam eats it up, drawing parallels to what he already knows.

'The pyramids of Giza? They were built by the Loric?'

'Partly us, but mostly the Mogadorians.'

'What about the Great Wall of China?'

'Humans.'

'Roswell, New Mexico?'

'You know, I've asked Katarina that once and she had no idea. So I don't know either.'

'Wait, how long have the Mogadorians been coming here?'

'Almost as long as we have,' she says.

'So, like, this war between you two, is it new?'

'Not necessarily. What I know is that both sides have traveled to Earth for thousands of years; sometimes we were here at the same time, and from what I understand, much of it was spent on friendly terms. But then something happened that ruined the relationship, and the Mogadorians left for a very long time. Beyond that I don't know much, and I have no idea when they started coming back.'

I cross the living room and plop the Chest in the middle

of the dining-room floor. Sam and Six glance up. Six grins, again giving me strange flutters. I smile back, but it feels insincere.

'I figure we might as well open this thing together.'

Sam begins rubbing his hands with a crazy look in his eyes.

'Jeez, Sam,' I say. 'You look like you're about to murder somebody.'

'Oh, come on,' he says. 'You've been teasing me with this Chest for almost a month now and I've been patient and I've kept my mouth shut out of respect for Henri and everything, but how often do I get to see the treasures from an alien planet? I just think about how the guys at NASA would die to be sitting where I am right now. You can't blame me for being so into this.'

'Would you be mad if this whole time it's been full of nothing but dirty laundry?'

'Alien dirty laundry?' Sam asks sarcastically.

I laugh, then reach down and grab hold of the lock. My hand instantly glows when touching the cold metal, and the lock again warms, shaking and twisting in my grip, protesting the ancient powers that keep it closed. When it clicks open I remove the lock, set it aside, and place my hand on the Chest's top. Six and Sam both lean forward in anticipation.

I lift the lid. The Chest is yet again ablaze with light that hurts my eyes. The first thing I do is remove the velvet bag holding the seven orbs that make up Lorien's solar system. I think of Henri and how we watched the light glow and pulsate at Lorien's core, showing that the

planet is still alive, albeit hibernating. I place the bag in Sam's hand. All three of us peer down into the Chest. Something else is lit up.

'What is that glowing?' Six asks.

'No idea. It never did that before.'

She reaches down and plucks a rock from the bottom of the Chest. It's a perfectly round crystal no bigger than a Ping-Pong ball, and when she touches it, the light brightens even more. And then it fades, and begins to slowly pulse. We watch the crystal, transfixed by the glow. Then, suddenly, Six lets it drop to the floor. The crystal ceases to pulse and resumes its steady glow. Sam reaches down to pick it up.

'Don't!' Six yells.

He looks up, confused.

'Something doesn't feel right about it,' she says.

'What do you mean?' I ask.

'It felt like pinpricks against my palm. When I grabbed hold of it I got a really bad feeling.'

'This stuff is my Inheritance,' I say. 'Maybe I'm the only one allowed to touch it?'

I bend down and carefully pick up the glowing crystal. Within seconds it feels as if I'm holding a radioactive cactus; my stomach compresses and acid climbs up my throat, and I instantly toss the crystal onto a blanket. I swallow. 'Maybe I'm doing it wrong.'

'Maybe we don't know how to use it. I mean, you said Henri kept you from seeing inside because you weren't ready. Maybe you're still not ready?'

'Well, that would be pretty lame,' I say.

'This sucks,' Sam says.

Six walks into the kitchen and returns with two towels and a plastic bag. She carefully grabs the glowing crystal with a towel and drops both into the bag, which she then wraps in a second towel.

'You really think that's necessary?' I ask. My stomach continues to gurgle.

She shrugs. 'I don't know about you, but the feeling I got when I touched it was bad news. Better safe than sorry.'

What's left in the Chest is everything comprising my Inheritance, and I'm not really sure where to start. I reach in and grab an object I've seen before, the oblong crystal Henri used to spread the Lumen from my hands to the rest of my body. It comes alive and bathes the dining room in its bright light. The crystal's center begins swirling with what looks like smoke, twisting and turning back on itself, as I have seen it do before.

'Now we're talking,' Sam says.

'Here,' I say, giving it to him. The crystal falls inert when it transfers hands. 'I've already seen it.'

Also inside the Chest are a few smaller crystals, a black diamond, a collection of brittle leaves bound with twine, and a star-shaped talisman the same pale blue as the pendant around my neck, which tells me it's Loralite, the rarest gem found only at Lorien's core. There's also a bright red oval bracelet and an amber-colored stone in the shape of a raindrop.

'What do you think that is?' Sam asks, pointing to a

flat, circular stone the same milky white color as a pearl that's stuck in the corner.

'Don't know,' I say.

'How about that?' he asks, this time pointing to a small dagger that looks to have a blade made of diamond.

I lift it from the Chest. The handle fits snug in my hand as though it was made for it, and I suppose it was. The blade isn't more than four inches long, and just by seeing the way the light glints along its edge, I can tell it's far sharper than any razor one might find on Earth.

'What about that thing?' Sam asks again, pointing to something else, and I have no doubt he'll ask the same question over and over until he's inquired about every object inside.

'Here,' I say, setting the dagger down and removing the seven orbs in an effort to keep him occupied. 'Check this out.'

I blow on them, and tiny lights flicker across their surfaces. Then I toss them up in the air, and they instantly spring to life, spinning in orbit around the orange-sized sun in the center.

'It's Lorien's solar system,' I say. 'Six planets, one sun. And this one here,' I add, pointing to the fourth orb, which remains the same various shades of ashen gray as the last time I'd seen it, 'is Lorien as it looks today, at this very moment. The glow at its center is what's left.'

'Wow,' Sam says. 'NASA dudes would be crapping themselves right now looking at this.'

'And watch this,' I say, illuminating my right hand. I

sweep the light over the orb, and all at once the surface changes from its depressing gray tones to vibrant blues and greens of the forests and oceans. 'This is the planet as it was the day before the attack.'

'Wow,' Sam says again, staring in awe with his mouth hanging open; and while the rotating planets have him transfixed, I look back in the Chest.

'Do you know what any of this is? Or what it does?' I ask Six, who doesn't respond. I turn and see she's just as amazed as Sam by the solar system spinning two feet above the floor. Since Henri had told me they weren't part of my Legacy, which means they weren't locked in the Chest, I had wrongly assumed she'd seen them before. But it makes sense she hasn't; they can only be activated after the first Legacy develops.

'Six,' I say again. She comes back to reality, turns to me and I find myself looking away once we make eye contact. 'Do you know what any of this stuff is?'

'Not really,' she murmurs, running her hands over the stones' surfaces. 'This is the healing stone Henri and I used at the school,' she says, pointing out a flat, black rock I've seen before. Then she freezes, a faint gasp escaping her lips. Sam and I exchange confused expressions. She lifts a pale yellow stone, its surface waxy and smooth, from the Chest and holds it up to the light. 'Oh my God,' she marvels, flipping it over.

'Tell me,' I prod. She looks me right in the eyes.

'Xitharis,' she says. 'It comes from our first moon.'

She brings the small stone to her forehead, squeezing

her eyes shut. The faint yellow shade of the stone darkens slightly. She opens her eyes and hands the stone to me. I frown and take it from her, my fingertips grazing the palm of her hand. Sam inhales sharply.

'What the . . .' He looks terrified, groping for me like he's blind.

'What's going on?' I ask, slapping Sam's hands away from my face.

'You're invisible,' Six says quietly. I look down at my lap, and it's true: I've completely vanished. I drop the Xitharis on the floor like a hot potato, and instantly become visible.

'The Xitharis,' Six explains, 'allows one Garde to transfer a Legacy to another, but only for a short period of time. An hour, I think, maybe two. I can't say for sure. All you have to do is charge it by focusing your energy on the stone. Put it to your forehead, and *bam*, it's ready to go.'

'Charge it, like a battery?' Sam asks.

'Exactly, and it won't start using the Legacy until it's touched again.'

I look at the stone. 'Sweet. Looks like somebody other than you is taking a trip into town.'

'And somebody other than *you* is going to be resistant to fire,' she says playfully.

'If you're nice to me, then it's definitely a possibility,' I say.

Sam picks the stone up and clenches his entire body in deep concentration. Nothing happens. 'Oh come on,' he says to the stone. 'I promise to use it for the power of good. No girls' locker rooms, I swear.'

'Sorry, Sam,' Six says. 'I'm pretty sure this stuff only works on us.'

He sets the Xitharis down and we dig through the rest of the Chest to see if anything else is activated by touch; but after an hour of studying and holding all seventeen artifacts, blowing hot air on them, squeezing them tightly, nothing else engages aside from the glowing crystal wrapped in the towel, the larger oblong crystal with the smoky center, and the solar system still rotating above us. The healing stone, however, does cure the cuts and bruises Six has been stamping my body with.

'Man, I've waited most of my life to open this thing; and now that I have, a lot of it seems useless to me,' I say.

'I'm sure their uses will reveal themselves in time,' Six assures me. 'Things like this need to be slept on. It's usually when they've left your mind completely that answers finally come.'

I nod, looking back at everything lying around the Chest. Six is right; forcing an answer only guarantees that no answer will come.

'Yeah, maybe some of it only activates with further Legacies. Who knows,' I say with a shrug. I put everything back inside, feeling compelled to keep the glowing crystal covered with the towel. I leave the solar system out, which continues its circular march. I close and lock the Chest and carry it down the hall.

'Don't be discouraged, John,' Six says behind me. 'As Henri said, you're probably not ready to see it all yet.'

14

I can't sleep. partly because of the Chest. For all I know, one of the gems inside could give me power to morph into different creatures like Bernie Kosar, or one could create an iron barrier around me impossible to penetrate by enemy attack. But how will I know without Henri? I feel sad. Defeated.

But mostly I can't stop thinking about Six, can't stop picturing her face hovering inches above mine, or the sugary scent of her breath, or the way the setting sun had made her eyes glow. In that moment I had an irrepressible desire to stop training and to simply wrap my arms around her and squeeze her down onto me. A pang of longing to do that even now, hours later, has anchored itself in my heart, and that's what's really keeping me up. That, and the overwhelming guilt I feel about my attraction to her. The person I'm supposed to be longing for is Sarah.

There's too much on my mind to expect sleep, too many emotions: pain, desire, confusion, guilt. I lie another twenty minutes before giving up on sleep. I whip aside my blanket and pull on a pair of pants and a gray tee. Bernie Kosar follows me from the room and down the hallway.

I poke my head into the living room to see if Sam's asleep. He is, wrapped up in a blanket on the floor like a worm in a cocoon, and I turn and walk back. Six's room is directly across the hall from mine, and her door's ajar. I stand looking at it, and I hear Six rustle on the floor.

'John?' she whispers.

I cringe, and my heart immediately races.

'Yeah?' I reply, still standing outside.

'What are you doing?'

'Nothing,' I whisper. 'I can't sleep.'

'Come in,' she says. I push open the door. Her room is pitch-black, and I can't see anything. 'Is everything okay?'

'Yeah, everything's fine,' I say. I barely turn on my Lumen, and the faint glow is like a night-light. I keep my eyes off her and on the carpet. 'Just too much on my mind, you know. I was maybe thinking of going for a walk or a run or something.'

'Well, that's kind of dangerous, don't you think? Don't forget you're on the FBI's Ten Most Wanted List with a fat reward on your head,' she says.

'I know, but . . . it's still dark out, and you could make us invisible, couldn't you? I mean, that's if you wanted to come along.'

I increase the lights on my hands and I can see Six sitting on the floor with a couple blankets over her legs and her hair's pulled back with loose strands falling around her face. She shrugs, then tosses the blankets aside and stands. She's wearing black yoga pants and a white tank. I can't stop myself from staring at her bare shoulders.

I look away when I'm hit with the absurd suspicion that she can feel my eyes on her.

'Sure,' she says, pulling the band from her hair and rewrapping her ponytail. 'I always have a hard time sleeping. Especially on the floor.'

'I hear that,' I say.

'Do you think we'll wake up Sam, though?'

I shake my head. She responds with a shoulder shrug and lifts her hand. I take it immediately. Six disappears, but my hand still glows and I can see her foot imprints in the carpet. Then I extinguish my hand and we tiptoe from the room and down the hallway. Bernie Kosar follows, and when we reach the living room, Sam lifts his head from the floor and stares right at us. Six and I stop, and I hold my breath to remain silent. I think about Sam's obvious crush on Six and how he'd be devastated if he saw us holding hands.

'Hey, Bernie,' he says groggily, then drops his head and rolls over with his back facing us. We remain silent for a few seconds, and then Six leads us across the living room and into the kitchen to leave through the back door.

The night is warm, and filled with the sounds of crickets and swaying palm fronds. I inhale deeply as Six and I walk hand in hand. I find it odd that Six's hand seems so small and delicate in mine, despite her amazing physical strength. I love the way it feels. Bernie Kosar races through the heavy brush lining the gravel drive while Six and I stroll silently down its center. It dead-ends into a narrow road and we turn left.

'I can't stop thinking about what you went through,' I finally say, but what I would rather tell her is that I can't stop thinking about her. 'Being held prisoner for half a year, having to witness Katarina being – well, you know what I mean.'

'Sometimes I forget it happened. And other times it's all I can think about for days,' she replies.

'Yeah,' I say, drawing out the word. 'I don't know; I guess it goes without saying that I miss Henri, and it kills me that he's gone. But after hearing your story I realize how lucky I really am. I mean, I got to say good-bye to him and everything. Plus, he was there while I went through my first Legacies. I can't imagine going through that alone like you did.'

'It was really, really hard, that's for sure. I could have used her the day I started to gain my invisibility Legacy. I could have used her even more for girl talks when I was growing up. They were pretty much our parents on Earth, right?'

'Right,' I say. 'What I find funny is that now that Henri's gone, the things I remember most about him are the things I usually hated. Like when we would leave some place behind and we'd drive for hours and hours and hours down the highway headed someplace I'd never even heard of when all I wanted to do was just get out of the car. Now, the conversations we had on those trips are the ones I remember most. Or when we started training in Ohio, and he made me do the same thing over

and over and over again . . . I hated it so much, you know? But now I can't look back on any of it without smiling.

'Like one time after my telekinesis finally came, we were training in the snow and he was throwing all these objects so I could learn to deflect them. I had to redirect them back at the source, and he heaved a meat tenderizer really hard at me, and I used its own velocity to whip it back at him; and at the very last second he had to jump headfirst into the snow to keep from being hit,' I say, smiling to myself. 'The pile of snow was actually a snow-covered rosebush with all these thorns. You would not believe the noise he made. Stuff like that I won't ever forget.'

A car approaches on the side of the road and we scoot off into the ditch until it passes. It whips into a stone driveway of a nearby house, and a man in a black leather jacket jumps out. He pounds on the front door, yelling for whoever is inside to open up.

'Jesus. What time is it?' I ask Six.

Six moves towards the man and the house, my hand still in hers. 'Does it matter?'

As we creep within ten feet of him, the smell of alcohol hits me. He stops pounding his fist against the door to yell, 'You better goddamn open this door, Charlene, or you don't wanna know what I'm gonna do!'

Six sees the revolver in his waistband the same time I do and she squeezes my hand. 'Screw this guy,' Six whispers.

He pounds again and again until the lights in the front

window turn on. Then, through the door, a woman shouts, 'Get out of here! Just get out of here, Tim!'

'Open the door right now!' he yells back. 'Or else, Charlene! Or else, you hear me?'

We're within touching distance of him. I can see the faded tattoo below his left ear is a bald eagle holding a snake in its talons.

She yells back, her voice shakier than before: 'Just leave me alone, Tim! Why are you here? Why won't you just leave me alone?'

He pounds and yells even harder. I'm about to put him in a choke hold, squeeze that bald eagle and snake right off his neck, when I see the gun slowly crawl up his lower back until it floats away from him in Six's invisible hand. She puts the barrel of the gun up against the back of the man's head and buries it in his brown hair. She cocks the hammer with a loud click.

The man stops pounding on the door. He stops breathing, too. Six pushes the gun even harder into his skull and then she pushes it stiffly to the right, spinning the man around. The sight of the floating gun in front of his face makes him go white. He blinks and shakes his head violently, expecting to wake up in his bed or in the back alley of whatever bar he came from. Six moves the gun side to side and I wait for her to say something, to really spook the hell out of him, but instead she suddenly turns the gun towards his car. She shoots, and a radius of broken glass appears on the windshield. He screams, shrilly, and bursts into tears.

Six aims the gun at his face again and he quiets down, letting a stream of snot hit his upper lip. 'Please, please, please,' he says. 'I'm sorry, God. I, I, I'm gonna leave right now. I swear. I'm leaving.' Six cocks the hammer again. I see the curtain of the front window move to the right, and expose the face of a large blond woman. I squeeze Six's hand and she squeezes back. 'I'm leaving right now. I'm leaving, I'm leaving,' the man sputters to the gun. Six aims at his car again and empties the chamber with a loud bang; the rear driver's side window explodes into a thousand pieces.

'No! Okay, okay!' the man shouts. There's suddenly a wet spot on the inner thigh of his jeans. Six motions the gun at the front window, and he makes eye contact with the blond woman inside. 'And I'll never come back. I'll never, ever, ever come back.' The gun bobs to the left twice, indicating he can leave. The man rips his car door open and dives in. Stones spit out from under his tires as he reverses out of the driveway and then barrels down the road. The woman in the window continues to stare at the handgun that's floating next to her front door, and that's when Six flings it over the house with such force that it's sure to land in the next county.

We run back to the road and then we continue to run until there isn't a house in sight. I wish I could see Six's face.

'I could do that kind of stuff all day,' she finally says. 'It's like being a superhero.'

'Humans do love their superheroes,' I say. 'Do you think she'll call the police?'

'Nah. She's probably going to think it was all a bad dream.'

'Or the best dream she's ever had,' I say. Our talk turns to all the good things we could do for Earth with our Legacies if we weren't busy being hunted or hated.

'How did you train yourself, anyway?' I ask. 'I can't imagine learning the things I did if it hadn't been for Henri pushing me so much.'

'What other choice did I have? Either we adapt or we perish. So I adapted. Katarina and I trained for years before we were captured, but obviously never once after my Legacies developed. When I finally got out of that cave I promised myself that her death wasn't going to be in vain, and the only way to do that was to seek revenge. So I picked up where we had left off. It was hard at first, especially on my own, but little by little I began to learn and grow stronger. Besides, I've had more time than you. My Legacies came sooner than yours, and I'm older than you.'

'You know,' I say, 'my sixteenth birthday – or at least the day I celebrated as my birthday with Henri – was two days ago.'

'John! Why didn't you tell us?' she asks, then lets go of my hand and playfully shoves me away, making me instantly visible. 'We could have celebrated.'

I smile and reach for her, feeling blindly in the dark. She takes my hand and interlocks her fingers in mine, allowing my thumb to rest over hers. The thought of Sarah

comes into my head, and I find myself instantly pushing it out.

'So what was she like?' I ask. 'Katarina?'

A moment of silence passes. 'Compassionate. She was always helping others. And she was funny. We used to joke and laugh a lot, which probably seems hard to believe, seeing how serious I usually am.'

I chuckle. 'I didn't say it, you did.'

'But hey, no changing the subject. Why didn't you say anything about your birthday?'

'I don't know. I actually forgot about it until yesterday, and then it just seemed pointless with everything else going on.'

'It's your birthday, John; it's not pointless. Every birthday any of us are lucky to have is cause for celebration, considering what's hunting us. And anyway, had I known I might have even taken it easy on you in training.'

'Yeah, you must feel terrible beating up a guy like that on his birthday,' I say, and then nudge her. She nudges me back. Bernie Kosar leaps from the brambles and trots beside us. Several burrs are stuck to his fur like Velcro, and I let go of Six's hand to pluck them all off.

We reach the end of the road. Tall grass and a winding river lie ahead of us. We turn around and amble back towards the house.

'Does it bother you that you never got your Chest?' I ask after a few minutes of silence.

'In a way I think it fueled me that much more. It was

gone; there was nothing I could do about it. So I did what I thought was smart and chose to focus on finding the rest of you. I just wish I could have found Number Three before they did.'

'Well, you found me. I can't imagine I would have survived this long if you hadn't. Or Bernie Kosar, for that matter. Or even Sarah.' As soon as I say Sarah's name, Six's grip loosens a little. Guilt rises in my chest as we make our way back to the house. I do love Sarah, but it's hard to imagine a life with her when I'm so far away, on the run, with no sense of where the future will take me. The only life I can imagine right now is the one I'm living. The one with Six.

We reach the house, and I find myself wishing our walk wasn't over. I try to stall, slowing my steps, hovering at the end of the driveway.

'You know, I only know you as Six,' I say. 'Did you have a name at one time?'

'Of course I did, but I didn't use it very often. I didn't go to school like you. Well, I did for a little while, but then we decided I was better off staying home.'

'So, what was your name?'

'Maren Elizabeth.'

'Whoa, really?'

'Why do you sound so surprised?'

'I don't know; Maren Elizabeth seems kind of dainty and feminine. I think I expected you to have something strong and mythic, like Athena, or maybe Xena, you know, like the warrior princess? Or even Storm. Storm would have suited you perfectly.'

Six laughs, and the sound of it makes me want to pull her to me. Of course I don't, but I *want* to, and maybe that's what's most telling.

'I'll have you know, I used to be a little girl who once wore ribbons in her hair.'

'Yeah, what color?'

'Pink.'

'I think I'd pay money to see that.'

'Forget it, you don't have enough.'

'I'll have *you* know,' I say, mimicking the same playful voice she just used, 'I have a whole Chest of rare gems at my disposal. Just point me in the direction of a pawn shop.'

She laughs, then says, 'I'll keep my eyes open for one.'

We continue to stand at the mouth of our driveway, and I look up at the stars and the moon, which is three-quarters full. I listen to the wind and to Six's feet on the gravel as she shifts her weight from one leg to the other. I take a deep breath.

'I'm really glad we went for that walk,' I say.

'So am I.'

I look where she's standing, wishing she were visible so I could read her expression. 'Could you imagine if every night were like this, living your life without having to worry about what or who might be lurking out of sight, without always having to peer over your shoulder to see if you're being followed? Wouldn't it be amazing to be able to forget, just once, what's peeking over the horizon?'

'Of course it'd be nice,' she says. 'And it *will* be nice when we finally have that luxury.'

'I hate what we have to do. I hate the situation we're in. I wish it were different.' I look for Lorien in the sky and release her hand. She makes herself visible. I grab her by the shoulders and turn her towards me.

Six inhales deeply.

Just as I duck my head towards hers, an explosion rocks the back of the house. Six and I scream and tumble to the ground. A plume of fire lifts up over the roof, and flames instantly spread inside.

'Sam!' I yell. From fifty feet away I rip the front windows out. They shatter against the concrete walkway. Smoke comes billowing out.

Before I know it I've burst into a dead sprint. I take a deep breath and leap, crashing into the house and splintering the door from its hinges.

15

Each night lately I lie awake for hours, my eyes open, ears attuned to the sounds of silence around me. Every so often I lift my head when I hear a distant noise – a drop of water hitting the floor, a person shifting in her sleep – and sometimes I crawl from bed and go to the window to be assured there's nothing out there, an obvious attempt to feel some semblance of security, however flimsy it might be.

Each night passes with less sleep than the night before. I've grown weak, exhausted to the point of delirium. I have trouble eating. I know worrying doesn't do me any good, but no amount of willing myself to rest or eat does anything to change how I feel. And when I finally do sleep, nothing keeps away the terrible dreams that wake me up again.

There's been no sign of the mustached man in the week since I saw him in the café, but I can't dismiss the notion that just because I haven't seen him doesn't mean he isn't out there. I keep returning to the same questions: who was in my cave; who *or what* was the mustached man in the café; why was he reading a book with the name *Pittacus* on the cover; and, most importantly, why did he let me go if he's Mogadorian? None

of it makes sense, not even the title of his book. I've turned up nothing other than a brief summary of the plot online: a Greek general given to short, pithy statements defeats an Athenian army when they were on the verge of attacking the city of Mytilene. What does it have to do with anything?

The questions of the cave and book aside, I've come to two conclusions. The first is that nothing was done to me because of my number. For the time being, it's keeping me safe, but for how long? The second is that the crowd of people in the café kept the Mogadorian from making a move. But from what I know of them, a Mogadorian wouldn't let a few witnesses deter him. I've stopped rushing to and from school ahead of the others and have instead attached myself to their large group. To keep Ella safe, I've stopped walking with her in public. I know it hurts her feelings, but it's for the best. She doesn't deserve to be mixed up in my problems.

But there's one thing that has given me a shade of hope in all this. A noticeable change has occurred in Adelina. Worry creases her forehead. There's a nervous twitch to her eyes when she thinks nobody's watching, and they dart from one section of a room to another like a scared, threatened animal, the same way they used to years ago when she still believed. And while we haven't spoken since I fell into her arms after rushing from the café, it's these changes in her that have me thinking I might have my Cêpan back.

Darkness. Silence. Fifteen sleeping bodies. I lift my head and glance across the room. Instead of seeing a small lump in Ella's bed, the covers are thrown aside and her bed is empty. It's the third night in a row I've noticed her missing, and yet I never hear her leave. But I have bigger things to worry about than where she's gone off to.

I drop my head on the pillow and glance out the window. A full moon, bright and yellow, hangs just outside. I stare at it for a long time, entranced by the way it hovers there. I take a deep breath and close my eyes. When I reopen them, the moon has turned from bright yellow to bloodred and it seems to shimmer, but then I realize it's not the moon I'm staring at, but rather its reflection, shining brightly in the dark waters of some great pool. Steam rises off its surface, and the air reeks of pungent iron. I lift my head again, and only then do I see I'm standing amid a ravaged, bloodied battlefield.

Bodies are strewn everywhere, the dead and dying, the aftermath of some war in which there are no survivors. I instinctively bring my hands to my body, feeling for puncture wounds or cuts, but I'm unscathed. That's when I see her, the girl with the gray eyes I've dreamed about, the one I painted on the cave's wall beside John Smith. She lies motionless at the base of the shore. I rush to her. Blood gushes from her side and soaks into the sand and is carried out to sea. Her raven hair clings to her ashen face. She's not breathing, and I'm completely and utterly anguished to know

there's not a single thing I can do about it. And then behind me comes a deep, mocking laugh. My eyes close before I slowly turn around to face my enemy.

My eyes open and the battlefield disappears. The familiar bed in the darkened room has returned. The moon is normal and bright yellow. I get up and walk to the window. I scan the dark terrain, still and quiet. No sign of the mustached man, or anything else, for that matter. All the snow has melted, and the moon glistens on the wet cobblestones. Is he watching me?

I turn away and crawl back into bed. I lie on my back, taking deep breaths to calm myself. My whole body is tense and rigid. I think about the cave and how I haven't been back since the boot prints appeared. I roll to my side with my back towards the window. I don't want to see what's out there. Ella still isn't in her bed. I try to wait up for her to return, but I fall asleep. No further dreams come.

When the morning bell rings I raise my head off the pillow, my body stiff and sore. A cold rain beats against the window. I glance across the room and see Ella sitting up, lifting her arms towards the ceiling, yawning deeply.

We shuffle from the room together, saying nothing. We coast about our Sunday routines and sit through Mass with our heads hung. At one point I nudge Ella awake, and twenty minutes later she returns the favor. I survive the El Festín lunch line, doling out food while looking for anyone suspicious. When everything appears normal, I can't decide if I'm relieved or disap-

pointed. What saddens me most is that I don't see Héctor.

Towards the end of cleanup, La Gorda and Gabby begin horsing around, spraying each other with the hose attached to the kitchen sink as I dry dishes. I ignore them, even when I get splashed in the face. Twenty minutes later when I've just finished drying the last dish, carefully placing it atop the tall stack, a girl named Delfina slips on the wet floor and bumps into me, causing me to fall into the stack and send all thirty plates back into the dirty water, where some of them break.

'Why don't you watch what you're doing,' I say, and I push her with one arm.

Delfina spins around and shoves me right back.

'Hey!' Sister Dora barks from across the kitchen. 'You two, knock it off! Right now!'

'You're going to pay for that,' Delfina says.

I can't wait to be officially done with Santa Teresa.

'Whatever,' I say, still scowling.

She nods at me, a malicious look upon her face. 'Watch your back.'

'If I have to come over there, Lord help me, you are going to regret it,' Sister Dora says.

Instead of using telekinesis to toss Delfina through the roof – or Sister Dora or Gabby or La Gorda, for that matter – I turn back to the dishes.

When I'm finally free I walk outside. It's still raining and I stand under the eaves and look towards the cave.

The mud will be thick on the mountainside, which means I'd get filthy. I use that as an excuse for why I won't go, though I know that even if it weren't raining I wouldn't have the courage, despite my curiosity of whether or not new boot prints have been made in the mud.

I walk back inside. Ella's Sunday duties require her to clean the nave after everyone leaves, wiping down pews. But when I go there, everything has already been cleaned.

'Have you seen Ella?' I ask a ten-year-old girl named Valentina. She shakes her head. I walk back to our bedroom, but there's no sign of Ella there. I sit on her bed. The bounce of the mattress causes a silver object to peek from beneath Ella's pillow. It's a tiny flashlight. I flip it on. The light shines brightly. I turn it off and put it back where I found it so that the Sisters won't see it.

I walk the halls, peeking in rooms as I go along. Because of the rain, most of the girls have stayed in, milling about in their small groups, laughing and talking and playing games.

On the second floor, where the hallway splits and leads to the church's two separate wings, I go left, down a dark, dusty corridor. Empty rooms and ancient statues cut into the rock wall and arched ceiling, and I stick my head in the doorways, looking for Ella. No sign of her. The hallway narrows and the dusty odor segues to a damp, earthy smell. At the corridor's end stands a padlocked oak door I jimmied open a week and a half ago

looking for the Chest. Beyond the door is a stone stairway that circles around the narrow tower leading up to the north belfry, which holds one of Santa Teresa's two bells. The Chest wasn't there either.

I surf the internet for a while but find nothing new about John Smith. Then I go to the sleeping quarters, lie in bed, and feign sleep. Thankfully La Gorda, Gabby, and Delfina don't come into the room, and I don't see Ella either. I crawl from bed and walk down the hall.

I enter the nave and find Ella in the back pew. I sit beside her. She smiles up at me, looking tired. This morning I had put her hair into a ponytail, but now it's come loose. I pull the band free, and Ella turns her head so I can redo it.

'Where have you been all day?' I ask. 'I was looking for you.'

'I was exploring,' she says proudly. I instantly feel terrible all over again for ignoring her on our walks to school.

We leave and go to our room, say good night to one another. Slipping beneath the covers, waiting for the lights to be shut off, I feel hopeless and sad, wanting to simply crawl into a ball and cry. So that's what I do.

I wake in the middle of the night and I can't tell what time it is, though I assume I've slept at least a few hours. I roll over and close my eyes again, but something feels off. There's some change in the room I can't quite explain, and it amplifies the same anxiety I've felt all week.

I open my eyes again, and the second they adjust to the dark, I realize a face is staring at me. I gasp and bolt straight backwards, crashing into the wall behind me. *I'm trapped,* I think, *trapped in the far, back corner. How stupid of me to have wanted this bed.* My hands tighten, and just as I'm about to scream and kick at the face, I recognize the brown eyes.

Ella.

I instantly relax. I wonder how long she's been standing there.

Very slowly she brings her tiny index finger to her lips. Then her eyes widen and she smiles as she leans forward. She cups her hand around my ear.

'I found the Chest,' she whispers.

I pull away, look earnestly into her radiant, upturned face, and know immediately she's telling the truth. My own eyes widen. I can't contain my excitement. I pull her to me and give her the tightest hug her small body can endure.

'Oh Ella, you have no idea how proud I am of you.'

'I told you I'd find it. I told you, because we're a team and we help each other.'

'We do,' I whisper.

I let go of her. Her face brims with pride. 'Come on. I'll show you where it is.' She takes me by the hand, and I follow her around the bed, tiptoeing quietly.

The Chest – a bright ray of hope when I'd least expected it, when I'd needed it most.

16

We flee the room, and I have the urge to sprint to wherever Ella's leading me. She glides swiftly and soundlessly across the cold floor. The corridor is dark; and while I see everything clearly, every so often Ella flicks on the flashlight to orient herself, then quickly turns it off.

When we reach the nave I think she's going to head towards the north tower, but she doesn't, and instead guides me up the center aisle. We skitter past the rows of pews. At the nave's front, stained glass saints line the curved wall and the moonlight behind them brings a celestial radiance that gives each a more biblical appearance than they've ever had before. Water drips in a constant patter somewhere.

Ella cuts a right turn at the front pew and sweeps towards one of the many open recesses that run the length of both walls. I follow. The air is cooler here than in the nave, and a tall statue of the Virgin Mary looms over us with arms lifted from her sides. Ella goes around her, and when she reaches the back left corner, she turns to me.

'I'll have to bring it down to you,' she says, putting the flashlight in her mouth. She takes hold of the stone pillar and scoots up it like a squirrel clawing up a tree.

All I can do is watch in amazement, so impressed by her mobility.

When she's almost at the ceiling, she pauses and then swings around the column, disappearing into a tight little nook that's almost invisible from where I stand.

I never noticed the nook before. Lord knows how Ella did. I crane my head to listen, hearing the rough friction of her shoes scrape along the rock, which means there's just enough room for her to crawl. Some kind of tunnel. I can't help but smile. I knew the Chest was here, somewhere, but I would have never found it in a million years if it weren't for Ella. I laugh at the thought of Adelina scaling the same column with the Chest so many years ago. Ella has stopped; I hear nothing. Twenty seconds pass.

'Ella,' I whisper. She sticks her head out and looks down. 'Should I come up?'

She shakes her head. 'It's stuck, but I almost have it. I'll bring it down to you in a minute,' she whispers back, and then yanks her head back in and disappears. I can't take the suspense of not knowing what's going on up there. I look at the base of the column and take hold of it; and just before I'm about to try climbing it, I hear a noise behind me that sounds like somebody kicking a pew. I spin around. The Virgin Mary blocks my view. I walk around her and scan the nave, but I don't see anything.

'I got it!' I hear Ella exclaim.

I rush back around the statue and look up, waiting

for her to appear. I can hear her grunt and struggle to drag the Chest to the nook's opening, and I have no idea if it's because the Chest is heavy or because the tunnel is so narrow. Little by little the dragging continues. I feel nothing short of ecstasy at finally having the Chest in my possession, and I don't even consider the problem of getting it open. I'll cross that bridge when I come to it. Just as Ella is almost to the opening, I hear something else behind me.

'What are you doing up?'

I whip around. Divided equally on each side of the Virgin Mary, Gabby and Delfina stand under the statue's left arm while La Gorda and a wiry Bonita, the champion of the dock game that almost got me killed at the lake, position themselves beneath the right arm.

I glance over my shoulder and see two small eyes peering down at us from the nook's opening.

'What do you want?' I ask.

'I wanted to see what the little tattletale was up to, that's all. You know, it's funny because I saw you sneak out of the room and I thought that I would get up and *finally* see what it was you're always looking at on the computer, but you weren't there.' Gabby paints a sarcastic, confused look on her face. 'You were in here, which is really weird.'

'Really weird. It's really weird,' La Gorda says. To my relief, I don't hear Ella dragging the Chest anymore.

'Why do you even care?' I say. 'Seriously. All I ever do is keep to myself and keep my mouth shut.'

'I care a lot about you, Marina,' Gabby says, stepping forward. She flips her long dark hair. 'In fact, I care so much that I worry about you hanging out with that loser drunk, Héctor, all the time. Do you get drunk with him?' She pauses. 'Do you drink from his bottle?'

I don't know if it is because she called Héctor a loser, or because she thought our friendship was anything more than just that, or because she is snooping on what I'm doing at the computer, but it just happens. I close my eyes and reach out with my mind, grabbing all four of them at once. La Gorda screams, while the other three whimper in shock. I pick them up off the ground – their bare feet kicking at the air, their shoulders smashed against each other's – and thrust them all across the smooth floor until they bounce off the steps leading to the raised dais at the back of the nave.

La Gorda slaps the floor with her open palms and gets to her feet like an angry bull ready to charge the conquistador. I run to her instead, making up the ground in a matter of seconds. La Gorda swings a wild punch and I duck, only to spring up and jam my right fist into her chin. She falls backwards with a gasp, and her head thuds against the floor. She's out cold.

Bonita jumps on my back and pulls at my hair. Someone punches me in the left cheek, and the other kicks me in the shin. Bonita slides down my back and hugs my upper arms so I can't move. Delfina swings and I duck. The punch glances off Bonita's mouth and

she loosens her grip enough for me to twist away. I grab Bonita's right arm in my hands and I drive her towards Gabby.

'You're dead, Marina! You are so dead!' Bonita shrieks, and I pull her sideways and knee her in the gut, knocking the wind out of her. I shove her to the ground next to La Gorda.

Delfina's confidence is broken. She looks for the door. 'You ready to leave me alone?' I ask her.

'Doesn't matter. I'm going to get you tomorrow,' she says. 'Right when you're not looking.'

'You're going to wish you didn't say that.' I fake right and lunge left, tackling her around the waist. Gabby tries to grab my hair but I whip Delfina around to block her. Then I pivot on my heels and release Delfina down the middle aisle of the nave. Her back hits the first step at the altar, and her groan echoes off the vaulted ceiling.

Gabby circles me. 'I'm telling Sister Dora. You're going to be in *so* much trouble.' I turn my body to keep my eyes on her. She stops right next to the column. I can tell she's about to charge and I'm ready for it.

Suddenly I see a flash of white above Gabby's head. It takes me a second to recognize that it's Ella, and she's jumped from the nook all the way down onto Gabby's shoulders. Gabby flails around until she can get her hands on Ella; and when she does, she tosses her onto the floor with a horrible cracking sound.

'No!' I yell, and then I punch Gabby in the sternum

as hard as I can. Her feet leave the ground and she hits the wall, knocking dust from the stone wall's mortar.

Ella's on her back, wailing, writhing in pain, but I notice she keeps her right leg completely still. I kneel beside her and pull up the bottom of her nightgown to see a sharp white bone sticking out of her skin just below the knee. I don't know what to do. I put my hand on her shoulders to try to console her, but she's in so much pain, she doesn't feel it.

'I'm right here, Ella,' I say. 'I'm here right beside you, and everything is going to be okay.'

Her eyes open and she gives me a pleading look. It's then that I see the damage done to her right hand. Her tiny fist is mangled, crooked; blood seeps out between her index and middle fingers. *Her talent.*

'Oh my God, Ella. I'm sorry,' I cry. 'I'm so, so sorry.'

She just cries. I feel myself begin to sweat. Never in my life have I felt so useless.

'Try not to move,' I say, knowing it's a futile plea. The nearest hospital is a half-hour drive. She'll pass out from the pain by then.

She starts to rock in a rhythm from side to side. I hover my shaking hands over the shard of bone sticking out of her leg, not knowing if I should apply pressure or try to push it back under the skin. I decide on applying pressure, and the second my fingers touch her skin, Ella stutters with a sharp intake of breath. An icy tingle inches up my spine, a feeling much like the times I've brought life back to the flower in the

computer room, and the feeling spreads throughout the rest of me. Is it possible that my ability to heal plants applies to people as well? Ella stops crying and starts breathing rapidly, her tiny chest rising and falling, rising and falling. I can feel the iciness concentrate in my palms and circulate outward from my fingertips. 'I think, I think I can fix you.'

Her chest continues to rise and fall at an abnormal speed, but her face takes on a look of peacefulness, of detachment. I'm afraid to, but I place my hands over the piece of bone that sticks out from her leg. I feel its pebbly, broken end; and soon it begins to retreat back under the skin. The puncture wound turns from red and white back to the color of her skin; and I can see the jagged contours of her broken bone move and shift within her leg, setting itself back in place. I'm amazed at what I've just done. This could be my most important Legacy yet.

'Keep still,' I say. 'One more thing.'

I close my eyes and wrap my hands around her thin right wrist. The iciness flows again through my fingertips. I open my eyes to watch her palm rise and her fingers spread away from each other. The cut between her index and middle fingers closes, and I see two broken knuckles straighten and mend. Ella clenches her hand and relaxes it.

I've done what Lorien has intended me to do, and that's to undo damage that's been inflicted on those who don't deserve it.

Ella turns her head to the right to look at my hands wrapped around her wrist. 'You're fine,' I say. 'You're better than fine.' She raises her head off the ground and props herself up onto her elbows. I pull her into my arms.

'We're a team,' I whisper into her ear. 'We take care of each other. Thanks for trying to help.'

She nods her head. I squeeze her and then pull away. I look around at the girls, all of them unconscious but breathing. Sticking out of the opening of the nave, I see the edge of the Chest.

'I'm so proud of you for finding the Chest. You have no idea,' I say. 'Let's get it tomorrow morning after we've had some rest.'

'Are you sure?' Ella asks. 'I can climb back up and get it.'

'No, no. You go wash up in the bathroom, and I'll be right there.'

When she's finally out of my sight, I raise my eyes to the Chest. Concentrating, I float it silently down to my feet. Now I just need to get Adelina to open it with me.

17

As I burst through the burning door and land on the melting brown carpet of the living room, several things race through my mind. Sam. Henri's letter. The Chest. Henri's ashes. I engulf myself purposefully in flames in order to move easily from room to room. 'Sam?' I yell. 'Where are you, Sam?'

Past the living room, I see that the entire back wall of the house is burning. The house could collapse in a matter of a minute. I dart into the bedrooms calling Sam's name. The bathroom door explodes with my kick. I check the kitchen, the dining room; and just when I'm about to try the living room again, I look out the window and see the Chest and a pile of our belongings, including the laptop, the coffee can of Henri's ashes, and the unopened letter, on the lip of the pool. Something small bobs in the middle of the water; it's Sam's head. He sees me and waves his arms.

I crash through the window and knock over the grill. I dive into the pool, the flames surrounding me hissing into gray and black smoke. 'You okay?'

'I, I think so,' he says. We pull ourselves out of the water and stand over everything Sam was able to save.

'What happened?'

'Dude, they're here. They're totally here. The Mogadorians.' The moment he says these words I feel sick to my stomach. My jaw quivers. Then Sam says, 'I saw them in the front window and then, *boom*, the house is on fire. I grabbed what I could . . .'

There's movement on the roof. Between fissures of rising flames, I see a huge Mogadorian scout in a black trench coat, hat, and sunglasses marching down the decline, his feet sinking into the soft tiles with every step. He carries a long gleaming sword.

I kneel and grab ahold of the Chest's lock, and it yields under my glowing grip. Brushing aside the crystals at the bottom of the Chest, I pick up the dagger with the diamond blade. Flames dancing from the house reflect in its sharp edge. To my surprise, the handle extends and wraps itself around my entire right hand. 'Get back,' I say to Sam.

The scout reaches the metal eave of the collapsing roof, and he drops onto the patio below, his feet cracking the concrete when he lands. He slices the sword in the air in front of him and it leaves a glowing trail. I control my breath and go over the last week of training in my mind.

The moment my feet push me forward, the scout roars and rushes at me with his trench coat billowing behind him. I see myself in his sunglasses the second before his sword swings across my body. I lean back far enough for him to miss me; but when I right myself, I enter the glowing trail the sword left behind. Pain

attaches itself to my neck and travels to my waist. I'm knocked backwards and into the pool.

When my head surfaces I see Sam squaring off with the scout. His bare hands are up and out; he bobs his shoulders left and right. The scout laughs and drops his sword to the concrete, and he then mimics Sam's fighting stance. Before I can heave myself out of the pool to help, Sam drops his weight onto his left foot and circles his right behind him. His sopping right shoe comes back around and connects with the scout's face with a force that staggers him back several feet.

The dazed scout picks up his gleaming sword. I'm up out of the pool before he can reach Sam, and I lift my dagger to block the plummeting sword. The blades meet, and there is a ball of light so bright I can't see for an instant. When the light fades, the scout's sword breaks at the exact spot my dagger collided with it. Not wasting the moment of surprise, I plunge the blade of my dagger into his chest and rip it downward. He turns to ash and it covers my feet.

The house finally collapses – beams of wood crack in different directions, windows pop and explode from the walls – the roof flattening over it all like a book with a broken spine. A storm cloud appears overhead and a lightning bolt slices through the sky, landing just on the other side of the house.

'We have to get to Six!' Sam shouts. He's right; the proximity of the lightning can only mean she's in the middle of a battle. Or finishing one. With my one free hand, I

heft the Chest up and over the backyard's brick wall after making sure the coast is clear. Sam tosses the rest up to me and I then pull him to the wall's cement top. We jump and roll on the moist grass beyond the wall. Securing everything behind a thick bush, we run around to the front yard.

In the middle of the driveway, just feet from our SUV, Six has a scout in a headlock, the muscles in her arms pulsing in the squeeze. Two more scouts are approaching. One aims a long, cylindrical tube right at me and a green light blasts me backwards. I can't breathe. I can't see. I roll into the high grass and feel the heat from the house.

When I'm able to open my eyes, I see the scout with the tube standing above me. I slowly regain some feeling in my arms and legs; my breathing returns to normal. The handle of the dagger still encases my right hand. The scout adjusts a knob on the tube, perhaps going from stun to kill, and then he steps on my right wrist. I try swinging my legs up and over me, but they don't react the way I want them to, still sluggish from the paralyzing blast I just endured. The barrel of the tube is set between my eyes, and I think about the gun Six turned on the drunk man just an hour ago. *This is it,* I think. *The Mogadorians' mission is a success. Number Four, check. On to Number Five.*

I watch hundreds of lights in the tube spark to life, swirling until they become one; just as he puts his finger on the trigger, Bernie Kosar clamps down on his thigh. The scout wobbles above me for a second before his

head is separated from his body by a bolt of lightning. It rolls in the grass right next to mine; our noses touch before the head crumbles into a pile of ash, and I do everything I can not to breathe it in. The body above me falls over and covers my jeans with ash.

'Get up already,' Six yells, suddenly in the exact spot the scout had been.

Sam appears above me, too, his face stern and dirty. 'We have to leave *right* now, John.'

The sound of sirens pierces the night. A mile away, maybe less. Bernie Kosar licks my left temple and whimpers.

'What about the third one?' I whisper.

Six looks over at Sam and nods. 'I got a hold of his sword and used it against him. Best moment of my life,' he says.

I'm draped over Six's shoulder, and she dumps me into the backseat of the SUV. Bernie Kosar settles himself on my shins and licks my lifeless right hand. Sam takes the keys and gets behind the wheel while Six retrieves our stuff. As soon as we're on the highway and I no longer hear sirens, I'm able to relax and concentrate on my right hand. The dagger's handle transforms and retreats from my knuckles and wrist. I drop the dagger in the foot well.

Fifteen minutes later, Six tells Sam to pull over, and we screech into the lit parking lot of a closed diner. She jumps out before the car has come to a complete stop, leaving the door open.

'Help me,' she orders.

'Six, I don't want to be a dick right now, but I can't really move my arms and legs.'

'Dude, just really try. We have to get them off our tail,' she says. 'If we don't, then you're dead. Think about it.'

I struggle into a seated position and feel blood circulate to my legs. I climb out of the car and waver there in my burned clothes, having no idea what she needs help with.

'Find the bug,' she says. 'Sam, keep the car running.'

'Roger,' he says.

'Find the what?' I ask.

'They use bugs to track vehicles. Trust me. They did it with me and Katarina.'

'What does it look like?'

'I have no idea. But time is short, so look fast.'

I almost want to laugh. There isn't a single thing in the world I think I could do fast right now. But nonetheless, Six goes racing around the SUV while I slowly drop to a knee and manage to crawl beneath it, flashing my hands on its undercarriage. Bernie Kosar gets to sniffing, starting at the bumper and moving his way forward. I spot it almost immediately, a small circular object no bigger than a quarter stuck to the plastic cover of the gas tank.

'Got it,' I yell, plucking it off. I pull myself out and hand the device to Six while remaining on my back. She briefly studies it, then drops it in her pocket.

'Aren't you going to destroy it?'

'No,' she answers. 'Check again. We have to make sure there isn't a second, or a third.'

I crawl back under with my hands blazing, scooting from the back of the SUV to the front. I don't see anything.

'You're sure?' she asks when I stand.

'Yes.'

We get back in and speed away. It's two o'clock in the morning, and Sam heads west. With Six's instructions, he keeps the SUV between eighty-five and ninety, and I can't help but worry about police. After thirty miles, he jumps onto an interstate and drives south.

'We're almost there,' she says. Two miles later she tells Sam to get off the interstate. 'Stop! Right here, stop!' Sam slams the brakes beside an idling semi whose owner is pumping gas. Six goes invisible and steps out, leaving the door ajar.

'What's she doing?' Sam asks.

'I don't know.'

After a few seconds the open door slams shut. Six reappears and tells Sam to get us back onto the highway, this time heading north. She's relaxed a bit, no longer holding a white-knuckled grip on the dashboard.

'Are you really going to make me ask what you just did?' I say.

She glances over. 'That truck was on its way to Miami. I stuck the tracking device on the underside of its trailer. Hopefully they'll lose a few hours trailing him south while we drive north.'

I shake my head. 'Should be an interesting night for that trucker.'

Once we're past the Ocala exits, Six tells Sam to get

off and park behind a strip mall a few minutes from the interstate.

'We sleep here tonight,' Six says. 'Actually, we'll take turns sleeping.'

Sam opens his door and turns his body sideways to dangle his feet out of the SUV. 'Um, guys? I probably should have mentioned this earlier, but well, I got cut pretty bad back there and it's really starting to hurt and I think I'm about to pass out.'

'What?' I scramble out of the vehicle and stand in front of him. He pulls up the dirty right leg of his jeans to reveal a wound above the knee that's slightly smaller than a credit card, though probably an inch deep. Dried and fresh blood cover his knee and shin.

'Good lord, Sam,' I say. 'When did that happen?'

'Right before I got ahold of that Mog's sword. I kind of pulled it out of my leg.'

'All right, come on, get out of the car,' I say. 'Get on the ground.'

Six shoves her head under Sam's armpit and helps him to the ground.

I open the back and retrieve the healing stone from the Chest. 'Better hold on to something, man. This might . . . sting.' Six offers her hand, and he takes it. The second I press the stone to his wound he writhes in agony as every muscle tightens. It seems like he's going to pass out. The skin around his wound turns white, then black, then to the bright red color of blood; and I immediately regret attempting to use the stone on a human.

Did Henri ever say it won't work on them? I'm trying to remember as Sam lets out a long-winded groan that empties him of air. The outer edge of the wound seals inward and then disappears altogether. Sam relaxes his grip on Six's hand, and he slowly regains his breath. After a minute he's able to sit up.

'Man, do I ever want to be an alien,' he finally says. 'You guys get to do way too many cool things.'

'You had me worried there for a second, buddy,' I say. 'Wasn't sure if it would work on you since some of the other stuff from the Chest doesn't.'

'Me neither,' Six adds. She leans over and kisses him on his dirty cheek. Sam lies back down and sighs. Six laughs and rubs her hand over his head of stubble, and I'm surprised by how much jealousy bubbles inside me.

'Do you want to go to the hospital?' I ask.

'I want to stay right here,' he says. 'Forever.'

'You know what? We were pretty lucky we were out on that walk,' Six says after we settle back into the SUV.

'You're right,' I say.

Sam places his right cheek on his headrest so he can look at both of us. 'Why were you guys out walking in the first place?'

'I couldn't sleep. Neither could Six,' I answer, which technically is the truth, but it doesn't take away the guilt. I know that Sarah is the girl for me, but I can't seem to stop these new feelings I have.

Six sighs. 'You know what this means, right?'

'What?'

'They've probably opened my Chest.'

'You don't know that for sure.'

'No, I don't. But after I grabbed that rock from your Chest and it started pulsing and hurting my hand, I haven't been able to shake the feeling I got from it. And it just now came to me that it probably has something to do with my Chest.'

'They've had your Chest for three years now,' I say. 'So you think it's possible for them to open the Chests without us, without us being dead?'

She shrugs. 'I don't know. Maybe? But I have this feeling that they got into mine and that when I touched that stone it somehow led the scouts to our house.'

'Why send so few?' Sam asks between yawns. 'I mean, why not wait for reinforcements before attacking?'

'Maybe they got scared and panicked?' Six offers.

'Maybe one of them wanted to be the hero,' I say.

Six rolls down her window and listens. When she's satisfied, she says, 'Regardless. Next time there will be more of them. Pikens and krauls and whatever else they can throw at us.'

'You're probably right,' Sam whispers. He's drifting off. 'I'll tell you one thing. This being on the run is really wearing me down.'

'Try doing it for eleven years,' I say.

'I think I'm a little homesick,' he mumbles.

I lean forward and see that in his lap he's holding his father's old glasses, the ones with the thick lenses he used to wear in Paradise.

'It's not too late to go back, Sam. You know that, right?'

He frowns. 'I'm not going back.' It's with far less conviction this time around than when he had first said it in the North Carolina motel. 'Not until I find my dad. Or until I at least learn what happened to him.'

His dad? Six mouths to me, confused.

Later, I mouth back.

'Fair enough,' I say. 'We'll figure it out eventually.' I turn back to Six. 'So, where do we head tomorrow morning?'

'Now that it seems they opened my Chest, I guess we'll see where the wind carries us. It hasn't let me down yet,' she says in a wistful sort of tone, then glances over at me. 'Did you know that if it wasn't for the wind and my need for caffeine one night in Pennsylvania, the night before the attack in Paradise, I'd have never gotten there in time?'

'What are you talking about?' I ask.

'I was drifting through the Midwest, sensing you guys were in Ohio or in West Virginia or Pennsylvania after I found some news online of what I thought was probably the handiwork of Mogs in Athens near that college; but after a few weeks of coming up empty, I was certain I'd lost your trail. I figured you guys had taken off for California or Canada by that point. So there I was, standing in the parking lot of this strip mall, tired and lost, practically broke, when this huge gust of wind ripped past me and blew open the door to a coffee shop on my left. I thought I would refuel and get back out there and figure something out, but in the corner of the shop was an open

computer for customers. I bought a large coffee and started searching the internet. Sure enough, I found an article about the house on fire that you jumped out of.'

I'm embarrassed to know how easy it was to find me. No wonder Henri wanted to keep me home or at school all the time.

'If it wasn't for that gust of wind opening that door, I would have probably ended up in a diner instead, sipping coffee until daylight. I wrote down all the information I could find on you guys and then I ran down the street looking for an all-night copy place. That's when I sent the fax and the letter with my number, to try to warn you guys or, at the very least, to tip you off so you could brace yourselves until I got there. And I arrived just in the nick of time.'

18

The wind carries us north to an Alabama motel where we stay two nights, again thanks to Sam using one of my identities. From there we drive west and spend a night beneath the stars in an open field in Oklahoma, which we follow up with two more nights in a Holiday Inn on the outskirts of Omaha, Nebraska. And from there, for no apparent reason – at least for no reason she'll admit to – Six drives one thousand miles east to rent a log cabin nestled in the mountains of the Maryland panhandle, a mere five-minute drive to the West Virginia border, and three short hours from the Mogadorian cave. We're exactly 197 miles from Paradise, Ohio, where our journey first began. Half a tank of gas from Sarah.

Before my eyes even open, I can already feel it's going to be a tough day, one of those days when the reality of Henri's death will hit me like a sledgehammer and no matter what I do, the pain won't leave. I've been having these days more often. Days filled with remorse. Filled with guilt. Filled with a genuine sadness to know I'll never talk to him again. The thought cripples me. I wish I could change it. But as Henri once said, 'Some things can never be undone.' And then there's Sarah, and the terrible guilt

that's crept in since leaving Florida for allowing myself to get so close to Six that I almost kissed her.

I take a deep breath, finally opening my eyes. The pale morning light enters the room. *Henri's letter*, I think. I have no choice but to read it now. It's too dangerous to delay it any longer. Not after almost losing it in Florida.

I slip my hand beneath the pillow and remove the diamond-bladed dagger and the letter. I've been keeping both of them close to me. I stare at the envelope for a moment, trying to imagine under what circumstances the letter was written. Then I sigh, knowing it doesn't really matter and that I'm just wasting time, and with the dagger I make a clean cut along the envelope's seal and remove the pages. Henri's perfect handwriting fills five yellow legal-sized sheets with thick black ink. I take a deep breath, and then let my eyes fall upon the top sheet.

January 19

J –

I've written this letter many times over the years, never knowing whether it might be my last, but if you're reading this now, then surely the answer is yes. I'm sorry, John. I truly am. We Cêpans who came, our duty was to protect you nine at all costs, including our lives. But as I put down these words at our kitchen table, mere hours after you saved me in Athens, I know it's never been duty that has kept you and me together, but rather love that will always be a stronger bond than

any obligation. The truth is that my death was always going to happen. The only variables were when and how, and if it hadn't been for you, then I would have certainly died today. Whatever the circumstances of my death, please don't blame yourself. I never expected to survive here, and when we left Lorien all those years ago, I knew I'd never be going back.

In the time between me writing these words and you reading them, I wonder how much you've discovered. I'm confident you now know that I kept a lot from you. Probably more than I should have. For most of your life I wanted you to stay focused, to train hard. I wanted to give you as normal a life on Earth as I could. I'm sure you'll find that idea laughable, but to know the full truth would have added a world of stress during an already-stressful time.

Where to begin? Your father's name was Liren. He was brave and powerful, and he lived his life with integrity and purpose. As you witnessed during your visions of the war, he carried out these traits until the very end, even when he knew the war was unwinnable. And that's about all any of us can really hope for, to die with our dignity, to die with honor and valor. To die knowing we did everything we could. That was the epitome of who your father was. It's the epitome of who you are, too, even if you don't necessarily believe it.

I sit up, my back flat against the headboard, rereading my father's name over and over. The lump in my throat

expands into a rock. I wish Sarah was here urging me to read on, her head on my shoulder. I focus my eyes on the next paragraph.

When you were just a small child, your father came around even when he wasn't supposed to. He adored you, and he could sit for hours watching you play in the grass with Hadley (I wonder now, have you discovered Bernie Kosar's true identity?). And while I'm sure you don't remember much of those youthful days, I can safely say you were a happy boy. For a brief while, you had the sort of childhood all children deserve, though not all receive.

While I spent considerable time with your father, I met your mother only once. Her name was Lara and, like your father, she was reserved and maybe even a little shy. I tell you this now because I want you to know who you are and who you come from. You come from a simple family of simple means, and the truth that I've always wanted to share with you is that we didn't leave Lorien because of where we happened to be that day. Our being at the airfield, it wasn't sheer happenstance. We were there because when the attack began, the Garde rallied together to get you there. Many sacrificed their lives in the process. There were supposed to be ten of you, though as you know only nine made it off.

Tears blur my vision. I slide my fingers over my mother's name. Lara. Lara and Liren. I wonder what my Loric

name was, if it also started with an *L*. I wonder, if there wasn't a war, if I would have had a younger sister or brother. So much has been taken from me.

When the ten of you were born, Lorien recognized your strong hearts, your wills, your compassion, and in turn she bestowed the ten of you with the roles you're all meant to assume: the roles of the original ten Elders. What this means is that, in time, those of you left will grow to be far stronger than anything Lorien has ever seen before, far stronger even than the original ten Elders from whom you've received your Inheritances. The Mogadorians know this, which is why they're hunting you so feverishly now. They've grown desperate and have flooded this planet with spies. I never told you the truth because I feared it might drive you to arrogance and that you might be led astray, and there's far too much danger out there looking for you to risk that. I urge you . . . become strong, grow into the role you are meant to assume, and then find the others. Those of you left, you can still win this war.

The last thing I have to tell you is that we didn't move to Paradise by chance. Your Legacies were delayed and I had begun to worry, and when my worry grew to a full-out panic when the third scar appeared – knowing you are next – I decided to seek out the one man who might hold the key to finding the others.

When we arrived on Earth there were nine humans waiting for us who understood our situation and our

need to scatter. They were allies of the Loric, and the last time we were here – fifteen years ago – they were all given a transmission device that would turn itself on only if it came into contact with one of our ships. They were there that night to provide us guidance in the transition from Lorien to Earth, to help us get started. None of us had ever been here before. When we stepped off the ship, we were each given two pairs of clothes, a packet of instructions to help us learn this planet's ways, and a slip of paper with an address on it. The addresses were a place to start, not to stay, and none of us knew where the others were headed. Ours led us to a small town in Northern California. It was a nice, quiet place fifteen minutes from the coast. I taught you to ride a bike there, and fly a kite, and more simple things like tying your shoes, which I had to first teach myself. We stayed six months, and then we went about our way, as I knew we must.

The man who met you and me, our guide, was from here, from Paradise; and I sought him because I was desperate to know where the others first went. But when we arrived here, the dark stars must have fallen, because the man was already gone.

This man who met us that first day, who gave us a cultural guide to follow and who set us up in our first homes, his name was Malcolm Goode. Sam's father.

What I'm telling you now, John, is that I believe Sam was right; I believe his father was abducted. For Sam's sake, I can only hope he's still alive. And if

Sam's still with you, I ask that you tell him this information, and I hope he finds comfort in hearing it.

Become who you're meant to become, John. Grow strong and powerful and never forget for a minute the things you've learned along the way. Be noble, confident, and brave. Live with the same sort of dignity and valor that you inherited from your father, and trust in your heart and your will, as Lorien trusts in it still to this day. Never lose faith in yourself, and never lose hope; remember, even when this world throws its worst and then turns its back, there is still always hope.

And I'm certain, someday, you'll make it back home.

With love,
Your Friend and Cêpan,
-H

Blood pounds in my ears; and despite what Henri has written, I know in my heart that if we'd left Paradise when he'd wanted to, then he'd still be alive. We'd still be together. He came to the school to save me, because it was his duty to, and because he loved me. And now he's gone.

I take a deep breath, wipe my face with the back of my hand, and then walk from my room. Despite his bad leg, Sam insisted on taking the second floor, even when Six and I offered to take it instead. I go up the stairs now and knock on his door. I enter and flip his bedside lamp on, and I see his father's old glasses on the nightstand. Sam stirs.

'Sam? Hey, Sam. Sorry to wake you up, but there's some major shit you need to know.'

That gets his attention and he pulls off the blanket. 'Tell me then.'

'First, you have to promise not to get mad. I want you to know that I had no idea of any of what I'm about to tell you until just now. And whatever Henri's reasons were for not telling you to your face, you have to forgive him.'

He scoots up the mattress until his back rests on the headboard. 'Damn, John. Tell me already.'

'Promise me.'

'Fine, I promise.'

I hand him the letter. 'I should have read it sooner, Sam. I'm really sorry I didn't.'

I leave the room and close his door to give him the privacy he deserves. I'm not sure how he'll react. There's no telling how a person will accept the answer to the question they've asked most of their life, the question that's haunted them.

I walk down the stairs and slip out the back door with Bernie Kosar, who runs into the forest. I sit on the top of a picnic table. I can see my breath in the cool February air. Darkness is pushed to the west, while the morning light bleeds in from the east. I stare up at the half-moon and wonder if Sarah is looking at it, or if any of the others might be seeing it. Me and the others, the five still alive, are meant to assume the roles of the Elders. I still don't entirely understand what that means. Then I close my eyes and lift my face towards the sky. I stay that way until the door slides open behind me. I turn, expecting to see Sam, but it's

Six. She climbs up on the picnic table and sits next to me. I offer her a weak smile, but she doesn't return it.

'I heard you walk out here. Is everything okay? Did you and Sam have a fight or something?' she asks.

'What? No. Why?'

'All I know is he's crying on the couch downstairs and he won't talk to me.'

I pause before telling her. 'I finally read the letter Henri left behind. There's some stuff about Sam he and I haven't told you. It's about his dad.'

'What about his dad? Everything okay?'

I turn my body so our knees touch. 'Listen. When I met Sam in school he was pretty obsessed with the disappearance of his dad, who just didn't come home from the grocery store one day. They found his truck and his glasses on the ground next to the truck. You know those glasses that you see him carrying around all the time?'

Six turns to look inside the back door. 'Wait. Those are his dad's?'

'Yeah. And so the deal is that Sam is pretty convinced he was abducted by aliens, which I always thought was crazy; but I, I don't know, I let him go on believing it because who am I to crush the dude's hope of finding his dad again? I was waiting for Sam to tell you all this, but I just read Henri's letter, and you wouldn't believe what was in there.'

'What?'

I tell her everything, about Sam's dad being a Loric ally who met Henri and me when the ship landed, why Henri moved us to Paradise.

Six slides off the top of the picnic table and lands awkwardly on the bench. 'That is just so totally random that Sam is here. In there.'

'I don't think it is. I mean, think about it. It just so happens that of *all* the people in Paradise I'm drawn to for a best friend, it happens to be Sam? I think we were destined to meet.'

'Maybe you're right.'

'Pretty cool that his dad helped us that night, right?'

'The coolest. Remember when he said he had these feelings growing inside him about being with us?'

I do. 'But here's the thing. In Henri's letter he says that Sam's dad actually *was* abducted, or maybe even killed, by the Mogadorians.'

We sit in silence watching the sun slowly come up over the horizon. Bernie Kosar jogs out of the forest and rolls onto his back to have his belly rubbed. 'Hey there, Hadley.' He flips onto his feet instantly when I say it, tilting his beagle head. 'Yeah,' I say, jumping down to scratch his chin with both hands. 'I know.' Sam walks out. His eyes are red. He sits next to Six on the bench.

'Hi, Hadley,' Sam says to Bernie Kosar. BK barks in response and licks his hands.

'Hadley?' Six asks.

The dog barks again in approval.

'I always knew it,' Sam says. 'Always. From the day he disappeared.'

'You were right all this time,' I say.

'Do you mind if I read the letter?' Six asks. Sam hands

it to her. I aim my right palm at the front page and turn on its light. She reads the letter in its radiance, then folds the pages and hands them back.

'I'm really sorry, Sam,' she says.

I add, 'Henri and I wouldn't have survived if it wasn't for your dad.'

Six then turns to me. 'You know, it's ridiculous that your parents were Liren and Lara. Or it's ridiculous I didn't realize that myself. Do you remember me from Lorien, John? Your parents and my parents – their names were Arun and Lyn – they were best friends. I know we weren't around our parents all that often, but I remember going to your house a few times. You were just a toddler at the time, I think.'

It takes me a few seconds to remember what Henri once told me. It was the day Sarah had gotten back from Colorado, the day we confessed being in love with one another. After she left, Henri and I were eating dinner and he said, *Though I don't know her number, or have any idea where she is, one of the children who came to Earth with us was the daughter of your parents' best friends. They used to joke that it was fate that the two of you would end up together.*

I almost tell Six what Henri said, but remembering how that conversation came about because of my feelings for Sarah brings back the same guilt I've felt since Six and I went for our walk.

'Yeah, that is pretty crazy. I don't really remember it, though,' I say.

'Regardless, this is some heavy stuff about the Elders and how we're supposed to assume their roles. No wonder the Mogs are so relentless,' she says.

'Definitely makes sense.'

'We have to go back to Paradise,' Sam interrupts.

'Yeah, right.' Six laughs. 'What we need to do is find the others somehow. We need to get back on that laptop. Train some more.'

Sam stands. 'No, I'm serious, guys. We have to go back. If my dad left something behind, that transmission device, I think I know how to find it. When I was seven, he told me that my future was mapped on the sundial. I would ask him what he was talking about, and he'd just say that if the dark stars ever fell, I was supposed to find the Ennead and read the map by my birth date on the sundial.'

'What's an Ennead?' I ask.

'It's a group of nine deities in Egyptian mythology.'

'Nine?' Six asks. 'Nine deities?'

'And what sundial?' I ask.

'It's starting to make sense to me now,' Sam says. He begins walking around the picnic table as he puts it together in his head, Bernie Kosar nipping at his heels. 'I used to get *so* frustrated because he was always saying all this weird stuff that only he understood. A few months before he disappeared, my dad dug a well in our backyard and he said it would collect the rainwater from the gutters and whatever; but after the concrete was poured, he put this elaborate-looking sundial on the stone

lid. Then he stood looking down at the well and he said to me. "Your future's mapped on the sundial, Sam." '

'And you never checked it out?' I ask.

'Sure I did. I twisted the sundial around, trying my date and time of birth and a few other things, but nothing ever happened. I thought it was just a stupid well with a sundial on it after a while. But now that I read Henri's letter, the part about the dark stars, I know that it has to be some kind of clue to all this. It's like he told me without telling me,' Sam beams. 'He was so smart.'

'So are you,' I say. 'This could very well be suicide, us going back to Paradise, but I don't think we have much of a choice now.'

19

I wake with clenched teeth, a sour taste in my mouth. I tossed and turned all night, not only because the Chest is finally in my possession and I'm anxious to try to talk Adelina into opening it with me this morning, but also because I revealed too much to too many people. I put my Legacies on full display. How much would they all remember? Will I be exposed before breakfast? I sit up and see Ella in her bed. Everyone is still asleep in the room, except for Gabby, La Gorda, Delfina, and Bonita. Their beds are empty.

My feet are about to touch the ground when Sister Lucia appears in the doorway, her hands on her hips, her mouth twisted into a frown. We make eye contact and I lose my breath. But then she takes a couple steps backwards and allows the four girls from the nave to wobble into the room, dazed and bruised, their clothes ripped and dirty. Gabby stumbles to her bed and falls face-first onto it, the pillow enveloping her head. La Gorda rubs her double chin and lies back onto her bed with a grunt, and Bonita and Delfina slowly crawl under their covers. As soon as all four girls are motionless, Sister Lucia yells that it's time to get up. 'And that means everyone!'

As I try to pass by Gabby on the way to the bathroom, she flinches.

La Gorda stands at the mirror inspecting the discoloration of her skin. When she sees my reflection over her shoulder, she immediately turns on the faucet and tries to focus on washing her hands. I can get used to this. I don't really want to intimidate people, but I like the idea I might be left alone.

Ella skips out of one of the bathroom stalls and waits her turn at the sinks to wash up. I worry that she's going to be scared of me because of what I did in the nave, but the moment she sees me Ella dramatically flexes her right hand over her head. I lean into her ear. 'So you're okay?'

'Thanks to you,' she says loudly.

I catch La Gorda's eyes in the mirror. 'Hey,' I whisper. 'Last night is our little secret. Everything that happened last night is our secret, okay? Don't tell anyone.'

She puts her finger to her closed lips and I feel better, but there is something about the way La Gorda looked at me that doesn't sit well.

I'm so preoccupied by what might be in the Chest that I forego my morning internet search for news on John and Henri Smith. I don't have the patience to wait for morning Mass to see Adelina so I walk from room to room looking for her, but she's nowhere to be found. The first bell rings for morning Mass.

I shuffle in beside Ella in one of the last rows and wink at her. I locate Adelina in the front row. Halfway

through Mass, Adelina looks over her shoulder and makes eye contact with me. When she does, I point up to the nave's nook where she hid the Chest so many years ago. Her eyebrows raise.

'I couldn't understand what you were saying,' Adelina says after Mass. The two of us stand under a stained glass window of Saint Joseph on the left side of the nave, and we're bathed in a patchwork of muted yellows, browns, and reds. Her eyes match the seriousness of her posture.

'I found the Chest.'

'Where?'

I nod my head up and to the right.

'I am the one who was supposed to decide when you're ready, and you are *not* ready. Not even close,' she says angrily.

I pull my shoulders back and set my jaw. 'I was never going to be ready in your eyes because you stopped believing, *Emmalina*.'

The name catches her off guard. She opens her mouth and stops before letting loose whatever tirade is on her tongue.

'You have no idea what I'm going through in here with these other girls. While you're walking around holding onto your Bible and praying and counting the beads on your rosary, you don't care at all that I'm getting bullied, that I have just one friend, that all the Sisters hate me, and that there's a whole world out there that I'm supposed to be defending! Two worlds,

actually! Lorien and Earth need me and they need you, and I'm holed up in here like an animal in the zoo and you don't even care.'

'Of course I care.'

I start to cry. 'No you don't! No you don't! Maybe you cared back when you were Odetta and maybe a little when you were Emmalina; but ever since you've been Adelina and I've been Marina, you haven't cared about me or the other eight or what we're supposed to be doing here. I'm sorry, but I can't stand you talking to me about salvation when that's *all* I'm trying to achieve. I'm trying to protect us. I'm trying to do so much good, and you act as if I'm evil or something!'

Adelina takes a step forward, her arms open for a hug, but something causes her to retreat and take a step back. Her shoulders bounce as she starts to cry. My arms immediately wrap around her and we embrace.

'What's wrong? Why isn't Marina in the cafeteria?'

We turn to see Sister Dora with her arms crossed over her chest. A copper crucifix hangs over her wrists.

'Go,' Adelina whispers. 'We'll talk about this later.'

I wipe my face and rush past Sister Dora. As I leave the nave I can hear snippets of a heated argument brewing between Sister Dora and Adelina, their voices echoing off the vaulted ceiling, and I run my hands through my hair in hope.

Before sneaking back into the sleeping quarters last night, I floated the Chest down the narrow dark hallway to the left of the nave, past the ancient statues cut

into the rock wall. It now sits hidden atop the narrow tower of the north belfry, secure behind the padlocked oak door. It's safe there for the moment; but if I can't convince Adelina to open it with me soon, I'll have to find another location.

Ella is nowhere to be found in the cafeteria, and I worry that my Legacy has somehow backfired and she's at the hospital.

'She's in Sister Lucia's office,' a girl says when I ask the girls at the table nearest the door. 'There was a married couple with her. I think they're going to adopt her or something.' She pours a spoonful of soggy eggs onto her plate. 'So lucky.'

My knees buckle, and I catch myself from falling to the ground by gripping the edge of the table. I have no right to be so upset at the thought of Ella leaving the orphanage, but she's my one friend. Of course I knew she would be on the Sisters' short list of adoptable girls; Ella is seven and sweet and cute and wonderful to be around. I truly hope she finds a home, especially after losing her parents; but I'm not ready to let her go, regardless of how selfish it is.

It was determined when Adelina and I arrived that I'd never be adopted, but I sit there now wondering if it might have been better if I was eligible. Maybe someone would have fallen in love with me.

I realize that even if Ella is adopted today, it'll take some time for all the paperwork to be reviewed and accepted, which means she'll be here a week, maybe

two, maybe three. But it still breaks my heart, and makes me even more determined to leave this place as soon as I get the Chest opened.

I slump out of the cafeteria and find my coat, then sneak through the double doors and march down the hill, not caring that I'm skipping school. I keep an eye out for the man with the Pittacus book, staying on the sidewalk behind the vendors on Calle Principal, bouncing from shadow to shadow.

As I walk past El Pescador, the village restaurant, I look down the cobblestone alley and see the lid of a trash can teeter and then crash to the ground. The trash can itself begins to quake and wobble, and I hear something scraping at its insides. A pair of black-and-white paws curl over the lip of the can. It's a cat, and when he struggles over the edge and lands on the alley floor, I see a long gash running along his right side. An eye is swollen shut. It looks as though he is about to fall over from exhaustion or starvation, and he just lies in a pile of trash as if he's given up.

'You poor thing,' I say. I know I'm going to heal him before I take my first step down the alley. He purrs when I kneel down next to him, and when I place my hand on his fur there isn't resistance. The iciness flows quickly from me to the cat, quicker than it did to Ella or my own cheek, and I don't know if the Legacy is getting stronger or if it works faster on animals. His legs straighten and paws spread wide, and his breathing picks up until it melts into a loud purr. I gently turn

the cat over to inspect his right side and see that it's completely healed and covered with a lush coat of black fur. The eye that was swollen shut is now open and looking up at me. I name him Legacy and say, 'If you want a ride out of town, Legacy, then we should talk. Because I think I'm leaving soon, and I could use the company.'

I'm startled by a figure appearing at the end of the alley, but it's just Héctor pushing his mother in the wheelchair.

'Ah, Marina of the sea!' he yells.

'Hi, Héctor Ricardo.' I walk towards them. His mother looks slumped and distant, and I worry she's gotten worse.

'Who is your friend? Hello, little man.' Hector bends down to scratch Legacy's chin.

'Just some company I've picked up along the way.'

We walk quietly, chatting about the weather and Legacy, until arriving at Héctor and his mother's front door. 'Héctor? Have you seen the man with the mustache and book at the café recently?'

'No, I have not,' he says. 'What is it about this man that bothers you so much?'

I pause. 'He just looks like somebody I know.'

'Is that everything?'

'Yes.' He can tell I'm lying but also knows enough not to pry. I know he'll be on the lookout for the man I believe is a Mogadorian; I just hope he doesn't get hurt.

'It was good to see you, Marina. Remember that

today is a school day.' He winks. I nod sheepishly, and he unlocks his front door, backing inside, pulling his sick mother along with him.

The coast is clear over my shoulder and I continue with my walk for a while, thinking about the Chest, when I will be able to talk again with Adelina. I also think about John Smith on the run, Ella and her possible adoption, my fight last night in the nave. At the end of Calle Principal, I stare at the school building, hating the front door and the windows, angry at all the time I've spent inside when I should have been on the move, changing my name with each new country. I wonder what I would name myself in America.

Legacy meows around my feet as I make my way back through the village. I am still walking in the shadows, studying the street blocks ahead of me. I peek inside the window of the café, hoping and not hoping to see the Mogadorian with the thick mustache. He's not there, but Héctor already is, and he's laughing at something the woman at the next table just said. I'm going to miss Héctor just as much as I'll miss Ella. I have two friends, not one.

Ducking under the window as I pass, I can't help but look down at Legacy's lush black-and-white fur coat. Less than an hour ago the cat was lying in an alley, bleeding on a pile of trash, and now he's a ball of energy. My ability to heal and breathe new life into plants and animals and humans is an enormous responsibility. Fixing Ella made me feel more special than I

ever had before, and it wasn't because I felt like a hero, but because I helped someone who needed it. I slink a few doors down the street and Héctor's laugh travels through the café window and wraps itself around my shoulders, and I know what I need to do.

The front door is locked, but when I go around to the back of Héctor's house, the first window I try opens with ease. Legacy licks his paws as I climb up and through the window. Jitters attack; I have never broken into someone's house before.

The house is small and dark inside, and the air is heavy. Every foreseeable surface is covered with Catholic figurines. I find Héctor's mother's room in no time. She lies on a twin bed in the far corner, her blankets slowly rising with each breath. Her legs are twisted at unnatural angles, and she looks frail. Pill bottles line a small nightstand, along with rosary beads, a crucifix, a miniature statue of the Virgin Mary with her hands held in prayer, and ten or so saints I don't know the names of. I drop to my knees beside Carlotta's sleeping body. Her eyes flutter open and scan the air. I freeze and hold my breath. I've never talked to her before, though when she finds me crouching beside her, a glint of recognition registers. She opens her mouth to speak.

'Shhh,' I say to her. 'I'm a friend of Héctor's, Señora Ricardo. I don't know if you can understand me, but I'm here to help you.'

She accepts what I have told her with fluttering eyelids. I reach up and caress the side of her cheek

with the back of my left hand, and then I rest it on her forehead. Her gray hair is dry and brittle. She closes her eyes.

My heart's pounding, and I can see a noticeable shake in my hand when I lift it and place it on her stomach; and it's then that I can feel how weak and sick she really is. The cold tingle crawls up my spine and spreads down my arms and into the tip of each finger. I grow dizzy. My breathing quickens, and my heart beats even faster. I begin to sweat despite the prickly chill turning my skin cold. Carlotta's eyes open, and a low groan escapes her open mouth.

I close my eyes. 'Shhh, it's okay, it's okay,' I say to comfort the both of us. And then, with the icy chill radiating from me to her, I begin to pull the sickness away. It retreats stubbornly, clinging tightly to her insides, reluctant to loosen its grip; but finally even the stubborn bits let go.

Slight tremors cause Carlotta to convulse and shake, and I do my best to hold her down. I open my eyes just in time to see the ashen color of Carlotta's face change to a pink glow.

Vertigo sweeps through me. I lift my hands from her body and fall backwards to the floor. My heart thuds so violently that it scares me, like it's about to break free from my body. But in time it slows, and when I finally pull myself to my feet, I see Carlotta's sitting up with a bewildered look, as though trying to remember where she is and how she'd gotten here.

I rush into the kitchen and drink three glasses of water. When I walk back, Carlotta is still gathering her bearings. I make another quick decision – I go to the nightstand and rifle through the ten or so pill bottles, finding the label I'm looking for: WARNING: MAY CAUSE DROWSINESS. I open it, take four pills, and shove them in my pocket.

'What's going on?' Carlotta asks. She is frantic. 'Where am I? Who are you?'

I don't answer her, and instead walk from the room. But before I leave, I turn and look at Carlotta once more. She's watching me with her healed, untwisted legs dangling over the bed as though she's about to stand.

I rush out of the house and find Legacy sleeping underneath the back window. Keeping to the alleys and side streets, I make my way back to the orphanage with the cat in my arms, wondering how Héctor will react when he finds his mother cured. The problem, however, is that in a village this small, secrets don't last very long. My only hope is that nobody saw me come or go, and that Carlotta won't remember what really happened.

Outside the double doors, I unzip my coat halfway and carefully place Legacy inside. I know just where I can keep him safe: up in the north belfry with the Chest. *The Chest,* I think. *I have to get it open.*

20

Being in love is a very strange thing. Your thoughts constantly drift towards this other person, no matter what you're doing. You could be reaching for a glass in the cupboard or brushing your teeth or listening to someone tell a story, and your mind will just start drifting towards their face, their hair, the way they smell, wondering what they'll wear, and what they'll say the next time they see you. And on top of the constant dream state you're in, your stomach feels like it's connected to a bungee cord, and it bounces and bounces around for hours until it finally lodges itself next to your heart.

That's how I've felt since the first day I met Sarah Hart. I can be training with Sam or trying to find my shoes in the back of our SUV, and the thought of Sarah's face and her lips and ivory skin take over me. I can be giving directions from the backseat and *still* be one hundred percent focused on the way it feels when the top of Sarah's head rests just under my chin. And I can be surrounded by twenty Mogs, my palms just starting to light up, and I'll be analyzing every line of conversation from Thanksgiving dinner at Sarah's.

But what's even more insane is that as we drive the speed limit towards Paradise at nine o'clock at night, as

we drive right towards Sarah and her blond hair and blue eyes, I'm also thinking about Six. I'm thinking about the way she smells, the way she looks in her training outfits, how we almost kissed back in Florida. My stomach also hurts because of Six. Not only because of her, but because of the fact my best friend also has a crush on her. I need to buy some antacids the next time we stop.

While Sam drives we debate Henri's letter and talk about how cool Sam's dad is for not only helping the people of Lorien but also for giving Sam a riddle to find the transmitter device in case anything were to happen to him. And still I'm going back and forth between Sarah and Six in my head.

We're two hours from Paradise when Six asks, 'But what if it's nothing, though? I mean, what if there's nothing down in that well but some weird birthday present or *anything* else but the transmitter. We're risking a lot, like *a lot* a lot, by showing up in Paradise like this.'

'Trust me,' Sam says. He drums his thumbs on the steering wheel and turns up the stereo. 'I've never been so certain of anything in my entire life. And I get straight As, thank you very much.'

I think the Mogadorians are there waiting, in far greater numbers than what we faced in Florida, watching everything that might lead them to us. And if I'm going to be honest with myself, the only reason I'm willing to take this risk is because of the possibility of seeing Sarah.

I lean forward in the backseat and pat Sam's right

shoulder. 'Sam, no matter what happens with that well and sundial, Six and I owe you big-time for what your dad did for us. But I really, really, really, really hope that it leads to a transmitter.'

'Don't worry,' Sam says.

Highway lights come and go. Bernie Kosar's floppy ears fall from the edge of the seat as he sleeps. I'm nervous about seeing Sarah. Nervous about being so close to Six.

'Hey, Sam?' I ask. 'You wanna play a game?'

'Yeah, sure.'

'What do you think Six's Earth name is?'

Six whips her head over her shoulder, her raven hair slapping her right cheek, and she frowns at me in mock anger.

'She has one?' Sam laughs.

'Just guess,' I say.

'Yeah, Sam,' Six says. 'Guess.'

'Um, Stryker?'

I laugh so hard Bernie Kosar jumps up to look out the nearest window.

'Stryker?' Six yells.

'Not Stryker, then? Okay, okay. I don't know, something like Persia or Eagle or . . .'

'Eagle?' Six yells. 'Why would I be Eagle?'

'You're such a badass, you know.' Sam laughs. 'I just figured you would be like a Starfire or like Thunder Clap or something really badassy.'

'Exactly!' I shout. 'That's totally what I thought, too!'

'So what is it then?' he asks.

Six crosses her arms and looks out the passenger-side window. 'I'm not telling you until you make a real guess with a real girl's name. Eagle, Sam? Give me some credit.'

'What? I'd name myself Eagle if I had the chance,' Sam says. 'Eagle Goode. That sounds pretty awesome, right?'

'It sounds like a brand of cheese,' Six says. We all laugh at that.

'Okay. Uh, Rachel?' Sam says. 'Britney?'

'Ew, yuck,' she says.

'Fine. Rebecca? Claire? Oh, I know. Beverly.'

'You are insane.' Six laughs. She punches Sam's thigh, and he howls and rubs at it dramatically. He hits her back, a couple of knuckles on her left bicep, and she feigns severe pain.

'Her name is Maren Elizabeth,' I say. 'Maren Elizabeth.'

'Aw, you gave it away,' he says. 'I was going with Maren Elizabeth next.'

'Yeah, right,' she says.

'No, I was, I was! Maren Elizabeth's pretty cool. Do you want us to start calling you that? Four goes by John, right Four?'

I scratch Bernie Kosar's head. I don't think I could get used to calling him Hadley, but maybe I could get used to calling Six Maren Elizabeth. 'I think you should take on a human name,' I say. 'If not Maren Elizabeth, then something else. I mean, at least for when we're in front of strangers.'

Everyone grows silent, and I reach behind me into the Chest for the velvet bag holding Lorien's solar system. I set the six planets and the sun in my palm and watch them hover and glow to life. As the planets begin to orbit their sun, I find that I am able to dim the brightness of their glow with my mind. I intentionally lose myself in them, successfully forgetting just for a few moments that I might be seeing Sarah soon.

Six turns to look at the faint solar system that floats in front of my chest, and then she finally says, 'I don't know; I still like the name Six. Maren Elizabeth was when I was a different person, and right now Six just feels right. It can be short for something if someone asks.'

Sam looks over. 'For what? Sixty?'

I set out seven mugs and a kettle on the stove. While waiting for the water to boil, I crush three of the pills I stole from Héctor's mother into a fine powder with the rounded back side of a metal spoon. Ella stands beside me watching as she always does when it's my turn to make the Sisters' nightly tea.

'What are you doing?' she asks.

'Something I'm probably going to regret,' I say. 'But something I have to do.'

Ella flattens a piece of crumpled paper on the table and places the tip of her pencil on it. Immediately she's drawing a perfect picture of the seven teacups I've lined up. From what I can get out of her, she met with a couple in Sister Lucia's office who said they had

'a lot of love to give.' I'm not sure how long the meeting lasted, but Ella says they're coming back tomorrow. I know what it means and I pour the boiling water from the kettle as slowly as I can, trying to prolong my time with her.

'Ella? How often do you think about your parents?' I ask.

Her brown eyes grow wide. 'Today?'

'Sure. Today, or any other day?'

'I don't know . . .' She trails off. After a pause, she adds, 'A million times?'

I bend down to hug her, and I don't know if it's because of how sorry I feel for her or how sorry I feel for myself. My parents are dead, too. The victims of a war I'm supposed to continue someday.

I scoop the crushed pills into Adelina's teacup, regretting that I've resorted to drugging her. There's no other choice. She can stand by and wait for death if that's what she chooses, but I refuse to give up or to go down without a fight, without doing everything within my power to survive.

With the tray teetering in my hands, I leave Ella at the table and make my rounds. One by one I hand the tea out around the orphanage, and when I'm ushered into the Sisters' quarters to deliver Adelina her tea, I carefully shove her cup towards the front edge. She takes it with a polite nod. 'Sister Camila is feeling ill this evening and I have been asked to sleep in the children's quarters tonight for her.'

‘Okay,’ I say. As I think about the possibilities of Adelina and me being in the same room tonight, I watch her take a long sip from her teacup. I can’t tell if I just made a huge mistake or helped my cause immensely.

‘I will see you soon then,’ she says. Then she winks at me. I’m taken aback, almost dropping the two remaining cups from my tray to the floor.

‘O-okay,’ I stutter.

When curfew comes a half hour later, nobody falls asleep right away, and instead many girls whisper to one another in the dark. I lift my head every few minutes to look at Adelina lying on her bed across the room. Her wink has left me confused.

Ten more minutes pass. I can tell most everyone is still awake, including Adelina. She’s usually quick to fall asleep when she’s on duty, so the fact that she’s still up tells me that she’s also waiting for everyone in the room to fall asleep. Now I think her wink definitely meant she wanted to resume our conversation. The room falls silent, and I wait before I lift my head. Adelina hasn’t moved in the last half hour, so I move the left legs of her bed off the ground and tip her slightly. Suddenly she raises her left arm above her like a white flag of surrender, and she points to the doorway.

I toss the covers aside, stand, then tiptoe from the room. When I reach the hall I slink a few paces into the shadows, holding my breath, hoping this isn’t some

sort of trap Adelina and Sister Dora have set up. After thirty seconds, Adelina enters the hallway. Her walk is labored and she sways from side to side.

'Come with me,' I whisper, taking her hand. I haven't held her hand in years, and it brings back the memory of us huddling together on the boat to Finland, when I was sick and she was strong. We were once so close you couldn't slide a piece of paper between us. Now the mere touch of her hand feels alien.

'I'm so tired,' Adelina confesses as we climb to the second floor; we're halfway to the north wing and the belfry protected by the padlock. 'I don't know what's wrong with me.'

I do. 'Do you want me to carry you?'

'You can't carry me.'

'Not with my arms,' I say.

She's too tired to argue. I focus on her feet and legs, and a few seconds later I've lifted Adelina off the floor and begin to float her down the dusty corridors. We pass the ancient statues cut into the rock wall and enter the narrower hallway in silence. I worry that she's fallen asleep, but then she says, 'I can't believe you're using telekinesis to fly an old lady like me down the hall. Where are we going?'

'I had to hide it,' I whisper. 'We're almost there, I promise.'

I unlock the padlock and it falls from the oak door's handle, and soon I'm following a floating Adelina up the stone stairway that circles around the north tower

leading to the belfry. I can hear Legacy faintly meowing from the top.

I open the door to the belfry and set Adelina gently down next to the Chest. She props her left arm up on the Chest lid and leans her head against it; I can see she has just about lost her battle with the pills, and I'm angry with myself now for tricking her. Legacy climbs into her lap and licks her right hand. 'How is there a cat in here?' she mumbles.

'Don't ask. Listen, Adelina, you're almost completely asleep, and I need you to open the Chest with me before you are, okay?'

'I don't think I have . . .'

'Have what?' I ask.

'Have it in me right now, Marina.' Her eyes are closed.

'Yes, you do.'

'Put your hand on the Chest's lock. Put my hand on the other side.'

I press my palm against the side of the lock and it feels warm. I use telekinesis to pull her right hand away from Legacy's tongue and onto the other side of the lock. She interlocks her fingers with mine. A second passes. The lock snaps open.

'Uh, guys? Something is, uh, something's totally happening back here.' The seven orbs that hover in front of my Chest in the backseat of the SUV are speeding up, and I can no longer control them. It gets so bright that I have to cover my eyes.

'Hey, hey! Dude, cut it out!' Sam barks. 'I'm trying to drive up here.'

'I don't know what's going on!'

'Pull over!' Six yells.

Sam rips the vehicle onto the shoulder of the road and slams on the brakes, stone and gravel crunching and pinging us. The six planets and one sun dim in brightness, and the planets start to whip around the sun at such a rate that it's hard to focus on any single one. With each orbit the planets are absorbed into the sun until it's the size of a basketball. The new globe rotates as though on an axis, and then it produces a flash of light so bright that I'm momentarily blinded. It slowly dims, and sections of its surface raise and recede until what's left behind is a perfect replica of Earth itself, all seven continents, all seven seas.

'Is that . . . ?' Sam asks. 'That looks like Earth.'

The planet spins near my head, and on its third or fourth rotation I see a small pinprick of pulsing light.

'Do you guys see that little light?' I ask. 'Look at Europe.'

'Oh, yeah,' Sam says. He waits for another rotation and then squints. 'I would say that's in what? Spain or Portugal? Can someone reach the laptop? Hurry.'

With my eyes still on the globe and the tiny pulsing light, I crash my hand around behind me until I find the laptop. I hand it to Six, who hands it to Sam. He looks up at the globe hovering in the backseat, types and looks up. 'Well, it's definitely in Spain, and it looks to be close to . . . Well, the closest city seems to be a place called León.

But that's, that's slightly off. We're looking at the Picos de Europa Mountains for sure. Anyone ever heard of them?'

'Definitely not,' I say.

'Me neither,' Six says.

'Is that maybe our ship?' I ask.

'No way, not in Spain. Well, at least I highly doubt it,' she says. 'I mean, if it is our ship then why would it just start glowing now, showing us where it is? That wouldn't make any sense. Besides, you've looked at these things how many times?'

'A dozen,' I say. 'Maybe more.'

Sam hugs his headrest and raises his eyebrows. 'Right. So it's as if something just activated it.'

Six and I look at each other.

'It could definitely be one of the others,' Sam says.

'Could be,' Six says. 'Or it could be a trap.' She looks at Sam. 'Has there been any suspicious news from Spain?'

He shakes his head. 'Not as of five hours ago. But I'll check again right now.' He starts typing on the keyboard.

'Before you do that, let's get off the main road before someone notices there's a glowing planet of Earth floating in the car,' I say. 'We're pretty damn close to Paradise, remember?'

Adelina snores and I feel guilty, but for the first time in my life I see the Inheritance I should have received years ago. Rocks and gems of different colors, different sizes and shapes. A pair of dark gloves and a pair

of dark glasses, both made of materials I've never seen before. There's a small tree branch with the bark pared away, and under that there is an odd circular device with a glass lens and floating needle not unlike a compass. But it's a glowing red crystal that has me most intrigued. Once I look at it I can't look away, and I slowly reach down and take it in my hand; it's warm and tingly in my palm. For a brief second the red light brightens, and then it fades and begins to slowly pulse at the same rate I breathe.

The crystal grows hotter, brighter, and it begins to emit a low hum. I panic, nervous that one of my Legacies has activated a Loric grenade. 'Adelina!' I yell. 'Wake up! Wake up, please!'

She furrows her brow and her snoring intensifies.

With my free hand I shake her shoulder. 'Adelina!'

I shake her harder, and as I do I drop the crystal. It bounces hard on the belfry's stone floor and rolls towards the doorway. As it falls from the first stair to the second, the red light stops pulsing. As it falls from the second stair to the third, it stops glowing altogether. And as it falls to the fourth stair, I chase after it.

Sam zips us down a dark dirt road. The globe continues to whir in my face. The tiny pulsing light continues to try to tell us something. We come to a stop, and Sam kills the engine and lights.

'So, I'm thinking it's one of you guys,' Sam says, turning around. 'It's another number. And that number is in Spain.'

'We have no way of knowing that,' Six says.

Sam nods at the globe. 'Okay, look. You guys were meant to stay apart from one another when you first arrived, right? That's how it worked. You all go off in hiding until your Legacies develop and you train and everything. And then what? Then you get together and you fight together. So this light right here, maybe that's a signal to get together, or more likely, it's a distress signal from one of the remaining numbers. Or, guys, maybe Number Five or Number Nine just opened up their Chest for the first time, and because we have this thing running at the same time, we can communicate.'

'Maybe they see we're in Ohio, then?' I ask.

'Shit. Maybe. Possibly. But seriously, think about it. If the Elders were going to give you all this stuff in your Chests, then they'd give you something to communicate with each other. Right? Maybe we just unlocked the key somehow, and we've got the location of someone who needs our help,' he says.

'Or maybe one of the others is getting tortured and they're being forced to contact us and it's a trap,' Six says.

Just as I'm about to agree, the edges of Earth grow fuzzy and then the entire globe vibrates with a female voice that says, 'Adelina! *¡Despierta! ¡Despierta, por favor!* Adelina!'

I'm about to yell back, but the globe suddenly shrinks, re-forms into the seven orbs and returns to normal.

'Whoa, whoa, whoa! What just happened?' I ask.

'I'd say the signal has been cut,' Sam says.

'Who was that girl? And who's Adelina?' Six asks.

I catch the stone after it bounces off the ninth stair, but no matter what I do it doesn't glow like it did before. I shake it in my palm. I blow on it. I set it in Adelina's open hand. It doesn't change from its new faint blue color, and I'm worried I broke it. I carefully set it back inside the Chest and pick up the short tree branch.

With a deep breath, I stick the branch out one of the two windows and I concentrate on the opposite end. There's a bit of a magnetic force happening; but before I can really test it or figure it out, I hear the oak door at the bottom of the tower creak open.

21

While we drive, I try a few more times to regain the signal with the globes, but every time I get the solar system up and running they just orbit like normal. It's almost midnight and I'm about to rifle through the other stones and objects in my Chest, but it's then I see the scattered lights of a town on the horizon. A sign passes on my right just like it did a few months ago when Henri was behind the wheel:

WELCOME TO PARADISE, OHIO
POPULATION 5,243

'Welcome home,' Sam whispers.

I press my forehead against the window and recognize a dilapidated barn, an old sign for apples, a green pickup still for sale. A warm feeling comes over my entire body. Of all the places I've ever lived, Paradise has been my favorite. It's where I made my first best friend. It's where I developed my first Legacy. It's where I fell in love. But Paradise was also where I met my first Mogadorians. Where I had my first real battle and felt real pain. It's the place where Henri died.

Bernie Kosar jumps onto the seat next to me, and

his tail wags at an amazing rate. He shoves his nose through the small crack in his window, and he sniffs furiously at the familiar air.

As we take the first side road on the left and make several more turns, backtracking here and there, making sure we're not being followed, finding the best and least conspicuous place to leave the SUV, we go over the plan once more.

'After we get the transmitter we go right back to the car and we leave Paradise immediately,' Six says. 'Right?'

'Right,' I say.

'We don't make contact with *anyone* else; we just go. We leave.'

I know she's referring to Sarah, and I bite my lip. Finally after all these weeks on the run, I'm back in Paradise and I'm told I can't see Sarah.

'Got it, John? We leave? Right away?'

'Lay off already. I know what you're getting at.'

'Sorry.'

Sam parks the SUV on a dark street under a maple tree two miles from his house. My shoes drop to the asphalt, my lungs take their first real breath of Paradise air and I instantly want to go back to how it was, back to Halloween, back to coming home to Henri, back to sitting on my couch next to Sarah.

We don't take any chances of losing my Chest in an unguarded car, so Six opens the back door and lugs it onto her shoulder. Once comfortable, she makes herself invisible.

'Wait,' I say. 'I want something out of there first. Six?'

Six reappears and I open the Chest and retrieve the dagger, slipping it into the back pocket of my jeans. 'Okay. Now I'm ready. Bernie Kosar, buddy, are you ready?'

Bernie Kosar transforms into a small brown owl, and he flaps his way onto a low branch of the maple tree.

'Let's do this already.' Six picks up my Chest and disappears again.

Then we run. With Sam trailing at a good pace, I jump a fence and pick up speed on the edge of the nearest field. After a half mile, I'm veering into the forest, loving the way the branches break off my chest and arms, how the tall patches of grass whip my jeans. I look over my shoulder often, and Sam is never farther than forty yards behind me, jumping over logs, sliding under branches. There is a noise beside me, but before I can reach for my dagger Six whispers that it's just her. I see a swatch of grass part down the middle and I follow.

Luckily, Sam lives on the outskirts of Paradise with large yards separating each neighbor. I stop just inside the lip of the forest when his house comes into view. It's a small, modest house with white aluminum siding and black shingles, a thin chimney on its right side, a tall wooden fence enclosing the backyard. Six materializes and sets down my Chest.

'That it?' she asks.

'That's it.'

Thirty seconds later, Bernie Kosar lands on my shoulder. Four minutes go by until Sam lumbers through a line

of brush and stands next to us, out of breath, his palms planted firmly on his thighs. He looks up at his house in the distance.

'How are you feeling?' I ask.

'Like a fugitive. Like a bad son.'

'Think about how proud your dad would be if we pull this off,' I say.

Six turns herself invisible to run reconnaissance, checking the shadows of the nearby houses, the backseats of every car on the street. She returns and says everything looks okay, but there are some motion sensor lights on the house on the right. Bernie Kosar flies away, perching himself on the highest point of the roof.

Six grabs Sam's hand and they turn invisible. I tuck the Chest under my arm and quietly follow them to the back fence. They reappear, and Six goes over first, then Sam. I toss the Chest over and climb quickly after. We duck behind an overgrown shrub, and I survey the backyard and its trees, high grass, a big tree stump, a rusty swing set, and an antique wheelbarrow on its side. There's a back door on the left side of the house and two dark windows on the right.

'There it is,' Sam whispers, pointing.

What I first thought was a tree stump peeking out of the middle of the yard is actually, upon closer inspection, a wide stone cylinder. Squinting, I see a triangular object sticking up off its top.

'We'll be right back,' Six whispers to Sam.

My hand in Six's, I turn invisible and say, 'Okay, Eagle

Goode. Guard that Chest as if my life depends on it. Because it does.'

Six and I carefully walk through the high grass towards the well, and then kneel in front of it. Numbers border the circumference of the sundial – one through twelve on the left side and another one through twelve on the right, zero at the top – and the numbers are surrounded by a series of lines. I'm about to grip the middle triangle and twist randomly when I hear Six gasp.

'What?' I whisper, raising my eyes to the dark back windows.

'In the middle. Look. The symbols.'

I study the sundial again, and my breath is caught in my throat. They're faint and easy to overlook, but in the middle of the circle are nine shallow Loric symbols. I recognize the numbers one through three because they match the scars on my ankle, but the others are new to me.

'What's Sam's birthday again?' I ask.

'January fourth, nineteen ninety-five.'

The triangle clicks like a lock as I turn it right to the Loric number one. I turn it left, swallowing hard as I aim it at what must be number four. My number. Then I rotate the triangle to one, nine, back around to nine again, and five. Nothing happens for a few seconds, and then the sundial begins to hiss and smoke. Six and I step back and watch as the stone lid of the well flips back and opens with a loud echoing crack. When the smoke clears, I see a ladder inside.

Sam is jumping up and down near the fence. One hand over his mouth, the other raised in a fist.

One of the dark windows of the house turns yellow. Bernie Kosar lets out two long *hoo*s from the roof. Before I can think, Six yanks me forward, and soon I'm visible and descending the ladder inside the well. Six follows, pulling the lid almost closed above her. I illuminate my palms and see we're twenty feet from a cement floor.

'What about Sam?' I whisper.

'He'll be fine. Bernie Kosar's up there.'

We reach the floor and find ourselves in a short hallway that curves to the left. The air is musty. I shine my palms back and forth as we walk through the curve; and when the hallway straightens again, we see there's a room ahead with a cluttered desk and hundreds of papers pinned to the wall. I'm about to run inside, but that's when my lights catch a long white object in the doorway.

'Is that . . .' Six trails off.

I'm stuck in my tracks. It's an enormous bone. Six pushes me forward and I pull the dagger from my back pocket.

'Ladies first?' I offer.

'Not this time.'

With a running start, I jump over the bone and immediately light up the room with my hands. A yell escapes my mouth as I take in the skeleton sitting against the wall. Six jumps inside, and when she sees it, she stumbles backwards into the desk.

The skeleton is over eight feet tall, with giant feet and hands. Thick blond hair falls from the top of its skull and reaches past its wide shoulder blades. Around its neck hangs a blue pendant similar to mine.

'That's not Sam's dad,' Six says.

'Definitely not.'

'Then who is it?'

I step forward and examine the pendant. The blue Loralite stone is slightly larger than mine, but everything else is the same. I stare at it and feel an overwhelming connection to whoever this was. 'I'm not sure, but I think he was a friend.' I reach over his head and retrieve the pendant, handing it to Six.

We move to the desk. I don't know where to start. A heavy layer of dust covers stacks of papers and writing utensils. The writing on the papers pinned to the wall above the desk is in every language but English. I recognize a few Loric numbers, but nothing else. A white electronic tablet sits on a dilapidated wooden chair, and I pick it up and press my fingers over its black screen. Nothing happens.

Six opens the top drawer to find more papers, and as she grabs the second drawer's handle, an explosion aboveground knocks us off our feet. A long crack travels along the room's ceiling and then the concrete buckles. Chunks fall all around us.

'Run!' I yell.

With the pendant around her neck, Six tears a dozen papers from the wall and I stuff the white tablet in the

back of my waistband. We scramble up the ladder and peek out the sliver of space between the well and the sundial. Dozens of Mogs. Smoldering fires. Bernie Kosar has transformed himself into a tiger with the curling horns of a ram. A Mog's arm is in his teeth. Sam is no longer at the fence, and neither is my Chest.

I'm about to burst out of the well when Six launches herself past me in a tornado of clouds. The sundial lid whips backwards, and she rips through a huddle of five Mogs, sending them across the yard. I pull myself out of the well and close it as she picks up a gleaming Mog sword, turning invisible.

I use my telekinesis to toss three armed Mogs standing near the well against the house. They explode into thick ash, and when I turn I see a shirtless man frozen in the back door with a shotgun in his hands. Behind him stands Sam's frightened mom in a nightgown.

Six materializes next to two Mogs running at me with glowing cannons, and she swings the sword through both their necks. Then she uses her telekinesis to throw the wheelbarrow at another, turning him into a pile of ash. I toss two Mogs against another, and Six impales all three in one quick motion. Bernie Kosar leaps into the middle of the yard and digs his teeth into a few Mogs struggling to their feet.

'Where's Sam?' I yell.

'Here!'

I twist to see Sam lying on his stomach under a charred shrub. Blood runs down his scalp.

'Sam!' his mom yells from the doorway.

He struggles to his knees. 'Mom!'

His mom yells again, but a Mog reaches down and pulls Sam up by his shirt. I concentrate and uproot the rusty swing set, but before one of its metal poles can spear the Mog in the chest, he tosses Sam over the fence.

With an intensity I've never seen in her before, Six slices through the remaining Mogs. She's covered in ash when she jumps over the fence after Sam. I leap onto Bernie Kosar and we follow.

Sam is on his back in the neighbor's yard. Motion sensor lights flood over him. I jump off Bernie Kosar and pick him up.

'Sam? Are you okay? Where's my Chest?'

He opens his eyes halfway. 'They got it. I'm sorry, John.'

'There!' Six points to several Mogs running through a field towards the forest.

I set Sam on Bernie Kosar's back, but he pushes himself off. 'I'm okay. I swear.'

From the other side of the fence, Sam's mom yells, 'Sam!'

'I'll be back, Mom! I love you!' And then he's the first to run towards the Mogs. Six and I catch up easily, but she veers right to plunge her sword into an approaching Mog. Four more are thirty yards ahead of her; and with the large pendant bouncing around her neck, she charges, with Bernie Kosar at her heels.

Sam and I enter the muddy field, and two Mogs cut off our path. Over my shoulder I see two more separating

and marching in our direction at strategic angles. The others have entered the forest at two different sections, and I can't see who has the Chest. I pull the dagger out of my back pocket. The handle wraps around my hand.

I run ahead, and the two Mogs in front of me run, too, their swords bouncing and cutting into the empty field behind them. When we're less than five yards apart I leap with my dagger above my head. As I start to fall, a huge tree zips underneath me, ramming both Mogs and killing them. Six. As I hit the ground again I turn to see her running towards Sam and the two Mogs who circle him.

The one on Sam's left tackles him around the waist. Six tears the Mog off and throws him far into the field, where he immediately gets back on his feet and charges.

I sneak up behind the other Mog and hammer my dagger into the back of his neck, pulling it out at an angle that slices down through his shoulder blade. He falls to a pile of ash that blows onto my shoes.

Bernie Kosar pounces on the other Mog and quickly he has a tongue coated in thick ash.

'We have to get back to the car and get out of here,' Six says. 'There must be more on their way – they were waiting for us.'

'We have to get my Chest first,' I say.

'Then we're going to have to split up,' Six says. With her soot-covered sword, she points at the two sections of forest the Mogs disappeared into. 'Bernie Kosar, you're with me.' Bernie Kosar shrinks into a hawk, and he and Six head left.

Sam and I enter the forest in the other direction. Soon we hear twigs cracking, and we run in that direction. I speed ahead and hurdle a series of dead trees to see four Mogs trying to escape through a small clearing. In the moonlight, I still can't see if any of them hold my Chest.

I slide down the hill on my side, crushing saplings, creating a small landslide of loose rock. I hear Sam crashing after me.

They're halfway through the small clearing. It's dense, with grass six feet tall, and I run through it at full speed. Sam yells for me to tell him what direction I'm headed in, but instead I keep running and aim my lit palm straight up into the sky as a beacon. 'Okay! Got it!' he yells.

Finally, right before the clearing becomes forest again, I can almost reach one. I dive for his legs and slice through the bottom of his muddy khakis and sever his Achilles tendon, causing him to roar onto his back. I climb up his flailing body and stab him in the chest, killing him.

Sam trips over my legs and falls on his face. 'You get it?'

'No. Come on!'

Using one hand as a flashlight and the other as a machete, I race through the forest with ease, not caring how close Sam stays behind me. In less than a minute, I see another Mog struggling over a fallen log. From twenty-five yards away, I lift the log high off the ground, tip it, and force the Mog to teeter and fall headfirst. I crash through weeds to find him motionless on his stomach.

I can already tell he doesn't have my Chest. I kill him with two stabs of my dagger.

'John?' Sam yells in the darkness. 'Dude?'

I again shine my palm in the air, and I'm scanning the trees when Sam arrives.

'Tell me you got it?'

'Not yet,' I say.

'No Chest,' Sam mutters.

'I just hope Six had better luck.' I reach behind me and pull the white tablet out to show Sam. 'But I do have this.'

He grabs it out of my hand. 'From the well?'

'That's not all we found. Wait until I tell you what else –' I suddenly recognize where we are. I stop walking. I even stop breathing.

Sam grabs my shoulder and says, 'Whoa, dude. What's going on? You feeling something? Like maybe somebody just opened your Chest?'

As far as I can tell, my Chest hasn't been opened. The feeling brewing inside me is something entirely different. 'We're near Sarah's house.'

22

After the door at the bottom of the tower creaks open, I hear footsteps. I hear echoed breathing. Whoever it is, it'll be impossible to hide a drugged Adelina, a cat, and a Chest stuffed with alien weapons and artifacts. I slowly set the branch back into the Chest and close the lid. Legacy creeps to the edge of the belfry floor and then sits and stares down into the darkness. We're all silent, but then Adelina rolls out a long, droning snore.

The footsteps in the circular stairway speed up. I give Adelina a few shakes to wake her up. She falls onto her side.

What do I do? I mouth to Legacy. The cat jumps on top of the Chest and then jumps back off again only to purr around my feet. It isn't an answer, but it does give me an idea. I lean down and set Legacy on top of the Chest and then scramble up into one of the two windows where the cool air penetrates my pajamas and instantly causes my teeth to chatter. The footsteps are getting closer.

With my mind, I raise the Chest high in the air, and Legacy's claws scrape at the lid for a safe footing. I have to duck as I float the Chest up and over me and out the window. Immediately after I set the Chest quietly on

the frosty lawn ten stories below, Legacy jumps off and runs into the darkness. I then float Adelina up and over me, her nightgown brushing the top of my head, and carefully I set her down next to the Chest.

The footsteps are loud now. I swing my legs over the edge of the window. Using whatever concentration I can still muster, I am able to levitate myself a few centimeters above the cold stone. I push out into the swirling wind. Before I lower myself away from the tower, I see the mustached Mogadorian from the café round the last turn of the stairway and stomp into the belfry.

My concentration buckles and then snaps into a million little pieces. I go into a wild free-fall until the last moment, when I press my hands in front of my chest and set my mind on floating like a feather. My right knee lands a hair from Adelina's shivering body.

I panic. I either have to try to get the Chest and Adelina down into the village for hiding – but it is the middle of the night and we are in our nightclothes and I can only see a few lonely windows lit in town – or I have to quickly find a place to hide us within the orphanage. It will take the Mogadorian less time to descend the tower than it did for him to race up it, but he still has a long hallway to travel and another flight of stairs to run down to make it to the first floor. I stick my head through the double doors, and once I see the coast is clear, I drape Adelina over the Chest and float them into the nave. My strength is waning immensely,

but I am somehow able to summon just enough power to get the Chest, Adelina and me tucked away up into the farthest recess of the drafty, cold and damp nook where the Chest had originally been hidden.

I am beginning to think I led the Mogadorian right to me by opening the Chest. Perhaps the red pulse of the crystal I dropped is some kind of transmitter. Adelina will know what it is, what to do. To combat the fear that an evil alien race is coming directly for me, to somehow apologize to Adelina for drugging her, and to gather a little warmth, I rest my head on Adelina's chest and wrap my arms around her waist.

Hours later, I hear Adelina grunt and shuffle her legs underneath mine.

'Adelina?' I whisper. 'Are you awake?'

'Who is that? Marina?'

I whisper, 'Adelina, you have to be really, really quiet.'

'Why?' she whispers. 'And where are we?'

'We're in the nave where you hid the Chest. But please listen to me. They're here. The Mogadorians came for me last night after I opened the Chest, and I had to hide us.'

'How did you open up the Chest by yourself? It doesn't work that way.'

'You told me how to do it. You were sleep-talking,' I lie. I could tell her I drugged her, but I'm not ready for that argument.

Her confusion is evident in her voice. 'I don't remember . . . I, I remember getting out of bed and then . . .

I guess that's about it. You opened up the Chest? What was inside?'

'A lot of things, Adelina. So much. There are all these stones and all these jewels, and one of them lit up in my hand and started flashing, and I think that's why the Mogadorian showed up.'

'What Mogadorian? What happened?' Adelina tries to sit up, but I stop her before she hits her head on the low ceiling.

I whisper, 'I saw a man in the café a few days ago who had a book about Pittacus, and he kept staring at me. He had this hat on and this big mustache, and I could just tell he was from Mogadore. And then last night after I opened the Chest in the north belfry, he showed up.'

'How did we escape?'

'I used my telekinesis to float us out the window and into the yard, and then I used it to get us up here.'

'We have to get out of here,' she whispers. 'We have to leave Santa Teresa immediately.'

My excitement is immediate. I hug her in the dark, and to my surprise she hugs me back. Adelina crawls to the lip of the nook and I follow her with the Chest hovering behind me. When the nave appears empty, Adelina asks me to lower her to the floor. Then I carefully drop the Chest over the lip and set it silently next to Adelina's bare feet. I'm about to levitate down when Sister Dora appears at the back of the nave and marches towards Adelina.

'Where have you been?' she barks. 'You left your

post all night. How could you do such a thing? And what is this luggage doing in here?'

'I had to get some fresh air, Sister Dora,' Adelina says softly. 'I'm sorry I left my post.'

I can see Sister Dora's eyes narrow. 'With Marina?'

'What?'

'I had four girls wake me up in the middle of the night saying that Marina snuck out last night and that you left with her.'

Adelina starts to speak, but Ella suddenly appears behind Sister Dora and tugs on her dress.

'Sister Dora? I just saw Marina,' she lies.

'Where?'

'In the bedroom, sleeping.'

Sister Dora bends down and snatches Ella by the arm, and the terrified look on Ella's face causes something to shift inside me. 'You're a little liar! I just came from the sleeping quarters, and *no* one is in there. You're making up excuses for her.'

'Sister Dora, that's enough,' Adelina says.

But Sister Dora begins dragging Ella away so forcefully that her feet hardly touch the ground. 'We're going up to the office, and you're going to learn that you don't lie here.'

Tears stream down Ella's cheeks. From the nook's opening, I stare at Sister Dora's hand and pry her fingers away from Ella's bicep. Sister Dora yells in pain, and then peers down at Ella with surprise and confusion. She grabs Ella again.

Adelina jogs over to them, and before I can send Sister Dora all the way down the main aisle on her back, Adelina grabs her wrist.

Sister Dora rips her arm away. My heart jumps into my throat with Adelina's newfound alliance to me and my friend.

'Don't you ever touch me again,' Sister Dora challenges her. 'You don't even belong here, Adelina. And neither does that juvenile demon you brought with you.'

Adelina smiles calmly. 'You're right, Sister Dora. Perhaps Marina and I don't belong here, and perhaps we will leave this very morning. But would you please be so kind as to let go of Ella first?' Her voice, while cordial and patient, contains a hint of venom.

'How dare you!' Sister Dora scoffs. 'Why, you're no more than an orphan yourself. We took you in when no one else wanted you!'

'We're all the same in the Lord's eyes. Surely you acknowledge as much?'

Sister Dora moves to take another step, but Adelina again grabs her arm. The two women stare into each other's eyes.

'I will be talking about this with Sister Lucia. You will be thrown out of here so fast you won't have a chance to pray for forgiveness.'

'I already said I'd be leaving this morning. And I will *always* have the chance to pray for forgiveness.' Adelina reaches her hand out to Ella, and she takes it. Sister Dora hesitates before reluctantly letting go of Ella's

arm. 'I'll not only pray that Marina forgives me for being such a terrible guardian, but I'll also pray that God forgives you for forgetting your purpose here.'

They continue to stare into each other's eyes for a few more seconds before Sister Dora pivots and huffs out of the nave. Once she's out of sight and Ella has her back to me, I float to the ground.

'Hi, Ella,' I say.

'Marina!' She lets go of Adelina's hand, runs and hugs me. 'Where were you?'

'Adelina and I had to talk alone,' I say, pulling away from her. I look up at Adelina. 'We had to talk about our future.'

Adelina squints, then looks down at her dirty night-gown and becomes embarrassed. 'Marina, go pack your things and put that Chest somewhere safe. We're leaving very soon.'

When Adelina walks away, Ella grabs my hand and squeezes it. 'The bad men were here last night, Marina.'

'I know, I saw him. That's why we're leaving.' As soon as I say it I know I will ask Adelina if we can take Ella with us.

'I saw all three of them,' Ella whispers.

I gasp. 'There's three of them?'

'They were at the window last night, looking at your bed.'

A shiver runs up my spine. I float the Chest back up into the nook and run to the sleeping quarters, dodging

huddles of girls in the hallway whispering to each other about something that happened in the village.

'They were right there,' she says, pointing at the window.

'Three of them, you're sure?'

She nods her head. 'Yes, and they saw me at the window watching them. Then they ran away.'

'What did they look like?' I ask.

'They were tall and had really long hair. And their jackets went almost to their shoes,' she says.

'With mustaches, right? They had mustaches?'

'I don't think so. I don't remember mustaches,' she says.

I'm confused, but I know I don't have much time before Adelina shows up with a bag of the belongings she's collected over the past eleven years. I'm about to race into the shower when Analee, another girl, stops me in my tracks.

'School is canceled today. That girl Miranda Marquez was found strangled inside the school this morning.'

I sit down on my bed, shocked. Miranda Marquez is a dark-haired girl who lives in the village and sits beside me in Spanish history class. Our teacher, Maestra Muñoz, often confuses us for each other because Miranda is skinny and tall like me, and her hair is the same length as mine. It takes me a second to realize that whoever killed Miranda might have mistaken her for me. Someone might have tried to kill me last night.

'This is really . . . this is bad,' I whisper.

Analee says, 'Plus, I heard one of the Sisters say that some villagers saw people flying through the air last night and now there are all these news vans out there doing a report on it.'

This is all happening so fast. The Mogadorians have found me. They found my cave. I was being reckless with my Legacies and witnesses saw me and Adelina leave the belfry window. A girl from my school might be dead because of me, and Adelina and I are leaving the orphanage in the middle of winter without a place to stay.

I take the fastest hot shower of my life and wait for Adelina.

23

'We're not going to Sarah's,' Sam says, following me along the edge of the forest. 'We got this tablet thing, possibly the transmitter we were after, and we're going back to help Six.'

I step towards him. 'Six can handle herself. I'm right here and Sarah's right here. I love her, Sam, and I'm going to see her. I don't care what you say.'

Sam backs down, and I keep walking towards Sarah's house. Sam says, 'Do you really love her though, John? Or are you in love with Six? Which one?'

I twist around and shine my palm in his face. 'You think I don't love Sarah?'

'Hey, come on!'

'Sorry,' I mutter, lowering my palm.

He rubs his eyes. 'It's a valid question, man. I see you and Six flirting all the time, *all the time*, and you do it right in front of me. You know I like her, and you don't even care. *And* to top it all off you already have like the hottest girlfriend in Ohio.'

'I do care,' I whisper.

'You care about what?'

'I care that you like Six, Sam. But you're right – I like

her too. I wish I didn't, but I do. It's stupid and cruel to you, but I can't stop thinking about her. She's cool and she's beautiful and she's Loric, which is like, extracool. But I *love* Sarah. And that's why I have to see her.'

Sam grabs my elbow. 'You can't, man. We have to go back and help Six. Think about it. If they were waiting for us at my place, then even more of them are waiting for us at Sarah's.'

I gently pull my elbow away from his grip. 'You got to see your mom, right? You saw her in the backyard?'

'Yeah,' he sighs. His eyes find his shoes.

'You got to see your mom, so I get to see Sarah.'

'That doesn't make as much sense as you think it does. We got the transmitter, remember? This is why we're in Paradise. It's the only reason.' Sam hands me the tablet, and I stare at its blank screen. I touch every inch of it. I try telekinesis. I hold it to my forehead. The tablet remains off.

'Let me try,' Sam says. As he fumbles with the tablet, I tell him about the ladder, the huge skeleton with the pendant, and the desk and wall covered in papers.

'Six grabbed a handful of the papers, but it's not like we can read them,' I say.

'So my dad had a secret underground lair?' Sam smiles for the first time in hours, handing the tablet back. 'He was so cool. I'd really like to look at the papers Six took.'

'Absolutely,' I say. 'Right after I see Sarah.'

Sam opens his arms in astonishment. 'What can I do to change your mind? Just tell me.'

'Nothing. There's nothing you can do to stop me.'

The last time I was at Sarah's house it was Thanksgiving Day. I remember walking up the driveway and seeing Sarah wave from the front window.

'Hey, handsome,' she said when she opened the door, and I turned around to look over my shoulder to pretend she meant it for someone else.

Her house looks completely different at two in the morning. With every window dark, with the garage doors closed, the house looks cold and empty. Uninviting. Sam and I are on our bellies in the shadow of a house on the corner, and I don't know how I'm going to talk to her.

I pull the prepaid cell phone I've had turned off for days out of my jeans. 'I could text her until she wakes up.'

'That's actually a pretty good idea. Just do this already so we can get out of here. I swear, Six is going to kill us, or worse, maybe she's about to be killed by a swarm of Mogs and we're here lying in the grass about to go through a scene from *Romeo and Juliet*.'

I power up the phone and type: **I promised I'd come back. U up?**

We count to thirty after I send it, and then I type: **I love you. I'm here.**

'Maybe she thinks you're pranking her,' Sam whispers

after we wait another thirty seconds. 'Say something only you would know.'

I try: **Bernie Kosar misses you.**

Her window lights up. Then my phone buzzes with a text: **Is it really you? You're in Paradise?**

I pull up a handful of grass, I'm so excited.

'Chill out,' Sam whispers.

'I can't help it.'

I respond: **I'm outside. Meet me at the playground in 5?**

My phone buzzes immediately: **I'll be there. :)**

Sam and I are hiding behind a Dumpster at the end of the street when Sarah takes her first steps onto the concrete playground. From the moment I see her, I'm breathless, flooded with emotions. She's twenty yards away, wearing dark jeans and a black fleece jacket. A white winter hat is pulled over her head, but I can still see her long blond hair, and it brushes over her shoulders in the slight wind. Her flawless complexion glows in the lone playground bulb, and I feel instantly self-conscious about being covered in dirt and Mog ash. I take a step away from the Dumpster, but Sam grabs my wrist and holds me back.

'John, I know this is going to be really hard,' he whispers. 'But we have to be back in those woods in ten minutes. I'm serious. Six is counting on us.'

'I'll do my best,' I say, not even thinking of the repercussions at this point. Sarah is right there, and I'm so close I can practically smell her shampoo.

I watch Sarah turn her head back and forth looking for

me. Finally she sits down on a swing and twists herself, the ropes above her becoming taut. Sarah starts to spin slowly, and I shuffle around the perimeter of the playground, pausing behind trees, watching her. She looks so beautiful. So perfect.

I wait until she's facing the other direction before stepping out of the shadows, and when she twists around again, there I am.

'John?' The toes of Sarah's sneakers scrape on the concrete to stop her from twisting back around.

'Hey, beautiful,' I say. I can feel my smile reaching the corners of my eyes.

Sarah covers her mouth and nose with her hands.

I walk towards her and she tries to get off of the swing, but its ropes are too taut for her to escape.

I jump forward and catch the swing's ropes in my hands. I twist her towards me and raise my arms, lifting her and the seat so her face lines up with mine. I lean in and kiss her, and the instant our lips meet, it's as if I'd never left Paradise.

'Sarah,' I say into her ear. 'I've missed you so, so, so much.'

'I can't believe you're here. This can't be real.'

I kiss her again, and I don't stop while I twist us both around and around until the ropes above her separate. Sarah pushes off from the seat and lands in my arms. I kiss her cheeks and her neck, and she runs her hands over my head, gripping my short hair between her fingers.

I set her down and she says, 'Somebody got a haircut.'

'Yeah, it's my whole tough-guy-on-the-run look. What do you think? You into it?'

'I am,' she says, pressing her palms to my chest. 'But you could be bald for all I care.'

I take a step back to cement this image of Sarah. I note the brightness of the stars behind her, the tilt of her winter hat. Her nose and cheeks are red from the cold; and as she bites her lower lip and stares at me, a small cloud of breath floats from her mouth. 'I've thought about you every single day, Sarah Hart.'

'I promise I've thought about you twice as much.'

I lower my head until our foreheads touch. We stay this way wearing ridiculous grins until I ask, 'How are you? What are things like for you around here right now?'

'Better now.'

'It's so hard being away from you,' I say, kissing her cold fingers. 'I'm constantly thinking about what it feels like to touch you and hear your voice. I've come close to calling you every single night.'

Sarah cups my chin and runs her thumbs over my lips. 'I've sat in my dad's car so many times just wondering where you are. All I needed to know was which direction and I would've started to drive.'

'I'm right here. Right in front of you,' I whisper.

She drops her hands. 'I want to come with you, John. I don't care. I can't go on like this.'

'It's way too dangerous. We *just* finished battling fifty Mogs over at Sam's place. That's what life is like with me right now. I can't put you in the middle of all this.'

Her shoulders shake, and tears dot the corners of her eyes. 'I can't stay here, John. Not with you out there and me not knowing if you're dead or alive.'

'Look at me, Sarah,' I say. She raises her head. 'There's no way I'm going to die. Knowing that you're here waiting for me, it's like a force field. We're going to be together. Soon.'

Her lip quivers. 'It's so hard. Everything is awful right now, John.'

'Everything's awful? What do you mean?'

'People are jerks. Everyone's saying hateful things about you, and they say a lot of things about me, too.'

'Like what?'

'That you're a terrorist and a murderer and you hate the United States. Guys at school call you names like Bomb Smith. My parents say you're dangerous and I'm never supposed to talk to you again no matter what; and as an added bonus, there's a reward on your head, so people are always talking about shooting you.'

She puts her head down. 'I can't believe you have to put up with all that, Sarah,' I say. 'At least you know the truth.'

'I've lost almost every friend I had. Plus I'm at a new school where everyone just thinks I'm this weirdo.'

I'm devastated. Sarah was the most popular, most beautiful, most liked girl at Paradise High School. Now she's an outcast.

'Things won't always be this way,' I whisper.

She can't hold back the tears any longer. 'I love you so

much, John. But I can't imagine how we're going to get out of this mess. Maybe you should turn yourself in.'

'I'm not turning myself in, Sarah. I just can't. We'll get out of it. Of course we will. My one and only love, Sarah. I promise, if you wait for me, things will get better.'

But the tears don't stop. 'How long do I wait, though? And what happens when things do get better? Will you go back to Lorien?'

'I don't know,' I finally say. 'Paradise is the only place I want to be right now, and you're the only person I want to be with in the future. But if we're able to somehow defeat the Mogadorians, then yes, I have to go back to Lorien. But I don't know when that will be.'

Sarah's phone buzzes in her pocket, and she pulls it halfway out to check the screen.

'Who's texting you so late?' I ask.

'Just Emily. Maybe you should just turn yourself in and tell them you're not a terrorist. I don't want to lose you over and over, John.'

'Listen to me, Sarah. I can't turn myself in. I can't sit in a police station and try to explain how an entire school was destroyed and how five people were killed. How am I supposed to explain Henri? Those documents they found in our house? I can't get arrested. I mean, Six would absolutely kill me right now if she knew I was here talking to you.'

Sarah sniffs and wipes her tears away with the backs of her hands. 'Why would Six kill you if she knew you were here?'

'Because she needs me right now and it's dangerous for me to be here.'

'She needs you? *She* does? I need you, John. I need you here to tell me everything is going to be okay, that all this is worth it.'

Sarah walks slowly over to a bench marked with initials. I sit down next to her and lean my shoulder onto hers. We're out of the light and I can't see her face very well.

I don't know where it comes from, but Sarah leans away from me and says, 'Six is very pretty.'

'She is,' I agree. I shouldn't have, but it just fell out of my mouth. 'Not as pretty as you, though. You're the prettiest girl I know. You're the prettiest girl I've ever seen.'

'But you don't have to stay away from Six like you have to with me.'

'When we go on walks we have to be invisible, Sarah! It's not like we can just hold hands and walk down the street. We have to hide from the entire world. I'm hiding just as much when I'm with her as when I am with you.'

Sarah shoots off of the bench and turns around. 'You go on walks with her? *Do you* hold her hand when you two walk down the street?'

I stand up and approach her with my arms out, the sleeves of my coat still caked with dirt. 'We have to. It's the only way I can be invisible.'

'Have you kissed her?'

'What?'

'Answer me.' There's something new in her voice. It's

a mixture of jealousy and loneliness, and enough anger to give each word a kick.

I shake my head. 'Sarah, I love you. I don't really know what else to say. I mean, nothing's happened.' A tsunami of discomfort crashes into me, and I rifle through my vocabulary to piece together the right words.

She's furious. 'It was a simple question, John. Have you kissed her?'

'I haven't kissed Six, Sarah. We haven't kissed. I love *you*,' I say, and then I cringe at the acidity of the words, the sentence sounding far worse than I thought it would.

'I see. Why was that question so hard for you to answer, John? My life just keeps getting better and better. Does she like you?'

'It doesn't matter, Sarah. I love you, so Six doesn't matter. No other girls matter!'

'I feel like such an idiot,' she says, crossing her arms.

'Stop, please. Sarah, you're misinterpreting everything.'

'Am I, John?' she asks, turning her head and staring fiercely at me with tears in her eyes. 'I've gone through so much for you.'

I reach out and try taking Sarah's hand, but she snatches it away the instant our fingers touch.

'Don't,' she says, a hard edge in her voice. Her phone buzzes again in her jacket pocket, but she doesn't make a move to check it.

'I want to be with you, Sarah,' I say. 'Nothing I say right now seems to come out right. All I can really say is that I've spent weeks missing you terribly, and there hasn't

been a single day that I didn't think about calling you or writing a letter.' I feel wobbly. I can tell I'm losing her. 'I love you. Don't doubt that for a second.'

'I love you, too,' she cries.

I close my eyes and breathe in the cool air. A bad feeling rushes over me; a prickly feeling that starts in my throat and claws its way into my shoes. When I open my eyes, Sarah has taken several steps away from me.

There's a noise to my left, and I whip my head to see Sam. His eyes are downcast, and he bobs his head in a way that tells Sarah and me that he'd rather not be approaching but he has to.

'Sam?' Sarah asks.

'Hey, Sarah,' he whispers.

Sarah wraps her arms around him.

'It's really good to see you,' he says into her hair. 'But, Sarah, I'm sorry. I'm really, really sorry and I know you guys haven't seen each other in a long time, but John and I need to go. We're in a lot of danger. You have no idea.'

'I sort of do.' She pulls off of him, and just as I prepare to start reassuring her how much I love her, just as I'm about to start saying good-bye, chaos erupts.

Everything happens so fast I'm unable to take it all in completely, the scenes randomly skipping like a movie reel gone mad. Sam is tackled from behind by a man in a gas mask. The blue jacket he wears has the letters FBI on the back. Someone wraps their arms around Sarah and whisks her away from me. A metallic shell skids across the grass and lands at my feet, and the white

smoke billowing from both ends burns my eyes and throat. I can't see. I hear Sam gag. I stumble away from the canister and fall to my knees next to a plastic slide. When I lift my head I see over a dozen officers surrounding me, all with guns drawn. The masked officer who tackled Sam has his knee on Sam's back. A voice through a megaphone blasts: 'Don't move! Put your hands on the top of your head and get on your stomach! You are under arrest!' As I place my hands on the top of my head, cars that have been parked on the street the entire time we were there suddenly come to life; their headlights turn on, red lights flash from dashboards. Cop cars screech around the corner, and an armored vehicle with SWAT written on its side jumps the curb and slams on its brakes in the middle of the basketball court. Men yell and pile out of it at an alarming rate, and that's when someone kicks me in my stomach. Handcuffs are clicked around my wrists. Above me I hear the whir of a helicopter.

My mind grabs hold of the only explanation it can come up with.

Sarah. The text messages. That wasn't Emily. The police were talking to her. What little of my heart that didn't break when Sarah backed away from me now shatters.

I shake my head with my face against the concrete. I feel someone remove my dagger. Hands take the tablet from my waistband. I watch as Sam is pulled off the ground by his arms, and our eyes meet for a brief second. I can't tell what he's thinking.

Cuffs are slapped around my ankles, and a chain connects to the cuffs around my wrists. I'm jerked up from the ground. The cuffs are too tight and dig into my wrists. A black hood is pulled over my head and secured around my throat. I can't see a thing. Two officers grab my elbows while another shoves me forward.

'You have the right to remain silent,' one of them begins as I'm led away, and I'm thrown into the back of a vehicle.

24

After five minutes, I get up off my bed and look in the wardrobe to see if there are any clothes I want to take with us. I'm holding a black sweater when I decide I can't leave without saying good-bye to Héctor.

I rip another girl's jacket from the wall, one with a hood, and write a quick note to Adelina: *Had to say good-bye to someone in town first.*

The double doors open into the chilly air, and once I see the police cars and news vans lining Calle Principal, I feel better. The Mogadorians wouldn't try anything with so many witnesses. I walk through the gate with the hood over my head. The door to Héctor's house is cracked open, and I knock softly on the door frame. 'Héctor?'

A woman answers. 'Hello?'

The door swings open and it's Héctor's mother, Carlotta. Her black-and-gray hair is pinned carefully around her head, and her face is pink and smiling. She's wearing a beautiful red dress and a blue apron. The house smells like cake.

'Is Héctor home, Señora Ricardo?' I ask.

'My angel,' she says. 'My angel has returned.'

She remembers what I did for her, how I cured her

disease. I feel embarrassed by the way she's looking at me, but she bends down for a hug and I can't resist. 'My angel has returned,' she says again.

'I'm so happy you're feeling better, Señora Ricardo.'

The tears that fall from her eyes are almost too much, and soon my own eyes swell with water. 'You're welcome,' I whisper. There's a meow behind Carlotta, and I lean over to see Legacy trotting towards me from the kitchen with milk dripping from his chin. He purrs against my shins and I bend down to pet his coat.

'When did you get a cat?' I ask.

'This morning he comes to my door, and I think he is so sweet. I've named him Feo.'

'It's good to see you, Feo.'

'He's a good cat,' she says, her hands now on her hips. 'Very hungry boy.'

'I'm so glad you two found each other. Carlotta, I'm very sorry but I have to leave. I need to speak with Héctor. Is he home?'

'He's at the café,' she says. The disappointment of Héctor drinking so early in the morning must be evident on my face, because Carlotta adds, 'Only coffee now. He's drinking coffee.'

I hug her good-bye and she kisses both of my cheeks.

The café is packed. I reach for the door, but just before I pull it open, something stops me dead in my tracks: Héctor's sitting at a small table, but I notice him only in my periphery. My eyes are glued to who's sitting in the chair opposite him – the Mogadorian from

last night. He's now clean shaven, and his black hair has been lightened to a chestnut color, but there's no mistaking him. He's just as tall and muscular as before, just as broad shouldered, just as dark and brooding, with the same heavy brows. I don't need the killer's description to know he matches it perfectly, with or without the dyed hair or missing mustache.

I let go of the door and step backwards. *Oh Héctor,* I think. *How could you?*

My legs shake; my heart pounds. As I'm standing there watching them, the Mogadorian turns and sees me at the window. My flesh turns cold. The world seems to stop; I'm stuck, rooted in place, incapable of moving a muscle. The Mogadorian watches me, causing Héctor to turn my way as well, and it's only upon seeing his face that I'm shocked into action.

I stumble backwards then, turn and run, but before I've made it far, I hear the café door open. I don't turn around. If the Mogadorian is following me, I don't want to know.

'Marina!' Héctor yells. 'Marina!'

Four officers ride with me. I touch my fingertips to the heavy chains. I'm certain I could break them if I wanted to, or I could simply unlock the cuffs with telekinesis; but the thought of Sarah empties me of the energy required for such an undertaking. *She couldn't have turned me in. Please don't let it have been her.*

The first drive takes twenty minutes, and I have no idea

where we are. I'm pulled out and shoved into a second vehicle which I assume is more secure, meant for longer transport. The second drive takes forever – two hours, maybe three – and by the time we finally stop and I'm again jerked out, the sickness over what Sarah may have done has grown to the point that it's nearly unbearable.

I'm guided into a building. After each turn I have to wait for a door to be unlocked. I count four of them, and the air changes with each new corridor, becoming staler the farther I'm led. Finally I'm pushed into a cell.

'Sit,' one of them orders.

I sit on a bed. The hood is removed but the shackles remain. Four officers exit and slam the door shut. The two larger ones take seats outside my cell, while the other two leave.

The cell is small, ten feet by ten feet, and contains the bed I'm sitting on, covered in yellow stains, and a metal toilet and sink. Nothing else. Three of its four walls are solid concrete, and there's a small window at the very top of the back wall.

Despite the filthy mattress, I lie down, close my eyes, and wait for my mind to slow down.

'John!' Sam's voice yells out.

My eyes snap open. I rush to the front of the cell, grabbing hold of the bars. 'Right here,' I yell back.

'Shut up!' the larger of the two guards yells, pointing his nightstick at me. Down the corridor, somebody yells at Sam, too. He doesn't say anything else, but at least I know he's close.

I reach my hand through the bars of my cell and press my palm against the flat metal surface of the lock. I close my eyes, focus my telekinesis to feel its inner workings, and yet I feel nothing other than a vibration that hurts my head the harder I concentrate.

The cell – it's electronically controlled. I can't open it with telekinesis.

I run as fast as I can back to the orphanage, the hood ballooning with air behind me, and as I gain speed the clouds and blue sky above me melt into a bright white.

I burst through the double doors and run to the sleeping quarters. Adelina's sitting on my bed, the note folded on her lap. A small suitcase sits at her feet. When she sees me, she jumps up and hugs me.

'You have to look at this,' she says, handing me the paper. I unfold it to see that it's not my note after all but a photocopied picture.

It takes me a second to realize what the picture is of, and when I recognize it my heart sinks. Someone has burned an enormous and intricate symbol into the side of a nearby mountain. With its careful lines and sharp angles, it's an exact replica of the scars around my ankle.

The sheet falls from my hand and slowly floats to the ground.

'That was found yesterday, and the police are handing these copies out looking for information,' Adelina says. 'We have to go now.'

'Yes, absolutely. I need to talk to you about Ella first,' I say.

Adelina tilts her head. 'What about Ella?'

'I want her to come with –'

Before I can finish my sentence, I'm rocked off my feet by a thundering crash. Adelina falls as well and slams her shoulder into the ground. There's been an explosion, somewhere within the orphanage. Several girls run into the room screaming; others run past the doorway looking for refuge elsewhere. I hear Sister Dora yell for everyone to go to the south wing.

Adelina and I get to our feet and head for the hallway, but then another explosion hits, and suddenly I can feel cold wind. I can't hear what Adelina is saying above the screams, but I follow her gaze to the roof, where there's now a jagged hole the size of a bus. As I'm staring, a tall man in a trench coat with long red hair walks to the edge of the hole. He points at me.

25

The interrogation room is warm and pitch-black. I rest my head on the table in front of me and try not to fall asleep; but after being up all night, I can't help myself. Instantly, I feel a vision forming and hear the whispers. I feel myself floating up through the darkness, then, as if shot through a cannon, I blaze through a shadowy tunnel. Black turns to blue. Blue turns to green. The whispers follow me, growing weaker the farther down the tunnel I go. Suddenly, I'm jolted to a stop and everything falls silent. A gust of wind appears with a bright light, and when I look down, I realize I'm standing on the snowy peak of a mountain.

The view is spectacular, with mountains stretching for miles. There's a deep green valley below me and a crystal blue lake. I'm drawn to the lake and begin descending when I see tiny bursts of light surrounding it. As if I'm wearing binoculars, my vision is suddenly magnified and I see hundreds of heavily armed Mogadorians shooting at four running figures.

My anger is immediate and colors blur as I run down the mountain. A few hundred yards from the lake, the sky growls above me with a black wall of clouds. Bolts of lightning crash into the valley and thunder roars. I'm

knocked off my feet as lightning strikes all around me, and that's when I see the glowing eye form and stare down from the clouds.

'Six!' I yell, but the thunder drowns me out. I know it's her, but what is she doing here?

The clouds part, and someone drops into the valley. My vision magnifies again, and I see that I was right: Six stands furious between the advancing army of Mogs and two young girls and two older men. Her arms are above her head, and a steady sheet of rain falls.

'Six!' I yell again, and a pair of hands grabs my shoulders from behind.

My eyes snap open and I whip my head off the table. The lights in the interrogation room are on, and there's a tall man with a round face standing above me. He's wearing a dark suit with a badge clipped to his belt. In his hands is the white tablet.

'Chill out, kid. I'm Detective Will Murphy, FBI. How we doing today?'

'Never better,' I reply, dazed by the vision. Who was Six protecting?

'Good,' he says. The detective sits, a pen and legal pad in front of him. He carefully displays the tablet on the left side of the table.

'So,' he begins, slowly drawing it out. 'Six what? What do you have six of?'

'What?'

'You were yelling the number six in your sleep. You want to tell me what that's all about?'

'It's my golf handicap,' I say. My mind tries to conjure up the faces of the two girls behind Six in the valley, but they're fuzzy.

Detective Murphy chuckles. 'Yeah, right. How about you and me have a little chat? Let's start with the birth certificate you gave to Paradise High. It's counterfeit, John Smith. In fact, we can't find a single thing about you prior to you showing up in Paradise several months ago,' he says, squinting as though expecting some reply. 'Your social security number belongs to a dead man in Florida.'

'Was there a question there?'

His grin turns into a smirk. 'Why don't you start by telling me your real name.'

'John Smith.'

'Right,' he says. 'Where's your father, John?'

'Dead.'

'How convenient.'

'Actually, it's probably the most inconvenient thing that's ever happened to me up until now.'

The detective writes something on the notepad. 'Where are you originally from?'

'The planet Lorien, three hundred million miles away.'

'Must have been a long trip, John Smith.'

'Took almost a year. Next time I'm bringing a book.'

He drops his pencil on the table, interlocks his fingers behind his head, and leans back. Then he pushes forward again and holds up the tablet. 'You want to tell me what this thing is?'

'I was hoping you could tell me. We found it in the woods.'

He holds it by its edge and whistles. 'You found this in the woods? Where at in the woods?'

'Near a tree.'

'Are you going to be a wiseass with every question?'

'That depends, detective. Are you working for them?'

He sets the tablet back on the desktop. 'Am I working for who?'

'The Morlocks,' I say, the first thing I remember from English class.

Detective Murphy smiles.

'You can smile, but they'll probably be here soon,' I say.

'The Morlocks?'

'Yes, sir.'

'Like from *The Time Machine*?'

'That's the one. That's like our Bible.'

'And let me guess; you and your friend, Samuel Goode, you're members of the Eloi?'

'The Loric, actually. But for our purposes today, the Eloi will be fine.'

The detective reaches into his pocket and slams my dagger on the table. I stare at its four-inch diamond blade as if I've never seen it before. I could easily kill this man just by moving my eyes from the blade to his neck, but I need to free Sam first. 'What's this for, John? Why would you need a knife like this?'

'I don't know what knives like that are for, sir. Whittling?'

He picks up his notepad and pencil. 'Why don't you tell me what happened in Tennessee.'

'Never been,' I say. 'I hear it's a nice place, though. Maybe I'll visit when I'm out of here, take a tour, see the sights. Any suggestions?'

He nods, tosses the notepad onto the table, and then launches the pencil at me. I deflect it without lifting a finger, sending it bouncing against the wall; but the detective doesn't notice, and leaves through the steel door with the tablet and my dagger.

Soon I'm shoved back into my old cell. I have to get out of here.

'Sam?' I yell.

The guard who's been sitting outside my cell jumps off his chair and swings the nightstick at my fingers. I let go of the bars just before they're crushed.

'Shut up!' he orders, pointing his nightstick at me.

'You think I'm afraid of you?' I ask. Getting him inside my cell sounds like a pretty good option.

'I couldn't give a damn, peewee. But if you keep it up, you're gonna regret it real fast.'

'You couldn't hit me if you tried; I'm too quick and you're too fat.'

The guard chuckles. 'Why don't you just sit back on your bed and shut your mouth, huh?'

'You know I can kill you any time I want to, right? Without even lifting a finger.'

'Oh yeah?' he replies. The guard steps forward. His breath smells rancid, like stale coffee. 'What's stopping you then?'

'Apathy and a broken heart,' I say. 'Both of those will go away eventually, though, and that's when I'll just get up and leave.'

'I can hardly wait, Houdini,' he says.

I'm extremely close to taunting him inside, and as soon as he unlocks the door, Sam and I are as good as free.

'You know who you look like?' I ask.

'Tell me,' he says.

I turn around and bend over.

'That's it, punk!' The guard reaches for a control panel on the wall, and as he's stomping towards the door of my cell, an earsplitting blast rattles the entire jail. The guard stumbles into the bars and smacks his forehead, falling to his knees. I drop and instinctively roll beneath the bed. Pandemonium erupts – yells and gunshots, clanking metal, and loud bangs. An alarm goes off, and a blue light flashes in the corridor.

I roll onto my back and twist my hands to get a firm grip on the chain binding my wrists. While using my legs as leverage, I straighten myself and snap the chain binding my hands and feet in two. I use telekinesis to unlock my cuffs and drop them to the floor. I do the same with the pair around my ankles.

'John!' Sam yells from down the hall.

I crawl to the front of the cell. 'Right here!'

'What's going on?'

'I was going to ask you the same thing!' I yell back.

Other prisoners shout through their cell bars, too.

The guard who fell in front of my cell grunts and struggles to his feet. Blood flows from a gash on his head.

The ground shakes again. It's more violent and lasts longer than the first time, and a fog of dust barrels down the corridor from the right. I'm temporarily blinded, but reach my hand through the bars and yell to the guard, 'Let me out of here!'

'Hey! How'd you get your cuffs off?'

I see he's disoriented, wavering a few steps to his right, a few to his left, ignoring the other guards who run by him with guns drawn. He's covered in dust.

A thousand gunshots come from the right end of the corridor. A roar of a beast answers them.

'John!' Sam screams in a pitch I've never heard from him before.

I make eye contact with the guard and yell, 'We're all going to die in here if you don't let me out!'

The guard looks towards the roars and terror spreads across his face. He slowly reaches for his gun, but before he can touch the grip it floats away from him. I know that trick – I saw that in Florida on a midnight walk – and I watch as the guard spins in confusion and runs.

Six becomes visible in front of my door, the large pendant still around her neck, and from the second I see her face I know she's pissed at me. I also see that she's in a very big hurry to get me out of here.

'What's down there, Six? Is Sam okay? I can't see anything,' I say.

She looks down the corridor and concentrates on

something, and a set of keys comes floating down the corridor, right into her hands. She inserts them into a metal panel on the wall. My door unlocks. I run out of my cell and I'm finally able to see down the corridor. It's extremely long, with at least forty cells between me and the exit. But the exit is gone, as is the wall it should be on, and I'm staring at the giant horned head of a piken. Two guards are in its mouth, and drool mixed with blood falls from its razor-sharp teeth.

'Sam!' I yell, but he doesn't answer. I turn to Six. 'Sam's down there!'

She disappears before my eyes, and five seconds later I watch another cell slide open. Sam rushes towards me. I yell, 'Okay, Six! Let's trash this thing!'

Inches from my nose, Six's face appears. 'We're not fighting the piken. Not here.'

'Are you kidding me?' I ask.

'There's more important stuff we have to do, John,' she barks. 'We have to get to Spain immediately.'

'Now?'

'Now!' Six grabs my hand and pulls me after her until I'm running at a full clip. Sam is right behind me, and we're able to get through two sets of doors with Six's keys. As the second one is flung open, we're faced with seven Mogs running with cylindrical cannonlike tubes and swords. Instinctively, I reach for my dagger, but it's not there. Six throws me the guard's gun then holds me and Sam back. She lowers her head in concentration. The lead Mog is spun around, and his sword slices across the two behind

him, turning them to ash. Six then kicks the Mog in the back and he falls on his own sword. She's invisible before he dies.

Sam and I duck the first tube's blast, and the second one singes the collar of my shirt. I shoot, emptying my pistol as I slide into the piles of ash. I kill one Mog and then pick up his dropped tube. Hundreds of lights spark to life the second my finger finds the trigger, and a green beam cuts through another Mog. I aim for the last two, but Six has already appeared behind them, lifting both to the ceiling with telekinesis. She slams them against the ground in front of me, then back to the ceiling and then again on the ground. My jeans are covered in their ash.

Six unlocks another door and we enter a large room with dozens of cubicles on fire. Holes smolder in the ceiling. Mogs are shooting at police, and police are firing back. Six wrestles a sword away from the nearest Mog and cuts off his arm, and then she jumps over a burning cubicle wall. I blast the stumbling one-armed Mog in the back with my tube, and he falls into a black heap of ash.

I see an unconscious Detective Murphy on the ground. Six darts through the maze of cubicles, swinging her sword so fast it blurs. Mogs turn to ash all around her. Police retreat through a door on the far left as Six slices through a circle of Mogs closing in on her. I shoot and shoot, destroying those on the perimeter.

When the room is clear, we run down an empty hallway under a shower of sparks.

'There!' Sam points to a giant hole leading out into a

parking lot. We don't hesitate, each one of us jumping through sparks and smoke; and before I sprint into the cold morning, I see my dagger and the tablet sitting on the desk in the office. I reach over and scoop them both up, and seconds later I'm following Six and Sam into a deep ditch that provides us plenty of cover.

'We're not going to talk about that right now,' Six says, her arms pumping fast. She dropped the sword a mile back. I tossed the Mog tube under a bush.

'But do you have it, though?'

'John, not right now.'

'But do you –'

Six comes to an abrupt halt.

'John! You want to know where your Chest is?'

'In the trunk of the car?' I ask, my eyebrows raised in apology.

'Nope,' she says. 'Try again.'

'Hidden in a Dumpster?'

Six lifts her arms above her head and a gust of wind sends me flying until I hit a massive oak tree. She marches towards me, fists at her sides. 'How is she?'

'Who?' I ask.

'Your girlfriend, you asshole! Was it worth it? Was it worth leaving me surrounded by Mogs fighting to get *your* Chest back to see precious little Sarah? Was it worth getting arrested for? Did you get enough kisses to make up for getting your face slapped all over the news again?'

'No,' I mumble. 'I think Sarah turned us in.'

'I think so, too,' Sam says.

'And you!' Six spins around to raise her finger at Sam. 'You went along with it! I thought you were smarter than that, Sam. You're supposed to be some kind of genius, and you think it's a good idea to go to the one place in the whole world that the police would definitely be watching?'

'I've never called myself a genius,' Sam says, picking up the tablet I dropped, brushing dirt from it. Six keeps walking. 'And, Six, I had no choice. Seriously. I tried as hard as I could to get John to go back and look for you and help.'

'He did,' I mutter, standing. 'Don't blame Sam.'

'Well, John, while you two lovebirds were hugging and kissing, I was getting my ass kicked doing you a favor. I would have died if Bernie Kosar didn't grow into this giant elephant-bear animal and help. They have your Chest. And I'm sure by this point it's sitting right next to mine in the cave in West Virginia.'

'Then that's where I'm going,' I say.

'No, we're going to Spain. Today.'

'No, we're not!' I shout, brushing off my sleeves. 'Not until I have my Chest back.'

'Well, I'm going to Spain,' she says.

'Why now?' Sam asks.

Our SUV comes into view. 'I was just online. It's serious over there. Somebody burned a huge symbol into the mountainside over Santa Teresa and it looks exactly like the brands around our ankles. Someone needs our help and I'm going.'

We hop in the car and Six drives slowly down the road,

and Sam and I hide in the footwells of the backseat. Bernie Kosar barks from the passenger seat, happy to be riding shotgun for a change.

Sam and I pass the laptop back and forth, both of us reading the article about Santa Teresa twice, three times. The burning symbol on the mountain is no doubt Loric. 'What if it's a trap?' I ask. 'My Chest is more important right now.' It might be selfish, but before I leave the continent, I want my Inheritance. The possibility that the Mogs might open my Chest is just as urgent to me as whatever is going on in Spain.

'I need to know how to get to the cave,' I say.

'John! Get real. You're really not going to come with me to Spain?' Six asks. 'After reading all that, you're going to let me and Sam go alone?'

'Guys, get this. Also out of Santa Teresa, there's a woman reported to have been cured, out of the blue, of an incurable degenerative disease. Santa Teresa is, like, an epicenter of activity right now. I bet every member of the Garde are on their way,' Sam says.

'If that's the case,' I say, 'then I'm definitely not going. I'm getting my Chest back.'

'That's insane,' Six says.

I scramble over the passenger seat and open the glove compartment. My fingers find the stone I'm looking for, and I drop it in Six's lap before hiding in the footwell again.

She lifts the pale yellow stone above the wheel, turning it over in the sunlight, and laughs. 'You had the Xitharis out?'

'I figured it might come in handy,' I say.

'These don't last long, remember,' she says.

'How long?'

'An hour, maybe a little more.'

The news is discouraging, but it could still give me the advantage I need. 'Can you charge it, please?'

When Six holds the Xitharis to her temple, I know she's agreed to let me go after the Chests while she heads to Spain.

26

I do it without even thinking. The second the man points at me from the edge of the hole in the roof, I send two metal bed frames rocketing towards him. The second one is a direct hit. He falls forward and into the sleeping quarters; and when he hits the stone floor, to my amazement, he turns into a pile of dirt or ash.

'Run!' Adelina screams.

We crash into the hallway, pushing against the flow of the other girls and Sisters heading to the south wing for safety. I take hold of Adelina's hand and guide us to the nave and down the center aisle.

'Where are we going?' Adelina yells.

'We're not leaving without the Chest!'

Another explosion rocks the foundation of the orphanage and my hip crashes into a pew.

'I'll be right back,' I whisper, releasing her hand, floating towards the nook.

Six tells us we're close to Washington, DC, and that makes sense. I am considered an armed and dangerous terrorist; no wonder I was taken to the nation's capital for questioning.

'There's a flight leaving Dulles International in less

than an hour,' she says, turning the wheel. 'I'm getting on that plane. Sam, are you with me or are you with John?'

Sam places his forehead on the backseat and closes his eyes.

'Sam?' Six asks.

'I'm thinking, I'm thinking,' he says. After a minute, he raises his head and looks right at me. 'I'm going with John.'

I mouth *Thank you.*

'It'll be easier for me to get there alone, anyway,' Six says, but she sounds hurt.

'You'll be fighting with more experienced Garde members,' I reassure her. 'Plus, it's probably going to take two of us to get both of our Chests out of there.'

Bernie Kosar barks from the front seat.

'Yeah, buddy,' I say. 'You're a part of this team, too.'

The Chest is gone. My entire body sweats with panic. I almost vomit. Did the Mogadorians know it was up here the whole time? Why didn't they trap me in here when they had the chance? I float back onto the nave floor.

'It's gone, Adelina,' I whisper.

'The Chest?'

'It's gone.' I hug her and bury my face in her shoulder. She pulls something up over her head. It's a pale blue, almost transparent amulet attached to a beige cord. She carefully slips it over my hair until the amulet touches my neck. It's both cold and warm at the same time against my skin, and then it glows brightly. My breath is taken away.

'What is it?' I ask, covering the glow with my hands.

'Loralite, the most powerful gem on Lorien, found only at its core,' she whispers. 'I've hidden it this whole time. It's yours, and there's no use in hiding it any longer. *They* know who you are, with or without the amulet. I'll never forgive myself for not training you properly. Never. I'm sorry, Marina.'

'It's okay,' I say, feeling tears well up behind my eyes. All these years, this was all I had wanted from her. Understanding. Companionship. The acknowledgment of shared secrets.

We get closer to the airport, and the fear of splitting up weighs heavily on us. Sam tries to distract himself by studying the papers Six took from his dad's office. 'I wish I could spread these out in some library's reference section.'

'After West Virginia,' I say. 'I promise.'

Six gives me and Sam careful instructions on how to find the map that'll take us to the cave. The rest of the trip passes in silence. We pull into a McDonald's parking lot a mile from Dulles.

'There are three things you guys have to know.'

I sigh. 'Why do I have the feeling that none of these things are going to be good?'

She ignores me and writes something on the back of a receipt. 'First, here's the address that I'll be at in exactly two weeks at five p.m. Meet me there. If I'm not there, or, if for some reason you aren't, then return in another week and I'll do the same. If one of us doesn't make it

after the second week, then I think we can assume the other isn't coming.' She hands it to Sam, who reads it and shoves it into his jeans pocket.

'Two weeks, five p.m.,' I say. 'Got it. The second thing?'

'Bernie Kosar can't go into the cave with you.'

'Why not?'

'Because it'll kill him. I don't understand it completely, but the Mogadorians control their beasts by filtering some sort of gas throughout the cave that only affects animals. If one leaves its designated place, it drops dead. When I finally got out, there was a heap of dead animals right at the cave's entrance. Animals that had gotten too close.'

'Gross,' Sam says.

'And the last thing?'

'Their cave is equipped with every detection device you can think of. Cameras, motion detectors, body temperature gauges, infrared. Everything. The Xitharis will allow you to get past everything; but once it's out of juice, look out, because they're going to find you.'

'Where do we go?' I ask Adelina. Now that the Chest is gone, I feel directionless. Even with the amulet around my neck.

'We go to the belfry, and you use your telekinesis to get us into the yard. Then we run.'

I take her hand and start running when a ball of fire suddenly roars from the back of the nave. The fire takes hold of the back pews and rages towards the

high ceiling. The nave is now brighter than it is during Sunday Mass. A man in a trench coat with long blond hair walks confidently out of the northern hallway, our path to freedom, and every muscle in my body seems to come unwound at the same time; every inch of skin breaks out with goose bumps.

He stands watching us, the flames attacking several more rows of pews, and then a sneer slowly breaks across his face. From the corner of my eye, I can see Adelina reach into her dress and remove something, but I can't tell what it is. She stands beside me, her eyes aimed at the back of the nave. And then, ever so gently, she reaches up and pushes me behind her.

'I can't make up for lost time, or for the wrongs that I've done,' she says. 'But I'm certainly going to try. Don't let them catch you.'

Just then the Mogadorian comes charging towards us, right down the center aisle. He's far larger than he looked from a distance, and he lifts a long sword that glows a fluorescent green color.

'Get as far from here as you can,' Adelina says without turning. 'Be brave, Marina.'

Six places the Xitharis into the console's cupholder and then slides out of the SUV. 'I'm running late,' she says as she closes her door.

Sam and I both exit the vehicle after carefully studying the parking lot, the other cars, the people milling about.

I round the front of the hood and watch as Six hugs Sam.

'Kick some ass over there,' he says.

They separate and she says, 'Sam, thank you for helping us even when you don't have to. Thank you for being so amazing.'

'*You're* amazing,' he whispers. 'Thanks for letting me tag along.'

To my surprise and Sam's, Six steps forward and kisses him on the cheek. They smile at each other, and once Sam sees me over Six's shoulder, he blushes, opens the driver's door, and climbs inside.

I don't want her to go. As much as it pains me to admit it, I know I might never see her again. She looks at me with a certain tenderness that I'm not sure I've ever seen from her before.

'I like you, John. For the past few weeks, I've tried convincing myself that I don't, especially because of Sarah and how much of an idiot you can be . . . but I do. I do like you.'

The words knock me over. I hesitate, then say 'I like you, too.'

'Do you still love Sarah?' she asks.

I nod. She deserves the truth. 'I do, but it's all really confusing. She may have turned me in, and she may never want to see me again because I told her I thought you were pretty. But Henri once said that the Loric fall in love once in their life. And so that means I will always love Sarah.'

Six shakes her head. 'Don't take offense at what I'm about to say, okay? But Katarina never told me that. In fact, she told me stories about *multiple* loves she had on Lorien over the years. I'm sure Henri was a great man, and there's no doubt that he loved you with everything he had; but it sounds like he was a romantic and wanted you to follow in his footsteps. If he had one true love, then he wanted you to have one, too.'

I'm silent, taking in her theory and pushing Henri's to the side.

She can tell I'm struggling with her words. 'What I'm saying is, when the Loric fall in love, a lot of times it is for life. Obviously, it was for Henri. But not always.'

And with that last sentence, Six steps towards me and I step towards her. The kiss that eluded us at the end of our walk in Florida now connects us with a passion I thought I'd reserved for Sarah and Sarah alone. I never want this kiss to end, but Sam turns on the engine and we separate.

'Sam likes you, too, you know,' I say.

'And I like Sam.'

I cock my head. 'But you just said you like me.'

She pushes me on my shoulder. 'You like me *and* Sarah. I like you *and* Sam. Deal with it.'

She turns invisible, but I can sense she's still in front of me.

'Please be careful over there, Six. I wish we could all stay together.'

Her voice comes out of the air. 'Me, too, John; but whoever is in Spain needs help. Can't you feel it?'

I can tell she's already gone by the time I say, 'Yes.'

I try to move, but I'm rooted in place. A glint of light in Adelina's hand catches my gaze, and I realize that what she removed from her dress was a kitchen knife. She runs towards the Mogadorian, and I start running down a pew the other way. With precision I've never seen before from her, she drops to the ground as the Mogadorian leaps and swings his sword for her throat. He misses her entirely, and as she comes back up she catches him flush with the knife's blade across his right thigh. Dark blood spurts out, but it does little to slow the Mogadorian; he turns and brings the sword back down. Adelina rolls forward, and it's with nothing short of awe that I watch her pass the knife across the Mogadorian's other leg as the momentum pushes her to her feet. How can I leave Adelina to fight alone?

I stop running, clench my hands into fists, but before I can do anything the man's left hand is wrapped around Adelina's throat, lifting her off the ground. His right hand drives the sword through her heart.

'No!' I yell, jumping on top of the pew's bench, rushing down the wood towards them.

Adelina's eyes shut, and with her very last breath, she thrusts her arm up and the knife's blade cuts an arc in the air in front of her. It falls from her hand and clatters to the floor. For a second I think she's missed,

but I'm wrong. The cut was made so cleanly that a full two seconds pass before the dark blood spills out. He drops Adelina and falls to his knees, both hands clutched to the front of his throat to stop the bleeding, but the blood simply cascades through his fingers. I walk towards him and take a deep breath. I raise my hand and lift Adelina's knife from off the floor. I let it hover for a brief moment, and just as his eyes widen at the sight of it, I plunge it into his chest. He disintegrates before my eyes, his body turning to ash and spreading across the floor.

I drop to my knees and take Adelina's lifeless body into my arms, cupping the back of her head and pulling her to me. Our cheeks touch and I begin to cry. She's gone, and regardless of my recently discovered Legacy, I know there isn't anything I can do to bring her back. I need help.

27

A growl comes from my left, and I lift my head to see another man in a trench coat with long brown hair. I rush to my feet as the Mogadorian lifts his hand. A flash of light comes from it and hits me hard in the left shoulder, sending me flying backwards. The pain is instant and blinding. It runs down my arm, white-hot as though electricity has hit the bone and travels through it. My left hand feels dead, and with my right I reach up and touch the new gash on my shoulder. I lift my head and look up hopelessly at the Mogadorian.

The charm, I think. Adelina told me when we traveled that I couldn't be killed unless it was in the order set by the Elders. This wound could be bad enough to kill me. I look down at my ankle to see if there are six scars instead of the three I've been living with for the last several months, but nothing has changed. Then how can I be killed? How can I be hurt this badly . . . unless *the charm has been broken.*

My eyes meet the Mogadorian's, and he bursts into a heap of ash. For a crazy moment I think the intensity of my own thoughts is what killed him, but then I see that standing just behind him is the Mogadorian from

the café. The one with the book, the one I've been running from. I don't understand. Does their selfishness run so deep that they'll kill one another to be the one who kills me?

'Marina,' he says.

'I, I can kill you,' I say in a shaky voice full of sorrow. The blood continues flowing from my shoulder and runs down my arm. I look over at Adelina's body and start to cry.

'I'm not who you think I am,' he says, jogging over to me and reaching out his hand. 'Time is extremely short,' he says. 'I'm one of you, and I'm here to help.'

I take his hand. What other choice do I have? He pulls me up, and from the nave before any others arrive. He leads me down the northern hallway and to the second floor, heading towards the belfry tower. My shoulder screams in pain with each step.

'Who are you?' I ask. A hundred different questions race through my head. If he's one of us, then why did it take him so long to tell me? Why torture me into believing he was one of them? Can I even trust him?

'Shhh,' he whispers. 'Keep quiet.'

The musty hallway is silent, and as it narrows, I hear dozens of heavy footsteps on the floor below us. Finally, we reach the oak door. It opens just a crack, and a girl's head sticks out. I gasp. Auburn hair, curious brown eyes, small features. She's older by years, but there's no mistaking that it's her.

'Ella?' I ask.

She looks eleven years old, maybe twelve. Her face, which brightens at the sight of mine, is more slender now. Ella pulls the door open so we can enter.

'Hi, Marina,' she says in a voice I don't recognize.

The man pulls me in, shutting the door. He wedges a thick wooden board between the door and the bottom stair, and the three of us rush up the circular stone steps. When we get to the belfry, I take another look at Ella. All I can do is stare at her, wide-eyed and confused, no longer feeling the blood rolling down my arm, dripping from my fingertips.

'Marina, my name is Crayton,' the man says. 'I'm sorry about your Cêpan. I wish I had gotten there sooner.'

'Adelina's dead?' the older version of Ella asks.

'I don't understand,' I say, still staring at Ella.

'We'll explain it all to you, I promise. There isn't much time. You're losing a lot of blood,' Crayton says. 'You can heal people, correct? Can you heal yourself?'

With all the confusion and running, I hadn't considered healing myself, but when I place the palm of my right hand over the gaping wound, I try it. The iciness tickles as the gash closes itself and the dead numbness is pushed from my hand and arm. After thirty seconds, I'm as good as new.

'Please be more careful with this,' Crayton says. 'It's far more vital than you know.'

I look to where he's pointing. 'My Chest!'

There's an explosion nearby. The tower sways, and dust and rocks drop from the ceiling and walls. More

rocks fall as another blast takes me off my feet. I use my telekinesis to stop their descent, and I fling them out the window.

'They're searching for us, and it's not going to take long until they realize where we are,' he says. He looks at Ella, and then at me. 'She's one of you. A member of the Garde from Lorien.'

'But she's not old enough,' I say, shaking my head, unable to replace the younger version I've come to know with this older one. 'I don't get it.'

'Do you know what an Aeternus is?'

I shake my head.

'Show her, Ella.'

While standing in front of me, Ella begins to change. Her arms shorten and her shoulders narrow; she loses twenty centimeters of height, and her weight drops significantly. The shrinking of her face shocks me the most, and quickly she looks like the tiny girl I've come to love.

'She's an Aeternus,' Crayton says. 'She's able to move back and forth between different ages.'

'I – I didn't know that was possible,' I stutter.

'Ella's eleven years old,' he says. 'She came with me on a second ship from Lorien that left after yours. She was just a baby, only hours old. Loridas, the last remaining Elder, sacrificed himself so that Ella could assume his role and grow into his powers.'

As I'm looking at Crayton, Ella slips her hand into mine as she's done so many times before; but it feels

different now. I glance over and see that she's returned to the older, taller version of herself. Recognizing my discomfort, Ella shrinks back down, the four years quickly melting away until she's seven again.

'She's the tenth child,' he says. 'The tenth Elder. We created a rumor about her backstory, her parents dying in a car accident, and we sent her here to live with you to watch over you and be the eyes I needed.'

'I'm sorry I couldn't tell you the truth, Marina,' she says in her soft voice. 'But I'm the best secret-keeper in the whole world, just like you said.'

'I know you are,' I say.

'I was just waiting for Adelina to give you your Chest,' she says, smiling.

'Do you know who the tenth Elder was?' Crayton asks. 'Changing his age is how Loridas was able to live as long as he did, even after the other Elders had passed away. Each time he grew old, he made himself young again, and assumed the vitality that comes with it.'

'Are you Ella's Cêpan?'

'Only in the surrogate sense of the word. Since she was just born, she hadn't been assigned a Cêpan yet.'

'I thought you were a Mogadorian,' I say.

'I know, but only because you misinterpreted the clues. This morning when I was talking to Héctor, I was trying to show you I was a friend.'

'But why didn't you just come and get me when you arrived? Why send Ella in?'

'I tried approaching Adelina first, but she cast me

out the second she knew who I was, and we needed you to have your Chest. I couldn't pull you away without it,' he says. 'So I sent Ella in, and she started looking for it even before you asked her to. The Mogadorians have known your general location for a good while now, and I've done my best to keep them off your trail. Killing some, well, killing most, but also planting stories in villages hundreds of miles away, about kids doing amazing things, like about a boy who lifted a car above his head and a girl who could walk across a lake. It was working until they discovered you were in Santa Teresa; but even then, they still didn't know which one you were. Then Ella found the Chest and you opened it, and that's when I came here, to talk to you in private. When you opened the Chest, it led the Mogadorians right here.'

'Because I opened the Chest?'

'Yes. Go ahead, open it up now.'

I let go of Ella's hand and grab hold of the lock. I'm sick thinking that I'm able to open it on my own, now that Adelina is dead. I remove the lock and toss the lid open. The small crystal is still glowing a faint blue.

'Don't touch that,' he says. 'The fact that it's glowing means a Macrocosm is in orbit somewhere. If you touch it now, it will tell them exactly where you are. I don't know whose Macrocosm is operational, but I'm pretty sure the Mogadorians have stolen somebody's,' he finishes. I haven't the slightest idea of what he's talking about.

'Macrocosm?' I ask.

He shakes his head, frustrated. 'There isn't time to explain it all,' he says. 'Relock it.' He opens his mouth to say more, but is interrupted by banging on the door at the bottom of the stairs. We can hear muffled bursts of foreign voices.

'We have to go,' Crayton says, rushing to the back of the room and grabbing a large black suitcase. He flings it open, revealing ten different guns, a handful of grenades, several daggers. He shrugs his coat to the floor and reveals a leather vest, and he rushes to strap every piece of weaponry to it before slipping his coat back on.

The Mogadorians ram the door below with a heavy object, and we hear footsteps enter the stairwell. Crayton removes one of the guns and snaps a clip into it.

'The burning symbol on the mountain,' I say. 'Was it you?'

He nods. 'I waited too long, I'm afraid, and when you opened the Chest it became impossible to slip away under their gaze. So I created the biggest beacon I could, and now we have to hope the others have seen it, and that they're on the way. Otherwise . . .' He trails off. 'Well, otherwise we're out of options. We have to get to the lake now. It's our only chance.'

I have no idea what lake he's talking about, or why he wants to go there, but my whole body is trembling. I just want to get away.

The footsteps are closer. Ella grabs hold of my

hand, back to her eleven-year-old self. Crayton pulls the slide on the gun, and I hear a bullet clicking into place. He aims it at the belfry's entryway.

'You have a very good friend in town,' he says.

'Héctor?' I ask, suddenly understanding why the two of them were talking in the café this morning. Crayton wasn't spreading lies, but rather telling the truth.

'Yes, and let's hope he keeps his word.'

'Héctor will,' I say, certain that's true regardless of what Crayton has asked him to do. 'It's in his name,' I add.

'Grab the Chest,' Crayton says.

I reach down and take the Chest in my left arm just as we hear the footsteps reach the last curves of the stairwell.

'Both of you, stay close to me,' Crayton says, his eyes moving from Ella to me. 'She was born able to change ages, but she's young and hasn't developed any Legacies yet. Keep her close. And don't let go of that Chest.'

'Don't worry, Marina. I'm fast,' she says, smiling.

'You two ready?'

'Ready,' Ella says, tightening her hand around mine.

'They're all going to be wearing body armor that would stop almost every bullet here on Earth,' Crayton says, 'but I've soaked mine in Loricyde, and there isn't a shield here that could stop them. I'm going to mow every damn one of them down.' His eyes narrow.

'Keep your fingers crossed that Héctor's outside the gates waiting for us.'

'He'll be there,' I say.

Then Crayton pulls the trigger, and he doesn't let go until every bullet's been fired.

28

We keep the windows down, saying little, unnerved by the task ahead. Sam keeps a firm grip on the wheel as the highway winds through Virginia.

'You think Six will make it?' Sam asks.

'I'm sure she'll make it, but who knows what she'll find.'

'That was a hell of a kiss you two had.'

I open my mouth and then shut it. A minute later I say, 'She likes you, too, you know.'

'Yeah, as a friend.'

'Actually, Sam, she *like-likes* you.'

Sam blushes. 'Sure. I could tell by the way she shoved her tongue in your mouth.'

'She kissed you, too, dude. I *saw* it.' I slap him in the chest with the back of my hand, and I can see he's replaying the kiss in his mind. 'After I kissed her I asked if she knew you liked her and –'

We're jerked over the double yellow line on the road. 'You did *what*?'

'Dude, relax. Don't kill us.' Sam glides us back onto our side of the road. 'She said she liked you, too.'

A devilish grin spreads across Sam's face. 'Interesting. It's kind of hard to believe this,' Sam finally says.

'God, Sam. Why would I lie about it?'

'No, I can't believe that this whole thing is real. That you're real or that Six is real, or that a hostile race of aliens has scattered themselves across the planet and nobody seems to know it. I mean, they've hollowed out a mountain in the middle of the state. How has it not been found? What did they do with all the dirt and rocks they removed? Even as scarcely populated as parts of West Virginia are, surely somebody had to stumble across it at some point. Hikers or hunters. Pilots of small planes. What about satellite imaging? And who knows how many other base camps or outposts or whatever you want to call them they have on Earth. I just don't understand how they move about so freely.'

'I agree,' I say. 'I don't know how either, but something tells me we probably don't know the half of it. You remember the very first conspiracy theory you told me?'

'No,' Sam says.

'We were talking about an entire Montana town being abducted, and you said the government allowed abductions in exchange for technology. Remember now?'

'Vaguely. Sure.'

'Well, that makes sense now. Maybe technology has nothing to do with it, and maybe the government isn't allowing abductions; but I really think some agreement has to be in place. Because you're right, there's no way they're traveling unnoticed. There are way, way, way too many of them.'

Sam doesn't respond. I look over and see that he's smiling.

'Sam?' I ask.

'I was just thinking of where I might be at this exact moment if you guys hadn't come along. Probably alone in my basement, collecting more conspiracy theories and wondering if my dad's still alive. That's how it was for years. But what's awesome is that I really do believe he's alive now. He's somewhere, John. I know it. And I know it because of you guys.'

'I hope so,' I say. 'It's pretty cool that Henri came to Ohio to try to find him, and you and I became friends almost immediately. It's like fate.'

Sam smiles. 'Or a cosmic aligning.'

'Nerd,' I say.

After a pause, Sam asks, 'Hey, John? You're positive that skeleton in the well wasn't my dad, right?'

'Absolutely, dude. He was Loric and huge. Bigger than any human.'

'What's your best guess, then? Who was it?'

'I really don't know. I just hope he wasn't too important.'

Four hours pass, and finally we see a sign pointing the way to Ansted, six miles ahead. We fall silent. Sam makes the turn and navigates a precarious two-lane road that twists up the mountain until we pass the town's border. We drive through it and turn left at the only stoplight in town.

'Hawks Nest, right?'

'Yep, a mile or two down the road,' Sam says, and it's there we'll find the map that Six drew three years ago.

The map is exactly where Six said it would be, hidden at Hawks Nest State Park, overlooking the New River. Exactly forty-seven steps down the Gysp Trail, Sam, Bernie Kosar, and I reach a tree with *E6* deeply carved into its side. From there, we leave the trail, taking thirty steps past the tree to the right. That's followed by a hard left turn, and then, a tenth of a mile away, we see a tree that towers over the others. In the small gap at the base of its twisted trunk, safely tucked away in a black plastic box, is the map that leads to the cave.

We make our way back to the SUV and drive another fifteen miles, ultimately pulling down a muddy, deserted road. It's the closest any road can get us, five miles due north of the cave. Sam takes the address Six wrote out of his pocket and puts it in the glove compartment. 'On second thought.' He removes it and puts it back into his pocket. 'As safe as anywhere,' he says.

I drop the Xitharis and some duct tape into Six's backpack that she left behind, and Sam slips the bag over his shoulders. I flip my dagger over in my hand and then stuff it into my back pocket.

We step out and I lock the doors, Bernie Kosar running circles around my legs. There's only a few hours left of daylight, which doesn't leave us much time. Even with the benefit of my hands, I can't imagine finding the cave without the sun to help us along.

Sam holds the map in his hands. At its right side Six has drawn a heavy X. A winding path five miles long connects the X with where we are now, marked on the map's left side. Along the way we'll skirt a riverbed while passing various landmarks noted for their physical descriptions, all of which are carefully marked to keep us on track. Turtle Rock. Fisherman's Pole. Circle Plateau. King's Throne. Lover's Kiss. Lookout Point.

Sam and I lift our heads at the same time, and we both see the rock a quarter mile away with an uncanny resemblance to a turtle's shell. Bernie Kosar barks.

'I guess we know which direction to head first,' Sam says.

And off we go, following the path set by the map. There's no trail, nothing that might allude to these mountains having been trampled by beings of another world, or even by beings of this one. Once we reach Turtle Rock, Sam spots a fallen tree that hangs over the cliff side at a forty-five degree angle, and thus looks like a fishing pole patiently waiting for a bite. And we hike on, following the trail as the sun lowers in the western sky.

Each step taken is another chance to turn around and walk away. But neither of us does. 'You're a hell of a friend, Sam Goode,' I tell him.

'You're not so bad yourself,' he replies. And then, 'I can't stop my hands from shaking.'

After passing King's Throne, which is a tall slender rock that looks like a high-back chair, I immediately spot two tall trees leaning against one another at slight angles, their

branches appearing like arms wrapped around each other in an embrace. And I smile, for a brief moment forgetting how terribly scared I am.

'Only one more to go,' Sam says, pulling me back into the clutches of reality.

We reach Lookout Point five minutes later. All told, the hike has taken an hour and ten minutes, and the shadows are long and stretched as the last light of dusk drains away. Without warning, a deep growl bellows beside me. I look down. Bernie Kosar's teeth are flashed, his fur bristling along his spine, his eyes pointed in the direction of the cave. He begins backing away from it.

'It's okay, Bernie Kosar,' I say, patting his back.

Sam and I drop to the ground and lay on our stomachs, both staring across the small valley at the cave's almost indiscernible entrance. It's far larger than I'd imagined, probably twenty feet wide and tall, but also much better hidden. There's something covering it, a net or a tarp maybe, making it blend in with its surroundings; you'd have to know it's there to be able to see it.

'Perfect location,' Sam whispers.

'Totally.'

My nervousness quickly turns to full-blown terror. As mysterious as the cave is, one thing I know for sure is that there'll be no shortage of things – weapons, beasts or traps – that could kill us. I could die within the next twenty minutes. And Sam could, too.

'Whose idea was this, anyway?' I ask.

Sam snorts. 'Yours.'

'Well, I have some stupid ideas sometimes.'

'True, but we have to get your Chest somehow.'

'There's so much in there that I don't even know how to use yet . . . but maybe they do,' I say. Then something catches my eye.

'Look at the ground in front of the entrance,' I say, pointing to a smattering of dark objects by the cave's entrance.

'At the rocks?'

'Those aren't rocks. Those are dead animals,' I say.

Sam shakes his head. 'Great,' he says.

I shouldn't be surprised since Six told us about it, but the sight of them fills me with even more dread, which I didn't think possible. My mind races.

'All right,' I say, sitting up. 'There's no time like the present.'

I kiss the top of Bernie Kosar's head, then run my hand down the length of his back, hoping this won't be the last time I ever see him. He tells me not to go, and I communicate back that I have to, no other choice. 'You're the best, BK. I love you, buddy.'

Then I stand. I take the bottom of my shirt in my right hand so I can remove the Xitharis from the bag without touching it.

Sam messes with the buttons on his digital watch, putting it in stopwatch mode. We won't be able to read its face once we're invisible, but when the hour is up, the watch will beep – though I imagine by then we'll have figured it out.

'Ready?' I ask.

Together we take our first step, then a second, and then we're hiking down the trail that may very well lead to our imminent doom. I turn around only once, when I've nearly reached the cave, and see Bernie Kosar staring at us.

29

We get as close to the cave as we can without being seen, and we duck behind a tree. I place the Xitharis stone on the sticky side of a section of duct tape. Sam watches with his fingers pinched around his stopwatch.

'Ready?' I ask.

He nods. I press the Xitharis and the tape to the very bottom of my sternum. I vanish instantly and Sam hits the watch's button, eliciting a soft digital beep. I snatch Sam's hand, and together we lurch around the tree and speed to the cave. It's all about the task at hand now, and with that in mind I'm no longer as nervous.

The cave is covered with a large camouflage tarp. We navigate through the graveyard of dead animals, being careful not to step on any, which is hard to do without the luxury of seeing your feet. There are no Mogs outside, and I hurry forward and flick the tarp aside a little too forcefully. Sam and I stumble in and four guards jump up from their seats and raise cylindrical cannons like the one that was held to my forehead that night in Florida. We stand as still as statues for a brief moment, and then quietly sneak past, hoping they'll attribute the tarp's sudden disturbance to the outside wind.

There's a cool breeze coming from a ventilation

system and the air is oddly fresh, which I hadn't expected considering it's laced with poisonous gas. The gray walls are polished smooth like flint; electrical conduit connects dim lights evenly spaced twenty feet apart.

We pass several more scouts and slither by undetected. The anxiety of the ticking clock racks us both with stress. We jog, we sprint, we tiptoe, we walk. And when the tunnel narrows and declines steadily, we side-step down it. The cool air grows hot and stifling, and a crimson glow at the end of the tunnel comes into view. We shuffle towards it until finally reaching the cave's beating heart.

The cavernous hall is far larger than I'd imagined based on Six's description. A long, continuous ledge runs along the circular walls and spirals all the way, from top to bottom, giving the overall appearance of a beehive; and the place is every bit as busy as one, too – there are literally hundreds of Mogs in sight, crossing the precarious stone arched bridges, entering and exiting tunnels. The deep floor and the vast ceiling are separated by a half mile, and Sam and I are situated very close to the middle. Two massive pillars sprout up from the floor and reach all the way to the ceiling, keeping the whole thing from caving in. The number of passageways around us is endless.

'My God,' Sam whispers in awe, taking it all in. 'It'd take months to explore this entire thing.'

My eyes are drawn to the lake of glowing green liquid down below. Even from so far away, the heat off of it

makes it hard to breathe. But despite the near roasting temperatures, twenty to thirty Mogs work around it, retrieving carts full of the bubbling stuff and quickly taking it away. Past the green lake, my eyes focus on something else.

'I think we can pretty much guess what we'll find down that tunnel with the giant bars,' I whisper. It's three times the height and width of the passageway that carried us here, and a checkered pattern of heavy iron bars covers it, keeping caged whatever beasts are inside. We can hear them howl from below, deep and almost sorrowful. One thing is immediately clear: their numbers are far from few.

'It'll literally take months,' Sam says again in a disbelieving whisper.

'Well, we have less than an hour,' I whisper back. 'So we better hurry.'

'I think we can put a big X through all those dark narrow tunnels that look obstructed.'

'I agree. We should start with the one directly across from us,' I say, looking at what appears to be the central room's main artery, wider and better lit than the others, the one with the greatest number of Mogs coming and going. The bridge over to it is just a long arch of solid rock that, at most, is two feet wide. 'Think you can make it across that archway?'

'We're about to find out,' Sam replies.

'Lead or follow?' I ask.

'Let me lead.'

Sam takes his first few steps uncertainly. Since we have to keep our hands locked, for the first forty feet or so we shuffle along sideways. It takes forever, and if we're to get to the other side and back again, there's no way we can do it at this pace.

'Just don't look down,' I say to Sam.

'Don't be cliché,' he responds, squaring his body. We move ahead slowly, and I wish I could see my feet for just this obstacle. I'm so focused on not falling that I don't feel Sam stop ahead of me, which causes me to stumble into him, nearly knocking us both off the bridge.

'What are you doing?' I ask, my heart thudding in my chest. I look up and see why he's stopped. Racing towards us is a Mogadorian soldier. He comes charging across in a jog, and he's already so close there's hardly time to react.

'There's nowhere to go,' Sam says. The soldier continues forward, cradling a wrapped bundle in his arms, and when he's close enough I feel Sam crouch. A second later, the Mog's feet are swept out from under him, completely catching the soldier off guard. He falls over the side of the bridge and catches himself with one hand as the bundle he was carrying drops away. The Mog cries out in pain as my invisible foot crushes his fingers, and he lets go and drops through the air, splattering far below with a sickly thud.

Sam races us forward before any further calamities arise. Every single Mog in the area has stopped in mid-stride, staring at one another with confused expressions.

I wonder if they believe what just happened was an accident, or if they're now on alert.

Sam squeezes my hand in relief when we've made it across, and he lurches ahead, having gained a world of confidence from killing the soldier.

The next corridor is wide and busy, and it doesn't take long for Sam and me to realize we're heading in the wrong direction; the rooms we pass are exclusively private, and the entire wing seems to be where the Mogs live: caves with beds, a large open cafeteria with hundreds of tables, a shooting range. We rush down a nearby corridor, but the result is the same. And then we try a third.

We follow the winding tunnel deeper into the mountain. Several tributaries lead away from the main drag, and Sam and I randomly turn down them based on nothing more than gut feeling. Aside from the main hall we entered, the rest of the mountain is nothing more than an interconnected network of damp stone corridors, off of which various rooms house research centers with examination tables, computers and shiny, sharp instruments. We pass several scientific laboratories that we both wish we had the time to investigate further as we rush by. We've probably run a mile, maybe two, and with each new corridor that turns up nothing, stress floods my veins.

'We can't have more than fifteen minutes left, John.'

'I'm aware of that,' I whisper, desperate and irritated and quickly losing hope.

When we take the next turn and rush up a steady

incline, we pass the thing I'd feared most: a room full of prison cells. Sam stops in midstride and keeps a firm grip on my hand, causing me to stop as well. Twenty to thirty Mogadorians guard more than forty cells, all lined up in a row, with heavy steel doors. In front of each door, there's a bubbling blue force field pulsing with electricity.

'Look at all those cells,' Sam says. I know he's thinking of his dad.

'Wait a second,' I say, the solution flashing into my head from out of nowhere. It's so obvious.

'What?' Sam asks.

'I know where the Chest is,' I say.

'Seriously?'

'So stupid of me,' I whisper. 'Sam, if you could pick just one place in this entire hellhole where you'd absolutely refuse to go, where would that place be?'

'In the pit with the howling beasts,' he answers without a second's hesitation.

'Exactly,' I say. 'Come on, let's go.'

I lead him back up the corridor that'll empty out at the cave's center; but before we've left the cells behind, a door clangs open and Sam jerks his hand to stop me.

'Look,' he says.

The nearest cell door stands wide-open. Two guards enter. They speak angrily for ten seconds in their native tongue, and when they exit they're clutching the arms of a pale, emaciated man in his late twenties. He's weak to the point of having trouble walking, and Sam's grip tightens as the guards shove him forward. One of

them unlocks a second door, and all three disappear through it.

'Who do you think they have locked up in there?' he asks as I pull him forward.

'We gotta go, Sam,' I say. 'We don't have the time.'

'They're torturing humans, John,' he says when we finally reach the central hive. 'Human beings.'

'I know,' I say, scanning the mammoth room for the quickest route down. There are Mogs everywhere, but I've become so used to passing by them that they no longer bother me. And besides, something tells me I'm about to find far scarier things than scouts and soldiers.

'People with families who probably have no idea where they've disappeared to,' Sam whispers.

'I know, I know,' I say. 'Come on, we'll talk about it when we're out of here. Maybe Six will have some sort of plan.'

We sprint around the spiral ledge and start down a tall ladder, but find it's nearly impossible to do so while holding the person's hand above you. I look down. There's still a far way to go.

'We have to jump,' I say to Sam. 'Otherwise it'll take ten minutes to get all the way down there.'

'Jump?' he asks incredulously. 'It'll kill us.'

'Don't worry,' I assure him. 'I'll catch you.'

'How the hell are you going to catch me if I'm holding your hand the whole time?'

But there isn't time to argue or debate. I take a deep breath, and leap from the ledge a hundred feet above the cave's bottom. Sam howls, but the continuous clatter

of manufacturing drowns out the noise. My feet hit the unyielding stone, and the force knocks me backwards; but I keep a firm grip on Sam, who lands on top of me.

'Never again are we doing that,' he says, standing.

The ground floor is so hot it's nearly impossible to breathe, but we sprint around the green lake towards the massive gate keeping the beasts locked away. When we reach it, a cool wind gusts through the bars, and I realize that the regular blasts of fresh air prevent any of the gas from entering this tunnel.

'John, I really don't think there's any time left,' Sam pleads.

'I know,' I say, letting a group of ten or so Mogs exit ahead of us.

We enter a dark tunnel. The walls look mucus covered, and barred chambers line each side of the shaft. Down the middle of the ceiling ten huge industrial fans blow, all pointed towards the entry we just came through, keeping the air cool and moist. Some of the locked chambers are small, though others are large, and bursting out of them all are feral and ferocious sounds. In the cage on our left are twenty to thirty krauls jumping over one another while letting loose shrill yips. Imprisoned on our right is a pack of demonic-looking dogs the size of wolves, with yellow eyes and no hair. Beside them stands a creature that looks like a troll, complete with a wart-covered nose. In a larger cell across the way a massive piken not unlike the one who busted through the prison wall that morning paces back and forth, sniffing the air.

'We might as well not even bother with these smaller rooms,' I say. 'If my Chest is here, it'll be in the biggest room at the end of this tunnel. I don't even want to take a guess at what kind of beast needs a door that large to fit through.'

'We're down to seconds, John.'

'We better hurry then,' I say, pulling Sam forward while quickly taking in the different horrors corralled here: gargoylelike winged creatures, monsters with six arms and red skin, several more pikens standing twenty feet tall, a wide reptilian mutant with trident-shaped horns, a monster with skin so transparent that its internal organs are on display.

'Whoa,' I say, stopping at a group of rounded tanks and vessels, most of which are silver, though two are copper colored and lined with heat gauges. Some kind of boiler room, I guess.

'So that's what's keeping this place going,' Sam says.

'This has to be it,' I reply. The tallest silo goes to the ceiling, and every tank is connected with heavy pipes, spouts, and aluminum ducts. Beside the silo, a control panel is affixed to the wall with a heap of electrical wires pouring out.

'Come on,' Sam says, impatiently jerking my hand.

Together we run the rest of the way to the tunnel's end. There's a massive door, forty to fifty feet tall and wide, made entirely of steel. To its right is a small wooden door. It's unlocked, and instantly I see why.

'Holy God,' Sam whispers, taking in the beast's enormity.

I'm momentarily stunned myself, and all I can do is stare at it: a hulking mass slumped in the room's far corner. Its eyes are closed and it breathes rhythmically. The beast must be fifty feet tall when standing, and from what I can tell its dark body is shaped like a man's, but with much longer arms.

'I want nothing to do with this place,' Sam says.

'You sure?' I ask, nudging him so his gaze leaves the monster. 'Look.'

There, in the center of the room, at eye level atop a thick stone pedestal, is my Chest. And right beside it sits a second one, almost identical in appearance. Both of them there for the taking. Except for the iron bars around them, which are housed beneath a humming and crackling electrical force field surrounded by a moat of the steaming green liquid. And the slumbering giant.

'That's not Six's Chest,' I say.

'What are you talking about? Who else's would it be?' Sam asks, confused.

'They found us, Sam. In Florida, they found us by opening Six's Chest.'

'Right, I know.'

'But look at the padlock on it. Why would they put the lock back on a Chest that they probably had a hell of a time getting into in the first place? I think that one's never been opened.'

'Maybe you're right.'

'It could be any of ours,' I whisper, shaking my head

while staring up at them both. 'Number Five's or Nine's or anyone's who isn't dead yet.'

'So they stole the Chest and didn't kill the Garde?'

'Like they did with me. Or maybe the Mogs caught one of them and they're being held here like Six was,' I say.

Sam doesn't get a chance to answer, because just then the alarm on his wristwatch begins to beep. Three seconds later it's followed by the whine of a hundred sirens echoing off the walls of the cave.

'Aw hell,' I say, turning my head. 'I can see you, Sam.'

He nods, a panicked look on his face. He lets go of my hand. 'I can see you, too.'

When I look over Sam's shoulder, the beast's eyes have come open – blank and white – narrowing in our direction.

30

The gunfire makes my ears ring long after it's stopped. Smoke rises from the end of the barrel, but Crayton wastes no time and drops the gun's clip and snaps another in place. Heaping mounds of ash have given the air a thick haze. We stand waiting, Ella and I behind Crayton. He keeps the gun raised, his finger hovering on the trigger. A Mogadorian climbs into the entryway with a cannon of his own, but Crayton fires first, cutting him in half and hurling him backwards. The Mogadorian explodes before he hits the wall. A second jumps into view, wielding the same flashing weapon that tore my shoulder downstairs, but Crayton disposes of it before any light comes forth.

'Well, they know where we are now. Come on,' he yells, rushing forward and down the stairs before I can offer to float us out the window. Ella and I follow, still holding hands. Crayton stops after the second curve of the stairwell, pressing his fingers to his eyes. 'There's too much ash in my eyes. I can't see anything,' he says. 'Marina, take the lead. If there's anything up ahead, yell and get the hell out of the way.'

I keep the Chest tucked beneath my left arm and Ella stays in the middle, holding my hand and Crayton's.

I lead them down and out the broken oak door just as the tower above us explodes.

I scream, ducking down and pulling Ella with me. Crayton instinctively begins firing. The gun unloads a rapid stream of ammunition – eight to ten bullets per second – and I can see an entire group of Mogadorians drop. Crayton stops firing.

'Marina?' he asks, nodding his head forward without seeing me.

I turn and study the hallway, thick with ash. 'I think it's clear,' I say; and the second the words leave my mouth, a Mogadorian leaps out of an open doorway and fires, sending a flashing white meteor raging towards us too bright to look at. We drop just in time, and the white death misses us by a hair. Crayton quickly lifts the gun and returns a barrage of bullets, killing the Mogadorian instantly.

I lead us forward. I have no idea how many of them Crayton just killed, but the ash stands thick on the floor, covering our feet and ankles. We pause at the top of the steps. Light from the windows comes through the fading ash, and Crayton has cleared his eyes. He takes the lead position, clutching the gun tightly to his chest while staying hidden behind the corner. Once we turn, all that separates us from the door leading outside are these steps, a short hallway, the back of the nave, and the main vestibule. Crayton takes a deep breath, nods his head, and then turns, dropping the barrel of the gun, ready to fire. But there's nothing to fire at.

‘Come on,’ he grunts.

We follow him and he escorts us across the nave’s rear, which is black with fire damage. For a brief moment I glimpse Adelina’s body, looking small from as far away as we are. My heart aches seeing her. *Be brave, Marina,* her words echo.

An explosion erupts against the outside wall on our right side. The stones blow inward, and I instinctively lift my hand and prevent any of them from hitting Ella and me. But Crayton gets hit hard, and he smashes against the wall to our left, landing with a grunt. The gun rattles away from him, and a Mogadorian enters the cathedral through the newly created hole. He’s holding a cannon; and in one fluid motion, I heave the Mogadorian backwards with my mind, bring Crayton’s gun into my hand, and pull the trigger. The gun’s kick is a lot harder than I expected, and I almost drop it; but I recover quickly and keep firing until the Mogadorian is reduced to ash.

‘Here,’ I say, pushing the gun into Ella’s hands; and in the comfortable way she takes it, I can tell she’s no stranger to firearms.

I rush to Crayton. His arm is broken, and blood seeps from gashes on his head and face. But his eyes are open and he seems alert. I slap my hands on his wrist and close my eyes, the iciness crawling over my body and extending to Crayton. I watch the bones in his arm move under the skin, and the gashes on his face seal and disappear. His chest expands and contracts so fast I

think his lungs are going to explode, but then he's calm again. He sits up and moves his arm fluidly.

'Nice job,' he says.

He takes the gun from Ella, and we climb through the hole in the wall and out into Santa Teresa's front grounds. I don't see a single person as Ella and I run ahead and pass through the iron gates while Crayton sweeps his gun back and forth, looking for any reason to fire it. My eyes are drawn over Crayton's left shoulder to a quick burst of red from the cathedral's roof. With a loud blast, the discharged rocket surges towards Crayton. I stare at the rocket's tip and raise my hands, concentrating harder than I ever have, and at the very last instant I'm able to slightly alter the rocket's path. It misses him and angles off towards a mountain, where it hits it with a plume of fire. Crayton rushes us through the gates with eyes alert and the gun aimed. He pulls up and spins around.

He shakes his head, and from behind us we hear the church doors thrust open.

'He isn't here,' Crayton says, and just before he turns around to begin firing, the sound of squealing tires pierces the air. The plastic covering that had kept the truck concealed falls off and its back side fishtails as Héctor, wide-eyed behind the wheel, floors it. He comes racing our way and slams on the brakes when he reaches us. The truck screeches to a halt, and Héctor reaches across the seat and throws open the passenger-side door. I toss my Chest beside Héctor, and Ella and I jump in. Crayton stays out just long

enough to empty his gun at the Mogadorians emerging from the church door. Several drop, but there are far too many to get them all. Crayton jumps in and slams the door, and the tires bite into the cobblestones in an attempt to find traction. There's the sound of another rocket nearing, but the tires catch and we go racing down Calle Principal.

'I love you, Héctor,' I say. I can't help it; the sight of him behind the wheel fills me with such warmth that it brims over the edge.

'I love you, too, Marina. I always told you, stick with Héctor Ricardo; he'll take care of you.'

'I never doubted it once,' I say, which is a lie; I had doubted it this morning.

We reach the bottom of the hill and fly past the signs announcing the town limits.

I twist around to peer out the back window as Santa Teresa quickly fades behind us. I know it's the last time I'll ever see it and though I've waited years to leave, it now holds the sacredness of being Adelina's last resting place. Soon the town is gone, left behind.

'Thank you, Señorita Marina,' Héctor says.

'For what?'

'I know it was you who cured my dear mother. She told me it was you, that you were her angel; and I'll never be able to repay you for it.'

'You already have, Héctor. I was very happy to help.'

He shakes his head. 'I haven't yet, but I'm sure going to try.'

While Crayton refills both clips and takes inventory of his ammo, Héctor navigates the windy and unpredictable road. We bounce and skid along the sharp turns and sudden hills. But despite the speed, it doesn't take long for a convoy of vehicles to be seen in the distance behind us.

'Don't worry about them,' Crayton says. 'Just get us to the lake.'

Even though the truck is barreling down the road, the convoy closes the gap. After ten minutes, a flash of light sails just over the truck and explodes into the countryside ahead of us. Héctor instinctively jerks his head down.

'My God!' he says.

Crayton turns around and breaks the back window with the butt of his gun, then fires. The lead vehicle is upended, which makes us all cheer in celebration.

'That should keep them far enough back,' Crayton says, quickly reloading the gun's clip.

And it does for a few minutes, but as the road grows more precarious and twists down the mountain at sharp declines, the vehicles catch right back up to us. Héctor mutters under his breath as he whips around each bend, the gas pedal buried, the truck's back tires swinging frighteningly over the edge of the towering cliff.

'Careful, Héctor,' Crayton says. 'Don't kill us before we get there. At least give us a chance.'

'Héctor is in control,' Héctor replies, bringing no

comfort whatsoever to Crayton, who keeps a white-knuckled grip on the headrest in front of him.

The only refuge is the road's perpetual turns, which keep the Mogadorians from getting a straight shot, though they try anyway.

As we race around a particularly sharp bend, Héctor can't turn us quickly enough and we go off the edge of the road. At a seventy-five-degree angle, the truck races down the dense mountainside, smashing through saplings, bouncing off boulders, barely avoiding thick trees. Ella and I scream. Crayton yells as he flies forward and slams into the windshield. Héctor doesn't say a word; he clenches his teeth and maneuvers us around and over obstacles until we miraculously land on another road. The truck's hood is severely dented and smoking, but the engine is still running.

'This is a, uh, shortcut,' Héctor says. He tries the gas pedal, and we quickly rumble down the new road.

'I think we lost them,' says Crayton, looking up the cliff.

I pat Héctor's shoulder and laugh. Crayton sticks the barrel of his gun out the back window and waits.

Eventually the lake comes into view. I wonder why Crayton believes the lake will save us.

'What's the big deal about the lake?' I ask.

'You didn't think I'd come to find you with just Ella, did you?'

For a moment I think to tell him that up until a few hours ago I thought he had come to kill me. But soon

the Mogadorians appear behind us again, and Crayton turns around while Héctor's eyes dart up to the rear-view mirror.

'This is going to be close,' Crayton says.

'We'll get out of it, Papa,' Ella says, looking at Crayton; and hearing her call him that fills my heart with affection. He smiles warmly at her, then nods. Ella squeezes my hand. 'You'll love Olivia,' she says to me.

'Who's Olivia?' I ask, but she doesn't get a chance to answer before the road turns at a ninety-degree angle and declines sharply towards the lake ahead. Ella tenses in my arms as the road ends, and Héctor barely lets up on the gas as the truck rams straight through a chain-link gate that surrounds the lake. We hit a slight bump, and the truck's tires leave the ground entirely before landing with a thud and bouncing on the shore. Héctor speeds straight for the water, and just before we reach it, he slams on the brakes and brings us skidding to a stop. Crayton shoulders open the passenger-side door and dashes towards the lake, rushing straight into the water until it reaches his knees. With the gun still in his left hand, he hurls an object as far as he can with his right and begins muttering something in a language I don't understand.

'Come on!' he screams, thrusting his hands up in the air as though offering encouragement. 'Come on, Olivia!'

Héctor, Ella, and I rush out and run up near him. I have the Chest under my arm and in an instant I see that the water has begun to crest and bubble in the lake's middle.

'Marina, do you know what a Chimæra is?'

But I don't get to answer, because just then a lone Mogadorian vehicle, a tanklike Humvee with a gun mounted on top, erupts onto the scene and speeds down the hill. As it comes right at us, in the water, Crayton unloads a barrage of bullets into the windshield. The vehicle instantly goes out of control, crashing straight into the back of Héctor's truck. It creates a deafening bang, followed by the crush of grinding metal and breaking glass. As the dozens of other vehicles in the convoy rumble down the last hill and begin firing, the world erupts in fire and smoke as explosions rock the beach, causing all four of us to hit the ground. Sand and water rain down, and we scramble back to our feet. Crayton snags me by the collar.

'Get out of here!' he yells.

I take Ella's hand and we run as fast as we can around the left side of the lake. Crayton begins firing; but it's not one gun that I hear but two, and I can only hope it's Héctor's finger pulling the second trigger.

We race towards a cluster of trees sloping down from the mountainside, jutting out all the way to the water's bank. Our footsteps slap on the wet stones, and Ella's accelerated pace matches my own. Gunfire continues to rattle through the air; and just as it lets up, a loud animal roar booms over our heads, causing me to stop short. I turn to look at the creature able to create such a paralyzing call, knowing it's not of this world. A long, muscular neck protrudes ten or fifteen

stories out of the water, the flesh a gleaming gray. At the end of it, a giant lizard head separates its pebbled lips to show an enormous set of teeth.

'Olivia!' Ella cheers.

Olivia rears her head and lets loose another earsplitting roar, and in the middle of it, a series of high-pitched yipping sounds roll down from the mountain. I look up and see a pack of small beasts descending towards the lake.

I gasp. 'What are those?' I ask Ella.

'Krauls. Lots of them.'

Olivia's neck is fully emerged and thirty stories high now, and as the rest of her body surfaces, her neck widens and her torso thickens. The Mogadorians immediately fire at her, and Olivia slams her head down on several at a time, creating large piles of ash. I can see the dark figures of Crayton and Héctor, both with guns blazing. The Mogadorians fall back as a hundred krauls enter the lake and swim towards Olivia. The creatures leap out of the water and attack. Many claw their way up Olivia's back and rip at the base of her neck. The lake water is soon streaked with blood.

'No!' Ella screams.

She tries running back, but I grab hold of her arm.

'We can't go back,' I say.

'Olivia!'

'That's suicide, Ella. There're too many.'

Olivia roars in pain. She whips her head at her sides and back, trying to crush or bite the black krauls that

have blanketed her. Crayton aims his gun at the beasts, but he lowers his weapon when he realizes he would most likely shoot Olivia in the process. He and Héctor instead fire on the army of Mogadorians lining up and preparing for a new attack.

Olivia wavers left and right, howls at the mountains, and backs herself up into the middle of the lake and slowly sinks in a wave of red. The krauls detach and swim towards the Mogadorians.

'No!' I hear Crayton yell above the chaos. I watch him try to enter the lake but Héctor pulls him back onto the shore.

'Duck!' Ella screams, pulling me down by the arm. A whoosh of air passes over us. A giant black hoof smashes the ground next to me, and I look up to see a horned monster. Its head is as large as Héctor's truck, and when the giant roars, my hair flaps in my face.

'Come on!' I yell. We race towards the trees.

'Split up,' Ella says. I nod and dart left, towards an ancient beech tree with gnarled limbs. I set the Chest down and instinctively lift my hands and then pull them apart. To my surprise the beech trunk opens, creating a hollow space that looks just big enough for two people and a Chest to fit.

I look over my shoulder to see the creature chasing Ella through a dense line of trees. I toss the Chest in the open trunk, and with telekinesis I pick up two trees and send them like missiles at the creature's back. They splinter against its dark skin with a loud crash, knocking

it to its knees. I run and grab Ella's shaking hand, pulling her in the other direction. The beech tree with my Chest comes into view.

'The tree, Ella! Get inside!' I yell. She sits atop the Chest and tries to make herself as compact as she can, shrinking down to a younger age.

'That's a piken, Marina! Get in!' she pleads; and before she can say another word, I close the trunk up around her, leaving just enough room so she can see.

'I'm sorry,' I say through the small crevice, hoping the giant didn't see where I've stashed the Chest and hidden my friend.

I turn and run trying to lead the piken away, but it soon catches up and knocks me from behind. The force of the hit is shocking, and I fall down a steep slope until my arm finds a boulder to hook around. I look over my shoulder to see that I'm less than a meter from a rocky cliff.

The piken appears at the top of the slope. There it shuffles sideways until it's positioned directly above me. It roars so loudly my mind blanks. I hear Ella scream my name in the distance, but I can't breathe, let alone yell back.

It marches down the slope. I raise one of my hands and uproot a small spindly tree near me and launch it at the giant's chest. It impales its chest, and it's enough for the piken to lose its footing; and it falls sideways, shrieking and barreling right at me. I close my eyes and prepare for the impact; but instead of smashing me

under its weight and knocking me over the cliff, its body hits the boulder I'm holding on to and then bounces *over* me. I whip my head over my shoulder to see the piken fall down the rocky cliff.

I'm finally able to concentrate enough to float myself up the slope. I hurry back towards the beech tree – to Ella and my Chest – and I hear the cannon's blast a split second before I'm shot. The pain is double anything I've felt before, and all I can see is red and flashes of white. I roll around uncontrollably, writhing in agony.

'Marina!' I hear Ella scream.

I roll onto my back and stare at the sky. Blood drips out of my mouth and nose. I can taste it. I can smell it. A few birds circle overhead. As I wait to die, I watch as the sky is taken over by a colossal group of dark, heavy clouds. The clouds crash and roll on top of each other, pulsing as if they're breathing. I think I'm hallucinating, seeing visions before I die, when a massive drop of water hits me on the right cheek. I blink as another hits me above my eyes, and then a bolt of lightning splits the sky in two.

A huge Mogadorian in gold-and-black armor stands over me smiling. He presses a cannon against my temple and spits on the ground; but before he pulls the trigger, he looks up at the looming storm. I quickly place my hands on the gaping wound in my abdomen, feeling the icy familiarity surge under my skin. Then the oncoming rain washes over me as the clouds become a solid wall of darkness.

31

By the look on Sam's face I can tell he's just about lost all faith in getting out of here alive. My own shoulders sag as I stare into the massive white eyes of the beast that's rising to its feet in front of us. It takes its time, stretching its muscular neck, veins as thick as Roman columns protruding on both sides. The dark skin on its face is dry and cracked like the stone jutting above its head. With its long arms, it has the look of an alien gorilla.

By the time the giant has pushed itself into a full standing position, fifty feet tall, the handle of my dagger has melted itself around my right hand.

'Flank it!' I yell. Sam runs left and I dart right.

Its first move is towards Sam, who immediately turns and runs along the circular edge of the moat. The beast lumbers after him, and that's when I sprint towards it and slide my dagger right and left, cutting small chunks from its calves. It rears its head and smashes its nose against the ceiling, and then swings a hand down at me, one of its fingers connecting with my back leg. I'm sent spinning into the wall, where I land on my left shoulder, dislocating it.

'John!' Sam yells.

The giant swings for me again, but I'm able to jump

out of the path of its fist; the giant may be powerful, but it's slow. Still, the cave we're in is not large enough to run very far so, slow or not, it still has the advantage.

I don't see Sam anywhere as I stagger from boulder to boulder. The giant has a hard time following me; and once I figure I have enough time, I slowly raise my left arm above my head and rotate my hand so my palm is on the back of my head. The pain shoots from my neck to my heels; and before I give in to it, I keep reaching and feel my dislocated shoulder pop back into place. A sense of relief comes over me, but it's short-lived as I look up to see the giant's palm right above my head.

I raise my dagger and its blade punctures the beast's palm, but it's not enough to stop it from wrapping its fingers around me. It picks me up, and the strength of its squeeze causes the dagger to fall to the ground. I hear its diamond blade clang; and as I'm turned upside down, I search for it so I can use my telekinesis to retrieve it.

'Sam! Where are you?'

I'm disoriented as the beast turns me right side up again, and it holds me a few feet above its nose. Then I see Sam emerge from a fissure in the wall. He runs and picks up my blade, and a second later the giant squeals in shock and pain. It squeezes me hard, and I push back against its fingers as much as I can. As it stumbles backwards, I'm able to free my shoulders, arms, and hands. I turn on the lights of my palms and shine my Lumen directly into its eyes. It's instantly blinded and backs into a

wall, and that's when I'm able to pull the rest of my body free and jump.

Sam tosses me my dagger and I charge at the beast, plunging the blade into the skin between every toe. The giant howls. It bends over, and when it does I shine my Lumen again into its eyes. It loses its balance, and I make a boulder behind it dislodge and slam into its lower back. The beast pitches forward, its long arms straight out to break its fall. Its massive hands land in the moat of steaming green liquid – and the sound of its searing flesh comes a second later. I watch as the beast crashes into the base of the electrical force field and the thick stone pedestals holding the Chests. The crash disrupts the force field and sends the pedestals flying across the room, breaking against the stone. The beast lies unmoving.

'Tell me you planned that,' Sam says, following me towards the Chests.

'I wish I could,' I say.

I open my Chest to find everything inside, including the coffee can of Henri's ashes and the volatile crystal that's wrapped in the towel. 'Looks good,' I say. Sam picks up the other Chest.

'What happens when we go through that door?' Sam says, nodding to the small wooden door we came in through.

We killed the beast and we have the Chests, but we can't turn ourselves invisible and just stroll by a hundred Mogs. I open my Chest and handle different crystals and

objects, but again I have no idea what most of them do, and the ones I do know how to use can't exactly get me through a mountain of aliens. Looking around the room, I'm losing hope. But it's after studying the giant's melting skin and disintegrating bones that I get an idea.

With my dagger back in my jeans pocket, I slowly approach the moat of bubbling green liquid. I take a deep breath and carefully dip a finger in it. Just as I'd hoped, it's scalding hot but merely tickles my skin like fire. It's like green lava.

'Sam?'

'Yeah?'

'When I say open the door, I want you to open it and get out of the way immediately.'

'What are you going to do?' he asks.

Visions of Henri running the Loric crystal over me as I lie on the coffee table, my hands in open flames, run through my mind, and I dunk my hand into the moat and pick up a dripping scoop of the green lava. I close my eyes and concentrate, and when I open them the liquid is hovering over my hand in a perfect flaming ball.

'This, I guess,' I say.

'Wicked.'

Sam runs over to the wooden door, and I nod to show him I'm ready.

He rips the door open and dives to his right. A cluster of heavily armed Mogs are running our way; but when they catch sight of the fiery green ball coming their way, they try to turn around. As the ball is about to splash on

the chest of the first Mog, I use my mind to spread it out like a fiery blanket. Several Mogs are hit, and after a moment of burning torture, they turn to ash.

I wing ball after ball of green lava at more Mogs, knocking them down. Sam collects a pile of their guns, and once there's a lull in the advancement, I grab two more balls of green liquid and run out the door. Sam follows me with a long black gun under each arm.

The number of Mogs running down the dark tunnel is staggering; and with the flashing lights and piercing sirens, it's a sensory overload. Sam pulls both triggers and mows down row after row of Mogs, but they keep coming. When he's out of bullets, Sam grabs two more guns.

'I could use some help here!' Sam yells, mowing down another line of Mogs.

'I'm thinking, I'm thinking!' The mucus-covered walls of the tunnel don't appear to lend themselves to spreading a decent fire, and I don't have enough of the green lava in my hands to do enough damage. To my left are the silver gas tanks and silos with their heavy pipes, spouts and aluminum ducts. Next to the tallest of the silos I eye the control panel with electrical wires pouring out. I can hear the screams and roars of the beasts in the barred chambers farther down the hall, and wonder how hungry they are.

I toss a flaming ball at the control panel and it disintegrates in a storm of sparks. The bars of the chambers lining the walls begin to rise, and that's when I toss the other green ball at the base of the gas tanks and silos.

I grab hold of Sam and sprint with him back into the giant's chamber. As the explosion erupts, I whip Sam against the stone section between the wooden door and the rising steel gate, and allow the advancing wave of flames to sweep over me. My ears are flooded with the crackle and hum of fire.

Dozens of krauls burst from their open chamber and attack a series of unsuspecting Mogs from behind; several pikens stomp into the tunnel with roars and swinging arms; the reptilian mutant with horns charges towards the back of the tunnel, ploughing over Mogs and krauls under the legs of the pikens; the gargoylelike winged creatures buzz at the ceiling, swooping down to take a bite out of anything they can; and the monster with transparent skin sinks its rows of teeth into the calf of a piken. That all happens in a matter of seconds, then they're overtaken by a sea of fire.

After a few minutes, once the fire escapes up the spiral cavern at the end of the tunnel to continue to wreak havoc throughout the mountain, the long corridor in front of me is littered with ash piles and black monster bones. I extinguish the fire surrounding me and brush my hands off onto my thighs.

Sam is singed, but otherwise okay.

'Brilliant, dude,' he says.

'Let's just try to get the hell out of here, and *then* we can celebrate.'

I stick my Chest under my arm and Sam picks up the other. We race through the fire's destruction; the stench

of death is choking. The charred ladder at the end of the tunnel appears stable, and with only one free hand apiece, we climb with difficulty. Our feet hit the burned and blackened spiral ledge, and we sprint around and around until we reach the cave's center.

The inferno I unleashed did much more damage than I thought it would, and we see piles upon piles of ash; but we also see hundreds of Mogs crawling out of different corridors and tunnels on their hands and knees, burned or still on fire, barking in pain, unable to pick up their guns, unable to do anything as we jump over them. There are other soldiers racing above us on ledges, some with weapons in their arms, others with the wounded.

I'm confused which way the exit is; and as I lead us through a series of tunnels with my pendant swinging around my neck, Sam and I each pick up a discarded gun. We run with them chest high, firing at anything that gets in our way. Even though we don't know where we're going, we don't stop moving until we come to the cells with human prisoners. That's when I know for certain we've gone the wrong way. I pull Sam in the other direction, but he plants his feet and stops me. I can see the concern and hope on his face. The cells have their steel doors stuck a foot above the floor and the bubbling blue force fields have disappeared.

'They're open, John!' he yells, tossing his Chest at my feet. I drop my gun and pick up the other Chest, and Sam finally says what I knew he was thinking: 'What if my dad's here?'

I look into Sam's eyes, and I know we have to check. He runs along the left side of the corridor, yelling into each cell for his dad. I'm investigating the cells on the right when a boy my age with long black hair sticks his head under a door. When he sees me, he puts a hand cautiously into the corridor.

'The force field is really gone?' he shouts.

'I think so!' I yell.

Sam hoists his gun over his shoulder and ducks his head under the boy's cell door. 'Do you know a man named Malcolm Goode? Forty years old, brown hair? Is he here? Have you seen him?'

'Shut up and stand back, kid,' I hear the boy say. There's a grittiness to his voice, something that makes me uneasy, and I immediately pull Sam to the side. The boy grips the bottom of the door and rips it from the wall, tossing it into the corridor like a Frisbee. The ceiling cracks and boulders fall, and I use telekinesis to shield Sam and me from being crushed. Before I can say a word, the boy emerges clapping the dust off his hands. He's taller than I am, shirtless and muscular.

Sam steps forward, and to my surprise he aims his gun at the boy's head. 'Just tell me! Do you know my dad? Malcolm Goode? Please!'

The boy looks past Sam and his weapon, focusing on the Chests under my arms. That's when I notice the three scars on his leg. They're just like mine. He's one of us.

I drop the other Chest to the ground in shock. 'What number are you? I'm Four.'

He squints at me and then offers his hand. 'I'm Nine. Good job staying alive, Number Four.'

He reaches for the Chest I've dropped. Sam lowers his gun, retreating down the corridor, stopping every few seconds to look inside a cell. Nine places his hand on the Chest's lock and it instantly shakes and snaps open. A yellow glow lights up his face when he opens the lid.

'Hell, yeah.' He laughs, placing a hand inside. Nine pulls out a tiny red rock and shows it to me. 'You have one of these?'

'I don't know. Maybe.' I'm embarrassed by how little I understand the items in my own Chest.

Nine places the rock between his knuckles and aims his fist at the nearest wall. A white cone of light appears, and instantly we can see through the wall and into an empty jail cell.

Sam runs in our direction. 'Wait! You have X-ray vision?'

'What number is the nerd?' Nine asks me, digging around in his Chest again.

'That's Sam. He's not Loric, but he's our ally. He's looking for his dad.'

He tosses Sam the red rock. 'This will make shit go faster, Sammy. Just aim and squeeze.'

'He's human, dude,' I say. 'He can't use this stuff.'

Nine places his thumb on Sam's forehead. Sam's hair blows upward and I can smell electricity in the air.

Sam stumbles backwards. 'Whoa.'

Nine ducks his hands back into his Chest. 'You've got about ten minutes. Get to it.'

I'm amazed that Nine has the ability to transfer powers to humans. Sam runs down the corridor, inspecting cells with a flick of the wrist. When he gets to the large metal door at the end, he aims the rock at it, exposing more than a dozen armed Mogs on the other side, and one is twisting together exposed wires in an open keypad.

'Sam!' I yell picking up my gun. 'Get back!'

Whoosh. The door rises and the Mogs rush forward. Sam sprints away, firing over his shoulder.

'You have any other Legacies yet?' I ask Nine over the sound of my gun.

He winks, and then he's gone, running along the cracked ceiling at super speed. The Mogs don't notice Nine until he's dropped behind them, and by then it's too late. He's a tornado, ripping through them with a ferocity I didn't know Loric possessed; even Six would be impressed. Sam and I stop firing, letting Nine dismember each Mog with his bare hands.

When he's finished, Nine runs back along the left wall of the corridor before circling to the ceiling and then to the right wall, a cloud of ash trailing him.

'Antigravity,' Sam says. 'Now *that's* a cool Legacy.'

Nine skids to a stop in front of his Chest and kicks it shut. 'I can also hear pretty well. For miles.'

'Okay, let's go,' I say, scooping up my Chest. Nine easily places his on his huge shoulder and grabs a gun from the floor.

'What about those other cells?' he asks Sam, pointing

down the corridor. A hundred or more cell doors line the walls past where the Mogs had entered.

'We have to go,' I say, knowing we're already pushing our luck. It's only a matter of seconds before we'll be surrounded. But there's no persuading Sam.

He runs under the large door, still holding the red rock. Another dozen Mogs suddenly emerge from a hidden tunnel entrance between us. Sam braces himself against the wall and fires. I see a few of the Mogs burst into ash, but then my view is blocked by a swarm of drooling krauls.

Focusing my thoughts on a boulder, I whip it at the krauls, smashing all but a few. Nine catches a kraul by its back legs, and slams the beast against the wall. He crushes another two, and when he's done he turns to me, laughing. I'm about to ask him what's so funny when he launches a boulder right at me. I barely jump out of the way, and a moment later my back is covered with black ash.

'They're everywhere!' He laughs.

'We have to get to Sam!' I try to run past Nine when an enormous piken hand snatches us both.

'Sam!' I yell. 'Sam!'

Sam doesn't hear us over the sound of his gun. The piken pulls us in the other direction, and, in what feels like slow motion, I lose sight of my best friend. Before I can yell again, the piken throws us down the opposite tunnel. I hit the wall and land on one Chest and the other lands

on top of me. The wind is knocked out of me; and when I look up, I see Nine spitting blood out. He's grinning.

'Are you crazy?' I ask. 'You're enjoying this?'

'I've been locked up for over a year. This is the best day of my life!'

Two pikens duck into the tunnel, blocking our direct path back to Sam. Nine wipes the blood from his chin and opens his Chest. He pulls out a short silver pipe, and it expands violently at both ends until it's over six feet long and glowing red. He runs toward the pikens with the pipe over his head. I stand to join him but feel a jolt of pain in my ribs. I dig inside my Chest for my healing stone, but by the time I find it Nine has killed both pikens. Running back along the ceiling, he twirls the pipe at his side, and when he's twenty feet away he yells for me to move. The glowing red pipe sails over my head like a javelin, impaling a piken in the stomach.

'Don't mention it,' Nine says before I can utter a word.

More pikens squeeze into the far end of the tunnel, and when I turn around to run, a flock of transparent birds with razor-sharp teeth is flying towards us. Nine grabs a strand of green stones from his Chest and flings it towards the flock. It hovers in the air and, like a black hole, sucks the birds into it.

He closes his eyes and the stones zip towards the pikens, spinning and unleashing the flock of birds into their faces. Nine points at me and yells, 'Boulder them!'

I follow his lead, rocketing boulder after boulder at the

mayhem. The pikens and the birds collapse under our barrage.

Several more pikens push their way into the tunnel, roaring. I grab Nine's arm to keep him from charging.

'They're just going to keep coming,' I say. 'We have to find Sam and get out of here. Number Six is meeting us.'

He nods and we run. At the next opening we veer left, unsure if we're making progress or getting even more lost. More and more enemies appear behind us with every new turn. Nine trashes every tunnel we pass through, bringing down ceilings and collapsing walls with telekinesis and perfectly thrown boulders.

We come to a long, low-arching bridge of solid rock, similar to the one Sam and I shuffled along earlier, and below is a steaming pool of green lava. Charging across the other side of the narrow bridge is a thick line of Mogs, and behind us several pikens are racing down the tunnel, straight towards us.

'Where do we go?' I shout as we step onto the bridge.

Nine says, 'We go under.'

Nine grabs my hand as we reach the peak of the bridge, and my world literally flips upside down until we're running along the underside of the arch. Without warning Nine lets go of me, but my shoes still firmly grip the belly of the bridge somehow. I reach over my head and scoop up a pile of the green lava, and by the time we're standing on the other side of the room, I have a perfect green ball of fire in my hand. I wing it at the Mogs on the

bridge and visualize it spreading over them. I can hear the sizzling of their flesh when we duck into another cave.

I'm out of breath when we reach a steep decline. I'm judging the grade of the drop when I'm hit with a blast from behind. I topple forward and fall at an amazing speed, and when the ground finally levels out, my recently dislocated shoulder hits it first.

I roll onto my stomach in unimaginable pain. The blast hit me square in the back, and my muscles are stuck in an uncontrollable spasm. I can hardly breathe, let alone search my Chest for my healing stone. The only thing I can do is stare at the slivers of moonlight that appear and disappear at the end of the tunnel. The tarp. It's flapping in the forest wind. I'm back to where I started.

I hear the sound of rocks crumbling behind me. I'm in more pain than I thought imaginable, and all I can think about is leaving the mountain. 'Straight ahead. It's the exit. We can regroup out there,' I manage.

If we can make it outside, then I can heal myself, hide our Chests in the forest. And maybe BK can come back in with us now that we've destroyed the gas tanks. The four Mogs who guarded the entrance are gone, and Nine jumps out through the tarp and into the forest. I follow. The stench from the dead animal carcasses hits us fast, and we both gag as Nine jogs into a line of trees. I collapse against a trunk. I need five minutes, I think. Then we're going back in for Sam. Guns and hands blazing.

Nine digs around his Chest and I close my eyes. Tears

roll down my face. I'm startled by something rough touching my left hand. I open my eyes to see it's Bernie Kosar in his beagle form, licking my fingers.

'I don't deserve that,' I tell him. 'I'm a coward. I'm cursed.'

He notices my injuries and tears, and then sniffs Nine's face before expanding into a horse.

'Whoa!' Nine jumps back. 'What the hell are you?'

'Chimæra,' I whisper. 'He's a good guy. He's Loric.'

Nine quickly pets BK's muzzle and then presses a healing stone to my back. As it works through my system, I notice a menacing storm brewing over the mountain.

The sky suddenly rages with lightning and booming thunder, and I'm so grateful Six has returned that I stand, ignoring the remaining pain in my back. The clouds shift and stretch in a way I've never seen before, though, and the sky feels suddenly evil. This isn't Six. She's not back to help.

I watch the funnel cloud that I've only seen in my worst visions form.

Bernie Kosar rears backward as a perfectly spherical spaceship, milky white like a pearl, sweeps down through the tornado's eye. The ship lands right in front of the mountain's entrance, sending tremors through the ground. In the same way as I had seen in my visions, a door appears from out of nowhere on the ship's side, simply melting away. The Mogadorian leader from my visions, he's here.

Nine gasps. 'Setrákus Ra. He's here. This is it.'

I'm silent, frozen in fear. 'So that's his name,' I finally whisper.

'That *was* his name. For every day they tried to torture me and my Cêpan, I'm going to stab him with this.' The red pipe glows in Nine's hand. Its ends expand with rotating blades. 'I'm going to kill him. And you're going to help me.'

Setrákus Ra walks towards the cave's entrance but stops before going in, one massive silhouette, stark and spectral. Through the raging wind and torrential rain, he turns, lifting his gaze in our general direction. Even from as far away as I am, the faint glow of the three pendants is unmistakable around his thick neck.

Nine and I charge out of the trees with Bernie Kosar galloping behind, but it's too late. Setrákus Ra has disappeared into the cave and the same bubbling blue force field that covered the prison cell doors appears over the entrance.

'No!' Nine yells. He slides to a stop and stabs the ground with his pipe.

With my dagger in my hand, I keep going. I hear Nine scream for me to stop, but all I can think about is killing Setrákus Ra, saving Sam and his dad and ending this war, right here, right now. When I hit the blue force field, everything goes black.

32

Thunder rolls, followed by brilliant streaks of lightning, and in their glare I see the clouds expand and drop. Rain falls in heavy sheets, and the armored Mogadorian looks down at me. He presses the cannon against my blue pendant and says something I can't understand. My wound in my stomach has almost healed, and I hear Ella yell my name over the thunder.

If I'm going to die, then I need to release Ella first. One of us needs to live to tell the others. I cautiously lift my hands and envision the trunk separating, when a bolt of lightning cracks in the distance. Less than a second later, the bolt strikes the Mogadorian standing over me, and he turns to ash and is swept away in the wind.

I climb to my feet and see that I've opened the beech tree's trunk halfway. I continue to separate the tree as I run towards it. 'Ella? Are you okay?'

She spills out of the trunk and falls into my arms. 'I couldn't see you,' she says, squeezing me. 'I thought I lost you.'

'Not yet,' I say, grabbing my Chest. 'Come on.'

We turn to run, and see Crayton and Héctor coming towards us. Héctor's been hurt, and his arm is over Crayton's shoulders for support. The wind and rain are

raging. Behind them, the first wave of Mogadorians and krauls are charging up the shore after them. When I see this, I break away a large limb from a dead tree and hurl it hard at the closest pack of krauls. It knocks down several, but they're back up again in no time. A Mogadorian soldier throws a grenade that I intercept midair with my mind and send right back into his stomach. It explodes, throwing several Mogadorians and krauls to the ground in soggy bits of ash. I send tree after tree, rock after rock, knocking many to the ground, killing more.

'Help me!' Crayton yells.

I rush to take Héctor from him. He has a bite wound in his stomach and a bullet hole in his arm, and both are bleeding badly.

'Come on, everyone!' Crayton yells, pulling bullets from his coat pocket and quickly sliding them into his gun's empty clip. 'We have to get to the dam!'

I open my mouth to respond, but an enormous lightning bolt snaps over us. It spreads across the sky like the veins of the gods, leaving the distinct taste of metal in the air. A deafening clap of thunder reverberates off the mountains. The wind and rain cease, and the clouds rotate around and around in a massive maelstrom, until a dark, glowing eye forms, staring at us from high over the mountaintops. The Mogadorians are just as mesmerized as we are. The wind kicks up again, and the dark clouds and the thunder and lightning come with it, slow at first, but quickly gaining

speed, heading our way. A perfect storm, beautiful at its cataclysmic heart, unlike anything I've ever seen before. All any of us can dō is watch the thick clouds rolling towards us with a deep growl.

'What's happening?' I scream over the gale force winds.

'I don't know!' Crayton replies. 'We're going to need to find some cover!'

But he doesn't move, and neither does anyone else. Héctor seems to have forgotten all about the pain of his wounds as he watches, too.

'Go!' Crayton finally yells, and then he spins around and fires on the Mogadorians to cover us as we run over a slight hill and then down into a valley. I see the dam on my right, which connects two lower mountains. It's too far away to realistically believe we'll reach it. Héctor's face has turned white and he's fading fast, and I start looking for a place to rest so I can heal him. Crayton's gun falls silent. I look behind me fearing the worst, but he's merely out of ammo. He chucks the gun over his shoulder and catches up to us.

'We're not going to make it to the dam!' He yells. 'Run to the lake!'

The rain starts up again as the four of us change direction. Bullets zip into our grassy footprints and ricochet off boulders. The clouds shift over us with a roar. A second later it's as if we've gone under a bridge: the rain just stops. I look over my shoulder and see that just a few paces back, the rain still falls heavy and hard. The wind picks up significantly, and suddenly

the Mogadorians behind us are stuck in the worst rainstorm I've ever seen. They completely disappear in a blur.

Our shoes slip over the sand on the shore, and Ella and Crayton dive into the water headfirst.

'I can't do it, Marina,' Héctor says, stopping before his feet reach the water.

I drop my Chest and grab his arm and say, 'I can fix you, Héctor. You can make it.'

'It wouldn't make any difference. I don't know how to swim.'

'I'm Marina of the sea, Héctor. Remember?' I allow the iciness to spread from my fingertips to the bullet hole in his arm. I watch it turn from black and gray and red to a tan patch of wrinkled skin. I quickly concentrate on the bite wound on his stomach beneath his shirt, and Héctor suddenly stands up straight with energy. I look into his eyes. 'As the Queen of the sea, I will swim with you.'

'But you have that,' Héctor says, pointing at the Chest.

'You'll have to hold it then,' I say, dropping it into his arms.

We jog into the water until our feet no longer touch the lake floor, and then I wrap my right arm around Héctor's chest and paddle with my left. Héctor hugs the Chest to his stomach, and he floats on his back, his head just above water. Ella and Crayton tread water in the middle of the lake, and I pull Héctor towards them.

The clouds overhead dissipate, shrinking into a hundred wispy lines of gray in the sky. The advancing Mogadorians are no longer a blur in a rainstorm, and the moment they can see they charge at the lake with dozens of krauls yipping in front of them.

A tiny black speck falls from above as the last cloud disappears, and the closer the speck gets, the more it appears to be a human.

Wearing a large blue pendant around her neck, she lands on the shore, rippling the sand. It's a strikingly beautiful girl with raven-colored hair; and the second I see her I know she's the one I've been dreaming of, the one I painted on the cave's wall.

'She's one of us!' I shout.

The girl looks around, we make eye contact, and then she vanishes a moment later. I'm shocked, crushed, believing I must have imagined her.

'Where'd she go?' Ella asks.

The moment I realize Ella saw her, too, that I hadn't imagined her, I watch as the two nearest krauls are somehow yanked backwards in the air. They're hovering, yipping and snarling at something behind them, and then they slam into each other until they fall limp. One kraul goes sailing into the legs of two soldiers, and the other is swung in the air, connecting with other krauls and soldiers.

'Invisibility. She has the Legacy of invisibility.' Crayton breathes.

She's invisible? I'm amazed and jealous at the same

time, but most of all I'm grateful. Every kraul that touches the water is yanked backwards by an unseen hand and slammed into the hard sand or a Mogadorian soldier. A dropped cannon rises from the grass and starts firing in all directions. Kraul after kraul is destroyed. Dozens of Mogadorians burst into clouds of ash.

Cannon blasts come from the other side of the lake, and I spin to see twenty or more Mogadorians wading in up to their waists. Rays of light hit the water all around us, creating enough steam that I can barely see Héctor in front of me.

'Ella?' I shout.

'Over here!' she yells from my left.

'Take Héctor.'

She wraps her arm around Héctor's chest. 'Why?'

'Because I'm not going to stay out here while that girl fights all by herself. This is my war, too.'

Before anyone can stop me, I sink below the surface and the water instantly tickles my lungs. I swim deeper until the green-blue color of the lake becomes gray. I see the hulking body of Olivia below me; she's lying lifeless on the lake floor, clouds of blood billowing from the hundreds of bite wounds on her back.

I head towards the opposite shore and after a minute I can see the legs of the Mogadorians. I swim next to the one farthest on the left. I plant my feet in the muddy bottom and launch myself out of the water. The Mogadorian doesn't have enough time to react as I toss him towards the middle of the lake with my

mind. I float his cannon into my hands, shoot him, and never let go of the trigger. The Mogadorians along the lake burst into ash, and when I've killed them all, I aim towards the hundreds near the vehicles.

There's movement in the water behind me and I'm too slow; a kraul jumps and sinks its teeth into my side. The pain is immediate and horrible, as if someone was holding a hot branding iron to my ribs. The beast whips me headfirst into the water and then against the sand of the shore. I catch my breath and scream as it arcs me back over and into the water again. I'm sure this is how I will die, but suddenly the kraul's mouth widens and releases me. I fall onto my stomach on the shore and watch as the kraul's mouth continues to widen until I hear bones snapping. The raven-haired girl materializes before my eyes, her hands on the beast's quivering lips. She looks back at me before yanking the jaws completely vertical, killing the kraul.

'Are you okay?' the girl asks me.

I lift up my shirt and place a hand on my wound. 'I will be in a second.'

She ducks a blast from a cannon. 'Good. What number are you?'

'Seven.'

'I'm Six,' she says before vanishing.

The iciness spreads from my fingers over my body, but I know I won't be able to heal myself completely before the oncoming wave of Mogadorian soldiers reaches me. I roll into the lake and stay underwater.

My wound is almost healed when I rise above the surface.

Number Six is on top of one of the armored Humvees with a glowing sword. She's fighting several soldiers at once: hacking off body parts, blocking cannon fire with her blade, using telekinesis to aim a floating cannon high above her so it blasts through dozens of Mogadorians on the formation's edge. She then hurls her sword into a crowd, impaling three soldiers at once. Number Six grabs the large gun mounted on top of the vehicle and mows down dozens of Mogadorians in seconds.

There are only twenty or thirty soldiers left. Maybe four krauls. Number Six holds one hand over her head while the gun in the other shoots and destroys the Humvees along the shore. Dark clouds form over the mountains and bolts of lightning crack and split the ground near her. The Mogadorians show fear for the first time, and I watch a few drop their weapons and run towards the woods.

'Out of the water!' I yell, fearful of the lightning. Ella drags Héctor to the edge of the lake and Crayton follows.

I reach the shore near Number Six and pick up two cannons. I struggle to keep my footing as I press both triggers, turning more soldiers to ash, destroying two of the krauls. An injured soldier hiding behind a wrecked Humvee tosses a grenade at Number Six's back, but I'm able to shoot it in the air. The explosion

rotates Number Six and the mounted gun, and a moment later the injured soldier is nothing but ash.

I can't keep my eyes off of Number Six. Her strength is mesmerizing. The blue pendant bounces around as the gun in her one hand cuts down more and more soldiers. She rotates to her left and blows a kraul into bits, and then she rotates to her right and takes out several more Mogadorians with a bolt of lightning.

The valley is bright and smoky. It's damp and charred. I look around me and can't believe that victory will be ours in just a matter of seconds. Crayton races over and I toss him one of my guns, and instantly he's killing soldiers retreating into the woods. Héctor runs with my Chest, and soon he and Ella stand behind me. I nod towards Number Six and smile at my friends, thinking that the worst is over; but that's when Ella raises her eyes over my head and her face turns white.

'Pikens!' Ella yells.

Four of the horned monsters run down the mountainside at full speed. Directly below them, Number Six is preoccupied with the few remaining soldiers and the kraul. I uproot as many silver firs as I can and send them like rockets. Four hit the lead one and it falls backwards into the path of the other three, and it's crushed and killed in the stampede.

'Number Six!' I shout. She hears me, and I point to the pikens rumbling down into the valley. She spins with the gun and blows the knees off the monster on the left. It tumbles down faster than the other two can

run, and Number Six jumps from the Humvee a moment before the dead piken flattens it with an echoing crunch.

Crayton and I shoot our cannons at the other two, but they're too fast, splitting up when they reach the valley floor. The clouds roar when Number Six stands, and an enormous bolt of lightning crashes into one of the pikens, cutting off its arm. It bellows and falls to its knees, but quickly regains its balance and charges ahead with blood spurting from its side. The other piken dodges Crayton's fire and rushes in from the other direction. We all run towards Number Six, but Héctor is too slow with my Chest in his arms. The piken closes in, and before I can help, the one-armed monster reaches down and snatches Héctor and my Chest in its fist.

'No!' I scream. 'Héctor!'

I'm in such shock that when the piken throws a lifeless Héctor and my Chest into the lake, I don't use my telekinesis to stop either from sinking.

Number Six has killed the other piken. She turns towards us now and holds both hands up to the sky. A lightning bolt severs the monster's head from its body.

For the first time all day, there is silence. I lean into Number Six, look at Ella and Crayton and the fire and destruction behind them, and I know that these quiet moments are about to become rare in my life.

'Your Chest, Marina,' Crayton says. 'You have to go get it.'

I turn to Number Six and hug her. 'Thank you. Thank you, Number Six.'

'I'm sure we'll get a chance to do it again sometime.' She wraps her arms around my shoulders. 'And just call me Six.'

'I'm Marina. This is Crayton and Ella. She's Number Ten.'

Ella steps forward and shrinks to her seven-year-old body. She extends her small hand towards Six, who has her mouth open, speechless.

Crayton starts to explain Ella and the second ship to Six as I walk into the lake. I feel its coolness for the first time. I swim to the middle and dive, descending until the water is devoid of any light and my feet touch the muddy floor. I circle the bottom until I see my Chest. I rock it back and forth to dislodge it from the mud's suction. Swimming with one arm, I start to ascend. When the water turns blue, I see Héctor's body and wrap my other arm around his waist.

Ella and Crayton stand with Six on the shore. I drop the Chest and slap my wet hands on Héctor's shin, arm, neck, all around his crushed back, hoping and praying the icy feeling will arrive in my fingers.

'He's dead,' Crayton says, pulling on my shoulders.

I don't give up. Hating myself for not trying the same thing on Adelina, I touch Héctor's face. I run my hand through his gray hair. I even levitate him a few centimeters off the sand and try it all over again, but it's true. He's gone.

33

I'm hovering over grass. I'm floating over a river. I feel wretched and stiff, and every time I dare to open my eyes, I'm either bouncing over a log or gliding up a rocky hill. There's a constant noise, and it takes me several minutes to realize it's the sound of Bernie Kosar's hooves. I'm draped over his back and we're moving quickly through the mountains.

'You awake?' Nine asks. I raise my head to see him sitting behind me, both of our Chests under his arms.

'I don't know what I am,' I say, closing my eyes. 'What . . . what happened?'

'You ran right into the blue stuff. That's the last thing on Earth, or Lorien, or anywhere, you want to do.' He sounds pissed, like I just tore him away from his own birthday party.

'What about Setrákus Ra?' I ask.

'Somewhere in the mountain, the coward. I couldn't find another way in. And I looked.'

I push myself up BK's hide in a panic. 'Where's Sam?'

'Not a chance, Four. Your buddy is either long gone, or he's hanging upside down staring at the wrong end of a knife.'

I vomit. Bernie Kosar quickly lowers himself so I can

slide off his back, and then I vomit some more. Nine tries to explain the sickness will go away soon, that he's gone through it several times when he tried to escape his cell, that the healing stone seems to be powerless against the force field's effects, but I'm too dizzy with visions of Sam being tortured to listen. My sickness is from my betrayal, not from some Mogadorian force field. I don't think I'll ever be able to forgive myself. It's my fault he went in there, and it's my fault he was left behind. I turned my back on my best friend.

'We have to go back,' I say. 'Sam would go back for me.'

'Not a chance. Not yet. You're too much of a mess and like you said before, we need numbers.'

I pull myself to my feet but fall onto my hands and knees almost immediately. 'You don't even know where we are.'

'We're a couple of miles from your car,' Nine says. He must see the confusion on my face, because he smiles and pats Bernie Kosar's back. 'Turns out I can talk to animals. Who knew? Bernie Kosar here is leading the way. Let's jet.'

I'm too weak to protest and I climb back up. Bernie Kosar gallops as fast as he can, his belly brushing the tops of shrubs and felled trees as he hurdles us over obstacles. My body aches and I clutch his side as we zig-zag up and down the mountains and hills, splashing through two fast-moving rivers. The stars slowly reveal themselves, high in the sky, and I know that one of them, far, far away, is the slight glimmer of Lorien's own sun, shining its bright light upon a hibernating planet.

‘So, what’s our next move?’ Nine asks as we trot among the shadows.

I’m silent, wondering what Henri would say our next move would be. I wonder what kind of look would be on his face. Would he beam with pride over me retrieving the Chests, rescuing a member of the Garde and killing so many Mogs in the process, or would he be disappointed in me for not taking on the leader when I had the chance, and for leaving Sam behind?

Visions of Sam locked behind one of those steel doors come to me every few seconds, and I watch my tears glide down BK’s neck. I hate to think it, but I’d rather he die than be tortured for information about me.

I try to blame Sarah for turning us in to the police, but I can only blame myself for contacting her when everyone told me not to. I keep quiet and dig my heels into Bernie Kosar’s hide and he picks up the pace.

Six is somewhere in Spain, hopefully with another member of the Garde. Part of me wants to get on a plane, to go directly to her, but with my escape from a federal facility and my face still on the FBI’s Most Wanted List, I don’t see how it’s possible.

We make it to the SUV, and I painfully dismount. I unlock the back door and Nine quietly loads both Chests into the trunk. Crawling across the backseat, disgusted with myself, I ask Nine if he’ll drive.

‘I was hoping you’d ask,’ Nine replies. I hand him the keys and feel the engine come to life.

Something is under my body, and I shift to my side to

find Sam's dad's glasses. I hold them above my head, and I let the moon reflect in the lenses. I suck in a deep breath and whisper, 'We'll see each other again soon, Sam. I promise.' And then, when I think things can't get much worse, it hits me almost harder than the blue force field. 'Oh shit! Six's address for when we meet. It was in Sam's pocket. I'm so stupid! How are we going to find each other now?'

Over his shoulder, Nine says, 'Don't worry, Four. Things are happening for a reason. If we're supposed to meet up with Six or Five or whoever, we will. And if Sam is supposed to still be a part of all this, he will be.'

Bernie Kosar jumps into the backseat in his beagle form and licks my cheek. I pat his head and let out a long-drawn sigh, in utter disbelief that after everything that's gone wrong in the last forty-eight hours, I've also managed to lose the address Six had written down. I look out the window to see the wind is blowing to the north, and I wonder if it might be telling me something, or, at the very least, pointing me in the right direction as Six believes it's done for her.

'Head north,' I say. 'I think north would be good.'

'You got it, boss.' Nine steps on the gas and I look over at Bernie Kosar, who has curled up and fallen asleep.

We bury Héctor's body at the bottom of the dam, where the white concrete meets the grass.

'He once told me that the key to change is letting go of fear,' I say, looking into the eyes of Ella, Crayton

and Six. 'I don't know if I've let go of fear just yet, but the change is happening. It's definitely happening. And I can only hope that you all can help me through it.'

'We're a team,' Ella says. 'Of course we will.'

After we say our good-byes, we climb the dam's ladder. We stand on top of the dam, peering down into the valley and the lake. On the other side of the dam is a series of locks holding back a much larger lake, and I can't help but think it's a metaphor for the way I'm feeling right now. In front of me lies my past, small and distant and dotted with carnage, threatened to be flooded at any time. Behind me and my fellow Garde members, the future is massive and held back by unnatural forces.

I turn to Six and ask, 'Do you know a John Smith in Ohio? Is he one of us?'

Her smile is wide. 'I do know John. He's Number Four.'

I reach for Ella's hand on my right and Six's on my left, and we stand there letting the mountain breeze whip our hair around our faces. Ella looks over at Six and asks, 'Can we go to America?'

'The charm is broken. I don't see why we can't all be together now.' Six shrugs, turning back to the lake below.

Crayton joins us. 'I hate to say this, but it's the calm before the storm, ladies. We're winning far too many battles for them to ease up now. You're getting too strong for them, and they'll be throwing everything they have at you. No more small armies with a few

hundred soldiers and a couple of clumsy beasts. Their ruler will be here soon. Setrákus Ra.'

'Who?' I ask.

'Setrákus Ra.' Crayton shakes his head. 'And I don't think we're ready for him.'

'Then it's settled,' I say. 'We're going to Ohio to be with John Smith.'

'West Virginia, actually. In exactly two weeks,' Six says.

'I'm not sure that's wise just yet.' Crayton begins walking away. 'We need to gather the others first.'

Six walks after him. 'That sounds good and all, but I have no idea where they are.'

'I do,' Crayton says, not turning around. 'I also know where our Chimæras are. If Setrákus Ra thinks this is going to be easy, he's got another thing coming.'

We follow him, taking the first of many steps down the opposite side of the dam.

The battle continues in the third thrilling instalment of The Lorien Legacies:

The Rise of Nine

Read on to discover what happens next . . .

1

I shake my head when I unfold my plane ticket, unsure if Crayton bought me this seat on purpose, or if it's just a coincidence. It's seat 6A, and I'm half expecting Marina to sit behind me in row seven, and Ella to make her way back to row ten. Instead the two girls drop quietly down beside me and lean towards the aisle to study every person entering the plane. When you know you are being hunted you are constantly on guard, and we never know if the Mogadorians are following us or if they've found us. I raise the shade to watch the ground crew hustle back and forth under the plane and see if anything looks suspicious, the city of Barcelona a faint outline in the distance. Crayton will board last, only after he feels the flight is absolutely secure.

Marina's knee bounces up and down furiously against mine. On top of everything else – the battle at the lake, the death of her Cêpan and finding her Chest – it's her first time on an airplane and she's nervous. It's actually the first time in almost ten years since she's left the town where she spent her childhood. A town and a convent that got destroyed by the Mogs. Thankfully there was no video of the incident or

there's no way we'd be able to leave. Right now we just look like three students going away on a trip.

'Everything okay?' I ask. My newly blond hair falls into my face and startles me. I keep forgetting I dyed it this morning. It's just one of the many changes to happen in the last forty-eight hours.

'Everyone looks fine,' Marina whispers, keeping her eyes on the crowded aisle. 'We're safe, as far as I can tell.'

'Good, but that's not what I meant.' I gently set my foot on hers and she stops bouncing her knee. She offers me a quick apologetic smile before looking back to study the passengers. A few seconds later, I feel her knee bouncing against mine again.

Marina's been locked up in an isolated orphanage with a Cêpan who refused to not only train her, but to remind her why she's here on Earth in the first place. I'm doing my best to help her, to show her how to control her strength and when to use her developing Legacies. I'm also trying to show her that it's okay to trust me. Not only did she just lose her best friend Héctor back at the lake, but like me she lost her Cêpan right before her eyes, something that will scar us both forever. The Mogadorians will pay for what they've done to those we've loved, on Earth and on Lorien. It's my personal mission to destroy every last one of them, and I'll be sure Marina gets her revenge too.

'How is it down there, Six?' Ella asks over Marina.

The five men below the plane begin to clear away their equipment, conducting a few last-minute jobs. 'So far, so good.'

My seat is directly over the wing, which is comforting. On more than one occasion I've had to help a pilot out of a jam. Once, over southern Mexico, I used my telekinesis to push the plane a dozen degrees to the right, moments before crashing into the side of a mountain. Last year I got 124 passengers safely through a vicious thunderstorm in Kansas by surrounding the plane with an impervious cloud of cool air. We shot through the storm unharmed like a bullet through a balloon.

When the ground crew disappears from the tarmac, I kick my backpack under the seat in front of me and wait impatiently for Crayton to board the plane. Every seat has been filled but the one behind Ella. I look out at the wing, checking for anything out of the ordinary.

'Six?' Marina asks. I hear her buckle and unbuckle her seat belt nervously.

I look away from the wing and accidentally kick my backpack again. Crayton bought it for me at the airport. The three of us need to look like normal teenagers, Crayton says, like students on a field trip. That's why there's an open biology text book on my lap.

'Yeah?' I respond.

'You've flown before, right?'

Marina is a year older than I am, and with her almond face and with her new haircut, with it falling just below

her shoulders, she can pass for an adult. Right now, however, she bites her nails and pulls knees up to her chest like a scared child.

'Yes,' I say. 'It's not so bad. In fact, it's kind of awesome.'

Sitting on the plane, I can't help but think of my Cêpan, Katarina. When I was nine, after a close call in a Cleveland alley with a Mogadorian that left us both shaken and covered in a thick layer of ash, Katarina moved us to Southern California. Our crumbling two-story bungalow was near the beach, practically in the shadows of Los Angeles International Airport. A hundred planes roared overhead every hour, interrupting Katarina's teaching, drowning out my play dates with my only friend, a skinny girl next door named Ashley.

I lived under those airplanes for seven months. They were my alarm clock in the morning, screaming directly over my bed as the sun rose, and at night they were ominous ghosts telling me to stay awake, to be prepared to rip off my sheets and jump in the car in a matter of seconds. And because Katarina didn't let me stray far from the house the airplanes also filled my afternoons. On one of these afternoons as an enormous plane shook the lemonade in our plastic cups, Ashley asked, 'Have you ever been on a plane?'

'Not really,' I said.

'What do you mean, "Not really"? You've either been on a plane, or you haven't.'

I remember feeling my face burn with embarrass-

ment. I finally said, 'I've never been on an airplane.' I wanted to elaborate, to tell her that I'd been on something much bigger, much more impressive than a little airplane. That I had come to Earth on a ship from another planet called Lorien and that the trip had covered more than a 100 million miles. I didn't though, because I knew I had to keep the Lorien secret.

Ashley laughed at me and then finished her lemonade. Without saying goodbye, she left to wait for her dad to come home from work.

'Why haven't we ever been on a plane?' I asked Katarina that night as she carefully peered out the blinds of my bedroom window.

'Six,' she said, before correcting herself. 'I mean, Veronica. It's too dangerous for us to travel by plane. We'd be trapped up there. You know what could happen if we were thousands of miles in the air and Mogs followed us on board?'

I knew exactly what could happen – the chaos, the other passengers screaming and ducking under their seats as a couple of huge alien soldiers barreled down the aisle towards us with swords. We would meet them and try to kill them before they killed us. I could see what might happen as we fought, and potentially brought down a plane with innocent passengers, all of whom would die. Still, those possibilities, and others that might happen, didn't stop me from wanting to do something so normal, so human, as fly from one city to the next. My silence the following days must have

cut through Katarina, because to my surprise she bought us two round-trip tickets to Denver. I couldn't wait to tell Ashley.

'Do you know how stupid this is?' Katarina asked as we stood outside the airport on the day of the trip.

'Just once. I just want to do it once,' I said, smiling, knowing it was unfair to ask Katarina for anything more than she'd already given me. Her entire life revolved around keeping me safe and making me strong. For me to ask for something on top of that was selfish. And I knew it, but I couldn't stop myself. 'We don't even have to get off the plane if you don't want to. We'll just stay on and fly right back here.'

Katarina ran her hand through her short black hair. She had dyed and cut it the night before, just after making herself a new I.D. A family of five walked around us on the curb, dragging heavy luggage, and to my left a tearful mother said goodbye to her two young daughters. I wanted nothing more than to join in, to be a part of this everyday scene. 'No,' Katarina finally said. 'We're not going. I'm sorry, Veronica, but it's not worth it.'

We walked home in silence, letting the screaming engines of the planes passing overhead speak for us. When we turned the corner of our street, I saw Ashley sitting on her front steps and the humiliation was almost too much to bear. She looked at me walking towards our house and mouthed the word *liar*. And no matter what I said, there was no way I could change

her mind. She thought I'd made up the trip, and the next day she told all the other kids at school. From that point forward I was known as a liar. And it hurt because it wasn't true. We were supposed to go on the trip. I just couldn't explain why we didn't.

And the irony in the whole situation was that I was a liar. All I had ever done since landing on Earth was tell lies about my name, where I was from, where my father was, why I couldn't stay the night at another girl's house in fear of being hunted and killed by unspeakable monsters. Lying was all I knew and what kept me alive. But when Ashley called me a liar the *one* time I thought I was telling someone the truth, I got so angry and upset that I walked to my room and slammed the door, and without thinking, I punched the wall. To my surprise, my fist went straight through.

Katarina ripped open my bedroom door with a kitchen knife in her hand, thinking it must be Mogs. When she saw what I had done to the wall, she lowered the blade and smiled said, 'Today's not the day you get on a plane, but it is the day you're going to start your training.'

Seven years later, sitting in this plane with Marina and Ella and nowhere to run, I can hear Katarina's voice in my head. I've flown dozens of times now, and everything has gone fine, though this is the first time I've done it without using my invisibility Legacy to sneak on board. Katarina would never have allowed this, but as guilty as that makes me feel, I know I'm

much stronger now. And I'm getting stronger by the day. If a couple of Mog soldiers charged at me from the front of the plane, they wouldn't be dealing with a meek young girl. After all the events of the last years, I've become a soldier, a warrior, someone they should fear instead of hunt.

Marina lets go of her knees and sits up straight, releasing a long breath. In a barely audible voice, she says, 'I'm scared. I want to get in the air.'

'Stay with me and you'll be just fine,' I say in a low voice.

She smiles, and I smile back at her. On the battlefield yesterday in Spain, when she was pushed to her limits, Marina proved herself to be a strong ally with amazing Legacies. She can breathe underwater, see in the dark and heal the sick and wounded. Like me, she's also developed telekinesis. And because we're so close in order – I'm Number Six and she's Number Seven – our bond is special. When the Charm still held and we had to be killed in order, the Mogadorians would have had to get through me if they wanted to get to her. And they never would have gotten through me.

Ella sits silently on the other side of Marina. As we wait for Crayton, she opens the biology book on her lap and stares at the pages. I've never seen someone concentrate so hard to keep up a charade, and I'm about to tell her she doesn't actually have to read the book, but then I realize she's not reading at all. Ella is trying to turn the page with her mind, but nothing's

happening. She's still young. Her next Legacy will come in time.

Ella was on another ship, one I didn't know existed until John saw it in his visions. She was just hours old at the time, which means she's almost twelve now. Crayton says he is her unofficial Cêpan because with the Mogadorians attacking and Ella being just born, there wasn't time for him to be officially appointed to her, but like all of our Cêpans he has a duty to help Ella develop her Legacies. In their ship was also a small herd of Chimaera, Loric animals capable of shifting forms and battling alongside us.

Even though Ella's only developed one Legacy – she's what Crayton calls an Aeternus, someone with the ability to move back and forth between ages – I'm happy she's here. After Number Three died, only six of us remained. With Ella, we're seven. Lucky number seven, if you believe in luck. I don't, though. I believe in strength.

Finally, Crayton squeezes down the aisle, carrying a black briefcase. He's wearing fake glasses and an oversized brown suit. Under his strong chin is a blue bow tie. He's supposed to look like our teacher.

'Hello, girls,' he says, stopping next to us.

'Hi, Professor Collins,' Ella whispers.

'It's a full flight,' Marina says. That's code for everyone on board looks okay. There is no imminent danger.

To tell him everything on the ground appears normal, I say, 'I'm going to try to sleep.'

He nods and takes his seat directly behind Ella. Then he leans forward between Marina and Ella and says, 'Use your time on the plane wisely, please. Study hard.'

That means not to let our guards down.

I didn't know what to think of Crayton when we first met. He's stern and quick-tempered, but his heart seems to be in the right place. And from years of sitting in front of the computer while watching over Ella, his knowledge of the world and current events is incredible. Official or not, he has taken his Cêpan role seriously. He says he would die for any one of us. Anything to save Lorien, he says. Anything to defeat the Mogadorians, anything to exact our revenge. I believe him on all counts.

Yesterday, on top of the dam overlooking the carnage at the lake, Crayton told us that Setrákus Ra, the Mogadorian leader, would be on Earth soon, if he wasn't already. That Setrákus' arrival was a sign that the Mogadorians understood we were a threat, and that they were going to step up their campaign to kill us. Setrákus is more or less invincible. The only Lorien that could fight him was Pittacus Lore, but yesterday Crayton told us that one of us holds all the same powers that Pittacus did. 'I've read about a boy who seems to have extraordinary powers in India. High up in the Himalayas. Some believe him to be the Hindi god Vishnu reincarnated, others believe the boy is an alien imposter with the power to physically alter his form.'

'Like me, Papa?' Ella asked. Her father-daughter

relationship with Crayton took me by surprise, and I couldn't help but feel jealous.

'He's not changing ages, Ella. He's changing into beasts and other beings. The more I read about him, the more I believe he is a member of the Garde, and the more I believe he may have all of the Legacies, and be able to fight and kill Setrákus. We need to find him. We need to find him as soon as possible.'

I don't want to be on a wild goose chase for another member of the Garde right now. I know where John is, or where he is supposed to be, and I can hear Katarina's voice again, telling me we should connect with John first before anything else. It's the least risky move. Certainly less risky than going on Crayton's hunch and rumors on the Internet.

'It could be a trap,' I had said. 'What if those stories have been planted just for us to find?'

'I understand your concern, Six, but I'm the master of planting stories on the Internet. There are far too many sources pointing to this boy in India. He's been there for a long time. He hasn't been running. He hasn't been hiding. He's just being, and he appears to be very powerful. If he *is* one of you, then we must get to him before the Mogadorians do. We'll go to America to meet up with Number Four as soon as this trip is over,' Crayton said.

'Promise?' Marina asked.

The captain's voice comes through the speakers. 'We're about to take off.'

I dream of redirecting the plane towards West Virginia and John and Sam. Images of John held in a prison cell keep entering my mind. I never should have told him about the Mog base in the mountain, but John wanted to get his Chest back and there was no way I could convince him to leave it behind.

The plane rolls down the runway and Marina grabs my wrist. 'I really wish Héctor was here. He'd have something smart to say right now to make me feel better.'

'It's okay,' Ella says, holding her other hand. 'You have us.'

'And I'll work on something smart to say,' I offer.

'Thanks,' Marina laughs. I let her nails dig into my wrist. I give her a supportive smile, and a minute later we're airborne.

PENGUIN BOOKS

The Rise of Nine

Pittacus Lore is Lorien's ruling Elder. He has been on Earth for the last twelve years preparing for the war that will decide Earth's fate. His whereabouts are unknown.

The Power of Six

PITTACUS LORE

PENGUIN BOOKS

PENGUIN BOOKS

THE POWER OF SIX

Pittacus Lore is Lorien's ruling elder. He has been on Earth for the last twelve years preparing for the war that will decide Earth's fate. His whereabouts are unknown.

The Rise of Nine

PITTACUS LORE

PENGUIN BOOKS

PENGUIN BOOKS

Published by the Penguin Group
Penguin Books Ltd, 80 Strand, London WC2R 0RL, England
Penguin Group (USA) Inc., 375 Hudson Street, New York, New York 10014, USA
Penguin Group (Canada), 90 Eglinton Avenue East, Suite 700, Toronto, Ontario, Canada M4P 2Y3
(a division of Pearson Penguin Canada Inc.)
Penguin Ireland, 25 St Stephen's Green, Dublin 2, Ireland (a division of Penguin Books Ltd)
Penguin Group (Australia), 707 Collins Street, Melbourne, Victoria 3008, Australia
(a division of Pearson Australia Group Pty Ltd)
Penguin Books India Pvt Ltd, 11 Community Centre, Panchsheel Park, New Delhi – 110 017, India
Penguin Group (NZ), 67 Apollo Drive, Rosedale, Auckland 0632, New Zealand
(a division of Pearson New Zealand Ltd)
Penguin Books (South Africa) (Pty) Ltd, Block D, Rosebank Office Park,
181 Jan Smuts Avenue, Parktown North, Gauteng 2193, South Africa

Penguin Books Ltd, Registered Offices: 80 Strand, London WC2R 0RL, England

www.penguin.com

First published in the United States of America by Harper,
an imprint of HarperCollins Publishers 2012
First published in Great Britain by Michael Joseph and Razorbill 2012
Published in Penguin Books 2013

010

Set in 12.5/14.75pt Garamond MT Std
Typeset by Jouve (UK), Milton Keynes
Printed in Great Britain by Clays Ltd, St Ives plc

PAPERBACK ISBN: 978–0–141–04786–7
OPEN MARKET PAPERBACK ISBN: 978–1–405–91288–4

The Rise of Nine

I

6A. Seriously? I look at the boarding pass in my hand, its large type announcing my seat assignment, and wonder if Crayton chose this seat on purpose. It could be a coincidence, but the way things have gone recently, I am not a big believer in coincidences. I wouldn't be surprised if Marina sat down behind me in row seven, and Ella made her way back to row ten. But, no, the two girls drop down beside me without saying a word, and join me in studying each person boarding the plane. Being hunted, you are constantly on guard. Who knows when the Mogadorians might appear.

Crayton will board last, after he's watched to see who else gets on the plane, and only once he feels the flight is absolutely secure.

I raise the window shade and watch the ground crew hustle back and forth under the plane. The city of Barcelona is a faint outline in the distance.

Marina's knee bounces furiously up and down next to mine. The battle against an army of Mogadorians yesterday at the lake, the death of her Cêpan, finding her Chest – and now, it's the first time in almost ten years that she's left the town where she spent her childhood. She's nervous.

'Everything okay?' I ask. My newly blonde hair falls into my face and startles me. I forgot I dyed it this morning. It's just one of many changes in the last forty-eight hours.

'Everyone looks normal,' Marina whispers, keeping her eyes on the crowded aisle. 'We're safe, as far as I can tell.'

'Good, but that's not what I meant.' I gently set my foot on hers and she stops bouncing her knee. She offers me a quick apologetic smile before returning to her close watch of each boarding passenger. A few seconds later, her knee starts bouncing again. I just shake my head.

I feel sorry for Marina. She was locked up in an isolated orphanage with a Cêpan who refused to train her. Her Cêpan had lost sight of why we are here on Earth in the first place. I'm doing my best to help her, to fill in the gaps. I can train her to learn how to control her strength and when to use her developing Legacies. But first I'm trying to show her that it's okay to trust me.

The Mogadorians will pay for what they've done. For taking so many whom we've loved, here on Earth and on Lorien. It's my personal mission to destroy every last one of them, and I'll be sure Marina gets her revenge too. Not only did she just lose her best friend, Héctor, back at the lake, but, like me, her Cêpan was killed right in front of her. We will both carry that with us forever.

'How is it down there, Six?' Ella asks, leaning over Marina.

I turn back towards the window. The men below the plane begin to clear away their equipment, conducting a few last-minute checks. 'So far, so good.'

My seat is directly over the wing, which is comforting to me. On more than one occasion I've had to use my Legacies to help a pilot out of a jam. Once, over southern Mexico, I used my telekinesis to push the plane a dozen degrees to the right, only seconds before crashing into the side of a mountain. Last year I got 124 passengers safely through a vicious thunderstorm over Kansas by surrounding the plane with an impervious cloud of cool air. We shot through the storm like a bullet through a balloon.

When the ground crew moves on to the next plane, I follow Ella's gaze towards the front of the aisle. We're both impatient for Crayton to board. That will mean everything is okay, at least for now. Every seat is full but the one behind Ella. Where is he? I glance out at the wing again, scanning the area for anything out of the ordinary.

I lean down and shove my backpack under my seat. It's practically empty, so it folds down easily. Crayton bought it for me at the airport. The three of us need to look like normal teenagers, he says, like high school students on a field trip. That's why there's a biology textbook on Ella's lap.

'Six?' Marina asks. I hear her buckle and unbuckle her seat belt nervously.

'Yeah?' I respond.

'You've flown before, right?'

Marina is only a year older than I am. But with her solemn, thoughtful eyes and her new, sophisticated haircut that falls just below her shoulders, she can easily pass for an adult. Right now, however, she bites her nails and pulls her knees up to her chest like a scared child.

'Yes,' I say. 'It's not so bad. In fact, once you relax, it's kind of awesome.'

Sitting there on the plane, my thoughts turn in the direction of my own Cêpan, Katarina. Not that I ever flew with her. But when I was nine years old, we had a close call in a Cleveland alley with a Mogadorian that left us both shaken and covered in a thick layer of ash. Katarina moved us to Southern California after that. Our crumbling, two-story bungalow was near the beach, practically in the shadow of Los Angeles International Airport. A hundred planes roared overhead every hour, always interrupting Katarina's teaching, as well as the little free time I had to spend with my only friend, a skinny girl next door named Ashley.

I lived under those airplanes for seven months. They were my alarm clock in the morning, screaming directly over my bed as the sun rose. At night they were ominous ghosts telling me to stay awake, to be prepared to rip off my sheets and jump in the car in a matter of seconds. Since Katarina didn't let me stray far from the house, the airplanes were also the sound track of my afternoons.

On one of those afternoons, as the vibrations from an enormous plane overhead shook the lemonade in our plastic cups, Ashley said, 'Me and my mom are going to visit my grandparents next month. I can't wait! Have you ever been on a plane?' Ashley was always talking about all the places she went and things she did with her family. She knew Katarina and I stayed close to home and she liked to brag.

'Not really,' I said.

'What do you mean, "Not really"? You've either been on a plane, or you haven't. Just admit it. You haven't.'

I remember feeling my face burn with embarrassment. Her challenge hit its mark. I finally said, 'No, I've never been on an airplane.' I wanted to tell her I've been on something much bigger, something much more impressive than a little airplane. I wanted her to know I came to Earth on a ship from another planet called Lorien and the trip had covered more than 100 million miles. I didn't, though, because I knew I had to keep Lorien secret.

Ashley laughed at me. Without saying goodbye, she left to wait for her dad to come home from work.

'Why haven't we ever been on a plane?' I asked Katarina that night as she peered out the blinds of my bedroom window.

'Six,' she said, turning to me before correcting herself. 'I mean, Veronica. It's too dangerous for us to travel by plane. We'd be trapped up there. You know what could happen if we were thousands of miles in the air and *then* found out Mogs had followed us on board?'

I knew exactly what could happen. I could picture the chaos, the other passengers screaming and ducking under their seats as a couple of huge alien soldiers barreled down the aisle with swords. But that didn't stop me from wanting to do something so normal, so human, as to fly on a plane from one city to the next. I'd spent all my time on Earth unable to do the things other kids my age took for granted. We rarely even stayed in one place long enough for me to meet other kids, let alone make friends – Ashley was the first girl Katarina even allowed over to our house. Sometimes, like in California, I didn't even attend school, if Katarina thought it was safer.

I knew why all this was necessary, of course. Usually, I didn't let it bother me. But Katarina could tell that Ashley's superior attitude had gotten under my skin. My silence the following days must have cut through her, because to my surprise she bought us two round-trip airline tickets to Denver. The destination didn't matter – she knew I just wanted the experience.

I couldn't wait to tell Ashley.

But on the day of the trip, standing outside the airport, Katarina hesitated. She seemed nervous. She ran her hand through her short black hair. She had dyed and cut it the night before, just before making herself a new ID. A family of five walked around us on the curb, dragging heavy luggage, and to my left a tearful mother said good-bye to her two young daughters. I wanted nothing more than to join in, to be a part of this everyday scene. Katarina watched everyone around us while I fidgeted impatiently by her side.

'No,' Katarina finally said. 'We're not going. I'm sorry, Veronica, but it's not worth it.'

We drove home in silence, letting the screaming engines of the planes passing overhead speak for us. When we got out of the car on our street, I saw Ashley sitting on her front steps. She looked at me walking towards our house and mouthed the word *liar*. The humiliation was almost too much to bear.

But, really, I *was* a liar. It's ironic. Lying was all I had done since I'd arrived on Earth. My name, where I was from, where my father was, why I couldn't stay the night at another girl's house – lying was all I knew and it was what kept me alive. But when Ashley called me a liar the *one* time I was telling someone the truth, I was unspeakably angry. I stormed up to my room, slammed the door, and punched the wall.

To my surprise, my fist went straight through.

Katarina slammed my door open, wielding a kitchen knife and ready to strike. She thought the noise she'd heard must be Mogs. When she saw what I had done to the wall, she realized that something had changed with me. She lowered the blade and smiled. 'Today's not the day you get on a plane, but it is the day you're going to start your training.'

Seven years later, sitting on this plane with

Marina and Ella, I hear Katarina's voice in my head. 'We'd be trapped up there.' But I'm ready for that possibility now, in ways that Katarina and I weren't.

I've since flown dozens of times, and everything has gone fine. However, this *is* the first time I've done it without using my invisibility Legacy to sneak on board. I know I'm much stronger now. And I'm getting stronger by the day. If a couple of Mog soldiers charged at me from the front of the plane, they wouldn't be dealing with a meek young girl. I know what I'm capable of; I am a soldier now, a warrior. I am someone to fear, not hunt.

Marina lets go of her knees and sits up straight, releasing a long breath. In a barely audible voice, she says, 'I'm scared. I just want to get in the air.'

'You'll be fine,' I say in a low voice.

She smiles, and I smile back at her. Marina proved herself to be a strong ally with amazing Legacies on the battlefield yesterday. She can breathe under water, see in the dark, and heal the sick and wounded. Like all Garde, she also has telekinesis. And because we're so close in order – I'm Number Six and she's Number Seven – our bond is special. When the charm still held and we had to be killed in order, the

Mogadorians would have had to get through me before they could get to her. And they never would have gotten through me.

Ella sits silently on the other side of Marina. As we continue to wait for Crayton, she opens the biology book on her lap and stares at the pages. Our charade does not demand this level of concentration and I'm about to lean over and tell her, but then I see she isn't reading at all. She is trying to turn the page with her mind, trying to use telekinesis, but nothing's happening.

Ella is what Crayton calls an Aeternus, someone born with the ability to move back and forth between ages. But she's still young and her Legacies have not yet developed. They will come in their own time, no matter how impatiently she wills them to develop now.

Ella came to Earth on another ship, one I didn't know existed until John Smith, Number Four, told me he saw it in his visions. She was just a baby, which means she's almost twelve now. Crayton says he is her unofficial Cêpan, since there wasn't time for him to be officially appointed to her. He, like all of our Cêpans, has a duty to help Ella develop her Legacies. He told us that there was also a small herd of Chimæra on their ship, Loric animals capable of shifting forms and battling alongside us.

I'm happy she's here. After Numbers One, Two,

and Three died, only six of us remained. With Ella, we number seven. Lucky number seven, if you believe in luck. I don't, though. I believe in strength.

Finally, Crayton squeezes down the aisle, carrying a black briefcase. He's wearing eyeglasses and a brown suit that looks too big for him. Under his strong chin is a blue bow tie. He's supposed to be our teacher.

'Hello, girls,' he says, stopping next to us.

'Hi, Mr Collins,' Ella responds.

'It's a full flight,' Marina says. That's code for everyone on board looks okay. To tell him everything on the ground appears normal, I say, 'I'm going to try to sleep.'

He nods and takes his seat directly behind Ella. Leaning forward between Marina and Ella, he says, 'Use your time on the plane wisely, please. Study hard.'

That means, don't let your guard down.

I didn't know what to think of Crayton when we first met. He's stern and quick tempered, but his heart seems to be in the right place and his knowledge of the world and current events is incredible. Official or not, he has taken his Cêpan role seriously. He says he would die for any one of us. He will do anything to defeat the Mogadorians; anything to exact our revenge. I believe him on all counts.

However, it's with reluctance that I'm on this plane headed to India at all. I wanted to get back to the United States as soon as possible, to get back to John and Sam. But yesterday, standing on top of the dam overlooking the carnage at the lake, Crayton told us that Setrákus Ra, the powerful Mogadorian leader, would be on Earth soon, if he wasn't here already. That Setrákus's arrival was a sign that the Mogadorians understood we were a threat, and we should expect them to step up their campaign to kill us. Setrákus is more or less invincible. Only Pittacus Lore, the most powerful of all the Lorien Elders, would have been able to defeat him. We were horrified. What did that mean for the rest of us then, if he was invincible? When Marina asked this, asked how any of us could possibly stand a chance of defeating him, Crayton told us even more shocking news, knowledge that all the Cêpans had been entrusted with. One of the Garde – one of us – was supposed to hold the same powers as Pittacus. One of us was supposed to grow as strong as he had been, and would be able to beat Setrákus Ra. We just had to hope that that Garde wasn't One, Two, or Three, that it was one of the ones still alive. If so, we had a chance. We just had to wait and see who it was, and hope that these powers showed themselves soon.

Crayton thinks he's found him – the Garde who holds Pittacus' powers.

'I've read about a boy who seems to have extraordinary powers in India,' he told us then. 'He lives high up in the Himalayas. Some believe him to be the Hindu god Vishnu reincarnated, others believe the boy is an alien imposter with the power to physically alter his form.'

'Like me, Papa?' Ella had asked. Their father-daughter relationship took me by surprise. I couldn't help but feel a touch of jealousy – jealousy that she still had her Cêpan, someone to turn to for guidance.

'He's not changing ages, Ella. He's changing into beasts and other beings. The more I read about him, the more I believe he is a member of the Garde, and the more I believe he may be the one to possess all of the Legacies, the one who can fight and kill Setrákus. We need to find him as soon as possible.'

I don't want to be on a wild goose chase for another member of the Garde right now. I know where John is, or where he is supposed to be. I can hear Katarina's voice, urging me to follow my instincts, which are telling me we should connect with John first before anything else. It's the least risky move. Certainly less risky than flying around the world based on Crayton's hunch and rumors on the Internet.

'It could be a trap,' I said. 'What if those stories were planted for us to find so we would do exactly this?'

'I understand your concern, Six, but, trust me, I'm the master of planting stories on the Internet. This is no plant. There are far too many sources pointing to this boy in India. He hasn't been running. He hasn't been hiding. He's just *being*, and he appears to be very powerful. If he *is* one of you, then we must get to him before the Mogadorians do. We'll go to America to meet up with Number Four as soon as this trip is over,' Crayton said.

Marina looked at me. She wanted to find John almost as much as I did – she'd been following the news of his exploits online and she'd had a similar feeling in her gut that he was one of us, a feeling I had confirmed for her. 'Promise?' she asked Crayton. He nodded.

The captain's voice breaks through my reverie. We're about to take off. I want so badly to redirect the plane, to point it towards West Virginia. Towards John and Sam. I hope they're okay. Images of John being held in a prison cell keep entering my mind. I never should have told him about the Mog base in the mountain, but John wanted to get his Chest back and there was no way I could convince him to leave it behind.

The plane taxis down the runway and Marina grabs my wrist. 'I really wish Héctor was here. He'd have something smart to say right now to make me feel better.'

'It's okay,' Ella says, holding Marina's other hand. 'You have us.'

'And I'll work on something smart to say,' I offer.

'Thanks,' Marina says, though it sounds like something between a hiccup and a gulp. I let her nails dig into my wrist. I give her a supportive smile, and a minute later we're airborne.

2

I've been in and out of consciousness for the past two days, rolling back and forth in a hallucinating sickness. The effects from the blue force field outside the Mogadorians' mountain have lingered far longer than Nine told me they would, both mentally and physically. Every few minutes, my muscles seize and sear with pain.

I try to distract myself from the agony by looking around the tiny bedroom of this decaying, abandoned house. Nine couldn't have picked a more disgusting place for us to hide. I can't trust my eyes. I watch the pattern on the yellow wallpaper come to life, the design marching like ants over patches of mold. The cracked ceiling appears to breathe, rising and falling at frightening speeds. A large jagged hole in the wall separates the bedroom and living room, as if someone tossed a sledgehammer through it. Smashed beer cans are strewn around the room, and the baseboards have been torn to shreds by animals. I've been hearing things rustling in the trees outside the house, but I'm too weak to be alarmed. Last night I woke to find a cockroach on my cheek. I barely had the energy to swat it off.

'Hey, Four?' I hear through the hole in the wall. 'You awake or what? It's time for lunch and your food's getting cold.'

I heave myself to my feet. My head spins as I stumble through the doorway into what used to be the living room, and I collapse on the dingy gray carpet. I know Nine's in here, but I can't keep my eyes open long enough to find him. All I want is to lay my head in Sarah's lap. Or in Six's. Either one. I can't think straight.

Something warm hits my shoulder. I roll over to see Nine sitting on the ceiling above me, his long black hair hanging down into the room. He's gnawing on something and his hands are greasy.

'Where are we again?' I ask. The sunlight coming through the windows is too much and I close my eyes. I need more sleep. I need something, anything, to clear my head and regain my strength. My fingers fumble over my blue pendant, hoping to somehow gather energy through it, but it remains cold against my chest.

'The northern part of West Virginia,' Nine says between bites. 'Ran out of gas, remember?'

'Barely,' I whisper. 'Where's Bernie Kosar?'

'Outside. That one is *always* on patrol. He is one cool animal. Tell me, Four, how did *you* of all the Garde end up with him?'

I crawl into the corner of the room and push my back up against a wall. 'BK was with me on Lorien. His name was Hadley back then. I guess Henri thought it would be good to bring him along for the trip.'

Nine throws a tiny bone across the ceiling. 'I had a couple of Chimæras as a kid too. Don't remember their names, but I can still see them running around our house tearing stuff up. They died in the war, protecting my family.' Nine is silent for a moment, clenching his jaw. This is the first time I've seen him act anything other than tough. It's nice to see, even if it's short lived. 'At least, that's what my Cêpan told me, anyway.'

I stare at my bare feet. 'What was your Cêpan's name?'

'Sandor,' he says, standing up on the ceiling. He's wearing my shoes. 'It's weird. I literally can't remember the last time I said his name out loud. Some days, I can barely picture his face.' Nine's voice hardens, and he closes his eyes. 'But that's how it goes, I guess. Whatever. They're the expendable ones.'

His last sentence sends shockwaves through me. 'Henri was not expendable, and neither was Sandor! No Loric was ever expendable. And give me back my shoes!'

Nine kicks my shoes into the middle of the floor, then takes his time walking first along the ceiling and then down the back wall. 'All right, all right. I know he wasn't expendable, man. Sometimes it's just easier to think of him that way, you know? Truth is, Sandor was an amazing Cêpan.' Nine reaches the floor and towers over me. I forgot how tall he is. Intimidating. He shoves a handful of what he's been eating in my face. 'You want some of this or not? Because I'm about to finish it off.'

The sight of it makes my stomach churn. 'What is it?'

'Barbecued rabbit. Nature's finest.'

I don't dare open my mouth to respond, afraid that I might get sick. Instead, I stumble back towards the bedroom, ignoring the laughter that follows me. The bedroom door is so warped it's nearly impossible to close, but I wedge it into the doorframe as tightly as I can. I lie down on the floor, using my sweatshirt as a pillow, and think about how I ended up here, ended up like this. Without Henri. Without Sam. Sam is my best friend, and I can't believe we left him behind. As thoughtful and loyal and supportive as Sam is – traveling and fighting alongside me for the last several months – Nine is so very not. He's reckless, arrogant, selfish and just flat-out rude. I picture Sam, back in the Mog cave, a gun rocking against his shoulder as a dozen Mogadorian soldiers swarmed him. I couldn't get to him. I couldn't save him. I should have fought harder, run faster. I should have ignored Nine and gone back to Sam. He would have done that for me. The immense amount of guilt I feel paralyzes me, until I finally fall asleep.

It's dark. I'm no longer in a house in the mountains with Nine. I no longer feel the painful effects of the blue force field. My head is finally clear, although I don't know where I am, or how I got here. When I shout for help, I can't hear my voice even though I feel my lips moving. I shuffle ahead, hands out in front of me. My palms suddenly start to glow with my Lumen. The light is dim at first, but quickly grows into two powerful beams.

'John.' A hoarse whisper says my name.

I whip my hands around to see where I am, but the light reveals only empty darkness. I'm entering a vision. I angle my palms towards the ground so my Lumen will light my way, and start towards the voice. The hoarse whisper keeps repeating my name over and over. It sounds young and full of fear. Then comes another voice, gruff and staccato, barking orders.

The voices become clearer. It's Sam, my lost friend, and Setrákus Ra, my worst enemy. I can tell I'm nearing the Mogadorian base. I can see the blue force field, the source of so much pain. For some reason, I know it won't hurt me now, and I don't hesitate to pass through it. When I do, it's not my screams I hear, but Sam's. His tortured voice fills my head as I enter the mountain and move through its maze-like tunnels. I see the charred remains of our recent battle, from when I tossed a ball of green lava at the gas tanks at the mountain's bottom, sending a sea of fire raging upwards. I move through the main cavernous hall and its spiraling ledges. I step onto the arched stone bridge Sam and I so recently crossed under the cloak of invisibility. I keep going, passing through tributaries and corridors, all while being forced to listen to my best friend's crippling howls.

I know where I'm going before I get there. The steady incline of the floor lands me in the wide room lined with prison cells.

There they are. Setrákus Ra is standing in the middle of the room. He is *huge* and truly revolting looking. And there's Sam. He's suspended inside a small spherical cage next to him. His own private torture bubble. Sam's arms are stretched high above his head and his legs are splayed, held in place with chains. A series of pipes are dripping steaming liquid onto various parts of Sam's body. Blood has pooled and dried under the cage.

I stop ten feet away from them. Setrákus Ra senses my presence and turns around, the three Loric pendants from other Garde children he has killed dangling from his massive neck. The scar circling his throat pulses with a dark energy.

'We missed each other,' Setrákus Ra growls.

I open my mouth but nothing comes out. Sam's blue eyes turn in my direction, but I can't tell if he sees me.

More hot liquid drips from the pipes, hitting Sam in the wrists, chest, knees and feet. A thick stream flows onto his cheek and rolls down his neck. Seeing Sam tortured finally gives me a voice.

'Let him go!' I shout.

Setrákus Ra's eyes harden. The pendants around his neck glow and mine responds, lighting up as well. The blue Loralite gem is hot against my skin, and then it suddenly bursts into flames, my Legacy taking over. I allow the fire to crawl along my shoulders.

'I'll let him go,' he says, 'if you come back to the mountain, and fight me.'

I glance quickly over at Sam and see that he has lost his battle with the pain and has blacked out, chin resting on his chest.

Setrákus Ra points to Sam's withered body and says, 'You must decide. If you don't come, I'll kill him and then I'll kill the rest of them. If you do, I'll let them all live.'

I hear a voice yelling my name, telling me I have to move. Nine. I sit up with a gasp and my eyes snap open. I'm covered in a thin layer of sweat. I stare through the jagged hole of broken drywall and it takes me a few seconds to get my bearings.

'Dude! Get up!' Nine yells from the other side of the door. 'There's a ton of stuff we need to do!'

I get to my knees and fumble around my neck for my pendant. I squeeze it as hard as I can, trying to get Sam's screams out of my head. The bedroom door swings open. Nine stands in the doorway, wiping his face with the back of his hand. 'Seriously, bro. Get your shit together. We need to get out of here.'

3

The air is thick and heavy as we leave the airport in New Delhi. We walk along the curb, Marina's Chest under Crayton's arm. Cars inch past on the congested roadways, horns blaring. The four of us are on the alert for signs of trouble, even the slightest indication we're being followed. We reach an intersection and are jostled on all sides. Women shove by with tall baskets balanced on their heads; men with buckets of water draped over their dark shoulders shout for us to get out of the way. The smells, the noise, the physical proximity of the busy world around us could overwhelm us. We stay vigilant.

There's a bustling market on the other side of the street that looks like it stretches for miles. Children crowd us with trinkets for sale, and we politely turn down their wood carvings and ivory jewelry. I'm amazed by the organized chaos of it all, happy to see life moving along in what seems to be routine, happy for this moment away from our war.

‘Where do we go now?’ Marina asks, raising her voice to be heard above the noise.

Crayton scans the crowd crossing the street. ‘Now that we’re away from the airports and its cameras, I suppose we can find a –’ A taxi skids to a stop in front of us, a cloud of dirt billowing from its tires, and the driver pushes the passenger door open. ‘Taxi,’ Crayton finishes.

‘Please. Where can I take you?’ the driver asks. He’s young and looks nervous, like this is his first day on the job. Marina must either relate to his mood or be desperate to get away from the crowds, because she jumps right into the back of the car and scoots all the way over.

Crayton gives the driver an address as he folds himself into the front seat. Ella and I pile into the back, next to Marina.

The driver nods, and then promptly slams his foot down on the accelerator, throwing us all back against the cracked plastic seat. New Delhi becomes a blur of bright colors and fleeting sounds. We zip past cars and rickshaws, goats and cows. We take corners so fast I’m surprised it isn’t on two wheels. We miss clipping pedestrians by a hair’s breadth so many times I lose count. Then I decide it’s probably best if I don’t look so closely. We’re tossed back and forth against each other. The only way we keep ourselves from falling onto the car’s dirty floor is by clinging to one another and anything else we can grab.

The taxi jumps a curb at one point, shooting down a stretch of narrow sidewalk to avoid stalled traffic. It's totally crazy and I admit I love every second of it. Years of running, hiding, and fighting have turned me into a total adrenaline junkie. Marina plants her hands on the headrest in front of her, refusing to look out the windows while Ella leans over her, trying to take it all in.

With no warning, the driver jerks the taxi violently down a road that runs behind a long row of warehouse buildings. The street is flanked by dozens of men with AK-47s. Our driver nods at them as we fly past. Crayton looks over his shoulder at me. His concerned face makes the knot in my stomach grow larger. The road is suddenly and noticeably absent of traffic.

'Where are you taking us?' Crayton demands of the driver. 'We need to go south and you're headed north.' Marina's head jerks up and she and Ella look over at me questioningly.

All of a sudden the car screeches to a halt and the driver dives out the door, rolling away from the taxi. A dozen vans and covered trucks surround the car. Each vehicle has a similar smudge of red paint on the doors, but I can't quite make out what it is. Men in street clothes jump out of the vans, machine guns ready.

Now the adrenaline really starts to flow. It always kicks in before a fight. I look over at Marina and see the terrified look on her face, but I know she will take her cues from me. I keep myself calm. 'You guys ready? Marina? Ella?' They nod.

Crayton puts his hand up. 'Wait! Look at the trucks, Six. Look at their doors!'

'What?' Ella asks. 'What's on their doors?'

The men come closer, their shouts growing urgent. I'm too focused on the imminent danger to consider what Crayton is talking about. When people with guns threaten me, or the ones I love, I'll make sure they regret it.

Marina looks out the window. 'Six, look! Are those number –'

I finally see what they're all staring at just as the door next to Marina is whipped open. The red smudges on the truck doors are all eights.

'Out!' the man yells.

'Do as he says,' Crayton says under his breath, voice calm. 'For now, we do what they want.'

We carefully get out of the taxi, our hands up, all four of us transfixed by the red numbers painted on the truck doors. We must be moving too slowly because one of the men leans forward and impatiently yanks Ella forward. She loses her balance and falls down. I can't help myself. I don't care if they're with Number Eight or not, you don't knock a twelve-year-old girl to the ground. I heave the man into the air with my mind, tossing him onto the roof of a warehouse across the street. The other men panic, whipping their guns around and screaming to one another.

Crayton grabs my arm. 'Let's find out why they're here and if they know where Number Eight is. If we need to, we'll strike with full force then.' Still furious, I shake off his hand but I nod. He's right – we don't know what they want with us. Better to find out before they're unable to explain.

A tall bearded man wearing a red beret steps out of one of the covered trucks and slowly walks towards us. His smile is confident, but his eyes are wary. A small pistol sticks out of his shoulder holster.

'Good afternoon and welcome,' he says in thickly accented English. 'I am Commander Grahish Sharma of the rebel group Vishnu Nationalist Eight. We come in peace.'

'Then what are the guns for?' Crayton asks.

'The guns were to convince you to come with us. We know who you are and would never engage in a battle with you. We know we'd lose. Vishnu told us you are all powerful like him.'

'How did you find us?' Crayton demands. 'And who is Vishnu?'

'Vishnu is the all-pervading essence of all beings, the master of the past, present and future, the Supreme God, and Preserver of the Universe. He told us you would be four in total, three young girls and one man. He asked me to convey a message to you.'

'What's the message?' I say.

Commander Sharma clears his throat and smiles. 'His message is: "I am Number Eight. Welcome to India. Please come and see me as soon as you can."'

4

The sky is gray and heavy. The woods are dark and cold. Most of the leaves have fallen from the trees and lie dead on the ground. Nine walks ahead of me, scanning the landscape for game. 'You know, that rabbit was better than I thought it would be.' He produces a short piece of vine from his pocket and pulls his shaggy black hair into a ponytail. 'I'll make it again tonight if you're interested.'

'I think I'll figure something else out.'

He looks surprised at my squeamishness. 'Scared of fresh kill? You have to eat if you want to get your strength up. I don't know why, but our healing stones don't do jack shit for your pain. And, you know, this sickness thing of yours is a real drag. Time's a-wasting, dude. We need to get you better and we've got to get out of here.'

I know how weak my body is by how tired I feel as we walk. We're only a couple of hundred yards from our ramshackle house and I'm exhausted already. I want so badly to be back there, sleeping. But I know I won't feel normal again if I don't get off my butt and move.

'Hey Nine, let me tell you about this dream I just had,' I say.

He snorts. 'A dream? No thanks, man. Well, unless it was about girls. *That* you can tell me *all* about; in detail.'

'I saw Setrákus Ra. I talked to him.' Nine pauses, then keeps walking. 'He offered me a deal.'

'Oh, yeah? What kind of deal?'

'If I go back to him and face him, he said he'll let everyone else live, including Sam.'

Nine snorts. 'That's a load of crap. Mogadorians don't make deals. At least, they don't make deals with any intention of keeping up their end of the bargain. And they don't show mercy.'

'I figure, why not just pretend I'm taking him up on it? I have to go back to the cave anyway to get Sam out.'

Nine turns to me, his face a mask of disinterest. 'Hate to break it to you, dude, but Sam's probably dead. The Mogs don't care about us, and they don't care about humans. I think you had a bad dream, and I'm sorry you got all scared and felt the need to bore me with it. But even if you did channel Setrákus Ra, that kind of offer is obviously a trap and you'll die walking into it. In fact, you'll die going within ten miles of that place. I guarantee it.' He spins around and walks away from me.

'Sam's not dead!' I say, anger welling up inside of me, giving me a strength I haven't felt in days. 'And the dream *was* real. Setrákus Ra was torturing him! I watched his skin sizzle from boiling liquid dropping onto it! I'm not going to just sit around here and let it continue to happen.'

He laughs again, but this time it isn't with a sneer. Not exactly reassuring, but definitely more gentle. 'Listen, Four. You're too weak to even run in place, never mind fight the most powerful being in the galaxy. I know it sounds heartless, dude, but Sam is *human*. There's no way you can save them all, so stop wasting your time and energy. It's not like you have an unlimited supply of either.'

The Lumen in my palms starts to light up. I'm in control of it now, a definite improvement. I'm hoping the glow is a sign the effects of the blue force field are wearing off. 'Look. Sam is my best friend, Nine. You need to get that and keep your opinions about my *energy* to yourself, okay?'

'No, you look,' says Nine. His voice sounds flat. 'This isn't playtime. We're at war, dude: *war*. And you can't make this about your feelings for Sam, if it makes everyone else less safe. I will not let you abandon the rest of us to face Setrákus Ra, just for Sam. We're going to wait until you feel better, whenever the hell that is, and then we're going to meet up with the others and train until we're ready. If you don't like it, then you'll have to fight me to get out of here. And I'm *so* ready for a fight, so, really, bring it on. I could use the practice.'

He lifts his hand and aims it at something through the trees. A second later I hear a quick yelp.

'Got it.' Nine smiles, clearly proud of his telekinetic hunting skills. I follow him, refusing to give up.

'Isn't there anyone you would die for? Anyone you'd risk your life to help?'

'I'm risking my life to help Lorien,' Nine says, fixing me with a stare that makes me listen. 'I'll die for Lorien and anyone who's Loric. And if I die, and that's a big "if," I plan on doing it with two Mog heads smashed between my palms and another one under my foot. I'm not looking forward to feeling your symbol burned into my leg just yet, so grow up, stop being so naïve and think about more than yourself already.'

His words hit me hard. I know that Henri would agree with him, but I will not turn my back on Sam again. I don't know if it's Nine's arrogance or the urgency of the vision I just had or the fresh air and the walking, but my mind seems to be clear and strong for the first time in days.

'Sam saved my ass more than once, and his dad was there to meet our ship when we landed on Earth. His dad may even have died for us, for Lorien. You owe it to both of them to go back to the cave with me. Today.'

'Not a chance.'

I step towards him and Nine doesn't hesitate. He grabs me and throws me against a tree. I pull myself to my feet and I'm about to swing at him when we hear twigs cracking behind us. Nine turns towards the noise. I flatten myself against the tree, dimly lighting my palms to be ready to blind whoever it is with my Lumen. I hope I haven't overestimated how much of my strength is truly back.

Nine looks over at me, and whispers, 'Sorry about you and the tree. Let's go find whoever's tracking us and kill them before they kill us.'

I nod, and we step forward. The noise came from a patch of pines, thick with needles and offering excellent cover. If it were up to me we'd wait and see who or what we're facing, but not Nine. He's wearing a strange little smile as we move towards the pines, ready to destroy whatever emerges. The pines rustle again, and one of the lower branches moves. But what we see isn't a Mogadorian cannon or gleaming sword. Instead, the small black nose of a brown and white beagle emerges.

'Bernie Kosar,' I say, relieved. 'Good to see you, buddy.'

He trots over and I bend down to pet his head. He's the one creature who has been with me since the beginning. Bernie Kosar tells me he's happy to see me back on my feet.

'He took long enough, right?' Nine says. I'd forgotten Nine had also developed the Legacy to communicate with animals. I know it's immature, but it bothers me to share that power with him. He's already the biggest and strongest Garde I've ever seen, has the ability to transfer powers to humans, an antigravity Legacy, super speed and hearing, telekinesis, and whatever else he hasn't told me yet. My Lumen sets me apart from the rest, but unless I find a source of fire to combine it with, it's practically useless. My ability to talk to animals was something I was looking forward to developing further, but now I'm sure Nine will find a better use for it before me.

Bernie Kosar must see the disappointment on my face because he asks if I want to go for a walk with him. Alone.

Nine hears him and says, 'Go for it. You're all BK talks about anyway. Whenever he wasn't patrolling the perimeter, he was in the bedroom looking after you.'

I keep petting his head. 'That was you, huh?'

Bernie Kosar licks my hand.

'My other best friend,' I say. 'I'd die for you, too, BK.'

Nine groans at the display of emotion. I know we're supposed to have each other's back in this massive intergalactic war, but sometimes I wish it *were* just BK and me. And Sam. And Sarah. And Six. And Henri. Really, I'd take anyone but Nine.

'I'm going to find whatever it was I killed out there, make sure we have some food for tonight,' Nine says as he walks away. 'You guys go have your special walk. When you get back, we need to talk about finding the rest of the Garde. Now that you're functioning.'

'And how exactly are we going to find them? The address Six gave us for a meeting point was in Sam's pocket. For all we know, the Mogs have it and are waiting for Six to show up. That sounds like even more reason to find Sam, if you ask me,' I say pointedly.

Bernie Kosar agrees. It sounds like he wants to look for Sam almost as much as I do.

'We'll talk about it over dinner. I'm thinking possum, maybe a muskrat,' he says, already heading into the woods to find his prey.

Bernie Kosar tells me to follow him and he leads me through the trees and down a tall grassy hill. The land levels out for a few feet before rising again. We move quickly and the exercise feels amazing now that my strength is returning. Two huge trees lean into each other up ahead. I focus and push them apart with my mind. As soon as there's a space between them, BK jumps through and I chase after him, remembering our early-morning runs to school back in Paradise. Life was so much easier then, when my days were spent training with Henri and my free time was spent with Sarah. It was exciting, finding out what I was capable of, how my powers would help me do what needed to be done. Even when I was frustrated or scared, there was so much *possibility* and I could just focus on that. I had no idea how good I had it.

My back is sticky with sweat by the time we reach a small peak. I'm better, but still not one hundred per cent. The view is spectacular, a panoramic scene of the Appalachian Mountains wrapped in fir trees, bathed in the late-afternoon light. I can see for miles.

'I gotta say, buddy, this is pretty awesome. Is this what you wanted me to see?' I ask.

Off in the distance, down on the left, he says. *Do you see it?*

I scan the landscape. 'In that deep valley?'

Beyond it, he says. *Do you see that glow?*

Squinting, I look past the valley. There's a cluster of thick trees and the faint outline of a rocky riverbed. Then I see it. Through the bottom of the trees on the far left is a glowing sliver of blue light. It's the force field at the bottom of the Mog's headquarters.

It can't be more than two miles away. Bernie Kosar says we can go back right now if I want. He'll join me inside this time, now that Sam and I have disabled the system that sent a deadly gas to animals through the mountain.

A shiver runs down my body as I stare at the blue light. Sam is in there. And Setrákus Ra. 'What about Nine?'

Bernie Kosar circles my legs twice before sitting at my

feet. *It's up to you,* he says. *Nine is strong and fast, but he's also unpredictable.*

'Have you taken him up here?' I ask. 'Does he know how close we are?'

Bernie Kosar cocks his head as if to say, *yes*. I can't believe he knew and didn't tell me. That's enough. I'm done with Nine.

'I'm going back to the house. I'll give Nine the option of coming with us, but whatever he says, it's time for me to face Setrákus.'

5

We bounce along a pothole-riddled road in a military transport truck. We're on the outskirts of the city and I look around. I see a massive mountain range looming in the distance, but that doesn't tell me much. Vehicles full of soldiers are in front of us and behind us. My Chest is at my feet and Six is sitting next to me. That makes me breathe a little easier. After the battle in Spain, the only time I feel even slightly safe is when Six is near.

I didn't think I would ever miss the Sisters of Santa Teresa, but right now, I'd give anything to be back at the convent. For years, all I thought about was escaping their rules and punishments, but now that I have escaped, all I want is something familiar, even if it comes in the form of religious discipline. My Cêpan, Adelina, is dead, murdered by Mogadorians. My best and only friend, Héctor Ricardo, is also dead. The town and convent are both gone, obliterated by the Mogs. The deaths weigh heavily on me; I was the one Adelina and Héctor were fighting to protect. God, I hope I'm not a curse. I hate the idea that my inexperience and lack of training might hurt anyone else. I don't want to put this mission in India in jeopardy just by my presence.

Finally Commander Sharma turns around to give us the lay of the land. 'This trip will last a few hours. Please, get comfortable. Help yourself to water in the cooler behind you. Don't draw attention to yourselves; don't engage with anyone. Not even to smile and nod. We're wanted.'

Crayton nods.

'So what do you think about all this?' Six asks Crayton. 'You think he's really up there?'

'I do. It makes sense.'

'Why's that?' I ask.

'The mountains are the ideal place for a Garde member to hide. For years, people have been scared to go near the glaciers north of China. Stories of alien sightings are enough to frighten the locals, and the Chinese military have been unable to investigate the reports because a mysterious lake appeared in the valley and blocked their access. Who knows what's true, and what's a rumor, but either way it's an excellent place to hide.'

'Do you think there are other aliens up there beside Number Eight?' says Ella. 'You know, like, Mogadorians?'

I was wondering the same thing.

'I don't know who else is up there, if anyone, but we'll find out soon enough,' says Crayton. He wipes sweat from his brow and touches my Chest with the tip of his finger. 'In the meantime, we should start learning how to use what's in here to help prepare us, if Marina is kind enough to share.'

'Sure,' I say quietly, lowering my eyes to the Chest. I'm not opposed to sharing my Inheritance, but I'm embarrassed by how little I understand what I have. My Chest was supposed to be shared between me and Adelina. It was her job to explain how to use everything, how it could save my life. But that never happened. After a beat, I say, 'I don't know what any of it does, though.'

Crayton reaches forward and touches my hand. I meet his solemn, yet encouraging eyes. 'It's okay that you don't know. I'll show you whatever I can,' Crayton says. 'I'm not just Ella's Cêpan now; I'm all of yours. As long as I'm alive, Marina, you can count on me.'

I nod, and place my palm against the lock. Now that Adelina is dead, I can open my Chest on my own and it's a bittersweet power. Six watches me, and I know she understands exactly how I'm feeling, having also lost her Cêpan. The cold metal lock shakes against my skin. With a click, it falls to the floor of the truck. The dirt road we're driving on is covered with potholes and debris, constantly jostling me and making it hard for me to steady my hand as I reach inside the Chest. I'm careful not to touch the glowing red crystal in the corner that caused me so much trouble in the orphanage's belfry, the one I worried was a Loric grenade, or worse. I reach for a pair of dark glasses.

'Do you know what these are for?' I ask Crayton. He examines them for a second but hands them back to me, shaking his head.

'I don't know for sure, but they may give you the power to see through things, like X-ray vision. Or they could be thermal detectors, good for seeing at night. There's only one way to find out, you know.'

I place the glasses on my face and look out the window. Aside from dulling the brightness of the sun, nothing else seems to happen. I check my hands but they're just as solid as before, and when I look up at Crayton's face, there aren't any thermal hot spots.

'So?' asks Six. 'What do they do?'

'I don't know,' I say, checking the barren landscape out the window again. 'Maybe they're just ordinary sunglasses.'

'I doubt it,' Crayton says. 'They have a use that you will discover, just like everything else in there.'

'Can I see them?' Ella asks. I hand them over.

She slides the glasses up her nose, then twists around and looks out the back window.

I turn back to my Chest.

'Wait – everything looks a little different somehow but I can't figure out why. It's almost like seeing everything a little delayed . . . or maybe sped up . . . I can't decide.' Suddenly Ella gasps, then shouts, 'Rocket! Rocket!'

We follow her line of vision, but I don't see anything but crystal-blue sky.

'Where?' Crayton yells. Ella points up at the sky. 'Get out of the truck! We have to get out right now!'

'There's nothing there.' Six squints into the horizon. 'Ella, I think those glasses are messing with you, because I don't see anything.'

Ella doesn't listen. She scrambles over me with the glasses still on and opens the door. The shoulder of the road is lined with sharp rocks and dead shrubs. 'Jump! Now!'

Finally we hear it, a faint whistling in the air, and a black speck suddenly comes into view, right where Ella was pointing.

'Get out!' Crayton yells.

I grab my open Chest, and jump. My feet hit the hard dirt road and sweep underneath me, and the world instantly becomes a swirl of browns and blues and sharp pains. The back tire of our truck grazes my arm, and I barely change direction in time to roll out of the way of the next speeding truck. My head hits a sharp stone and I flip over one last time, landing on my Chest. The impact knocks the wind out of me, and the contents of my Chest have scattered in the dirt. I hear Ella and Six coughing somewhere nearby but I can't see them in the haze of dust that surrounds us. A second later the rocket smashes into the ground just behind the speeding truck we dived from. The explosion is deafening, and with Commander Sharma still inside, the truck flips forward onto its roof in a cloud of smoke. The careening jeep behind it is unable to swerve.

It hits the edge of the chasm caused by the rocket, and dives right into the tremendous hole. Two more rockets hit the convoy. The air is so thick with dust that we cannot see the helicopters overhead, but we can hear them.

I blindly grope the area around me, trying to gather everything that spilled out of my Chest. I know I'm probably collecting just as many stones and twigs as pieces of my Inheritance, but I can sort through it later.

I've just grabbed the red crystal when I hear the sound of gunfire tear through the air. 'Six! You okay?' I shout. Then I hear Ella scream.

6

I'm frantic, pulling open closet doors, looking under what little furniture there is, when I hear someone come noisily into the house. I assume it's Nine because Bernie isn't growling.

'Nine,' I yell. 'Where'd you hide my Chest?'

'Look under the kitchen sink,' he calls back.

I walk into the kitchen. The curling linoleum floor looks like a decrepit chessboard someone's spilled coffee all over. The handles to the cupboard under the sink are loose, and when I pull on them I hear a click.

'Wait, Four!' Nine yells from the other room. 'I made a –'

The cupboard doors blow open and I fly backwards.

'Trap!' Nine finishes.

A dozen sharpened sticks are shooting straight at me. They're inches away when my instincts kick in and I'm able to deflect them with my telekinesis. The sticks ricochet left and right, stabbing the walls.

Nine stands in the doorway laughing. 'So sorry, dude. I totally forgot to tell you I rigged that up.'

Furious, I jump to my feet. Bernie Kosar skids in and growls at Nine. While he berates Nine for his stupidity, I focus on pulling the sticks out of the walls. I will them to hover in the air, aimed at Nine. 'You don't sound sorry.'

I'm seriously considering launching the little spears at him when he uses telekinesis to break the sticks into two, four and then eight pieces and they fall to the floor.

'Hey, I really did forget,' he says, shrugging. He turns around to head into the other room. 'Anyway, grab your Chest and get in here. We have to jet, so start pulling your stuff together.'

My Lumen lights up the moldy cupboard and I carefully stick my head under the sink. At first I don't see anything and think Nine is messing with me. I'm about to march into the living room to demand he return my Chest to me when I notice something. The left side of the cupboard goes deeper than the right. I feel my way around and pull away the false plywood wall. Jackpot. There it is. I grab the Chest and carry it out of the kitchen.

In the living room Nine's digging in his own Chest, the Chest we rescued from the Mog cave. 'Good to see you, old friend,' he says when he pulls out a short silver staff. Next he grabs a round yellow thing covered with small bumps. It looks like a strange fruit and I half expect him to squeeze it to produce juice. He sets it in his palm, and before I can ask what it is, he whips it down at the floor and quickly backs himself up against the wall. It bounces high after hitting the carpet and changes from yellow to black, expanding to the size of a grapefruit. When it reaches shoulder height the small bumps explode, turning into razor-sharp spikes. I duck and roll in BK's direction to avoid getting impaled.

'What the hell?' I shout. 'You could have warned me!

This is the second time in less than five minutes that you've almost killed me.'

Nine doesn't flinch when the spikes retract violently back into the ball just before it returns to his palm.

'Hey, hey, hey, would you please relax?' Nine says. He holds the ball close to his eye, causing me to hold my breath. 'I knew nothing would hit you. I can control it with my mind. Well, I can control it partly. Usually.'

'Partly? Are you kidding me? I didn't see a lot of control just now. I had to jump out of the way.'

Nine takes the ball away from his eye, looking a little chagrined. Not enough, though. 'Right now, I can only control the color.'

'That's it?' I'm incredulous. He shrugs.

BK tells him to stop fooling around.

'Hey, I'm just checking to make sure I remember how everything works. Everything I know how to use, at least,' Nine says, dropping the ball back into the Chest. 'Because you never know.' He pulls out the strand of green stones he used back at the Mog cave and flings it into the air. It hovers in a perfect circle and sucks debris off the ground like a black hole. It spins towards a back window and glows white, and when Nine snaps his fingers the debris explodes out of the circle, breaking whatever was left of the window.

'Check that one off,' he laughs.

I open my own Chest. Nine thinks that there's something in our Chests that can help us find the others. The first thing I see is the blue coffee can holding Henri's ashes and I suck in my breath. I'm instantly transported back to the forest in Paradise, walking with Sarah through the melting snow to see Henri's dead body. I promised Henri I would take him back to Lorien, and I still plan on it.

I carefully move the coffee can to the floor next to the Chest and grab the dagger with the diamond blade, letting the handle extend and wrap itself around my fist. I turn it over, looking at the blade. I release the dagger and continue to sift through the items. I try not to dwell on the objects I don't know – the star-shaped talisman, the collection of brittle leaves tied with twine, the bright red oval bracelet – and I stay away from the crystal that's double-wrapped in towels and stuffed into a plastic bag. The last time I touched that crystal, my stomach convulsed and acid climbed up my throat.

I push aside the smooth yellow Xitharis rock that transfers Legacies and pick up an oblong crystal that is full of memories. Its surface is waxy with a cloudy inside, and it's the first thing Henri ever pulled out of the Chest to show me. When the cloud swirled, it meant my first Legacy was developing. This crystal was the beginning.

Then I see Sam's dad's glasses and the white tablet Six and I found in Malcolm Goode's office in the well. That's enough to snap me back to reality.

I look over at Nine. 'Maybe something in our Chests can get us through the blue force field. I think the effect of it is weakened, anyway. There may be a chance we can get to Sam tonight.'

'Would be nice if something in the Chest would help us do that, that's for sure,' Nine says in a casual tone, his eyes focused on the purple pebble he is balancing on the back of his hand. It disappears.

'What's that?' I ask.

He turns over his hand and the pebble reappears on his palm. 'I have no idea, but it would be a killer conversation starter with the ladies, don't you think?'

I shake my head and slide the red bracelet from my Chest over my hand. I hope it will propel me into the air or shoot a ring of lasers, but it just hangs there on my wrist. I wave my arm over my head, asking it to work, begging it to reveal its powers. Nothing happens.

'Maybe you should try licking it?' Nine laughs, watching me.

'I'll try anything,' I mutter, frustrated. I keep it on and hope something will just *happen*. Everything in my Chest came from the Elders. Everything has a purpose, so I know it must do something. My hand brushes against the velvet bag holding the seven orbs that make up Lorien's solar system. I pull open the bag and drop the stones into my hand and show them to Nine, remembering the day that Henri first showed them to me. 'Are these what you're looking for to find the others? Henri had these. This is how we figured out another member of the Garde was in Spain.'

'I've never seen those before. What do they do?'

I blow softly on the stones and they glow, coming to life. Bernie Kosar barks at the sight of the orbs hovering over my palm. They have become planets and orbit the sun. Just as I'm about to shine my Lumen onto Lorien to see it in its lush, green state as it was the day before the

Mogadorian attack, the orbs once again speed up and brighten and I can no longer control them.

Nine comes closer and we watch as the planets collide one by one with the sun until there is just a large single ball in front of us. The new globe rotates on its axis and flashes a light so bright we have to shield our eyes. Eventually, the globe dims and sections of its surface rise and recede until we're looking at a perfect replica of Earth.

Nine is mesmerized. The Earth rotates and we immediately see two pinpricks of pulsing light, one on top of the other. Once we can orient ourselves, we see they are in West Virginia.

'There we are,' I say.

The ball continues to rotate and we see there's another pulse of light in India; a fourth is moving north quickly from what looks like Brazil.

'When I was showing Six and Sam our solar system a few days ago in the car, the same thing happened. It turned into a globe of the Earth. It was the first time it ever did that,' I say.

'I'm confused,' Nine says. 'There are only four dots on this thing and there are supposed to be six of us left.'

'Yeah, I'm not sure about that. When this happened before, a dot showed up in Spain,' I say. 'Then the globe went all fuzzy and we heard someone who sounded panicked yelling the name Adelina. We assumed she was another member of the Garde. That's when Six decided to go to Spain, to try to find her. I figured this was how you planned to contact the others, but I guess not if you've never seen it before.'

Nine's eyes go wide. 'Wait. Oh my God, man. I haven't seen this thing before, but I think Sandor told me about it. To be honest, when we opened my Chest the first time, the silver staff and the yellow porcupine ball were so amazing I only half listened to anything he said after. But now I remember, he told me some of us had a red crystal – which I do, and that's what I thought I'd use to communicate with the others – and some of us have the solar system.'

'I don't get it.'

He turns to his Chest, grabs a glowing red crystal the size of a cigarette lighter, slams the lid of his Chest, and turns back to me. I glance at the solar system and gasp. One of the blue dots in West Virginia has disappeared.

'Whoa, hold on. Open up your Chest again. I want to see something.'

Nine obeys and a second blue dot reappears on the globe in West Virginia.

'Okay. Now, close it.'

He closes it and the dot disappears again. 'This is boring,' he says. When Nine speaks, the Earth globe grows fuzzy and vibrates with a half-second delay of his voice. 'Wait, what was that? Why is my voice echoing?' The Earth vibrates again.

'This is not boring. *This* is incredible,' I say, staring at the globe. 'The reason we don't see all six of the Garde members on the globe is because the orb only reveals the members of the Garde who have their Chests open at that exact moment. Watch.' I lift the lid of Nine's Chest.

Nine whistles. 'Very cool, Four, very cool.' Half a second later we hear his voice through the globe again. Nine puts his crystal down, having figured it out.

'But judging by the speed of this guy here,' I say, pointing to the dot in motion, 'whoever is in South America has to be on a plane. It's covering too much ground too fast to be doing anything else.'

'Why would they have their Chest open on a plane?' Nine asks. 'That's stupid.'

'Maybe they're in trouble. Maybe they're hiding in the bathroom trying to figure out what all this stuff actually does, just like we are.'

'Can they see us right now, too?'

'I don't know, but maybe they can hear us. I think if you hold onto that red crystal, any of us with this macrocosm Earth can hear you.'

'If half of us have a crystal, and the other half have the power to get this big glowing globe up and running, then –'

'The only way for us to actually communicate back and forth would be if a couple of us teamed up first,' I interrupt. 'Well, now that we're together, maybe we should try to talk to the others. You know, in case their macrocosms are going,' I say. 'Maybe another pair has gotten together like us.'

Nine grabs the red crystal and holds it near his mouth like a microphone. 'Hello? Testing one, two, three.' He clears his throat. 'Okay, if any of you Garde members are out there standing in front of a glowing ball, listen up. Four and Nine are together and we're ready to meet up with you. We want to train and end all this bullshit and get back to Lorien. Pronto. We're not going to say exactly where we are in case any Mogs are listening in, but if you have your macrocosm going you'll see two dots together, and they are, uh, us. So, um . . .' Nine looks at me and shrugs his shoulders. 'That is all. Over and out and stuff.'

The skin on my wrist suddenly feels numb under the bracelet. I shake it and my arm begins to tingle. 'Wait. Say we're about to get out of here and for them to make their way to the United States. That's where Setrákus Ra, the Mogadorian leader, is. Tell them we're going after him and we're going to rescue our friends as soon as we can.'

The Earth in front of me buzzes to life with Nine's echoing voice. 'Everyone come to America ASAP. Setrákus Ra has shown his ugly face over here and we're aiming to smash it in and take him down *real* soon. We'll send out another message tomorrow. Stay tuned.'

Nine drops the red crystal back into his Chest, looking way too pleased with himself, then kind of embarrassed that he just talked into a ball. I frown. My right arm has gone ice cold, and I'm about to rip off this bracelet before putting the orbs back into the velvet bag when the Earth grows fuzzy again. Then there's the sound of an explosion, followed by a voice I know well. It's the same girl I heard before, the girl Six went to Spain to seek out. She's yelling. 'Six! You okay?'

We hear a scream and two more explosions rock the

fuzzy edges of the globe. I grab Nine's crystal out of his Chest, frantic to try to communicate with her.

'Six!' I yell. I would jump into the thing if I could figure out how. 'It's me, John! Can you hear me?'

There's no response. We hear the faint sounds of the blades of a helicopter before the globe goes silent again and the Earth's edges grow solid. The pulsing light in India is now gone. Suddenly, the globe shrinks and reforms into the seven orbs, each of which falls to the ground.

'That did *not* sound good,' Nine says, scooping up the stones. He drops them back into my Chest, and takes his crystal out of my frozen hand.

Six is in trouble – the kind of trouble that involves explosions and helicopters and mountains. And all of this is happening now, halfway around the world. How am I going to get to India? Where can I get on a plane?

'Six is the chick who gave you the map to the mountain? The one who abandoned you and your boy to jet off to Spain?' Nine asks.

'That's her,' I say, kicking my Chest shut, fists clenched tight. My head is swimming. What's wrong with Six? Who is the other girl, the one I've now heard twice? I notice my arm still feels strange. Hearing her voice distracted me so much I forgot about the growing discomfort there. I try to remove the bracelet from my wrist, and it burns my fingers. 'Something's going on with this thing. I think something may be wrong with it.'

Nine shuts his Chest and reaches over. 'The bracelet?'

As soon as he touches it he rips his hand away. 'Damn! It zapped me!'

'Well, what do I do?' I try snapping my arm out, hoping I can fling the bracelet off.

Bernie Kosar trots over to smell the bracelet, but stops midstride and jerks his head up to stare at the front door. His ears rise and the fur on his back bristles.

Someone's here, he says.

Nine and I look at each other and start to back slowly into the room, away from the door. We'd been so engrossed in everything in our Chests, and in hearing the voice through the globe, that we'd let our guard down, and weren't paying attention to our surroundings.

Suddenly, the door is blown off its hinges. Smoke bombs fly through the windows sending glass shards everywhere. I want to fight, but the pain from the bracelet is now so intense I can't move. I fall to my knees.

I see a flash of green light and hear Nine shout out in pain. He falls down next to me. I've seen that green light before. That is the unmistakable green light of a Mogadorian cannon.

7

Bullets whistle by, exploding in the dirt all around us. Ella and I take cover behind the wreckage of one of the trucks. The bullets seem to be coming from everywhere, from every direction, from every angle. Ella's been hit. The air is so thick with dust from all the commotion, I can't even see her wounds. I gently run my hands over her body until I feel the wet, sticky blood and find a bullet hole in her lower thigh. When I touch it, she cries out in pain.

I use the most soothing voice I can muster, given the circumstances. 'It's going to be okay. Marina can help you. We just need to find her.' I pick Ella up and start carefully moving away from the truck, shielding her with my body. I almost trip over Marina and Crayton, who are huddled behind another piece of debris.

'Come on! Ella's hurt! We have to get out of here!'

'There are too many of them. If we try to run now, they'll kill us. Let's treat Ella first, then fight back,' Crayton says.

I set Ella down next to Marina. She's still wearing the dark glasses. I can see her wound clearly now; her blood is flowing steadily. Marina places her hands on Ella's leg and closes her eyes. Ella inhales sharply, her chest beginning to rise and fall at a rapid pace. It really is amazing to see Marina's Legacy in action. Another explosion sounds nearby and a blast of dust sweeps over us just as Ella's wound contracts, pushing the bullet out of her flesh. The gash turns from black and red back to the color of her pearly-white skin. An outline of a small bone shifts just below the surface of her skin and Ella's body slowly begins to relax. I rest my hand on Marina's shoulder, relieved, and say, 'That was incredible, Marina.'

'Thanks. It was pretty cool, wasn't it?' Marina removes her hands from Ella, who slowly props herself up onto her elbows. Crayton gives her a hug.

A helicopter roars overhead and decimates two trucks with a spray of bullets. A chunk of metal lands close to me; it's a piece of smoldering truck door, the red number eight just barely visible. The sight of it fills me with anger. Now that Ella is healed, I'm ready to fight back.

'Now we move on them!' I yell at Crayton.

'Is it the Mogadorians?' Marina asks, clicking the lock of her Chest shut.

Crayton looks over the top of the debris heap we've been hiding behind, and ducks back down to report. 'It's not the Mogs. But there are a lot of them and they're coming closer. We can fight here, but it would be better to take it to the mountains. Whoever they are, if they aren't here to attack us but are battling Commander Sharma, I see no reason to reveal your powers.'

An explosion behind us pushes another cloud of dirt our way, and I watch the helicopter circle back around and head straight for us. Marina and I look at each other and we can tell we're both thinking the same thing. There's no way to honor Crayton's request that we not use our Legacies and do what we need to do. She takes control of the helicopter and reverses its flight path. Its passengers will never understand what happened but we know it's out of our way. And regardless of who's inside, we don't want anyone to be in danger's path unnecessarily. Ella and I cheer with relief as we watch the spinning blades disappear into the distance while Crayton watches with a frown. Then Commander Sharma dives behind our cover.

'Thank God, you're alive,' he says. I'm tempted to say the same thing to him. I thought he was killed when that first rocket struck. Blood trickles from a large cut on his temple, and his right arm hangs awkwardly at his side.

'I'm holding you responsible for this,' I say, glaring at him.

He shakes his head. 'Those are soldiers of the Lord's Resistance Front. They are who we were trying to avoid.'

'What do they want?' I ask.

Commander Sharma scans the horizon before looking me in the eyes. 'To kill Vishnu. And destroy all of his friends. Like you. More are on their way.'

I move to a crouching stance and carefully peer over the demolished truck. A large brigade of heavily armed vehicles is moving towards us, several helicopters hovering above them. Tiny flashes of light appear from the long line of the trucks and jeeps, and seconds later I hear the bullets zip past us.

'Let's go kick some ass,' I say.

'It's not possible to defeat them here,' Commander Sharma says, picking up a machine gun with his good hand. 'No more than twenty of my men are still fighting. We must take it to higher ground if we want a chance to survive this.'

'Just let me handle it,' I say.

'Wait, Six,' Crayton says, scooping up Marina's Chest. 'He's right. The mountains will give us more cover. You can still take out every single one of them. It just won't be as visible, which is good for us. We don't need the Mogs picking up on this right now.'

Marina puts her hand on my arm. 'Crayton's right. We need to be smart. Let's not draw more attention to ourselves than we have to.'

'The Mogs?' Commander Sharma asks, confused. We'll need to be more careful around him.

Before anyone can answer, two low-flying helicopters zip in with their guns blazing. Several of the commander's soldiers are mowed down, their weapons blown to useless shards of metal. If we're going to run, it's now or never. I use my telekinesis to pull on the tail of one of the helicopters, tipping the nose down. It looks like a rodeo horse trying to buck its rider as the pilot struggles furiously to level the copter out. We watch the pilot give a particularly hard yank to the joystick and two men bounce right out of the cabin. They weren't very high in the air, so the fall shouldn't injure them – much.

I look over at our fleet of stalled SUVs and see smoke rising faintly from one of the tailpipes. An engine is still running! I shout, 'Let's go! Now!'

Everyone rushes from behind the cover; Commander Sharma yells for his few remaining men to retreat. The brigade is less than a hundred yards away. As we run I feel a bullet zip through my hair. Another one rips through my forearm, but before I can scream, Marina is right next to me, her icy hands tending to my injury as we run. All but one of the commander's soldiers follow his orders to retreat. That lone soldier follows the commander, running with us.

We reach the SUV and get inside – the four of us, plus Commander Sharma and the one soldier. Crayton steps on the gas and whips us onto the road. Bullets tear through the tail end of our truck, shattering the back windshield, but we're able to manoeuvre around a small rock formation and evade the relentless gunfire.

This is not a road built for speed. It's full of potholes, rocks and other debris, and Crayton struggles to keep us from careening off the shoulder. The SUV is overflowing with guns – I find a shotgun and crawl into the back, waiting for a target. Marina follows suit, leaving her Chest with Ella.

Now that I have a moment to gather my thoughts, I'm angry. We thought if Number Eight remained in the mountains, we would be safe here, under the radar. Instead, we're being attacked because of him. If we survive this, I am *so* going to tear Eight a new one.

'Where are we going?' Crayton yells over his shoulder.

'Just stay on this road,' the commander says. I look over my shoulder and see the Himalayan Mountains through the windshield. They are slowly getting closer, their jagged tops growing more menacing. Up ahead, the brown desert ends, and a curving band of green surrounds the base of the mountains.

'Why do these guys want to kill Number Eight?' I ask Commander Sharma, the barrel of my shotgun bouncing off the frame of the back window.

'The Lord's Resistance Front does not believe he is Vishnu. They believe we are blasphemous, accepting this mountain boy as the Supreme God. They want to kill us in his name.'

'Six!' Ella yells. 'Incoming!' She's still wearing the glasses.

I look out the back window in time to see something fire out of the helicopter. It's a missile of some sort heading straight for us. I use my telekinesis and send it directly into the desert floor, where it explodes. The helicopter fires two more missiles.

'Time to take these dudes out!' I yell. 'Let's do this one together, Marina.' She nods and instead of directing the rockets into the ground this time, we loop them so they're heading directly back at the copter. We watch grimly as the helicopter explodes in a giant fireball. We never try to kill; but, given a choice between killing versus being killed, I will pick us every time.

'Awesome work, Six,' says Ella.

'Yippee-ki-yay, and all that,' I reply with a grim smile.

'Do you think they'll leave us alone now?' asks Marina.

'I don't think it's going to be that easy,' says Commander Sharma.

'She has all the same type of powers as the boy you call Vishnu,' says Crayton, motioning towards me. 'Will that be enough to dissuade them? Do you think they'd still try to fight him?'

'They would if they could find him,' says the commander.

'How many are there in the Lord's Resistance Front?' I ask Commander Sharma.

'In total? Thousands. And they have wealthy donors who support them in any way they need.'

'Hence the helicopters,' Crayton says.

'They have worse than that,' the commander adds.

'The best plan for us is to outrun them,' Crayton says to the commander. 'I'll drive as fast as I can. If we have to fight, we'll fight; but I'd like to avoid it.'

Five minutes pass in tense silence. Marina and

I monitor the brigade in the distance, and whenever we pass something large enough, we use our telekinesis to drop it in the path behind us. The tall trees that have begun to dot the sides of the road quickly form a thick line of defense. The car dips into an extremely narrow valley before beginning to ascend the mountain. We have just come to the base when Commander Sharma tells Crayton to stop. I lean forward in my seat and see dozens of small mounds in the dirt.

'Land mines?' I ask.

'I'm not sure,' the commander says. 'But they weren't there two days ago.'

'Is there another route to wherever we're going?' Crayton asks.

'No, this is the only path,' Commander Sharma says.

Suddenly, we hear the sound of helicopter blades, but I don't see them yet. They're hidden behind the tall trees. Of course, that means they can't see us, either, though it sounds like they aren't very far off anymore.

'We're sitting ducks if we stay here,' I say, my mind racing to figure out our next best move.

Crayton opens his door and steps out with a machine gun under his arm. 'Okay, this is it.' He points up and to our right. 'We either go up there and get behind a line of trees and fight, or we keep running straight up the mountain.'

I follow him out. 'I'm not running.'

'Neither am I,' says Marina, standing next to me.

'Then we fight,' says Commander Sharma. He points into the hills. 'Half of us set up on the left while the other half takes position on the right. I will take these two with me.' He indicates Ella and me.

Crayton and I look at each other and nod.

Ella turns to Crayton. 'You okay without me, Papa?'

Crayton smiles. 'Marina's Legacy will make sure whatever they do to me won't last long. I think I'll be okay.'

'I'll keep an eye on him, Ella,' Marina adds.

'Are you sure we should do this, Commander?' the soldier asks. 'I can go to fetch Vishnu, bring him back to help.'

'No, Lord Vishnu should stay where he's safe.'

Crayton turns to Ella. 'Keep those glasses on. Maybe you can be our eyes up there in the trees. I'm still not sure how they work, but let's hope they'll help now.'

I hug Marina and whisper into her ear. 'Be confident in your abilities.'

'I should heal Commander Sharma before you go,' she says.

'No,' I whisper. 'I don't trust him yet and he's less dangerous to us if he's injured.'

'You sure?'

'For now.'

Marina nods. Crayton taps her arm and beckons her to join him and the young soldier. The three of them scramble up the left wall of the valley, disappearing behind a boulder.

Commander Sharma, Ella, and I move up the right side of the hills, carefully avoiding the bumps on the ground as we move. We find a position behind some massive boulders, and settle in to wait for the brigade to arrive.

I turn to Commander Sharma. I feel slightly guilty about not letting Marina heal him, but for all I know, he's set this up as an elaborate trap. 'How's your arm?' I whisper to him.

With a grunt, Commander Sharma lies down and sets the barrel of his gun on a flat rock. He looks up and winks. 'I only need the one.'

Out of the corner of my eye I can see a helicopter buzz overhead but it leaves almost immediately. Either Marina took care of it, or the pilot couldn't penetrate the thick canopy of the valley. I look through the trees, hoping to manipulate the clouds surrounding the peaks of the mountains, but the afternoon sun has burned them off. With no wind, and no clouds, there aren't any elements to control. I can turn invisible if I need to, but I prefer to keep that hidden from the commander for now.

‘What do you see?’ Ella asks.

‘A whole lot of nothing,’ I whisper. ‘Commander, how far away is Number Eight?’

‘You mean Vishnu? Not far. A half-day’s walk, maybe.’

I’m about to ask him to tell me where, exactly. We should know in case something happens to the commander and we need to move forward without him. But I’m distracted when a rusty pickup truck swings into the narrow valley at full speed with a man standing in the open bed. Even from a distance, I can see he’s nervous as well as armed. He jerks his gun from side to side, frantically trying to be everywhere at once. As soon as our SUV comes into view, the pickup skids to a stop and the soldier in the back hops out. More vehicles appear and pull up behind the pickup. A soldier drops out of a red van and sets a rocket launcher onto his shoulder. I see an opportunity.

I nudge the commander with my foot. ‘I’ll be right back.’

I don’t give him a chance to argue as I run quickly into the woods. When he can’t see me any longer, I use my invisibility Legacy to disappear and sprint down into the valley. The soldier has our truck in his crosshairs, but before he can pull the trigger I rip the rocket launcher off his shoulder and slam one end into his belly. He doubles over and goes down with a scream. Hearing the commotion, the driver of the truck rushes over with a pistol in his hand. I point the rocket launcher at his face. The soldier takes a split second to decide if the free-floating launcher is about to do its thing, then turns and runs away with his arms above his head.

I aim at the now empty, rusty pickup and pull the trigger. The rocket flies out of my launcher and a wave of fire explodes under the pickup, blowing it thirty feet into the air. The burning truck lands hard, and bounces and rolls quickly forward, the momentum sending it into the back of our SUV with a crash. I watch it lurch forward, rolling slowly over the small mounds in the road that had stopped us from advancing. The next thirty seconds are filled with ear-splitting, rapid detonations, as soldiers fire blindly around them and the mounds in the road explode. Thousands of birds burst out from the trees all around us, their sounds quickly drowned out by the snap, crackle and pop of munitions doing their thing. I was right; they *were* land mines. And now our SUV is nothing more than a smoldering pile of metal.

Evidently, this was just the opening act. The main attraction – armored vehicles, small tanks, mobile missile units – is closing in on the mountain. There have to be a couple of thousand soldiers on foot. Five or six attack helicopters hover overhead. I hear a whirring and turn to see a missile launcher rising and rotating, going into operational mode. The tips of five white missiles turn up and towards the area where Marina and Crayton have taken cover. There's movement in the tree line, and the commander's young soldier runs down into the valley. He's unarmed and headed right for the missile launcher. At first I think he's going to sacrifice himself somehow to save my friends, but no one fires at him. He stops when he reaches the launcher and starts pointing higher up the side of the mountain, to where Crayton and Marina are hiding. The launcher rises another few feet and adjusts its aim.

He's a traitor, part of the group trying to kill us! The next thing I know, he is flying into the air, yanked upward by telekinesis. Marina must have realized the same thing. But it might be too late. He's already revealed her location.

I look towards the missile launcher and gather my strength so I can alter the flight of the missiles once they're fired. As I start to focus on it, another launcher whirs to life and aims its missiles directly at me. Though I'm invisible, the army knows a shoulder rocket was fired from where I'm standing. I only have the power to deal with one of them, and there's no time to run. I have a choice. Save Crayton and Marina or save myself.

The launcher pointed toward the mountain starts firing. The missiles come screaming out, heading straight for the hills. I get control of them and redirect them into the ground, where they explode, just as the second launcher fires. I turn and see their white tips moving towards me. I don't have time to do anything, but suddenly the missiles loop up and turn back towards the launcher that fired them and the brigade. They barrel into five different vehicles, all of which explode.

Marina. She saved my life. We are working together, just as we were meant to do, and the thought makes me feel more determined than before to get this pit stop over with and find Eight. I want to send a message to the remaining soldiers of the brigade so I stop using my invisibility Legacy and show myself. I focus and start to control the flames rising from where the missiles exploded with my telekinesis. I spread the fire down the road to engulf the rest of the brigade. One by one, the flames move down the row of vehicles and it's like exploding dominos. Message received. The remaining soldiers of the Lord's Resistance Front begin to retreat. For a second, I'm tempted to indulge in a little retribution. But that's cruel and unnecessary and exactly the kind of thing the Mogadorians would do. I know my fantasies of going medieval on their retreating asses are not going to help us now.

'That's right! Run! Because if you don't, that fire is just waiting to finish the job off!' When the last one disappears from view, I turn and start walking back towards the hills. I need to find my friends.

8

The smoke is thick but beginning to dissipate. From where I am on the floor, I can see dozens of legs and black boots. I raise my eyes and see almost as many rifles, all of them aimed at my head.

My eyes move from the heavy boots up to the gas masks, relieved to see they belong to humans and not Mogadorians. But what kind of humans have Mogadorian weapons? A gun barrel is pushed into the back of my skull. Normally, I'd use my telekinesis to rip it away and toss it a mile into the mountains, but the pain from the bracelet is too intense for me to be able to focus my energy on that. One of the men says something to me, but I can't concentrate enough to make out what he's saying.

I search for a focal point to help get me through the pain, and see Nine groaning on the carpet. From where I am, it looks as if he's having trouble breathing; it also looks like he can't move his arms and legs. I want to help him, and struggle to get up, but I'm kicked back down as soon as I start to move. I roll onto my back and immediately a long cylindrical tube is pressed into my left eye. There are hundreds of lights inside the tube, and I watch them swirl together to become one solid green beam. It's definitely a Mogadorian cannon, the same kind that paralyzed me outside our burning house in Florida. I focus my other eye past the side of the weapon and see a man in a khaki trench coat. He pulls back his gas mask to reveal a ring of white hair and a fat, crooked nose that looks like it's been broken more than once. I find myself looking forward to breaking it again.

'Don't move,' he growls at me, 'or I'll pull the trigger.'

I glance over at Nine, who seems to be recovering. He's sitting up, looking around, struggling to shake off his dazed expression. The man with the cannon pressed to my face looks over at him. 'What do you think you're doing?' he says.

Nine smiles up at him, clear eyed and calm. 'Trying to decide which one of you I'm going to kill first.'

'Shut him up!' a woman yells as she enters the house, also carrying a Mog cannon. Two men press their boots against Nine's shoulders and force him back to the floor. The woman motions at me, and someone takes me by the shoulders and pulls me onto my feet. Another man grabs my wrists to put me in handcuffs.

'Son of a bitch!' he cries as he touches my red bracelet. I may not know everything the bracelet does, but I like this part of it.

Once upright, I get my bearings. There are ten or twelve men in masks, all holding rifles. The man and woman who were speaking seem like they're in charge. I look for Bernie, but don't see him. Even so, I can hear him inside my head.

Just wait. Let's see what they want and what they know.

'What do you want with us?' I ask the man with the broken nose.

He laughs and looks over at the woman. 'What do we want, Special Agent Walker?'

'For starters, I want to know who your friend is over there,' she says, pointing the tube back at Nine.

'I don't know this kid,' Nine says. He blows his hair out of his face and offers a smile. 'I just stopped by to sell him a vacuum cleaner. The place looked like a dump and I thought he could use it.'

The man circles over to Nine. 'Is that what you have in these fancy chests here? Vacuum cleaners?' He nods to one of the other officers and says, 'Let's have a look at these vacuum cleaners, shall we? I may be interested in one myself.'

'Be my guest.' Nine's smile is menacing. 'I'm having a sale. Two for the price of three.'

For a split second, Nine and I make eye contact. Then Nine sweeps his eyes over to the wall, where a moth is hovering near the ceiling. Bernie Kosar. I'm sure Nine also heard BK's orders to wait to see where this is going. I wonder if he'll be able to control himself. One of the soldiers slaps a pair of handcuffs on Nine, and he quickly sits up again. I can see the handcuffs around his wrists are already broken. He's only holding his hands together to keep up the charade.

Nine's just waiting for the right time to attack. I don't know if he ever intended to do as BK asked. I pull my arms apart behind me, quietly and easily breaking my own handcuffs. Whatever is about to happen, I'd better be ready.

A bunch of the men have surrounded Nine's Chest. One of them is slamming the butt of his rifle over and over on the lock holding it closed, but it doesn't have any effect. He smashes it a few more times anyway, clearly frustrated.

'How about this.' Special Agent Walker pulls out a revolver. She fires at the lock and the bullet ricochets around the room, barely missing another officer's leg.

The broken-nose man grabs Nine by the back of his neck, pulls him to his feet, then shoves him forward. Nine can't maintain the ruse of his handcuffs and braces his fall, landing on his hands and knees. Realizing Nine's hands are now unrestrained, the man yells over his shoulder, 'Somebody get me some more handcuffs! We've got a broken pair over here!'

His chin tucked into his chest, Nine's whole body vibrates with laughter. He pops his legs out and does a pushup. Then he does another one. An officer kicks his right hand out from underneath him, but Nine doesn't miss a beat. He does another pushup with just his left hand. The officer kicks at his left hand, but Nine is too fast to let that knock him over. His right hand is down in a flash and his one-handed pushup shows off his perfect form. Four officers jump on him, each one holding a leg or arm, but Nine just keeps on laughing. Suddenly, I find myself joining him. His bizarre sense of humor is infectious. Man, I have to give him props.

Special Agent Walker turns to me. I slowly pull my arms out from behind me, the broken handcuffs dangling from my wrists. I wiggle my fingers and casually place both hands behind my head and start whistling.

She narrows her eyes and arranges her face in the most intimidating glare she has. 'Do you know what happens to kids like you in prison?' she asks.

'They escape? Like I did last time?' My eyes are wide and innocent.

I hear Nine howling with laugher at my performance from under the pile of officers. I have to admit, Nine does bring a weird kind of fun to the proceedings. My smile breaks wide now. I know these men are just trying to do their jobs. They think they're keeping their country safe. Right now, though, I hate them. I hate them for slowing us down and I hate this woman's tough-guy act. I hate that they have Mog cannons. But most of all I hate them for working with Sarah to capture Sam and me last week. I wonder what they promised her to get her to turn me in. Did they play on her sympathies? Convince her she would save me, by letting them take us? Did they say she could visit me, while I paid the price for my so-called mistakes? I look over at Bernie Kosar, but I don't see the moth anymore. That's when a fat brown and white cockroach scurries up my leg and burrows into my jeans pocket.

Nine will go along with this for a while longer, BK tells

me. *But I don't know how much longer. Find out everything you can, quickly.*

The lead guy claps his hands to get the attention of the other men. 'Okay! Let's get these guys out of here before our friends show up.'

'Who are your friends?' I ask him, though I'm already pretty sure that for some reason the U.S. government and the Mogadorians are working together. That's the only explanation for why they'd be using Mog weapons against us. 'Who don't you want to show up?'

'Shut up!' Special Agent Walker yells. She pulls out a cell phone and dials a number. 'We're bringing him in, plus another one,' she says into the phone. 'Two Chests. No, but we'll get them open. See you soon.'

'Who was that?' I ask. She ignores me as she puts her phone away.

'Hey, buddy, I thought you wanted to buy a vacuum,' Nine says to me. 'I really need this sale. My boss is going to kill me if I come home with a full box of Hoovers again.'

They pull Nine to his feet. He stretches his back and smiles, like a cat smug and full of mouse. 'It doesn't matter where you take us, there's no prison that can hold us. If you knew who we are, you wouldn't waste your time with this crap.'

Agent Walker laughs. 'We know who you are, and if you were as smart or as tough as you think you are, we would never have found you in the first place.'

Officers pick up our Chests and walk out the front door.

New handcuffs are slapped over our wrists. They use three pairs on Nine.

'You have *no* idea what we're capable of,' Nine says in a sickeningly sweet voice as they lead us through the front yard. 'If I wanted to, I could kill you all in a matter of seconds. You're damn lucky I'm being such a good boy. For now.'

9

We're at a gate. There is a narrow path beyond it and it goes straight up the mountain. Crayton asks me to cover the trail behind us while Six takes the lead with Commander Sharma. I wonder if his soldier's betrayal has had any effect on him. I wonder if he will question the loyalty of his troops when he returns to his command. I can't imagine asking him, not without somehow suggesting he should have known. Of course, maybe he should have.

I'm carrying the small tree branch from my Chest. I need to figure out what it does. The first time I'd held this – the first time I'd ever opened my Chest, back in Santa Teresa at the convent, when Adelina was still alive – I hadn't had time to figure out what it did. But I did remember that when I'd held it out the window, I'd felt some kind of magnetic force. Almost instinctively, I rub its smooth, pared surface with my thumb. After a while, I notice it has an effect on the trees we pass. I aim and concentrate on what I want from the trees, and soon I hear the creaking of their roots and the clattering of their branches. I turn and walk backwards up the path, asking the trees on the edges to keep us safe, and they bend and twist into each other, making it impossible for anyone to follow. I want so much to be of help, I want so much not to be a curse, and to put my Inheritance to use to help us, that every time a tree responds a huge wave of relief washes over me.

We walk mostly in silence. At one point, to break up the boredom of the hike, I tickle Six's face by lowering a branch right in front of her. She swats it away without breaking stride, too completely focused on what may lay ahead. As we walk I think about Six. About how fearless she was back with the soldiers. She's always so calm, cool and collected. She takes command and makes decisions as if it were the most natural thing for her to do. One day I'll be like her. I'm sure of it.

I wonder what Adelina would think of Six – and about me now. I wonder how much further along I'd be if she had trained me. I know all those years in the orphanage without guidance from her means I'm not where I should be. I'm not as strong and confident as Six. I'm not even as knowledgeable as Ella. I try to bury my resentment and focus on Adelina's final act of honor. She charged at the Mog fearlessly, armed with just a kitchen knife. I try to stop the memory before I get to the part where she dies. I almost never do. If only I'd had the courage to fight alongside her, or knew then how to use my telekinesis to unwrap the Mogadorian's hand from Adelina's neck. If I had, she might be walking with us right now.

'We rest here,' the commander says, his voice breaking through my reverie. He points to a couple of flat boulders bathed in the afternoon sun. Just beyond the rocks I can see a small stream of fresh water. 'Not long, however. We need to make a lot more progress up this mountain before nightfall.' He looks up at the midafternoon sky.

'Why? What happens at nightfall?' Six asks.

'Very strange things. Things you are not yet ready to see.' Commander Sharma takes off his shoes and socks, rolls up the cuffs of his pants in a fussy sort of way and wades into the stream.

Crayton removes his shoes and socks too, and follows him. 'You know, Commander, we're already taking a pretty big leap of faith just following you up this mountain. The least you could do is answer our questions when we have them. We have a very important mission. And we deserve your respect.'

'I do respect you, sir,' he says. 'But I follow Vishnu's orders.'

Crayton shakes his head in frustration and walks further upstream. I notice Ella has wandered away and is sitting alone on one of the boulders by the stream. She's been wearing the dark glasses from my Chest the entire hike, and she takes this moment to clean them carefully on her shirt. Seeing my gaze on her, she holds them out to me. 'I'm sorry, Marina. I don't know why I hung on to them. It's just that –'

'It's okay, Ella. They helped you see that attack before

any of us could. We may not know their full power, but you seem to be doing just fine with them.'

'I guess so. I wonder if there's anything more I can get them to do.'

'What *have* you seen as we've been walking?' Six asks.

'Trees, trees and more trees,' Ella says. 'I keep waiting for something to happen, or to see something unusual. I wish I knew for sure this meant there is nothing for me *to* see.' I can tell she is frustrated with herself, not the glasses.

With the small branch in my hand, I bend a large tree over to create shade on the boulders. 'Well, keep trying.'

Ella holds the dark glasses up to the light. As she turns them over it's almost as though I can read her thoughts, thanking me for making her feel like she's part of the team, doing some good.

I look over at Six, who has stretched out on the ground. 'What about you, Six?' I ask. 'You want to check out anything in my Chest?'

She stands, yawns and looks up the path. 'I'm okay, I think. Maybe later.'

'Sure,' I say. I walk down to the stream and splash water on my face and on the back of my neck. Just as I'm about to take a drink, Commander Sharma wades out of the stream and says it's time to go. We all get ready to continue up the mountain. I grab my Chest and balance its weight on my hip.

Immediately, the trail becomes much steeper. It's also surprisingly slick and absent of rocks, as if this path had been recently washed clear by a storm. We're all having difficulty keeping our footing. Crayton tries running to gain some momentum, but he slips and falls in the dirt.

'This is impossible,' he says, standing up and brushing himself off. 'We're going to need to cut through the forest to gain any kind of traction.'

'Out of the question,' the commander says, his arms out like a tightrope walker. 'We will not conquer our obstacles by running away from them. Speed does not matter, just that we do not stop.'

'It doesn't matter how slowly we go? This message brought to you from the guy who says *very strange* things happen at nightfall,' Six snorts. 'I think you need to tell us how much further we have to go, and if it's longer than three hours on foot, then I say we enter the forest and forgo these obstacles,' she says, staring him down.

I look at the small branch in my hand and an idea comes to me. I concentrate on the trees around us, lowering branches in from both sides. Suddenly we have a way to pull ourselves upwards, rope climbing the Lorien way. 'How about this?' I ask.

Six grabs the line of branches and tests their strength, moving up a few feet. Over her shoulder, she yells, 'Brilliant move, Marina! You rock!'

I continue to bend the trees as we climb. Still wearing the dark glasses, Ella watches the woods around us, occasionally glancing over her shoulder. Once the path levels out and it's easier to maintain our footing, Six digs in and starts to run up the trail ahead of us, circling back regularly to report on what she's seen ahead. Every time it's the same: 'It just keeps going.' Finally, she returns to say there's a fork up ahead. Hearing this, Commander Sharma looks confused and picks up the pace.

When we reach the fork in the dirt path, Commander Sharma frowns. 'This is new.'

'How can it be new?' Crayton asks. 'Both paths look exactly the same. Well traveled and equally so.'

The commander paces in front of the fork. 'I promise you the path on the left did not exist before. We are very close to Vishnu. We go this way.' He begins to walk confidently up the path to the right and Crayton follows.

'Wait,' Ella says, 'I see nothing up ahead on the right. The glasses are just showing me dark emptiness.'

'That's all I need to hear,' Six says.

'No. We go right,' the commander says to Six. 'I've traveled this many times, my dear.' Six pauses, then slowly turns to look at him.

'Do *not* call me dear,' Six warns.

As Commander Sharma and Six glare at each other my eyes are drawn to something scratched in the mouth of the path on the left. The figure is shallow and just a few inches long, and I have to look closely, but there is no question. It's the number eight.

'According to *this*, Ella's right. We go left,' I say, pointing at the number.

Six walks over to the markings and drags the toe of her shoe under the number eight. 'Good eye, Marina.' Crayton looks at it too, and smiles.

We fall back into our normal positions, with Six and a reluctant Commander Sharma up front and me taking up the rear. The path ascends slightly, turning rocky. Then, to everyone's surprise, a steady stream of water begins to flow from ahead of us, down the trail. The rocks under our feet soon become tiny islands. I jump from one rock to another, but in a few minutes the rocks are submerged. All of a sudden, we're walking through a river.

Ella is the first one to speak. 'Maybe the glasses were wrong? Maybe this path wasn't the right one after all.'

'No. This is correct,' the commander says, bending down to drag the tips of his fingers along the surface of the water. 'This is a sign I've seen before.' We have no idea what this cryptic comment means but we've gone this far, so we might as well keep going.

The river current becomes faster and it's harder to move against it. We trudge higher up the path until the water is to Ella's waist and I'm having trouble keeping my balance. But just as quickly as it began, the water slows and the land levels out and opens into a large pool of water. A jagged wall of stone stands high behind the pool, and four separate waterfalls descend from its top, crashing into the water.

'What's that?' Ella points.

In the middle of the giant pool, a white boulder juts

out of the surface. A gleaming blue statue of a crowned man with four arms rests atop the boulder.

'The Almighty Lord Vishnu,' Commander Sharma whispers.

'Wait. That's supposed to be Eight? A statue?' Six says, turning to Crayton.

'What's he holding?' Ella asks. I follow her gaze and see that there's an object in each of his four hands: a pink flower, a white shell, a gold wand, and on the tip of one of his index fingers, a small blue disc that looks like a CD.

The commander wades further into the pool. He's smiling and his hands are shaking. He turns to us. 'Vishnu is the Supreme God. In his left hands, he holds a conch shell to show he has the power to create and maintain the universe, and under that is a mace to signify his power to destroy materialistic and demoniac tendencies. In his right hands are the chakra, to show he has a purified spiritual mind, below that there is the beautiful lotus flower.'

'Which shows divine perfection and purity,' Crayton adds.

'Among other things, yes! That is right, Mr Crayton. Very good.'

I stare at the statue, at its serene blue face and gold crown and the objects in its hands, and I feel myself forgetting about everything else. About the battle at the base of the mountain and the carnage back in Spain. About Adelina and John Smith and Héctor. I forget about my Chest and Lorien and the fact that I'm standing in cold water. The energy flowing through me is magnificent. And judging by the peaceful looks on the faces of the others, the energy is contagious. I find myself closing my eyes and feeling blessed to be here.

'Hey! He's gone!' Ella yells. My eyes snap open to see her whipping off the dark glasses. 'Vishnu's gone!'

She's right – the white boulder in the middle of the lake is empty. I look at Six and Crayton and see they're on high alert, ready for danger. I glance around us. What is this, a trap?

'He will now test you,' Commander Sharma says, interrupting my thoughts. He's the only one among us who doesn't look shocked by Vishnu's disappearance. 'That is why I have brought you here.'

We all see it at the same time. Something is blocking the sun on top of the jagged wall above the pool, and a long, oddly shaped shadow is cast along the water. A figure walks slowly along the ridge until it stands directly above the farthest of the four waterfalls on the left.

'Commander?' I ask. 'Who is *that*?'

'*That* is your first test,' the commander says, stepping onto the grassy shore around the lake. We all follow, without taking our eyes off the figure.

A second later it dives gracefully off the cliff. I notice its legs are strangely short and it has a wide, circular torso. It falls slowly, almost floating, as if it can control gravity. When it breaks the surface of the pool, there is no splash. Not even a ripple. Six reaches up and squeezes the large blue pendant that hangs around her neck. Ella takes a few steps back, away from the lake.

'This could be a trap,' Crayton says quietly, voicing my fear. 'Prepare to fight.'

Six lets the pendant drop from her hands and rubs her palms together. I set my Chest down and begin to mimick her movements, but I feel ridiculous and glance around as surreptitiously as I can to see if anyone noticed. Good thing they are otherwise occupied. Fact is, Six knows how to fight, has trained for this her entire life. Everything she does has a purpose. I'm just rubbing my hands together. I slowly lower my hands back to my side.

'He'll test you one at a time,' says the commander. Six snorts.

'You don't make the rules. Not for us,' Six says. She turns to Crayton, who nods.

'Commander, this is not what we came here to do,' Crayton adds. 'We came here to find our friend, not to be tested or to fight.'

Commander Sharma ignores him, walks into a patch of short grass and sits. I never would have taken him for a guy who could pretzel himself into the lotus position. 'It must be one at a time,' he says serenely.

The being – or whatever it is – that dived into the lake is still under water. And I'm the only one with the Legacy to meet it down there. I know what I have to do.

Still, I'm surprised to hear the words come out of my mouth. 'I'll go first.'

I look over at Six. She nods at me and I dive into the lake. The cool water becomes darker the deeper I swim. My eyes are open, and at first I can only see a few inches of murky water in front of me. But my eyes soon adjust and my vision penetrates far into the lake, my ability to see in the dark coming in handy. I allow the water to enter my lungs, and a familiar calm sweeps over me. I start breathing normally, letting my Legacy take over.

I reach the muddy bottom and spin around, looking in every direction for the thing that dived from the cliff. Something moves over my right shoulder, and I turn to see a figure coming at me. He's wearing a golden crown over his short, jet-black hair. His eyebrows are perfect semicircles, and his nose is pierced with a gold ring. He is strangely beautiful. I can't take my eyes off him.

I stand perfectly still, waiting to see what he wants. He comes closer. When he gets within a few feet of me and I can see him more clearly, my jaw drops. What I thought was a strangely circular torso is, in fact, the body of a turtle. I'm mesmerized, watching to see what he will do next. So much so, I'm taken by surprise when he lunges towards me and hits me with his two right arms.

I go spiraling backwards, the force propelling me with a speed that stuns me. But I'm not in motion for long. My feet quickly find the muddy bottom and I twist around in a panic, trying to find him in the darkness, my senses on alert and on guard. Something taps my shoulder and I turn to see the blue turtle man. Damn, he moves fast. He winks at me, then swings both of his left arms, but this time I'm ready for him. I raise my forearm and knee in time to block them. Then I plant the bottom of my foot squarely on his chest and kick as hard as I can. I flip over and come at him from the back, wrapping my arms around his neck, and look around for something, anything, I can use as a weapon. I see a large rock sticking out of the mud in front of us, and I use my telekinesis to send it at this alien turtle, using all of my strength to pull it through the water. He sees the rock coming and when it's within inches of hitting him, he just disappears. Poof. The rock smashes me instead and I fall back in the mud.

I lie there dazed, waiting for him to appear again, but he doesn't come. Eventually, I decide to float to the top.

The first thing I see as I break the surface is Six, standing at the edge of the water, looking for me. 'What happened?' she calls.

'She passed.' Commander Sharma nods.

'You okay?' Ella shouts. 'I couldn't see anything through the glasses.'

'I'm good,' I yell back. And I really am.

'What do you mean, she passed?' Crayton demands of the commander. 'That was one of his tests?'

The commander just smiles serenely and ignores Crayton.

'Okay, who's next?' Treading water, my eyes follow the commander's finger high over my head. I turn to see a shadowy figure up on the jagged wall again. This time he's a giant bearded man with an axe in his hand.

Six wades into the water up to her knees as I climb out, wringing water out of my long, dark hair. She is all steely determination and confidence when she says, 'Me.'

The figure walks to the third waterfall and dives. This time he makes a massive splash when he hits the pool. We can see the ripple on the surface of the water as he moves towards Six under water. Then the tip of his axe comes out of the lake, followed by his giant head. Six doesn't flinch, doesn't change expression at all, even when he's fully emerged and stands at least four feet taller than her in the shallow water at the edge of the lake.

With a grunt and a howl, the giant swings the axe. Six leaps out of the way but before he can pull back, she kicks at the wooden handle, breaking it in half.

'Way to go, Six!' Ella yells.

The giant swings a fist at her, which she easily avoids with a bob and a weave. With the next beat, she lands a quick kick to his kneecap. As the giant bends over and howls in pain, Six grabs the end of the broken axe handle as it floats by and swings it at his head. The being disappears before it hits him.

'What the hell was that?' Six asks, whipping her head around wildly, on the alert for any kind of reappearance.

Commander Sharma smiles placidly. This guy is really starting to make me angry. 'That was another test, which you passed. There is one more.'

Before anyone can speak, we hear a roar. I reel back with horror at the creature I see emerging from the water. It's over ten feet tall and has the head of a lion and the body of a man. It has five muscular arms flexed at each of its sides. The creature shakes the water from its mane as it steps onto the shore and marches towards Ella, unleashing a second roar.

'Oh. My. God,' Ella says, mouth open and eyes wide.

'No,' Crayton says, stepping in front of Ella. 'You're not ready for this – it's too much.'

Ella rests a hand on Crayton's arm. A small smile breaks across Ella's face and she seems to transform from a scared kid into a Garde prepared to fight. 'It's okay. I can do this.'

Six comes to my side. We're both ready to fight if Ella needs us. The creature moves towards her; she slides my glasses back onto her face. Then, it attacks.

The creature swings all ten arms at Ella, but she ducks and avoids each one. It's as if Ella sees every punch before it happens. The tree behind her ends up taking the beating. Large chunks of wood fly around her, hitting the creature's face, bouncing off its chest. Not running away but not fighting back either, Ella circles the tree trunk, continuing to dodge the ten fists. The tree is getting pummeled.

Suddenly, Ella screams. 'Oh no! What have I done?'

Before I can figure out what Ella means, there's a loud *crack* and the heavy tree trunk tips forward. It's about to crush the creature when the figure disappears just like all the others. As the tree continues its fall to the ground, a branch swipes the dark glasses off Ella's face and they are crushed by a huge tree branch. 'Marina, I'm so sorry! I knew the glasses were going to be broken, but I couldn't do anything to stop it.'

Crayton, Six, and I run over to Ella, who's staring in horror at the fragments of the glasses by her feet. 'Ella! Don't worry about the glasses. You held your own and that thing disappeared. What's important is that you're okay. I'm so proud of you,' I tell her.

'Ella, that was amazing!' says Six.

'Congratulations,' the commander says, still sitting calmly, Buddha-like. 'You have just defeated three of Vishnu's avatars. You've passed his test. The first was Kurma, a half man, half tortoise who churned the ancient ocean so that other peaceful gods could regain immortality. The man with the axe was Parashurama, the first warrior saint. The last was one of the most powerful incarnations of Vishnu, the man-lion, Narismha. Now, we await Vishnu's arrival.'

'We're done waiting,' says Crayton, turning to the

commander, jaw set and fists clenched by his side. 'He'd better show himself, and fast.'

'Chill, chill, chill,' a boy's voice says, emerging from the high grass behind me. 'The commander was just following my orders. I was being cautious.'

From the grass we now see the statue of Vishnu step towards us, alive and smiling.

'I've been waiting a long time to meet you.'

10

Sitting on a metal chair, I'm in a Plexiglas cage in the back of a small truck. My hands are cuffed to the chair and my ankles are secured with heavy shackles. A strap of leather pulls my forehead back against the Plexiglas wall behind me. I'm facing the side of the truck, but can turn my head just enough to see Nine, also in a Plexiglas cage, a few feet away from me. In front of me a guard is watching us. I know I could free myself in an instant, but BK, who's still hiding in my pocket, is right. We need to see what they know and how it could help us. Nine must agree because he is even more capable of breaking the binds that hold him, but he, too, does nothing. There are a bunch of locks on our cages and the only way we can talk through the thick Plexiglas is through the eight tiny holes in the cage doors. The truck's engine is running, but we haven't moved an inch.

Special Agent Walker is sitting on a long metal bench near the front of the truck. She has one foot on my Chest, and the other on Nine's. A Mogadorian cannon lies across her lap. The man with the crooked nose is sitting next to her with the other cannon. Walker is whispering into a cell phone. Every so often she glances over at us. I can almost hear what she's saying, catching words like *boyfriend* and *powerless*. I remember Nine saying back in the mountain that he can hear for miles. I hope he's picking up more than I am.

'Hey, John!' Nine yells.

The guard turns towards Nine's cage and aims a rifle at Nine's head. 'You! Shut up!'

Nine ignores him. 'Johnny! When do you want to roll on out of here? I don't know about you, but I'm bored, I could use a change of scenery.' He does enjoy pissing people off. I'm beginning to understand the appeal.

Special Agent Walker closes her phone and pinches the bridge of her nose with her fingers. She looks like an aggravated parent or teacher, her exhaustion wiping away a lot of her authority. Then she takes a deep breath and sits up straight, as if she's made a decision. She knocks on the window, indicating the driver should start moving.

She stands and marches towards us, balancing herself with the cannon over her head. She comes to a stop in front of me. There's something in her eyes that wasn't there before. It's almost as if she's sorry she caught us. Or she's sorry about what she has to do next. Or both.

'How did you find us?' I ask.

'You know how,' she says.

I still have the bracelet around my wrist. It's been quiet for the last few minutes, but as soon as the agent speaks, it begins to buzz again.

Nine shouts, 'Hey, I wasn't kidding about being bored here. I don't feel like playing nice anymore. It's up to you, but you should know that you don't have long before I decide to amuse myself. You can tell us everything you know right now, or I'll kick my way out of here and make you tell me. Guess which one will make my day a little more fun?'

The man with the crooked nose rises slowly from the bench and aims his cannon directly at Nine. 'Who do you think you are, kid? You're in no position to threaten us.'

'Whatever you're planning, I promise, I've been through worse,' Nine says.

'I know exactly where you were before. Don't you get that? We *know*.' The man sounds annoyed by Nine's bravado.

'Agent Purdy,' Walker says to him. 'Lower your weapon. Now.'

The agent starts to lower it and I decide to have some fun. I guess Nine is rubbing off on me. Using my telekinesis, I rip the cannon out of his hands and toss it to the back of the truck. It hits the back door before landing on the floor with a clang. Just at that moment we take a sharp corner and Agent Purdy stumbles towards me, his right shoulder slamming against my cage. I use my telekinesis to keep him pinned in place.

'Son of a . . .'

'Don't you know you should always wear a seat belt, Agent Pretty?' Nine laughs. 'Safety first! Here, take one of mine. You just need to come on in here to get it.'

Agent Purdy says, 'However you're doing this, you better stop it.' He tries to sound scary, but it's hard to sound threatening in his position.

I lean forward, easily breaking the strap across my forehead. Playtime is over. 'Agent Purdy, do you know where Sam Goode is?'

'We have Sam,' Special Agent Walker says, turning towards me. Her voice is casual but her cannon is pointing right at me.

For a second, I'm so blown away by this new piece of information my mind goes blank, and I accidentally release Agent Purdy. He crashes into the aisle.

They have Sam? Setrákus Ra isn't torturing him in the cave like I saw in my vision? He's okay? I'm about to ask where Sam is when I notice the lights swirling in the tube of Special Agent Walker's cannon. Instead of green, these lights are black and red.

She grins at the alarmed look on my face. 'If you're lucky, *John Smith*, or whatever your name is, we'll show you a video of how we use our interrogation techniques on Sam. But if you're *really* lucky, we'll show you some footage of that little blonde girlfriend of yours. What's her name again?'

'Ooooohhhh, shit,' Nine says. I can hear the grin in his voice as he knows what is about to go down. 'Now you've gone and done it.'

It takes me a second to find my voice. 'Sarah,' I whisper. 'I know she's working with you. What did you have to tell her to turn her against me?'

Agent Purdy grabs his cannon and settles back into his seat. 'Are you kidding me? That girl wouldn't tell us a thing, and, believe me, we asked *many* things in *many* different ways. She had nothing to say to *us*. She's *in love*.'

Once again, I'm stunned. I was so sure Sarah was working with the government to bring me in. When I saw her last week in Paradise, she acted so strange. She met me in the park, but then started getting mysterious text messages – at two in the morning. Seconds later we were surrounded by agents and being slammed to the ground. I can't think of anything else that explains it. It had to have been those text messages; they must have been from the police. How else could they have known that Sam and I were there? Damn. Now I don't know what to think. *And* she's still in love with me?

'Where is she?' I demand.

'Far, far away,' Special Agent Walker says. Is she taunting me?

'Who cares, dude?' Nine yells, interrupting. 'Big picture, Johnny, big picture! She's not in it! Neither is Sam!'

I ignore him. Now that I know the U.S. government has Sam *and* Sarah, I'm determined to find them both. I'm thinking of my next move, my next question, when I feel Bernie Kosar crawling out of my jeans pocket.

It's almost time to go, he says. *We'll take the woman to lead us to Sam and Sarah.*

'Nine,' I say. 'You ready to get out of here?'

'God, yes. Been ready forever. I really have to pee.'

Special Agent Walker glances from me to Nine and back again. She doesn't know where to point the cannon, so she moves it back and forth between us. Agent Purdy stands again and does the same. The guard in the back of the truck points his rifle at us.

'If they move, shoot anything but a vital organ!' Agent Purdy says, moving to stand shoulder to shoulder with Special Agent Walker.

Bernie Kosar jumps from my lap and crawls up the glass door. He flitters his tiny cockroach wings at me and he says to count to five.

'Hey, Nine?' I ask.

'I'm already on three, my man,' he says.

Walker shouts at us to shut up. My bracelet vibrates and sends a thousand pinpricks up and down my wrist but I ignore it. Nine breaks all of his restraints as if they were nothing, and stands up. I do the same, though it takes more effort for me. Nine kicks the Plexiglas wall at the front of his cage and the whole thing pops easily out of its frame. As he steps out, the guard fires at him. With a smile he just raises his hand and stops bullets in midair. He lowers his hand, and the bullets fall to the floor one at a time.

He looks over at me, 'Need some help there, buddy?' He kicks in a wall of my cage, and I step out. BK scrambles back into my pocket.

Before the guard can do anything, I use my telekinesis to launch him to the ceiling and twist his weapon into a useless piece of metal. Agents Walker and Purdy both fire their Mog cannons at us, but Nine stops the streams that come out of them. He smiles, and shakes his finger at the two agents. 'No, no, no. You should know better by now.' He looks over at me. 'Get ready, Johnny, 'cause we are going for a spin!'

The truck immediately flies off the road and starts rolling. Without warning, Nine grabs me and links arms, pulling me along until I gain my footing. We run up the left side of the truck, moving like a hamster in a wheel so we can stay horizontal as the truck flips over and over. Metal crunches around us, sparks rain from every corner and the guard and agents look like rag dolls as they're tossed in all directions. The force of the crash causes the back doors to pop open and when the truck stops rolling, we jump out. There were a number of police vehicles trailing us and they've all come to a screeching halt with their sirens blaring.

'Hey, John?' Nine says, unfazed by any of it.

'Yeah?' I say, shaking my head as I try to lose the dizzy feeling from the spinning truck. Neither of us is taking our eyes off the blinking crowd of police cars.

He starts to step back towards the truck and I do the same. 'We gotta get our Chests back, dude, and do what BK said and get that woman agent.'

'Definitely.' I pat my pocket, making sure BK is still there.

'So why don't you take care of that, while I take care of this.' Nine telekinetically lifts two police cruisers off the ground, and the officers inside struggle to get out.

I dash back to the truck, now smoldering in the ditch. I jump inside, avoiding the guard and Agent Purdy, moaning on the floor, and find our Chests. Special Agent Walker sits against what remains of the metal bench, staring at the blood on her hands in a daze. Her red hair falls loosely down her shoulders, and there's a long scrape along the side of her face. The Mog cannon is now a shattered pile of parts under her legs. She watches me arrange the Chests under my arms, and I drop to a knee in front of her.

'You're coming with us.' I am not asking.

She opens her mouth to speak, and a trail of blood trickles out. It's then that I see the piece of metal sticking out of her shoulder. I put down one of the Chests and try picking her up, but she groans and coughs up more blood. I let go, afraid if I move her again she'll bleed out and die before I can find out where Sarah and Sam are.

'Where are they?' I ask. 'Tell me now! You are going to die any second, lady, and I'm trying to save Earth and my friends. Now, tell me! Where are Sam and Sarah?'

Special Agent Walker's head flops in my direction and her green eyes open wide, as if seeing me for the first time. The gunfire outside is getting closer. 'You . . . you're an alien,' she finally whispers.

I punch the side of the truck in frustration. 'Yeah, I am! But I'm here to help, if you would just let me! Now, before you run out of time, out of breath, tell me where they are. In Washington?'

Her breathing turns ragged and it's as if she can't see or hear me. I'm losing her. I'm losing her and I still don't know where Sarah and Sam are. My voice sounds small all of a sudden. 'Just tell me where they are. Please.' Our eyes meet and I can tell I've gotten through to her.

Special Agent Walker's mouth opens to speak and it takes a couple of tries to find her voice. 'Out west. In . . .,' then her voice trails off and her eyes close. Her bloody hands clench and then relax; her whole body goes slack.

'Wait! Hold on!' I frantically grab at my Chest, trying to get it open so I can get my healing stone. All I can think is, if I heal her she'll tell me where they are. I've just placed my hand on the lock of the Chest when a group of officers jump into the open end of the truck, guns drawn.

'Get away from the agent! Move! Or we'll shoot! Down on the ground! Hands behind your back! Now!' They are barking orders at me, but I can't obey. I don't want to obey. I need to get the healing stone. I need to hear what she was going to say. I reach to open the Chest and I hear the officers screaming, 'Hands up. HANDS UP. HANDS UP!' I reach into my Chest anyway.

I hear the first gunshot, immediately followed by dozens more. As the hail of bullets fly around me, my wrist starts to tingle more strongly than ever. It doesn't hurt anymore, and the bracelet starts to expand, covering my entire arm with a sheath of red material before spreading and popping open like an umbrella. I have no idea what is going on and I really don't care. I can only think of my healing stone and the limp body of Walker so close and yet so useless. Suddenly, I'm behind a six-foot-high shield that curls up over my head and under my feet. The bullets bounce right off it.

An orchestra of gunfire erupts, and countless bullets ricochet off my shield. After a couple of minutes, they become less and less frequent, like microwave popcorn that's almost done. When the gunshots finally stop, the red material compresses itself back into the arm sheath, and then shrinks into the tingling bracelet around my wrist, all of its own volition. I look down, amazed at how effective it is, how perfect its timing is.

Walker is still lying unconscious by my feet. The officers with their guns trained on the back of the truck just a moment ago are gone, but I hear gunfire outside. I'm torn between looking for my healing stone to revive Walker and going outside to see if Nine needs help. I want to wake her up, force her to tell me where Sam and Sarah are, but I can't leave Nine alone if he's in trouble. I decide that Walker will keep – she's clearly not going anywhere and I just have to hope she doesn't die on me. I take the opportunity to stuff a Chest under each arm and run out. As soon as I emerge I see the officers running in the opposite direction. I don't know what Nine did while I was in there getting to know my bracelet a little better, but they all look terrified.

'Ah, Nine?' I call over. 'What exactly did you do to them?'

He smiles. 'Just used my telekinesis to lift them all about thirty feet in the air. Then I offered them a choice: go higher or run away. I applaud the wisdom of their decision, don't you?'

'Looks like they made the right choice,' I say.

'Hey, I thought we were bringing the agent woman with us,' Nine says.

'She's still inside – she's unconscious and I was going to

use my healing stone on her, but I wanted to check on you first, make sure you were okay,' I tell him.

'Dude, you were worried about *me*? I *got* this. We need her to tell us where we're going! You're the one who refuses to go anywhere that isn't towards your friends. Remember?' Nine picks up an assault rifle and shoots it into the air. 'Get in there and get her! I'll be out here, playing with the soldier toys.'

Officers continue to retreat on foot, some hiding behind trees on the side of the road. Nine aims the gun above their heads. The rifle rocks against his shoulder and the bullets zip through the high branches. I can hear him cackling, enjoying the spectacle, as I move back to the truck.

I open my Chest and pull out my healing stone and duck into the truck to see how badly Walker is injured.

But she's not there. I look around, as if she might have gotten up and moved to a different part of the truck. I'm completely confused by what I'm seeing. What I am *not* seeing. There is no one there. The bodies that were there minutes ago are all gone. Shit.

I'm furious with myself. I can't believe how badly I've screwed this up. Not only do we still not know where they have Sam and Sarah, but it is likely that Purdy and Walker are still out there.

11

Number Eight is sitting in the grass. The lake is calm and still behind him. 'I am known by many different names. Some call me Vishnu, while others call me Paramatma or Parameshwara. I am also known by my ten avatars, three of whom you have met and battled. Quite successfully, I might add.'

'If they are your avatars, they are a part of you. Which means, *you* felt it necessary to declare war on three girls who were trying to reach you.' Crayton spits out. 'You're supposed to be impersonating a peaceful god, aren't you?'

'You have a lot of explaining to do,' Marina adds.

He is unmoved by our anger and remains seated. 'I had to be sure you are who you claim to be. I had to be sure you were ready to meet me. My apologies if your feelings, or anything else, were hurt. You all proved yourselves, if that makes you feel any better.'

I'm fed up. I'm tired and hungry. Not to mention I flew across the world *and* fought an army to get here. I want answers. I stand up, fists clenched at my sides. 'I'm going to ask a question, and if you don't answer me directly, we're leaving. This isn't a philosophical discussion; and you had no right to test us. Are you, or are you not, Number Eight?'

He looks up at me and purses his lips. His skin color changes from blue to a deep copper tone. When he shakes his head, the crown falls off and his black hair grows into a shaggy mop of curls. Two of his arms vanish, and in a matter of seconds, a shirtless teenage guy sits on the grass in front of us. Commander Sharma gasps.

He's kind of thin, but toned. With his full lips and thick black eyebrows, I must say he's kind of hot. Around his neck hangs a blue Lorien pendant.

He's one of us.

Ella looks over at Crayton, who exhales a long breath. He opens his mouth, about to say something, but the boy speaks first.

'My Cêpan originally named me Joseph, but I have gone by many names. In this region, most people know me by the name Naveen.' He pauses and looks at me, then pulls up the ragged leg of his pants to reveal the scarred Loric symbols of One, Two and Three on his ankle. 'If you want to get all Loric on me, then yes, you can call me Number Eight.'

The anger bubbling inside of me pops and disappears. We have found another member of the Garde. We just got stronger.

Crayton steps forward and offers his hand. 'We've been looking for you, Eight. We've traveled a long distance. I'm Crayton, Ella's Cêpan.'

Eight stands and shakes Crayton's hand. He's tall, and every muscle in his upper body and stomach is *very* well defined. He's clearly been training for years, surviving alone in the mountains.

Ella stands as well. 'I'm Ella,' she says. 'I'm Number Ten.'

'Whoa!' Eight says. He looks into her eyes. 'What do you mean, you're Number Ten? There're only nine of us. Who told you you're Number Ten?'

All of a sudden, Ella shrinks down to become a six-year-old girl. I guess there's nothing quite like having your identity being questioned by a former statue to give you a crisis of confidence. Crayton nudges Ella, and then, just as quickly, she transforms back into her tall, twelve-year-old self.

Eight responds by growing five feet taller to tower over her. 'That all you got, Ten?'

Determination covers Ella's face and it looks as if she's trying to grow another few years, but nothing happens. After a few seconds, she shrugs, 'I guess so.'

Crayton turns to Eight. 'I'll fill you in later, but there was another ship that left Lorien after yours. Ella and I were on that ship. She was just a baby at the time.'

'Is that it, or is there a Number Thirty-Two I should know about?' Eight asks, shrinking back down to his regular height. His voice is husky, but also kind. For the first time, I notice his eyes are the most amazing shade of deep green. By the look on Marina's face, she is noticing all of this too. I can't help but smile as she nervously tucks her hair behind her ears.

'Ella's the last,' Crayton answers. 'This is Six, and this is Marina, Number Seven. You appear to be able to shape shift. Anything else we should know about?'

In response, Eight expands into a two-headed giraffe, towering twenty feet above us this time. I try to suppress my smile.

'Indeed I do have that Legacy,' the head on the left says.

The head on the right lowers to the water and takes a drink before looking up and adding, 'Among other things.'

'Oh, yeah? Like what?' Marina asks.

Eight turns back into a boy and skips along the surface of the pool as if it were solid ice.

When he circles back to us, he begins to sprint before skidding to a stop, sending a wave of water towards Marina.

But Marina is not going to get shown up by the new guy. Without flinching, she lifts her hands and stops the water midair, then pushes it back at Eight with her telekinesis. He in turn blows the wave high into the air like a geyser. Not to be left out of whatever game it is they're playing, I take control of the wind and I use it to push the geyser across the pool until a wall of moving water surrounds Eight on three sides.

'What else ya got?' I shout, my voice daring him to keep things going.

Eight disappears from where I've trapped him behind the water and an instant later reappears on the jagged rocks above the pool. He disappears again and shows up inches from my nose.

Eight's sudden closeness is so jarring I reflexively throw a fist into his ribs. He grunts and stumbles backwards.

'Six! What are you doing?' Marina yells.

'Sorry,' I say. 'It was a reflex.'

'I deserved it,' says Eight, shrugging off Marina's protectiveness.

'So you can teleport?' Marina asks. 'That is *very* cool.'

He suddenly appears at her side and casually

leans an arm on her shoulder. 'I'm a fan of it.' Marina giggles and shrugs him off. *Giggles? Is she kidding me?*

Eight smiles, disappears and shows up again standing on Crayton's shoulders, balancing with exaggerated arm circles and wobbly legs. 'Sometimes I pick stupid places to land, though.' Eight is our jester, all of a sudden.

I'm struck by his playfulness, unsure if it's going to be an attribute or a liability. I decide to view it as a positive. I can just see the annoyance and confusion on the Mogadorians' faces moments before this kid turns them to ash. Crayton leans forward and, as if they'd rehearsed the routine in advance, Eight does a flip onto the ground, then claps his hands, obviously pleased with himself.

'Where's your Cêpan?' Marina asks.

Eight's cheerful face turns serious. We all know what this means. Instantly, my mind goes to an image of Katarina gagged and chained to a wall. I think of John and his Cêpan, Henri. I shake away the memories before tears form in my eyes.

'How long ago?' Crayton gently asks the question we are all thinking.

Eight spins to look out over the field of high grass beyond us. With his mind, he parts the grass left and right until there's a narrow path.

He raises his head at the setting sun. 'Listen, we have to get out of here. The light is going. I'll tell you all about Reynolds and Lola on the way.'

Commander Sharma runs up to Eight and grabs his wrist. 'What about me? What can I do for you? Please tell me.' He startles me. I've been so wrapped up in our little session of getting-to-know-you, and he's been so quiet, I completely forgot his role in all this.

'Commander,' Eight says. 'You have been a loyal friend to me and I want to thank you and your soldiers for all your hard work. Vishnu would be very happy with your devotion. I'm afraid now we must part ways.'

It's clear by the expression on the commander's face that he thought he was in this for the long haul.

'But I don't understand. I have done everything you have asked of me. I brought you your friends. My men have died for you.'

Eight looks Commander Sharma in the eyes. 'I never wished for anyone to die for me. That's why I refused to leave the mountain and walk with you in the streets. I'm sorry lives were lost, more sorry than you will ever know. Believe me, I know what it feels like to lose people. But, this is where we must go our separate ways.' He's firm, but I can see it's hard for him to do this.

'But –'

Eight cuts him off. 'Good-bye, Commander.'

The man turns, a look of despair on his face. Poor guy. But he is a soldier who knows when to take an order, when to accept how things are going to be. 'You're leaving me.'

'No,' Eight says. '*You* are leaving *me*. You are off to something bigger and better. A wise man once told me that only by leaving someone good can you meet someone better. You will be with your Vishnu, and you will only know him once I am gone.'

It's hard to watch. Commander Sharma opens his mouth to say something, but closes it when Eight turns and walks down the path without looking back. At first, I think Eight is being too harsh. Then I realize, this is the kindest way he can do what must be done.

'Hey! Wait!' Crayton calls after Eight. 'The base of the mountain is the other way. We have to get to the airport.'

'First, I need to show you all something,' he calls back. 'And we may not need an airport.'

'Where are you going? There are things you don't know yet. We need to sit down and talk, we need to make a plan!' says Crayton.

'I wish I didn't break those glasses,' Ella says. 'We can't just *follow* him without knowing where he's taking us or if it's a good idea. He thinks he knows everything, but he may *not*.'

We watch Crayton think about what to do. I know what *I* think we should do. We've finally found another member of the Garde, and we have to stick together now. I nod towards Eight's quickly disappearing figure. Crayton looks at me, then nods back. He scoops up Marina's Chest, and begins to walk after Eight. Without saying anything, Marina and Ella hold hands and start to follow him. I get in line behind them. I use my advanced hearing to listen for sounds of the commander moving from the spot where we left him. I hear nothing. I can picture him standing there, still and silent long after we've left. I understand why it had to be done, but I still feel sorry for the guy. Left behind, after all his loyalty. I look at Eight's back, ramrod straight ahead of me, and I feel bad for both of them.

Eight leads on. We follow him down a hill and find ourselves in a wide-open valley. Everywhere I look there are snow-tipped Himalayan Mountains. Closer by, there are patches of forest with fields of yellow and purple flowers in between. It's beautiful. We're all soaking it in as we walk when Crayton breaks the silence.

'So. Who were Reynolds and Lola?'

Eight slows so we can walk together. He reaches down to pick a handful of purple flowers only to crush them in his hand. 'Reynolds was my Cêpan. He laughed a lot. He was always laughing. He laughed when we were on the run and when we slept under a bridge or hid in someone's leaky barn in a monsoon.' He turns to look at us each in turn. 'Does anyone remember him?'

We all shake our heads, even Crayton. I wish I could. But I was only two years old when we made the journey.

Eight continues. 'He was a great Loric and an even better friend. But Lola ... Lola was a human he fell in love with when we first got here. That was eight years ago. They met at the market, and from that moment on they were inseparable. Reynolds was so in love. Lola moved in with us very quickly. She barely left our house.' Eight kicks a patch of flowers. 'I should have *known* she couldn't be trusted by the way she looked at me, how she always wanted to know where I was, what I was doing. I wouldn't let her near my Chest, no matter how many ways she tried. But Reynolds trusted her so much, he eventually told her who we were. He told her *everything*.'

'Not smart,' I say. John told Sarah, and look at where that got them. Trusting humans with our secret is too risky. Love only makes it more risky.

'I can't even describe how angry I was. When I realized what he had done, I lost it. He and I fought for days. We had never argued before. I trusted him completely, and it wasn't that I suddenly didn't trust *him*. It was *her*. That was when Lola started pushing us to come into the mountains with her to hike and camp. She said she knew the perfect place. She convinced Reynolds it would help him make peace with me, for us to *bond*. I thought Lola's plan to get Reynolds and me to kiss and make up was unlikely, but I went anyway.' He stops walking long enough to point at a mountain peak due north. 'We went to that mountain right there. I brought along my Chest. By that point I could teleport and I had telekinesis, plus my strength was off the charts – and I needed to train and figured the mountain air would help me get stronger, faster. But as soon as we arrived, Lola kept trying to separate us. She did everything to get Reynolds to leave me alone. In the end, she had to make do with Plan B.' He turns away and resumes walking. We give him a few steps to pull himself together.

'So what was Plan B?' Marina asks gently, trying to move him along. He needs to tell us all of this, but we don't have to torture him.

'On the third night in the mountains, she left to gather firewood, leaving me and Reynolds alone for the first time the whole trip. I knew something was wrong. I felt it in the pit of my stomach. Lola returned quickly – with a dozen Mogadorian warriors. Reynolds, he was so in love with her, he was heartbroken before he remembered to be scared. He screamed at her, begging her to explain why she would do this to him, to us, to me. Then one of the warriors threw a bag of gold coins in Lola's general direction. She was promised a lot of money by the Mogadorians to provide a *service*.' Eight sneers the word. 'Like a dog jumping on a treat, she dived at it. It all happened so fast. She dived, one of the Mogadorians raised a glowing sword and stabbed her in the back, and the bag of coins exploded at her feet. Reynolds and I just stood there, frozen, watching her die.'

I resist the urge to dash ahead, grab his hand, and squeeze it to show how much I understand how he feels. I look at his straight, proud back, watch the purpose in his long strides, and know what he needs right now is his space. At least, that's what I want when I think about Katarina dying.

His last word, *die*, hangs in the air. Finally, Crayton clears his throat and says, 'We don't need to hear any more right now. You can stop if you want.'

'They couldn't kill me,' Eight's voice gets louder, as if he's trying to drown out the sad memories. I know the trick. It rarely works. 'Even when they managed a direct hit with one of their swords, across my neck or into my stomach, I didn't die. But they did. The deadly cuts meant for me happened to them instead. They couldn't kill me because of the charm, and I did everything I could to protect Reynolds. But we were separated in all the chaos and I teleported too late. Reynolds was . . .' He pauses for a second. 'One of them took my Chest. I tried to stop him. I grabbed one of their swords and I tried to stab him through his stomach, but I missed by *this much.* Pretty sure I took off his hand, though. Anyway, he got away. Right after he ran into the woods, I saw a tiny silver ship shoot up through the trees. I killed the others.' His voice is so cold, so emotionless, I shiver.

'I lost my Cêpan too,' Marina says quietly after a moment.

'Me too,' I add. I glance over at Ella, who has moved closer to Crayton. At least she still has him. Hopefully we won't lose the last Cêpan that any of us knows.

The sky above us grows darker by the second.

Marina volunteers to walk in front so that she can lead the way with her Legacy of night vision. I smile when she takes Eight's hand, happy that someone tries to comfort him.

'I've spent so much time in these mountains,' Eight says.

'All alone?' Ella asks.

'I was alone for some of it. I didn't know where to go. And then one day I came across an old man. He was sitting under a tree with his eyes closed, praying. My Legacy to become other shapes had arrived months earlier, and I approached him in the form of a small, black rabbit. He felt my approach. He laughed before he even opened his eyes. There was something about his face that I trusted. I guess he reminded me of Reynolds, before Lola came into our lives. So I hopped into the bushes and teleported behind a line of trees in the opposite direction. When I approached him again, in my regular form, he offered me some lettuce. It was clear that he knew me, would always know me, no matter what form I took.'

'We're coming to another lake,' Marina says, interrupting Eight. Now that the talking has stopped, I can hear the lapping of water and a quiet waterfall beyond.

'Yes, we're close,' Eight confirms. 'We'll eat and sleep soon.'

'So, then what happened? With the old man?' Crayton asks.

'His name was Devdan and he was a very enlightened, spiritual person. He told me all about Hinduism and Vishnu. I clung to his stories. In my mind, they represented how we're trying to save Lorien. He taught me ancient forms of Indian martial arts, like kalarippayattu, silambam and gatka. I worked with my Legacies, my powers, to see how far I could take what I learned from him.

'One day, I went to meet him in our usual spot and he wasn't there. I went back day after day. But he never returned and I was alone again. It was many months later when I stumbled upon Commander Sharma and his army during a training exercise.' He hesitates before continuing. 'Unfortunately – or fortunately, I'm not sure yet – it was while I was in the shape of Vishnu and they vowed to protect me from any evils. I knew it was because I was in a form they worshipped, and I hated preying on their beliefs, but I couldn't resist. I guess I hated being alone even more.'

Marina starts to lead us around the lake. Eight tells her to head for the waterfall we can hear in the distance.

'Did the Mogs ever come back?' Crayton asks.

'Yes. They still return in the tiny silver ships

every so often, buzzing around the mountains to see if I'm still here. But I just turn into a fly or an ant and they keep going.'

Crayton says, 'That lines up with all of the reports of UFO sightings in this region.'

'Yes, that's them,' Eight says. 'With every visit, they become more careless about detection. I haven't seen one in a few days, but they've been much more frequent in the last six or eight months. I took this to mean the conflict was escalating.'

'It is,' I say. 'We've been finding each other, joining up. Marina, Ella, and I just met up in Spain a few days ago. Number Four is waiting for us back in America. And now we've found you. That just leaves Five and Nine.'

Eight is silent for a moment. 'I want to thank you for traveling all this way for me. It's been so long since I've had anyone to talk to. To talk about my real life.'

The waterfall is now just feet away. 'Now what?' I have to yell to be heard over the noise of the water.

'We climb!' Eight yells back, motioning to a sheer, stone wall in front of us.

I place my hand on the stone's smooth surface and tap my foot around to find a toehold. My foot immediately slips, and when I'm about to try it again, I hear Eight's voice far away, above me. He is already at the top, yelling something down at us. Teleportation is even better than I thought. It may even be better than invisibility. I wonder if we can combine them somehow.

'Just use your telekinesis to float your way up,' Marina says to me. 'You get Ella. I'll get Crayton.'

I follow her advice and we float up. It's actually much easier than I imagined. Up at the top is Eight's campsite. Soon we're sitting around a fire, cooking a vegetable stew in a large pot. The trees overhead form a thick canopy and, with the water below, it's a perfect spot to hide. Eight's mud hut is somehow both depressing and ideal at the same time. The walls are uneven and the door is a lopsided oval; but it's also warm and dry, and it smells of fresh flowers. Inside is a homemade hammock and a small table, and three colorful rugs hanging from the walls.

'Nice place you've got here,' I say, walking back to the fire. 'I've been on the run so long, I forget what it's like to have a home. Even a hut.'

'There is something about this place. There will always be a piece of me that remains here. I'm really going to miss it,' he says, looking around fondly.

'So, does that mean you'll come with us?' Marina asks.

'Of course I will. The time has come for us to be together, to work together. Now that Setrákus Ra is here, I have to go with you.'

'He's here?' Crayton asks, suddenly uneasy.

Eight takes his first bite of stew. 'He arrived a few days ago. He's been visiting me in my dreams.'

12

We jumped a freight train in West Virginia. I've been trying to sleep, but too many thoughts are swirling around in my mind. I squint as my eyes adjust to the morning sun coming through the slatted door. I'm relieved to see we're still headed west. That's all Special Agent Walker said before disappearing: west. So, that's where we're going. I try not to think about the possibility that she may have deliberately misled us, and instead focus on how she thought she was about to die and had nothing left to lose, and therefore no reason to lie to me.

I roll onto my back. The ceiling of the train car is dirty, stained a variety of colors. I stare at a dark blue spot directly above my head for so long, I finally drift off to sleep. I dream, which I often do. But this one is different, more of a nightmare than a vision.

I'm in West Virginia, back in the prison cell. Only this time, it is empty and brightly lit from above. The spherical cage that held Sam is now empty. The only indication he was ever there is a pool of still-wet blood on the floor. I walk into the middle of the cell, look around frantically and try to scream his name, but as soon as I open my mouth the bright lights from above are sucked into my throat, stealing my breath, choking me. I fall to my hands and knees, trying to get some air.

Still gasping, I look up. Now I am in a large arena, with thousands of Mogadorians going wild in the stands. They chant and throw things down at me while fights break out among them. The floor is a shiny black slab of rock. I rise from all fours shakily. When I take one step forward, the ground behind me falls away, leaving only a black abyss. Above me is a giant hole and through this hole I see a group of clouds moving across a blue sky. It takes me a moment to realize where I am – inside the peak of a mountain.

'Four!' It's Nine's voice. Nine! I'm not alone. I look around and try to yell back, but my throat is still clogged. A beam of light escapes my mouth. Instinctively, I twist around and try to aim the light until it finally lands on Nine. He's on the other side of the arena, but something is blocking my view of him. It's Sam. He's hanging between us, his wrists in shackles. Agent Purdy and Special Agent Walker stand below him, their Mogadorian cannons aimed at Sam's chest. I don't hesitate. I run to my best friend, the rock falling away behind me with every step I take. The roar of the crowd escalates until it's absolutely deafening.

When I've almost reached them, the black rock where the agents stand drops away, and they fall with it.

'Help! Help me, please, help me,' Sam yells, his body twisting, trying to break free from the shackles.

I try using my telekinesis to free him, but it doesn't work.

I try to use my Lumen, but my palms remain dark. My Legacies are failing me.

'Bring the rest, John,' Sam says to me. 'Bring them all.'

His voice sounds strange, like it's not his. It's almost like someone – or something – evil is speaking through him.

Suddenly the tan, thin boy who appeared in my last vision is next to me. Once again, he's transparent, like a ghost. When I see he's wearing a Loric pendant around his neck, I reach out for him. But he shakes his head at me and places a finger to his lips. The boy leaps onto Sam and climbs up his legs and body until he can get his hands around the chains. I watch him strain, trying to pull apart the shackles, and I can see the surprise on his face when he realizes he doesn't have the strength to do it.

In my last vision, he asked me what number I was, and I feel an enormous pull to speak to him. I cough, clear my throat, and I know my voice has finally returned. I yell, 'I am Number Four!' just as the arena falls silent.

'Have you made your decision?' Sam asks. He continues to twist and turn in his shackles, the other boy still struggling to break his chains above him. Sam looks right at me and I can see his eyes are a deep maroon color. This is not Sam, I tell myself.

All at once, Sam's body begins shaking so violently that the other boy loses his grip on him and I can only watch in horror as he falls and disappears into the same chasm that swallowed the agents. A purple glow then surrounds Sam, and the chains break of their own accord. Instead of falling, like the boy, like the agents, Sam floats, suspended in mid-air. A spotlight snaps on and I watch, disbelievingly, as Sam grows and transforms – into Setrákus Ra. The three Loric pendants around Setrákus Ra's neck glow brightly, as does the purple scar circling his throat. 'Do you want the human back?' he bellows.

'I will take him back!' I yell at him, furious. I'm rooted to the spot, nothing but abyss around me, nowhere to step on to get closer to him.

Setrákus floats slowly to the ground. He lands and the rocks show no sign of giving way as they have for the rest of us. 'This is your surrender? Fine. I shall accept your pendant now.'

I look down and my pendant is already gone. I look up again to see it hanging from Setrákus Ra's giant fist. His cracked lips open to reveal a sharp, crooked-toothed grin.

'No! I will not surrender!' The moment I say it, I feel a sudden weight around my neck. My pendant is back.

The other boy leaps from the chasm into which he fell and lands near Setrákus Ra, his head held high. The boy joins my cry, 'I will never surrender to you! Let Devdan go, and fight me!'

'Time is running out,' Setrákus Ra says and I now realize he is speaking to both of us – that he has been the whole time. He was trying to get both of us to surrender. Did he think he could convince us both to sacrifice ourselves in the belief that he would allow the others to live? I can only hope none of the others fall for his tricks.

The blue stain on the ceiling of the train car is suddenly

all I see, and I sit up abruptly, trying to shake off the dream that has left my brain fuzzy. I touch the bracelet around my wrist. Before I drifted off into my vision, my nightmare, I had discovered that by concentrating on the bracelet's abilities, I was able to remove it. But the moment it left my wrist, I felt unsafe without it and hurriedly popped it back on. I touch it again and wonder if my reliance on it is a good or a bad thing. All of a sudden, something small bumps against my back and I jump up and spin around.

Clearly I'm on edge from my dream. It's just Bernie Kosar, this time as a beagle, my favorite incarnation of him.

'Another nightmare?' Nine yawns from the corner. He sits on his Chest, absentmindedly carving symbols into the wall with a nail, the very picture of someone who is *not* on edge. The soles of his bare feet are black.

'They're getting really strange,' I say, and I hope I don't sound as shaken as I feel. Last thing I need is Nine seeing me as some kid, scared by bad dreams. 'And I think others are having them at the same time.'

Nine lifts the nail to examine it more closely. He tilts his head, as if it's a rare specimen and not the most ordinary object in the world. With his tongue sticking out of the corner of his mouth he looks as if he is concentrating all of his energies on this one nail. With a small smile, he bends it between his fingers, snapping it into two perfectly equal pieces. He turns to face me. 'And what does that mean? You think they are all having visions of some kind? Or, they are having the same action-packed nights you are?'

I shrug. 'I don't know. I keep seeing this really skinny kid with curly black hair. He's wearing one of our pendants, so I have to assume he's one of us. We are aware of one another, but things in the dream seem to be tailored for him in some ways and to me in others. I see *you* in these visions too.'

Nine frowns, then opens his Chest and digs around inside. I'm hoping he is going to pull out something that will help me decipher my visions, help me figure out what, if anything, I'm supposed to do with them. 'I'd like to try to contact the others with the red stone, but I guess the government has it tapped somehow. Which is total bullshit.' He sits back looking frustrated.

I walk across the empty car to where he's sitting. He has a yellow cube in his hand that I've never seen before. 'What do you think it means, if the government has your stone tapped? How do you think it happened? I mean, it must have been the Mogs, but how did they convince the government to work with them?'

Nine looks at me incredulously. 'Are you serious? Who cares why they're working together or what the Mogs had to say to get them on their side? The point is, they *are* working together. The U.S. government and the Mogadorians have teamed up! For them, it is official: *we* are the bad guys!'

'But the Mogs will destroy Earth – or worse – once they get rid of us. Doesn't the government know this? Isn't it obvious that we're the *good* guys?'

'Apparently not. Who knows how it happened? Maybe

they're just using one another; both trying to double cross the other. Whatever it is, the government *has* to be underestimating the Mogs. If they weren't, they'd be scared out of their freaking minds.' Nine places the yellow cube in his mouth. A look of satisfaction appears on his face.

'What is that?' I ask.

'Sustenance,' he says, his voice garbled. 'It's a food substitute. You suck on it and it fills you up for a little bit. Take a look. You might have one too.'

I unlock my Chest and poke around for a yellow cube. My hands pass over the white tablet we found in Malcolm Goode's hidden office in the well, and I take a second to press its buttons. Still dead. I push it aside. I don't find a yellow cube, but there's a blue one. I hold it out for him to see. 'Do you think this does the same thing?'

He shrugs. 'Dunno. Won't know till you try. Go for it.'

I hesitate for a few seconds, then place it on my tongue, and my mouth is immediately flooded with ice-cold water. I am only able to drink a little before some goes down the wrong way, causing me to cough the stone onto the floor. Nine spits his yellow stone into his hand and offers it to me, but I pass.

'You have to eat sometime,' he says.

Bernie Kosar walks over to Nine and opens his mouth. 'Sure, BK,' Nine says obligingly, placing the yellow cube on the dog's tongue.

'At least we're headed west, where Sam and Sarah are. I'm sick of running and hiding, running and hiding. First things first, we find them.'

'Yeah, well, speak for yourself. I've been locked up and tortured for the past year, man. Being in motion, in control of where I am and when I'm going there, is something I do not plan to give up anytime soon. Just relax, Johnny. I have an idea and you need to remember the plan. We're not wasting time finding your human friends. We contact the others and meet up, and when we're ready, we face Setrákus Ra. In that order.'

I turn and punch a hole in the side of the train car, and the impact causes the wheels on one side to momentarily lose their grip on the tracks below. I'm angry and I feel like I'm spiraling out of control. 'How exactly are we going to meet up with them when our only means of communication might be being monitored? I say we head for California, or whatever government facility is out west, and we demand they give up Sarah, or we'll start blowing stuff up! Or, we threaten to tell the media that the government is working with a bunch of evil aliens. We'll see how that goes over.'

Nine laughs, shaking his head. 'Um, no. That's not going to happen.'

'Well, shit, then I don't know what to suggest. What if we go back to Paradise to see if maybe Sarah's there. If I can just see that she's safe, I promise I'll drop it. We have to be close to Ohio by now, don't we?'

Nine walks over to the hole I've created in the wall and peeks out. His voice is quiet when he speaks. 'It all looks the same to me, man. You know, Earth has *nothing* on Lorien. Sure, Earth looks pretty nice in some places, but

Lorien was beautiful everywhere. It was the most beautiful planet in all the galaxies. You've seen how it used to be in your visions, right?' I'm surprised with how impassioned he's suddenly become. Talking about Lorien, his face is as happy and relaxed as I've ever seen it. For the first time I see a homesick kid. But it's fleeting. He quickly rearranges his face into its usual mask of snark and dismissal.

'We are *not* going to Ohio to see if another one of your *humans* is all cozy and safe. This is *not* our home, Four. These humans are not our brothers and sisters. Everything we do here on Earth is for our *real* home, for our *real* brothers and sisters; for the Elders who sacrificed their lives to put us on that ship.'

Nine steps back, swings, and punches another hole in the wall of the car, right next to mine. Unlike mine, his punch is so hard and so fast that the wheels underneath us don't shift. Nine sticks his head through the hole and he breathes deeply, his black hair blowing and flapping in the wind, then pulls his head back inside. He clenches his fists and turns to look at me. 'If you don't have Lorien in your heart, then you should say so right now. I won't run around with a traitor. Our *only* goal is doing everything we can to be at full strength so we can defeat Setrákus Ra and his army. That's it. Got it?'

I decide to remain silent. My feelings for Sam and Sarah will never subside. I know this. But Nine is right about what comes first. We are of help to no one if we do not increase our strength, and that only happens if we can find the others. I need to concentrate on Lorien. When we defeat

Setrákus Ra, Sam and Sarah – along with everyone else on Earth – will be okay. I nod.

Nine sits down and closes his eyes, hands clenching his knees so tightly his knuckles are white. 'We just passed a sign I recognize. We're a couple of hundred miles away from the safe house my Cêpan set up. We can go there, order a pizza, maybe watch a little TV. You can sit around and sigh and think sad thoughts about your poor, lost Sarah. I will go out, find some hot chick to make out with for an hour or so, *then* we'll figure out how to communicate with the rest in some other way.'

BK drops the yellow cube out of his mouth and looks up at me. He doesn't even have to ask. I place my blue cube on his tongue and he closes his mouth and sighs happily.

I look over at Nine. He is so sure of himself, so confident. 'And how are we going to do that? The macrocosms are tapped! We have no other way to communicate with them!'

'No, this is perfect,' Nine says, getting excited. 'Wait until you see my place, Four. It's totally badass. Whatever we want, we'll have. Whatever we need, we'll get. We'll rest and train, we'll be in the most amazing shape, ready for whatever comes at us. And we will figure out a way to get in contact with the rest of the Garde.'

13

I lie awake for hours, sitting and watching the fire outside the hut. Inside, Ella sleeps on the hammock; Six and Crayton snore under blankets on the floor. After a while, the fire goes from a raging and crackling blaze to glowing embers. I watch the smoke waft through the air, drifting to hang around beneath the canopy of trees. Eventually, the fire dies out entirely.

I just can't sleep. For so many years, I was alone with my envy and anger, trapped in that orphanage. Now, finally, I can let it go. Now I believe there's nothing we can't do with all of us together. So I don't know why I still feel this pit in my stomach whenever I get a moment to think. I know what the pit is, too; I feel lonely. But I'm not alone, I keep telling myself.

I look over at Eight, sleeping as close as he can to the fire for warmth. In the early morning light, all curled up, he looks small. He sleeps restlessly, under a thin blanket of twisted vines. I watch him toss and turn, running his hands through his already messy hair. I stoke the coals to create as much heat as possible and the crackle is enough to make him stir. I don't know why, but I feel protective of him. At the same time,

I think about his muscular arms and I want him to protect me. Must be something about opposites attracting. He is playful and I am, well, not.

Crayton's forehead is creased with worry when he finally gets up and wakes the others. We all try to shake off the sleep cobwebs as quickly as possible. I know Crayton is wondering how he's going to get us all on a plane.

My thoughts turn to Eight's vision of Setrákus. He poses the greatest threat of all, even more than a bunch of well-armed Mogs. I know Crayton doesn't think we're ready to face Setrákus. We haven't developed our Legacies, we haven't had a chance to learn how to fight together, and we must find Four, Five and Nine before we face a threat like Setrákus Ra. When I said as much last night, Eight shook his head, frustrated by all the skepticism. 'I know we could take him, together,' he said. 'I've seen him in my dreams and felt his power. I know what he's capable of; but I also know what *we* are capable of, and it is far greater than anything he could *ever* be. I believe in us. But it won't happen if we aren't all convinced.'

'I agree, we do need to bring down Setrákus Ra. But first we need to find the others. The chances of beating him are far better if you are all together,' Crayton had argued. I could hear the worry in his words.

Eight stood firm, clearly believing we're enough to take him. 'My dreams have guided me to you all. And they tell me we can do this; we can't run away, even if it is to find the others.'

Now Eight stands and stretches, revealing a bit of his stomach as his shirt lifts. He leans down and picks up a walking stick and twirls it in his hands. I can't take my eyes off him. It's such a new and unusual feeling for me and makes me feel shy and excited at the same time. 'So where do you want to go?' he asks, looking around at all of us.

'East coast, United States,' Six says. She kicks the bottom of his walking stick as it swings by and it flips up and into her hand. These two are quite the comedy duo. Six throws the stick back to him and he makes a big show of diving and missing it on purpose. Their play looks a lot like flirting. I have to admit, it makes me jealous. Even if I wanted to, I could never be this way with Eight, with anyone. This is just how Six is, easy. No wonder they're having so much fun.

'Okay, if that's where you want to go, we have a couple of options. A plane? Do we have enough money to buy tickets for all of us?'

Crayton pats his shirt pocket, nodding. 'That shouldn't be a problem.'

'Great. We head back to New Delhi, buy some tickets, and we can be in the United States in a day or so. *Or*, we could be in the state of New Mexico in just a few short hours.'

'We can't *all* teleport,' Six points out, drawing in the dirt with her toe.

'Maybe we can,' Eight says, a sly smile on his face. Six has drawn a circle and Eight reaches his foot over to add two eyes, a nose and a big smiley face. They grin at each other. 'We just need to take a short walk, then it's a simple matter of a giant leap of faith.' He is clearly enjoying keeping us in the dark; I see the others nodding at him, so caught up in his confidence they forget to ask for any details. I don't want to be the one to point out we have no idea what he has in mind.

'Sounds a lot faster than a plane,' Ella says. 'And a whole lot cooler.'

'You've got my attention,' Crayton says, hefting my Chest up onto his shoulder. 'You need to show us what you're talking about, the quicker, the better. If Setrákus Ra is already here on Earth, we've got to move fast.'

Eight holds up a finger, telling Crayton to be patient. Then, he pulls off his shirt and pants. Wow. 'Not before my morning swim,' he says.

Eight sprints to the edge of the cliff where the waterfall drops off. Without pausing, he dives with his hands out at the side. Like a bird, he seems to float, riding the waves of air. I rush to the edge of the cliff and look over the side, just in time to see him change shape and enter the water as a red swordfish, and then surface as himself. I suddenly get the urge to jump in too, and I follow him.

The water is startlingly cool when I dive in, but when I come up for air I can feel my face is flushed. What is going on with me? I'm not usually this impulsive.

'Nice dive,' Eight says, swimming over and treading water close to me. He shakes his head and his black, glistening curls whip around his head. 'So, do you prefer being called Marina or Seven?'

'I don't care. Whatever,' I say, feeling shy.

'I like Marina,' he says, speaking decisively for both of us. 'Is this your first time in India, Marina?'

'Yes. I was in Spain for a long time. In an orphanage.'

'An orphanage, huh? At least you had lots of kids around you; you could make friends. Not like me.'

I can see how lonely he's been. I decide not to correct him and tell him how all the other girls hated me and I had no friends until Ella showed up. I just shrug. 'I guess. I'm happier now.'

'You know what? I like you, Marina,' he says. It sounds like he is rolling my name around in his mouth, savoring it. 'You're quiet, but cool. You remind me of –'

Suddenly, there's a huge splash right between Eight and me. The waves rock us away from each other and I watch Six emerge, her wet blonde hair falling perfectly down her back. She doesn't say a word then dives back under the water, pulling Eight with her. I dive too, and watch them wrestle under water until Eight, laughing, begs for mercy and Six lets him go.

'Damn, you're strong,' he says as he breaks the surface, coughing.

'And don't you forget it,' she says, grinning. 'Now, can we please get out of here?'

The sight of Six and Eight all tangled up makes me jealous, but this is not the time for it. I duck my head under water to give myself a minute to pull myself together. I let the water enter my lungs and I sink and sink, until my toes touch the muddy and rocky floor. I sit down in the mush and try to collect my thoughts. I'm angry at myself for feeling so vulnerable. This is a crush! Nothing more. And do I *really* care if Eight prefers Six's perfect, blonde hair to my mop? I mean, *she* isn't a threat to me. We have to work as a team, trust each other. I don't want to be angry with Six, especially after everything she has done for me. For a minute I pace around the bottom, hoping to come up with something witty to say when I surface. *I can do this.*

I realize I'm directly under the spot where the waterfall enters the pool, where the water is clear and sparkling. The glint off something catches my eye. It's a long silver object stuck in the muddy floor.

I go to take a closer look. It's maybe fifteen feet long and, when I circle it, I'm stunned to realize it's some sort of cockpit behind a long windshield. That's when I see a Chest, just sitting there on the seat inside. I can't believe it – is it possible that this is the silver ship that Eight saw fly away the day that the Mogs attacked, the day that his Cêpan was killed? I hear a muffled cry and realize it's mine. I grab a handle on the fuselage, and pull. It doesn't budge. The pressure at the bottom of the lake is so strong, but I keep pulling and soon the cockpit door swings open. A rush of water mixes with water that was trapped inside. The Chest is slimy when I grab it and race for the surface.

The first thing I see is Six and Eight, sitting in the grass and talking. Ella is twirling Eight's walking stick over her head, then out in front of her. Crayton is watching Ella, his chin cupped in his hands. Ella sees me coming out of the water and spikes the stick into the grass.

'Marina!' she calls.

'Hey, there you are! Where'd you go?' Eight yells, coming over to the edge.

'Come on out, Marina,' Six calls. 'We really have to boogie now!'

I lift the Chest up and out of the water, holding it aloft so they can all see it. I don't even care the most revolting, mucky water is pouring off it and onto my head. I'm grinning so wide, my face hurts. I love the looks on their faces, mouths agape and eyes wide. I'm enjoying it so much I use my telekinesis to float the Chest over to Eight and Six and leave it there, in midair.

'Look what I found, Eight!'

Eight disappears from the grass and reappears up in the air next to the Chest. He wraps his arms around it and hugs it. Slime and all. Then he teleports back to the edge of the lake, the Chest still in his hands. 'I can't believe it,' Eight finally says. 'All this time, it was right here.' He looks stunned.

'It was inside a Mog ship at the bottom of the lake,' I say, walking out of the water.

Eight disappears again and teleports directly in front of me, our noses practically touching. Before I can register how nice his warm breath feels on my face, he picks me up and kisses me hard on the mouth as he twirls me around. My body stiffens and I suddenly have no idea what to do with my hands. I don't know what to do at all, so I just let it happen. He tastes salty and sweet at the same time. The whole world disappears and I feel as if I'm floating in darkness.

When he sets me down, I pull back and look into his eyes. One glance and I know this huge, romantic moment was a spontaneous and grateful gesture for him. No more, no less. I'm an idiot. I really need to let this crush go.

'I never swim over here. From the start, I always dived off on the other side there,' Eight says. 'Stuck in the same area.' He shakes his head. 'Thank you, Marina.'

'Um, you're welcome,' I whisper, still dazed by the first part of his thank-you.

'Now that you've hugged it hello, don't you want to open it?' Crayton asks. 'Come on, already!'

'Oh! Right, of course!' Eight yells, and he teleports back to the Chest.

Six walks towards me. 'Marina! That was so awesome!' She hugs me, then pulls away to shake me by the shoulders, smiling at me meaningfully. In a low voice, she whispers, 'And am I seeing things, or did you just get kissed?'

'Kind of weird, right?' I whisper, watching her for any signs of jealousy. 'But I don't think it means anything.'

'Not weird at all. I think it's kind of *great*,' she says, clearly thrilled for me, like a friend, or a sister. I'm ashamed of myself, for feeling jealous of her earlier. We both look over at Eight as Ella begins to make a drumroll noise to announce the Chest's opening.

Eight has his palms on the lock. Almost immediately, it shakes and the Chest falls open. He quickly dives in elbow-deep, trying to touch everything all at once. He's like a kid in a toy chest; he's so excited. We all crowd around and watch. I can see some of the stones look like mine, but other items are completely different. There's a glass ring, a curved antler, a black piece of cloth that shimmers blue and red when Eight touches it. He grabs a thin piece of gold the length of a pencil and holds it up. 'Ahh, good to see *you* again.'

'What is that?' Six asks.

'I don't know its real name, but I call it "the Duplicator."' Eight holds it above his head, like a wand. Then he snaps his wrist and it expands out, and down, like a scroll. Soon, it's the size of a doorframe. He lets go and the frame hovers in front of him. Eight steps behind and we can see the occasional pair of hands and feet when he starts doing jumping jacks.

'Okay,' Six says. 'That is the weirdest thing I've ever seen.'

Eight teleports to her side and stands there, head cocked to the side as he scratches his chin, like he's judging a show. Our heads snap back to the golden doorframe. The hands and feet are continuing their steady pace. Wait. There are *two* of him now! The one standing next to Six claps, opens his palm, and the piece of gold contracts and zips back into his hand. Immediately, the second Eight disappears.

'Impressive,' Crayton says, clapping his hands slowly and loudly. '*That* will come in very handy sometime soon. At the very least, you will make an excellent distraction.'

'I used it to sneak out of our house a few times,' Eight admits. 'Reynolds never figured out what I could do. Even before he died, I was *always* trying to figure out how to do the most with my Legacies.'

Crayton throws Eight's clothes to him, and picks up my Chest. 'Now, we *really* need to get going.'

'Aw, come on,' Eight says, pulling on his pants. As he hops about, he bats his eyes at Crayton and says in a wheedling voice, 'I just got my Chest back. Can't I get reacquainted with it? I've missed it so much.'

'Later,' Crayton says curtly. When he turns towards us, though, I can see he is smiling.

Eight drops the piece of gold inside the Chest and

pulls out a green crystal, stuffing it into his pocket. He closes the Chest and picks it up with a dramatic sigh. In his most pathetic voice he says, 'Oh, all right. Our reunion will just have to wait. Follow me, everybody.'

'How often has Setrákus visited you in your dreams?' Crayton asks. We've been walking more than five hours and we're making slow progress up the mountain. Eight is leading us up a winding path that is more ledge than road. There's a thin blanket of snow everywhere, and the wind is brutally strong. We're all freezing, but Six protects us with her Legacy, pushing the wind and snow out of our way. Weather control is one of the more useful Legacies, that's for sure.

'He's been talking to me for a while now, trying to trick me and get me to lose my temper,' Eight says. 'But now that he's on Earth, it's a lot more frequent. He taunts me, lies, and now he's trying to get me to sacrifice myself so that you can all go back to Lorien. He's been getting to me more than usual lately.'

'What does that mean, exactly? "Getting to you"?' Crayton asks.

'Last night in a vision he showed me my friend Devdan hanging from chains. I don't know if it's a vision of something that's actually happening or just a trick, but it's really messing with my head.'

'Four sees him, too,' Six chimes in.

Eight spins around with a surprised look on his face

and walks backwards, his mind clearly putting the pieces together. His foot comes dangerously close to slipping off the ledge, making me gasp and reach out nervously. But he never wavers as he continues, 'You know, I think I saw him last night. I forgot about it until now. He has blond hair? Tall guy?'

'And better looking than you? Yup, that's him,' Six says with a smile.

Eight stops backpedalling and looks thoughtful. The drop off to our left is almost two thousand feet. 'You know, I always assumed it was me, but guess I was wrong,' he says thoughtfully.

'Assumed you were what?' I ask, willing him away from the edge.

'Pittacus Lore.'

'Why would you think that?' Crayton asks.

'Because Reynolds told me that Pittacus and Setrákus were always able to communicate with each other. But now that I know Four can, too, I'm confused.'

Eight starts walking forwards again when Ella asks, 'How can *anyone* be Pittacus?'

'Each of us is supposed to take on the roles of the original ten Elders, so I guess that means one of us will take on Pittacus's role,' Six explains. 'Four's Cêpan told him so, in a letter. I read it myself. Eventually, we're supposed to become even stronger than them. That's why the Mogs are moving so quickly now, before we become more dangerous, better able to protect ourselves and attack them.' She looks over at Crayton, who is nodding as she speaks.

I feel like I'm the only one who knows so little – nothing, really – of my history. Adelina refused to tell me anything, to answer a single one of my questions, or even hint at what I would one day be capable of. Now, I'm so far behind everyone else. The only Elder I even know of *is* Pittacus, never mind knowing which one I might become. I just have to believe I'll figure out who I am when the time is right. Sometimes, I get sad when I think about everything I wish I already knew and when I think about what my childhood should have been. But there's no time for me to mourn what can't be changed.

Ella comes to walk with me, brushing her hand against mine. 'You look sad. You okay?'

I smile at her. 'I'm not sad. But I am mad at myself. I've always blamed Adelina for why I haven't developed my Legacies the way that I might have. But look at Eight. He lost his Cêpan, but took what he had and just kept working at it.'

We walk together in silence for a few more minutes, until Eight speaks. 'Do you ever wish the Elders had given us our Inheritance in locked backpacks instead?' He switches his Chest to the other arm.

I look guiltily at Crayton. I move to take my Chest from him, but he just pushes me away gently.

'I have it for now, Marina. Soon enough I'm sure

you'll need to bear its burden alone, but I'll help while I can.'

We walk for another few minutes until the path along the ridge suddenly ends at a steep cliff. We're a few hundred feet from the peak, and I stare over the Himalayas spread out on my left. The mountains are vast and seem endless. It's a breathtaking sight, one I hope I'll remember forever.

'So, now where?' Six asks, looking skeptically up at the mountain. 'There is no way we can go straight up the peak. There don't seem to be a lot of other options, though.'

Eight points at two tall, hulking boulders leaning against the mountainside, and then clenches his hand. The boulders separate, revealing a curved stone staircase that winds around and leads inside the rock face. We follow Eight up to the stairs. I feel both claustrophobic and vulnerable. If someone follows us, there's no way out.

'Almost there,' Eight says over his shoulder.

The stairs are so cold; their iciness seeps up through my feet and body. They finally lead us to a huge rock cavern that has been carved out of the mountain.

We pour into it, gazing around in awe. The ceiling is a couple of hundred feet high, and the walls are smooth and polished. Carved deep into one of the walls are two sets of vertical lines several feet high and spaced five feet apart. A small blue triangle sits between the two lines, with three more curved lines carved horizontally above it.

'Is that supposed to be a door?' I ask, following the lines with my eyes.

Eight steps aside, to let all of us see better. 'It's not supposed to be; it *is* a door. It's a door to the far corners of the Earth.'

14

I pull my hoodie up over my head and hunch my shoulders. Nine's wearing a dirty Cubs cap and cracked sunglasses, items he found in the train yard where we jumped off. After an hour's walk south, we're standing against the wall of a platform, waiting for another train. This one is elevated. The el, as Chicagoans call it. The Chests in our arms stand out against the other passengers' briefcases and backpacks, and I do my best to act casual. Bernie Kosar sleeps comfortably inside my shirt, now a chameleon. Nine is still kind of pissed that I was skeptical that anyone would put a *safe* house in such a densely populated area. I know Henri would never have chosen such an exposed place.

We don't speak as the train rumbles into the station. Bells chime, the doors slide open, and Nine leads me into the last car. When the train pulls away, we watch the city of Chicago slowly grow closer.

'Just enjoy the view for now,' Nine says. He looks more and more at peace the closer we get to the city. 'I'll tell you more when we get off.'

I've never been to Chicago before. We pass what feels like a million apartment buildings and houses as we clatter through the different neighborhoods. The streets below are full of cars, trucks, people, dogs being walked, babies being pushed in strollers. Everyone looks so happy, and safe. I can't help but wish I were one of them. Just going to work or school, maybe for a walk with Sarah to get a cup of coffee. A normal life. Such a simple idea, but it's almost impossible for me to picture. The train stops, people stream off and others push to get on. The train gets so crowded that two girls, a blonde and a brunette, are forced to stand practically leaning over us.

'Like I said,' Nine says, smiling happily, 'just enjoy the view.'

After a few minutes, the blonde kicks the Chest under my feet. 'Ow! Jeez, guys. What's with the ginormous boxes?'

'Vacuum cleaners,' I'm nervous and Nine's story from the other night is the first thing that pops into my mind. 'We're, uh, salesmen.'

'Really?' The brunette asks. She looks disappointed. I sag a bit; even I'm a bit disappointed in my fictional life.

Nine takes off his cracked sunglasses and elbows me in the ribs. 'That was a joke. My friend here, he thinks he's so funny. Actually, we work for an art collector and we're taking these artifacts down to the Art Institute of Chicago.'

'Oh, yeah?' the blonde asks. The two girls glance at each other and look pleased. As she turns back to us, she tucks her hair behind her ear. 'I'm a student there.'

'Seriously?' Nine says with a pleased smile.

The brunette bends down, looking curiously at the intricate carvings on the lid of my Chest. I hate that she's so close to it. 'So, what's inside? Pirate treasure?'

We should *not* be talking to them. We shouldn't be talking to anyone. We're no longer just teenagers trying to blend in with the humans around us. We are *alien fugitives* who just destroyed a fleet of government vehicles. There's a bounty on my head and I bet they're putting one together for Nine right now. We should be hiding in the middle of nowhere, back in Ohio, or even out west. Anywhere but sitting on a packed train in the middle of Chicago, flirting with girls! I open my mouth to say that the Chests are empty, to make them stop asking questions and leave us alone, but Nine talks first. 'Maybe my friend and I could swing by your place later this evening. We'd love to show you what's inside then.'

'Why don't you just show us now?' the brunette asks with a pout.

Nine looks left and then right. He's really hamming it up. 'Because I don't trust you yet. You two are kind of, ah, suspicious. You know that, right? Two beautiful girls like you, you're right out of a spy movie.' He winks at me. It suddenly dawns on me; he's just as bad around girls as I am. He overcompensates and looks kind of ridiculous doing it. It makes me like him more, even if he is totally embarrassing us both.

The girls look at each other and smile. The blonde digs into her purse, scrawls something on a scrap of paper and hands it to him. 'The next stop is ours. Give me a call after seven and we'll think about hooking up with you guys somewhere later. I'm Nora.' I'm stunned his stunt worked.

'I'm Sarah,' the brunette says. Of course that's her

name. I shake my head. If that isn't a blinking sign that we must end this conversation now, I don't know what is.

Nine reaches his hand out to shake theirs. 'I'm Tony, and this handsome stud next to me is Donald.' I clench my teeth and give them a polite wave. *Donald*?

'Cool,' Nora says. 'Well, talk to you later.' The train stops and they get off. Nine leans over and waves to them through the window. After the train pulls out of the station, Nine chuckles to himself. He is looking very smug.

I elbow him in the ribs. 'Are you nuts? Why would you deliberately draw that kind of attention to yourself – to us? You had no right to drag me into your stupidity. And, why *in the world* would you do anything to encourage them to look at our Chests? Let's hope any girl stupid enough to buy your crap is too stupid to think too hard about any of it!' I liked him a whole lot better when he just looked like a loser.

'Calm down, *Donald.* You think you could keep your voice from squeaking so loud? It's no big deal. Nothing is going to happen to us here.' He leans back, hands folded behind his head. When he speaks again, though, he doesn't sound so puffed up. 'Sandor would have been so damn proud of me just now, you know? I bet you'd never know it, but normally, I'm crazy nervous around girls. And the more I like them, the worse it is. No more. After what I've been through this past year, nothing really scares me anymore.'

I don't respond. I slump down in my seat and watch the city get taller and taller, the architecture more interesting. There are playhouses, shops and beautiful restaurants all wrapped in glass. Some of the buildings shine so bright in the sun I have to shield my eyes. Cars clog the roads below us, their honks reaching us up on the track. No place could be more different from Paradise, Ohio. Our train stops and starts up again through two more stations, then Nine tells me to stand up. We're next. A minute later we're walking east on Chicago Avenue, each of us carrying our Chest under an arm. Lake Michigan is straight ahead.

When the crowd around us thins, Nine says, 'Sandor loved Chicago. And he thought it was smart to hide in plain sight in a city like this. No chance of sticking out, always a crowd to disappear into, that kind of thing. I mean, think about it, where are you more anonymous than in a busy city?'

'Henri would never have allowed it. Being in a city like this would have freaked him out. He hated being anywhere he couldn't keep an eye on anyone who might have an eye on us. On me.'

'And that's why Sandor was the best Cêpan that ever lived. He had rules, of course. First and most important, "don't be stupid."' Nine sighs. Amazingly, he has no idea how infuriating, how insulting this talk about Sandor is.

I'm pissed and I don't care who knows it. 'Oh, yeah, if Sandor was so great, why did I find you in a Mogadorian prison cell?' I feel horrible the minute I say it. Nine misses Sandor, and we're in the last place they spent real time together, where Sandor told Nine he was safe. I know how powerful that kind of assurance is.

Nine stops dead, right in the middle of a busy corner

with people streaming past us. He steps up to me until our noses are inches apart. His fists are clenched, not to mention his teeth. 'You found me in that cell because *I* made a mistake. It was *my* mistake, not Sandor's. And you know what? Where's your Cêpan? You think yours was so much better than mine? Wake up, idiot! They're both *dead*, so I really doubt one was so much better than the other.'

I feel bad for what I said but I'm sick of Nine trying to bully me. I push him away. 'Back off, Nine. I mean it. Just. Back. Off. And stop talking to me like I'm your little brother.'

The light changes and we cross the street, both of us fuming. I follow him onto Michigan Avenue and we walk in silence. At first I'm too angry to pay attention to my surroundings, but slowly I become aware of the skyscrapers above me. I can't help it. This city is awesome. I look around. Nine sees me admiring the city, *his* city, and I can feel his mood softening.

'You see that big black one with the white spires on top?' Nine asks. He looks so happy to see this building I forget I'm pissed at him. I look straight up. 'That's the John Hancock Center. It's the sixth tallest building in the country. And that, *little brother*, is where we're headed.'

I snatch him by the arm and pull him to the side of the sidewalk. 'Wait a minute. *That's* your safe house? One of the tallest buildings in the city is where you think we're going to *hide*? You've got to be kidding me. That's *nuts*.'

Nine laughs at the incredulous look on my face. 'I know, I know. It was Sandor's idea. The more I think about it, the more brilliant I realize he was. We stayed here for over five years, no problems. Hiding in plain sight, baby, hiding in plain sight.'

'Right. Are you forgetting about the part where you got caught? We are *not* staying there, Nine. Not a chance in hell. We need to go back to the train, figure out a new plan.'

Nine rips his arm out of my grip. 'We got caught, *Donald*, because of someone I thought was my friend. She'd been working with the Mogs and I was too stupid to notice. She betrayed me and I couldn't see beyond her nice ass, so Sandor was captured. I watched him being tortured, and there was nothing I could do to stop it. The one person I loved more than anyone in the world. In the end, the only thing I could do for Sandor was put him out of his agony. Death. The gift that keeps on giving.' His sneer can't hide the pain in his voice. 'Fast-forward one year and I see your ugly face outside my prison cell.' He points up at the John Hancock Center. 'Up there, we were safe. It's the safest place you'll ever be.'

'We'll be trapped,' I say. 'If the Mogs find us up there, there's nowhere to run.'

'Oh, you'd be surprised.' He winks and then walks towards the building.

All of a sudden I am very conscious of just how many people are going by us. I'm nervous as hell, without a single clue where else I should be or go. One thing I know for sure, the Mogadorians keep getting better at blending in, so I have zero confidence we'd even know it if one just brushed by. This thought terrifies me so much I literally twitch as it occurs to me. And I have to assume there are thousands of cameras all over Chicago, and with the Mogs and the government working together, the Mogs probably have access to them. Great. We're on some predatory Candid Camera and there is nothing we can do about it. Inside, anywhere inside, is going to be safer than standing around out here. I put my head down and follow Nine.

The lobby is amazingly luxurious. There's a grand piano, leather furniture, and sparkly chandeliers. At the far end I see two security desks. Nine hands me his Chest and takes off his cap. One of the security guards is a large bald guy who is seated behind the desk, until, that is, he sees Nine. Then, he lets out a howl and leaps to his feet.

'Hey! Will you *look* at who the cat dragged in! You don't write, you don't call, where the *heck* have you been?' the man asks, shaking Nine's hand, his other hand clutching his arm. He just stands there, beaming at Nine. The long-lost son returns, and all that, I guess.

Nine is grinning at him with real affection and puts his other hand on the man's shoulder, 'Oh, I think a better question is, where haven't I been?'

'Next time, tell us when you're taking off. I worry! Now, where's that uncle of yours?' He looks over Nine's shoulder, as if expecting Sandor to come up behind him.

Nine doesn't miss a beat. 'Europe. France, actually.' No flinch, nothing. He's good. I know how hard this must be for him.

'He got some kind of visiting teaching gig?'

'Yup,' Nine says. He nods at me. 'It's a long gig, he's thinking about maybe even taking a permanent spot, so

I've been staying with my friend Donald on the south side. We need to hang upstairs for a while so we can work on a history project. Check out these boxes, man, we have work to last us months!'

I look down at the Chests in my arms and the security guard stands aside and lets us walk past. 'Sounds like you guys have yourselves a plan. Hey, nice to meet you, Donald. Good luck with your project!'

'Same here,' I say. 'And, thanks!' I'm trying to sound friendly, but it's hard. Nine is clearly fine with this guy knowing his comings and goings, noticing his absence, setting up a lie it might be hard to back up later on. But I hear Henri's voice in my head, warning me this is the exact *opposite* of what we should be doing. I try to shake off the nerves making my stomach do flips. Second-guessing things won't help.

We make our way to a small elevator bank and Nine presses a number. The light above one of the sets of elevator doors brightens with a big arrow pointing up.

'Oh, hey, Stanley?' The security officer jogs over just as we are about to step through the elevator doors, his keys jingling on his belt.

I look at Nine with a smirk. 'Stanley?' I mouth. That's worse than Donald!

'Not now,' he mumbles back.

'I've got a bunch of packages for you. We've been holding them in storage. We didn't know where you were and you didn't leave a forwarding address. You want me to send them up?'

'Give us an hour to settle in first, okay?' Nine asks.

'Absolutely, boss.' The guard salutes as we step into the elevator.

Once the doors are closed, I feel Bernie Kosar crawl from one of my shoulders to the other, and back again. He tells me he's tired of hiding. 'Just a few more minutes,' I say.

'Yeah, BK,' Nine says. 'We are just about home. Finally.'

'How could you be so confident this place would be yours to come back to? I mean, you've been gone a really long time.' There seems to be no situation, no idea that makes Nine second-guess what he believes. I wish I could be like that. Even if he isn't always right, it makes for a great team member and an even better warrior.

'Sandor set everything up. Payments for this place are made automatically from his account. We always kept things pretty vague about what he did. And we referred to his "teaching gigs" the other times when we went away for months. Clearly, people bought it.'

Nine presses a series of numbers into a small keypad below the floor numbers and the elevator rockets upwards. The numbers increase so fast I barely have time to think about how high we're going. We pass the eightieth floor and then start to slow down. We come to a stop and the doors open silently, and we step directly into an apartment. I look up at the huge crystal chandelier hanging above two couches in the living room. Everything seems to be bright white with gold trim.

'This is your apartment? You can't be serious,' I say.

'Yup, we've got our own private entrance,' he says in response to my amazed look.

I thought only people on TV lived like this. It's completely boggling my mind that this place belongs to a Garde member.

I see a camera in the upper right-hand corner of the room, pointed our way, and instantly shield my face. But Nine explains it's a closed-circuit camera that can be monitored only from inside the apartment.

'After you,' he says, bowing low and sweeping his arm in welcome with an exaggerated flourish.

'I can't believe you guys have the whole floor,' I say, looking around with my mouth agape.

I hear Nine's hand slide along the wall as he says, '*Two* whole floors, as a matter of fact.' Nine hits another switch and dozens of dark shades rise to reveal floor-to-ceiling windows. The room is bathed in sunlight. Bernie Kosar leaps out of my jacket and turns into a beagle. I walk over to the window and look out at the view. It's incredible. The whole city of Chicago is spread out below. Lake Michigan is a sheet of bright blue on the left. I set my Chest on a plush recliner and place my forehead against the window. As I look down on the roofs of other buildings, I hear something start to whir in the apartment behind me, then feel a whoosh of fresh air from the vents near my feet.

'Hey, you hungry?' Nine asks.

'Sure,' I say. It's weird, but from this height, everything looks fake: the cars, the boats on the water, the trains snaking around on the elevated tracks. To my surprise,

I do feel *safe*; I mean, *really* safe. I actually feel as if nothing can touch me, get me, up here. It's been a long time since I felt this way. It's almost strange.

I hear the door to a refrigerator open. 'I am so psyched to finally *relax*,' Nine calls from the kitchen. 'Hey, make yourself at home; take a shower, eat some frozen pizza. We even have time to chill, sleep, before it's time to call those girls. When was the last time you could say any of that? Man, it is good to be home.'

It's hard to turn away from the view; it's kind of mesmerizing. I want to just stand here, right here in this spot, and enjoy feeling safe. The only thing better would be if Henri and Sarah and Sam and Six were here with me.

Something soft and crinkly hits the back of my head. An energy bar.

'Let me show you around.' Nine's giddy, like he's psyched to show off his toys.

I munch on the bar as we walk through a living room filled with plush couches and leather recliners. A giant flat-screen television hangs above a marble fireplace, and on the glass coffee table stands a vase of fake orchids. There is a layer of dust on every surface. Nine says he'll get a cleaning service up to deal with it as he runs a finger over one particularly well-coated table. In the hallway, he opens the first door on the right.

My jaw drops. Standing there are two huge Mogadorian soldiers with alabaster skin and long black hair, wearing black trench coats. They stand just inside, guns poised and ready to shoot. The weeks of training with Six and

Sam surge through my brain and I rush the closest one and duck under his cannon, then I deliver an uppercut to his chin and follow that with a thrust kick to his abdomen. The Mog is stunned and falls straight backwards. I look around for something to stab him with, but all I see are free weights and punching gloves. That's when Nine runs in and playfully kicks the other Mogadorian in the groin before flicking its nose. His Mog wobbles on its heels before tipping sideways. It takes one more second before I realize these are just dummies. Nine doubles over and when he finally catches his breath, he slaps my back.

'My, my, those are some *fine* reflexes!' he howls.

My cheeks are blazing hot. 'You could have warned me.'

'Are you kidding? I've been thinking about doing that to you since we got on the el. Man, that was great!'

Bernie Kosar enters the room and sniffs at the rubber feet of the Mogadorian I leveled. He looks up at me.

'They're for training, BK,' Nine says, chest puffed proudly, sweeping an arm out wide. 'We call it the Lecture Hall.'

I take my first real look around. It's a huge, empty room. On the far end, there's a control panel, like a cockpit. Nine walks over and sits at the console and starts flicking switches and typing in commands. From the walls, the ceiling and the floor, combat situations and weapons. He spins the chair around to face me, eager to see how impressed I am. I'm immediately jealous of the time he must have spent here. And it shows.

'This is . . .' I raise my eyes to the ceiling. I can't even find the words. It makes me embarrassed about what I've been doing all this time. My so-called training space was the snow in my backyard, or with Six and Sam at the pool. Suddenly, I'm resentful about Henri moving us around so often, not giving me the kind of training I clearly needed to do my part. If we had made a place like this, then maybe I would be as confident and strong as Nine. Maybe Sandor really was the better Cêpan.

'You haven't seen the best part yet,' Nine says.

We move through the training room and he spins opens a vaultlike door in the back. There are shelves and shelves of weapons: guns, swords, knives, explosives and more. There's a whole wall just for ammunition.

Nine pulls a large automatic rifle topped with a scope off a shelf and aims it at me. 'You'd be surprised how easy it was to buy all this stuff. Gotta *love* the Internet.'

He walks towards me with the gun and pushes a button over my shoulder. The far end of the room separates to uncover a firing range longer than a bowling alley. Nine grabs a box of bullets and loads the rifle. Then I watch as he blows to bits a paper target ninety feet away. 'Don't worry. These rooms are pretty well sound-proofed, but we're so high up that no one could hear us anyway.'

A door down the hall leads to a surveillance room. He walks up to a light switch near the front door and flicks the switch while leaning down and placing his face close to it. A faint blue light scrolls over his eyes and the computers come to life. Retinal scan. Cool, very cool. Clearly, Sandor was able to set up a high-tech security system. There are a dozen computers and even more monitors. We're tapped into every camera in the John Hancock Center, all one hundred floors of it, plus what seems to be every camera around the city that's controlled by the Chicago Police Department. Nine touches something on a keyboard and the largest screen in the room comes to life, showing a photo of a muscular man in a black Italian suit, its beautiful cloth and perfect cut apparent even in the grainy picture. He has black hair and a thick beard, and he's holding two laptops. I look at Nine, wondering why he's showing me this.

'That's Sandor,' Nine says after a minute. His voice is different. I hear less bravado. He turns to me. I hear vulnerability. 'Come on. You have a decision to make, an important one.' He pauses for dramatic effect. 'Which room will you choose to stay in? There are a few of them to check out. Take your time. The pizzas won't take long.'

15

Crayton steps between Marina and Ella to get a closer view of the lines carved into the mountainside. He presses his palm in the center of the outlined door, then pulls his hand away. 'That's interesting. It's warm. And what, exactly, do you mean when you say it's a door to the far corners of the Earth?'

'Here's the deal,' Eight explains. 'At best, I can teleport two hundred feet. Maybe two-fifty. And the farther I go, the worse my accuracy is. One time I was aiming for a treetop a couple of hundred feet away and I landed in between a mountain lion and her cubs. That got ugly, fast. This teleporting Legacy is truly brilliant and has been incredibly useful so many times, but it's not as easy as it looks. *From inside this cave*, though, I can teleport around the *world*.'

I place my hands on the mountainside and I can feel the warmth move through me. 'How?'

Eight moves out of the way so Ella and Marina can touch the door. 'My best guess is that this is an ancient Loric cave, or maybe one of the Loric headquarters, and I was just lucky enough to find it, and I was even luckier to figure out what I could do here. Whatever it was, I am definitely not the first Loric to visit this place.'

His words are barely out of his mouth when I feel a surge of adrenaline and fear shoot through me. I know Crayton has the same thoughts when he whips his head back to look in the direction we came from, and then over at me. I do what he's about to ask, and move quickly down the passage, listening for movement. If this is an ancient Loric cave it would've been under surveillance by the Mogadorians. There could be soldiers waiting for us, or devices set to alert them about our arrival.

I turn to Eight. 'Are you out of your mind? Have you completely *lost* it? Actually, maybe we're the ones who've lost *our* minds. We're the idiots who blindly followed you to a known Loric hideout! This place could be crawling with traps!' As what I've just said sinks in, Marina and Ella move closer to us.

'Hey, hey! Look, I'm sorry,' Eight says, dropping his Chest. 'I've been here so many times without anything happening that I didn't think there was any risk.'

'Let's not waste time apologizing or criticizing,' Marina says, stepping forward. 'Just show us how to open it up, so we can get to the rest of the world. Or, at least, someplace else!'

Crayton nods, still glancing around suspiciously. 'Yes. Let's get in there, where we're less vulnerable.'

Eight pulls his pendant over his head. He reaches up to the blue triangle. 'Wait till you see what's next,' he says, smiling. Then he holds his pendant to the blue triangle.

Nothing happens at first, but after a tense moment the carved lines begin to deepen and spread towards each other. Eight lets the pendant drop down to his chest. Dust shoots into the passage and we move back a few feet. When all the lines touch and there is a perfect outline of a door, the right edge separates from the face of the cavern, and swings open. A blast of warm air hits us, and we all stand still, mesmerized by a blue glow coming from inside.

The energy I feel coursing through me is overwhelming and I become completely and utterly calm. 'What's the blue light?' I finally ask.

'That's what makes me able to teleport around the world,' Eight responds, as if this were the simplest concept to grasp.

Ella walks towards the opening. 'I feel weird inside.'

Marina says, 'Me too.'

With a smile, Eight ducks through the doorway;

Crayton and Ella are quick to follow. I bring up the rear. As we climb up another staircase Eight talks.

'A couple of years ago, as my Legacies grew, I started having these very vivid dreams, like the ones I'm having now with Setrákus and Four. I learned more about Lorien, and about the Elders. Learned about our history here on Earth, how we helped the Egyptians build the pyramids, how the Greek gods were actually Loric, how we taught the Romans military strategy, and so on. In one of the dreams, there was all this stuff about moving around on Earth, and how the Loric used to do it. *This* mountain was in my dream. We'd already moved to India and I recognized it. After the dream, I came up here and started looking around. That's when I found all of this.'

'That's amazing,' says Marina.

The stairs end in another room. The ceiling is domed and several jagged columns hold it up. I realize we're inside the peak of the mountain. The room is empty except at its very center, where an intricate set of rocks form a whirlpool-like pattern, radiating out from one central blue stone that's the size of a basketball.

'Loralite,' Crayton whispers. He walks towards the center of the cave and sets Marina's Chest down. 'That is the biggest Loralite stone I have ever seen.'

'Is the Loralite the reason you can go anywhere you want?' Marina asks, turning to Eight.

'Well, that's the thing,' Eight sighs. 'I can't go *anywhere* I want. More like six or seven far-off places. It took a lot of messing around and landing in places I didn't mean to before I figured out I can only teleport where there's another one of these big Loralite rocks around.'

'So where *can* we go?' I ask.

'Well, so far I've gone to Peru, to Easter Island, to Stonehenge, the Gulf of Aden near Somalia – but I really don't recommend that one for a lot of reasons – and I've ended up in the desert in New Mexico.'

'New Mexico,' I say immediately, turning to Crayton. 'If we go there we could be across the country and with John in less than a day. We know we can move around easily once we are in the U.S.'

Crayton walks over to the wall, looking around at some markings on it. 'Wait. You're saying you can't control where you go? That's not as promising as I had hoped.'

'No, but if we end up somewhere besides New Mexico – if that's where we want to go – we just teleport again until we get there. It's not so bad,' Eight says.

'And do you know if you can take all of us with you?' I ask. 'If it's anything like my Legacy of invisibility, we may have a problem. I can only turn other people invisible if they're holding my hands.'

'I don't know, to be honest. I've never tried to bring anyone else,' Eight admits.

'Maybe you can take two trips,' Marina suggests.

'These drawings are amazing,' Crayton interrupts, motioning us over to the cave walls. 'Maybe there are some clues for us here.'

He's right. The orange walls are covered with hundreds of symbols, paintings and carvings, reaching as high as the very tip of the dome.

I walk over and my eyes are drawn to a faint green painting of a planet. Instantly, I know it's Lorien, and a lump catches in my throat. Below it, scratched in blue, is a female figure standing over a male, and both are holding sleeping babies. Rays of interrupted white lines come off the bottom of Lorien, ending just above the four figures. Carved next to the female's head, in a different drawing style, are three columns of alien symbols. 'What the hell?' I whisper, confused.

A few feet to my left is a simple black sketch

of a triangular spaceship. There are intricate spirals and symbols on its wings, and a tiny, swirling constellation of stars on the blunt nose. Eight walks up next to me and points to the constellation. 'Do you see? It's the same pattern as the stones in here.'

I turn around to compare – he's right. Immediately, I wish Katarina were here to see all this. I wonder if she even knew about it. I turn to Crayton, who is examining drawings on the ceiling. 'Did you know about any of this?' I ask.

'We left Lorien in a very big hurry. The planet was under attack from the Mogadorians. We didn't have time to gather as much information as we should have. We knew places like this existed, but no one knew exactly *where* they were, or what they did. Clearly, for all the information we did manage to gather before we left, there were important things that we didn't get,' he explains.

'Follow me, everybody,' Eight calls out, gesturing for us to follow his lead towards a dark corner of the room. 'It just gets weirder and weirder.'

He stops in front of a huge carving. It is ten feet high and twenty feet long, split into different scenes. Kind of like a comic book. The first panel shows a spaceship with nine children standing in front of it. Their faces are drawn with detail, and I'm able to pick myself out immediately. The sight of me as a toddler rocks me back on my heels.

'Was this here when you first saw the cave?' Crayton turns away from the wall to ask Eight.

'Yes,' he responds. 'All of this was here, just as you see it now.'

'Who could have done it?' Marina asks, looking up and down the wall, her voice filled with awe.

'I don't know.' Crayton stands with his hands on hips, examining the wall. It's disconcerting to see him look so confused.

The next panel shows a dozen dark figures that I can only assume are Mogadorians. They hold swords and guns, and the figure in the middle is twice the size of the others. Setrákus Ra. The Mogs' tiny eyes and straight mouths are so accurate, so lifelike, I feel shivers run down my back. My eyes move right, and the next scene shows a girl lying in a pool of blood. I compare her face to those in the first panel, and it's obviously Number One. Number Two, also a girl but younger than One, is also down, under the foot of a Mogadorian. Dead. My stomach turns when I see Number Three, a boy, impaled by a sword in a jungle. The last panel in the top row shows Number Four running from two Mogadorian soldiers, jumping over a ray that's been shot from one of their guns. I gasp involuntarily. In the background is a large building on fire.

'Holy shit. That's John's school,' I say, pointing to the last panel.

'What is?' Marina asks.

I stab at the wall. 'That fire at John's school after we fought the Mogadorians. I was there! This is John's school!'

'Is that you in the sky, then?'

I look closer and see a small figure with long hair hovering over the school. 'Okay, that is really freaky. Yes. I don't understand. How did anyone –'

'Look, is this Number Five?' Ella interrupts, pointing at the first box of the bottom row. Standing on the top of a pine tree is a figure throwing something down at three Mogadorians on the ground.

'This is incredible. Everything is here. It's all laid out,' Crayton says. 'Someone foresaw it all!'

'But who?' I ask.

'Oh, no,' I hear Marina whisper. 'Who's that? Who else dies?'

I skim quickly over the next two panels, where we start to come together, to one that shows Marina and me standing next to a lake. And I see John running out of the mouth of a cave with another person. I don't know who it is, maybe

Sam. I can't tell because the boy's head is turned away. Then my eyes reach the panel Marina's looking at. With his or her arms out, a Garde is standing with a sword plunged all the way through its body. It's impossible to identify who it is because the face has been chipped away from the wall. Right below it, on the floor, are pieces of stone.

'What the hell is going on here?' I ask. 'Why is only *that* face missing?' Eight is silent, head down. 'Did you do that?'

'Nobody can dictate what's going to happen,' he says.

'So you thought you'd just destroy it? To do what, exactly? Make it less true?' Crayton asks.

'I didn't know what any of this was. I didn't know any of you. I thought it was a story, at least until –'

'Is it me?' Marina interrupts. 'Am I the one who dies?'

I have the same question. Am I the one with a sword through me? It's a chilling thought.

'We're all going to die someday, Marina,' Eight says in a strange voice.

Ella scoops up the pieces of rock and studies them, turning them over.

Crayton steps in front of Eight. 'Just because you destroyed it doesn't mean it's not going to happen. Withholding the information from us does not make it more or less true or destined to happen. Are you going to tell us who it is?'

'I didn't bring you all the way in here to examine a chipped section of the wall,' Eight says. 'You guys need to keep going – look at the last two panels.'

He has our attention again. We are not going to do anyone any good getting caught up on which of us gets killed with the sword. We turn our attention back to the wall. In the panel Eight is now pointing at, Setrákus Ra is lying on the ground with a sword held to his throat. The figure holding the sword is impossible to make out. On both sides of him, Mogadorians lie dead. In the last panel, there's an odd-looking planet cut in half. The top part looks like Earth, and I can see Europe and Russia, but the bottom half of the planet is covered in long, bumpy stripes. It looks dead and barren. A small ship approaches the top half of the planet from the left, and another small ship is approaching the bottom half from the right.

I'm trying to figure out what this means when I hear Ella gasp.

'It's Eight.'

We all twist around to see her holding the pieces of stone from the floor up to the Garde member's missing face. She managed to put the puzzle pieces back together. Number Eight dies in the picture.

'It doesn't mean anything,' he says firmly.

Marina gently places her hand on his arm. 'Hey, it's just a drawing.'

'You're right,' Crayton responds, softly. 'It is just a drawing.'

Eight pulls away from Marina, circling back to the center of the cave; the rest of us are still rooted to our spots in front of the massive wall that tells stories no one should or could possibly know. Someone has predicted Eight's death. Given the accuracy of the other panels, it's hard to come up with a convincing argument for only this one being wrong. No *wonder* he's always joking around; why he acts as if he has reason not to be quite as careful as the rest of us. He's trying to hide from fate, maybe fly in the face of it. I look back over the last two panels. At first I'm relieved to see Setrákus Ra with a sword to his throat. But the fact that he's still *alive* in the picture pisses me off. And what does the last panel even *mean*? It's showing a confrontation so clearly still in progress, the outcome unclear. And, why is the planet cut in half? What is it saying will happen?

Crayton picks up Marina's Chest, walks

towards Eight and puts his arm around him. He starts speaking quietly.

'What do you think he's telling him? What *can* he tell him that would make him feel better?' Marina whispers, turning to me.

Just as I'm about to go join Crayton in comforting Eight, an explosion rocks the cave, and a wave of fire enters the door. Marina grabs my arm as I hear Ella scream across the room. The jagged columns holding the ceiling up crack and begin to sway and break. A large section falls towards Ella, and I use my mind to shield her, propelling the crumbling stone away from her. I look over at Crayton and Eight just as Eight disappears.

'What's happening?' Marina screams, using her telekinesis to shield the two of us from the falling debris while I protect Ella.

'I don't know,' I say frantically, trying to see through the smoke and dust. Suddenly, Eight reappears in the middle of the room. Blood flows from a wound in his side, his face ashen. 'The Mogadorians!' he shouts. 'They're here.'

16

I'm lying in bed, enjoying my choice of room and the amazingly comfortable pillows I found there. I'm just drifting off when I hear the front door open and then Nine speaking to someone in a low tone. I sit up in alarm, my heart pounding in my ears. Then I realize – it must be the doorman bringing the boxes up. I lie back down. Bernie Kosar licks the bottoms of my feet and says he's going to get something to eat.

'I'll be there in a minute,' I tell him. I stare at the ceiling, hands folded behind my head.

The ceiling has a faint texture to it. My eyelids grow heavy again. The next thing I'm aware of I'm no longer looking at the ceiling. I'm outside and it's snowing.

'Concentrate, John!' I hear someone say from behind me. I turn to see Henri holding an armful of kitchen knives. He has one cocked above his shoulder.

'Henri! Where are we?' I call out to him.

'Did you hit your head?' Henri asks. He's wearing jeans and a white sweater, and both are torn and tinged with blood. There's a blue light somewhere behind him, but when I try to see what it is, craning my neck to peer around him, Henri gets angry. 'Come on, John! It's like you're not even here with me. I need you to start concentrating! Now!'

Before I can argue, Henri whips a knife at me and I'm able to slap it away from my face at the last second. He throws a second one at me, then a third, and a fourth. I block each one, but Henri seems to have an endless supply. I am keeping up, but it's getting harder. The knives are coming faster and faster; too fast.

'We didn't have to keep running!' I yell at him, dodging two knives at once.

Henri throws the next knife with such velocity that, when I slap it away, my hand starts to bleed. He yells, 'We can't all live in Chicago in the clouds, John!'

When the next knife comes, I snatch it by its handle and whip it into the snowy ground. The snow around it turns black. I catch another knife and slam it down, too. 'If we had found the right place, we could have had a real home! We never even tried! And you picked Paradise? Of all places?'

'I did my best! And that's where Malcolm Goode was! You found the tablet, John! You haven't even used it yet!' Henri shouts. The blue light behind him disappears, and the darkness in the snow starts to seep outward and spreads, until it's like we're wading in a black sea. Henri pulls a large knife over his head and wings it at me. When I try to defend myself, my hands feel stuck to my sides. I'm watching the knife fly through the air, flipping, end over end, and I know it's about to hit me right between the eyes. Once it's a couple of feet away, a huge hand reaches out and snatches it out of the air. It's Setrákus Ra. In one fluid motion he has the knife firmly in his grip and whips it over his shoulder and back down again, swinging it at me.

As the tip of the knife plunges into my skull, Setrákus Ra yells, 'Your pizza's getting cold!'

I sit up and I'm back in bed, in the Hancock tower. I'm drenched in sweat and gasping for air. Nine stands in the doorway with a whole pizza on a platter. His mouth is full and he continues to chew while he says, 'Seriously, man, you got to eat it while it's still hot. And I still want to get some training in before our double date.'

'I saw Setrákus Ra again,' I say. I know my voice sounds flat. My tongue feels sticky. 'And Henri.'

Nine swallows and waves his hand in the air, still holding half a slice. 'Oh, yeah? Forget about it, they're just dreams. That's what I tell myself, and it usually works out just fine.'

'And how, exactly, do you make that work?' I ask, but he's already gone. I slide off the bed and stumble down the hallway. I see Bernie Kosar attacking a defrosted steak on the kitchen floor. My pizza sits steaming on the table. I haven't dreamed about Henri in so long, I'm having a hard time shaking the vision off. While I eat my pizza, I think about the flying knives, the snow, how we were yelling at each other – when it hits me. Henri mentioned the tablet. I haven't done anything much but look at it. What little time I've spent with it, I've been annoyed by the fact that it doesn't seem to work. I grab my Chest off the chair and open it, taking the tablet out.

It looks as frustratingly blank as every other time I've

looked at it. It's nothing but a white metal square with a screen; blank, dead, useless. Nothing I do brings it to life. I turn it over and examine its few ports. They're triangular, unlike any I've seen before.

'Nine?' I yell.

From the direction of the surveillance room, he shouts, 'In here!'

I stuff a slice of pizza in my mouth and chew as I walk, bringing the tablet with me. Nine sits on a rolling chair with his feet up on the long table between monitors. Most of the screens are divided into quarters. Nine hits the keyboard in his lap and the screens rotate. None of them show us anything interesting.

Nine grins. 'Anything you want me to check on first?'

'Yeah. Enter a name, "Sarah Hart."'

Nine grabs his long black hair in his fists. 'Aaargh! Seriously, dude? You have the most incredibly one-track mind. With all this crazy shit going on, *that's* the first thing that comes to you?'

'It's the only thing that comes to me,' I say. 'Just do it.'

Nine types in her name, and to my disappointment, nothing comes up other than a list of school activities. I make him search for 'Paradise, Ohio,' 'Sam Goode,' 'John Smith,' and 'Henri Smith.' Everything that pops up are things I've seen before: the destroyed high school; the domestic terrorism charge; the reward offered for information leading to our arrest or capture. I slide the white tablet onto the desk in front of me and push it in his direction. 'Listen, Nine. I need your help with this.' I tell him about my vision, and about Henri talking to me about the tablet.

'Dude, you've *got* to *chill*,' Nine says. 'I forgot how personally you take these dreams. I'm going to try something with this tablet thing.'

'Be my guest,' I say with a sigh.

He turns it over a few times in his hands, touching every inch of the screen. Then he examines the ports on the back and clicks his tongue. 'I think . . .' he says, trailing off to spin in his chair. He walks over to the corner of the room where there's a stack of opened brown boxes. Nine digs through the top two, saying, 'I asked them to bring these up from storage when they delivered the stuff that arrived for Sandor. I wanted to see if there was something in one of them that could give me an idea for a new way to communicate with the others . . .' He puts aside the first two boxes and then yanks the third off the stack. He opens the top of it, pulls out the two new laptops inside and shouts, 'Bingo!' Nine stands, looking victorious, and holds up a thick black cord. One end of the cable is, amazingly, shaped like a triangle – the same as the triangle-shaped port on my tablet.

'Where did *that* come from?'

'I don't know. Sandor had all this stuff with him on the ship that brought us here. I never even had a chance to see most of it, never mind learn how to use it. I tried to figure out what this stuff does a couple of times, but Sandor was always protective of it, and I never got anywhere. I mean, most of the time, I can't tell the difference between the Earth stuff and ours, which really doesn't help.'

He takes the cord he's found and brings its triangle-shaped end to the triangle-shaped port on my tablet. We hold our breaths as Nine slides the end into the port. It fits and we both sigh in relief. Slowly, he puts the other end into the closest computer's USB slot. A black horizontal line appears on the tablet's screen, and seconds later we're looking at a map of Earth. One by one, seven pulsing blue dots appear: two in Chicago, four in India or China, and one in what looks like Jamaica.

'Um, bro,' Nine says, his voice hushed. 'I think that's us. As in, *all of us*.'

'Damn, you're right. There we are, there we *all* are,' I whisper. 'We don't even need the macrocosm with this thing.'

'Wait a sec, there are seven dots, but only six of us left,' Nine says, furrowing his brow.

I lean back. 'I told you there was another ship, right? '

'Right, right,' he says, suddenly the eager pupil paying close attention to me.

'Well, we know there was an infant inside. This might mean it made it to Earth, after all! And *that* means –'

'Setrákus Ra has seven of us to deal with, not six,' Nine interrupts. 'The more the merrier.'

While we're both taking this new information in, a small box appears in the upper-right corner of the tablet screen with a green triangle inside. I press the triangle and two small green dots show up on the map. One is in the American Southwest, and the other is in northern Africa, possibly Egypt.

'What do you think these are?' I ask. 'Do you think they're nuclear bombs? Mog bombs? Shit, you don't think they're going to blow up Earth, do you?'

Nine slaps my back. 'No. Think about it. A map that shows us is clearly geared for, well, us. Mog bombs are, like, a different category. I think these are our *ships*, dude!'

I'm speechless. It does kind of make sense. If that's true then something almost too wonderful to let myself think about might also be true. After Setrákus Ra has been killed and Earth has been saved, we could actually fly back to Lorien. We could help bring it out of hibernation. *We can go home*. All of a sudden, I'm desperate to know the exact location of the dot in the Southwest, the one closest to us. 'Where is this?' I ask, pointing to it.

Nine pulls up a map on a screen and says, 'The one out west is in New Mexico, the other one is in Egypt.'

Hearing him say 'out west' reminds me of Special Agent Walker's last words to me. My decision is instantaneous and final. 'That's where we need to go. New Mexico.'

17

The minute Eight appears in the middle of the room, gushing blood, I rush over and place my hands on his wound. His blood runs over my fingers and down my wrists, and when another explosion rocks the cave, we both fall to the ground. 'I'm sorry,' he whispers. 'This is my fault.'

'Shh. I can heal you. It's my Legacy. You just have to relax for a second.' The iciness flows from my fingertips to his ribs, and Eight immediately goes rigid with pain. The explosions keep coming and Eight winces with each one, but I stare deep into his eyes, willing him to stay with me. 'It's okay. Six is here. She can deal with this. We *will* be okay.' I sound absolutely certain, trying to convince both of us.

'Maybe this is when I die, maybe the drawing was just off,' he says.

I press down harder, finally feeling his wound start to shrink in response to my touch. I shake my head firmly. 'No, it isn't.'

Through the chaos, I see Six push Ella and Crayton behind a large pile of fallen rock. She looks over at Eight and me, and the next thing I know we're lifted off the ground and floated over to the rest of the group.

When Six sets us down, she says, 'All of you, just stay here while I turn invisible and check things out. Fix him up, Marina.' She winks at me. Her voice tells me we'll be okay if we all remember what we can do. The only way we'll survive is if we pull together.

'I'm trying,' I say, but she's already invisible. Below my hands, Eight's lungs struggle to keep up with my Legacy, and his face drains of color. I can feel his insides shifting, almost as if resisting my powers. That's not it, though. It can't be. He's just more wounded than I thought. Or, my Legacy is fading. But that is not an option. I begin to panic and I fight the sick feeling in my stomach. I need to focus on him, and not let myself get distracted by what is happening around us.

I hear gunfire and the distant screams of Mogadorian soldiers. I can only imagine what Six is doing out there. She is a merciless warrior when she needs to be, incredibly dangerous to any who threaten her – or us.

'How is he?' Crayton asks, hovering over Eight and glancing back and forth between the pain on Eight's face and the panic in mine.

Ella grabs Eight's hand and gets him to focus on her. 'It's okay. It's going to hurt, Eight, but then it will feel better. Trust me.' I watch her calming words wash over him and he begins to nod through his grimaces.

We hear a deafening crash overhead, and the cave's ceiling comes alive with cracks that spread fast and wide. The dome is a jigsaw puzzle of pieces that threaten to break free at any moment, and suddenly the first one falls, a stone the size of a car plunging down towards us. I don't want to withdraw my healing touch, but I have to remove my hands from Eight's side in order to focus all of my energy on deflecting the stone away with my mind. When I lay my hands back on Eight's wound, it feels like I'm starting all over again. I take whatever solace I can from the cave drawing. It may show him dying, but it does not show him dying here, this way.

'Where's Marina's Chest?' Ella asks. 'Maybe there's something in there that can help.'

Crayton stands. 'Both Chests are on the other side of the cave. I'll get them.'

'No!' Ella grabs the cuff of his sleeve, but Crayton races off. I watch, helpless. Pieces of the ceiling continue to fall and Ella yells for Crayton to come back, to wait for Six. My mind is racing. Six is out there battling single-handedly with a Mog army, and I know I need to forget all of it, and focus my energy on Eight. I can feel his body giving in to the pain and damage that I can't seem to heal quickly enough to save him. I squeeze my eyes shut, willing him to respond to my Legacy, when I see his wound has returned to its original size, as if I've not even touched him.

'Ella.' I look at her, my eyes filling with tears. 'It's not working. I don't know what to do!'

Ella's voice is determined. 'We need him, Marina. Just concentrate. You can do this.'

I try to catch my breath and see Crayton barely dodge

a jagged boulder. 'Eight. Hold on. I *will* do this, you *will* be better soon,' I say as he closes his eyes. I shut out the noise of the attack, I shut out the hysteria surging inside of me, and I tell myself, *I can heal Eight. I will heal him and Six will take care of the Mogs. We have a mission and this is not the end.* I sit up straight, my breath slows to a normal rhythm, and a ball of ice seems to form between my shoulder blades. It races down my spine and out to my fingers. The force of it nearly pushes me over, but my fingers stay firmly on Eight's wound. I can feel something happening inside of Eight and my breath quickens. My heart beats so fast I think it's going to explode, and then Eight opens his eyes.

'It's working!' Ella shouts.

Vertigo sweeps through me. I wobble but remain upright as Eight's wound closes. I can feel his broken ribs move back into place beneath my hands. After a few seconds I allow myself to sit back. I'm so exhausted I can barely keep my eyes open. I take a deep breath and Eight sits up. He touches where the wound was, feels his ribs, and then reaches out to take my hand.

'I have never felt *anything* like that,' Eight says to me, looking incredulous. 'I don't know how to thank you.' I open my mouth to respond when Six suddenly appears.

She has a Mogadorian cannon in her hand. Her face is covered in black ash. She's out of breath but in control. 'I've pushed them back, but I could use some help out there.'

Eight staggers to his feet. 'Right.'

'I was thinking of Marina,' Six says, surveying the scene and seeing immediately that Eight is in no condition to be of help to anyone. I'm honored she wants me to fight alongside her, but I know I'm too weak to stand. 'Where's Crayton?' she asks, looking around.

I've been so focused on healing Eight I'd forgotten about him. I whip around just in time to see him digging the Chests out from under some rubble. Then he picks up both Chests and starts to make his way back over to us. Just as Six moves to help, an explosion blows apart whatever was left of the ceiling. Huge chunks of snowy rock fall into the cave, followed by hundreds of bullets. Eight stands over Ella, using his telekinesis to deflect the debris and gunfire. Six starts firing into the exposed sky with the Mog cannon. There's another explosion high overhead, and a few seconds later a silver ship like the one I saw at the bottom of the pool crashes into the crumbling mountain just above us. A bleeding Mogadorian soldier tries frantically to extricate himself from the cockpit. I struggle to my feet as he punches a hole through the windshield, and before he can pull himself out, I use my telekinesis to bring two boulders up and smash him between them. A cloud of ash floats to the ground.

A rocket enters the cave, blasting the wall nearest Crayton. The panel carving we were all entranced by just moments ago is decimated. Crayton is thrown by the blast and he flies into the middle of the cave, landing next to the blue Loralite stone as the Chests skid across the floor. He isn't moving. I'm stunned – it all happened so fast.

'Papa!' Ella screams.

Even though the walls are crumbling around us, I race with Ella to Crayton's side. She takes one of his hands. I put mine on his body and close my eyes, trying to find a sign of life. I search for anything to work with, to heal, but there's nothing.

'Save him!' Ella yells at me, her small face twisted in anguish. 'Marina, please, you can do this! You can fix him!'

'I'm trying,' I say, but it comes out as a sob. He's dead. Her Cêpan is gone.

'Just concentrate like you did with Eight! You can do it again!' Ella is frantic, stroking Crayton's head and petting his hand.

Out of the corner of my eye I see Six charge towards us with her cannon firing into the sky. Eight teleports next to me. He leans over and says, 'You can fix him. Come on, Marina.'

I start to cry. I can't do it. I know there is nothing for me to heal, but I try and try to summon my Legacy, pleading for it to work. But Crayton is dead; there's nothing for my Legacy to connect with. I move my hands to his crushed chest and stomach. I can feel all of his broken bones beneath my hands. Ella gets behind me and pushes on my shoulders, pressing my hands harder onto Crayton.

Six stops shooting and grabs my arm. She looks me in the eye. I shake my head.

Ella falls to her knees, sobbing. She crawls over to Crayton and whispers into his ear, 'Let Marina fix you. Please don't go. Please, Papa.' She looks up at me, tears streaming down her cheeks. Her voice is angry. 'You didn't even try, Marina! Why won't you try?'

I wipe my tears on my shoulders. 'I tried, Ella. I tried, and there was nothing I could do. He was already gone. I'm sorry.' I sit back on my heels, but keep my hands on Crayton's body.

A rocket hits the far wall, separating it completely from the mountain. We know from our walk up that behind the hole is a straight two-thousand-foot drop. Cold wind sweeps in and over us. Eight turns to Six. 'Give me the cannon. I'll be right back.' Six hesitates for a second before handing it to him. Eight disappears, and I look up to see him sprinting along the crumbling lip of the hole, leaping from spot to spot as the rocks crumble away. Even in flight, he never stops shooting. Soon, two silver Mog ships explode into balls of flame.

I keep moving my hands across Crayton, but Six yanks me onto my feet. 'Stop. He's gone.' I look down at Crayton, his rugged face, his bushy eyebrows, and remember the first time I saw him at that café in Spain. I thought he was my worst enemy. Instead, he saved my life. I stretch out my hands to try one more time, but Six hugs me close to her. I feel her tears on my neck.

Her lips touch my ear as she whispers, 'There's nothing we can do.'

Sobbing, Ella reaches over and grabs Crayton's left hand. She kisses it and places it against her cheek. 'I love you, Papa.'

'I'm so sorry,' I say again.

She looks up at me and tries to speak, but she can't. Gently, she lays Crayton's hand on his chest and strokes it once more before standing. Eight teleports next to us and returns the cannon to Six. Another strong gust of freezing wind blasts over us and flips open one side of Crayton's jacket. We all see it at the same time – a white envelope in his inner jacket pocket. FOR ELLA is written on the outside.

Six grabs it and shoves it into Ella's hands. 'Ella. Listen to me. I know you don't want to leave him. None of us do. But if we don't leave right now we will die too. You know Crayton would want us to do what is necessary to survive, right?' Ella nods. Six turns to Eight. 'Right. Now, how do we teleport the hell out of here? Has too much of the mountain been destroyed for it to work?'

'Ella, you hold my Chest! Marina, get yours,' Eight says, ushering us towards the glowing blue Loralite. 'Six, you're going to have to hold on to someone's arm so we can all go at once.' He looks around grimly at the wreckage. 'I really hope this works.'

He grabs Ella's hand and mine. Six hooks her arm through my other elbow. I look around at the pieces of the walls that spoke to us about our future and our past.

I think about the many Loric who were here before us. I'm sad we'll be the last ones to see it. But I also think about the responsibility that being the last Loric puts on all of us. I take one last look at Crayton, thanking him for everything he did.

'Okay. Here we go,' Eight says. Then, everything goes black.

18

All of a sudden, Nine's at the edge of his seat. 'Holy shit! Four! Check it out. They've moved.'

'Who moved?' I take the tablet out of his hand. The blue dots that identify us have changed position. At least, some of them have. There is still one blue dot in Jamaica and two in Chicago. But there are now three off the coast of Africa, and one in New Mexico. My chest relaxes when I see there are still seven dots, but I'm confused by how they moved to these other places so quickly. 'How did they do *that*?'

'I have *no* idea,' Nine says. 'It's like they teleported or jumped through space. Maybe they found a stargate, or something?'

'Henri said stargates don't exist,' I said, shaking my head.

'Yeah, well, neither do aliens from another planet, according to *some* people. In fact, *many* people.'

He's right. Maybe Henri was wrong. 'One Garde is in New Mexico, Nine. Near what you think might be our ship. That can't be a coincidence. Do you think they're going after it?'

'Man, I hope not. It is *so* not time for that yet. We have a lot of shit to take care of before we leave Earth.'

I stare at the blue dot pulsing in New Mexico, and press the green triangle, revealing where the Lorien ships are hidden again. There is no way this one has accidentally landed so close to it. Add that to the fact I've been told Sarah is out west, possibly with Sam, and I'm convinced.

'I'm serious, Nine. That's where we are going. New Mexico. Now. Everything we've seen and learned points to it, tells us we need to go there right now.' I rush out of the room, slam my Chest shut and put it next to the front door. 'BK?' I call out. Bernie Kosar trots over with the steak bone in his mouth.

Nine follows me. 'Dude. Slow. Down. We are *not* going to up and fly off to New Mexico! *Especially* after what we just saw! These guys are teleporting around. By the time we get in the elevator, they could be in Antarctica! Or, Australia! There's too much we don't know yet. We don't even know for sure that's our ship. What if it's a trap?' Nine moves in front of the door and crosses his arms. I know I must look like a crazed lunatic, punching at the elevator button, trying to pretend Nine is not there blocking my efforts.

The words tumble out of my mouth. 'We have to go there anyway. Even if the Garde member we see now disappears before we get there. New Mexico is *still* the obvious and only place for us to go.' I'm desperate for him to get on board with this. 'We can take some of your guns.' My head is spinning. I sprint into the training room and head for the munitions cabinet. I'm leaping over the mats in the direction of the cabinet when I hear the metal rings clang overhead. Nine drops from above me, into my path, and puts his hand up.

'Whoa. Hold on there, bud. Take a breath,' he says with his hands up, palms out towards me. '*I* think we should go to Paradise.'

'Are you freaking kidding me? *Now* you want to go to Paradise?' I am going to kill this guy.

'I got to thinking while you were asleep. We need to go back to where you found the tablet. You said before there were a bunch of papers down there, not to mention that skeleton and some maps. I think we're missing something, something that is the key to beating Setrákus Ra.'

'You don't get it,' I say, pushing past him. 'Things are happening out west *this second*. Do you have a car?'

He shoves me hard in the back. I almost fall, but I catch myself. I stand there, back to him, fuming. 'I do have a car, *but* we're going to Paradise first. We need to find anything we can to help us fight.'

'Not a chance.' I turn and shove him back, and before I know it, our arms are locked over each other's heads. Nine kicks my feet out from underneath me and I fall to the ground.

Bernie Kosar barks, telling us to stop.

'Relax, BK,' Nine says, waving at him. 'Consider this a little light training before we head to Ohio.'

'Right. We're training now,' I spit, pulling myself to my feet. 'With everything we just learned.'

Nine throws a jab and I deflect it. But I can't do the same for his right hook. My ribs feel like they just got hit with a battering ram. I fall to my knees, clutching my middle, and he side-kicks my sternum, knocking me flat on my back.

'Come on, man!' he yells down at me. 'Step it up, why don't you? You think you can charge into the desert, take on whatever enemy comes your way, but you can't take me?'

I spring to my feet and surprise him with a clean punch to the gut. As he doubles over, I knee him in the mouth.

'*That's* what I'm talking about, Four!' Blood spills from his split lips, but he's beaming at me. We circle each other. 'Tell you what. Since you're showing signs of giving me a decent run, I'll make you a deal. You beat me, we go to New Mexico. Immediately. I'll even let you drive. But if I win, we spend a couple more hours here, figure some shit out, and come up with a *real* plan. *Then*, we go back to Paradise and head down that well.'

'And you call *me* a coward,' I say.

We continue to circle each other and we each land some devastating blows. I hear one of Nine's ribs snap when I connect with my right elbow. I swing around with my other elbow, but he delivers a hard kick to my left knee. Cartilage rips and pain sears through my leg. Limping, I'm able to throw a few more punches, but I can't move, giving Nine a huge advantage. He leaps behind me and kicks my other leg out from under me. My head hits the floor and the world goes white. When I get my bearings, Nine has my arms pinned to with his knees. The fight is over. And with it goes our chances for finding the Garde out west.

'I'll get a healing stone,' Nine says, slowly standing. With blurred vision, I watch him hold his side as he leaves the room. Bernie Kosar whimpers.

'This is bullshit, you know that?' I yell after him. 'You can't just decide things like this! That Garde in New Mexico could die on their own and you don't even care!'

Nine's voice booms through the apartment. 'We're soldiers, Johnny! And soldiers die. We were sent here to train and fight and some of us aren't going to make it. That's the nature of war.'

I slowly hop into the living room on my one good leg. I can see through the windows the sun is setting. BK sits on the floor, in the last patch of light, looking at me. He begs us to sit down and talk and plan our next move with level heads.

Nine walks in with a healing stone held to his ribs. He tosses it to me and I immediately place it to my left knee. Through the pain, I feel the cartilage slowly reconnecting. It doesn't take long for it to do its thing and soon the pain has disappeared completely. I plant a hand on the window frame and say, 'If we're not going to New Mexico, then let's deal with Setrákus Ra. Right now. You and me. Maybe if we take him out, the rest of the Mogs will die, and we'll save *two* worlds.'

Nine sits down on a leather couch and puts his feet up on the glass coffee table. He sighs and closes his eyes. 'Sorry, Johnny, but even if Setrákus Ra dies, the Mogs will still fight. Just like Pittacus Lore died and we still fight. Stop looking for an easy way out and face it. We're all going to fight until the last one is killed.'

I look out the window and gather the strength to say what I've wanted to say for weeks, ever since I read Henri's letter: 'Pittacus isn't dead. I'm Pittacus.'

'*What* did you say?'

I turn to face him. 'I said, I'm Pittacus Lore.'

Nine leans back laughing so hard he nearly flips over the couch. '*You're* Pittacus? Why on Earth would you think *you're* Pittacus Lore?'

'I feel it,' I say. 'It's why Lorien hibernates. Pittacus lives on through me.'

'Oh, yeah? You know what? I think I can I feel it, too,' he mocks, feeling his torso. He stands and marches over to me. 'But, hey, if you *are* Pittacus, the strongest, *wisest* Elder of Lorien, then I just kicked Pittacus's *ass*. I wonder what that makes me?'

'Lucky,' I say, regretting I said anything.

'Really? Sounds like *somebody* wants a rematch.'

Enough, Bernie Kosar says. *No more fighting. Save your strength.*

I ignore him. 'Fine. A rematch it is, then.'

'If you want to take me on again, then there's going to be a change of venue. And to make it even more interesting, *Pittacus*, I say we each get to use one item from our Chests.'

'Fine.'

I open my Chest, reaching immediately for the four-inch dagger. The handle vibrates the moment I touch it and quickly wraps itself around my fist. I see Mog ash still stuck in its grooves; the smell of it makes me hungry for another fight.

Nine grabs the short silver staff with his right hand. Okay, *that* makes me nervous; I saw how he decimated all those pikens in West Virginia with that thing. He waves his finger at me when he sees my dagger. 'Ah, ah, ah. I said only *one* item.'

'I have my dagger. That's it. And that's all I'll need.'

'And what about your cute little bracelet?'

'Uh, I forgot about it. It's probably the better choice for me. Thank you.' I toss the dagger back into my Chest.

'Follow me,' Nine says. Ignoring Bernie Kosar and his pleas to stop, I follow Nine through the apartment and into the elevator, both of us silent. I assume the fight will be in the building's dark basement among columns and cement walls, our powers hidden from the world. Instead, we ascend. The elevator doors open and Nine punches a key-pad by the door in front of us, and it clicks open. We're on the roof of the John Hancock Center.

'No way, no *freaking* way. Too many people can see us up here!' I say, shaking my head, turning back towards the door inside.

Nine walks out onto the roof. '*Nobody* can see us up here. That's what's so great about being at the top of one of the tallest buildings in the city.'

I don't want to look like I'm chickening out, so I follow, showing a lot more confidence than I feel. But I'm not pre-pared for the fierce wind that hits me hard, almost pushing me back into the doorway. Nine keeps walking, his black hair whipping around his head, seemingly impervious to the force of the wind. His white T-shirt balloons around his torso until he strips it off and lets it fly over the ledge. When he gets to the center of the roof, he snaps his wrist, expanding the silver staff at both ends until it's over six feet long and glowing red. He turns to me and curls his palm, beckoning me closer. Like a tightrope walker, I take a deep breath and put one foot in front of the other to walk towards him. We're in the giant shadow of the looming white spire at the far end of the roof and, just as I near him, Nine turns and runs towards it.

I have no idea what he is about to do, so I stop walking to watch his next move. Without breaking stride, he sprints straight up the spire until he reaches the top. The spire is swaying in the wind and I'm dizzy just looking at him, teetering up there. Nine pulls the red staff over his head and, before I can register what he is doing, he hurls it. The second it leaves his hand, Nine dives headfirst towards me, and I'm faced with dodging two flying objects at once. I just manage to roll away from the sharp staff as it nears me, and I watch as it plunges into a metal beam at an angle. I turn to deal with Nine's approach and as he's about to tackle, I land a blow so hard I send him flying across the roof.

I reach over and yank Nine's red staff out of the metal beam. Henri never trained me with anything like it, but I twist it over my head and charge anyway. Nine stands and steels himself for my attack. I swing the staff across his body, but he parries it away with his wrist and immediately moves to kick my newly repaired knee. I pull my leg back so he misses, but he's able to get his hands on the staff. We both struggle to gain control of it, circling and kicking, dodging and blocking. He uses his telekinesis to float my feet off the ground. I start to resist but then realize I can use it to my advantage with the strong wind up here. Carefully timing my moves with a hearty gust, I flip over the staff; in a fraction of a second, I'm behind Nine with the staff against his throat.

'We should be on our way to New Mexico,' I say, pulling us towards the door that leads back to the elevator.

Nine head-butts me with the back of his skull, right into my nose, and I lose my grip on the staff. He grabs it as I stumble backwards and slam into an electrical box.

'Is that you talking, Johnny? Or, is it *Pittacus*?' he says mockingly as he swings the staff. My bracelet expands just in time to deflect his blow. The electrical box I'm next to has been sliced in half by his near miss. Sparks fly everywhere, including inside my open shield and onto me. When they bounce onto my shirt, I let the fire catch and spread. My shield shrinks, and Nine stares, stunned at the sight of me consumed by flames.

He shakes the surprise off. 'Why didn't you turn into a human fireball when we were on the same team?' he shouts.

The fire around my body crackles and hums in the strong wind. I walk towards him. He may think this is all fun and games. I don't. 'Are we done now?'

'Not quite.' He smirks.

I form a small ball of fire in my palm. I figure I'll make my lack of humor about the situation clear enough if I bowl the ball of fire at his legs, but he knocks it away with the end of the staff like a hockey player. I skip two more fireballs down the roof, each one faster than the last, but he uses his mind to push them to the side. The first one rolls off and ineffectually burns out; the other makes its way to the edge of a fan casing. The heat melts it away, and the high winds tip the whole cover off the enormous fan, leaving it exposed.

I raise my hands over my head to create a fireball the size of a refrigerator, but as it grows, Nine charges at me with the staff over his shoulder. He plants one end of the staff in the ground and vaults himself, feetfirst, at my flaming chest. He screams in pain as the soles of his shoes connect with my burning body, and I'm sent flying backwards. The world that had been reds and yellows is now grays and blues. On my final rotation, I realize I'm flying directly into the exposed fan. At the last possible moment, I spread my arms and legs out and catch myself, mere inches from its blades. The fan is powerful enough to nearly extinguish what's left of my dwindling fire before I dive off and roll away.

'Trying to cool off?' Nine asks, hands on hips, as if simply observing my technique. He's kicked off his half-melted shoes.

'I'm just getting warmed up!' I leap to my feet to ready myself to respond to his next move.

Nine sprints to his left and I follow. He jumps over some pipes onto the raised ledge. Again I follow. We are now both inches from a thousand-foot drop onto the street below. To my utter shock, Nine then steps off the ledge. I yell and lean over to grab him, but when I do, I don't see him sailing to his death. He's standing, horizontal, on a window with his arms crossed, that same, big, smile on his face. I've leaned too far, trying to grab him, and I frantically wheel my arms to regain my balance. But I can't catch myself and suddenly I'm tipping further over the abyss. Nine sprints back up the side of the building and hits me with a powerful uppercut to my jaw. I'm knocked backwards but I don't have the chance to land. Nine catches me by the neck, spins and holds me over the ledge.

'Now, Number Four. All you have to do to get me to set you down, all safe and sound, is say it.' He holds the staff with his other hand over his head. 'Say you're not Pittacus.'

I kick at him, but he holds me out, just out of range. I end up swinging back and forth like a pendulum.

'Say it,' he repeats, his teeth gritted. I open my mouth, but can't bring myself to deny what I feel with such certainty to be true. I believe I *am* Pittacus Lore. I believe I *am* the one who can and will end this war. 'You want to go running to New Mexico to find our ship. You can't believe for even a second it might be a trap. Then you talk about taking on Setrákus Ra, but you can't even beat *me* in hand-to-hand combat. *You* are not *him*. You're not Pittacus. So, let's stop the bull right now. Just say it, Four.'

He tightens his grip on my throat. My vision blurs. I look

up into the cloudless sky and it turns red, just like the night the Mogadorians invaded Lorien. I see flashes of the faces of Loric who were slaughtered. Their screams ring in my ears. I see the explosions, the fire, all of the death. I see krauls with Loric children in their teeth. The pain I feel for all of them at that moment is so overwhelming that I know I can withstand whatever is done to me now, including Nine crushing my neck.

'Say it!'

'I can't,' I manage to squeak out.

'You've got to be delusional!' he yells, squeezing harder. Now I see the bombs falling on Lorien. I see the torn bodies of my people, my planet being destroyed. At the top of one mound of bodies, I see my dead father wearing his silver and blue suit. Nine shakes me violently, my feet swinging wildly. *'You're not Pittacus!'*

I close my eyes to escape the visions of carnage swimming in front of me, dreading whatever comes next. I can see Henri's letter in my mind: *'When the ten of you were born, Lorien recognized your strong hearts, your wills, your compassion, and in turn she bestowed the ten of you the roles you're all meant to assume: the roles of the original ten Elders. What this means is that, in time, those of you left will grow to be far stronger than anything Lorien has ever seen before, far stronger even than the original ten Elders from whom you've received your Inheritances. The Mogadorians know this, which is why they're hunting you so feverishly now.'*

Whatever it all means, I know Nine wouldn't actually kill

me. Each member of the Garde is too important, Pittacus or not. More than anything, coming together and fighting as one, as the Garde we were born to be, is more important than any fight he and I might have. That's small comfort, given the fact that my body is still swinging when I feel the wind change slightly. The hand around my neck opens and my stomach drops as I start to fall. Could I have been wrong? Instead I feel my feet touch down in less than a second. I open my eyes and find myself back on the roof. Nine walks away, his head down. He snaps his wrist and the long red staff shrinks into a piece of silver. Over his shoulder, he yells, 'Next time, I drop you!'

19

I'm facedown in scorching hot sand. It's in my mouth, up my nose, I can barely breathe. I know I should get up, try to roll over, but my bones ache too much. I squeeze my eyes shut, trying to block the pain all over my body. I finally muster the strength to rise, but when I place my hands down to push myself up, the sand burns them. I let myself fall back.

'Marina?' I groan.

She doesn't respond. I still can't open my eyes, but I listen carefully for any signs of life. All I hear is the wind and sand whipping against my body.

I try to speak again, but can only muster a whisper. 'Marina? Somebody, help me. Eight? Ella? Anyone?' I'm so confused I even call out for Crayton. As I wait and hope for a response, I'm hit with the memory of Crayton's dead body. I see it all happening again. Ella's tears. The Mog attack. Hooking my hand inside Marina's elbow and Eight saying, 'Here we go.'

The sun is so hot above me my hair feels like a blanket of fire on my neck and shoulders.

Finally, I manage to roll onto my back, and to lift my arm and shield my eyes from the blinding light. Slowly, blinking, I open them a bit at a time. I don't see anyone. Just sand. I struggle to my feet and hear Eight's voice echoing in my head: 'I really hope this works. I've never tried to bring anyone else.'

Well, it looks like it *didn't* work. Or, it worked, but not for me, for all of us together. Where did Ella and Marina end up? Are they together? Is Eight with them? Are we all in different corners of the world? Or am I the only one alone? My brain is frantically churning through all the different possibilities. If we've not only lost Crayton, but also been separated, torn apart, we are so much farther away from our goal. I feel *sick* with the frustration and panic. All we've worked for, everything we sacrificed to go to India and find Eight – it might have been for worse than nothing.

I'm alone under a cloudless sky and a sweltering sun, with no idea of where I am or how in the *world* I'm going to find another living soul, Garde or not. I scan every direction, hoping to see Marina stumble over a dune with her hand waving above her head, Ella not far behind, or a laughing Eight, cartwheeling across the sandy expanse, but all I see is a desolate desert.

I think about what Eight told us about how this teleporting thing works. Wherever it is that I've landed, I *know* I'm near one of the blue Loralite stones. Even if I don't have his teleporting Legacy, I'm hoping I could still use the Loralite in some way. I drop to my hands and knees and furiously start to dig. I have no way of knowing where the thing is, where to start looking, but I'm desperate. So desperate I barely notice the sand burning my fingers.

But the only rocks I find are tiny, cracked and ordinary. Out of breath, sweat pouring down my face and into my eyes, I finally stop and sit back. I can't afford to expend what little energy I have this way. I need to find water and shelter. I cock my head and listen to the wind, hoping for some kind of sign, but there's nothing and no one. Nothing but sand and dunes for as far as the eye can see. And that leaves nothing for me to do but walk. I look up at the sun, orient myself using my shadow, and start to trudge through the sand.

I walk north. With no protection from the blazing rays, my eyes stinging from my sweat running into them, and the pain of the hot sand whipping against my entire body, I feel vulnerable in a way I've never felt before. Everywhere I look, there is just an endless view of the same, and I know my body can't endure this intense sun for a long period of time. I struggle for a few more steps, then I turn invisible to escape the relentless heat. This will make it hard for anyone to find me, but I have no choice. Then I use my telekinesis to hover above the Earth, just to keep my feet away from the burning sand. The higher vantage point only confirms my long-distance assessment of sand, sand and more sand. I squint, hoping to see a road or sign of civilization of any kind each time I pass a dune. But the only thing that changes, the only variation in my endlessly sandy view, comes in the form of devilish flowering cacti and chunks of petrified wood. The clear, cloudless sky mocks me, offering not even a bit of white to manipulate into creating a thunderstorm. When I rip open the first cactus I come near, I am devastated to find it doesn't hold enough water to begin to quench my thirst.

Eventually, just as my energy and spirits are almost at their end, mountains appear on the horizon, giving me at least the prospect of some salvation. They look like they're at least another day's walk away, though it's hard to know for sure. They're definitely too far to reach today and that is enough to send my hopes plummeting. I know I need to find shelter.

I turn visible and hope someone will see me. I look up at the sky and see the first group of clouds of the day. My heart leaps and I feel a small surge of energy I did not know I even had. I concentrate on creating a storm, just a tiny one, above me. The rain is brief, but awesome nonetheless. It's the only reason I don't collapse and just give up.

I keep moving until I at last come across a low barbed-wire fence. Just beyond it I can make out a faint dirt road. It's the first sign of civilization I've seen, and I'm so overjoyed I can even pick up my pace to reach it. I follow the road for a mile or so before I reach a small hill, which I manage to get up and over. On the other side, miraculously, I see outlines of several small buildings. I can't believe it. Should I believe it? It has to be a mirage.

But, no. The closer I get, the more convinced I am these structures, these signs of life, are *real*. Unfortunately, the closer I get, I can also see the buildings are full of holes; crumbling, wooden skeletons abandoned to the relentless attack of the desert. These buildings represent what happens when you're stuck in a place like this. I've stumbled into a ghost town.

Before I let my disappointment bring me to my knees, I focus on what might have been left behind. Before the ghosts took over. Plumbing? A well? I stumble around, searching inside and outside the structures, trying to find some source of water. I have been reduced to that one, essential ingredient. I need to find water. Everyone needs water, so there *must* be some, somewhere, right?

No. Or, at least, there is none that I can find. I guess there must have been a well at some point, but there isn't one now. Buried by sand, ripped out by space aliens, who knows? The despair that comes over me is like nothing I've ever felt before. Alone, no water, no food, no proper shelter. I yell, as loud as I can, 'Is there anyone here? Please! Someone! Anyone!'

A wood beam creaks from somewhere on my right. It's not exactly the answer I'm looking for.

I look inside each building; as expected, each is emptier than the last. After I've confirmed just how alone I am, I pick the corner of what I believe was once a grocery store to rest for a bit. I try to imagine the building stocked with food and water, just to entertain myself. I pretend I'm going to cook a huge meal for the remaining members of the Garde. At the long table in my mind, Marina sits between Eight and Ella. I put John at the head, with me at the other end. I imagine Nine and Number Five are with us. They kid around with each other, and share stories about all the places they've been. Everyone is laughing, congratulating me on the feast I've prepared, and I tell them all I'm just happy they could make it out here.

'What's your favorite memory of Earth so far?' I imagine Marina asking the table.

'Right now,' John says. 'This one, right here. Safe, with all of you.'

We all agree, raising our glasses to successfully finding each other. Number Five gets up, leaves the room and reenters with an enormous chocolate cake. Everyone cheers and plates are passed around. When I take a bite, it's the most amazing thing I've ever tasted.

Of course, none of this has happened. I'm just a lone, crazy person, sitting in an abandoned, broken-down grocery store in the middle of the desert. I must be crazy, because as I come out of my dream of feasting with the Garde, I realize I am chewing. Chewing air with a satisfied smile on my face. I shake my head and will away my tears. I have not battled Mogs, survived a Mogadorian cell and watched Katarina die to have it all end in the middle of the desert, alone. I pull my knees up to my chest and rest my forehead on them. I have to figure out a plan.

It's still sweltering hot when I leave the ghost town. I've rested from the sun for a while, but I know I have to keep moving before I lose all of my strength. I've walked about a mile towards the mountains through the burning sand when

I feel the most intense cramping in my legs and stomach. I focus what little mental energy I have left on uprooting a few nearby cacti and manage to get a mouthful of water from them.

I concentrate on my Legacy and try to summon another thunderstorm from the few scraggly clouds overhead, but all I manage to create is a plume of sand that washes over me, burying me up to my knees.

For the first time, I'm not just nervous about what's to come; I'm scared I'm going to die out here. I have nothing left. The Elders chose me as a warrior to save our race, and I'm going to die in the middle of a desert.

I feel myself starting to panic, to truly lose it. I have just enough of a grip to know I can't lose it – I'm so vulnerable out here that it will be all over if I do. I'm so desperate I think back to last night, and my imaginary meal with the rest of the Garde. To keep myself focused I think about what I wish I could say to them right now.

Hey, Marina, how are things? Me? I'm in a desert heading to some mountain. I'm guessing I must be in New Mexico, based on what Eight said about where he was able to teleport to before. I'm growing weak, Marina. I don't know how much longer I can hold on. And I don't know where you are, but please, please find a way to get from wherever it is you landed and come and find me.

Ella? Do you know how sorry I am about Crayton? I know how much it hurt, watching him die, leaving him behind. I promise you, we will avenge his death, and I will be the one out front. If I make it out of this desert, I will avenge all of Lorien.

Eight, I couldn't find the Loralite. I see no sign of food, water, shelter, civilization, and I am alone. Can you tell me where the Loralite is? I want to get out of here; I want to find you guys.

I don't even feel stupid, chatting in my head to people who are almost certainly on the other side of the world. I close my eyes and desperately wait for someone to answer me. No one does, of course. So, I trudge on. It gets harder to place one foot in front of the other. I start to waver, listing to the right, then the left, almost falling but catching myself at the last moment. Eventually, though, I can't steady myself and I fall forwards. I resign myself to crawling and continue like this for a while with my eyes closed against the blinding sun. After a while I look up to check where the sun is in the sky and again think I'm imagining a mirage when I see a gate made of solid metal a few hundred feet away. It's over twenty feet tall, topped with spiraling barbed wire. Even from this distance, I can hear the hum of electricity. The fence is charged. This goes a long way towards convincing me it isn't a mirage.

Although I have no idea what's behind this gate, I need help, and I'm at the point where I don't care where that help comes from. I crawl over to the gate and manage to sit up. I wave my hands over my head, hoping it's monitored.

'Please help me,' I manage to whisper, my throat as dry as sandpaper.

The gates don't open and no one emerges. I let myself slide back down into the sand. I try to gather the last bit of strength I have to make one more go of it. I roll over onto my stomach and pull myself slowly up to my feet. I decide to test the fence. What's a little electricity after near starvation and life-endangering thirst? I look around and spot a small cactus. I float it up into the air, and drop it onto the fence, where it sizzles and pops. The charred remains fall to the ground, smoking.

I let myself fall first to my knees, then onto my side, then, finally, roll onto my back. I close my eyes. I feel blisters forming on my dry lips. I hear a faint mechanical noise behind me, but I can't lift my head to see what it is. I know I'm losing consciousness. There's a swirling echo in my ears and then a low drumming. A few seconds later, I swear I hear Ella.

Wherever you are, Six, I hope you're okay, she says.

A short laugh comes out of my mouth, followed by a sob. I'm sure there would be tears, if I had any moisture left in my body. *I'm dying in a desert, Ella,* I respond. *The one with the mountains. I'll see you on Lorien one day, Ella.*

I hear her voice again, but this time I can't make out what she's saying. She is drowned out by a new noise in my head, choppy and loud. And then I feel it. It's a high wind that whips my hair over my face. I slowly open my eyes to see three black helicopters hovering over me. Men yell for me to put my hands over my head, but all I can do is close my eyes.

20

Ella is floating above me. She is in a panic, eyes wide, bubbles shooting out of her mouth. I'm trying to figure out what's going on, how she got here, why there is so much water. I try to reach for her hand, but my arms won't do as I ask them. What happened to me when we teleported? I can tell my face is numb, and there's a pain behind my eyes that's unbearable. My legs won't kick no matter how hard I try. All I can do is watch Ella float higher and higher above me, away from me. Where did all this water come from? My left shoulder begins to rock violently, and it takes a second to realize someone is shaking my arm. Then I see Eight, his black curls hovering over his head like a halo. He hooks his arm under my armpit and I try not to let his look of concern scare me more than I already am. He tries to swim us towards the surface, but the Chest under my arm weighs us down.

I let the freezing water enter my lungs. It's the only thing I can do. Eight kicks the Chest out of my paralyzed arms and yanks me upwards. We start to rise. I look around wildly for a glimpse of Six, but I don't see her.

When my head breaks the surface of the water, the

first thing I'm aware of is a glaring, hot sun. Everywhere I look is water. I see Ella treading water nearby. A few minutes in the fresh air gets my limbs to start working, so I tread water as well. Eight appears fully occupied with cursing our luck.

'Where's Six?' I cry, coughing. I keep whipping my head around to see if I can spot her blonde head bobbing around on the surface.

'I couldn't find her down there!' Eight yells. 'I have no idea if she made it or not!'

'Why wouldn't she have made it?' Ella asks, a new panic rising in her voice.

Eight slowly rises out of the water until he's standing on the surface. It doesn't look as easy for him this time. He kicks the tip of a slow passing wave, pissed. 'Damn it! I knew I shouldn't have tried to teleport with so many people!'

'But where could she be? How do we find her?' Ella cries.

'I don't know. For all I know, she's still back at what's left of the cave.'

My limbs are still coming around slowly, and I'm struggling to just keep my head above water. 'What! She'll be killed if she's still there!'

Ella is also struggling to stay afloat. Eight pulls her over to him so she can get on his back, her arms wrapped tightly around his neck. 'Six could have ended up somewhere else, too,' Eight says, trying to sound more hopeful. 'I just don't know where, exactly.'

'Where are *we*?' I ask.

'That much I know.' Eight sounds relieved to have a definitive answer to something. 'We're in the Gulf of Aden. And that . . .' he points at the coastline in the distance that I didn't see before. 'That's Somalia.'

'How do you know?' asks Ella.

'I ended up here once before,' he says flatly. He doesn't elaborate, so there must be more to his story.

I don't know much about Somalia, other than it's in Africa and is in a perpetual state of brutal tribal and civil war, not to mention the poverty that keeps tempers high. I don't know if I have the strength to use my telekinesis or even to swim under water to get to that coastline; I'm even less sure if I want to. I need to think.

'You know what? I'm going to go under for a bit. I can save some energy down there while we figure out what to do,' I say. As I go down, I hear Ella call out.

'Look for Six!'

Her words give me a surge of strength. Just the possibility of finding Six puts new energy in my dive. I go deep and open my eyes. The water is relatively blue, even this far away from land. There's movement below me and I dive further to find a small school of tuna. I slowly twist around in circles, looking for even a glimpse of Six's dyed blonde hair, and more than twice I'm fooled by waving strands of seaweed. I look up and see the faint shadow of Eight's body on the surface. Feeling confident my strength will stay with me, I descend until I touch the bottom. Navigating my way along the sea floor and scanning the water ahead of me, I accidentally brush up against a mass of coral and cut my knee. The sharp pain stuns me for a second and I reach down and touch it, to heal it, and it takes longer than I expect for my Legacy to work. Whatever happens during teleporting must have some effect on our Legacies and our strength. Grateful that my breathing seems to be okay, I can only hope this doesn't last long – I don't want us to be vulnerable.

I keep moving and eventually find my Chest next to Eight's, and spot the large, blue Loralite stone a few feet away from them both. I try to pick up the Chests, but am too weak to budge them. I look up and see Eight's shadow still in the same spot and decide to ask for his help.

As I ascend I cut through a school of beautiful orange fish. I break the surface. 'No sign of Six, but the Loralite stone is down there, right next to our Chests,' I report. 'Let's get them and go. We'll teleport somewhere else, see if we can catch up to wherever Six has landed.'

'Don't we need to be *at* the Loralite to teleport? How will I get down there?' Ella asks. 'I can't hold my breath for that long.'

'You don't have to,' Eight says with a grin.

'Do you have a Legacy that turns you into a torpedo people can catch a ride on, too?' I ask.

'Better,' Eight says. He reaches into his pocket and grabs the green crystal he put there when his Chest was first returned to him. The crystal begins to glow, and then a crazy amount of wind starts to shoot out from it. Eight aims it at the ocean. A shallow crater forms in the water below him and he falls into it. 'Come on! Quick!'

Ella and I swim into the crater. Eight holds out his free hand and I take it; Ella grabs my other hand.

'Get ready. We're about to drop. Fast!' he says. 'You have to stay with me because the water will collapse behind us. When we get to the bottom, Ella, be prepared to hold your breath long enough for me to grab the Chests.'

'Everyone keep your eyes open for Six,' I say.

Ella squeezes my hand. 'If she's down there, we'll find her.'

Eight positions the crystal so it's aimed at the ocean floor. 'Here we go!' he yells. We fall fast, the wind from the crystal blasting a small circle of water out of our way until it unites again a few feet behind Ella. We're inside a bubble, shooting through the water. Eight howls in amusement; I can't help but join in.

Ella grabs my arm. 'Six is in trouble!' She says. 'She says she's in the desert!'

'What are you talking about?' I reply, as fish and sharks and squid pass us in a blur. 'How do you know that?'

Ella hesitates for a second before yelling, 'I don't really know! I just talked to her somehow in my head! She says she's dying!'

'If she's in the desert, then she's in New Mexico already!' Eight shouts.

'Eight, we've got to get there right away,' I cry.

We arrive on the ocean floor and try to run on the muddy bottom, but it's impossible to move quickly. Water rushes in behind our pocket of air and the crystal swiftly becomes useless, creating a small whirlpool in front of us. I look back to make sure Ella is okay and holding her breath. When I turn around, Eight has transformed into a black octopus. He swings two tentacles out and snatches up our Chests, and with two of his other tentacles he grabs our hands. Eight pulls us towards the glowing blue Loralite stone sticking out of the mud floor. Before I can look at Ella again, I'm engulfed in darkness.

21

Nine and I ride the elevator down in silence. I'm furious and utterly humiliated, and it's got nothing to do with the feelings welling up inside me. When we enter the apartment, Bernie Kosar jumps off the couch to ask if we are finished with all the nonsense.

'I don't think it's up to me. What do you say, Johnny?' Nine mutters. He opens the fridge and pulls out a slice of cold pizza. He flips the tip of it into his mouth, takes a huge bite and chews noisily.

I lean down and scratch BK's chin. 'I hope so, buddy.'

With a mouth full of pizza, Nine says, 'Pack up your doggie bags, BK, because we're hitting the road. We're heading back to Paradise city, where the girls are pretty. And, damn, Four, take a shower already. You smell like smoke.'

'Shut up,' I say, falling onto the couch. Bernie Kosar climbs into my lap and looks up at me with sad eyes.

Nine walks away, down the hallway. He calls back to me, 'A deal's a deal, man! We leave for Paradise in a couple of hours, so you may want to grab a quick nap after your shower. And, hey! It's a road trip! You can't be bummed about a road trip!'

I'm exhausted, but I slump towards my room. A deal *is*

a deal. The bed moans when I fall onto it, but after a few minutes, I can't bear my own smell. I drag myself into the shower. The water can't get hot enough on my skin, a side effect of my Legacy. As I stand under the spray, so tired I'm swaying on my feet, I replay the fight on the roof in my mind. I try to figure out how I lost against Nine, but I can't. I'm so tired. I think I'm mumbling to myself. I turn off the water and listen to the drops fall onto the shower floor. I grab a towel as I stumble back to bed. I need to rest.

I climb in between the sheets and using telekinesis, turn off the light. I hear Nine's thudding steps as he moves towards the surveillance room and I close my eyes. Sleep blankets my mind for a second before I hear a noise. Nine is lightly tapping on my open door. I have my back to him and I don't move, even when he clears his throat and starts to speak. 'Hey. Johnny? I'm sorry that I can be such a dick. I could blame it on being locked up for so long, that does something to you. But, honestly, I'm pushing here because I really do think I'm right. We *need* to go to Paradise. *Now.* So I hope we can be friends. I want to be friends. And I'm glad you're here.'

I haven't moved a muscle the whole time he's speaking and I'm stunned by this moment of sensitivity. I'm not sure what to say, even as I flip over. He's a slouched shadow leaning in the doorframe. 'I'm glad I'm here, too. Thanks.'

'Sure.'

Nine slaps the wall twice, looks down at the ground,

then turns and walks away. As his footsteps move down the hall, my eyes drift closed. After a few minutes, I hear faint whispers. I know a vision or nightmare is coming. I'm aware I'm in bed, yet I'm frozen in place. I feel myself floating, and when a dark doorway forms above me, I start to spin in the air incredibly fast. I rocket through the doorway and I'm moving through a black tunnel with my arms stuck to my sides. As the black turns to blue, the whispers grow louder, repeating the same thing, over and over, 'There is more to know.'

The blue tunnel turns to green, and green turns back to black. Then, bam, I fall out of the tunnel and my bare feet land on a familiar rocky floor. I swing my arms and find I have control of my body once again. I'm back in the arena at the top of the mountain. I whip my head around, looking for Sam, but he's nowhere to be seen. Neither is the other Garde member. The space is completely empty, even the bleachers.

But then, in the center of the arena floor, a black stone flips over, and on the other side crouches a large Mog soldier, wearing a ragged black cloak and black boots. His waxy pale skin shines and the sword he holds above his head shimmers, as if lit from within. When he sees me, he stands and points the sword at me menacingly. It's pulsing, as if somehow alive, an extension of the evil that wields it.

I don't hesitate. I rush right at him, my palms lighting up and emitting a powerful beam. When I'm ten yards away,

I aim the Lumen at my feet and light them on fire. The flames climb up my body as I leap. The soldier jumps at me and when we meet, I burrow a smoldering hole right through his chest. He turns to ash before hitting the ground.

To my right, another black stone flips over; it's another sword-wielding Mog. Two more flip to my left, and I hear others appear behind me. The stone under my feet starts to vibrate, and I dive away just as it rotates to produce a Mogadorian holding a cannon. After punching a hole through the closest soldier on my left, I start launching fireballs, battling with a newfound strength. My red bracelet comes to life, blasting open to sever the head of the giant soldier. In a minute, I wipe them all out. My adrenaline is pumping, and I'm listening for more stones to reveal my next round of suitors.

A dozen stones flip in front of me, and then fifty on both sides. The largest, best-equipped Mog soldiers I've ever seen surround me. I create a small ring of fire around myself and move backwards, the fire maintaining its perimeter until I'm against the wall of the arena. The fire burns between the Mogs and me. Somehow, though, I don't think my position is particularly secure.

I widen the ring of fire around me until it hits a row of soldiers. They catch fire, but don't turn to ash. In fact, they walk right through the fire with their weapons up. I throw dozens of fireballs, but this time they have no effect. Something red zips in the air over my head, and I watch it puncture the chest of a Mog soldier who continues to march forward. I recognize the item. It's Nine's staff. Nine drops out of the empty bleachers to the spot right next to me. Even in the middle of an attack, I feel relieved to see him. I immediately feel safer, more confident that even these fire-resistant Mogs will be defeated now that it is the two of us.

'Nice of you to join me!' I yell.

He stands right next to me but doesn't seem to hear my voice. 'Hey, Nine!' I try again, but he still doesn't react. He just keeps staring at the advancing Mogs.

When the soldiers are only a few feet away from us, the ground below our feet starts to tremble and quake. I try and hold onto the wall, but I can't keep my balance. Next thing I know, a tremendous *boom* shakes the opposite end of the arena and pieces of black rock rain down on us. Nine dodges a large boulder that slams into the wall behind me, leaving a giant hole that leads to the outside. Looking through, I can see blue skies.

From the swirling dust and flying debris a large stage rises out of the explosion. There, in the middle, is Setrákus Ra. *Like an evil rock star,* I can't help but think. The purple scar around his neck burns brightly above the three blue pendants on his chest. To my horror, the moment he appears, my fire goes out. I try to illuminate my legs with my Lumen, but my palms suddenly won't light. Setrákus Ra slams the end of his golden staff with the moving eye onto the ground and roars for silence. The soldiers in front of me snap to attention, turning from me and Nine to him. One by one, they rest their weapons at their sides.

'All of you have been chosen to end this fight!' Setrákus Ra yells. 'You will go forth and you will destroy the Loric children. When they are dead, you will bring me their pendants and their Chests. You will crush their human friends. *You will not fail me!*'

The Mog soldiers cheer and raise their fists in unison.

Setrákus Ra slams his staff down on the stone floor with another thundering bang. 'Mogadore will rule this galaxy! Everything, on every planet, will be ours!' The soldiers cheer and wave their weapons in the air.

'Together, we will fight. I will fight with you. Together, we will win this battle and annihilate all who live on Earth!'

I try again to light my Lumen but it still doesn't work. Then I try to lift a large sharp stone at my feet with my mind to launch at Setrákus Ra. It doesn't budge. My bracelet shield has retracted and shows no sign of kicking into action. My Legacies – and my Inheritance – have left me.

The soldiers have turned back around and once again aim their weapons at us. Without our Legacies, we're sitting ducks. We *have* to get out of here.

'Nine! This way!' I yell.

Finally, this seems to get through to him. He whips his head around and looks at me. We move towards the hole in the wall. Standing in a ray of cold sunlight at the lip of it, I peer down into a valley, thousands of feet below. I look over my shoulder; there are Mog soldiers charging at us.

'We'll walk on the side of the mountain,' Nine says. 'Here. Take my hand.'

I grab his hand. We've only taken a single step down the side of the snowy mountaintop when we realize Nine's Legacy has failed him too. Instead of feeling the mountain beneath my feet, there is only air. We're falling. I look over at a shocked Nine, his long black hair whipping all around his face. Below us, two dark doorways are approaching fast. I prepare myself for a painful impact, my stomach doing backflips as I fly through the air. To my utter amazement, I go headfirst through the door on the left and I keep falling until I find myself in a dark tunnel alive with booms of thunder, cracks of lightning. The whispering starts again, and as the tunnel turns to green to blue and back to black, the hoarse voice I heard when the vision began speaks again: 'New Mexico.'

My eyes snap open and I sit up, my face damp with sweat. I rip off the sheets that cling to me. *New Mexico.* I leap up and charge down the hall towards Nine's room, determined to convince him once and for all. If I have to fight him again, so be it. I will keep fighting until I win.

I stop in front of Nine's door and turn on my Lumen, needing to confirm that my Legacies really haven't abandoned me. I knock and push the door open. I'm surprised to find Nine sitting up in bed with his head in his hands.

'Nine,' I say, flipping on the light. 'I'm sorry, I know a deal's a deal and you did beat me. But we have to go to –'

'New Mexico. I know, Johnny. I know.' He shakes his

head. I'm not sure if he's trying to wake up or come to grips with his sudden reversal. Probably both. 'Just let me wake up a bit.'

'So, you've reconsidered?'

He plants his feet on the floor, one at a time. 'No, I haven't *reconsidered.* But when you're falling to your death off a mountain because your Legacies don't work and some ghost keeps repeating "New Mexico," you take the hint.'

'You had the same vision?' I ask. The comfort I felt when I saw Nine – it was because he was really there. It dawns on me that Nine and I have a connection and I should give him more respect than I have been. I have to stop seeing him as an adversary. Our lives depend on it.

Nine pulls on a shirt, and gives me a condescending look I know well. 'No, you idiot. Haven't you figured it out yet? I didn't have a vision *too.* We were in the *same vision.* It's been happening all week. Get a clue, would you?'

I'm flustered, and I don't hide it well. 'But whenever I talked about them you blew them off. You blew *me* off. You kept saying they're just dreams and all that. You could see how the dreams have been tormenting me, Nine! You've been acting like I'm nuts for taking them seriously!'

'First of all, you believe you're Pittacus Lore, so technically you *are* nuts. Second, I wasn't messing with your head. I did blow the visions off at first; mine *and* yours. Thought they were bullshit. When Setrákus Ra asked me to surrender, just like he asked you and that other kid, I figured the visions were a form of mind game or some trick, perpetrated by the Mogs. I didn't think we should trust them; I definitely didn't think we should do anything they suggested we do. In fact, I thought the safest bet was to do anything *but* what they wanted. But this time . . .' Nine pauses. 'This time, it felt like a warning. A warning we should take seriously. Now, I'm pretty convinced that there is some serious shit about to go down, Four.'

As relieved as I am that he has finally decided to listen, I'm frustrated it took so long. 'That's what I've been trying to tell you! Okay, then, let's go! Have you thought about how we're going to get there? Oh, man, please tell me you and Sandor have your own helicopter or airplane tucked away somewhere!'

'Sorry, dude, they were on our wish list.' he yawns and stretches. 'But I do have a car in the parking garage. And I *love* to drive. Fast.'

Nine and I grab as much as we can from the weapons room, stuffing two large duffel bags full of rifles, handguns, and grenades. I pick up a rocket launcher but Nine says it won't fit in the trunk. We need the remaining space for ammo. Next, we race to the surveillance room to grab the tablet.

Nine sits down and starts punching keys at one of the computers. 'I have to shut this sucker down. Wouldn't want any of it to be useful to someone who isn't welcome.

Do me a favor. While I'm dealing with this, check on the Garde with that tablet thing.'

I press the blue circle in the upper corner and wait. I see our two radiating blue dots in Chicago. Then I see one in northern New Mexico, and there's still one in Jamaica. I wait a few seconds for the other three to appear, but they don't.

'Um, Nine? I only see four,' I say, my voice rising in panic. 'There're only four blue dots!'

He rips the tablet out of my hand. 'Let me see it. They must somehow be off the grid,' Nine says. He doesn't sound so sure of himself all of a sudden. He presses the green triangle and the green pulsing dots show up on the map in New Mexico and Egypt, just like before. 'At least the missing three didn't take one of the ships.'

I look closer and press the blue circle again. I realize the blue dot in New Mexico is now at the exact same spot as the green dot. 'That Garde in New Mexico is on top of the ship, if that *is* a ship.'

'Hope whoever that is knows it would be one *lonely* flight,' Nine says. I shake my head at him and look back at the screen, trying to figure out what our next move should be.

Then it hits me. 'Wait. The government is involved in all this somehow, right? What else is in New Mexico? Area 51! Is that where this green dot is? The most well-known place for UFO sightings?' It's all starting to come together.

Nine pulls the keyboard closer and starts tapping even

more quickly. 'Cool your jets, cowboy. First of all, Area 51 is in Nevada. Second, we *aliens* know that place is just a decoy. It's a meaningless airplane hangar, give or take.' A map of New Mexico appears on the main screen and Nine zooms in on the northern half. 'Okay, wait a second.' He looks from the tablet back to the computer screen. 'Now *this* is interesting. You weren't that far off, after all. We may not be headed for Area 51, but we *are* going someplace just as secret.'

'What do you mean?' I ask, while I wonder why I'm always playing catch up with this guy.

Nine pushes his chair away from the desk with an annoyingly satisfied grin on his face. 'Holy shit. It all makes sense now.' He stabs the screen with his finger. 'In this part of New Mexico there's a town in the middle of the desert called Dulce. Is any of this ringing familiar? No? Dulce, as in the infamous underground Dulce Base, run by the one and only U.S. government. That *must be* where our ship is. Now I'm positive those are our ships, blinking away on that screen! In their perfect wisdom, the government feeds the rumors about Area 51 so all the UFO freaks stay away from the real deal in Dulce.'

I can't help but smile. 'So, now we're going to an underground government base?'

'I certainly hope so,' Nine says, shutting down the computer. He practically takes a bow, so pleased with himself for figuring all this out. 'Although it's supposed to be insanely secure and completely impossible to get into. And that's why it's the perfect place to hide our ship.'

'Or to hide the random aliens you find during the course of your travels,' I add.

It feels as if everything has been turned upside down since I woke up. We quickly get moving, piling the weapons, our Chests, and the supplies in the elevator. BK barely squeezes in with us as the elevator doors close. Nine surprises me with how gentle he sounds when he addresses the closed doors, 'You were a sweet home, Chicago. I hope I see you again.'

We descend rapidly. 'Hey, man,' I say. 'Remember, our *real* home is *so* much cooler.' He doesn't say anything, but I see his shoulders relax.

The elevator doors open into an underground garage. We pause and carefully look around before we start to unload. With the coast clear, Nine and I throw the bags over our shoulders and BK follows. As we turn a corner, I see we're headed for a car hidden under a dusty tarp. After the luxury of the apartment, I can only imagine what must lurk beneath it. I can picture a yellow Ferrari, or something equally flashy. Or maybe it's a white convertible Porsche or even a black Lotus.

Nine must have read my thoughts. He winks at me and yanks the tarp off to reveal our ride. There, in all its glory, sits an old, beat-up, beige Ford Contour. Not exactly the pimped-out ride I was expecting, but bling is now the least of my concerns; this thing doesn't look like it'll even start.

'Are you serious?' I ask, not even bothering to hide my disgust.

Nine looks at me innocently, even though he clearly

knew what I was expecting. 'What? You were hoping for a Camaro?'

'Not exactly. But I was hoping for something with less rust spots. Something that looks less determined to die,' I say.

'Shut up and get in, Johnny,' he says, tossing his bags into the trunk. 'You ain't seen nothin' yet.'

22

I wake to the sensation of rocking back and forth. Everything hurts. My whole body feels fried by the sun: my throat, my skin, my feet and my head. My lips are so dry and burned, I can't even put them together. My eyelids are the worst of all, and they refuse to open, no matter how desperately I want to see where I am. The rocking and swaying continues and it dawns on me I must be in a moving vehicle. A wave of nausea rolls over me. I try to lift my hands to my head, but that's when I discover they're tied down. So are my legs. Now I'm wide awake, and I force my eyes open and look madly around, but all I see is darkness. I close my eyes again. The desert sun must have left me blind.

I try to call out for help, but all I can do is wheeze and cough. My ears pick up an echo, and I concentrate on the air around me. I cough again, just to hear the echo once more. It's enough sound to understand I'm in a tight space, and that the space around me is made of metal. It feels like I'm in a coffin, and I almost wretch.

That's when I start to panic. What if I'm not blind? What if I'm really dead? I can't be. I am in way too much pain to be dead. But I feel buried alive.

My breath starts to come fast and furious when a man's voice stops my panic attack cold. It's loud and electronic, coming through a speaker. 'Are you awake?'

I try to answer him, but my throat is too dry. I tap my fingers on the bench and realize it's metal, too. A few seconds later there is a noise to my right, and I can sense something has been placed near me.

'There's a glass of water and a straw beside you. Take a sip,' the man says.

I turn my head and find the straw with my mouth. The skin on my lips cracks as I try to close them around the straw. When I take a sip of water, I can taste the metallic tinge of blood and I hear a low humming in my ears. It's the same hum I heard at the gate. The box I'm in must be flowing with electricity.

'What were you doing at that gate?' The man asks. Every time he speaks, I am struck by how neutral his voice is. It isn't friendly, but neither is it threatening.

'Lost,' I whisper. 'I was lost.'

'How did you get lost?'

I take another sip before saying, 'I don't know.'

'You don't know. I see. Your number is six, is it not?'

I cough and choke at the question, mentally chewing myself out for doing so. I'm usually cooler than this, but my mind is completely cooked by the sun. If he wasn't sure of the answer before, he is now. I resolve to get a grip, to stop making stupid mistakes.

The voice is back. 'Well, Number Six. You're pretty famous around here. The footage from the high school in Paradise and the way you took down those helicopters in Tennessee was impressive. And then there's the incredible show you put on in D.C. last week, breaking John Smith and Sam Goode out of a federal facility. You are quite the little warrior princess, aren't you?'

I'm still stuck on how he could know who I am; now he's talking like he had front-row seats to my life? My body sways hard to the left, and I realize I must be in a moving vehicle that just took a turn, taking me who knows where. I push against the strap over my forehead – nothing happens. I try using my telekinesis, but as soon as I even start to focus my thoughts pain rolls through my stomach so bad I almost throw up again.

'What you need to do is relax. Trying to fight isn't going to get you anywhere. You're dehydrated and most likely have heat stroke. You're going to feel pretty sick for a while.'

'Who *are* you?' I manage to ask, painfully.

'Agent David Purdy, FBI,' he says. I feel slightly better knowing I'm in the hands of the U.S. government, not captured by the Mogs. I couldn't go through that again, knowing what was coming, especially now that the charm that protected me the first time has been broken. With the FBI, my chances of survival have just skyrocketed. No matter how aggressive they are, they aren't monsters. All I need right now is a little patience; the opportunity to escape will come. Purdy doesn't know that, probably assumes it can't be true. Right now, I'll just follow his advice. Relax. Rehydrate. Wait. I might as well see what else he's willing to tell me about what he knows about me, what he knows about all of this.

'Where am I?' I ask.

The speaker squeals before Agent Purdy answers. 'You're in a transport. It's a short trip.'

Again I try to use my telekinesis to undo my

leg straps, but I'm still too weak and the attempt makes me nauseous again. I take another couple of sips of water to give myself time to think. 'Where are you taking me?'

'We've got a reunion planned for you with a friend, or maybe I should say a friend of John Smith's. Do you call him John? Or, do you call him Number Four?'

'I don't know what you're talking about,' I say. I pause before answering. 'I don't know anyone named John Four.'

All of a sudden, I remember what happened back in the desert, just before I blacked out at the gate. I felt half out of my mind, so much so I wasn't even sure the helicopters landing close by were even real. I remember hearing Ella's voice. No. I didn't just hear her voice; we *spoke* to one another. She asked, I answered. Given the fact that it's the FBI who has me, it's a pretty good bet there really were helicopters. If *those* were real, maybe I did communicate with Ella. Has a new Legacy kicked in? Just when I needed it most.

Ella? Can you hear me? I try again, just in case. *The FBI is holding me, some agent named Purdy has me locked up and we're in some kind of vehicle. Purdy says it isn't far, wherever it is we're going.*

'How did you get to the desert, Number Six?'

Purdy's voice interrupts. 'Weren't you just in India, with your friends? Remember that? Just like all the other kids, reading schoolbooks and being kidnapped at the airport.'

How does he know that?

'How did you know where the base was?' His voice is losing a bit of its neutrality. I think I hear just a hint of impatience.

'What base?' I ask. I'm having a hard time thinking straight.

'The one we found you dying outside of in the desert. How did you know where to find it?'

I try to turn invisible, but again, the moment I try testing my Legacy, my stomach erupts with a ferocious and immediate pain. I want so badly to curl up in a ball, but the straps hold me flat and the pain takes my breath away.

'Drink your water,' the agent advises again. His voice is back to its detached neutrality.

Just as I did the first time, I obey, take a sip and wait. The pain finally starts to dull, but then a powerful wave of dizziness washes over me. My mind feels like it's a car careening out of control, swerving this way and that. The thoughts, too many of them to be coherent, come fast and furious. The events from the last few days flash by me. I see myself taking hold of Marina's arm right before we teleported. I see Crayton lying motionless. I watch myself saying goodbye to John and Sam. I almost forget where I am. That is, until the voice forces me back to my present circumstances.

'Where is Number Four?' He is nothing if not consistent, this guy.

'Who?' I ask, forcing myself to focus on what he's saying. If I don't, I'm going to make another mistake like I did before.

All of a sudden, the calm voice is completely gone. He screams through the speaker, 'Where is Number Four?' I wince at the noise.

'Go to hell,' I spit. I'm not telling him anything.

Ella? Marina? Anyone? If anyone can hear me, you need to say something. I need help. I'm in some desert. All I know is I'm near a U.S. government base, and the FBI has me. We're going somewhere, but I don't know where. And there's something wrong with me. I can't use my Legacies.

'Who was with you in India, Number Six? Who were the man and the two girls?'

I stay silent. I picture Ella's face. The youngest Lorien left. I know how that must weigh on her. And now, she's without Crayton. It was just a day ago I was jealous of what they had, and now he's gone.

'What numbers were they? Who were the girls?' Agent Purdy sounds impatient, though his voice is calmer now.

'That's my band. I play the drums. They sing. I love *Josie and the Pussycats*, don't you? I like to watch retro cartoons. All the kids are doing it.' My lips crack and bleed again when I smile. I don't mind. I taste my blood on my tongue and smile wider.

'Six?' the man asks in a gentler voice. I guess he's going to try the Good Cop tactic. 'Was that Number Five and Seven you were with at the airport in India? Who is the older man? Who are the girls?'

Suddenly it's as if I can't control what comes out of my mouth. My voice doesn't even sound like mine when I say, 'Marina and Ella. They're sweet, sweet girls. I just wish they were a little stronger.' What am I saying? Why am I saying anything?

'Are Marina and Ella members of your race? Why do they need to be stronger? And what number is Marina?'

I catch myself this time before answering, shocked that I even opened my mouth to answer again. I concentrate all my energies to find my voice, to respond as I know I should. It's like I'm battling a war within me. 'I don't know what you're talking about. Why do you keep talking about numbers?'

Agent Purdy's voice blasts into the box. 'I know who you are! You're from another planet! I know you kids go by numbers! We have your ship, for Christ's sake!'

At the mention of our ship, my mind starts to spin. I flash back to the journey from Lorien. I see myself as just a kid, staring out the ship's windows at the emptiness of space as we travel towards Earth. I eat at a long white table and look at the other eight kids, each with their Cêpans. There's a boy with long black hair laughing and throwing food. A blonde girl sits next to him quietly eating a piece of fruit. The Cêpans at the end of the table watch the kids closely. I see a young Marina crying, her legs tucked up to her chest, sitting on the floor under a control panel. Her Cêpan is on her knees next to her, trying to coax her to stand up with her. I remember I got in trouble with a boy with short black hair.

The next face I see is a young Number Four. His blond hair is long and wavy. He's kicking the wall with his bare foot, angry about something. He turns around and grabs a pillow, slamming it to the floor. Four looks up, sees me watching, and his face turns bright red. I hand him a toy, something I've stolen from him. The guilt I felt back then rushes over me all over again, just as strong as it was when it first happened. The other faces in the room grow fuzzy.

Then I see myself in Katarina's arms when we landed on Earth. I remember the door of the ship opening.

Where have these memories come from? As hard as I tried before, I could never remember very much about our journey to Earth aside from a few small details. I've never had this vivid a flashback before.

'Are you listening to me?' Purdy yells. 'We have talked to the Mogadorians,' he says. That statement yanks me back to the present with a thud. 'Did you know that?'

'Oh, yeah? What'd they have to say?' I ask, trying to sound like I'm just making conversation, but I regret it instantly. Why would I admit knowing who the Mogs are? Before I can dwell on my mistake too much, my mind drifts back to the ship, to its doors opening, to the human with brown hair and large thick glasses standing, waiting to greet us. In his hands are a briefcase and a white tablet, and behind him sits a big box of clothes. Somehow I know that's Sam's dad. Sam. Oh, how I want to see Sam again.

'I want to see Sam,' I slur. Even though I don't

want to say anything more, reveal anything else to the agent, I can't help myself. I hear my voice, feel my brain thick and sluggish, and instantly I realize there must have been drugs in the water. That's why I can't hold a thought in my head, why I keep drifting into my past, and why I feel such pain when I try to use my Legacies.

I kissed Sam. I should have kissed him for real but I was too worried what John would think.

John. I kissed John, too. I would really like to kiss John again. My stomach gets kind of squirmy when I play back the moment when John grabbed me by the shoulders and turned me towards him. He lowered his face to mine, but just before our lips touched, the house exploded. I can feel my chin tilt upward as I replay the moment again and again. Except this time, when the house explodes, we kiss. The kiss is perfect.

'Sam?' Agent Purdy asks, interrupting my thoughts. I was really enjoying remembering that kiss. 'I'm guessing you mean Sam Goode, right?'

Sam's face is now all I can see and my head is spinning out of control. 'Yeah. Sure. I want to see Sam Goode.' I can hear my voice drifting off.

'Is he one of you? What number is Sam Goode?'

My eyelids grow heavy and I find myself falling asleep. The drugs are finally doing me some small favor.

'Six!' He shouts. 'Hey, Six! Wake up! We're not finished here!'

His shouts jar me so badly, I jerk up, only to be stopped by my restraints.

'Six? Six! Where is Sam Goode? Where is John Smith?'

'I'm going to kill you,' I whisper. My anger and frustration with being tied up and powerless is getting the best of me. 'When I find you, I am going to kill you.'

'I have no doubt you'll try.' The agent laughs.

I try to clear my head, to concentrate on where I am. Too quickly, everything begins to spin until I pass out.

The room is tiny and made of cement. There's a toilet and cement block with a mattress tied down on it and a blanket that's too short to cover me. I've been awake for two hours, maybe more. I'm having a difficult time putting thoughts together. I'm trying to establish some kind of timeline from when I found myself alone in the desert, to the gate, to waking up to my interrogation ride of horror. I need to figure out where I've been, how much time has passed and what information I let slip.

Unscrambling my brain isn't easy. Since the moment I regained consciousness in this cell, the overhead lights have strobed relentlessly. I feel a sharp, pounding pain in my head. My mouth is dry and I hold my churning stomach as I try to focus on the most important part of my recall, my conversation with the agent.

I manage to turn invisible, just to see if I can, but as soon as I do I'm attacked with that extreme nausea I felt on the ride, so I materialize immediately. Either the drugs are still in my system or this is being caused by something else.

I close my eyes for a few minutes to escape the flashing lights. They're so bright, it's impossible to block them out entirely. I remember Agent Purdy said he was in contact with the Mogadorians. Why would the U.S. government be talking to the Mogadorians? And why would he admit that to me? Don't they know the Mogs are the enemy? What I can't figure out is, how much does the government know about me, about my kind? As soon as the Mogadorians wipe out the Garde, the next thing they'll do is kill every last human on Earth. Doesn't the government know that? I'm guessing the Mogs have presented a very different picture of themselves.

I hear a man's voice come from somewhere above me. It's not Purdy, the agent who spoke to me in the container. I open my eyes to look for a vent or speaker, but I can't see anything with the strobe light flashing relentlessly.

'Prepare yourself for transport, Number Six.' A small panel in the middle of the metal door opens with a clang. I stumble over and find a plastic cup of purple liquid sitting on a shelf. My insides gurgle at the sight of it. Why is it purple? Is it drugged, like the water I was drinking earlier?

'You must drink the water to be transported. If you do not drink the water, we will be forced to inject you with it by any means necessary.'

'Go to hell!' I yell at the ceiling.

'Drink,' the voice repeats. It does not invite discussion.

I pick up the cup and walk to the toilet. I hold the cup high and tilt it, making a big show of pouring it out. The last drop has barely fallen when the cell door whips open. Several men with batons and shields rush in at me. Acid bubbles in my stomach as I try and steel myself for a fight because I know I'm going to have to use my Legacies. I decide that this time, I can do it. And maybe I can use the flashing lights to my advantage.

I greet the first officer with an open punch to the throat. As a baton swings down at me on my left, I catch the attacker's wrist and give it a good twist. I hear it snap. He screams and releases the baton. Now, I have a weapon.

The officers form a circle around me but in the flashing light, our movements look like they're happening in slow motion and are hard to follow. I pick a man at random and attack, cracking my baton across both his knees. He falls and I pounce on his neighbour. The physical exertion causes sickness to crawl up my throat, but I swallow it back down. Now that I've managed to push through once, hopefully it will become easier. I slam the butt of the baton on the man's temple. One of the remaining men hits me on the back of my head with something, and another one grabs a chunk of my hair and yanks. Using my telekinesis, I smash them against each other. The body slam makes both of them fall, and I kick them hard.

The once incapacitating sickness ebbs and flows, but my strength doesn't – it is *back*. Now armed with two batons, I fight off three more men. When they start firing Tasers, I freeze the sharp probes in the air before swinging them back towards the shooters. Finally, the doorway is clear and looks like it is staying that way. When I step outside the cell, I brace myself and turn myself invisible. The pain is the worst yet, but I know I can push past it. I just need to hold on for a little while longer, until I can get out, and find the others.

23

I come to facedown in wet grass. I lift my head and press my palms onto the ground to get my shoulders up. I hear Eight groan from somewhere nearby. Ella calls my name, but my head throbs too much for me to sit up and look for her.

'Six?' I whisper into the air. 'Are you here?'

'I don't see her anywhere, Marina,' Ella says, coming over and sitting down next to me. I lay my cheek back down on the grass and allow myself to just lie there for a few more minutes. Ella brushes a lock of hair off my cheek, but I'm numb and don't feel a thing. Sickness rises in my throat as I hear Eight continue to groan. Ella seems unaffected. I *never* want to teleport again.

I look around. My vision keeps doubling, and I struggle to bring it under control. Based on how green and lush it is, it's obvious we didn't land where we intended. 'This isn't New Mexico, is it?'

'Not even close,' Ella whispers.

I finally feel as if I can move, albeit slowly, and I look up at Ella. Her brown eyes are hard to read in the darkness, then I register it must be the middle of the night. I look past Ella and into the starry sky. I flash back to the blue ocean, to Eight turning into a black octopus.

Then I remember what Ella said just before we teleported.

'Ella. Did I imagine it, or did you say you *talked to Six*?' She nods. 'With your mind, right?'

Ella looks away. 'I'm sure you think I'm nuts. I keep asking myself if it really happened. Maybe I just wanted it so badly. . . .' Ella shakes her head and looks down at me, her face serious. 'No. I did *not* imagine it. I *know* I spoke to her. She said she was in a desert. That *must* mean she made it to New Mexico, right?'

'Ella, you're not crazy. I believe you and I think you're right,' I say, pressing my fingers against my pounding temples, willing away the pain and the fuzz that keeps me from thinking clearly. 'You must be developing a Legacy. What we need to do now is figure out how it happened that time so we can do it again. '

Ella's eyes widen. 'Really? You think it's a Legacy? What's it called?' she asks eagerly.

'Telepathy,' Eight's voice comes from behind me.

I roll over, grimacing from the pain, and look up at Eight, who's standing on a huge stone slab held up by two even larger gray boulders.

I sit up, roll over onto all fours, and get unsteadily to my feet. Hands on hips, I turn around and realize this place looks awfully familiar. But it isn't because I've been here before. I know this place from all the pictures, from textbooks. I look back up at Eight. 'Are we seriously at –'

'Stonehenge? Oh, yeah.'

'Wow,' I whisper, slowly turning around again to survey the scene. Ella walks over to a stone that must be twenty-five feet high, her head tipped back as she drags her hand across the surface. I understand the impulse to reach out and touch it. I mean, it's *Stonehenge.* I can't help but join her. The stones are cold and smooth, and just touching them makes me feel like I'm three thousand years old. Some are in perfect shape while others look like they must be mere shards of what they used to be. We all wander around for a while, seeing up close what most people only ever see in textbooks.

'Eight? What *is* telepathy, exactly? Do you know how to use it, and how I can control it?' Ella asks.

'Telepathy is the ability to transfer thoughts from one being to another. You're able to communicate with someone else's brain. Go ahead, try it with me.'

Ella circles around and comes to a stop in front of Eight. She closes her eyes. As I watch, all I can think is how amazing it would be if Ella *has* developed this Legacy. It would allow us to connect the Garde, no matter where any of them are, anywhere in the world. After a few seconds, Ella opens her eyes and looks at Eight. 'Did you hear me?'

'I didn't,' Eight says, shaking his head sadly. 'You just need to keep trying. It always takes time to figure out how to work with our Legacies. Telepathy will be no different.'

Her shoulders sag in disappointment anyway. 'Your Chests are over there, by the way,' she says, pointing.

Eight turns to me, stretching from side to side. 'I just need a little more time to recover from that last one. I want to be as strong as possible when we try again for New Mexico, okay?' He climbs up on a nearby rock.

'I don't know,' I sigh. 'I felt so horrible when I came out of that last one. Injuries are one thing – teleporting makes me feel sick. I don't know if I can do it again. And what's to stop us from ending up back at the bottom of the ocean? Meanwhile, it sounds like Six is in serious trouble, and we're bouncing around from place to place. We may never land in New Mexico!'

'I know, I know,' Eight says, hopping down from a stone and brushing off the dust from his pants. 'I know how frustrating this is. But doing something is better than nothing. And the only thing we can do is keep trying until we get where we need to go. We three will stick together, we will keep trying and we *will* find Six.' I don't know where he gets his calm, his conviction.

Ella wanders off behind a grouping of stones as I say, 'You know, there are other ways of getting from one place to another. We could just find an airport and fly there from here.'

Eight scratches his chin, deep in thought as he starts to walk. I follow him to the center of the monument. 'If Six really is in trouble, an airplane isn't the solution. It would take us forever to get to her.' He stops for a minute and turns to face me. 'Besides, I see us finding her.' I look at him quizzically, but he just grins and shrugs. What does he mean?

'Eight. Did you have a vision? What else did you see? Who else did you see?'

He shrugs. 'I can't really tell you more than that. I just see it; or, I feel it. I think it's a Legacy I haven't figured out yet. The only way I can describe it is that it feels like a sixth sense.'

'Is that how you knew we were coming to India?' I ask.

'Yeah,' he says. 'I don't have any control over it. These flashes, images, just come to me.'

We continue to walk through the group of massive stones and find Ella off by herself, sitting against a rock. When we approach, she looks up and says, 'I keep trying to talk to Six again, but nothing happens. Maybe it never *did* happen.'

I kneel beside her and put my arm around her shoulders. 'Legacies take time, Ella. I know when mine appeared for the first time, it was usually when I was upset or in danger. They come at a time when they are of the most use, when they might save us. My Legacy that allows me to breathe under water came as I almost drowned. Also, the teleporting may have affected you, so maybe it will take a while to work again.' I give her shoulders a squeeze.

'It's true. The first time I teleported,' Eight says, 'my Cêpan was about to get run over by a taxi. I just appeared next to him, like that.' He snaps his fingers. 'It's the only reason I was able to pull him out of the way.'

'I miss Crayton so much, right now,' Ella says. 'He

always helped me with this stuff. What if I'm never any help to the Garde? Sometimes, I wish I was never chosen by the Elders.' Her voice trails off and she slumps down, looking absolutely dejected.

'Ella.' Eight takes a step forward. 'Ella. Look at me. You can't think that way. We are *so* happy you're here. We need you. If you weren't here, we would be looking for *you*. You are exactly where you should be. Right, Marina?'

'Ella, do you remember what we used to say, back in the orphanage? We are a team. That means something important. We take care of each other.' As I'm talking, I realize that my aversion to teleporting is selfish. The only hope we have of finding the others is by getting to New Mexico. The safest, fastest way to get there is by teleporting, even if it means landing in the wrong place a few more times. I will not allow my fear to endanger anyone. When one of us is weak, the rest of us need to be that much stronger. I give her shoulder another squeeze. 'We will get to New Mexico, find Six, and we will continue to fight.'

Ella nods but remains quiet.

We all wander off, lost in our thoughts. I know I need some time to clear my head, to be as strong mentally as I feel physically, before we move on. This place is so peaceful, and it's so quiet, that it's the perfect setting in which to think. An hour or so later, I walk into the center of the circle to see Eight leaning down and picking a stone up before dropping it.

'Eight! What do you think you're doing?' I yell, alarmed. 'Do you remember where we are? This is a sacred, historic, *ancient* place! You can't just kick rocks around! Put them back where they were!'

Before he even has a chance to return the stones, I use my telekinesis to do it myself. Stonehenge may not be my history, but it is someone's, and that deserves more respect than Eight is showing right now. I want to leave this place exactly as we found it.

Eight looks up at me, surprised by my anger. 'I'm looking for the Loralite stone. I know it's half buried around here, under one of these stones, and we have to find it if we're going to go anywhere,' Eight says.

'Well, just make sure you put them back *exactly* where you found them when you're done looking,' I grumble. 'Stonehenge is one of the most famous places on Earth. Let's not ruin it.' I am tired of leaving destruction behind.

Eight makes a big show of peeking delicately under a rock and returning it gently to its place. 'I would just like to say that Stonehenge is only here in the *first* place because of the Loric. Reynolds said we built it as a cemetery for those who died fighting on Earth.'

'Really? This is a graveyard?' Ella asks, walking up behind me and looking around curiously.

'It was,' Eight says, patting a large boulder. 'For thousands of years, at least. And then humans started poking around, doing all that research they love so much. There is nothing like a quest to understand everything, even if there is nothing to know. Whatever. I will *honor* the placement of the rocks.' He continues to move as if tiptoeing through a bed of tulips.

'Let me help.' I walk carefully among the stones, helping Eight look for the Loralite, floating several rocks inches above the ground before setting them back down exactly as they had been. As I move on to another group of stones I hear shouts in the distance. I lean around a stone to see two men in uniforms running towards the monument, flashlight beams bouncing in the darkness. Ella and I duck down behind the biggest, closest rock formation.

'Shoot,' I whisper. 'Everybody hide.'

We can see the beams from their flashlights scan the ground, and whenever one gets close to us, we shift our position around another stone just in time.

'I know I heard something out here. Kids' voices,' the smaller of the two guards says.

'Okay. Well, where are they?' the other guard asks, looking around. There is a distinct note of disbelief in his voice.

Both men are silent for a moment. I peek around the stone to see the larger guard looking around, annoyed by the lack of evidence of intruders. Then something catches his eye, but I can't see what it is. I'm worried. What could he have found? 'Bill? Come over here and look at this. Where do you think these came from?'

'Huh. Don't know. They sure weren't there earlier,' the other says.

I nearly jump out of my skin when Eight materializes next to me. 'They found our Chests,' he whispers. 'I'll just toss the guards into the pasture, okay? We need to find the Loralite, so we can get the hell out of here, and that's not going to happen until those guys leave. And I am *not* letting them leave with our Chests.' His voice is grim.

I'm about to say no when my brain begins to buzz. After a brief echo of static I hear Ella's voice in my head: *I can distract them while you find the Loralite.* I look over at her in shock, eyes wide.

Ella squeezes my hand and whispers, 'I can distract them –'

'I already heard you,' I interrupt. 'Ella, I heard you in my head!'

She smiles widely. 'I *thought* it worked this time. Wow! I did it!' she whispers excitedly.

'Hey, you two, keep it down,' Eight whispers. 'Do we have a plan?'

'I have an idea,' Ella responds. Shrinking herself into a six year-old, she runs wide, out past the outer circle of the stones, then walks back towards the men. She puts on her best little girl voice as she calls out, 'Daddy? Where are you?'

'Hello?' One of the guards calls back. 'Who's out there?'

Eight teleports away while I watch Ella. She is standing still, shielding her eyes from their flashlights. She's quite the actress. She sounds legitimately lost and worried. 'I'm looking for my daddy. Have you seen him?'

'What in the world are you doing out here, little girl? Where are your parents? Do you know what time it is?'

As they approach her, Ella starts to sob, stopping the men in their tracks. 'Now, now, just calm down, no need for tears,' the larger one says in a soothing tone.

Ella turns up the waterworks and says, louder now, 'Don't touch me!'

'Hey, hey, nobody's touching you,' the other says in alarm. They are looking at each other, both confused and at a loss as to what to do with her.

'Psst, Marina,' Eight whispers. He's behind me with a Chest under each arm. 'We have to find the Loralite. Now! She can't hold their attention forever!'

We run into the center of Stonehenge. Eight and I start checking under every rock we can find, as quickly as we can. There are only a few left to check when we hear the men coming back towards us, Ella in tow, still sniffling.

'Okay, I think it's time for another distraction,' Eight says, disappearing again. He reappears by the outer circle of stones, plants his hands on an upright slab, and pushes hard. All I can do is watch in horror, frozen to the spot. The huge stone wobbles and then slowly tips backwards, then the horizontal slab on top falls too, and that's when Eight starts yelling, 'Help! Help! The stones are falling over! Stonehenge is falling down!' I will *kill* him. I clench my fists at my side, which is when I realize I still have a small rock in my hand. I lean down and carefully, pointlessly, return it to its spot.

The guards break into a sprint towards Eight's voice, and when their flashlights catch the falling stones, they scream in panic. The smaller guard runs to get in between two vertical stones, but it's too late. They connect and collectively tip to the right. The horizontal slab that was over them lands on the ground with a thud. My mouth falls open as the stones tip, one by one, going over like dominos.

'Code Black! Code Black!' the large guard screams into his walkie-talkie, then tosses it to the ground. He wraps his arms around one of the massive vertical stones remaining upright, trying with all his might to stop it from going over with the others. But it's pointless. The massive stones keep falling.

Eight appears back by me and tips over two small stones, and suddenly a faint blue glow lights up his legs. 'I found it! Over here!' he whispers excitedly. I'm relieved to hear he's found the Loralite, but I'm too focused on the demolition of Stonehenge to be excited. I can't believe he did this. I'm furious. Ella runs past me as I dart under one of the few slabs still in place and use my telekinesis to slow down the boulders in motion.

The larger guard slams his back against a stone that's next in line to tip, and the other guard joins him. I wrap my mind around their stone and hold it steady. When it's hit with another falling boulder, I don't let it tip. The guards slide away from the stone and fall to the grass, shocked by their sudden show of strength. Next I reverse the domino effect so the fallen boulders push each other back up, and I stabilize them in their original positions. Then, using what little strength I have left, I slowly lift the horizontal slabs off the ground and set them back on top of the boulders.

The guards watch all this, mouths agape, too stunned to respond to the crackling, concerned voices squawking from their walkie-talkies.

'Marina,' Ella whispers. 'Hey. Marina, we need to go. Now. Come on.'

I walk backwards towards the center of the monument, relieved and able to leave, now that I've managed to put everything back together.

I stalk over to Eight and yank my Chest from him. Still furious and unable to look at him, I grab hold of his hand. Ella carries Eight's Chest while clinging to his other hand. We stand, joined together, over the blue Loralite. The last thing I hear before the darkness comes is the larger guard – defeated and ready to be done with this particular adventure – responding into his retrieved walkie-talkie, 'False alarm.'

24

I hide behind a row of lockers in a long dark hallway while I turn visible. The pain from using my Legacies is so intense I curl myself up into a ball, pressing the two batons into my ribs to get some relief. I push my sweaty head against the cool cement wall and try to catch my breath, hoping the pain will subside quickly. I've been going up and down hallways, but I worry I'm just running in circles. So far, I've found an empty hangar and a lot of electronically locked doors. I know from when Sam and John were caught by the police before that our telekinesis doesn't work with electricity. I think about John and Sam, Marina and the others. I hope they're okay; or, at least, in less pain than I am. I picture John and Sam waiting for me at our rendezvous point. We were supposed to meet there in a few days. What will they think when I'm not there? I am so frustrated – and scared – I feel breathless. I know this kind of thinking isn't helpful, so I try to refocus my attention on how to get the hell out of here.

Almost on cue, an alarm sounds. The bleating overhead feels relentless as soon as it begins. I know what this means and I know I need to get it together. Fast. Everyone is looking for me. Armed soldiers zip down the long hallways in small open vehicles. Each time one passes, I'm tempted to pluck the men out, hop in, and take off. But I'm sure I wouldn't get very far and I'd give up the one advantage I have right now. They don't know where I am.

I've stopped trying to communicate with Ella. Clearly, I was just delusional. I'm on my own. I need to stop talking to myself and find something to blast through a door and get out of here. I think I'm underground. I just wish I knew how deep.

The lights go on in the hallway. As I discovered earlier, I know this means the motion-sensors have been triggered. A moment later, I hear a vehicle coming my way. I clench my stomach, turn invisible, and get the anticipated wrench of pain. Tears silently flowing down my face from the agony, I press myself up against a wall and watch the cart crawl towards me carrying three soldiers. As it passes in front of me, I hit the driver in the face with one of the batons. Man, do head wounds bleed *a lot.* Nose, mouth, forehead, all gushing geysers. His (seemingly) spontaneous injury causes him to slam his foot on the gas pedal and veer straight into a wall. The driver is out cold and the other two soldiers spill onto the cement floor. They take in the driver's face and see absolutely nothing around that might have caused it, and grab for their walkie-talkies. But I'm expecting this, and I've stepped into position to slam the closest man's head into the hood of the vehicle and kick his legs out from underneath him. The third soldier starts over to see what happened, and I slam his head down too. Then I grab one of their badges and run.

I need to figure out where to go from here and I need to do it fast. I can't stay invisible too much longer.

I use the swiped badge to get past an electronically locked door and find myself in a hallway completely different from the others I've seen so far. I have to stop the pain, so I turn visible and immediately feel relief. I look around and try to figure out where I am. The hall is wider than the others, with a high ceiling that's domed and carved out of sandstone. Two thick yellow pipes crawl along the ceiling, flanked by drooping electrical lines. I come to a turn in the hallway and peek around the corner. I don't see anyone, so I flatten my back against the wall and ease around the corner. I'm facing a red door with a sign that reads:

DANGER. AUTHORIZED PERSONNEL ONLY. SHUTTLE ONE.

I try using my telekinesis to open the door, pushing through the pain, but another electric lock keeps it shut. I'm about to try the badge again when I hear footsteps coming fast in my direction. I turn invisible again, but it makes my stomach churn so violently I fall to the floor. I can't survive another round of this, no way. Around the corner someone yells, 'I think I hear something this way!'

From the ground, barely able to stay invisible, I grab a guard by the ankle as he runs by. He goes facedown onto the floor, giving me enough time to swipe my stolen badge through the electronic lock. The door pops open and I slip inside.

I'm on a grated metal platform, high above three sets of train tracks that disappear down a circular tunnel. A three-car tram, plastered with several different symbols of the U.S. government, sits empty on the set of tracks closest to the platform. Outside the door behind me, I hear the guard I disabled yelling to a group of men who have just arrived on the scene. I stumble down a narrow set of stairs and jump inside the open doors of the tram, pulling down on the first lever I see.

My head snaps back as the tram takes off like a rocket. The circular tunnel blurs with red lights and long dark shadows, and twice I zip under grated platforms like the one where I entered without slowing down. The tracks suddenly dip and curve to the right, and then I'm rolling high over a long canal filled with water. I'm hoping this will shoot me out into the desert. Instead, the tram slows down and stops below another platform. There must be points at which there are automatic stops. The doors open and I jog up the stairs. I've let myself turn visible again and appreciate how pain-free my stomach is, knowing it won't stay that way for too much longer. I'm going to need my Legacies to get out of here.

I take a deep breath and carefully try the door at the top of the stairs. It's unlocked. Slowly, I open it just a crack to peek and see what is on the other side. My eyes have barely focused when the door is slammed open, clipping my shoulder painfully. I'm now face to face with a guard with a familiar weapon hanging from his shoulder – a Mogadorian cannon. As soon as the guard reaches for it the cannon buzzes to life with a spark of lights. But before he can press the trigger, I dive at him and we crash into a stone wall. The guard rushes forward and tries to grab me by wrapping his thick arms around my waist. Instead, I move just out of his reach and tackle his legs, pulling them out from under him. His skull makes a horrible cracking sound when it hits the ground. I cringe, but I can't stop to think about it. I quickly shove his body just through the door into the tunnel and close it. I grab his cannon and bolt.

I look around to get my bearings. There are enormous, smooth columns holding up the ceiling of the winding tunnel, and I weave in and out of them, keeping an ear out for more guards. My mind is racing, sorting through what I've seen, trying to piece it together. First on the list, *why* did that soldier have a Mogadorian cannon? Did he get it from a captured Mog? Or are the Mogs supplying the government with their weapons? The tunnel forks and I slow, trying to decide which way to go. I see nothing to help me choose, so I think of the last time I encountered a fork in a road. It was in the Himalayas, the one that surprised Commander Sharma. I go left.

The first door I spot on the left is all glass. Through it I can see scientists in white coats and masks moving around what look like large gardens brimming with tall green plants. Hundreds of powerful bright lights hang low over them from the ceiling.

A red-haired woman in a dark suit enters through another door and walks over to one of the guys in a white coat at the front of the room. Her right arm is in a sling and she has bandages on her cheek. She watches the scientist pour a vial of liquid over a section of the closest garden. I am stunned to see the plants instantly grow several feet taller and their tips split open. White vines spread in every direction, creating a thick canopy over their heads. The scientist writes something on his clipboard, and then looks up to talk to the woman. I don't have time to duck out of the way and we make eye contact through the glass door. I slowly raise the Mog cannon at him and shake my head. I have to hope he considers himself a noncombatant and wants to stay out of the action. No such luck. I watch him slip his hand into his pocket. Damn. He's triggering something. There's a noise over my head and a thick sheet of metal nearly hits me as it falls in front of the glass door, protecting it. Alarms sound and I know the whole area is going into lockdown. I can't get captured. I brace myself for the pain about to take over my body and make myself invisible.

Just in time. Soldiers pour into the tunnel and I inch along the wall to avoid them. The pain and the wave of sickness doesn't come. Whatever drug they gave me must have worn off. The relief I feel is profound, though I don't have time to enjoy it. A door clicks open on my right. Without thinking, I jump through it and find myself in a narrow white hallway lined with more doors. Halfway down the hall a lone soldier is backing out of one of them.

'Please. Just shut *up* already,' he calls into the room. 'And you should really eat something.'

He pulls the door shut and starts to turn and walk away. But I'm right there and drop him with a right hook to the jaw. I see his keys hanging from his belt, pull them off and frantically shove them into the lock of the door he just closed, one after another, until I find the one that works. I am guessing whoever he was talking to is no friend of his, and I could use an ally right now. I push the door open to see if today is the day I make a new friend.

I suck in my breath, shocked at what I see. I don't know what I expected, but it wasn't the girl I see cowering in the corner. She's covered in grime and there are thick red welts on her wrists, but I recognize her instantly. Sarah Hart. John's girlfriend, and the one who turned

John in to the police the night we went back to Paradise.

She pulls herself shakily to her feet, using the walls on either side for support. She is steadying herself to face whoever walks through the door. The fear in her eyes tells me only bad things happen when the door opens. I remain invisible long enough to drag the unconscious soldier from the hall inside the room. Leaving him just invites others to investigate, and I don't need any company. I shove him into a corner, hoping that he's out of sight if there are cameras in here. I close the door.

'Sarah?' I say quietly.

She spins around, looking towards my voice but visibly confused. 'Who is that? Where are you?'

'It's Six,' I whisper. She gasps quietly.

'Number Six? Where are you? Where's John?' she asks, her voice shaking.

I'm still speaking softly, not sure if we're alone. 'I'm invisible. Just sit back down like you were and pretend I'm not here. Put your head down so we can talk. I'm betting they have you on camera.'

Sarah sinks back down into the corner, pulling her knees to her chest. She lowers her head, her hair falling forward and blocking her face entirely. I walk over and sit down next to her on the floor.

'Where's John?' she whispers.

'Where's John?' I can't keep the anger out of my voice. 'Right now, you can forget about John, Sarah. You should know where John is; after all, you set him up, right? Because of you, he went to jail. And then, *I* got him out. What I want to know is, what are *you* doing here?'

'They brought me here,' her voice trembling.

'Who brought you here?'

Sarah's shoulders shake as she cries softly into her knees. 'The FBI. They keep asking me where John is and I keep telling them I don't know. You need to tell me where he is. I have to tell them or they're going to kill everyone I know!' She sounds desperate.

I can't say I'm very sympathetic. 'That's what happens when you switch sides, Sarah. You knew how John felt about you; you knew he trusted you. And you used that to help these people. And now, they're using you. Now, quickly, tell me what you told them about John!'

'I don't know what you're talking about,' Sarah says, and she starts to sob even harder. I can't help it; it kind of breaks my heart seeing her like this. What have they done to her? Her long hair covers her face and arms and she looks so small and young. I feel my anger melt away and I rest my hand on her back.

'I'm sorry,' I whisper.

She catches her breath at my touch and turns her head to look in the direction of my voice. I can just make out her blue eyes; they're red and bloodshot. To give her the strength to do what we need to I make myself visible for a split second, show her the Mog cannon in my hands, and disappear again. I see a tiny smile cross Sarah's face before she turns her face back to her knees. She sighs, takes a deep breath and in a much firmer voice says, 'It's good to see you. Do you know where we are?'

'I think we're in New Mexico in an underground base. How long have you been here?'

'I have no idea,' she says, wiping away a tear that has fallen on her leg.

I stand up and go over to listen at the door. I don't hear anything. I know I'm wasting precious minutes, but I have to ask. 'I don't get it, Sarah. *Why* did you turn John in? He's in love with you. I thought you cared about him.'

She flinches as if I've slapped her. Her voice is wobbly, but she looks me right in the eye when she responds. 'Really, I have no idea what you're talking about, Six.'

I have to close my eyes and breathe a few times to keep my voice from rising, to keep my anger from returning. 'I'm *talking about* the night he came over to profess his undying love for you. Remember? Your phone buzzed at two a.m., and the police arrived a minute later? *That's* what I'm talking about. You broke John's heart when you turned him in.' She starts to raise her head to respond, but I make a noise to remind her to keep her head down.

She resettles her head on her knees and speaks in a flat voice. 'That's not what I was trying to do. I didn't have a choice. Please. Where is John? I need to talk to him.'

'I'd like to talk to him too. I'd like to talk to all of them! First, though, we have to figure out a way out of here.' My voice is urgent.

She sounds defeated when she speaks again. 'There is no way out of here. Not unless you want to fight a thousand Mogadorians.'

'What?' I circle back to her. What is she talking about? This is a U.S. government facility, not a Mog base. 'You've seen them? The Mogs? They're here?'

A glazed look washes over Sarah's face. She no longer looks like the girl I met in Paradise, the human girl who John fell in love with and was willing to do anything for. I don't even want to think about what the FBI and the Mogs have done to her. 'Yes. I see them every day.'

I feel as if the wind has been knocked out of me. It was one thing to suspect this was the case – another to have it confirmed. 'Well, *I'm* here now,' I announce, trying to make one of us feel more confident. 'I promise, the next Mog you see will have my foot up his ass.'

Sarah laughs quietly into her legs. Her shoulders relax a bit for the first time since I walked in. 'Sounds good to me. Six, please, can you tell me where John is. Is he okay? Will I be able to see him?'

I know she's worried about Four, but her constant questions about him are beginning to really annoy me. 'To be perfectly honest, I haven't seen him recently, Sarah. We split up. He went with Sam and Bernie Kosar to get his Chest back, and I went to Spain to find another one of us. We were supposed to meet up in three days, but I don't see that happening right now.'

'Where? Where are you supposed to meet? I need to know. It's killing me, not knowing where he is.'

'Right now, it doesn't matter where we were supposed to meet because *I won't be there*,' I explode. 'We need to focus on how we're going to get out of here.'

Sarah flinches at the anger in my voice. She tries again. 'Where are the others? Where's Number Five?' Sarah asks.

I ignore her – she is clearly not listening to me. I walk back to the door and put my ear to it again. I hear footsteps – definitely more than one person – coming down the hallway. I consider my options. I can either lure them into the cell or I can take them down where they are. Either way, I know I need to deal with them, turn Sarah invisible, and pick a direction for us to get out of here.

Sarah stands up. 'What about Numbers Seven, Eight and Nine? Where are they? Are they together?'

If she doesn't quiet down, she's going to get us captured, or worse. I hiss at her, 'Sarah! Enough! Stop!' I put my ear against the door again and instantly know something is wrong. It sounds like the hallway is packed with men. We're trapped. I spin around to tell Sarah, but she looks like she's in the middle of a seizure. I am frozen seeing her body convulse and flop around the floor of the cell.

'Sarah!' I let myself become visible and run over to try and keep her head from slamming down on the cement floor. Has she been drugged?

Sarah's body starts to shake so fast she becomes a blur. I can only watch helplessly as a white outline appears around her body. I reach out to touch it but before my fingers reach it, the line turns black. I focus on Sarah with my mind to try and stop her convulsions with my telekinesis, but as soon as I try my brain feels like it's burning, like an enormous amount of dark energy is invading my skull. The next thing I know, I am falling backwards, holding my throbbing head, my eyes squeezed shut. When I open them again, I can't believe what I'm seeing. Sarah Hart is growing taller, and darker, until she's at least seven feet tall. Her blonde hair shortens until it's a short black buzz cut. Her face morphs into a demonic monster's. A purple scar appears on one side of her now thick neck; then it slowly elongates until it reaches the throat. When the scar finally stops growing, it begins to glow.

Did I just watch Sarah turn into Setrákus Ra? I've never seen him, but I've heard enough to have a pretty good idea of what, or who, I'm looking at.

The door bursts open and I am momentarily blinded by a flash of blue light. The next thing I know, a dozen Mog soldiers rush in, cannons up and ready.

I try to turn myself invisible, but nothing happens. I don't have time to figure out why. I grab the cannon I had set down to help Sarah, jump up, and fire it at one of the Mogs. He falls to my feet in a cloud of ash. I keep shooting, killing two more, but as I turn to find my next victim, I'm yanked backwards and choked by my pendant. I can turn my head enough to see I'm being held by the beast who was once Sarah. He spins me around, swats the cannon out of my hands with his other massive paw and yanks me towards his face. Up this close, I can see his dark skin is a sea of small scars, like he's been raked by razor blades.

I focus my mind on lifting my weapon off the ground but it just sits there. None of my Legacies are working! Without my Legacies, I'm vulnerable. I'm worse than vulnerable. I've got nothing to fight with. But I am not giving up.

'Tell me where they are!' Setrákus Ra roars. He pulls my chain tighter around my throat. I watch his purple scar brighten as he asks, 'Where are they, Number Six?'

'It's too late,' I whisper as bravely as I can. 'We're too strong now and we're coming for you. Lorien will live again and we will stop you.'

The slap is so hard that I can't feel the side of my face and my ears are ringing. I force myself to keep staring at him. He curls his cracked lips to reveal two rows of sharp, crooked teeth. He's so close that my vision is slightly blurred, so I look for something I can concentrate on. I pick a tooth that's broken in half and leaking a thick black liquid. I'm not sure why, but this has the strange effect of making him less scary. It's just so gross.

'Tell me where you're supposed to meet Number Four in three days.'

‘On the moon,’ I say.

‘You will die in front of them. I will kill you myself.’

I don’t respond. I don’t acknowledge he’s even spoken as he tightens his grip. The pendant John and I found in the well in Ohio, the one that was on the massive skeleton, cuts into the back of my neck as it is pulled tighter and tighter. As he pulls the chain even more, I think of John’s face as we trained together, I see the Garde sitting around the white table on the ship and I smile. I’m proud to have been chosen by the Elders. Out of respect to them, I will not beg for my life.

‘So, there you are, Number Six.’ I know the voice immediately. Agent Purdy. I open my eyes to see an old man. He has a cast on one arm and his face is covered in bruises. When he walks towards me, I see he’s limping.

When he gets close enough, I spit at his leather shoes. Setrákus Ra laughs right into my ear.

Agent Purdy looks over my head to speak to him. ‘Did you get the information you were looking for? Do you know where they are?’

Setrákus Ra growls and I’m whipped against the wall as an answer, my knees striking the cement first. When I hit the ground, I’m immediately pulled back to my feet by the pendant chain. I can feel my ribs have taken some of the impact; I think a couple of them are cracked. I'm having difficulty breathing. I try again to use my mind to lift the cannon on the floor, but it doesn't budge.

'So nice of you to join us here, Six,' Purdy says. 'I see you've met Setrákus Ra.'

'You're a coward,' I whisper. Legacies or no, I am going to take him down or die trying.

'Coward? *You* are the one who runs from me,' Setrákus Ra objects dismissively.

I stare hard into his maroon eyes. '*This* is cowardly. You must think you won't be able to kill me if I am at my full power. And that is what I call a *coward*.'

Setrákus Ra's scar glows again, the brightest yet. To my surprise, the chain around my neck loosens. 'Put her with the girl,' he says, pulling the pendant over my head. My stomach drops when I see it hanging from his hand. He looks at me, and smiles. 'I will fight you, Six. Alone. And you will die. Very soon.'

I'm dragged out of the cell and the top of my feet sweep across the cement. Then something hard hits the back of my head. I close my eyes – better for them to think I'm out cold so it's easier to focus on where they're dragging me. One right and two left turns. I hear a door open and I'm pushed forward. I stumble until I hit something soft. Or until something soft hits me. I haven't opened my eyes yet when I feel arms wrap around me. When I open my eyes I'm surprised, for the second time in an hour, to see Sarah Hart.

25

Our beige Ford Contour barrels down the highway with Nine behind the wheel. I stare at the long rows of corn in the fields and I try to picture what they'd look like from space. I can't stop thinking about our ship sitting somewhere in the New Mexico desert. After all these years, after all the running and hiding and training, everything is nearly in place. Members of the Garde have developed their Legacies and are coming together, Setrákus Ra came to Earth to fight, and when it's all over we will have a ship to fly us back to Lorien.

'I'm bored,' Nine says. 'Tell me a story. Tell me about Sarah. How hot is she, anyway?'

'Forget it. She's out of your league,' I say.

'Four, if *you* could get anywhere near her, I'm pretty sure I'd have a shot. Especially in *this* car.'

This car. Nine let me wallow pitifully when I first saw it sitting there. I mean, given everything else that I'd seen about how Sandor and Nine had lived, it was understandable that I pictured our ride as something with a whole lot more bling to it. Turns out, looks can be deceiving. The Ford was just hiding its assets.

From the outside, the car does look like something most likely found on cinderblocks. But inside it has to be the most technologically advanced thing I've ever seen. I feel like James Bond. There's a radar detector, a laser jammer, and bulletproof tinted windows. When Nine wants a break from driving, the car does the driving for him. With the push of a button, a gun turret with large barrels pops out of the hood. This, of course, is controlled with the steering wheel. Nine demonstrated all of it on a lonely stretch of highway in southern Illinois, squeezing off a few rounds at an abandoned barn. My firsthand experience of cars was limited to the beat-up pickups and other throwaways Henri found for us – the kind of cars we would have no problem ditching at the last minute. He never would have gone for something like this. There would be too much evidence if it got left behind. It just goes to show again how different each Cêpan was.

Nine takes his hands off the wheel and puts them together like he's praying. 'Please, I'm begging you. Just tell me again what she looks like. After this many hours of corn, I would do anything for something pretty to think about.'

I look back at the fields, lips pressed together. 'No way.'

'Dude, you'd think she hadn't, you know, turned your ass in to the police. Come on! Why are you so protective?'

'I don't even know if she *did* turn me in. I don't know who to believe anymore. But if she did, I have to think she had her reasons. Maybe she was lied to or pressured into it.' So many questions about Sarah have been running through my mind. If only I could see her, talk to her.

'Yeah, yeah. Forget that stuff for a minute. Just tell me

what she looks like. I really want to know. And I promise not to say a word.' I can tell he's not going to give this up. 'I swear on the Loric code, if there is such a thing.'

'Of course there's such a thing! You and Sandor were just too busy living this cushy life, playing with your toys, to bother with anything as basic as Loric code,' I retort. We ride in silence for a few minutes. 'Okay, I'll tell you this about Sarah. You know when you're talking to a beautiful girl and she's focused only on you and everything is going great?'

'Yeah.'

'And you think you're with the hottest girl in the state, maybe in the country, *maybe even on Earth*. Just by walking in a room, she lights it up. Everyone wants to be her best friend, wants to marry her, or both. Can you picture her?'

Nine's smile widens. 'Yeah. Okay. I can picture her.'

'Well, that's Sarah. She's the hot girl who lights up the room. She treats you like you're the most important person she's ever met. When she smiles at you, oh man, it's the best, and nothing else matters. On top of all that, she's the sweetest, smartest, most creative person I've ever met. And she loves animals and once –'

'Dude. I don't *care* if she's nice to puppies. Just give me her deets, her look, her style.'

I've never known anyone so relentless. I sigh. 'Blonde hair, blue eyes. Tall and thin – and you should see her in this one red sweater she has. It's not even fair how gorgeous she looks in it.'

Nine howls at the ceiling, waking Bernie Kosar up in the back seat. I point at him. 'Hey! You're not supposed to say anything, remember? On the Loric code?'

'Okay, okay, okay,' Nine says. 'Thank you for that tidbit. She sounds like a total babe. Now, tell me about Six.' He rubs his hands together, grinning in anticipation.

'No way!'

'Aw, come on, Johnny.'

I laugh. It's impossible not to want to talk about her. 'Okay. Six. Let's see. Well, first of all, she's the strongest person I've ever met.'

He snorts. 'Give me a break. I'm sure I could kick her ass.'

'I don't know, man. Wait until you meet her.'

He fixes his hair in the mirror. 'Huh, I can't wait.'

'And she's got long black hair, and she always looks like she's pissed off –'

'Have you ever noticed, there's something kind of exciting when a girl is mad at you? ' Nine muses, tapping his chin as if he were really giving it deep thought.

I suddenly feel guilty. I shouldn't be talking like this, with Nine of all people. And I definitely shouldn't be comparing Six and Sarah this way, as if it's a competition – especially since they hate each other. Sarah hates Six because of everything I said about Six the night she turned me in, and Six hates Sarah because I risked our lives going to see her when Six needed my help. And because she thinks Sarah betrayed us. 'I don't feel right talking about Six. I think I'll just let you meet her, come to your own conclusions.'

Nine shakes his head. 'You are such a wuss, dude.'

For a while, we ride along in silence. Road signs announce where we are. I check the tablet again, grateful for Nine and Sandor's love of electronics. If I couldn't plug it into the car's computer, I would have no way to see if the three Garde members have reappeared. I see the blips representing me and Nine in eastern Oklahoma; there's still one in New Mexico, and a fourth is moving quickly north over the Atlantic Ocean. The other three showed up in England, and I still don't know how they could have gotten there so quickly from India. I decide to give myself permission to check again in five or ten minutes.

I look out the window, examining the signs as they go by. We're more than halfway to New Mexico when I notice the gas gauge is perilously close to EMPTY. I point to it and Nine pulls in to a truck stop. He asks me to open the glove compartment. Two rolls of hundred-dollar bills roll out and into my lap.

'Damn,' I say, catching them.

'Let me have one of those, will ya?' Nine asks.

I peel off a bill and hand it to him. He pops the gas tank and climbs out of the car. I put a few of the bills in my pocket and tuck the rest of it back in the glove compartment. Exhausted, I pull the lever to recline the seat, put my head back and close my eyes. Bernie Kosar leans forward and licks my cheek, making me chuckle. I am bone-weary tired, but I fight the sleep that tries to wash over me. I can't deal with what comes with sleep. I'm sick of taking on Setrákus Ra in my dreams.

I let my mind wander to Sarah and Six; I hope they're both okay. Then I think of Sam. I still can't believe I abandoned my best friend. I tell myself I had no choice. The blue force field had incapacitated me to the point where going back in would have been suicide. No matter how true all of this is, it still feels bad.

I'm startled from my thoughts by the loud click of the gas pump finishing its fill. I breathe deeply, eyes still closed, to appreciate every last second of silence before Nine gets back into the car. Except, the silence continues. Nine doesn't hop in and start to chatter away. I open my eyes and look back at the pump, but no one is there. Where is he? I look around the gas station. Nothing. I'm immediately worried. I get out, Bernie Kosar hopping out behind me, and lock the doors.

First I head inside the station – he's not there. Next, I go out to the parking lot which is full of semi-trailers. With my advanced hearing, I pick up Nine's voice, and I can tell he's good and pissed off. Bernie Kosar and I run towards his voice, weave around several trailers, and find him standing between two young guys with blood on their T-shirts. In front of Nine are three big truckers, all of them shouting in his face.

'*What* did you just say to me?' the trucker in the middle asks Nine. Under his yellow cap, a bushy red beard covers the man's face.

'Are you deaf?' Nine says, over-enunciating as if speaking to an idiot. 'I said, "You have girl arms." I mean, look at your wrists.' Why does he insist on *looking* for trouble?

'Uh, what's up?' I interrupt, walking over.

The trucker on the right, a tall guy wearing aviator sunglasses, looks at me. He points his finger in my face and yells, 'Mind your own business, asshole!' As I join the group, the trucker on the left spits a long stream of brown juice at my feet.

'As far as *I've* figured out,' Nine turns to explain to me, 'these fat guys are angry at these little guys. The little guys were hitchhiking and caught a ride with one of them, promising money they didn't have. So now, the fat guys are trying to beat up the little guys with their puny girl arms.'

I turn to the truckers, the fat guys, and try to make nice. 'Okay, well, none of this has anything to do with us, and we need to get on the road. So, guys, let me apologize for my friend, who clearly doesn't know when to mind his own business.'

'Yeah,' the bearded trucker growls at Nine. 'Just get the hell out of here, punk, and let us deal with these lowlifes.'

I take my first real look at the hitchhikers. They smell like they've been on the road for a while. They couldn't be more than eighteen, probably younger. As the truckers move towards them menacingly, they glance at each other with real panic in their eyes. Next thing I know, Nine is stepping in front of the little guys and saying, 'I don't care who promised what to who. You touch these kids again and I'll break *all* your goddamn arms.'

I squeeze in between Nine and the three now truly pissed-off truckers, holding both sides back. Bernie Kosar barks threateningly. 'Okay, okay, just stop.' I turn to Nine, willing him to listen to me. 'We can't do this right now. We have somewhere *very important* we have to get to. *Now*,' I say. I dig into my pocket and turn to the truckers. 'Listen, how much did these guys say they would give you?'

'A hundred bucks,' the one wearing the aviators says.

'Fine,' I say, pulling one of the bills out of my pocket. The truckers' eyes widen at the sight of such a big bill and I instantly know things just got worse.

'Why would you give *anything* to these guys, Johnny?' Nine asks.

I feel the meaty hand of a trucker on my shoulder. He squeezes my shoulder as he says, 'Did I say a hundred bucks? I meant a thousand. *Johnny*.'

'That's crazy!' one of the hitchhikers shouts. 'We never said we'd give you any money!'

I spin back to the truckers, waving the bill like it was flag. 'A hundred bucks, guys, just take it. Consider it a tip for good service, or payment in lieu of a beating, I don't really care what you call it. Just take it!'

'I said a thousand,' the man on the left says, spitting again, this time directly on the top of my shoe. 'Are you deaf?' A low growl starts deep in Bernie Kosar's throat.

Nine moves forward, but I push him back and turn to face him. 'No! It's not worth it, man!' I put my face right up in his. He has to understand how serious I am. I will not let him do this. 'Please. Think of what Sandor would want you to do. He'd want you to walk away. *I* need you to walk away.' I whisper.

'You guys aren't getting *shit*!' Nine yells over my shoulder at the truckers.

I use my body to shove him backwards, towards the car. I spin around just in time to see the bearded trucker pull a knife out of his pocket. 'All of your money. Now.' The other two men step up to flank me.

'Listen,' I say, lowering my voice, trying to get control of the situation. 'You will take the hundred bucks and you will walk away. If you don't, I'm not going to hold my friend back anymore. Believe me, you don't want that. You have no idea what he can do and you don't want to know.'

I'm not entirely surprised when the answer comes in the form of a fist. It comes from my right and I easily dodge it. I grab the trucker's wrist, and throw him down. BK looms over him, still growling, and the man shrinks back.

'My turn!' Nine says gleefully, pushing me out of the way.

The bearded trucker swings his knife wildly at Nine, who steps lightly out of range. On his next swing, Nine ducks under the blade and hooks his arm beneath the man's armpit, slamming him to the ground. He kicks the knife out of the trucker's hand and it goes skidding under a truck. 'Dude, you should listen to my wise pal over there. You *seriously* do *not* want to mess with us.'

'All right, all right. We're done here,' I say, placing my hand on Nine's shoulder. 'And now, we're *all* going to walk away. Let's go.'

I hear the hammer of a gun click. We freeze. The trucker with the aviator glasses waves a .50-caliber Desert Eagle at us. I don't know everything about guns, but I know this one packs a very big punch. He sounds pretty serious when he asks, 'Which of you wants to die first?'

Of course Nine steps forward, crossing his arms over his chest. 'Me.'

He raises the gun towards Nine's face and laughs at what he thinks is just bravado. 'Don't tempt me, punk. Killing you would be the highlight of my day.'

'Well, then, shoot. No reason to put off the highlight of your day. You don't look like you get a lot of them.' Nine says. I sigh, knowing this is all going to end badly. And after, there will be attention we don't need.

At this point things begin to move really fast. First, a sudden and very loud blast from a nearby truck startles the gun-touting trucker, who fires off a shot. Nine stops the bullet with his mind, just inches from his nose. With a grin and a tilt of his head, he spins the bullet midair and sends it racing back at the shooter. He sees the bullet coming his way and turns tail and runs as fast as his legs will take him.

I turn to look at Nine. This guy is having *way* too much fun. I know what he's going to do and I know it is a bad, bad idea. 'No. Nine. Don't do it,' I say, shaking my head, knowing he is going to do it anyway.

Nine laughs and feigns innocence. 'Do what? This?'

He and I both turn to look at the bullet that is still hovering where Nine stopped it near the trucker. He gives a little chortle and sends the bullet racing after the fleeing trucker, right into his ass. He goes down, screaming his head off. Nine turns to the other truckers, including the one BK has decided to let off the ground. They look like they are about to pee in their pants they're so scared. Nine smiles at them and I know he's still not done messing with their heads. He says to the two truckers, 'You know what? I think you two should make up for your rude friend. Here is what you are going to do. You are going to reach into your pockets, *very slowly*, and take out your wallets. Then, you are going to give every dollar you have to these nice guys here. You know, for their trouble,' he says, motioning to the hitchhikers. 'I don't think you want to hear what I'll do if you do not cooperate. Quickly.' Both truckers nod and reach into their pockets.

The hitchhikers look totally stunned by all they've just seen. 'Uh, thanks, man,' one of them says.

'No problem,' Nine says as the money is exchanged. Everyone's hands but ours are visibly shaking.

'Just so you know, we never promised that guy any money. They were trying to shake us down. We're absolutely broke,' the other says.

'I believe you. And, you're not broke anymore,' Nine says, smiling. 'Let's just say, I know what it's like, on the road and on the run. It can be hard for a kid to figure out a way to get some cash.' He turns to me for confirmation. I smile at the kids but look back at Nine and make it clear I am more pissed off than I've ever been. He shrugs. 'Hope the next ride you catch goes better!' He turns and walks away, and BK and I follow.

We get to our car, climb in, and pull away in silence.

After a minute or two, Nine reaches over and flicks on the radio. He drums his fingers on the wheel in time to the song.

'What the *hell* were you doing back there?' I yell, punching his shoulder. 'And don't give me any crap about the poor little boys and the mean, mean trucker men, either! You're just entertaining yourself and showing off! And you know what? That's putting us *both* in danger, not to mention keeping us from getting where we need to go. C'mon, Nine! Get it together!'

Nine is gripping the steering wheel so tightly his knuckles are white and I can see his jaw is clenched so hard his muscles are twitching. 'I was *not* showing off and I was *not* entertaining myself.' I wait for him to continue, to explain, but it's clear he is not going to say anything else. What does *he* have to be mad about?

'What, you were just standing up for two humans who were getting pushed around? Even though you said humans aren't worth the time or energy?' He flinches when I throw his words back at him.

'I don't like bullies. No one has a right to take or to hurt, just because they can. I wasn't going to let them do that. And I made damn sure they wouldn't do it again.' His voice is flat. He looks over at me, at the surprised look on my face, and turns back to the road. 'Don't know why you look so shocked. I'm a humanitarian, man.'

I shake my head. Every time I think I have Nine figured out, he does something to turn it around and I end up liking him even more. I shrug, lean my head back, and turn to watch the landscape whip by the window. I drum along with the music on my armrest. 'I didn't know, that's all,' I say.

He relaxes into his seat and smiles in a satisfied way that is more like the Nine I'm used to. 'Yeah, well, now you do, man. Now you do.'

26

My head is in Sarah Hart's lap, the real Sarah Hart, and she strokes my hair with her fingers. I stare blankly at the ceiling. I reach up and touch my neck. The cut that runs all the way around it is deep. I want to sit up, but my bruised ribs and knees won't allow it.

I'm humiliated by how easily I was overtaken by Setrákus Ra. How weak I was in the face of his tremendous strength. I've killed so many Mogadorian soldiers. I've cut off their heads while mowing them down with weapons I controlled with my mind. Since I received my Legacies, I have always been ready to fight; no fear, no matter who or what I faced. Until now. Setrákus Ra tossed me around by my pendant like I was a rag doll. I was helpless against him. He even made my Legacies disappear. I had the opportunity to kill Setrákus Ra, to save Lorien and end the war, and I was swatted down like an annoying gnat.

'Six? Can you tell me if John is still alive?' Sarah asks cautiously. 'I know you're in pain, but can you tell me that?'

'Yes. He's alive,' I whisper. I can feel her sigh with relief against me.

After a pause, she asks, 'Are you okay?'

'I don't really know,' I say. I turn my head so I can look up into Sarah's tired eyes. I try to smile. I'm exhausted. My eyelids are already fluttering when I open my mouth to speak, 'He was you, he tricked me into thinking he was you, the monster.'

Sarah takes this in without any sign of confusion. She shakes her head and looks away. 'I know. He showed me. A couple of days ago he came into my cell. I thought he was there to take me back to the room where . . .' She trails off for a minute, then clears her throat and straightens up. 'This room with all these machines and strobe lights. I feel like I'm crazy in there and everything hurts. It's hard to explain. But he wasn't here to take me anywhere. He just stood there, not saying anything. Then he started jerking around, like he was having a seizure. Then he started to shrink, and, bam! – it was like I was looking into a mirror. When he finally did speak, it wasn't his voice. It was mine. I tried to hit him and rip out his eyes, but he beat me so badly that . . . Well, the first time I could stand was when I caught you when you were thrown in here.'

'I'm flattered.' I try to laugh, but it gets caught in my throat. 'No, seriously, thank you.'

'Well, you're *welcome.*' She's smiling down on me, and I think she must have been terrified. I was more scared than I've ever been just now, and I was born and raised to do this. This is my life. It isn't Sarah's, not by a long shot.

'I don't get something. How did he know so much about you? How could he trick me for so long?'

'They know everything, Six,' she says, her voice deadly serious.

I slowly begin to roll out of her lap, to push myself off the ground. I try to ignore my ribs begging me to stay down. 'What do you mean, everything? About who? And what do *you* know? About any of this?'

Sarah looks away. 'What little I know, I told them all of it,' she says after a minute. 'I couldn't help it. They kept taking me to that room, strapping me down, and they injected me with drugs. They asked me the same questions, over and over; after a while my mouth moved even though I told it to stop. I just couldn't stop talking.' Sarah puts her face in her hands and sobs. 'I told them everything, repeating whole conversations word for word.'

I sit against the wall and let the pain wash over my body. 'If John sees Setrákus Ra and believes it's you, I don't know what will happen.'

Sarah suddenly sounds frantic. 'We have to

get out of here! We have to stop him! Is there any way we can warn John?'

'I don't know if I'm ready to break out of here.'

'What? Why?' she asks, shocked.

I stagger to my feet, clutching at my ribs. 'Now that I've met Setrákus Ra, I want another chance at him. He let me live, and now, I'm going to kill him.' This would sound more lethal if I weren't swaying slightly, but I mean it from my very core.

Sarah stands, and I get a good look at her for the first time. Her face is covered in dirt and bruises, her blonde hair limp on her shoulders, but she's still beautiful. The bottom of her red sweater is torn and she's not wearing any shoes. She's swaying a bit herself. She stares at me, incredulous. 'Look at yourself, Six. You're hurt. You're *really* hurt. Do you know what you're even saying? It would be nuts for you to fight him alone. John will come; just wait for him. Please. He'll come, and he'll rescue us, *and* Sam. I know he will.'

'Sam's here? Are you sure? Have you actually seen him?'

Sarah clenches her jaw. 'They tossed him in here with me once. He was unconscious, all cut up and bruised. Like me.' Then the energy drains out of her and her voice drops. 'But I know I can't believe anything I see or hear anymore.'

Picturing a bloody Sam in this very cell makes my stomach twist with anger. What happened in that Mog cave? I punch the cement wall, surprised to see it chip away. My strength is returning. No pain. My Legacies are coming back. I look directly into Sarah's eyes. 'Sarah, did you turn John in that night at the playground? You need to tell me.'

Without hesitation she answers. 'Absolutely not. I love him. Yes, I was confused about, well, about everything, and it was a lot to take in. But I would never betray any of you, especially John.'

I see her tear-filled eyes, and know she's telling the truth. 'Even though he's an alien, you still love him? You don't care?'

Sarah smiles. 'I can't explain it. I can't explain how love feels to me, how it fills me up inside and keeps me going, but I know that it's strong and beautiful and I know it's how I feel about John. I love him, and I will always love him.' Just saying the words aloud has her standing up straighter; she looks stronger and more determined.

Her conviction moves me. I think about what happened between me and John, the kiss and everything. I don't love John like Sarah does.

She clearly believes John is the only one for her, in the entire universe.

'I've been having these flashbacks, you know, about our trip to Earth. He and I were always fighting,' I say, my voice soft.

'You were?' she asks, hungry for anything I can tell her.

'Well, not really fighting so much as me pushing him around and taking his toys.'

We laugh and she takes my hand. I'm sorry she's here because of us. I'm not going to let her down. She has so much faith in what we do, who we are, I can see it on her face. 'I'm going to get you out of here, okay? I'm going to get you back to John,' I say.

'I hope so,' she says softly.

'And we'll find Sam and get him out of here too; then we'll meet up with Seven, Eight and Ten, find Five, and we'll figure everything out as a team.' Her hand in mine gives me even more strength, more certainty than ever.

'Hang on. Number Ten? I thought there were just nine of you guys.'

'There are a lot of things you don't know, things we've learned recently,' I say, touching the cut around my neck. It still hurts, but feels like it's already starting to heal. I wonder vaguely if I'm gaining a new Legacy.

Sarah hugs me, but our moment is brief. The

door whips open, and a dozen Mog soldiers march into the room, cannons aimed at my chest.

'Turn invisible,' Sarah whispers under her breath. 'Go.'

I test my ribs and roll my neck. I feel better than I did five minutes ago. It has to be good enough. 'No. I'm done running.'

The red-haired woman I saw in the garden room limps into the cell. I look at her arm in the sling and the bandages over her cheek, and can't help but wish I was the one who did all that to her. Anyone who would join up with the Mogs and torture kids in a secret bunker, deserves everything she got, and more. Does she know who the Mogs really are? What they intend to do? The woman purses her pale lips and stares at me. 'So. You're the one who will fight Setrákus Ra?'

I step forward. 'Yes. Who are you?'

'Who am I?' she asks, shocked that I would dare to ask such a thing. I guess she isn't used to people questioning her right to be anywhere, asking her to explain who she is.

'Yeah, *you*, asshole.' Does she have me confused with someone who has any respect for her *position*? 'I asked you a question. Who are you and why the hell would you be working with *them*? Do you know what the Mogadorians are going to do? What their plan is? They will destroy Earth, but only after they get what they want. And you are not only helping them, you are putting out the damn welcome mat! Did they tell you why they're here? Did you even ask?' I am furious and desperate; this woman has got to listen to me. She needs to understand what is at stake here.

Her face remains unchanged. 'I know all I need to know. They are *here* because they're looking for you and your friends. In exchange for our help, they will help *us* with matters that are vital to our security. And I'll let you in on a little secret. I look forward to finding that Number Four again, and his freak alien friend. I have first shot at them, and I will take it, with pleasure.'

Sarah and I exchange a glance. Alien friend? Who is she talking about? Has John met up with another Garde?

'What *things* are the Mogadorians going to help you with?' I ask.

'Well, for starters,' she says, motioning to the Mog's cannon, 'we get these. Thousands and thousands of alien weapons with capabilities impossible to create here on Earth, that none of our enemies have access to. With their technology, the Pentagon will be light years ahead of any other army on Earth. We will be invincible.'

I'm disgusted and I make sure it shows. 'Setrákus Ra has also been supplying us with iridium, a chemical that's incredibly rare on Earth, and we've made scientific breakthroughs with it that will make this country billions of dollars. Also, the United States government is very interested in finding other life-sustaining planets, and the Mogadorians have already shared information about that.' When she stops talking, she rocks back on her feet, and crosses her arms over her chest defiantly.

'Did they tell you what they do when *they* find other life-sustaining planets? I'll tell you what they do. They destroy them,' I shout in her face. 'You picked the wrong side, this time. My friends and I are trying to stop them.'

'That's enough. Your presence is requested by Setrákus Ra. This way. Now.' The woman moves aside to let me pass.

I know I could take this woman and every one of these soldiers. But that would just delay getting to what I really want – to defeat Setrákus Ra. 'As tempting as it is to kill you all right now, I think I'll save you for Number Four and his freak alien friend,' I sneer. 'If Ra wants to do this now, let's go.' I push past her and walk out of the cell.

'Six!' Sarah calls after me. 'Please! Be careful!'

I walk down the hall, my enemy flanking me.

We walk down hallways, through several doors, and after a few minutes, I'm standing inside a huge room. It's big enough for an army of tanks. It's also big enough for an epic fight.

The door slams and I hear it lock behind me. It's so dark now that I can barely see two feet in front of me, never mind the other end of the room. I walk towards what I think is the center of the room, testing my telekinesis as I go by levitating off the ground. The pain I felt earlier is gone. When I think I'm in the middle of the room, I close my eyes and turn around, feeling the air with my mind. I sense there are about two dozen or so beings silently entering the room. I'm disappointed. I wanted this to be one on one.

When I open my eyes, they've almost adjusted to the dark. I wish I had Marina's Legacy to be able to see in the dark, but I can make out enough for now. There are Mog soldiers lined up against the back wall. They're wearing ragged black cloaks and black boots, and whip their swords across their bodies. They're bigger than most of the Mogadorians I've fought before, but I know I can kill them just the same. A door opens behind me, and another dozen soldiers enter.

'Hey! What is this? Setrákus Ra!' I yell to the ceiling, turning around to make sure the Mogs can all see me and know they do not have some cowering human here. 'I thought you wanted to fight me!'

A section of the wall explodes in the back of the room, and the Mogadorian leader appears. The three Loric pendants swing from his grotesque neck. I plan on taking all of them back. Setrákus Ra opens his arms and yells, 'You must first earn the right!'

I guess this is the command to charge, because all at once, the soldiers let out a battle cry, and rush at me. I start at my right and begin to pick them off, one at a time.

27

Wind, hot sand and punishing heat, along with a pounding headache, welcome me to our next teleporting destination. I try to shield my eyes from the blinding sun as I lie on my back, recovering. Welcome to New Mexico.

'Oh, yeah,' Eight groans, but he sounds satisfied. 'We made it.'

I smile but stay where I am to give the pain in my head time to lessen before I try to move.

'Ella?' I call out.

'I'm right here, Marina,' she calls over. 'Look where we are! New Mexico!'

'Finally. Can you try communicating with Six again?'

'I already have. No luck yet.'

I slowly stand up. Eight is on his hands and knees at the bottom of the sand dune, dry heaving. The teleporting seems to have affected him more severely than it did the last couple of times. Ella has her hand on the back of his neck. The two Chests sit nearby. I rotate 360 degrees and all I see in every direction is sand, sand and more sand. And the occasional cactus. 'Which way should we go?'

Ella and Eight climb up the dune and stand next to me. After a minute, Ella points north and says, 'Look! Six said something earlier about dying in a desert with mountains.'

Squinting, I see where she's pointing. The faint outlines of mountains ripple in the afternoon haze.

'That's where we're going then,' Eight says. 'We can cover the distance in short hops once my teleporting comes back. For now, we walk.'

We pick up the Chests and head north. 'Ella,' I say, 'you need to keep trying Six. If you can't reach her, maybe you can try Four, or even try one of the others, Five or Nine.' We've lost so much time just getting here. Maybe Ella can find something out that will save us some time now.

Nine examines the map he's brought up on the screen in the middle of the steering wheel. He looks around at the endless desert surrounding us. The car's GPS has picked up an underground tunnel nearby; now we just need to find the entrance. When I press the green triangle on the tablet, it shows we're only a mile or two from the ship. I push the blue circle and shout, 'Nine! They're here!'

'Who's here?' Nine asks, scanning the horizon.

'The other three blue dots. They're here in New Mexico!'

Nine rips the tablet out of my hands and lets out a loud hoot. 'Holy shit, bro. This is really all about to go down.' He looks at me, his eyes shining.

'I think this is it. The beginning of the end.' As much as I'm looking forward to finally getting a chance to do what we need to do, it's dawning on me that this is going to be the fight of our lives.

'This right here, *this* is when we rise to the occasion,' Nine says. 'You will fight harder than you ever have, Four. You're going to be a beast. And me? I'm going to rip Setrákus Ra's head off, wrap it up and send it back to Mogadore with a giant red bow on it. And then Lorien is going to rise from the ashes.' His voice is shaking with emotion, with all the pent-up anger and fight he has been carrying around with him.

Bernie Kosar barks from the backseat and Nine turns around to look at him with a smile. 'You, too, BK. You, my friend, are going to kick some major ass.'

I imagine what it will feel like to meet up with all the Garde members, something I haven't let myself do for so long. I look out over the horizon. My mind is clear and open to all possibilities. It feels good. And that's when I hear a girl's faint voice echo in my head. It's soft and broken like a bad radio signal at first, but it becomes clearer.

Four? Number Four? Can you hear me?

'Yes, yes! I can hear you!' I yell out loud, whipping my head back and forth. 'Who is that? Where are you?'

Nine looks at me, confused. 'Um, dude. I *hope* you can hear me. I'm right here.'

'Not you. I heard a girl. Did you hear her? A girl was just talking to me.'

Number Four? It's Number Ten. Can you hear me? This may be hopeless, I don't know if I'm talking to anyone. Maybe I'll never figure this out without Crayton.

'There it is again,' I say excitedly. Nine is looking at me like I've completely lost my mind. 'Nine! She just said something else! Did you hear her? She said she's Number Ten! I think she's in my head somehow.'

'Number Ten! The baby from the second ship! Well, don't just sit there staring at me! Talk back to her, dumbass!'

That's easy for him to say. She didn't know if it was working. I'm guessing it's a new Legacy kicking in – for both of us! – it takes training to know how to make a Legacy work when, and how, you want it to. I know I don't have much time to waste figuring it out. I take a deep breath and block out the noise in my head and around me, and focus. I try to re-create the feeling I had right before I heard the voice a few minutes before. I feel calm, open, and somehow . . . connected.

I can hear you, I try saying in my head. Nothing. I wait a moment and try again. *Number Ten?*

Number Four! You can hear me?

'She heard me!' I laugh out loud and look at Nine, victorious.

'Tell her we're about to ride into town and save the day,' Nine says. 'Tell her we'll swing by and pick her up on our way to Lorien, wherever she is.'

Where are you? I hear her ask. *I'm with Seven and Eight in the desert, in New Mexico. We're trying to find and rescue Number Six.*

'What's she saying?' Nine yells. I know it's making him crazy not being able to hear our conversation, but I can't talk to him now. I need to concentrate on hearing Ten's voice, on responding to her.

What do you mean? Where is Six? We're in New Mexico too. I'm with Nine and we're in the desert looking for an underground base.

I look out at the mountains. 'We have to find that tunnel, fast,' I say to Nine.

'Did she say where they are?'

'She just said she's here, in the desert, with Seven and Eight and they're trying to rescue Six. That must be who we saw show up on the map earlier. I know I shouldn't worry – if anyone can take care of herself, it's Six. But still – I'm worried.'

'She's got to be inside Dulce. Let's go find her.' Nine's fingers speed over the screen. The map changes color and looks to be scanning the area, finally zooming in on the trunk of a five-pronged cactus about a quarter mile away from where we are. Below it, I can see the outline of an underground tunnel. 'Ha! Nice try, you sneaky government bastards. Tell Number Ten to get her butt over here!'

Can you tell me where you are, Ten? We found a tunnel to get inside the base where we think Six is being held. We're in a brown car, pulling off on a side road.

After a pause, she says, *We can teleport to you. How do I find you?*

'They don't know how to find us,' I report to Nine.

'Maybe we can send up a signal somehow? Damn it! We should have brought that rocket launcher!' He hits the steering wheel with the palm of his hand and stares out the window, shaking his head.

'We don't need a rocket launcher,' I realize, jumping out of the car. I aim my palms into the blue sky and light my Lumen, swaying the beams back and forth.

Look for the beams of light in the sky, I instruct Ten. I don't hear anything for a minute. I hope we haven't lost our connection.

We see them! Ten finally says.

'They're on their way,' I yell into the car, keeping my Lumen in the air. I want to give them as much time as possible to see exactly where we are. 'We just need to sit tight.'

'I'll try,' Nine says, studying the screen on the steering wheel again, but already starting to twitch. 'Man, I can't believe we found them!'

I finally turn off my Lumen and climb back in the car. I almost can't believe this moment has come, that we're about to fulfill the destiny the Elders laid out for us. We're coming together to defeat the Mogadorians and resurrect Lorien from its hibernation.

Suddenly, we hear the unmistakable noise of a helicopter.

'Um, Johnny?' Nine says. 'They're not getting here by helicopter by any chance, are they?'

'Shit,' I say. Bernie Kosar jumps into my lap, putting his front paws on the door to look out the window. The three of us watch several helicopters climb into the sky from the hazy horizon. The cluster of choppers moves together and stops to hover directly above us. I use my mind to focus on the one out front and send it spiraling off back where it came from. Then I bring it down, hard enough that it won't go up again anytime soon.

'It must be the Feds. They're getting on my nerves almost as much as the Mogadorians. They must have been looking for us and saw your lights!' Nine yells. The gun turret in the hood of the car pops up. Nine aims, then shoots warning shots to the right of the remaining choppers, then the left. As soon as he stops shooting they lower down, hovering just above us. I'm about to get rid of another one with my telekinesis when Nine lets out a yelp.

'Check out the road,' he says. I look to my left and see an enormous dust cloud rising from a long line of black vehicles. Bernie Kosar barks and scratches at the door. I open it and he changes into an enormous hawk and ascends into the sky. I run around to the trunk of our car and open it with a pound of my fist. I unzip one of the duffels and pull out four automatic rifles, dropping two next to Nine's door. Gunshots are already firing from the faraway vehicles, and I scramble on top of the car and take aim while Nine continues to unleash a barrage at the incoming helicopters. Out of the corner of my eye, I see Bernie Kosar swoop into the side of a helicopter. He's got one of the pilots with his talons. He yanks and pulls at him, using his powerful beak to rip out the safety belt holding him in the seat. When the pilot is free BK drops him onto the sand below. His helicopter falls and bursts into flames on impact. The caravan of black cars swerves around the wreckage and I hold down the triggers of my two guns, taking out the front tires of the first two cars. It doesn't stop the convoy, but at least it slows them down.

The remaining helicopters spread apart in the sky and come at us from different angles. Pockets of sand explode all around us. One helicopter flies directly overhead, and I roll out of the way of its line of fire.

I struggle to clear my mind. It isn't easy, but I'm getting the hang of what it takes for me to go inside my head to communicate. I take a few deep breaths and quiet my mind. *Number Ten? Where are you? We're under attack.*

We can hear it, she says. *We're coming.* Her thoughts are calm, with an edge of worry. It feels good just to hear it, though, to know others are on their way.

I shift around and see two black helicopters bank left and head in the opposite direction, firing missile after missile at a new target. That has to be them! I can only redirect three of the rockets, but someone else deflects the rest.

'Ten and the rest are almost here!' I yell down to Nine through the driver's window. Next thing I know the gun turret on the front hood has exploded, sending hot metal flying over my head. I roll off the roof of the car just as it's split in half by a new hail of bullets.

Nine jumps out of the car and grabs the two rifles I set in the sand by his door. 'Looks like we've got a real fight on our hands. I've been waiting for this my *whole life.*'

The helicopters circle back and line up over the faraway vehicles, forming a united front. Nine lifts his palm and the lead black truck is suddenly ripped straight up in the air like a shuttle rocketing into outer space. Nine flips his hand and the car falls back down again. We can hear the men screaming from where we are. The car comes to a stop right before it hits the ground, then smashes down hard. We watch the men scramble out on shaky legs and look for somewhere to run. At the sound of the impact, Bernie Kosar, still in the form of a hawk, dives and lands behind the twisted car on the road, and transforms into a beast. The trailing vehicles swerve into the desert to avoid him, some spinning completely around. Bernie Kosar roars.

Nine ducks into the backseat of the car and throws our Chests into the sand. Opening his, he pulls out the string of green stones and the silver staff, and as he jogs backwards towards the chaos, he yells, 'You wait for the others. BK and I will be right back!'

I shout back, 'Don't look like you're having too much fun! And make sure you don't blow up the entrance to the military base!' A helicopter swings in from my right, and just as I yank on its nose with my mind, something rips into my left leg. I fall headfirst into the sand, blinded by pain. It feels all too familiar and I roll on the ground screaming at the top of my lungs. I know what this means. A scar is searing itself into my leg. Another member of the Garde is dead.

Everything stops. The thought of another one of us dying sweeps through my body and I'm paralyzed by grief so deep it feels like I'm sinking into the sand. There is one less soldier to reclaim Lorien, one less soldier to fight to save Earth and every living thing on it. Two missiles slam into our car, blowing it to bits.

Gunfire rains down on me and just in time my bracelet expands into a shield. I take some solace in the fact that my Inheritance is in tune with the dangers that face me – although I don't know why it didn't protect me from the first onslaught of gunfire. The bullets are hitting close and constant. When I finally manage to examine the new scar wrapped around my ankle, I'm shocked to see two gaping bullet wounds instead. I don't know that I've ever been so happy to be wounded and bleeding. I'm so relieved that it's not another scar that I don't even care that my hands are covered in blood. As I apply pressure to stop the bleeding, the desert goes strangely silent. My bracelet retracts.

I manage to flip myself over and look up. Standing over me are three teenagers. The boy is tall and tan with curly black hair, and the two girls hold Loric Chests. I recognize the boy immediately from my visions. He nods and smiles, saying, 'Nice to see you again, Number Four. I'm Eight.' Before I can respond, he disappears.

One of the girls is short with auburn hair and tiny features. She looks no older than twelve, and I know this must be Number Ten, the Garde from the second ship. She drops the Chest and kneels by my side. The other Garde, a tall girl with shoulder-length brown hair, sets her Chest down and, without saying a word, kneels beside me as well and lays both her hands on my wounds. An iciness rushes over me and my body convulses on the desert floor. Just when I think I am about to pass out from the pain, it's gone. I look at my ankle and see my wounds are completely healed. It's amazing. The girl stands, offers me her hand, and pulls me to my feet.

'That's one hell of a Legacy you've got there,' I manage to say.

'John Smith.' She's staring at me and looks kind of starstruck. 'After all this time, I can't believe you're standing here in front of me.'

I'm about to respond, but over her shoulder I catch sight of a missile screaming towards us. I shove the girls to the ground, falling on top of them, and a dune behind us erupts like a volcano, sending a sand cloud high over our heads. When it dissipates Eight reappears next to us.

'Everything good here? Everyone ready to fight?' he says.

'Yeah, we're good,' the taller girl says, nodding towards my leg. Ten had said she was with Seven and Eight, so this must be Number Seven. Before I can introduce myself properly, Eight disappears for the second time.

'He can teleport,' says Number Ten, smiling at my look of wonder. I can hardly believe that so many of us are finally together. I smile back at her.

In the distance, I can see Eight again, fighting alongside Nine and Bernie Kosar. They wreak havoc on each approaching vehicle; flipping and disabling heavy military equipment like cheap plastic toys. Nine's glowing red staff slices open the underside of a low-flying helicopter. Eight teleports next to a black Humvee and flips it over with his hands. Two helicopters swing low and collide into a fireball.

A new sense of urgency comes over me to get to Six as fast as I can. 'So I'm guessing you're Seven and Ten; what can you do?' I say as I find our rifles in the sand and hand them each a gun.

'You can call me Marina,' the girl with the brown hair says. 'And I can breathe under water and see in the dark and heal the wounded. And I have telekinesis.'

Call me Ella, I hear Ten's voice say in my head. *Aside from my telepathy, I can change ages.*

'Awesome. I'm Four, that nut job with the long black hair is Nine, and the beast is my Chimæra, Bernie Kosar.'

'You have a Chimæra?' Ella asks.

'I don't know what I'd do without him,' I say. What's left of the brigade finally separates, and a dozen vehicles bounce off the road and race towards the three of us. A small plume of smoke escapes from the top of one of the vehicles, and I turn the rocket it just fired around with my mind, slamming it into a sand dune. The other trucks and SUVs keep speeding ahead.

I start picking up pieces from Nine's destroyed car and whipping them towards the oncoming brigade. I launch tires, doors, even a mangled seat at them. Marina does the same, and we're able to stop three or four vehicles from advancing. Still, there are a half dozen or more to deal with.

Suddenly Eight, Nine and BK pop up in front of us. Eight

lets go of Nine's hand and reaches forward to shake mine. 'Number Four.'

'You have no idea how happy we are that you guys are here,' I say.

Nine shakes Ten's and Seven's hands, and says, 'Hello, ladies. I'm Number Nine.'

'Hi,' Ten says. 'You can call me Ella.'

'I'm Number Seven, but I go by Marina,' she offers.

I wish there was time to talk to these people I've waited so long to find, to hear their stories, to know where they've been hiding, to know their Legacies, and what's in their Chests. But there are more helicopters on the way.

'We can't stay here and defend this same piece of desert forever,' I say. 'We have to get to Six!'

'Let's take out these bad boys,' Nine says, pointing to the oncoming cloud. 'And then we can find Six and get on with it.'

We all turn to watch the approach. Several new helicopters now dot the sky. I look over at my fellow Garde, and each one looks ready to fight. We've never had so many of us together. Never before have things looked so possible. After all this, we're never splitting up again.

'They'll just keep coming,' I say. 'We should just go get Six.'

'Okay, Johnny. The tunnel is that way,' Nine says, pointing behind us. 'I'll take up the rear and deal with anything that needs handling. You know, snap a few necks, shake things up a bit.'

Those of us with Chests pick them up. I take the lead, heading in the direction Nine pointed. I scan for traps and move everyone towards the five-pronged cactus. Seven and Eight are on my heels, with Ten close behind them. There is a steady stream of gunfire behind us as Nine does his thing. He sounds like he's having a party with himself back there, hooting and hollering. Only he would consider this fun.

We pick up the pace and don't stop running until we get to the cactus. Nine gleefully fires shot after shot while Eight and I try to deal with the prickly plant, the only thing that stands between us and where Six is being held. The map showed that the tunnel is right where the cactus stands. Finally, we manage to blow it to pieces using our telekinesis. Beneath it is a thick brown door with a metal handle in the middle of it. As I stand there looking at the entrance to the tunnel, the other Garde by my side, I remember what Nine said earlier: 'I've been waiting for this my whole life.' We've all been waiting for this – waiting for the moment when we'd find each other, when the nine of us would rise up and defend the legacy of Lorien against the Mogadorians. As it turned out, all nine of us didn't make it, but I know that the six of us who are left, as well as the addition of Number Ten, will do whatever it takes to survive what's to come.

28

An enormous Mog charges at me, gleaming sword swinging. I duck under the blade and connect my fist with his throat. He drops his weapon, gasping for air. No sooner has the metal clanged to the ground than I pick it up and behead him. A cloud of his ash engulfs me as three more charge. The ash hides me. I crouch low, slicing Mog legs off at the knees as soon as they approach. When I stand, another massive Mog tries to get me from behind. I backflip over him, driving my sword through his midsection as I land. I step through his cloud of ash to find myself surrounded by a dozen more. I don't see Setrákus Ra.

I turn invisible. After ripping through another round of Mogs, I look again for Setrákus Ra. I see him at the far end of the room and don't hesitate. I run straight at him. More Mogs appear; I lose count of how many. I leave them all a pile of dust. When I'm within thirty feet of Setrákus Ra, he raises a fist and points it at me, almost as if he can see me. Blue electricity shoots from his hand and crackles along the ceiling of the room and I feel myself turn visible. Once again, he's taken away my Legacies. I knew this could happen, but I feel a pang of loss anyway. Still, I'm ready for whatever he has for me.

Soldier Mogs come at me from all sides, but I just keep moving towards Setrákus Ra. When a Mog steps into my path, I rip my sword through his neck. Another grabs me from behind and I cut off his arm. Another comes screaming towards me and I shove my sword through his midsection. At this point, I'm so focused on where I will ram my blade through Setrákus Ra's neck that I barely notice killing off the Mogs.

The next thing I know, he's right next to me and he grabs my neck. He raises me up with one hand until my feet are dangling off the ground and once again our faces are only inches apart.

'You fight well, little girl,' he breathes into my face. I wince from the stench.

'Give me my Legacies back and you'll see how well.' My voice is strangled.

'If you were as strong as you think you are, I wouldn't be able to take them away in the first place.'

‘Don’t give me that, you coward! If you’re so sure you can take me, why don’t you do it? Show me how big and tough you are. Give me back my Legacies and fight like a man!’ I shout.

His voice echoes as he bellows, ‘You use your powers, and I’ll use mine!’

He tosses me back into the middle of the room, but I barely notice the pain of the impact when I hit the floor. My sword clangs to the ground and skitters away. A soldier sends his sword spinning at me at high speed. My first instinct is to try to stop it with my mind, but my Legacies are still gone. Even so, my strength and reflexes are with me, full force. I am going to kill Setrákus Ra, with or without my powers. I reach out with both hands and slap them over the oncoming blade, trapping it inches from my chin. The next second I’m tackled around the waist and, as I fall onto my back, I rotate the sword between my palms and sink it into the attacking Mog. I’m covered in a blanket of ash as I hit the ground. More Mogs come. I’m destroying them with their weapons, and the justice of that is awesome. I feel stronger with every one I reduce to nothing. I’m also more pissed off. If I have to go through every Mog on Earth to get to Setrákus Ra, I’ll do it.

Setrákus Ra is just standing there, watching

the show. He roars so loud I can feel the vibrations in my chest. My years of training were all leading up to this moment. The only way I could feel stronger is if the rest of the Garde were here; we should be fighting him together. I shake off the thought. I will take him out for all of us.

After I finish off the last soldier, Setrákus Ra moves into the middle of the room to where I stand. He reaches behind his back and produces a massive double-headed whip that he snaps against the ground. It lights up with orange flames.

I don't even flinch. There is nothing he can do to scare or stop me now. I race forward, yelling, 'For Lorien!'

He flicks the whip over my head, sending a thick blanket of flames over me. I dive under its edge and roll in the direction of his feet. As I dodge his stomping boot, I see several scars branded around his ankles. I register them but don't have time to think if there's a connection between his scars and mine. My sword slashes his calf just above the highest scar on his left leg and then I spring to my feet. The mark I made immediately hardens and fades to another scar. He is completely unaffected by the wound, he doesn't even limp a single step.

He snaps the whip at me again and I try to cut off one of its two tails but when the flames touch my sword, the blade melts. I throw the remains of the sword at him. He raises his hand and halts the weapon in midair. It twirls and glows and as he stretches open his fingers, the melted blade climbs back above the handle, reforming into a gleaming sword again. He smiles and lets it fall to the ground.

I dive for the sword, but when I reach down to grab it, his whip snaps across the top of my right hand. My skin boils and opens and, instead of blood, a hard black substance appears in the gash. I look at it and know I should feel unbelievable pain, but I'm numb. I stagger forward and finally get hold of the sword. Weapon in hand, I circle back around to face the Mog leader. But something is terribly wrong with my right hand now. It won't move.

Setrákus Ra cracks his whip again and I jump out of the way as it flies past me, leaving a trail of flames in its wake. When he raises his arm to pull the whip back over his shoulder again, I see an opening and take it. Gripping the sword in my left hand, I rush at him and plunge it deep into his ribcage. I yank it downwards, ripping his waxy skin apart until the sword is lodged at the bottom of his torso. I fall backwards, looking up at him and desperately hoping I've delivered the final blow, that I've ended the war.

No such luck. Though Setrákus Ra grimaces for the first time, instead of turning into a pile of ash he just reaches down and pulls the sword out of his body. He examines the blade, watching his thick black blood dripping off of it. Then he puts the blade in his mouth and bites down on it, breaking it in half, and lets it drop to the ground. It's like he's playing with me. What's going on? I rise to my feet, calculating quickly what my next move should be. Step one is avoiding Setrákus Ra long enough to figure it out. I wish, more than ever, that my Garde was standing with me.

Ella? Can you hear me?

Nothing.

I continue to back away from Setrákus Ra, trying to put more distance between us to give myself a fighting chance. That's when I notice my right hand is starting to tingle. I look down and see the skin around the whip's wound has turned black. As I watch, the discoloration spreads to my knuckles and fingernails; in a matter of seconds my entire right hand is black up to my wrist. The tingling sensation vanishes. My hand feels incredibly heavy. Like it's turned to lead.

I look up at Setrákus Ra. The purple scar on his neck begins to pulse with a bright light. 'Are you ready to die?' he asks me.

Ella? If you're coming, now is the time. In fact, it's now or never.

I want so much to hear her voice in my head, telling me that she and the others are just outside the door. We should be together, fighting Setrákus Ra with our Legacies, the gifts the Elders bestowed upon us, until there is nothing left to him but the worthless, powerless, pile of ashes all of the other Mogs have become. Instead, I'm here alone, my hand injured and useless, playing cat and mouse with Setrákus Ra. And he's just standing here in front of me, fire whip in hand, having rendered my Legacies useless, toying with me. *What* is going on?

I take one more look around at the desert, then reach for the wheel on the brown door and give it a spin. After one rotation, I decide to speed things up and just yank it off its hinges. A steel ladder goes down into a black hole.

'I can see in the dark,' Marina volunteers. 'I'll go first.' I stand aside to let her get by.

Marina climbs down the ladder into the darkness and drops out of sight. Eight tosses her Chest down after her.

'It's about twenty feet down. Looks like there's a long tunnel,' Marina calls up. 'All clear so far. I don't see anyone.'

Nine looks at Ella and me and says, 'Ladies first.' Ella starts down the ladder, and when she disappears, Nine smirks at me and says, 'Well, okay, but I was referring to you, Four.'

I shake my head at him. He's nothing if not consistent. He gestures for me to go down next. 'You know I love you, man. Get in there.'

Using telekinesis, I let Bernie Kosar, back in his beagle form, down first, then tuck my Chest under one arm and awkwardly climb down using just the other hand. It's musty and cold inside the tunnel. Ahead of me, I can hear Ella and Marina walking and BK's toenails clicking on the cement. I turn the Lumen on in my free hand and sweep the concrete tunnel for a few seconds, getting my bearings.

I use my Lumen to illuminate the distance between our location and a sharp turn far up ahead, then I turn it off. 'Marina, you can see to keep us moving, right?' Eight and Nine have now caught up with us. She nods and we all start to follow her down the dark passageway. We haven't gone very far when I almost slam into Ella, who has stopped dead in her tracks.

'Oh no! I finally got through to Six. She needs us! She says it's now or never!'

'Let's pick up the pace, people!' Nine calls out from the rear.

We run as fast as we can through the dark. I flash my Lumen every few seconds to keep us from running over each over. We make a sharp turn and I wave my hands again to light up the tunnel and reveal what's ahead. The next hundred yards slope downward, and my Lumen lights up a concrete door at the end. I slide my Chest down ahead of me until it slams against the door. Still sprinting, I turn on both of my palms to give us all a better view.

Nine quickly rips open his Chest and pulls out the yellow ball covered in small bumps. Like a magician, he holds it in his fingers and then whips it at the door. It bounces just a few inches off the metal before expanding while turning black. Long, razor-sharp spikes explode out of it and the door is blown inward on impact. The spikes instantly retreat until it's just a yellow ball again, lying innocently on the floor. Nine leans down, grabs it, and tosses it back into his Chest, which he closes with a loud snap.

'I was hoping that would happen,' Nine says admiringly. If I were him I'd have taken advantage of my Chest of wonders to see through the door first, to know what we were about to get to. But this is no time to critique anyone's decisions.

We all bolt through the doorway. As soon as we enter, motion-sensor lights come on above us. Red lights flash and sirens blare, attacking our senses. At the end of this shorter passageway, we come to another large concrete door. This one rises as we approach it, revealing dozens of enormous Mogadorian soldiers with cannons and swords up and ready to use.

'Mogs? What are they doing here?' asks Eight in disbelief.

'Yeah. Bad news; the government and the Mogadorians have teamed up,' I say.

'Easy pickings,' Eight says. Nine nudges me and makes an exaggerated gesture of approval at our new-found Garde member.

I feel a surge of adrenaline pump through my body that I've only felt in my visions. All of a sudden I know what to do. I look over at the others.

'Follow my lead!' I yell. They nod back at me. I drop my Chest, light the Lumen in both palms, and rush straight ahead. The last thing I see out of the corner of my eye is Ella scooping up my Chest.

Just like in my vision, I aim the Lumen at my feet as I run and they catch on fire. The flames climb up my legs and engulf my body just as I reach the first soldier. When I jump, I'm a fireball that burns right through him. He turns to ash and I keep running.

The Mogs I pass swing around 180 degrees to shoot at me, but my flames offer the perfect protection. I lower my head and run with my arms stretched out, effectively keeping any other soldiers away. Marina, Eight, and Ella are on the heels of the soldiers, picking them off from behind as I race ahead. Nine has run up onto the ceiling and is battling the Mogs from above. I toss fireballs at the closest ones to me and in a matter of seconds, they're all torched, leaving a thick cloud of ash and smoke hanging above. I slow my pace when I see the last one go down. When we reach the back of the room, I launch a large ball of fire at the door, blowing it to pieces. I take a second to admire how well that worked, BK even getting his share of Mogs, though this is clearly neither the time nor the place for self-congratulation. Maybe Nine's rubbed off on me. We all turn to see what's next.

Setrákus Ra has done something to me. I can't move at all and stand rooted in place. At first, I wonder if it's just all the punishing battle or the bizarre wound on my hand, or both. Then I realize there is something seriously wrong, something stopping me from being able to move. I force my chin up to look at Setrákus Ra looming before me. Setrákus Ra has produced a golden cane with a black eye on the handle. He holds it out and the eye opens, blinks, rolls left and then right before it finds me. Then the eye slowly closes, and snaps back open to emit a crazy-bright, blinding, red light. As the beam crawls over my helpless body, it leaves behind a weird, buzzing sensation on my skin. I really need to move. I need to get away from that creepy light, away from whatever it's doing to me, but I'm immobilized. My hand weighs a ton. I am vulnerable and I need to get control – of the situation, of myself. But I can't.

The light from the eye is now purple and it rolls over my face. I lick my lips and taste something burned. Setrákus Ra moves towards me until he's a few feet away. I close my eyes and tighten my jaw, thinking of John and Katarina and Sam and Marina and Ella. I see Eight and Henri and Crayton, and even Bernie Kosar. I will *not* give Setrákus Ra the honor, the pleasure, of looking at him while he kills me. Something hot and soft touches my forehead, like a blast of air. I steel myself for whatever is about to happen; brace myself for the certain agony it will bring. When nothing happens, I open my eyes to see Setrákus Ra just standing there. Well, not exactly. There are bands of red and purple light shining out of the head of his cane and crawling up and down his massive body.

Setrákus Ra starts to shake and a white light outlines his shoulders and arms. He falls to his knees, convulsing, his huge head jerking up and down. Then his dull, waxy skin pulls away from the muscle and bone. When the skin snaps back down onto his shrinking body, it has a new, olive tone. Long blond hair grows out of his scalp until he has a full head of hair. When he looks up at me, I am more desperate than ever to attack but I still can't move. He's me – gray eyes and high cheekbones and dyed blonde hair.

'For me to be you, you must stay alive,' he says in my voice, 'but only for now.' He lifts a palm into the air and, as if there was one magnet in the ceiling and another in my now-black hand, I shoot off the ground, slam against the ceiling, and dangle there, fifty feet off the floor. I feel a painful buzzing in my brain. I try again to call for Ella in my head, but I can't even hear myself think. When I touch my free hand to the one stuck to the ceiling, it, too, turns black. The heavy stiffness that weighed down my hand is now spreading. The only things I can move at this point are my eyes. My entire body is now black. Black rock.

29

Once again I take the lead. Marina trails me and a growling Bernie Kosar runs alongside her. Ella still has my Chest, with Eight and Nine following close behind. My fire has made me invincible, and my flames instantly consume every Mogadorian soldier that comes charging around a corner or through a door. The fire has not only taken over my body, but also my mind. I have never felt so confident, so determined, so ready to defeat our enemies before.

'She still hasn't responded to me!' Ella yells as we enter another hallway filled with sirens and flashing lights. 'I don't know if she can hear anything I'm saying.'

'Well, she isn't dead yet because we don't have any new scars,' Nine says, sticking out his leg as if to admire it.

My fire is getting higher and wider, licking the walls and ceiling of the corridor as I pass through. It's hard to describe my energy, how I am barely able to contain it, like I might explode with it. I'm ready to fight Setrákus Ra and I know the others feel the same way. Nine and Eight are like wrecking balls swinging down the hall, pounding soldiers into oblivion, bouncing from one Mog to the other, and Marina is fighting fearlessly, using all means available to toss soldiers into the air. Ella, with fewer powers revealed, looks on a bit enviously as we swat away the soldiers.

I wish I had the time to stop and tell her how vital she is, how important her ability to communicate telepathically was to our all coming together. How she, as the youngest Loric, represents our long life and the power of our Garde. We're ready to take back Lorien and that's only possible because of everything we bring to the fight, each one of us. The hallway splits off and we need to quickly decide which way to go. Separating is never going to be an option again.

'Okay, Fire Boy, which way?' Nine asks.

Marina steps up and says, 'This way.' Her ability to see in the dark is better than the limited view my Lumen offers, so I extinguish my fire and we all follow her to the left.

Marina doesn't even hesitate at the entryway of a long wide room filled with tall brown columns. Neither do the rest of us. We have our weapons ready when we first hear the noise of people marching in on the far end of the room. I nudge Marina's arm. 'Hey, can you see who that is?'

'Yeah. I'm guessing they're government soldiers. They're definitely not Mogs. There are a lot of them. I don't know, twenty, thirty? There could be more than that.' She turns and moves towards them. We all do the same. We can toss them aside easily, twisting their guns with our telekinesis. We blow through the big room, pass another corridor door, and turn left, where we find a dozen government soldiers dressed in black, protecting a heavy metal door. As soon as they see us, they step into formation to fully block the passageway and start firing. As if prearranged,

Marina and Eight both raise their hands, stopping the bullets as they are fired, inches away from their barrels. Immediately, Nine joins the action and uses his mind to rip the guns out of the soldiers' hands and lifts the soldiers up, dangling from the domed ceiling. We each grab a gun.

Nine wedges the tip of his staff into the doorframe they were guarding and rips it off its hinges.

Behind the doorway is another hallway, this one lined with doors on both sides. Nine runs ahead to each of the doors and briefly presses his ear to each one.

He reports one unmanned control room after another. Further down the hall we find what look like empty prison cells. I wonder if we're getting closer to finding Six. She could be behind any one of these doors.

I spot a trail of blood in front of one of the doors. From ten feet away I rip the door out of its frame. The cell is pitch black inside. Before I have a chance to use my Lumen, Marina pushes by me. 'There's a person in here!' she cries.

We hear a whimper from the back corner and I flash my lights into the darkness. There, scared and dirty, is someone I thought I would never see again. Sarah. I fall to my knees, my lights glowing dimly. I open my mouth to speak, but only a squeak comes out. I try again: 'Sarah.' I can't believe she's sitting in front of me. I can't believe we found her.

After a quick glance up at me Sarah hugs her knees to her chest and looks afraid. Afraid of me. She drops her head into her knees and sobs. 'Please don't do this to me, please don't trick me anymore. Not like this. I can't take it, I can't take anymore.' She's shaking her head over and over. I don't think she's even registered I'm not alone. I can feel everyone standing behind me, cloaked in darkness.

'Sarah,' I whisper. 'It's me, John. We're here to take you home.'

Nine hangs back, but I can hear him say to someone, 'So this is the famous Sarah; girl looks good, even dirty.'

Sarah pulls her legs to her chest even more tightly and peeks over her knees. She looks so vulnerable and scared; I just want to scoop her up. But I move slowly, ready for anything. This could be a trap. I haven't come this far only to act without thinking. When I touch her shoulder, she screams in panic. I can feel everyone behind me flinch with the sudden noise, the sheer terror in her voice.

She presses her back against the wall, her hair sticking to the rough concrete. Then she lifts her face to the ceiling and cries, 'Don't trick me anymore! I've told you everything. Please don't trick me anymore!'

Marina steps forward so she is standing next to me. She grabs my arm and gives me a shake, then pulls me to my feet. 'John, we can't stay here; we have to get moving. We need to take Sarah with us!'

Sarah finally looks beyond me and sees the others. I watch her take in Marina standing there, looking down at her. Her eyes widen and she looks back at me, then she looks around at the others who have stepped closer.

Tears streak the thick layer of dirt on her cheeks. 'What's happening? Are you really here? Are all of you really here?'

I kneel down next to her again. 'It's me. It's us. I promise. Look, even Bernie Kosar wants to say hi.' He trots over and licks her hand, his tail wagging.

I lay my hands on hers, and when I see the bruises running up and down her wrists, my eyes fill with tears. I press her fingers to my lips. 'Sarah, listen to me. I know I left you once. I promise you, I will never do that again. Do you hear me? I will *never* leave you.' She is still looking at me as if I might disappear or turn into a fire-breathing monster.

A thousand other things I've been thinking about for so long race through my mind and I struggle to say more. I flash back to our last conversation at the playground, moments before the police took me away. 'Hey, Sarah. Do you remember when I said that I think about you every day. Do you remember that?' She looks at me and nods. 'Well, I did and I do. Every day.' She allows herself a tentative smile. 'Now do you believe it's really me?' She nods again. 'Sarah Hart, I love you. I love only you. Do you hear me?'

She looks so relieved, it makes me want to pick her up and tell her it's over and I will keep her safe. Always. She kisses me, her hands on each side of my face.

'Four, come on! We have to move,' Eight shouts. He and the others have moved to the door, anxiously looking both directions of the hallway.

There's an explosion in the hallway and Eight runs out to see what it is, followed by Ella and Marina. 'What the hell is taking so long, man?' Nine shouts to me, gesturing madly towards the door. 'Stand the girl up and let's get going! Sarah Hart, it is *awfully* nice to meet you, but we *really* need you to move! Now!'

Nine rushes over and helps me get Sarah to her feet. Once she's fully upright, he gives her a quick hug. She looks surprised by the warm welcome, and I have to wonder about the wink he gives me over her head. 'Sarah freaking Hart! Do you have any idea how much this jerk talks about you?' I smile at Sarah, then Nine.

'No,' Sarah laughs quietly, leaning into me and winding her fingers through mine.

'Okay, okay. Come on, you two,' Nine says, turning to head back to the door.

I stare into Sarah's blue eyes. 'Before we go, I have to ask you something. And you need to understand that I *have* to ask it. You're not working for them, are you? The government and the Mogs?'

Sarah shakes her head. 'Why does everyone keep asking me that? I would never betray any of you.'

'Wait. Who's everyone? Who else asked you that?' I ask.

'Six,' Sarah says, looking surprised I would even need to ask. Her blue eyes widen. 'You didn't find her?'

'You've seen Six?' Marina speaks up, excited. 'When? Where?'

'She's fighting Setrákus Ra,' Sarah says, starting to panic again. 'They took her away a while ago.'

'What? No way! That's *my* fight!' Nine yells.

'Don't worry, man, if we move fast, maybe you can get a piece of him,' I say. Then I look down the hall to find Eight, Marina, and Ella running back towards us.

'That way,' Marina shouts.

I grab Sarah's hand and pull her behind me. Everyone races down the hall where we find Bernie Kosar standing in front of a metal doorway that's the size of a loading-dock entrance, barking uncontrollably.

This time Nine does use his rock to look through the door. Like before, a white cone of light appears, then we can see right into a huge room. 'Looks like there's something going on in there. I see movement in the shadows,' Eight says. 'I'll teleport through and scout it out.'

'Wait a sec, Eight.' I hold up my hand to stop him. 'No scout. We should just do this, all of us.'

Eight looks at me for a second, then nods. 'You're right. This is for all of us.'

When we're all gathered at the door, I look down the line of determined faces. Even Sarah. She's gone from weepy rescue-girl to warrior in a heartbeat. Pretty impressive. Of course, she hasn't got a *clue* what we are pretty sure is about to happen. It's likely this is going to be an epic battle, if not *the* battle. I have a feeling in my gut that everything has led up to this moment. This could be what we've been working towards.

'Whatever's inside, whatever happens,' I say, lighting the Lumen in my palms, 'we *will* kill Setrákus Ra, no matter what.' I'm saying this for me, not them.

'We're all on this, dude,' Nine says.

I hold a glowing palm over the door, and just as I'm about to blow it inwards, a woman with red hair and an arm in a sling comes hobbling through a door at the far end of the hall. She and I gasp at exactly the same time; then she turns and darts back through the door.

'Wait! Agent Walker!' I shout after her.

'Walker? Are you kidding me?' Nine asks, incredulously. 'The chick soldier who tried to capture us?' The others just look on, confused for a beat, before Eight speaks up.

'I'll get her for you,' he says, and then disappears. When he materializes a moment later he's got her, arms twisted behind her back. The first thing I do is rip off the gold badge on the front of her shirt.

Nine plucks the badge out of my hand and makes a great show of examining it carefully. 'Well, well, well. Who do we have here? Special Agent Walker?' Nine laughs. 'Lady, you look awful!' He hands the badge back to me as if it suddenly has cooties.

'Do you know how pathetic you are?' I yell. 'Cutting deals with the Mogs, doing their dirty work, for what? They are going to *destroy* you!'

'I'm doing my job,' she says stiffly. Eight has a tight grip on her. 'We are doing what's best for this country.' She stares back at me defiantly, but I know we will make it clear how much she has to fear from us soon enough.

Sarah points at her. 'I've seen you before. John, she was there when Six was taken away.'

Nine grabs Agent Walker by her shirt's lapels like some gangster from a movie. Eight never loosens his grip on her arms. Nine shoves his face right into her face. 'I want this one, I get to kill her.'

Walker is now frantically struggling to back away from Nine and free herself of Eight. 'Wait! I know where your ship is!' Special Agent Walker pleads. 'I know you want it and you'll never find it without me.'

'Our ship is here?' Marina asks, clearly uncertain if she can trust what Agent Walker says.

The agent narrows her eyes. 'I'll show you if you let me go.'

'What do you think, Four?' Nine asks.

'John? What happens when you find your ship?' asks Sarah, grabbing my arm.

'We don't have time for this!' Marina says. 'I know Six is inside this room. The fact that this woman will say anything to keep us from going in tells me I'm right! Forget about her! Who cares if or where our ship is, until we have Six!'

Nine says, 'I'll handle her.' Walker floats up into the air and hangs by her belt hook on the light fixture high above us, red-faced with fury. Nine looks at us, winks and flicks the fingers of one hand behind his back, blowing the door open. 'Marina's right. Six and Setrákus Ra come first. Shall we?'

He smiles at Sarah. 'You're pretty badass from what I've heard from Johnny here,' he says, handing her Walker's Mog cannon. 'Think you can handle her?'

Sarah takes the cannon. 'If she moves from that light, I'll blast her. Gladly.'

I look at the rest of the Garde. 'It's time.'

We rush inside. We don't have to figure out who's doing what. We just know. It's quiet and dark and an awful stench permeates the air. All I can think of is the arena that kept appearing in my visions. Is this it? I look around, trying to see if I can tell. The center of the large room is dimly illuminated. Nine runs into the circle of light and yells, 'Time to come and play, Setrákus, you piece of shit!'

'Where's Six?' Marina says. She joins Nine in the center of the room, along with Eight. They quickly drop their Chests and start to look around.

'You guys! There's something up on the ceiling,' Ella says, her voice echoing around the room. I look up to see a small formation of rocks hanging from the ceiling.

I shine my Lumen on the object, and bathed in its glow, it almost looks like a statue. 'This isn't right. I don't know why, but there's something wrong here,' I say in a low voice.

While we watch the shadows for any sign of movement, Nine uses his anti-gravity Legacy to run up onto the ceiling and look at the rock formation. When he starts to get close I hear a familiar voice yell, 'Stop!'

I whip around to see Six standing alone in the doorway. A loop of thick rope hangs from her hip, and in her hand is a jagged blue sword. She looks unharmed. Now *that* is the Six I remember; confident and strong. Did she do it? Is it possible that Six has already killed Setrákus Ra?

'Six! Oh, my God, it's you!' Marina cries. 'You're okay!'

'It's over,' Six says. 'Setrákus Ra is dead. That formation on the ceiling is Mogadorian poison. Stay away from it.'

The relief in the air is palpable. Eight teleports to Six's side and wraps his arms around her in a huge hug.

Six was always the strongest of us, stronger than even me or Nine. She just saved Lorien, Earth, and possibly the universe. I want to pick her up, put her on my shoulder, and parade her back to Lorien.

I start towards her too, but Ella grabs my wrist and pulls me back. I hear her in my mind. *John. Something's wrong.*

The next few moments happen in what feels like slow motion. Six pulls the jagged blue sword back and thrusts it forward. Horrified, I watch Eight become rigid, then the tip of the sword breaks through the middle of his shoulders. He slumps forward. Six pushes Eight's body off her sword and he falls to the floor, motionless.

'No!' Marina screams from behind me and rushes towards Eight.

I'm paralyzed with shock until my instinct to fight kicks in. I look down and a massive fireball has formed in the palm of my right hand. Whatever confusion I was just feeling has cleared and I know what I need to do. This can't be Six. And whoever this really is, I need to kill them.

'Six,' I say, rolling the fireball on the tips of my fingers. 'What did they do to you?'

She laughs and raises her other hand into a fist. Blue lightning shoots out between her knuckles and spreads along the ceiling of the room. My fireball disappears. What's going on?

'Four!' I look up to see Nine flying through the air from above me. His anti-gravity Legacy must have failed him too. I manage to catch enough of him to stop him from slamming down on the ground and help him get to his feet.

Marina stands protectively over Eight, guns aimed and ready to fire. Eight is still on the ground and I can't tell how badly he's injured. At least I know he's alive, since I don't have a new scar. Marina lets loose a burst of bullets, but they stop inches from Six's face and drop uselessly to the concrete. I try to light myself with my Lumen again, but nothing happens.

With her sword held high, Six's body starts to convulse and blur with a quick flash of white. She grows taller and her long blonde hair shrinks into a small patch on top of a large skull. Her face elongates and morphs, and somehow I know she's changing into Setrákus Ra even before the glowing purple scar appears on his neck. Two battalions of Mog soldiers silently emerge from doors on the sides of the room and flank him. Without a word, Nine, Marina, Ella, and I move closer to one another, standing over Eight, to make it clear we will face him together.

'All of you in one place. How convenient for me. I hope you're ready to die,' he snarls.

'I think you have that wrong,' I reply.

'That's what Number Six thought, too. But *she* was wrong. Very wrong.' He smiles, his revolting and stained teeth glinting in the dim light.

Nine looks over at me and rubs his hands together, all eager anticipation. 'Johnny boy, have we discussed how important oral hygiene is to me?' He looks back at Setrákus Ra, 'Dude, brush your teeth before you even think about threatening me!' He extends his glowing red staff, turns to Setrákus Ra and charges. Thankfully we still have the power of our Inheritance.

30

Out of the corner of my eye, I see Nine charging Setrákus Ra. I turn back to Eight, to see if I can heal him. I keep my hands on Eight's chest wound, waiting for my Legacy to start working again. Nothing. I beg Eight to hold on, to fight through the pain, but his brown eyes roll back, and his breath becomes more and more shallow. Panicked, I flash back on the drawing from the Loric cave, the one where Eight is killed by Setrákus Ra's sword. Is the prediction coming true? I desperately keep pressing my hands all over his chest.

'Marina!' John shouts. 'We have to get you and Eight out of this room, now! I have a feeling if we can get away from Setrákus Ra, our Legacies will start working again. If I'm right, you can still save Eight.'

'He's almost gone,' I manage to choke out. 'It might be too late, no matter what we do.' I can't bring myself to tell him about the cave drawing. I wonder if Eight is able to think about any of this, to remember the drawing, to know what this moment might be. I hope not.

'Then we should hurry,' he says, handing me a Mog cannon and picking up Eight. 'Shoot anything and everything that's not one of our friends.'

We try to cover the hundred or so yards to the door as quickly as we can, while keeping an eye on the others who are locked in battle. With every Mog I turn to ash on the way, I feel stronger and stronger. I try not to think about where Six – the real Six – is, or what's happened to her. I *knew* that wasn't Six. I wish I had killed that *thing,* even before it revealed itself. I scan the room. Nine is fighting Setrákus Ra, clearly treading water, his staff clashing with Ra's sword. As strong as Nine is, it almost looks like Setrákus Ra is toying with him, just waiting for the right moment to strike and kill.

Every ounce of confidence and strength I felt a moment ago drains out of me. There are simply too many of them and too few of us. And we are without our Legacies, which means we're just *kids*. Kids fighting an organized, alien army. I hate to leave the others, but I know John is right. I know I need to get out of here if I'm going to have any hope of healing Eight. And saving Eight is the only choice.

We're almost at the door when two dozen Mogs come right at us. Some of them have cannons, some of them have swords, and they all appear terrifyingly unstoppable. I try to shoot them, but the cannon blasts I send their way don't even make a dent in the advancing mob. There are just too many of them. John manages to set Eight down just outside the door, then he joins me, charging them and wielding his sword. I fight alongside him. I will not let John down no matter how bad the odds appear. We protect one another and we draw strength from each other when we feel weak. It's why we've survived this long, and why we will win. We are stronger when we unite.

John mows the Mogs down, one at a time, methodically and fast. I shoot steadily as I maneuver to block the doorway and protect Eight. I duck outside the door to check on Eight's condition. I feel his pulse, which is faint, and I can tell my Legacy has not returned. I lay my hands on him and whisper fiercely, 'You can't die, Eight. Do you hear me? I am going to heal you. My Legacy will return and I will heal you.'

I realize the Mogs that had charged us are all gone – destroyed – and the abrupt silence startles me.

'We have to hurry. More will come,' John says urgently.

We hear a deafening scream – through the door we can see Bernie Kosar has transformed into a beast and is surrounded by Mogs who are trying to slash at him, but he jumps in and out of their reach. The Mogs can't get him, but he isn't able to do much damage to them, either. We step back into the room in time to see Setrákus pull out a whip. Its tips begin to flame and he strikes Nine in the arm. The wound immediately begins to turn black. John turns to say something to me when I hear a shot. Before I can even tell what happened, John's body convulses and he falls to the ground.

I'm stuck to the ceiling, entombed in black stone. I watch as the rest of the Garde fight for their lives and I can't even feel my own body, never mind let them know I'm up here. I'm helpless and it's killing me. I've trained every moment of my life, learning how *not* to be helpless. Setrákus Ra is no great fighter. He's only taking us down because he is able to render us powerless. I want to be standing down there with his head in my hands for all of the Mogs to see. I would make sure they witnessed the destruction of their leader, and then I'd leave them in the same pile of ash.

Am I watching the dream of Lorien die? We thought we were so strong and so smart and so prepared. We thought we were going to end the war and fly back home to Lorien. We were fools, arrogant fools. We knew of Setrákus Ra, the great and terrible Mogadorian leader, but we didn't know anything about how he fought, the powers he would bring to the battle. In retrospect it seems obvious that he would have the power to take our Legacies.

I wish I could communicate with my fellow Garde – I'd be able to direct them well from this vantage point. For one thing, I can see that while the Mogs are stupendously strong physically, they bring little if anything in the way of mental technique. These guys are almost as dumb as the rock I've become. They reveal their movements before they act. Their plan of attack is easy to read because they don't have one. This is a game of numbers and brute force, and that is an enemy that can be beat if you know what you're dealing with. But when you're in the thick of it, it's impossible to see. I wish I could tell the Garde to focus all of their energies and strength on Setrákus Ra. Otherwise I fear the battle will be short, the Mogs almost sure to win.

I watch Bernie Kosar get slashed. He's transformed himself into an enormous beast, the same kind he became back in Paradise. His body is thick and muscular, his teeth and claws are sharp and jagged, and two curled horns have sprouted from his head. I see Setrákus Ra hit Nine with his whip and Nine's arm turn black, which I can only assume means he'll be in the same position as me soon. John has been shot, and he goes down writhing in pain. Marina picks up a cannon and starts firing on the advancing Mogs.

Ella's sneaking out of the room. Does she have a plan?

I'm distracted from watching Ella by the sound of BK roaring in pain. I see he's fallen to his knees. Though he's still fighting, still killing Mogs, he's bleeding heavily from his wounds. It's agonizing watching him being slowly destroyed, in so much pain.

I'm bleeding out; I can feel my blood and my strength running out of me and there's nothing I can do about it.

Wave after wave of Mogs just keep coming. I have no idea how many we've killed so far today, but it doesn't seem to make any difference. Without our Legacies, it's like trying to stop a tsunami with a pile of Swiss cheese.

Marina is behind me, firing on the Mogs. I look over at Bernie Kosar and see the Mogs have ropes around his horns and are dragging him out of the corner.

'Coward, you're nothing but a coward! You have to paralyze us just to beat us!' I hear Nine scream. I see him in the center of the room, one of his arms black and hanging heavy and useless, as Setrákus rears his whip back.

Setrákus Ra smiles. 'You can call me whatever names you want. It's not going to change the fact that you're about to die.' He snaps the whip forward. Nine tries to block the flaming tips with his staff, but with only one arm, it's impossible. One of the tips hits Nine's hand, sending the staff flying, and the other tail of the whip hits Nine's face. He screams out in pain as his hand and face both start turning black. Setrákus advances on him. I have to do what I can before I'm totally useless, or dead, so I start firing my cannon at Setrákus Ra from my position on the ground. At best, I'm a distraction, but I will do whatever I can. He stops each one of the projectiles I fire in midair, and tosses them aside like they're nothing.

I hear a new source of cannon fire. I turn towards the door and see Sarah moving into the room, firing on Mogs, Ella behind her. Sarah. She hasn't been trained. There's no way she can survive a battle with the Mogs and Setrákus Ra! 'Sarah!' I scream. 'You've got to get out of here! This is not your fight!'

Sarah ignores me and keeps moving deeper into the room. Nine is trying to move away from Setrákus Ra, but his arms, both of which are now completely black, weigh him down. His face is quickly turning as black as his arms. Setrákus strikes Nine again, this time getting him with both tips of the whip right in the middle of his chest. Nine cries out and Setrákus shouts, 'I had heard you might be my greatest challenge, but look at you, you are *nothing*!'

As Setrákus Ra brings his whip back once more to deliver a fatal blow to Nine, Ella darts out from behind Sarah and throws something at him, something that looks like a small red blur. It hits Setrákus in the arm and he looks down, shocked, before letting out a deafening roar.

I feel something change inside of me. It's immediate and enormously powerful, like someone plugged me into an energy source. I focus on my hands and try, just once more, to light my Lumen. To my amazement, it works. Our Legacies have returned.

From behind me I hear Marina cry out and she races over to Eight, who's still just outside the doorway. I see her run her hands over his chest, working on his wound. She looks at me through the doorway. 'What just happened?'

I shake my head. 'I have no idea, but now we've got ourselves a real fight.'

My palms glowing, I turn towards the center of the room where Setrákus Ra is clawing at his arm, trying to pull out the small red object Ella threw at him. He finally succeeds and turns to snap the whip at Ella and Sarah, who is still firing the cannon. They don't move out of the way fast enough and the whip makes contact. They both go down.

As soon as the dart hits Setrákus, I feel the change. My Legacies are back. My strength is starting to return. I have a chance to get out of here and help the others.

I start struggling within the black casing and can now feel myself move slightly within it, but not enough to break out.

As I continue to struggle, I look below me. John is with Sarah and Ella, both down. He's left a trail of blood behind him as well as piles of ash. Marina has run back outside to Eight. Bernie Kosar is still in the corner, but now he is tearing apart the Mogs that were dragging him a second ago. In the middle of the room, Nine is still facing off with Setrákus Ra and he's been able to break his hands and face free from the black rock that was taking over his body.

Seeing that gives me hope that I can break out of my own stone prison and I continue my struggle until I feel the casing start to give way. I'll be out soon. I am frantic to free myself. The only thing I want right now is to show Setrákus

Ra what it feels like to have a real fight on his hands.

Just when I was giving up hope that I would ever be able to help Eight, my Legacy returned. I put my hands on the wound in the center of his chest and feel it start to work. With every second that passes, his heart beats stronger and stronger. I've never felt anything so good in my life, that steady *bump bump bump*. If I weren't in the middle of the fight of our lives, for our future, I think I would start crying right now, but I stay strong, and keep my emotions in check.

I look down and see Eight's eyes flutter open, then look up at me. 'You need to know . . . Six tried to –' he starts to say.

I cut him off. 'That wasn't Six. It was Setrákus Ra. I don't know how, but it was him.'

'But . . . ?' The confusion in Eight's eyes makes my heart break.

'Eight, I can't explain everything right now. How do you feel? Can you stand? We have to get in there, join the others and fight. Are you ready? I need to heal John and I need you to run interference. Got it?'

He nods and I start to get up, but there's just one thing I need to do before it's too late. I look into his eyes, his beautiful brown eyes, take a deep breath, and kiss him. He looks shocked as I pull back. I shrug at him and smile. 'Hey, there's no time like the present, right?' Before he can say or do anything, I turn to find

John. I need to heal him, fast. He took three cannon blasts protecting me. If I don't get to him now, he'll die.

There's a trail of blood where John dragged himself across the floor, and Eight and I follow it. A heavy cloud of smoke is hanging in the air from all the cannon blasts. When we get to John he's on his knees, shooting balls of fire from his hands at a massive gang of Mogs trying to get to Ella and Sarah. As we move towards him, the Mogs fire at us. But now that I'm able to use my telekinesis I can deflect their shots, and Eight begins fighting back too. I run to John's side and begin to heal his wounds. He's breathing heavily and is very pale. He's lost so much blood.

'John! You need to stop for a minute so I can heal you!' I have to shout to be heard over the chaos and commotion. I grab his chin and force him to look at me.

He shakes his head, trying to release my grip, 'If I stop, the Mogs will kill Sarah and Ella.'

'If you don't stop, *you'll* die. Eight is healed now, he can do defense while I work on you. Please! John! We need you.' I feel him stop struggling.

I look more closely at the wounds on his legs. They're similar. Both legs are bleeding steadily from gaping holes. I work on the right one first, and can immediately tell Four's thigh bone is also broken. He can't help but scream while it kneads itself, but the sound is absorbed by everything else going on. His hands ball into fists as I continue.

The second leg isn't as bad and I'm able to heal it more quickly. John is already breathing easier. I reach for his arm and yell into his ear, 'You are looking a whole lot better!'

I place my hand on the wound on John's upper arm and can feel the muscles, the biceps and triceps, have been shredded. It's going to take a minute or two for them to heal. Eight is still firing away at the constant stream of Mogs, but they are coming almost faster than he can keep up with.

I feel John's muscles finally knit together and he's healed. He looks at me and I nod. He leaps to his feet and races over to help Eight protect Ella and Sarah, who are still down.

I feel strong. Good. Sarah and Ella did something miraculous that got us our Legacies back, made it possible for us to fight, but now they're both hurt. I will turn every last one of these Mogs into ash for hurting my friends.

I rush towards them, whipping balls of fire from my hands at the Mogs. I know it should never feel good to kill a living creature, but right now, it feels *great.* Now that I'm up Eight is teleporting all over the room, appearing in front of Mogs and slicing them to pieces with a sword. Nine is still fighting Setrákus Ra, but the two of them are moving so fast they're just a blur. I need to get in there and fight, but I also need to stay here and help Sarah and Ella.

Suddenly, one of the Mogs advancing on me turns in a

different direction. He's not aiming his cannon at me. It's pointed directly at Sarah and Ella, who are still lying motionless. He fires and their bodies start to convulse, and I begin to scream.

I watch in horror as Ella and Sarah's prone bodies are hit with Mog cannon fire. John reaches them and I rush to his side. He's kneeling next to them and holding their hands as their bodies shake. We're too late.

After all of this, after we made it this far and we all found each other at last, it looks like we're about to lose another member of the Garde. And Sarah. John just found her again, and he's going to lose her. I close my eyes as well, bracing myself for another scar to burn itself into my leg, a scar for Ella. I know this one is going to hurt the most.

But nothing happens. Is there something different about Ella that her death won't cause a scar? That can't be. I open my eyes and look at John, who's still hunched over Sarah and Ella, still intently squeezing their hands.

I look closer at the girls and can't quite believe what I'm seeing. Their wounds – cannon blasts to their bodies and hideous burns on their faces – are healing. 'What's happening? How are *you* doing this?' I ask John, looking at him in wonder.

'I have no idea,' he says, shaking his head. 'I didn't know I could do this. I saw Sarah on the ground and I wasn't going to let her die, or Ella. Not another one of the Garde. I won't let that happen, especially now that we're together. I took their hands and thought about how much I wanted their injuries to heal, how much I wished I could heal them . . . and it suddenly just started to happen.'

'You've developed a new Legacy!' I cry, squeezing his shoulders.

'Or, I just wanted it so badly, a miracle happened. Whatever it is, they're both healing.' He lets out a laugh, filled with exhaustion and relief. John looks to the center of the room, where Nine continues to fight. 'Marina, this is not the time we're going to bring Setrákus Ra down. Even though our Legacies have come back, I don't think we can defeat him just yet, and I don't want to take the chance of losing another Garde member. We have to find Six. Then we need to figure out a way to get the hell out of here, regroup, and come up with a plan. We'll kill him together or die together. But we do it on *our* terms, when we *know* we're ready to do it.'

We hear a moan, and look down at Sarah and Ella. Their eyes are open and color is coming back into their cheeks. John leans over and kisses Sarah.

The casing is finally breaking off. I flex my arms and kick my legs and start to fall as the last of it crumbles. I use my telekinesis to lower myself to the ground.

I lie there for a second, trying to catch my breath. The smoke is so thick my eyes are watering. All of a sudden, a huge explosion rocks the room. An alarm goes off, red lights flash, and a piercingly loud siren fills the air. I can see John's Lumen burning and I make my way through the haze towards it. Ella, Marina and Sarah are standing next to him, and as I get closer Eight appears, teleporting to Marina's side. Bernie Kosar has turned back into a beagle and he limps over to John.

Ella cries out when she sees me and throws her arms around me. I return her hug and then look at John. Seeing his face again is like a dream come true. He touches my arm. 'You okay?'

I nod. 'What about you?' I ask, and I know I sound as exhausted and beaten down as I feel.

'We're all alive so far – but where's Nine?' he replies, looking around as we all realize simultaneously that the battle sounds have disappeared. We run towards the center of the room, towards the area where Nine had been battling Setrákus Ra, keeping him at bay. Nine is lying on the ground, motionless, and Setrákus Ra is nowhere in sight. Marina falls to her knees next to him and frantically starts running her hands over his body while I spin in circles, trying desperately to see through the haze to make sure Setrákus Ra isn't hiding, waiting to capture and kill us when our backs are turned. Aside from the shrill sound of the alarms, the room is eerily quiet and I realize there are no Mogadorians anywhere.

'He's alive!' Marina cries. 'He's just stunned.' Nine sits up, shaking his head groggily.

'What happened?' he asks.

'I was going to ask you that,' Eight says. 'There was an explosion and everyone but the seven of us have disappeared.'

'I don't know – I didn't see where he went. One second I was trying to hold my own, fighting him off, the next thing I knew I was here on the ground.'

'What do we do now?' Sarah asks.

'We have to get of here,' says John. 'Setrákus Ra could reappear at any second, and this could be a trap. Even though this is a government base, it clearly isn't safe.'

'Anyone know a way out of here?' I ask. They all look at each other grimly.

'We have to go back the way we came in,' says Eight. 'My teleporting Legacy won't work with so many of us.'

'Okay,' John says. 'We don't know what we'll face on the way out and we may have to fight our way through more Mogadorians, or human soldiers, but we need to stay together now. We're never splitting up again.'

Nine steps over and stands next to me, then looks me up and down. 'I don't believe anyone introduced us, proper like. It's nice to officially meet you, sweetheart. I'm Nine,' he says, winking at me. I roll my eyes and John snickers.

I look around for a second. It's a miracle we're all together, all still alive. Every living Loric on Earth but one is standing within a few feet of each other.

We're alive and we're fighting and that means we still have a chance. And we *will* meet Setrákus again, and soon. Next time, he will *not* get away from us.

Want to know where it all began? Read on for an extract from the first thrilling book in the series

I Am Number Four

to find out.

The door starts shaking. It's a flimsy thing made of bamboo shoots held together with tattered lengths of twine. The shake is subtle and stops almost immediately. They lift their heads to listen, a fourteen-year-old boy and a fifty-year-old man, who everyone thinks is his father but who was born near a different jungle on a different planet hundreds of lightyears away. They are lying shirtless on opposite sides of the hut, a mosquito net over each cot. They hear a distant crash, like the sound of an animal breaking the branch of a tree, but in this case, it sounds like the entire tree has been broken.

'What was that?' the boy asks.

'Shh,' the man replies.

They hear the chirp of insects, nothing more. The man brings his legs over the side of the cot when the shake starts again. A longer, firmer shake, and another crash, this time closer. The man gets to his feet and walks slowly to the door. Silence. The man takes a deep breath as he inches his hand to the latch. The boy sits up.

'No,' the man whispers, and in that instant the blade of a sword, long and gleaming, made of a shining white metal that is not found on Earth, comes through the door and sinks deeply into the man's chest. It protrudes six inches out through his back, and is quickly pulled free. The man grunts. The boy gasps. The man takes a single breath, and utters one word: 'Run.' He falls lifeless to the floor.

The boy leaps from the cot, bursts through the rear wall. He doesn't bother with the door or a window; he literally runs through the wall, which breaks apart as if it's paper, though it's made of strong, hard African mahogany. He tears into the Congo night, leaps over trees, sprints at a speed somewhere around sixty miles per hour. His sight and hearing are beyond human. He dodges trees, rips through snarled vines, leaps small streams with a single step. Heavy footsteps are close behind him, getting closer every second. His pursuers also have gifts. And they have something with them. Something he has only heard hints of, something he never believed he would see on Earth.

The crashing nears. The boy hears a low, intense roar. He knows whatever is behind him is picking up speed. He sees a break in the jungle up ahead. When he reaches it, he sees a huge ravine, three hundred feet across and three hundred feet down, with a river at the bottom. The river's bank is covered with huge boulders. Boulders that would break him apart if he fell on them. His only chance is to get across the ravine. He'll have a short running start, and one chance. One chance to save his own life. Even for him, or for any of the others on Earth like him, it's a near impossible leap. Going back, or going down, or trying to fight them means certain death. He has one shot.

There's a deafening roar behind him. They're twenty, thirty feet away. He takes five steps back and runs – and just before the ledge, he takes off and starts flying across the ravine. He's in the air three or four seconds. He screams, his arms outstretched in front of him, waiting for either safety or the end. He hits the ground and tumbles forward, stopping at the base of a mammoth tree. He smiles. He can't believe he made it, that he's going to survive. Not wanting them to see him, and knowing he needs to get farther away from them, he stands. He'll have to keep running.

He turns towards the jungle. As he does, a huge hand wraps itself around his throat. He is lifted off the ground. He struggles, kicks, tries to pull away, but knows it's futile, that it's over. He should have expected that they'd be on both sides, that once they found him, there would be no escape. The Mogadorian lifts him so that he can see the boy's chest, see the amulet that is hanging around his neck, the amulet that only he and his kind can wear. He tears it off and puts it somewhere inside the long black cloak he is wearing, and when his hand emerges it is holding the gleaming white metal sword. The boy looks into the Mogadorian's deep, wide, emotionless black eyes, and he speaks.

'The Legacies live. They will find each other, and when they're ready, they're going to destroy you.'

The Mogadorian laughs, a nasty, mocking laugh. It raises the sword, the only weapon in the universe that can break the charm that until today protected the boy, and still protects the others. The blade ignites in a silver flame as it points to the sky, as if it's coming alive, sensing its mission and grimacing in anticipation. And as it falls, an arc of light speeding through the blackness of the jungle, the boy still believes that some part of him will survive, and some part of him will make it home. He closes his eyes just before the sword strikes. And then it is over.

I

In the beginning there were nine of us. We left when we were young, almost too young to remember.

Almost.

I am told the ground shook, that the skies were full of light and explosions. We were in that two-week period of the year when both moons hang on opposite sides of the horizon. It was a time of celebration, and the explosions were at first mistaken for fireworks. They were not. It was warm, a soft wind blew in from off the water. I am always told the weather: it was warm. There was a soft wind. I've never understood why that matters.

What I remember most vividly is the way my grandmother looked that day. She was frantic, and sad. There were tears in her eyes. My grandfather stood just over her shoulder. I remember the way his glasses gathered the light from the sky. There were hugs. There were words said by each of them. I don't remember what they were. Nothing haunts me more.

It took a year to get here. I was five when we arrived. We were to assimilate ourselves into the culture before returning to Lorien when it could again sustain life. The nine of us had to scatter, and go our own ways. For how long, nobody knew. We still don't. None of them know where I am, and I don't know where they are, or what they look like now. That is how we protect ourselves because of the charm that was placed upon us when we left, a charm guaranteeing that we can only be killed in the order of our numbers, so long as we stay apart. If we come together, then the charm is broken.

When one of us is found and killed, a circular scar wraps around the right ankle of those still alive. And residing on our left ankle, formed when the Loric charm was first cast, is a small scar identical to the amulet each of us wears. The circular scars are another part of the charm. A warning system so that we know where we stand with each other, and so that we know when they'll be coming for us next. The first scar came when I was nine years old. It woke me from my sleep, burning itself into my flesh. We were living in Arizona, in a small border town near Mexico. I woke screaming in the middle of the night, in agony, terrified as the scar seared itself into my flesh. It was the first sign that the Mogadorians had finally found us on Earth, and the first sign that we were in danger. Until the scar showed up, I had almost convinced myself that my memories were wrong, that what Henri told me was wrong. I wanted to be a normal kid living a normal life, but I knew then, beyond any doubt or discussion, that I wasn't. We moved to Minnesota the next day.

The second scar came when I was twelve. I was in school, in Colorado, participating in a spelling bee. As soon as the pain started I knew what was happening, what had happened to Number Two. The pain was excruciating, but bearable this time. I would have stayed on the stage, but the heat lit my sock on fire. The teacher who was conducting the bee sprayed me with a fire extinguisher and rushed me to the hospital. The doctor in the ER found the first scar and called the police. When Henri showed, they threatened to arrest him for child abuse. But because he hadn't been anywhere near me when the second scar came, they had to let him go. We got in the car and drove away, this time to Maine. We left everything we had except for the Loric Chest that Henri brought along on every move. All twenty-one of them to date.

The third scar appeared an hour ago. I was sitting on a pontoon boat. The boat belonged to the parents of the most popular kid at my school, and unbeknownst to them, he was having a party on it. I had never been invited to any of the parties at my school before. I had always, because I knew we might leave at any minute, kept to myself. But it had been quiet for two years. Henri hadn't seen anything in the news that might lead the Mogadorians to one of us, or might alert us to them. So I made a couple friends. And one of them introduced me to the kid who was having the party. Everyone met at a dock. There were three coolers, some music, girls I had admired from afar but never spoken to, even though I wanted to. We pulled out from the dock and went half a mile into the Gulf of Mexico. I was sitting on the edge of the pontoon with my feet in the water, talking to a cute, dark-haired, blue-eyed girl named Tara, when I felt it coming. The water around my leg started boiling, and my lower leg started glowing where the scar was imbedding itself. The third of the Lorien symbols, the third warning. Tara started screaming and people started crowding around me. I knew there was no way to explain it. And I knew we would have to leave immediately.

The stakes were higher now. They had found Number Three, wherever he or she was, and Number Three was dead. So I calmed Tara down and kissed her on the cheek and told her it was nice to meet her and that I hoped she had a long beautiful life. I dove off the side of the boat and started swimming, underwater the entire time, except for one breath about halfway there, as fast as I could until I reached the shore. I ran along the side of the highway, just inside of the tree line, moving at speeds as fast as any of the cars. When I got home, Henri was at the bank of scanners and monitors that he used to research news around the world, and police activity in our area. He knew without me saying a word, though he did lift my soaking pants to see the scars.

In the beginning we were a group of nine.

Three are gone, dead.

There are six of us left.

They are hunting us, and they won't stop until they've killed us all.

I am Number Four.

I know that I am next.